Airship 27 Productions

TM

Wu Dang Chronicles

Wu Dang: Fist of the Wanderer © 2018; Wu Dang: Exile of the Wanderer ©2020; Wu Dang: Return of the Wanderer ©2021 Barbara Doran

Collection © 2022

Published by Airship 27 Productions
www.airship27.com
www.airship27hangar.com

Interior illustrations © 2018, 2020, 2021 Gary Kato
Cover illustration © 2022 Rob Davis

Editor: Ron Fortier
Associate Editor:
Production Designer: Rob Davis
Promotions Manager: Michael Vance

ISBN: 978-1-953589-27-9

Printed in the United States of America

10 9 8 7 6 5 4 3 2 1

by Barbara Doran

Table of Contents

Chapter 1: Metal –
Obedience Leads to Great Power

The Chinese were fighting again.

Captain Jake Burton was accustomed to Shanghai's constant noise; drunken sailors going to and fro, street vendors hawking their wares, horses and mules clopping through the streets, dragging carts and carriages. The street fights, on the other hand, were a new and disconcerting development. They were also a dangerous one for any foreigner fool enough to wander onto the battlefield.

The trouble found Burton in Old Town, the part of Shanghai reserved for native Chinese and a place he usually avoided. Americans—especially six foot tall Americans with light brown hair and blue eyes—stood out like a sore thumb here. He was conscious of being the center of attention, though no one was rude enough to stare outright. "Trouble with you, Jake, is you're too greedy," he muttered to himself.

Still, Burton's would-be client was obviously rich. The courier who'd brought the invitation had been dressed in fine dark blue silk, his carefully shaved forehead polished to near mirror smoothness. Everything about him had suggested wealth and importance. Whoever Lang He Xiao was, he was obviously a member of China's ruling class. No Manchu courier would work for a Han, no matter how rich and influential.

Burton was nearing his destination when a howl of rage came from a nearby alley, followed by the sound of shattering wood. Knowing better than to hang around when someone started shouting slogans and breaking things, he turned down another alley. He chose poorly, walking straight into a small gang of men in grey trousers, their lean torsos bared to reveal tattoos of butterflies, each carrying heavy cleavers.

"I don't suppose any of you speak English?" Burton asked, backing up. He understood Chinese, could even speak it—badly—but this wasn't the time for comic translation errors.

Someone shouted angrily behind Burton and he didn't need to look to know he was pinned between the first gang and another so similarly dressed the only way to tell the difference were their headbands; the words Heaven's Fist written on them in Chinese. Both gangs were Han, with the characteristic queue required by Qing law.

Burton was an experienced sailor and he wasn't afraid of a few cuts and bruises. He did draw the line at being outnumbered. Besides, it was obvious he wasn't their target. He searched for an escape route, while the two groups shouted at each other. Threats, mostly, with descriptions of ancestors and mating habits that didn't need translation.

The fight began when one of the Heaven's Fist gang shoved one of the Butterflies, knocking him to the ground. Immediately, the others jostled for position, swinging their blades and yelling incoherently. Blood spurted and men shrieked as each side did their best to slice the other. Disinclined to be fileted with the rest, Burton pressed back against the wall and struggled to get past. He could see the main road—and safety— mere feet away. All he had to do was reach it.

Something tugged Burton's trouser leg. A quick glance downward showed him a young man peeking out through a narrow crack in the wall. The youth beckoned quickly, adding, "Come," in Chinese. It wouldn't be easy to follow, Burton being bigger and heavier than his would-be rescuer. It was also his best chance.

Forcing his way down to join the stranger, Burton followed the youngster through the wall. As he'd feared, it was tight, but the bricks crumbled as he pushed, slowly giving way and letting him through into a badly run-down courtyard.

The young man pulled Burton to his feet with easy and surprising strength. He was skinny and short—barely coming to Burton's shoulder—but his grip was rock hard. Before Burton could say a word of thanks, his rescuer turned and headed for the open doorway of an old Chinese house. Once again he called, "Come."

"Hey. Wait. Who are you?"

The youth didn't answer, leaving Burton to decide whether he should cooperate. With some rare exceptions, Westerners weren't welcome in Chinese homes. Moreover, the young man was the oddest Chinese Burton had ever encountered. Roughly dressed in patched trousers and an equally patched short robe, his general appearance was at odds with what Burton had become accustomed to.

He'd seen the queues Han Chinese wore. He'd seen the carefully shaven foreheads of the Manchus. He'd even seen utterly bald Buddhist monks. But this man's unshaven black hair fell to his waist, as straight and silky as a young girl's. Indeed, Burton might have mistaken him for a woman if not for his dry tenor. Well, that, and most women didn't have such strong features.

Ordinarily, Burton would have taken his own risks and headed elsewhere. This time he couldn't. There wasn't anywhere to go and the young man had come to his aid in a time of need. Distrustfully, aware of being out of his depth, Burton trailed behind the youth, letting him lead the way inside.

ᴏᴏᴏ

Yi Xiao hurried through Old Man Fang's mansion, hoping to reach the front door before anyone noticed him. Or, rather, before anyone noticed his giant-sized companion. Alone, he could have escaped easily. With Burton along, his chances dropped significantly. Especially since the man would not stop talking.

Behind Yi Xiao, Burton commented on the furnishings. "A little bit tatty, that hanging, but it'd fetch a pretty penny back in New York." His voice was rumbling thunder and sure to attract attention. Or would if the latest battle between the Heavenly Fist Society and their long term rivals, the Butterfly Blades, weren't more interesting.

"And my sister is quite fond of the porcelain dishes. Though the last set I brought back for her shattered on the way home."

Yi Xiao stopped and glared at his companion, making the silencing gesture he'd learned from his father's second wife. "Will you please be quiet?"

A startled expression crossed Burton's face. "You speak English? Perfect British English?"

"Not now!" Yi Xiao snapped. "We have to get out of here. Master says, save your breath for when it's needed."

"I don't even know where here is! Or who this master is you're talking about…" Burton trailed off. "Wait. This isn't your home?"

Yi Xiao sighed, indicating his ragged clothes. "Do I look like I belong to a rich merchant's family?"

"How'd you get in then? Are you a thief?"

"I climbed the wall and no. Will you come?"

"I don't know. I might be better off throwing myself on the mercy of… whomever it is that lives here. Who does live here, by the way?" Burton eyed the furnishings. "And are you sure they're rich? This place looks a bit run down."

"Pawn Merchants like Old Man Fang don't waste their money on fripperies," Yi Xiao retorted. "Bodyguards, on the other hand…" He gestured sharply behind Burton as two big, overly armed and armored men approached. In Chinese, he added, "So sorry to have disturbed. We were just passing through."

The attempt to ease the bodyguards' minds had exactly the effect Yi Xiao expected. Which was to say, none at all. He grabbed Burton's wrist and dragged him towards the front of the building. "Run!"

Burton might be irritating and incapable of doing anything without running off at the mouth but he knew where he wasn't wanted. "If you aren't a thief," he grumbled, following behind Yi Xiao, "Why are you here?"

Yi Xiao ducked past a third bodyguard, just coming around the corner as his fellows shouted for help. "To get you out of that mess, Captain Burton."

Naming the foreigner was a mistake. Burton stopped in his tracks, nearly dragging Yi Xiao off his feet. "You know who I am? Were you following me?"

"Yes, I know. Yes, I was." Before Burton could demand more, Yi Xiao dodged behind him, catching hold of the nearest bodyguard's wrist and redirecting the man's attack before he could grasp hold of Burton's collar. Flinging the bodyguard against the wall he drew on his inner strength and thrust the base of his palm into the man's side. Padded armor, strong enough to take most blows, proved useless. A rib snapped in a most satisfying way beneath Yi Xiao's blow.

The bodyguard growled a curse and slammed Yi Xiao backwards, or tried to. Giving way to the blow, Yi Xiao slid sideways and under the man's arm. At the same time he hooked the man's knee and dropped him to the ground.

Unexpectedly, Burton sided with Fang's bodyguards, striking Yi Xiao from behind with something hard and heavy. Unprepared for the attack and focused on the other men, Yi Xiao went down, only dimly aware of Burton saying, "Now gentlemen, that proves he isn't with me. I don't suppose you'd let me go?"

The sound of a bodyguard's fist hitting Burton's jaw was oddly satisfying.

ooo

When Burton came to, he and his erstwhile rescuer had been tied up and stuck in a cellar. At least, he assumed the other person in the musty darkness was his erstwhile rescuer. Someone was breathing a short distance away from Burton, shallow ragged breaths like a sailor coming off a bender.

"I expect an apology, you realize?" the young man said suddenly.

"Why should I? I get caught in a fight and you conveniently show up to drag me through some rich sod's house to get caught by his bodyguards? You know who I am when we've never even met? What am I supposed to think?"

The fellow went silent. Then he asked in a puzzled way, "Sod? Why would you call Old Man Fang a lump of dirt?"

For the first time Burton realized the limitations of his companion's English. His near perfect British accent had fooled Burton into talking to him like a native speaker. "It's slang. For sodomite."

"I... see." The young man paused, then said in a defeated way. "No. I don't see. What is a sodomite?"

Now Burton was embarrassed and he decided to end the conversation. "Ask your tutor. I'm not here to give you English lessons." He took a deep breath and fell to coughing at the stench of something old, moldy and somewhat sulfurous. "Never mind. How do you know who I am? And who are you, anyway?"

"I know who you are because I was sent to make sure you arrived safely, Captain Burton. As for who I am; I am called the Wanderer, my surname is Lang, my personal name is Yi Xiao, and I am the youngest and least worthy grandson of Lang He Xiao. Along with being your guide in this nonsensical adventure, I am but a humble would-be priest of no particular note."

If it hadn't been entirely too dark to do so, Burton would have glared at his companion. "You? A priest? With all that hair?" He was certain the fellow wasn't Christian. Nothing about him suggested such a thing.

"You're thinking of Buddhist priests. I am, or try to be, a follower of the *Dao*." By now Yi Xiao was beside Burton, undoing the ropes binding him. "Not successfully, I admit, or you wouldn't have been able to strike me, earlier."

Burton didn't waste time scoffing. "So you were protecting me? Why?"

"Because a *guilao* in Old Town sticks out like a pine in a rice field."

It took Burton a moment to remember what *guilao* meant. 'Ghost' or 'Foreigner'. The word many Chinese used for Westerners. "Well, yes, I suppose that's true. But if your boss didn't want me to stick out, maybe he should have met me elsewhere." There were plenty of places in Shanghai where people could meet privately.

"My... boss... is elderly and doesn't care for the foreign districts of Shanghai." Yi Xiao sighed. "In any event, all this is getting us nowhere. Old Fang has sent for the city guards and I'd rather not attract their attention." Cloth rustled as he rose to his feet.

"How do we get out of here?"

"Fortunately, this is a storage cellar beneath Old Fang's kitchen. They've probably set a guard but I can deal with one or two men. Given, of course, no one knocks me unconscious from behind."

Burton refused to be embarrassed. No one had told him to expect a guard after all. As Yi Xiao moved around the room, searching for the exit, Burton asked, "What about that fight? Was it what you were protecting me from?"

"It's over and yes. Not because you were their target. Things are a trifle up in the air these days. The Daoguang Emperor's illness has set China reeling. Every triad, every society, every citizen of the rivers and lakes are vying for dominance." Yi Xiao shifted again, adding, "Now be quiet a moment, if you can. I'm not good enough to do this while distracted. Master says, silence is worth its weight in gold."

Burton was just about to complain that he could, so, be quiet when it occurred to him that he'd be proving the opposite. He waited, listening to Yi Xiao's breathing, puzzled by its slow cadence. What was the man doing? And why did he feel like he could see Yi Xiao's outline in the darkness ahead of him? He'd just decided there must be some faint light after all when the man let loose a sharp cry.

Wood smashed above them and light flared. Somewhere in the distance a man shouted angrily. Burton didn't need Yi Xiao's urging to run for it.

ooo

With the fight outside Old Man Fang's mansion over, Yi Xiao thought it safe to leave by the back gate, rather than attempt the house again. This, however, meant explaining himself to Burton, who had a regrettable tendency to demand answers without thinking for himself. "I was hoping to use the distraction of the fight to escape through the front. I didn't know you have more words than a pond has carp."

The insult set Burton's jaw going twice as fast as it had before. Yi Xiao was a rude bastard, a brat with no consideration for a lost foreigner, an arrogant boy who didn't know how to treat his betters. Being busy watching for trouble, Yi Xiao ignored the nervous babblings of a frightened man.

When trouble came, it came from an unexpected source. Yi Xiao was watching for someone to take offense to his charge's presence. Instead, he found himself face to face with an angry stranger, this one heavy-set, wild-haired and clearly looking for a fight. From his accent, he was Taiwanese. From his clothes, he was a dockworker searching for adventure. From his expression, Yi Xiao was the adventure he searched for.

"You!" the man shouted, waving his fist within inches of Yi Xiao's nose. "I know you!"

"My dear sir, I'm afraid I don't know you at all." Yi Xiao tried to nudge Burton off to the side. The man didn't cooperate. "Where is it you think we've met?"

Another swipe, this one close enough to set Yi Xiao's hair fluttering. "Don't play the fool with me, you damn Manchu bastard! You stole my woman at Golden Phoenix in Soochow four months ago!"

Yi Xiao couldn't help being side-tracked. "The Golden Phoenix? However did you manage to get in? You don't look like you can afford their prices. Besides, whomever you met, it wasn't me. I've been training on Heng Shan for the last two years."

"Weren't you just telling me not to judge a person by their possessions?" Burton commented. "And shouldn't you mention you weren't there before quibbling over details?"

"Possibly." Yi Xiao noted the American understood Chinese. He'd have to warn his grandmother. "I tend to forget myself sometimes."

"Given he's ready to break that long nose of yours, you might not want to do that."

Yi Xiao returned his attention to his would-be attacker. "May I suggest the French Quarter? I'm sure a fine gentleman like yourself can find plenty of willing companions there. Cheaper, too."

The man growled, about to swing his fist again, but Yi Xiao raised a hand, "One moment. I have a rule about fighting."

"Yeah, he's a priest, you know. You don't expect a man of God to know how to fight."

Yi Xiao ignored Burton's base canard, asking his would-be opponent, "What's your name?"

"Feng. Feng Mei Sheng!"

The man wasn't familiar. If he was part of the martial world—and Yi Xiao doubted it—he wasn't important. More likely he was a street tough looking for a reason to fight. "Very well, Mei Sheng, I charge a hundred *tael* for every blow you land."

Both Mei Sheng and Burton stared at him. "What?!"

"You're a strong fellow and medicine's expensive," Yi Xiao pointed out. "If you hit me, I'll be needing to see a doctor."

Infuriated, Mei Sheng took a step forward and struck hard. Yi Xiao twisted sideways, just as the man's fist brushed his shoulder. "Of course, you do have to hit me first. I won't charge if you miss. That wouldn't be fair."

Now Mei Sheng was utterly furious, slamming his fists into Yi Xiao as hard as he could. Or, rather, slamming his fists into thin air. Yi Xiao was not yet a true master, but a poorly trained and foul-tempered streetfighter would need luck or carefully hidden skill to get a blow past his evasions.

Mei Sheng had both. His next flurry of attacks drew Yi Xiao's attention in the wrong direction, giving the man an opening. He took it without hesitation, his kick strong and high. Stocky though he was, the man's reach was unexpected and disconcerting. Yi Xiao was sent flying, landing in the dirt and rolling backwards to his feet. Someone in the gathering crowd yelled an insult; he'd lost a bet thanks to Yi Xiao's inattention.

"Master says, don't get cocky," Yi Xiao reminded himself ruefully. Then he was dodging his attacker again, paying attention to the man's lower body. He ought to have known better than to ignore it before. Even the least experienced fighter's attacks could be read in the movement of their feet and hips.

This time he spotted the shift in weight heralding another kick. This time he twisted out of its way. This time he caught hold of Mei Sheng's leg and lifted it higher, dropping its owner onto his back. The man slammed into the dirt, to the great amusement of their growing audience.

"You dirty bastard! You rotten little pig-swiver!" The flow of invective was educational, but Yi Xiao already knew most of it. He dropped one knee into the man's throat, controlling the urge to shatter his windpipe. Unaware of how close he'd come to death, the man howled, "Get off me!"

"No. Listen to me carefully. This foolishness is going to get attention. The city guards are busy cleaning up another fight, but once they have, they'll be headed here." Yi Xiao tapped the man's nose lightly. "Now, who sent you to attack me?"

A startled look filled Mei Sheng's eyes. "How'd you... I mean, no one!"

"That's a lie. You're a better fighter than you look. More importantly, I doubt any dockworker would hold a grudge over one of Mrs. Song's girls. Not for four months. So who hired you?" Yi Xiao pressed his knee a little harder against the man's sternum to keep his attention.

Wilting, Mei Sheng admitted, "I didn't get his name. But he said you took the girl he was going to buy."

The whole thing made no sense. Yi Xiao had never been in the Golden Phoenix, though his brother, horrible gossip that Yi De was, had mentioned the place in his letters. Not that his staid elder brother ever went there. It was their cousin, ever given to slipping off and evading his keepers, who liked the place. With a sense of inevitability, Yi Xiao asked, "How'd you know it was me?"

The man reached up and Yi Xiao caught his hand quickly. "In my pocket," Mei Sheng protested. "A drawing. I've been following your trail all around the country."

Yi Xiao found a tattered sheet of paper with a face painted on it. Mirror familiar features gazed back at him; long face, thin straight nose, narrow lips. The only real difference was the hairstyle. He grasped hold of his long forelocks. "Do you think this is four months growth?" Most Manchu men shaved the front of their heads, keeping only enough hair for their braids. Yi Xiao, as a priest of the *Dao*, hadn't had a razor near his scalp for two years now.

Mei Sheng looked embarrassed. "I... er... well..."

Standing up and pulling the man to his feet, Yi Xiao said, "I hold no grudge. Here." He put a hundred *tael* coin into his erstwhile opponent's hand. "Go find yourself a doctor."

"Wait. Why?"

"I'm a priest, not a street fighter." Admittedly and embarrassingly, Yi Xiao had enjoyed himself rather too much. But that didn't change the fact that a seeker of the *Dao* shouldn't be brawling in the street like a common thug. He hesitated, torn between secrets he could not reveal and the knowledge that this man's quest would get him killed. "Take the money and some advice. Drop this matter. Repay your benefactor if you have to but don't keep hunting for the man in this painting. You won't survive."

Mei Sheng snorted. "Why? Is he that good? Better than you?"

"No. Quite the opposite." Yi Xiao handed the picture back. "But he's too well protected.

If you did get to him, you'd never escape the consequences. The death of a thousand slices might be the least of your worries. Even I dare not raise a hand to him."

It took Mei Sheng a moment to understand. He folded the paper up carefully and said, "We'll see. You may be right after all."

As Mei Sheng turned and walked away, Yi Xiao returned his attention to his companion, who'd been watching the fight with a mix of confusion and amusement. In English, he added, "Come along, Burton. You have an appointment and it's high time you got to it."

∞

Burton couldn't help being annoyed. Accustomed to command, he didn't like being dragged around like a toddler. Admittedly the most recent fight had been Yi Xiao's own problem but he'd felt a fifth wheel, waiting for the pair to finish their argument. He was also glad not to have to fight Yi Xiao himself. There'd been a moment when it'd looked like the man would kill his attacker.

"That picture did look like you," he commented as Yi Xiao led him towards a large round entranceway through a white wall. A shorter wall blocked their path inside, forcing them to go around it; another example of Chinese evasiveness and circuitous thinking.

"It wasn't."

They entered a large courtyard where a dozen Manchurian men were doing their afternoon exercises. Burton had seen this sort of thing before, visiting his Chinese contacts in the business district. Apparently it both kept the servants fit and too tired to get into trouble.

"A relative?" Burton pressed, sensing weakness and finding it irresistible. He ignored the fists and staffs striking through the air, though some came within half a foot of him as they passed. "Your twin brother, maybe?"

"I don't have a twin." An elderly servant greeted Yi Xiao and at a word from the young man, went back inside. "We need to clean up. I've sent for someone to take you to your room."

Burton hadn't intended to stay but he didn't get a chance to argue. Yi Xiao headed off in another direction and two pretty young maids came out to persuade Burton into slippers and lead him into the house. Deciding not to argue, he let the pair take him to an attractive little room with a bowl for washing his hands and a plain blue silk robe for him to put on over his clothes.

"Please will you change?" one of the girls asked, bowing. "The Elder should be respected."

Cleaning up only took a few minutes. The robe covered the worst of Burton's sins and the rest, his hands and face, weren't so dirty as to be noticeable. All he had to do was scrub them quickly and make sure his fingernails were clean. As for his hair, it was generally a tousled mess no comb had ever tamed. He doubted anything could be done about it this late in the day.

Once Burton dressed he stepped out and looked around. Now this was the sort of place he expected a rich merchant to own. The halls were ivory tinted plaster. The ceiling was covered in elaborately carved tiles. The floor was fine and well-varnished wood. More tellingly, there were paintings and other *objet d'art* decorating every flat surface, from walls to counter. If he could bring these things back with him to New York he'd be set for life.

"There you are." Yi Xiao had changed to a simple mauve robe. He'd even tied his hair back into a sleek knot at the top of his skull. Accustomed as Burton was to the ubiquitous queue, the hair style was mildly startling. "Come along."

They walked through elegant halls to a small room towards the back of the house, its walls covered in bookshelves. A desk stood across from Burton and he had a queasy flashback to his first ship, his first captain and his first and nearly last mistake. At least this time he wouldn't be blamed for having forced his fellow crewmembers to cut a necessary rope before it could drag him straight into the deep.

There was a thin, elderly, woman sitting at the desk, dressed in padded dark silk embroidered with chrysanthemums. Her hair was completely grey and her eyes were slightly clouded, but she had a look that made Burton think she must have been quite spirited and headstrong when she was younger.

The lady was reading an English newspaper with a dark frown. She muttered under her breath, then slammed the paper down with a cold snort. Tall as he was, it was easy to see what she'd been reading. Something about the Daoguang Emperor's illness. Yi Xiao had said the man was sick and now Burton remembered there was a very young and inexperienced heir waiting in the wings. What was the youngster's name? Oh, yes, that was right. Yi Zhu.

Looking up at her grandson, the woman raised a brow. "Where is your willow leaf knife?" she demanded in Chinese.

"Grandmother," Yi Xiao bowed three times then went to his knees and abased himself against the floor. "I greet you."

"Rise, youngest grandson. Introduce me to the foreigner. Do not bother with my titles. We don't have time for that nonsense."

Yi Xiao obeyed. "Grandmother, this is Captain Jake Burton." In English, he added, "Captain, this is the head of the Lang family, He Xiao. You may refer to her as Madam Lang."

Burton was startled, but he bowed nonetheless, not bothering with the kowtow. He didn't regard it as shameful the way some did, but it also wasn't his style. He wasn't even sure how many he might be expected to offer, especially to someone who—despite not wishing to mention it—was clearly some sort of nobility. A mere merchant wouldn't have titles to omit.

Haltingly, because he understood Chinese better than he spoke it, Burton said, "Pleased meeting you, ma'am." His limit reached, he added in English, "Er... am I right, thinking she's the one who invited me?" Women back home weren't so forward. Hell, women in China usually weren't either. But this lady, lean, elderly and austere, might be a queen or a princess. She wasn't the sort to leave her business to others.

Yi Xiao was about to answer when Madam Lang interrupted. "You distracted me. Where is your willow leaf knife?"

Cheeks bright with embarrassment, Yi Xiao told her, "I'm done with weapons. I left it back at Heng Shan."

Madam Lang's expression might have frozen boiling water. She was so coldly angry Burton knew his presence alone prevented her from telling her grandson what she thought of his decision. Guessing defending the youth wouldn't help, Burton held his tongue.

"Do not think you are safe simply because this foreigner is with you," the old woman stated calmly. "We will discuss your feckless irresponsibility to the rivers and lakes later."

"Yes, Grandmother." Yi Xiao bowed his head, then turned an embarrassed look at Burton. "Private business," he added in English. "No need to worry about it."

"No doubt. I don't suppose you'd like to get to the point now? I am a busy man."

The old woman's English was probably no better than Burton's Chinese but she understood enough. "Assist me," she ordered Yi Xiao. "We must not keep our guest waiting."

Another bow and Yi Xiao moved to stand behind Madam Lang. Once he'd done so, his grandmother began to speak and he to translate. "You are the captain of the *Henrietta Marie*."

"I am. And a fine barque she is, too." Burton had scrimped and saved for her, borrowing heavily from his family back in New York. He was as proud of the little vessel as if she were his own child. "I've already filled her hold, though, so if you're hoping to sell me something…"

"I am not a merchant, Captain Burton. I have nothing to sell you. Rather, I must send a package to San Francisco. It is valuable; one of our family's greatest treasures, but it cannot remain in China. The risk is too great."

Burton frowned. "I'm not going to San Francisco, ma'am. I'm headed to San Diego and south from there to Panama."

With a smile, the old woman inclined her head. "San Diego is sufficient, Captain. The package can find its way to San Francisco on its own."

Yi Xiao stared at his grandmother with a confused expression. He plainly had no idea what the endangered treasure was she wished to send away. The boy obviously knew better than to ask, but he was desperately curious.

For that matter, so was Burton. Packages, especially important and valuable packages, generally didn't travel on their own. "It's rude to inquire, but how exactly do you plan on getting it from San Diego to San Francisco safely?"

"Given he's been walking all over Heng Shan's peaks these past two years, I believe he can find his way unassisted. Can't you, grandson?"

ooo

Yi Xiao prided himself on staying calm through the strangest of circumstances. Yet the news he was being sent to America made him forget his manners. Instead of translating his grandmother's last words, he demanded, "WHAT?" in a voice that broke in a way it hadn't for years.

"Do not stop translating, boy. The Captain is a busy man and we don't want to waste his time." His grandmother's voice was ice and stone and he knew he'd done wrong to question her in front of an outsider.

Another man might have argued. Another man might have walked out on the whole mess. Another man was not the youngest male descendant of the Imperial Princess He Xiao. He'd been raised to filial piety. Hell, his personal name—like hers—meant that very thing. Besides, he loved her, despite her autocratic and tyrannical ways.

Obediently, Yi Xiao told Burton, "My grandmother is sending me to America and wishes you to transport me."

Burton, who'd obviously understood already, frowned. "Madam Lang, the *Henrietta Marie* is a cargo ship. We've carried passengers in steerage before—twenty American dollars a head—but it's hardly the place for a young noble like your grandson. Surely you can find another, more comfortable, way to get him where he needs to go?"

The suggestion made Yi Xiao scoff, but he didn't say what he was thinking. He'd spent most of the last two years cultivating his Self on Heng Shan's peaks. Alone except for his chosen master, he'd sat in a cave, or atop the mountain or even in the middle of a racing stream. All to teach his soul the ways of the *Dao*. A ship's steerage, dark and crowded though it might be, would be unpleasant but survivable.

Rather than explain, all Yi Xiao asked was, "You've carried passengers that way before. Have any died?"

"I'm pleased to say they have not."

"If they can survive the journey I can as well. My family is, as you say, one of the noblest. We are not pampered pets who can hardly bear sunlight, much less a few days…"

"Months. The trip is at least two and half months, if the winds and weather are with us."

"Months, then. I won't pretend it will be easy, yet I can do what I must. Little though I might wish to." The last escaped Yi Xiao's lips before he could hold them back, eliciting a glare from his grandmother. He flinched, adding, "When do you sail?"

"I plan on leaving in a day or so. The weather may or may not cooperate but if you expect to leave with us, you'd better be on board before then. Time and tide wait for no man, no matter how noble his blood."

ooo

With an agreement made, Madam Lang was kind enough to offer Burton dinner and a place to sleep. He gladly accepted; he hadn't eaten for hours now and he needed a rest. Besides, his curiosity was up. There had to be a reason Madam Lang was sending her grandson away, so clearly against his wishes. Burton wanted to know why. It didn't matter to him, but it was a mystery and experience had taught him carting a mystery around unexamined was how one found oneself neck deep in trouble.

Dinner was a great pot of boiling soup set up in the middle of the table. Everyone, from the smallest and most excitable daughter to Madam Lang herself, was responsible for dropping raw meats and vegetables into the pot and retrieving what they wanted to eat. There were odd sauces; raw egg, soy sauce, vinegar and many different spices. Burton made mental notes. He doubted his sister back home would care for this style of eating but he might persuade his crew to try it sometime.

As for the company, it was strangely familiar and comfortable. He'd always found his loud, boisterous and obstreperous crew to be better companions than his own flesh and blood. The Langs weren't nearly as crude or socially inept as the crew of the *Henrietta Marie* but they had their own ways. The children—easily half a dozen little girls—ran around the dining hall, babbling loud and fast about their lessons and their play. Meanwhile their elders talked over them, ignoring them except when they nearly pulled the pot down atop themselves.

The previous generation were only a little quieter. They kept Yi Xiao busy, asking him all sorts of odd questions about what he'd been doing. Burton didn't understand what 'cultivating' meant, nor why cinnabar fields were important, but he could tell it was impressive; at least to Yi Xiao's many sisters. Burton wondered how the family kept them straight, for each and every ones' names began with 'Yi'. It was apparently a tradition, where children of the same generation bore the same syllable in their name.

As for Yi Xiao's father, mother, elder brother and sister-in-law, they seemed busy going over some sort of engine plans. They barely acknowledged Burton's existence, not rudely, but because they were focused on their own interests. Burton, whose youngest brother had a similar bent, would have understood.

There were two members of the household whose presence pleased and confused Burton. Yi Xiao's English tutor was, apparently, a member of the family, despite her obviously British origin. Red-haired and grey-eyed, Grace Smythe-Barnes was governess, secretary and all around household assistant. Ordinarily, Burton would never expect to find a white woman working for a Chinese family, no matter how noble they obviously were.

" . . . IMPRESSIVE; AT LEAST TO YI XIAO'S MANY SISTERS. "

The woman's daughter, Yi Jin, explained everything. The girl was obviously half-Chinese, her light brown hair and slender hazel eyes combined with ivory skin and high-cheekbones. It didn't take Burton long to realize she was Yi Xiao's half-sister, a situation some might find scandalous. Burton, knowing Chinese society as he did, was only surprised Mr. Lang's second wife was white, not that he had one at all.

As they ate, Burton answered Yi Jin's many questions about his travels, which in turn elicited an apology from her mother. "Please don't let her overwhelm you." The woman gave Yi Jin a warning look, adding, "She can be terribly pushy sometimes."

"I'm just practicing my English, mother. Like you wanted me to."

Burton chuckled and waved off the apology. "She's also being kind, keeping the English speaker entertained. I do know a bit of Chinese, but not nearly enough for a proper conversation."

"Even so…"

"Even so, how about I ask a possibly rude and pushy question myself." The second Mrs. Lang smiled, waving for him to go on. "I realize it may be family business and something you'd prefer not to discuss, but given I have to transport him; why is Yi Xiao's grandmother sending him off with a flea in his ear? Did he embarrass the family somehow?"

Burton knew the question was risky. It was obvious from the elderly matriarch's attitude that her plans were secret. But he'd once had to race all the way from Bangkok to London, pursued by pirates and fake officials. He didn't like mysterious treasures with unknown troubles attached. He still didn't know what'd been in that box, either.

It was Madam Lang who answered her English far better than she'd pretended earlier. "It is a family affair, Captain. Yi Xiao, himself, has done nothing wrong. But there are those who would use him to bring trouble to others."

Seeing that was all he'd be told, Burton was about to try a different tack when Yi Xiao interrupted, frowning puzzledly. "What did you mean, 'flea in my ear'?"

Chuckling, Yi Xiao's… second mother? step-mother? aunt?… told him, "It's an idiom, Xiao Xiao. It means to send someone off with a rebuke." She added for Burton's benefit, "The whole family understands formal English, but idioms like those are difficult to teach."

Almost perkily, Yi Xiao agreed. "Like what you said earlier. The word you said I should ask my tutor about." Before Burton could stop him, he turned to the second Mrs. Lang. "Sod, I think it was. Short for sodomite?"

Burton felt his cheeks go bright red as Mrs. Lang turned a hard, cold, look on him. "I'm a sailor," he said weakly. "I was upset."

There was an odd and nearly identical expression on both Madam Lang's face and Yi Xiao's. A faint trembling of the lips suggested they were scant inches from bursting into laughter. The second Mrs. Lang glanced from one to the other, lips tight. Finally she shook her head. "Yi Xiao, you may ask Mr. Burton to explain the meaning of the word later when you are in less polite company than this."

Softly, the old lady murmured, "Cutting the sleeve isn't quite as impolite, grandson. But I wouldn't suggest using that phrase where you're going, either."

Comprehension dawned in Yi Xiao's eyes. "Oh. Oh, I see. I had a feeling it was something rude, given the circumstances. But he did tell me to ask you, Mama Grace."

"I'm sure he did. I also sure you knew you shouldn't." Mrs. Lang sighed, catching hold of a rapidly moving girl as she passed. "Take warning, Captain Burton. Mischief does not run in this family, it trots, gallops and capers through it."

The conversation turned to other, less significant things, but Burton found himself wondering just what he was getting himself into, transporting a man like Yi Xiao anywhere.

OOO

It was impossible to sleep. The shock of his grandmother's plans left Yi Xiao confused and frightened. He was painfully conscious that he shouldn't be so disturbed. "Master says, confusion is as natural as order. Move with it and it will come to rest," he reminded himself, sitting in a quiet corner of the garden.

He wished he understood why he was being sent away; with or without a flea in his ear. Grandmother had made it clear it wasn't his actions that had brought about his exile, but neither had she told him what had. She was still angry at him for leaving his sabre behind, even though a priest of the Wind and Rain sect had no need of such things.

Yi Xiao's meditation was interrupted by movement on the path beyond his hiding place. Burton, clumsy and unafraid, coming back from a trip to the toilet. No surprise. The foreigner had drunk several whole pots of tea at dinner. Not to mention eaten far more food than anyone Yi Xiao had seen before.

Burton stopped in his tracks and a faint sound rustled. Yi Xiao didn't move, but he focused his *qi*, tuning his awareness to the world around him. Now he knew there was a third man in the garden, creeping stealthily through the underbrush towards the house.

The stranger was using his own inner awareness to help him find his way past the house guard. No doubt that was how he'd gotten so far past Yi Xiao. Admittedly, Yi Xiao's inattention had helped, yet only a trained warrior could have managed such a feat even assisted by Yi Xiao's distraction.

There were places where Yi Xiao would have ignored an intruder. His grandmother's Shanghai home was not one of them. He stood, intending to interrupt the stranger's slow progress, but Burton got there first. "Hey! Are you supposed to be here?" When Burton reached out to grab the man, the stranger sent him flying. He lay, gasping for air, while the stranger dropped a heel into his sternum.

As the Captain stared blearily at his attacker, muttering Yi Xiao's name, the man drew his sword, placing it at Burton's throat.

Yi Xiao moved quickly, fingers striking the intruder's spine, the back of his ear and collarbone. Immediately, the man went still, though his voice did not. "How dare you lay hands on me?"

The voice and arrogance were familiar. Unimpressed, Yi Xiao retorted, "You're the one sneaking around grandmother's garden, Zhu Zhu. What did you expect would happen?" He helped Captain Burton to his feet. "Go inside and tell a servant to fetch my grandmother. Tell them I said we have an important guest."

"How about I give him a taste of what he gave me instead?"

"Do as I say. Now." Yi Xiao deepened his voice, gazing levelly at the Captain. Somehow, by some miracle of sense, Burton stopped arguing. Maybe nearly getting his spine snapped and his throat cut had had a salutatory effect on his mobile tongue. He hurried inside silently.

Once Burton had gone, Yi Xiao returned his attention to his prisoner, undoing the paralysis. "Now, cousin, I'm sure you have an explanation for this. I'm equally sure you think it's a good one. I'm not certain my grandmother will agree."

OOO

Ordinarily, Burton would never have walked away from a fight. The blow to his head must have shaken him up. Well, that and Yi Xiao's resemblance to his grandmother went further than skin deep. The youngster had an unexpectedly commanding side to him, one that defied argument.

Finding a servant took several minutes. Getting her to understand the situation was only resolved by the second Mrs. Lang's arrival. "Whatever is going on out here? Mr. Burton, you're making quite a fuss. Is something wrong?"

"There's an intruder who looks just like Yi Xiao."

Burton was exaggerating but the resemblance was marked. They were both fine-featured, with long noses and thick brows. The newcomer wore his hair in the same style as most Manchus, but his forehead was covered in a thick dark stubble, as if he hadn't had a chance to shave recently. The greatest difference lay in attitude. The stranger had an arrogant, self-assured, air that Yi Xiao lacked. Yi Xiao's voice of command aside, the boy always seemed to be sniggering up his sleeve at the world.

"An intruder? Who looks like Yi Xiao?" The second Mrs. Lang gave quick, sharp, orders to the servant who immediately ran off into the twisted maze of hallways. Then the woman returned her attention to Burton. "How was he dressed?"

Ruefully, Burton admitted, "I didn't notice much else about him. A hooded robe over the usual street clothes, I think. Something grey, maybe a black vest?"

"Nothing embroidered? No dragons?"

Burton tried to think. "No. Nothing like that. He looked like a merchant. Respectable. Even staid... aside from a regrettable tendency to throw people over their shoulders."

Madam Lang came down the hallway, her spry steps belying her age. She barely gave her daughter-in-law a glance. "Where is my grandson and the intruder?"

"Still out back, I think." There was a shout and a crash, quickly followed by the sound of flesh striking flesh. A moment later Yi Xiao came flipping down the hallway, calling back something incomprehensible. Whatever language he spoke, it was neither formal Chinese nor the informal dock-tainted dialect Burton understood best.

The other man skidded down the hallway, expression calm and hard as he aimed a blow at Yi Xiao's chin. It missed, for Yi Xiao evaded him with that same slippery snake movement from earlier. Burton had never seen anyone fight the way Yi Xiao did but it was effective, albeit aggravating for the one trying to hit him.

Blow after blow narrowly missed as Yi Xiao called out what sounded like insults. His opponent didn't like them, that was certain. His nose flared and his lips tightened every time Yi Xiao opened his mouth. Yet throughout all this he stayed calm, just shifted, struck and kicked so fast his limbs were a blur in the dimly lit hallway.

For some reason Yi Xiao seemed unwilling to strike his opponent. He kept his hands safely behind his back, as if to keep himself from instinctively reacting to the stranger's attacks. "What's the matter, Zhu Zhu? Can't move fast enough?" He was grinning dangerously, a daredevil flirting with the edge of disaster.

Madam Lang had had enough. "Stop this nonsense right this minute," she ordered calmly in Chinese. "Both of you."

Yi Xiao might have been enjoying the fight but he obeyed immediately. The intruder was less submissive. He used the moment of Yi Xiao's distraction to land a blow straight in the middle of the young man's belly.

Some men would have fallen over immediately, the breath knocked out of them. All Yi Xiao allowed himself was a soft, "Oof." Then another and another as his attacker let loose with a flurry of blows that ought to have broken every rib he had. Burton was impressed. Most men would have been falling over their own feet under such punishment.

Madam Lang smacked the intruder's head with her cane. "Young man, you will cease this behavior this minute." Her tone was the very one Burton's mother used when her children had gone too far. It had the same effect, ending the game immediately.

"Aunt He Xiao! He attacked me first. After sending the foreigner after me!" The young man sounded whiney, even to himself and he readjusted his tone, bowing slightly to Madam Lang. "I'm incognito, I admit it, but he of all people should have recognized me."

"Cousin, your hood hid your face. I didn't recognize you until after I'd disabled you." Yi Xiao brushed himself off, gesture resembling a cat cleaning himself after a clumsy tumble. "And our guest didn't attack you."

Burton almost spoke up, but a sharp glance from Madam Lang stopped him. The old lady was a fearsome figure. If she'd been a man, she'd be Emperor. Instead of arguing, he stepped back and let her do her work.

"Daughter. Take the Captain back to his room. I shall handle these two miscreants." When the stranger looked offended, she added, "You broke into my garden and started a fight with my guest. Do not dare pretend you have no responsibility for what happened."

Burton raised a hand. "Madam Lang, does this have to do with my upcoming trip, and my cargo?" When the old woman raised a brow, he added, "If so, I have some part in this matter. Besides, your nephew did nearly break my back throwing me over his shoulder."

After several long seconds of careful thought, Madam Lang said, "It isn't fair to set you a task that might turn dangerous. Ignorance may be bliss, but it is an unaffordable pleasure right now."

Returning her attention to the others, the old lady ordered, "Come with me. Explanations are in order." Then, without bothering to make sure she was obeyed, she walked away, cane thumping on the floor softly as she went.

ooo

Yi Xiao walked beside his cousin, deliberately aping the other man's stately mannerisms. Zhu Zhu always was a trifle full of himself even when they'd been children. Back then, Zhu Zhu hadn't realized just how much of Yi Xiao's imitation was mild mockery. Now, he was deeply annoyed.

"Stop teasing your cousin," Grandmother Lang said sharply. "I don't need to look to know you are. You always do."

Knowing he'd been pinned to the wall and hung up to dry, Yi Xiao simply said, "Yes, Ma'am. Sorry, Zhu Zhu." He sneaked a look at his cousin and was surprised and pleased by a momentary look of glee turned his way. So Zhu Zhu had learned a little bit of humor after all. Not enough to make him any less stiff and self-important, but a little.

To Yi Xiao's surprise, his grandmother didn't take them to her office. Instead she led them downstairs into the practice room. His cousin was equally surprised, asking, "Auntie, are we to duel to settle our differences?"

It was a fair question; she'd had them do so before, after all. But now Yi Xiao was a priest of the Wind and Rain and his cousin was practically untouchable. Yi Xiao meant it when he'd said he hadn't realized who Zhu Zhu was until after he'd struck. Once he'd recognized his cousin all he could do was evade. Which, fortunately, was one of the first things his master back in Heng Shan had taught him. Zhu Zhu's martial arts had improved immensely since they'd last met.

"Not at all." Grandmother Lang took the only seat in the room and gestured for everyone else to come closer. "I want privacy and this is the most secure room in the house. After all, we practice our secret technique here."

Burton coughed. "Err. Secret technique?"

Zhu Zhu looked disdainful and tightened his lips while Yi Xiao looked away innocently. He wasn't sure his grandmother was right to bring this outsider into their business but he certainly wasn't going to be the one to explain the secrets of the martial world.

To his deep surprise, however, Grandmother Lang told the man, "Our family practices a martial art called Blade of the White Wolf. As one of the leading families of the *jianghu*, it's our duty to use what we learn here to guide and protect our country."

A confused expression crossed Burton's face. "Leading families of the rivers and lakes? I don't understand."

It took Yi Xiao a moment to realize the trouble. "The word *jianghu* translates literally to rivers and lakes, but it's an idiom meaning the martial world. There are families, clans and societies who train their members to fight or use other techniques." He had a feeling—based on what second mama had taught him—that Burton either wouldn't understand or would scoff at those skills. Given they didn't have time to explain, it was easier to just gloss over the whole thing.

When it looked like Burton was going to press for more, Zhu Zhu interrupted. "Foreigner, you're allowed to be here only because Imperial Princess He Xiao says so. May I suggest you shut your mouth and use your ears to actually learn something?"

The Captain turned a quick look Grandmother Lang's way. "Imperial Princess? Impressive. I figured you were important, but not that important. Are you the Emperor's sister, then?"

Before Zhu Zhu could show his anger at Burton's lack of manners, Grandmother Lang told the man, "I am a great deal too old for that. I am his father's sister." She made a gesture at Zhu Zhu, adding, "Allow me to handle the situation, nephew. I would much rather know what you are doing here, rather than heading for Beijing. Even if you have been irresponsible enough to spend your days carousing in brothels and wandering the cities incognito, you cannot be so blind to your duty as to remain away while your father lies gravely ill."

Zhu Zhu flushed bright red. "I had more purpose to my wandering than carousing," he said softly. "And I've been trying to get home, I swear it. My enemies have blocked my path at every turn."

As if to prove Zhu Zhu's point, a servant came running into the room. "Madam Lang! Madam Lang! General Hwei is in the main hall. He demands your presence!"

The news didn't surprise Grandmother Lang. Her lips tightened as she told the servant, "Provide the General with tea. Tell him he must be patient with an old woman woken suddenly from sleep. It may take me some time to grant him the audience he desires."

Once the servant had run off, Grandmother Lang turned to Zhu Zhu. "We must act fast and you must do as I say, without hesitation or argument." Seeing Zhu Zhu about to do that very thing, she tapped him on the nose with her index finger. "If you would reach your father before he dies, you must obey me."

Unwillingly, Zhu Zhu inclined his head. "What do I do?"

"Let your hair hang loose. It's fortunate you haven't had time to properly shave your scalp. Also, remove your robes."

That nearly made Zhu Zhu rebel, but Yi Xiao interrupted. "And I cut my forelocks and give him my clothes?" Now he understood the plan and the part he was to play.

"Good boy. Yes." Madam Lang turned to Captain Burton. "You've guessed?"

"I think so. He's the heir, Prince Yi Zhu, isn't he? And this General Hwei wants to keep him from reaching the Emperor before he dies."

Yi Xiao ignored the discussion, preparing himself for his rôle. With only the slightest regret, he began hacking his forelocks down as short as he could. There wasn't time to shave, but it didn't matter. The enemy would think his cousin was trying to disguise himself as a Han.

"I don't understand," Zhu Zhu muttered, untying his braid and spreading his hair down his shoulders. "What is she up to?"

Yi Xiao grinned, taking off his robe. "It's simple. You're running away to sea." As his cousin stared at him in outraged disbelief, he added, "Or, rather, I am for you."

Zhu Zhu's glare was immediately distracted by the sight of Yi Xiao's naked shoulders. The mark of the storm, painful proof of his training, forked its way along his arm and torso. He pointed. "You…"

"Don't you remember I was training on Heng Shan?"

"You never said you were training with the Storm Hermit."

Most people didn't try to learn from the Storm Hermit. It took a great deal of courage to approach her lightning guarded fastness. Yi Xiao, whose courage often masqueraded as foolhardy overconfidence, had been among the few to reach her and the even fewer to convince her to let him learn.

"Now I know why you didn't dare strike me."

"Other than the fact that one doesn't strike the heir?"

"As if that's ever stopped you before."

"It does now and not just because I could kill you," Yi Xiao retorted, sliding into his cousin's robe and pulling the hood over his head. He turned to Grandmother Lang. "Madam…" His voice choked with emotion.

"Be well. Be safe. You have our blessings. Seek our old friend Chang when you reach San Francisco." The old woman handed Yi Xiao a pack, then set a hand in blessing on his head. "Go. General Hwei surely has men watching out for your cousin and you must lead them astray."

ooo

It took Burton embarrassingly long to work out the plan. In his defense, he was a foreigner, a mere ship's Captain, with no contacts among the high and mighty of Chinese society. Yet the situation was now painfully obvious. Even knowing as little as he did about Chinese politics he could guess the First Prince was in danger. Wandering around anonymously, he'd stayed away too long, giving his enemies time to take advantage of their Emperor's weakness. If Yi Zhu couldn't get back to court before his father died, he'd lose both throne and life.

It only took a few minutes to get to the other end of the passage beneath the Lang family's house. Dimly lit by Yi Xiao's lamp, there was something unnerving about the shadows and shifting breeze as it drifted past Burton's face. When they climbed a narrow set of steps into a small cemetery and a dozen bats dove past them, Burton came inches from telling Yi Xiao just what the boy could do with the pretty and valuable jade amulet Madam Lang had paid for his passage.

Fortunately for Burton's future bank account, Yi Xiao said sympathetically, "You don't have to take me if you're better off not accepting this job. I'll think no less of you if you tell me to find another way to reach America. Nor will I mind if you keep Grandmother's amulet. You didn't sign up for Chinese politics."

There were plenty of things Burton hadn't signed up for. However, "I accepted payment and agreed to the terms. Jake Burton keeps his word without needing it written down."

A quick, relieved, smile crossed Yi Xiao's face. The kid had been worried and rightly so. He was in a world of trouble by no fault of his own. None of this was fair. Yi Xiao hadn't done anything—aside from strongly resemble his cousin—to be forced into self-exile.

When Burton expressed sympathy, Yi Xiao shrugged it off. "I obey my family's needs. Besides, I can seek the *Dao* wherever I go."

Although Burton didn't understand at all, the question of what *Dao* was and why it mattered had to wait. The youngster strode along the middle of the road, making no effort to sneak around. He could have been a wanderer seeking a place to sleep or a messenger with no time to waste. Yi Zhu's enemies, however, knew what they were looking for.

Several dozen men stepped out of the shadows just as they neared the entrance to Old Town. Most wore the simple dark-blue uniforms of Chinese foot-soldiers; short tunics with a single character on them and trousers stuffed into padded boots. Armed with short spears, their grim expressions told Burton they weren't looking for a dance.

Yi Xiao paused as a broad shouldered man of medium height sauntered into sight. He had hard, grim, features, with a greying mustache and equally greying queue beneath an elegant black cap. His dark robes were the sort Burton had seen high-level officials wear, with a heavily embroidered square at the chest. Burton didn't know what the symbol meant but he knew this man was trouble. Big trouble.

The man sneered at the sight of them, stalking forward silently. "The General and I have been looking for you for quite some time, your Highness," he said in Chinese. "And here I find you consorting with foreign devils? Really, Yi Zhu, it's men like him who shamed your father."

"Hey. Don't blame me for the Brits," Burton snapped. He didn't know if the man spoke English but he couldn't help interrupting.

Both men ignored him, busy circling each other while the soldiers gathered round. While Burton tried to work out the best path for their escape, Yi Xiao said, in perfect imitation of his cousin's haughty tones, "Your master's failure to protect our waterways allowed the British to shame us, Colonel Tsang."

"What he said," Burton added, stepping closer to one of the guards. Immediately the man's spear sliced downwards, blocking his path. "Hey, careful. Those things are sharp."

Meanwhile, Tsang was growling furiously, cursing and threatening to feed his enemy his entrails. "If I could see you face the death of a thousand cuts, I would, you turtle dung!" At the same time he raised his hands, crooking his fingers in a strange gesture. Burton blinked, almost certain a flicker of purple fire crackled around the man's gauntlets.

"Didn't Colonel Bianshi try that last year? The youngest son of the Langs removed his head for him." Yi Xiao took a step backwards, so he was close to Burton. In English he said, "Don't interfere. Get me to the ship after he's gone."

Burton didn't understand, but agreed. Yi Xiao had some plan up his sleeve it seemed. All Burton could do was go along with it. Even if he had his pistol the best he could do was injure the enemy. A bullet might make it through the man's armor but it wouldn't do much damage. Nor could Burton fight so many people. Not even with the impressively skilled Yi Xiao there to help.

ooo

Colonel Tsang was stronger than he'd been the one time Yi Xiao had watched him fight. A follower of the Black Thunder sect, the Colonel transformed his inner energies to a particularly virulent form of negative *qi*. It was one step short of black magic and despised by most inhabitants of the martial world. Sadly, it was not yet illegal.

"Dare you raise your hand to me?" Yi Xiao demanded, keeping his voice deep. The Colonel had yet to realize he was attacking the wrong man and he needed to keep it that way. If Tsang, and thus his master Hwei, could be persuaded that he'd murdered the Prince he wouldn't go after the Yi Xiao traveling to Beijing with Grandmother Lang.

"Why not? You're a vagabond. A poorly dressed madman who attacked me in the streets." Colonel Tsang smiled at Yi Xiao's wide-eyed expression, "Yes, you fool. You thought your disguise amusing, no doubt. Thought its anonymity would protect you. But it also means no one will know you when you die. I'll leave you in the dirt for the scavengers."

Before Yi Xiao could open his mouth to argue, Tsang struck, hands covered with the dark energies of his *qi*. It seared through Yi Xiao, intensely cold and intensely painful. If he hadn't spent the last two years learning to redirect the Storm Hermit's lightning, he'd have been knocked unconscious in seconds.

Grounding the energies, Yi Xiao let loose a scream that probably woke the entire neighborhood. Not that anyone would be fool enough to try and find out what was going on. Those outside the martial world generally knew better than to poke their noses into it.

"Hah! Your skill is weak as ever!" Colonel Tsang didn't waste time gloating. He caught Yi Xiao's face by the jaw, sending his dark *qi* into his victim's body with furious glee. He didn't notice the same energy dissipating into the ground, redirected there by Yi Xiao's less visible aura.

Even partially defended, Yi Xiao was in agony. He'd experienced worse but not by much. Still, it was almost time to implement the next stage of his plan. He'd have to make it look good. Tsang wasn't a fool and if he noticed anything wrong about his victim's 'death' he'd surely realize how he'd been tricked.

Yi Xiao struggled to break free, grabbing at his attacker's wrist and kicking. He tried to wrap his legs around his enemy's torso, as if to take him down that way, only to find himself slammed down onto his back. Burton shouted incoherently and he was desperately glad the American didn't forget himself and use Yi Xiao's real name.

Help, unwanted and unneeded, came from another direction. Gasping, throat burning, lungs bursting, Yi Xiao barely heard the sound like a thousand arrows slicing the air. A willow leaf sabre struck the ground inches from his left hand, its curved surface engraved with ancient characters.

Yi Xiao ignored the blade in favor of trying to escape his attacker. Not because he wanted to but because that was what was expected of him. Except a moment later he was free, sprawled across the cobblestones, choking and wheezing as a white-clad figure whirled around the Colonel.

Blinking, he stared at the stranger, watching her long dark hair float on the breeze, entwined with robes of the finest opalescent silk, her face hidden by an equally diaphanous veil. "Take your sabre," she ordered, keeping Colonel Tsang's dark aura from touching her with a delicate gesture. It wasn't as easy as she made it look. Her lips were tight, her jaw clenched against the pain. "Defend yourself!"

The sabre was, indeed, Yi Xiao's; the one he'd left buried in a stone on the highest peak of Heng Shan. He wanted to demand how she'd found it, how she'd managed to get it free and, more importantly, why she'd brought it back to the man who didn't want it.

" A WILLOW LEAF SABRE STRUCK THE GROUND... "

That would mean admitting he wasn't who he pretended to be. Right that moment he didn't dare.

"My sabre?" he croaked, watching her fight with a blade as slim and shining as she was. Elegant sweeps and strikes sent Colonel Tsang's attacks flying harmlessly away. She was good, though not quite as good as he'd been. "It's not my sabre."

"Of course it's your sabre. Whose else would it be?" Tsang got a strike in during her moment of distraction, sending her flying.

Yi Xiao rose to his feet. "It looks like... Yi Xiao's... sabre. But... he's given... it up." He hoped she'd believe him. He didn't have time to deal with whatever troubles she brought with her.

The woman dodged the Colonel's next blow, but she was starting to tire. Redirecting power like Tsang's took mental strength. "Given it up? Nonsense!"

Once again Tsang slammed his open palm into the woman's shoulder. "Fool girl," he growled. "Don't interfere in my business!" She fell, landing in a heap and struggling to rise. It was obvious from the blood staining her shoulder she could not. Black energy bubbled around the injury, stinking of decay and death.

"Burton, take care of her," Yi Xiao called out. He had to deal with Tsang and get the girl to safety quickly. Injured as she was, she didn't have much time before Tsang's poisonous *qi* killed her. Regretfully, Yi Xiao took his sabre. "Master says, when life is endangered, do what must be done," he reminded himself. Then he loosed a series of slashing cuts that forced Tsang backwards.

"White Wolf style, Yi Zhu? It won't save you. You can't have mastered it." The Colonel's dark aura sparked with purple shafts of lightning that Yi Xiao parried and redirected easily.

"Miss? Miss, are you all right?"

Knowing the girl couldn't last long, Yi Xiao began the elaborate pattern of strikes characteristic of the White Wolf Blade. Created by an illustrious ancestress, they required both speed and agility to perfect. Yi Xiao had abandoned the style in favor of his master's, but the skills he'd learned had not faded.

At the same time, Tsang drew his dark aura together, entire body crackling with black-tinted lightning. He was as good as Yi Xiao, certainly as fast, and the power he'd gathered would obliterate the *qi* of any living thing it touched. It was a race now. Yi Xiao couldn't attack and defend at the same time, but neither could Colonel Tsang.

Fortune, more than anything else, was on Yi Xiao's side. He flung himself forward, blade flashing as he struck, and reached Tsang just seconds before the Colonel could unleash his full power. Without hesitation he thrust his sabre deep, driving it into the man's belly and up into his heart.

ooo

The fight left Burton near speechless. He'd heard rumors of strange powers and magics, but he'd never seen such fireworks close up. Nor had he seen bloodlust like Yi Xiao's before and he hoped never to see it again. It almost made him run from the whole mess. Only the girl, lips covered in froth and body shuddering as the poison worked through her system, kept him where he was. She was so young and helpless, a mere child in desperate straits.

Knowing Colonel Tsang's death would bring more trouble; Burton hoisted the girl in his arms and shouted to Yi Xiao, "We have to get out of here!" He just hoped he wasn't carrying a corpse who hadn't realized she was dead yet.

"We will," Yi Xiao agreed, pulling his weapon from his victim's chest and cleaned it on

Tsang's robe. Turning, he glared at his enemy's soldiers. "You know who I am?"

They were staring, stunned and terrified by the look in the man's eyes. Not that Burton blamed them. They could easily be Yi Xiao's next victims. They dropped to their knees and began to kowtow. "Please, your Highness. Forgive us! He was our commander. We were bound to obey!"

"Go to Madam Lang and surrender yourselves to her. Tell her what happened and what I told you. Assist her return to Beijing safely and your sins may be forgiven." The order sent the soldiers scurrying off rapidly.

Yi Xiao snatched up the girl's sword and headed the other way, not bothering to make sure Burton followed. "Bring her along. I'll see to her injuries aboard ship. Can we leave immediately?"

"I think so. If the winds are with us, at least." Burton didn't like rushing off so quickly but he could tell this mess was going to spill onto him and his ship if he stayed. "By noon, I hope."

"The wind will be with us. I promise." Yi Xiao's expression, usually flighty and mischievous, was as stern and commanding as his Imperial cousin's. "Colonel Tsang is not the only one whose *qi* commands the elements."

"What was all that about, anyway? I've never seen anything like it."

Yi Xiao's old mischief returned in his voice. "If you ride the rivers and lakes you'll see it all the time. Would you like to learn?"

Burton thought about it. Thought about his ship and the nice, simple, life he led. Then, without hesitation, he said, "No. Not at all. I have better things to do than swinging a sword or turning people into lightning rods."

With a laugh, Yi Xiao said, "To tell the truth, Captain Burton. So do I." His expression turned distant as they headed towards the *Henrietta Marie*. "Master says, a true disciple of the *Dao* can find balance no matter where they are. Perhaps, if I'm fortunate, I will find it in America as readily as I would have found it here."

Chapter 2: Water –
Continuing towards Greater Order

It took days for Gan Han to realize she was at sea. Dazed and in pain as she was, it was about all she could do to keep from crying. A warrior of the Hua did not cry. The heir to the family's Lotus Blossom technique most especially did not cry. She refused to admit she was crying.

Her healer didn't help her mood. His utter refusal to admit to being Yi Xiao was bad enough. His cheery sense of humor only made her angry. The fact that he'd rescued her from a fight she probably shouldn't have joined was embarrassing. His calm disregard for her modesty as he healed her was humiliating. If she could have risen from her bunk and cut him down, she would have.

As the pain from her injury finally subsided and Gan Han realized where she was, she came the closest she'd come to panicking in her life. When her healer entered the tiny and horribly dark room, she attacked immediately. "Where have you taken me, you bastard?"

The man caught her arm and forced her back into her bed without effort. "Now, now. You're not strong enough for such nonsense."

"Answer me, Yi Xiao!"

"I'm just an itinerant priest," he said, checking her pulse. "Nobody important. Why do you want this Yi Xiao, anyway? Did he run away from marrying you? Silly of him if he did; you're far too pretty to leave behind, even with that scar."

Gan Han traced the twisted knot of flesh that marked her from cheekbone to chin. Then she slapped the man as hard as she was able. It was too dark to see much, but she knew it wasn't nearly hard enough, leaving barely a mark on his cheek. "How dare you insult me?"

"No, really, it's no insult," he insisted. "That scar healed well and the rest of your face is quite attractive."

The flattery made Gan Han nervous and she grabbed her coverlet, pulling it up over herself. It was pointless modesty. He'd surely seen far more of her than any man but a husband had a right to. Admittedly, it'd been to save her life, but that didn't make it any less embarrassing.

To her great relief, Yi Xiao didn't press the point. Instead, he set a bundle of cloth on the end of her bunk. "Having healed you, I now prescribe sunlight and fresh sea air. Both of which, I note, we have in abundance. You'll want to dress warmly. Even in full daylight, the wind is strong and cold out there. You can use that stick if you need something to lean on. Be careful coming outside. Captain Burton claims the sea is mild and pleasant at the moment. An inexperienced sea traveler, however, might not agree."

With that, the idiot left the room.

OOO

Sea travel was unexpectedly pleasant. Yi Xiao hadn't admitted it before, but he'd been a little worried. He'd heard travelers' stories about sea-sickness and difficulty walking. Perhaps it was his training, tied as it was to wind and storm that gave him the advantage.

Having done what he could for the young lady—whose name he still didn't know—Yi Xiao joined Captain Burton at the rear of the *Henrietta Marie*. The sun was warm against his back, the scent of the sea air was a heady mix of salt and fish and the cool wind ruffled his now collar-length hair.

"I thought you said you were going to convince her to come out?" Captain Burton asked. He was dressed much like Yi Xiao right then; a light linen shirt and trousers and a kerchief to protect his head from the sunlight. It was odd clothing to Yi Xiao, but it meant he fit in. Captain Burton's crew was a motley bunch from all corners of the globe. A Chinese sailor dressed in European clothes didn't stand out at all.

Yi Xiao leaned over the railing to see if the young lady was there yet. "I'm not sure she will," he admitted. "She doesn't seem to like me much."

"She doesn't trust you, you mean. Not that I blame her."

Since no one could blame someone in their guest's circumstances for distrusting a chancy fellow like Yi Xiao, he didn't argue. Of course, that was the way Yi Xiao preferred it. She was, as he'd said, attractive enough, but he didn't need the distraction. She was a problem and not just because he'd had to detoxify Colonel Tsang's dark aura from her system. The fact that she'd been looking for him made things even more awkward.

"I just wish I knew what she wanted of me."

"Is she your fiancée?" Burton held up his left ring finger for some reason. "Your people have arranged marriages, right?"

Yi Xiao was almost certain she wasn't. "My grandmother is autocratic and given to making decisions about our lives without consulting us. But she generally tells us her intentions, once she'd made up her mind."

"Perhaps you met her before and made her think you'd marry her?"

Now that was ridiculous. "That girl is barely fifteen. A mere child. She shouldn't even be out on her own—daughter of the martial world or no." He didn't mention he'd chosen to enter that world at fourteen, excited by the danger and eager to prove his skill against all comers.

"Juliet Capulet was thirteen, you know." Burton grinned, adding, "That's Shakespeare, in case your second mother never taught it to you."

"Mama Grace is English, I'll remind you. And Romeo and Juliet was set in Italy, at a time when such things were common," Yi Xiao pointed out dryly. "I admit, Grandmother did marry at fifteen, but that was because she wouldn't stop pestering her father." Grandmother Lang had loved her husband from the first, even after her father-in-law, the traitor Heshen, had been forced to commit suicide. It was her devotion and stubborn will that had saved the family from disgrace. That and the fact that she'd terrified her brother, the Jiaqing Emperor.

Burton chuckled. "I admit, if a lady like your grandmother wants something it'd take a pretty strong will to deny her." He returned his attention to the question at hand. "What about that sword she tried to give you? Is that what your grandmother meant by willow leaf knife?"

Yi Xiao sighed at the memory. He'd a feeling he wasn't going to be forgiven for leaving his weapon behind anytime soon. "It's a sabre, not a sword, but yes."

The distinction puzzled Burton immensely. "I don't understand."

"Swords like the one the young lady carries are called *jian*. They're two-edged and are considered weapons for elite warriors. My weapon, being single-edged, is a *dao* and is more common; a soldier's weapon."

"Oh. I see. Like a cavalry sword, back home?"

"I'm not sure. I've never seen western swords." Yi Xiao set aside his curiosity regretfully. He was not yet far enough along his path to think about such things. "Not that it matters."

"Your patient may disagree on that subject," Burton offered wryly. "Speaking of whom…" He pointed at the young woman stumbling out into the light.

Yi Xiao somersaulted over the railing and landed beside her. Dressed now in clothing much like his own, wrapped in a warm jacket and clutching her stick in a desperate attempt to stay upright, she looked a little like a street beggar. Her hair was a tangled mess and her eyes showed a mix of fear and anger. "You could have waited for me."

"I thought you'd prefer to dress alone."

"Why? You've seen it all." Her tone was sharp and bitter. The voice of one who wanted to believe she didn't care.

"I haven't, though. Just your shoulder. Hardly enough to mention." Yi Xiao helped her to the railing and pointed towards the horizon. "If you feel seasick, look out as far as you can. It'll help."

Annoyed, the girl snapped, "I was born on a boat, you bastard. I don't get seasick."

"I see." Yi Xiao considered the information, trying to think where he'd met her and what he'd done to set her after him. Realizing he still didn't know who she was, he asked, "So, what's your name? Unless I'm seriously mistaken, we haven't been introduced."

"I am Xihua Gan Han. We may not have met, but you surely know my name, Yi Xiao."

The family, at least, was familiar. "While I don't recognize you at all, I have to guess you're a member of the Death Flower clan?" Gan Han could be written as steel lotus, and the Death Flowers all went by such names.

Fury flickered in the back of Gan Han's eyes and she tried to take a step towards him, only to trip and nearly fall. He caught her and helped her grasp the railing. "How dare you not know me? Your name is flung in my face everywhere I turn. Yi Xiao's skill is the deftest. Yi Xiao's arm is the strongest. Yi Xiao's blade is the fastest."

It was an old and familiar song. Once a weapons master gained a reputation every other warrior in the martial world wanted to test themselves against it. Once, and not too long ago, Yi Xiao would have admired Gan Han's dedication. Now all he felt was despair. How was he to leave his past behind when it kept following him?

Calmly, or as calmly as he could, he pointed out, "Yi Xiao hasn't been in the martial world for two years, Lady Gan Han. I doubt he was nearly so great a warrior as to overshadow all who followed him."

She sneered. "Tell that to my mother. To my sisters. They saw you fight, saw you defeat the assassin attacking the Emperor's son just last year. Don't tell me you left the martial world two years ago when the truth is obviously not in you."

Yi Xiao hadn't forgotten the incident but he hated to remember it. His cousin had come looking for him, wanting Yi Xiao to join him on his wanderings. Exhausted and dejected by his lack of progress, Yi Xiao had gone with Yi Zhu to the nearby city of Hunyuan. Things hadn't gone well and Yi Xiao had been forced to kill his cousin's would-be murderer.

"Yi Xiao's actions were shameful," he told the woman grimly. "If he killed a man, even in the Prince's defense, he displayed a deplorable lack of self-control." Just as he had a week earlier, fighting Colonel Tsang. The worst of it was just how much he'd enjoyed the killing. "The martial world is a place of violence and greed. Yi Xiao is better out of it."

The statement clearly infuriated Gan Han. She slapped Yi Xiao, her blow still too weak to so much as mark him. "If that's how Yi Xiao thinks, then you're right. He doesn't deserve the name he made for himself. Fight me. I will prove my blade the strongest and send you on your way."

Yi Xiao raised a brow. He'd seen her skill back in Shanghai and while she was good, she wasn't good enough. Even without his sabre he was still the better fighter. Besides, "I am a mere wanderer, with no title except would-be priest. When this ship reaches San Diego, I will be leaving it and you, to go my own way. I suggest you take your pride and your desire for supremacy back to the martial world where it belongs and leave me to my own destiny."

He could feel her hot eyes on him as he walked away.

OOO

If Gan Han hadn't been so weak she would have argued the point with Yi Xiao long after he'd chose to ignore her. The damage the Black Thunder warrior had done her made it impossible. Even with the poison purified from her system, her physical strength wasn't up to the effort.

She tried exercising her way back to full health, exhausting herself in the process. Yi Xiao protested she wouldn't recover from her injuries any faster, but she refused to listen. The Captain—an annoying Westerner with a constantly moving mouth—tried to block her chosen exercise floor. The sailors, a mixed-bag of men from dozens of seaports, kept getting in her way. None of this stopped her.

It was Gan Han's own body that forced her to accept her limitations. One morning after a particularly difficult exercise, she found herself barely able to crawl out of her bed. Not even massage or sitting in the sun in the only quiet spot aboard ship made her feel any better.

Unable to exercise, she sat at the bow of the ship, enjoying the breeze despite herself. She even controlled her urge to growl when Captain Burton came up beside her with a pot of tea. "Now this better," he said in horribly accented Chinese. "You sit. Rest."

"You degrade our language just by setting it on your lips," she muttered, though she did take the tea. It wasn't very good. Of course, it was probably the low quality leaf they only sold to foreigners.

"If speak English, will be glad to criticize back," Burton retorted. Given she'd already told him she'd never learned his barbaric language and had no desire to do so; she ignored the suggestion, sipping her tea in grim silence.

At last Burton asked, "Why sad?"

"I'm not sad, you foolish Westerner. I'm angry. You and that idiot Yi Xiao practically kidnapped me. Now I won't see China again for weeks!" She corrected herself, remembering what she'd been told. "No, months."

"True, yes." Burton leaned against the railing, watching her thoughtfully. "And sorry for that. But we had to leave. He in danger. Enemies of state. He stay, he die. And you injured. Dying. Needed his help." The Captain looked thoughtfully towards the thing they called a crow's nest, where Yi Xiao sat, pretending to 'cultivate' himself. The damned fool couldn't even find a better lie to explain his cowardice. The mystic mumbo jumbo of the mountain sages was mere nonsense.

Everything Burton was telling her they'd told her before. Some of it might even be true. Gan Han's mother had said the young warrior resembled the Prince greatly. She'd even heard rumors that Yi Xiao was really the Prince's twin brother. He was born in the same place on the same day, after all. A twin to the Emperor's heir could only bring trouble to everyone around him.

"Stupid man," she muttered. "All he has to do is admit the truth and fight me."

"He fight you now, you die. Like Colonel Tsang."

"Who?"

"You not know who you fight, back Shanghai?" Burton shook his head at her ignorance. "Man who hurt you. He kill him. Still upset about."

The stupid man's lack of a spine was hardly Gan Han's problem. She waved off the implied criticism. "Why do you care, anyway? Don't you have something to be doing? A leak to stop? A sail to mend?"

"Could show you how," the Captain offered. "Would be something to do."

"I'd rather swim home." Noticing a faint dot on the horizon, she added, "Or you could find me a boat at that island up ahead." Not that she would have left. She couldn't go home until she'd defeated that idiot Yi Xiao.

"Island?" Captain Burton spun around, staring in the direction she'd indicated. Then, shouting something in English, he ran back to the mast, clambering up like the monkey he was.

Disinterested in whatever it was that'd upset the Captain, Gan Han sat back and sipped her tea, trying to think of some way she could get her desperately needed exercise again.

ooo

Captain Burton's sudden appearance in the crow's nest barely drew Yi Xiao's attention. He was having more trouble than usual calming his mind. It wasn't his destination bothering him, nor the reason for it. He'd already accepted the necessity and come to terms with it.

What he hadn't come to terms with was his own nature. He could lie to everyone else; tell them he was a man of peace, a follower of the *Dao*, seeking a balanced state of being. But he knew in his heart that his deep desire for those things was at odds with his love of danger and trouble. He'd liked fighting Colonel Tsang and had welcomed the excuse of Gan Han's condition to kill the man. Even now, several weeks after the fight, the memory of his blade sliding smoothly into Tsang's heart sang through his thoughts.

It sat ill with him, a bitter knowledge that the thing he'd tried so hard to erase from his heart simply would not leave him. How many would have to die before he gained control of his wolfish love of killing? "Master says, the heart feels as it must, but the brain and body need not follow."

"What the hell are you talking about? I said, why didn't you tell me about that island out there!?"

The Captain's demand finally got Yi Xiao's attention and he raised his eyes to the man. "Oh, that? It's been there for a little while now."

"And you didn't think to tell me?" Burton looked ready to shake him. "Damnit man…"

Standing, Yi Xiao peered at the faint dark mound in the distance. "Well, you said to watch for sails and ships, not islands."

"That's because there is no island out here!" Burton flung his hand at the sea in a broad gesture. Yi Xiao evaded easily, still eying the thing in the distance. "None!"

"Now that's just foolishness. It's quite obviously there…" Yi Xiao's answer trailed off as he took in Burton's meaning. "Oh. You mean it isn't on any of the charts?"

With an exasperated snort, Burton told him, "No. No, it is not. Which means we're off course! But how can we be off course? I checked it just an hour ago."

There was no pretending Yi Xiao understood the intricacies of naval navigation. "Could it be something other than an island? Some debris?"

Burton was already peering through his telescope so Yi Xiao waited and watched. Something moved at the edge of the horizon, a faint darkness rising above the shadowy mound. "Is that a ship?" he asked, pointing off to the side. If it was, it was in trouble, leaning sideways in the water.

"It is, damnit." Burton leaned over the edge of the crow's nest. "Ship ahoy. It's sinking! Twenty degrees starboard, now!"

It wasn't hard to guess what they were doing. Yi Xiao didn't know much about sea travel but it made sense that ships finding others in trouble would go to help. The one question he had was, "What about that island?"

"It looks a bit like a volcano, but I couldn't see any lava," Burton told him, keeping watch. "Don't know what's going on with it, but I'd bet my last dollar it has something to do with why that ship's in trouble. Wouldn't be the first time a volcano popped up out of nowhere to ruin some poor crew's day."

The description seemed inadequate, but Yi Xiao didn't argue. The *Henrietta Marie* was getting closer, so he could see the other ship's state without a telescope. Masts broken, sails rent, railing shattered, things were probably worse below decks. There was someone clinging to the only remaining mast, waving their free arm wildly.

"All hands!" Captain Burton roared. "We have a rescue!"

ooo

Ordinarily Burton's shouting wouldn't have drawn Gan Han's interest. She didn't like the man and would have happily ignored him. The fact the ship immediately changed course made her sit up and take notice. She looked around and spotted an odd shoal of sand surrounding an island that appeared to be formed of pure mud. Off to the side was another ship, this one smaller and lighter than Captain Burton's. It was better armed, too, with light cannons sticking out from every port.

Gan Han realized they were coming to the other ship's rescue and wondered if it were wise. Burton could be sailing straight into a trap. Admittedly, the closer they got, the more obvious the ship's damaged state became. Yet even injured men could turn on those who came to help them.

If she'd liked anyone aboard ship, Gan Han might have suggested rescue was risky. As it was, she welcomed trouble, if only to work off some of her anger. She shifted her position so she could watch the other vessel, expecting problems at any moment.

Burton's crew was already assisting survivors to escape their ruined ship. It took some time and Gan Han became more and more certain she didn't like the looks of the other crew. Neither did Burton's men, she was pleased to note. At least they weren't fool enough to blindly trust seeming helplessness.

One man, a short westerner with greying blond hair and a bright gold canine tooth, searched out Burton. He was speaking in English, what little Gan Han understood barely making sense. She thought he was thanking the Captain and asking if Burton would allow him to bring a chest aboard. Burton seemed to agree and the two men returned to the damaged ship with more assistants.

"It seems we're due some company," Yi Xiao said behind Gan Han, startling her into striking out at him. As usual, he wormed out of the way before she could touch him, so all she did was brush a bit of dirt from his shoulder. "Now, don't be that way."

"Don't sneak up on me, Yi Xiao!"

"I'm just a wanderer."

"I refuse to call you anything of the sort."

"Pity. I'm certainly not going to be anything else." Yi Xiao leaned against the railing, watching as the men dragged a heavily padlocked chest onto Burton's deck. "I wonder what's in the box. Gold? Tea? I hope not opium."

Westerners were always selling opium in China, causing more trouble with a few pounds of the drug than any thief or rebel. Gan Han refused to comment on it, saying only, "Why don't you ask?"

"I think I will...," Yi Xiao started to say, then paused, cocking his ear towards the ship. "Did you hear that?"

"Hear what?"

"Listen first," Yi Xiao said with annoying patience. When she shrugged, he added, "Someone shouted."

Again Gan Han shrugged. "So?"

"So there's still someone aboard."

It hardly mattered to her. "Maybe he's too injured to help and they left him there. Why do you care?" She was startled to see his concern. She was about to reach out to stop him but he was already over the edge of the ship and swimming for the damaged vessel. Within seconds he'd disappeared into the hole in its side, while Gan Han shrieked his name.

Burton, who'd been busy discussing something with the other ship's captain, raised his head. When he realized what Yi Xiao had done, he sighed and once again crossed over, yelling something incoherent as he went. Gan Han followed close behind. She wasn't going to be left out of the fun any longer.

∘∘∘

The wreckage made it easier for Yi Xiao to board the other ship; the *Southern Cross*, or so the nameplate said. Broken spars gave him something to grasp and climb and the gash in the ship's side gave him an entrance. Luckily the ship had listed the other way. She would have sunk already otherwise.

There was a sound somewhere in the darkness of the hold. Weaker than before, it was the same desperate cry Yi Xiao had heard earlier. Likely its owner had little time left. Possibly Yi Xiao was already too late. He slid into wreckage filled water, struggling through the mess and feeling his way with his bare feet. Accustomed to the sharpened rocks of Heng Shan's peaks, he found the effort strangely familiar.

Again someone called and Yi Xiao called back, "I hear you. I'm coming." He spoke in Chinese, then English, hoping his tone would calm the trapped victim even if they didn't understand him.

"Damnit, Yi Xiao. Do you have an ounce of sense in that head of yours?" Burton's voice came from the deck above, where the man was peering through one of the cracks.

"He can call you Yi Xiao. Why won't you let me?" Gan Han demanded through another crack.

Yi Xiao sighed. "Master says, if you cannot keep your balance when the world is flailing, you have not found the *Dao*." Before either of his undesired audience could respond, he added, "There's someone in here. Find a rope and help me get them out."

Gan Han didn't move from her spot, contenting herself with insults to Yi Xiao's personality, his appearance and his courage. When she started in on his parents, however, he drew a line. "You may insult me as much and as often as you like. Insult my family and you insult my ancestors. I think you know what an offense that is."

Although she sneered, Gan Han went silent on the matter. He was in no position to accuse her of offending the Emperor's ancestors, but she seemed to realize she'd gone too far. "You're an idiot."

"So I have been told by those around me for most of my life," Yi Xiao admitted. "Indeed, as far as I can tell, you may be right."

"Why risk your life for a foreigner who may be dying already?"

"Because he isn't dead yet." By this time Yi Xiao had found the trapped victim, a big man with broad shoulders, impressive muscles and features of such mixed ancestry no one could be sure what it consisted of. He was naked, chained to the wall, and looked as if he'd been severely beaten recently. That he'd survived this long spoke of stamina and stubborn determination. "And life is important."

"Hah!"

Ignoring her response, Yi Xiao focused his thoughts and examined the first chain, searching the metal for its weakest point. Then, drawing on his *qi*, he shattered the link with a single blow. He turned to the other chain and repeated the process.

Suddenly a rope dangled down, followed by Burton's voice. "Do you need me to come help?"

"Best not. I'll tie the rope around his waist and you can pull him up. Though you may need assistance, he looks heavy." Yi Xiao didn't mention the chain. He'd have to explain how he removed it and Burton didn't want to know more about Yi Xiao's skills than absolutely necessary.

"Right. Let me know when you're ready."

After a few deep breaths to recover himself, Yi Xiao tied a makeshift harness. "Pull him up," he called.

As the Captain tugged and strained to pull their rescue up out of the water, Yi Xiao saw the man's eyes were open, his stoic expression hiding some strong emotion. Anger? Hate?

Or was it fear?

ooo

" . . . HE'D BEEN SEVERLY BEATEN RECENTLY. "

When they dragged the last survivor of the wrecked ship over to Burton's deck, the other victims shifted uneasily. The one, the man Gan Han assumed was their Captain, said something to Burton in a worried sort of way. Whatever it was, it didn't please the American. He said something about sea law, in a tone so hard it was obvious he'd brook no argument.

Not that the other Captain didn't try. Gold tooth flashing as he tried to persuade Burton of something, he gestured broadly, voice getting a little deeper and a little angrier with every sentence. At last Burton put his foot down, ordering the rescued crew below decks. They went, but their expressions were worrisome. Trouble was brewing; it was only a matter of time.

"What was all that about?" Gan Han demanded, assisting Yi Xiao with the rescued man's injuries. Not out of sympathy but because she wanted to harangue Yi Xiao further. Having him trapped with his latest patient seemed the best time to do so.

"That man says our patient is an insane criminal being transported to Australia." Done cleaning the man's injuries, Yi Xiao opened the little bundle of tools he'd been carrying in his pack. A jar of ointment, a spool of fine silk, with a gold needle thrust into its top, scissors, a fine sharp blade and a candle. He threaded the needle, lit the candle and heated its tip. "He thinks we put everyone at risk, rescuing him."

The ship shuddered, reminding Gan Han of the strange island that'd been slowly rising from the ocean. "From the volcano?"

"I think they mean our patient."

The man lying between them didn't look like he could do much. Oh, he was huge, easily six-foot tall and solidly built. Awake and uninjured, he'd be a dangerous opponent. Right now, however, he was a mess. Cuts and bruises covered his body and his coarse black hair was partially torn from his scalp. He'd lost a fight already and was in no condition for another.

Yi Xiao set a hand to the man's face, about to pull the cut on his forehead together to sew the flap of skin shut. As he did so, a huge hand grabbed him by the throat. The other hand caught Gan Han's wrist, pulling her down towards its owner. "Sorcerer," the man growled in Chinese. "I'll kill you if you lay your spells on me."

Gan Han slid her hand free and punched the man's shoulder, striking the center of one of his larger cuts. "Touch me again, I slit your throat," she snapped in turn. She wasn't going to put up with another damned idiot making a fool of himself. Before he could grab her, she somersaulted backwards. Instead of landing on her feet as she ought to have, she stumbled and fell to the ground, sprawling.

"Enough," Yi Xiao said, prying the man's fingers from his throat. He was clearly exasperated with both of them. "Gan Han, you're in no condition for acrobatics. Sir, I'm not a sorcerer, nor am I using magic to heal you. Relieve your mind of that fear."

"I saw what you did back there." The man's voice was weak, as weak as Gan Han felt. "Sorcerer!"

"What I did was a basic application of *qi*. Anyone trained to channel their inner energies into a physical blow could do the same." Yi Xiao began sewing up his patient's injury, using his knee to hold the man down. At the same time he lectured, spouting the foolish nonsense so beloved of mountain mystics.

It wasn't so much that Gan Han didn't understand or believe in *qi*. But Yi Xiao's claims were far beyond anything any human could do. As for Gods and Immortals; they didn't exist. "I wish you'd stop deceiving yourself. What you're saying is impossible."

Her statement made Yi Xiao frown at her, the moment of distraction almost netting him a blow to the eye. "Stop that. I'm trying to help. Do you want something to drink?

It might make you feel better." When their patient simply growled a curse, he sighed, shifting position so he was kneeling on the man's arms, trapping them. "Gan Han, you were using your *qi* to protect yourself from Colonel Tsang's black aura. How can you claim you don't believe?"

"That's different." From the looks of things, this wasn't going to end quickly if someone didn't hold their patient down. She moved to his head and held it steady while Yi Xiao worked. "*Qi* flows through the body. All I was doing was redirecting his poison. And don't you dare bite me, you horrid man."

Again Yi Xiao frowned; though this time he kept his attention on his work. "His dark aura, you mean. Don't squirm." The last was directed at their unwilling patient.

"I mean his poison. You don't really think it was his spirit attacking me, do you?"

"Will the two of you let me go?"

"When I'm finished." Yi Xiao stitched up the wound crossing the man's forehead. "I do think that," he admitted to Gan Han. "But if you don't, there isn't much point in arguing the matter."

"I don't need help!" The man tried to kick his way out of Yi Xiao's hold but the idiot would-be priest was ready for that. He sat down hard on his patient's chest, knocking the wind from him.

"Good. Because I don't believe that and I refuse to be convinced. Better if you just give up the whole thing and return to the blade." Gan Han spread some of the ointment Yi Xiao gave her on their patient's injuries, adding, "Although you won't have it long because I will defeat you."

"You can't beat me, with or without a weapon," Yi Xiao retorted, sewing up the last of their patient's worst gashes. "Just drop the subject, Gan Han. It isn't happening."

Gan Han refused to argue the point any longer. He was right about one thing. She couldn't beat him yet. Her body was still too exhausted from her injuries. But they had over a month of travel left before they reached San Diego. Plenty of time for her to recover and show him exactly what she was made of.

Given, of course, they weren't all murdered in their sleep by the homicidal madman Yi Xiao had seen fit to rescue.

ooo

The rest of the day was spent getting the *Henrietta Marie* as far from the strange island as possible. With the excitement of the rescue over, the peculiarity of the thing made everyone nervous. Even Yi Xiao, born and raised miles from the sea, could tell the island was about as wrong as an island could be. For one thing, the vast majority of its surface had no solid ground beneath it. Rather it consisted of oddly light particles of sand, floating atop the water around a central cone of gushing mud.

"I've never seen anything like it before," Burton told him as the island receded in the distance behind them. "We're just lucky it wasn't a real volcano. We'd be charred ash otherwise."

That much was obvious. Of course, if it had been a volcano, Yi Xiao liked to think they wouldn't have been fool enough to get as close to it as they had. "It doesn't seem to be rising very fast, though. Do you really think it's dangerous?" Admittedly, he did, but he didn't know enough to be sure.

"I don't think it's safe, that's what I think." Burton glanced downwards though he couldn't see the other danger on his mind. "Anymore than that fellow you insisted on saving is."

Yi Xiao wouldn't argue the point of whether or not he should have saved the man. Whatever he was, murderer, madman or innocent victim, he was a living being. "Master says, life is important. Save it where you can."

"Your master isn't here to have her throat slit if he breaks free of the brig and murders us all in our sleep!" Burton said plaintively. "He's huge. I don't have the sort of chains needed to keep him under control."

"I don't know that we need any." Once the man—Hai Chan—had been patched up and given food and drink he'd sulkily cooperated with Yi Xiao. If he was to be believed, the *Southern Cross* was his own ship and Kramer and his men pirates who'd killed his crew. Hai Chan would've been next if that island hadn't erupted at exactly the wrong moment. The only reason Burton hadn't thrown them all in the brig was because he didn't have space. He'd decided to pretend Kramer was honest and keep close watch on him and his men.

"Do you believe he'll stay put?"

"His captors injured him badly. He's too weak to break free." Besides, Yi Xiao had given Hai Chan a dose of sleeping drug. Not from distrust, but because he—like Gan Han—had no sense when it came to rest.

Burton frowned at Yi Xiao curiously. "You're sure his injuries weren't from the accident?"

Some of the bruises and cuts certainly were, yet Yi Xiao, experienced in such matters from a lifetime in the martial world, recognized knife cuts when he saw them. The prisoner had been slashed repeatedly and beaten within an inch of his life. He said as much, adding, "It's a tribute to his stamina that he survived. Perhaps that's why they chained him; he frightened them so much they didn't dare risk his recovering enough to attack them."

That obviously didn't make Burton feel better. "It still doesn't prove he's innocent. He's dangerous, whatever the truth is." When Yi Xiao didn't answer, the Captain sighed. "I don't like casual killing, either, and I know you want to be done with that. We'll just have to keep an eye on him and the others."

"Wise choice." Years of training in the martial world had honed Yi Xiao's senses. If he was right, and his sense of danger was seldom wrong, then someone in their band of survivors was looking on the crew with killing intent.

The only question was, would they act on it?

ooo

Having more men aboard ship meant Gan Han had even less room for exercise than before. Worse, these newcomers—ill-mannered boors each and every one—spent their days idling around on deck, ogling her and getting in the way. The only times they weren't a constant bother, mispronouncing her name and pretending to court her, was from late at night to mid-morning, when they all lazed about in their bunks.

The only time the ship was truly quiet was in the early morning hours. Then all Gan Han could hear from her tiny room was the creaking of the ship's timbers, the flapping of its sails and the mutters of those few crewmen keeping watch. She knew Yi Xiao was up. The idiot practiced the style he claimed his master taught him in the early morning. Gan Han had watched him once, prancing around on deck wearing nothing but a pair of loose trousers as he waved a pair of scarves around. He'd looked a fool.

It finally occurred to Gan Han that she'd have the deck to herself if she rose earlier than Yi Xiao. It took several days of trying, but finally—about a week after they'd rescued the crew of the *Southern Cross*—she found the deck empty of everyone but the lookout. The skinny little boy was too shy to argue with her, leaving her to practice to her heart's content. As long as she finished before Yi Xiao came on deck, she could hide her techniques and her slowly recovered strength.

Over two weeks after the rescue, Gan Han came on deck for her usual practice and was surprised to find the young lookout missing. She'd have ignored the peculiarity if not for the fact that he was a responsible boy. He wouldn't have left his post unattended without good reason.

Lit by a few lanterns and no moonlight, the shadowy deck made her feel oddly nervous. The silence, broken only by the wind and lapping waves, seemed ominous. Was she imagining it? Or did she sense the faintest edge of a killing intent, somewhere near? If so, it wasn't aimed at her.

Gan Han walked around the deck and peered through the shadows. All she could see were the things she'd become accustomed to. A box here, a pile of carefully coiled rope there, a sleeping deckhand in a corner. With all the extra men aboard ship, everyone had had to find some place to bunk and this one had chosen an out of the way spot near the railing.

Yet there was something wrong about the figure. Gan Han stopped. Listened. Moved slowly and quietly closer. Even the quietest sleeper made some noise and this man was utterly still. It only took a moment to realize he was dead, his throat slit from ear to ear.

A hand slid around Gan Han's mouth and a stranger whispered something in a barbaric language. She didn't need to understand the words to know the intent. She was to remain still and make no sound. Otherwise the pinprick against her throat would turn into something worse.

The man—one of the *Southern Cross's* crew—dragged her off to the side. Some of his fellows were moving in the shadows, silent and cautious as they took up their positions. No doubt they were preparing to take over the ship and under some circumstances; Gan Han might not have cared who did what to whom. This time her own life was at stake.

Yi Xiao had yet to return Gan Han's sword to her, but that didn't make her helpless. Death Flower techniques incorporated both blade and weighted sleeve fighting. Besides, no true martial artist could depend entirely on having their chosen weapon to hand. She could attack whenever she chose, biding her time so as to make it count.

Several members of the *Southern Cross's* crew gathered together near the man holding Gan Han captive. One said something softly, tone faintly mocking as he eyed her. She didn't need to understand their foreign babble to guess at what they'd said, nor what they'd suggested for her. Or for the lookout another man had captured.

Gan Han's captor chuckled, tightening his grip in an ugly mockery of an embrace. Somehow, she managed not to react, not even to allow her expression to show her anger. She wasn't afraid of them. There were only four untrained fighters. Even without her sword she was sure she could handle them. She just needed the right moment.

Someone pushed open the hatch leading to the lower deck and shoved a mostly unconscious Hai Chan through. A voice spoke from beneath, saying something about being ready to start now. It was rare for Gan Han to regret her limited English. The foreign devils' babble was unseemly and unpleasant but knowing what her captors were up to would have been useful. No doubt they planned on taking over the *Henrietta Marie*. She just didn't know how.

One of the men chuckled and kicked Hai Chan in the side. Still groggy from Yi Xiao's medicines, he didn't react. A slightly harder kick barely elicited an "oof" and still failed to rouse him. Gan Han didn't bother trying to stop their abuse. Hai Chan wasn't her responsibility after all.

Another man spoke, suggesting it didn't matter. He said more, Hai Chan and Captain Burton's names, together with the word for death. Gan Han guessed the plan. They meant to make it look as if Hai Chan had broken free and murdered the Captain. Likely they'd kill him as well, so he couldn't protest his innocence.

One of the foreigners headed towards the door to Captain Burton's cabin, only to be interrupted by Hai Chan's gruff voice, his tone combining anger and triumph. "Bastards! You'll pay for what you've done!" He rolled sideways, out of the men's reach, and came to his feet.

At the same time one of the conspirators went flying, flung there by a strike between the shoulders. Yi Xiao called out, "Now, Gan Han!"

Recognizing her cue and appreciating the idiot warrior's trust in her good sense, Gan Han slammed her elbow into her captor's sternum, twisting just enough to keep his blade from slicing her throat open. Freed of his grip, she smashed her weighted sleeve into the man's temple. Bone shattered and he went down in a heap.

Hai Chan was knocking heads together. At the same time, Yi Xiao danced with the last pair of foreigners. At least, that was the only way Gan Han could describe his fighting technique. Slippery as a snake, he shifted and twisted, catching hold of wrists and sliding his feet between his opponents', tripping them. It was a cowardly style, unseemly for a man as skilled with the blade as he.

Gan Han saw another pair of foreigners climb out from a grate towards the bow of the ship. Rather than watch Yi Xiao make a fool of himself, she paused to snatch the stiletto from the man she'd killed, then rushed at the pair. The weapon wasn't her favorite choice, but it was all she had.

Dodging the first man, she sliced the tip of her blade across the other's cheek. As blood flowed and he shouted, she swung her long weighted sleeve. It wrapped itself around the man's wrist and she used it to spin him around, tangling him in the fabric's length.

The other man grabbed for her, but she evaded him easily, blocking his grasp with her blade. He screamed, blood spurting from his palm as her weapon cut deep. She was about to bury the blade in his chest when a loud bang startled her into turning.

The captain of the *Southern Cross* stood over Hai Chan with a huge cutlass in one hand and a pistol in the other. Yi Xiao, cowardly as ever, was backing away. Annoyed, Gan Han snapped, "Damn you, do your duty!"

"My duty doesn't include getting shot," Yi Xiao countered. "Especially with a magically enhanced weapon."

There being no such thing as magic, Gan Han disregarded the argument. "If you won't, I will." She stabbed her opponent, skewering him through the heart before he had a chance to shriek. She was about to go after the foreigner when Hai Chan flipped back to his feet and barred her path with an overly muscled arm.

"Get out of my way," Gan Han ordered.

"You're not up to it, little girl," Hai Chan growled. "The damned bastard's spell's more than I could handle, much less you." His chest and shoulder were blackened and charred as if someone had taken a torch and pressed it to his bare flesh. Another man would have been screaming in agony, but they'd already established that Hai Chan had immense reserves against pain.

"You're not a warrior of the Death Flowers." The very fact that this idiot sailor thought she wasn't his equal was an insult. "I'm more than a match for any so-called sorcerer."

Yi Xiao caught her wrist and pulled her back. "No. He's right. You were already hurt on my behalf. No need to repeat the experience."

This seemed a chance to force her rival into returning to his true and proper path. "In that case, get your sabre and fight him. Prove you're my better."

"I don't need a blade to prove myself." Yi Xiao's expression shifted, as if the boast were something to be ashamed of. "Just get back. We'll find a way to get rid of him."

"If you're so good you can fight that man without your sabre and win, I'll accept you've chosen the right path for yourself," Gan Han told him, knowing full well she couldn't keep her promise. "Show me your skill, Yi Xiao. Prove the value of what the Storm Hermit has taught you."

ooo

The bargain was one Yi Xiao yearned to avoid. Not because he doubted his skill against Captain Kramer's sorcery. The Westerner's magic, and magic it certainly was, required a focus to work. It also required time to use; enough time that Yi Xiao was fairly sure he could evade it. As for taking the man down without killing? Kramer might be a sorcerer, but he'd no skill in the martial arts. His movements proved that much.

No. It was the fact that Yi Xiao was forced to bargain at all that bothered him. He'd been unsuccessful in persuading Gan Han that he wasn't the man she'd been hunting for. Unsuccessful in persuading the girl that there was no need for the two of them to fight. Unsuccessful in persuading her that he'd left the martial world. A challenge like this risked rousing his love of fighting and bloodshed and he wanted so desperately to be done with all that.

Yet still, he seemed to have no choice but to fight. "Give me your sleeves," he ordered Gan Han. He'd left his own scarves with his things below, where he'd been guarding Hai Chan. When she glared at him, about to refuse, he pointed out, "You want me to show you my skill. I don't have to have them, but they'd be useful."

With a dour expression, Gan Han sliced her sleeves from her outer robe. "You'll replace them, you know." It wasn't a request.

"I will." Yi Xiao turned his attention back to Kramer, whose only reason for giving them time to prepare was that it gave him time as well. The man had been infusing his magic in bullet after bullet while they'd talked, so that now he had a dozen of the things.

Quick analysis told Yi Xiao why the enemy captain didn't carry his ensorcelled bullets around with him, ready for any eventuality. Why, too, the captain didn't give his spell to anyone else. It required its creator to maintain it. Which, in turn, meant Kramer couldn't be as strong as he wanted them to believe.

Oh, the spell was powerful. It'd injured Hai Chan badly after all. It wasn't, however, the work of a master sorcerer. The man had learned to imbue his spells into the bullets but had yet to learn to embed the magic the spell needed to operate. Any sorcerer worth their spells could do that much, yet Kramer clutched the bullets in his spare hand, obviously using his physical contact to maintain the magic.

So the first thing to do was to disarm his enemy of as many of his little toys as possible. Yi Xiao hefted Gan Han's sleeves, telling his allies, "Back up. Weighted, these things are deadly." Gan Han knew that already. She'd killed her captor with one blow, after all. Yet she didn't complain at Yi Xiao's including her in the order. She was too busy watching him closely, trying to understand what he was doing.

Kramer sneered. "You'll have to get to me first, Chinaman."

"True." Yi Xiao flipped sideways, a cartwheel that needed no hands to help him spin. When he landed, he let loose with one of Gan Han's sleeves, letting it brush his enemy's robe. Deliberately, he cursed, as if the blow had been intended to do much more and much worse.

The enemy captain loaded the first of his many bullets into his weapon, aiming it for Yi Xiao's heart, then fired at Gan Han instead. It burst into flame as it passed, forcing Yi Xiao to use one of the girl's sleeves to block it. Immediately the fabric caught fire, or tried to. Yi Xiao let his *qi* flow through the cloth, washing away the flames before they did more than sear it.

Kramer's bullets were far faster than anything Yi Xiao had dealt with so far. If he weren't using his *qi* to redirect any energy flung his way, he would have taken the next shot straight to the chest. There were those who claimed they could harden their skin against bullets but Yi Xiao wasn't one of them. Even if he became a true master of the Wind and Rain style he'd never manage such a feat.

Again Kramer loaded his weapon and again Yi Xiao redirected the shot with his *qi*. Behind him, Gan Han was yelling, telling him to stop prancing around like a street actor. Hai Chan remained silent, much to Yi Xiao's relief. Already they'd attracted attention as the rest of the crew, finally realizing there was trouble, began gathering on deck. Now he'd have to worry about them as well as himself.

The noise drew Captain Burton out, but all he said was, "Don't make a mess on my ship. A bigger mess, that is." He must have noticed Gan Han and Hai Chan's victims, their blood seeping into the deck behind Yi Xiao. Or maybe it was the burn marks from Kramer's magic. Yi Xiao ignored the complaint, dodging another bullet, this one coming within inches of his face as he arched backwards to evade it.

"This is a fight, not a dance," Gan Han snapped. "Do something useful. Preferably fatal."

It seemed Yi Xiao was in the minority. Gan Han, Hai Chan, the *Henrietta Marie's* crew, even Captain Burton, all seemed entirely agreeable with the idea of his killing Kramer. The fact that killing was a thing Yi Xiao wanted to be done with didn't matter to them in the slightest. Knowing his argument would fall on deaf ears, he countered, "I am a Priest of the Wind and Rain. Not a blood-thirsty murderer."

"Doesn't matter anyway. You're the one going to die." Kramer's knowledge of Chinese was unexpected but Yi Xiao supposed any man who sailed the Pacific was going to pick up at least a little of the local languages. "You and everyone else aboard this ship."

Burton asked reasonably. "How are you going kill us all? You're alone now."

"The hell I am."

"The hell you aren't. I knew you were up to something. My men were just waiting for yours to attack. Those they haven't killed already are all tied up down in the bilge. "

Yi Xiao used the man's moment of distraction to roll right in front of him, striking his gut as hard as he could. The *qi* enhanced blow knocked Kramer off his feet. Unfortunately, that wasn't enough to stop him. He rose unsteadily, catching hold of a gaff. It glowed under his touch and Hai Chan called out a warning. "Don't let him hit you."

That much was obvious. Apparently Kramer could imbue more than bullets with his magic. Yi Xiao had no doubts about the danger. He flipped backwards to avoid the weapon, using Gan Han's sleeves to distract his enemy. The man used the gaff, catching Yi Xiao's weapon and tangling it in the hook. His magic flowed into the sleeve and this time there was too much for Yi Xiao to block with his *qi*. The sleeve caught fire and burned away.

Kramer thrust his gaff at Yi Xiao again. Knowing better than to allow it, Yi Xiao raced at him and, instead of simply striking with his remaining sleeve, leapt into the air, somersaulting over the man and slamming the weight into the back of his head. Kramer fell forward and lay, half-stunned, on the blood-stained deck.

Relieved, thinking Kramer was done, Yi Xiao relaxed, about to turn to Captain

Burton and tell him to put the man in the brig. Except Gan Han cried out, "What's happening to him?" For the first time she actually sounded scared.

Yi Xiao's opponent seemed to be glowing. He spread his hands flat, the same glow seeping from his entire body and into the deck. A stain of reddish gold, the color of his magic, spread outwards. "I don't like the look of that," Burton murmured.

"Get back. All of you." Yi Xiao's warning didn't come fast enough. One of Burton's men, curious and unfortunately foolhardy, poked the stain with his dagger. Immediately the glow enveloped the blade and went straight up the man's hand and arm. Within seconds he was a glowing, screaming, struggling thing, trying to break free of whatever it was Kramer had created.

Yi Xiao moved quickly. He'd neither choice or time. He dropped into water summoning stance, shouting, "Get out of the way!" Then he drew on his inner power, gathering it together as he stepped in the slow, stately, pattern of the Mountain Dragon's Dance. His qi flowed along with him, flaring brilliantly in a profligate and dangerous use of power. He'd learned the pattern but he'd hardly come close to mastering it. If he got one thing wrong, failed his concentration, he'd be transformed and lost forever.

The power flowed through him, water and wind combining to form a cloud of chill vapor, tiny daggers of ice spinning around him in a whirlwind. It flowed across the deck, danced along with him, singing its ancient and wordless song. Someone screamed Yi Xiao's name but he ignored their call. He had to wash that stain of magic from this ship before it consumed it entirely.

Its heat and his swirling fog struck each other. Ice blades shattered and melted, flames smoked and faded. If Kramer had been a stronger or better sorcerer, Yi Xiao's qi storm could never have defeated him. As it was, it took just about all Yi Xiao had to force the burning magic—including its creator—to the center of his power. Then, knowing he was ending a life again, and grieving for it, he sent the whole seething mess overboard, to explode in the depths of the ocean.

As he let his qi fade, Yi Xiao fell to his knees. Burton was there a moment later, keeping him from landing on his face. Then Gan Han approached. "Is that proof enough?" he asked, but was too close to unconsciousness to comprehend her answer.

ooo

It wasn't possible. It couldn't be possible. Yet Gan Han couldn't deny what she's seen. "What was that?" she whispered, barely able to breathe.

"Sorcery, as I told you," grumbled Hai Chan. "What else?"

Yi Xiao had been just as insistent that he wasn't a sorcerer. Nor was it a point worth arguing. Whatever power it was the young noble had displayed, it wasn't natural. Was this how he'd become so skilled at the blade? It'd make Gan Han's life easier; after all, she could hardly be expected to outmatch a man whose talent was a mere cheat.

Still, easier though the revelation might be, she sensed she'd be wrong to assume it. The power Yi Xiao had wielded had nothing to do with his blade-work. No technique she could think of involved the strange leaps, spins and bounds the young man made use of. She'd seen his grandmother at work once, years ago. Wolf Fang style was rapid and direct, relying mostly on speed and offense. The only thing the Storm Hermit of Heng Shan's technique shared with the White Wolf Blade was incredible speed and agility.

"Hey! You help him. I have a ship to care for." Captain Burton again, his abysmal Chinese an affront to any native speaker. Gan Han swallowed her criticism. The idiot wasn't worth her time. Besides, he was right that Yi Xiao needed help and she doubted the man had a clue how to manage it.

Hai Chan called out to the Captain, "I'm no doctor. I'll help you. I know ships better than healing."

The foreign devil didn't look as if he liked the idea. Still, he obviously needed an extra hand. The fight with Kramer and his men had killed or incapacitated several of his men. Raised aboard her family's junk, Gan Han knew the *Henrietta Marie* didn't have many extra crewmen. Captain Burton would need as many hands as he could get.

As the others went to work getting the ship back in order and back on course, Gan Han dragged Yi Xiao's barely cooperating body to her berth. There wasn't a mark on him and aside from looking drawn and exhausted, he seemed unharmed. She corrected herself. Half-conscious though he was, there was a twist to his brows suggesting deep unhappiness. "What is it?"

His eyes fluttered. Opened briefly. "Master says, the true *Dao* makes killing unnecessary. I fail. Over and over I fail her. Over and over I fail myself."

Gan Han felt a surge of rage and jealousy towards the Hermit of Heng Shan. How had the woman managed to twist Yi Xiao so far out of his true and proper path as a weapons master? How had she managed to transform the deadliest killer the martial world had ever known to this... this... ineffectual crybaby?

"You don't have to find that stupid *Dao*."

"I want to find that stupid *Dao*," Yi Xiao said firmly, opening his eyes again and looking at her with strange and oddly powerful calm. "And if I fail now, I keep trying. I will not fight you, Gan Han. Not to prove a thing I no longer need."

Almost at a loss for words, all Gan Han managed was, "I'll follow you until you do."

"You're welcome to try." Yi Xiao turned his back to her. "But first you'll have to find my path."

Chapter 3: Wood –
Gathering Together with Limitations

The rest of the journey to San Diego was relatively uneventful by Hai Chan's standards. He'd been a sailor all his life and was accustomed to the little excitements of ocean life. Being boarded by pirates had been about the worst and he still felt he could have handled the bastards if their Captain hadn't been a sorcerer. The storms and long windless days, however, were as normal as the constant squabbles between dozens of strong personalities crowded together in close quarters. He gladly left the arguments to Burton.

Besides, Hai Chan had his own argument with Yi Xiao to pursue. Unlike that silly chit, Gan Han, he didn't need or want to fight the man. He knew what the martial world was, but he'd never been interested in joining it, any more than he wanted anything to do with sorcery. Making Yi Xiao admit the truth of what he did, however, would have been eminently satisfying.

Yi Xiao was a stubborn creature, though, and Hai Chan didn't know enough about sorcery to prove him wrong. Yet he couldn't believe the thing the priest called *qi* wasn't magic, no matter how often Yi Xiao patiently explained the difference. So what if *qi* was an internal power, born of the wielder's spiritual energy? It was still a power that could be directed beyond flesh to act on the world.

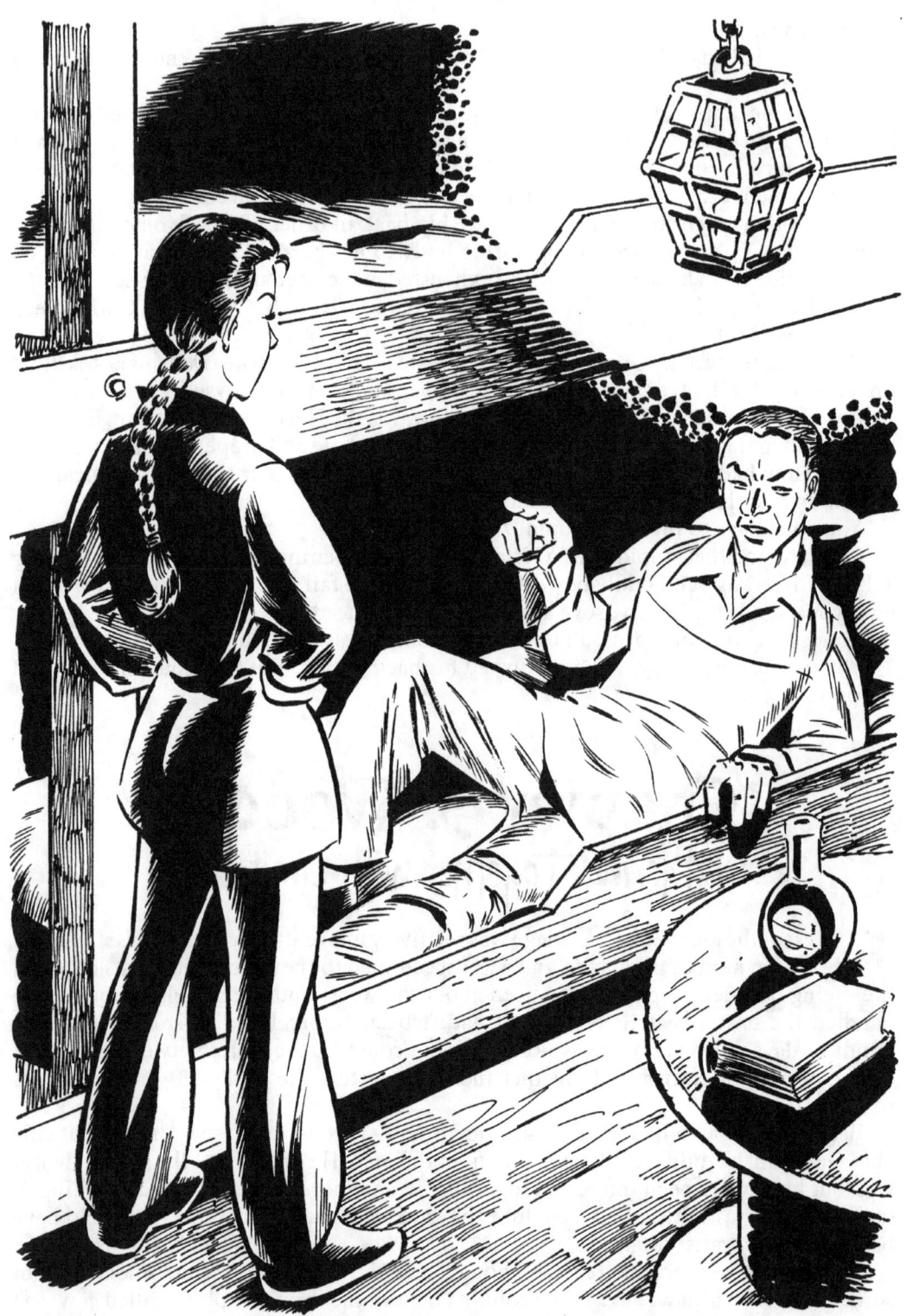

" I WANT TO FIND THAT STUPID *DAO.* "

At least Gan Han no longer pretended there was no such thing as magic. Kramer's sorcery had proved her wrong on that count. She didn't understand it any better than Hai Chan but at least she wasn't sneering at his childish belief in such things. She still sneered at his uneducated, uncomplicated and unconcerned ways, while he called her what she was; a self-absorbed, childish, and bloodthirsty little girl. The martial world seemed rife with people like her.

It made Hai Chan wonder how Yi Xiao, sweet-tempered and strangely imperturbable as he was, had avoided becoming like Gan Han. Any descendent of the Qing emperors, particularly one belonging to a powerful family in the martial world ought to have grown up knowing their place and power. Kindness, a desire to do no harm, those weren't things Hai Chan associated with men like Yi Xiao. He, himself, had been forced to flee his hometown because the local clans had started a war with each other.

Still, Yi Xiao was oddly likable, aside from his insistence that his magic was nothing of the sort. He was a facile conversationalist and amusing to watch, especially when he teased Gan Han. It made Hai Chan's plans for his own future easier to decide. "When we reach port I will go with you to San Francisco."

The young priest was puzzled. "I've no objection, but why? You're a sailor; why not remain aboard the *Henrietta Marie*? Captain Burton seems to have found some use for you."

Staying with Captain Burton would be profitable, certainly. The westerner might be annoyingly overconfident in some matters but he knew his job and he did it well. Still, "I was captain of my own ship. I intend to be again." At Yi Xiao's confused expression, he added, "You don't know how things are in California right now?"

"I don't," Yi Xiao admitted. "Enlighten me?"

"You've at least heard they found gold last year, somewhere near a place called Sutter's Mill?"

"I've been training on Heng Shan for the last two years," Yi Xiao pointed out.

The mountain range of Heng Shan was far enough inland that news from a barbaric place like America wouldn't reach that far. Moreover, if Yi Xiao's stories about his training were to be believed, a disciple of any mountain priest would have little to no contact with the outside world.

"Well, they did. So much gold, in fact, that miners and prospectors have been pouring into California ever since. It's gotten to the point that captains don't dare land in San Francisco. Their crews desert to go hunting for gold and their ships sit in dock, empty and useless."

Yi Xiao worked out Hai Chan's intentions quickly. "So you plan on absconding with an abandoned ship? How will you get a crew, if they're all mining for gold?"

"I'll find a way." It wasn't as easy to make one's fortune as gold-hungry prospectors thought. By now there'd be disaffected and disappointed would-be miners, beginning to realize just how futile their search really was. Hai Chan would find them and somehow persuade them aboard ship, then sail as far from San Francisco's golden trap as possible. He'd show them they'd profit more trading and hauling goods around the Pacific. There was no reason, no reason at all, why Americans and Englishmen should be the only ones to gain from the western appetite for tea and other Chinese goods.

All without trading a single ounce of opium.

ooo

Yi Xiao's return to land proved amusingly awkward. As he walked down the gangplank onto the relatively steady surface of San Diego's dock, he nearly fell into the water. He stumbled over his own feet before managing to steady himself by catching hold of a post and clinging tight. He grinned broadly at his own clumsiness. "I could do with a bath, but not that way."

"You are embarrassing," Gan Han grumbled. Her glare would have cut right through him if her sword had been involved.

"You were raised aboard your family's junk," Yi Xiao pointed out, chuckling as he recovered himself. "You knew to expect this. I didn't."

"Idiot," she muttered under her breath.

Ignoring the girl's complaints, Yi Xiao turned his attention to the broadly grinning Captain Burton. "I believe we part ways now."

"I'm afraid so. It's been interesting, traveling with you, but…"

"Excuse me! Sir? Excuse me?" The Captain broke off as a tall, rangy, black-haired westerner hurried towards him with an anxious and irritated expression. He was overdressed for the warm weather and his thick wool shirt was soaked in sweat. There were two men behind him, equally overdressed and sweaty.

Burton frowned. "Can I help you?"

"Sir, are you the captain of this fine vessel?" The westerner's accent was one Yi Xiao didn't recognize. There was a lilt to it, or a drawl, of a sort he'd never heard before. It sounded American, but not the same as Burton's.

"I am."

"Thank God you've come. I am Reverend Josiah Burns. I, and my companions, ten men in all, would travel with you to San Francisco. We have…"

Burton stopped the man from continuing. "Sir, I appreciate your desire, but the *Henrietta Marie* is headed to Panama after this. I have cargo promised to be there within the month and no time for any detours."

Burns tried to argue. "But we've been stranded here for two weeks!" He gestured north. "The fishing boat we hired in Panama abandoned us here. We've been hoping to find someone, anyone, to take us the rest of the way to San Francisco."

"Didn't you come around the Horn? You should have stayed with your ship."

Burns waved off the question. "We came to Panama through the Gulf and hiked across the isthmus." An irritated expression crossed his face as he added, "And it weren't no easy trip, I can tell you that."

Yi Xiao visualized the map and wondered why Burns was so annoyed. It was just around fifty miles across the isthmus. It wouldn't take much more than a week to make the trip, even through jungle. He didn't ask, contenting himself with listening and, he hoped, learning.

"I quite understand," Burton commiserated. "I've traveled that way once or twice myself. Jungle, not much trail to speak of and the mosquitoes. I hope you brought plenty of quinine."

"We did, and good thing, too. One youngster was so sick he nearly died." Burns shrugged off the concern, adding, "But you understand our frustration?"

Burton agreed. "I do. I'm guessing your plan was to avoid Cape Horn and spend less time asea?" he asked curiously and when Burns agreed, added, "What I don't understand is why you didn't hire a proper ship in Panama to take you all the way to San Francisco. Fishermen have better things to do with their time than ferry people several thousand miles from home."

With an angry snort, Burns explained, "There aren't any ships coming back from San Francisco. Word is as soon as they get there, their crews desert and leave their ships stranded."

"I see." Burton spread his hands helplessly, "You have my deepest sympathies but I can't help you. I've given my word."

Anger flashed across the man's face. "I and my companions are to starve here, then?"

Yi Xiao doubted they'd starve. San Diego looked to be a busy port, with plenty of jobs for able and willing men.

"I don't suggest that. You could go by land. El Camino Real is…"

"That so-called trail the Mexicans left us? Are you mad? It's over five hundred miles to San Francisco by land. And we have our gear and food to carry as well!"

Worried by the man's insistence and suspicious of the way they stared longingly at the *Henrietta Marie*, Yi Xiao rose to his feet, nearly overbalancing. Burton caught his arm, muttering, "This isn't the time for your circus act."

"I'm not even sure what that is," Yi Xiao countered, speaking in Chinese. "Never mind that. May I make a suggestion?"

Burns glared at the interruption, while Burton, guessing Yi Xiao didn't want what he said to be understood, responded in the same language. "What is?"

"They look desperate. They may try to take what is not given."

Burton considered that. "I won't disagree. What suggest?"

"They hired a fisherman to get them this far. Tell them to do so again. Even if they can't find someone willing to make the whole trip, they could hire fresh boats wherever they stop." Yi Xiao had been studying Burton's maps carefully, knowing he'd have to find his way north on his own. He'd considered doing the same thing himself, but he'd had quite enough of shipboard life. He yearned for the relative quiet of the road.

"What's that heathen Chinee servant of yours saying?" Burns demanded.

"He's not a servant. He's a passenger," Burton corrected. "He suggested you hire another fisherman. They might not get you all the way, but you could keep hiring boats until you're there."

The man scoffed. "What a waste of time and money!"

"Maybe, but otherwise you'll have to walk, or keep hoping to find a ship willing to risk its crew to the lure of the gold fields." Burton inclined his head politely, "And now, if you don't mind, I have business to settle. I'm sorry I can be of no further use to you."

"But…"

"Good day, sir. I wish you luck in finding your way." Burton turned his attention back to his own business, ignoring the way Burns' mouth worked. Once again speaking in Chinese, he told Gan Han, "As soon as my work done, will return you home. Wait here."

Without a word, Gan Han walked back aboard ship, ignoring Yi Xiao's cheerful farewell. Once she was out of sight, Burton ordered his second-mate to pull up the gangplank. "No one boards without my permission, no matter who it is nor how important."

"Understood sir."

"Yi Xiao, Hai Chan. Not know if we meet again, but if do, hope to find you well. Safe journey, you both."

Recognizing it was high time they were on their way, Yi Xiao headed into town. He didn't mind walking to San Francisco, but Hai Chan hadn't liked the idea when he'd proposed it earlier. They'd have to find horses and guidance. The Road of the King was supposed to be well-marked, but he knew little of local customs. He hoped to find someone to advise them.

ooo

The trouble with Yi Xiao was he kept so much of his thoughts to himself. Hai Chan didn't even know why the man was headed to San Francisco. Nor did asking help. Yi Xiao's only answer was, "Because I am a filial grandson."

By this time they were halfway through a pleasant little town of odd buildings built of wood and clay. Most were colored some light shade, with attractively painted windows and doors. All were strange to Hai Chan's eyes. There wasn't a single properly curved roof in sight. Indeed, some of the buildings didn't have true roofs at all, just flat tops with bars of wood sticking out.

Yi Xiao gawked unabashedly, ambling down the street with the loose limbed movement of one accustomed to long, slow walks. It was a difficult speed for Hai Chan. He was taller than Yi Xiao by several inches and had to adjust his steps to match his companion's. The priest could move quickly when he wanted, but this wasn't one of those times.

"Do you have the slightest idea what you're looking for?"

"A little, yes. Burton told me where the market was. We may not find horses or a guide there, but perhaps I can get someone to change my silver to something more useful." Yi Xiao paused to evade a group of children whose appearance reminded Hai Chan of Southern Chinese. They ran around Yi Xiao, screaming with laughter, especially when he pretended to trip and fall over them, performing a little dance to evade their rapid movements.

"I can see why that silly girl of yours gets so mad at you. You're a buffoon." Everything Yi Xiao did was surely an affront to Gan Han's dignity.

"She isn't my girl, you realize?"

"She seems to think so."

Yi Xiao snorted, "Not really. She's looking for her mother's approval, not a man's love." He looked thoughtful, adding, "I'm not the sort she'd want, anyway."

Thinking about it, Hai Chan supposed he might be right. He didn't need to ask why Yi Xiao behaved so oddly. The young man's nonsense kept people at a distance. There was a hidden part of his personality he wished no one to approach too closely. Hai Chan had caught a glimpse of it, that day when Yi Xiao had slain Kramer. The man played at being kind and gentle, even humorous, but there was an underlying violence to him, a love of killing terrifying in its intensity.

"She seems to have given up on whatever she wanted from you, at least."

"Thank the Gods, yes." Yi Xiao wiped his forehead in an exaggerated way. "I don't need to spend the rest of my days avoiding her. And before you ask why I don't just let her beat me, she'd know if I pretended to fight."

Well, yes. It'd be the worst sort of insult to a warrior of the martial world. Gan Han's pride would never have put up with such an affront. Likely she'd force Yi Xiao to kill her, out of sheer obstinacy. "Just as well she's going home, then."

Yi Xiao agreed as they entered a large open area full of carts and people. It looked like any number of Chinese markets and though the produce was strange and unfamiliar, as were some of the scents, it felt like coming home. Hai Chan had spent a great deal of his childhood in markets like this and it made him feel more comfortable in this strange land, with so many unfamiliar sounds, smells and faces.

"Excuse me. Does anyone speak English here?" A westerner, one with an accent similar to the Reverend Burns', was trying to talk to the traders, most of who stared at him with blatant dislike. He was over-dressed the same way Burns had been, though unlike Burns he'd let his shirt hang open and wasn't bothering with a hat to cover his bright red hair. "Please?"

A boy, not much more than twelve, peered out from behind the man, his cropped red hair proving their relationship. He was looking around nervously, grey eyes wide and scared. "Pa," he said. "Maybe them two?" He pointed at Yi Xiao and Hai Chan. "They don't look like they're from around here."

The boy's father looked over at them. "Don't be silly, Jo. Them two are Chinamen. They don't speak no English, guaranteed."

If it'd been up to Hai Chan, he'd have pretended not to understand a word, to avoid getting caught up in some strangers' problems. Especially strangers obviously associated with that Burns fellow. Yi Xiao, on the other hand, was perfectly willing to stick his long nose into trouble. He cocked his head and smiled, saying, "I actually do speak English. And French. And German. And a bit of Russian. And several dialects of Chinese, of course, including Taiwanese, Manchurian, Cantonese and Mongolian. Though I'm afraid the last two are no better than my Russian. Still, I'm fluent enough to annoy people in a number of different languages. Which would you prefer?"

The boy was giggling by now, though there was still a scared look in his eyes that made Hai Chan think he and his father were in some trouble. His father was staring at Yi Xiao with an expression of disbelief, which made Hai Chan elbow his companion. "Don't be so damned ridiculous," he said in Chinese. "This isn't the time for your nonsense."

"There's always time for my nonsense," Yi Xiao argued, but stopped grinning like an idiot to add, once more in English, "If I can help you, I will. Though I'm not at all sure how useful I'll be. I'm just as much a stranger to this town as you."

The man said, quite slowly and more than a little hopefully, "You're a Christian convert?"

Though Hai Chan had learned his English from a missionary, he mostly felt impatient with their earnest and naïve attempts to persuade their students to follow their God. He considered saying as much but decided it might be better if he kept his knowledge of English to himself. Playing the ignorant fool could prove useful on occasion.

Yi Xiao, having proved his foolishness in other ways, went on as he'd begun. "I'm afraid not. But I assure you, I'm harmless. I can even be helpful, if you'll allow me. What sort of assistance do you need?"

"I don't even know who you are, much less if I can trust you. You talk pretty for a Chinaman, but..."

Yi Xiao bowed. "Thank you. My second mother says I talk too much, really. I also forget my manners. My name is Lang Yi Xiao, a wanderer headed for the city of San Francisco. This is Hai Chan, a sailor also headed for that city."

Hai Chan bowed, saying in Chinese, "Pleased to meet you."

The boy tugged at his father's coat and pulled him close, whispering something urgently. Hai Chan wasn't sure, but he thought the child said something about liking Yi Xiao. Giving in, the father said, "I'm Hal Kraft, Mr. Shee-ow. And I guess it's pretty obvious my kid here and I are headed to San Francisco too."

"Lang," Yi Xiao corrected. "In China, we use our family name first. Which, I suppose, means I should call myself Yi Xiao Lang here in America? Master says, when in Rome, do as the Romans do."

Kraft almost let himself be dragged along by the current of Yi Xiao's nonsense. "I suppose," he agreed. "But you said you can help? Do you know any Spanish? I'm trying to find someone to sell me a horse and a pack mule. I think some of these people know what I'm saying but they act like they can't understand a word."

"Regretfully, Spanish is not one of the languages I've learned. There are similarities with French, of course, but not enough. I was hoping to find an English speaker here as well, for the same reason."

"I... see." Kraft sounded disappointed but unsurprised.

It was obvious the grim-faced merchants understood more than they pretended. Something about the way they were studiously and obviously ignoring the outsiders' discussion made Hai Chan certain they were refusing to cooperate. He said as much to Yi Xiao.

"Interesting," Yi Xiao murmured and returned his attention to Kraft. "Is there a reason they might..." He trailed off, eyes on something further down the way. "Er... I think someone is looking for you."

Hai Chan followed Yi Xiao's gaze and saw Reverend Burns staring around the market, his fury obvious. The man spotted his fellow westerner and strode towards them rapidly, calling out Kraft's name as if he were a child who'd wandered from its keeper.

At the same time Jo dove below the nearest cart and scurried behind it. The old woman who owned it started to complain, then stopped suddenly when the boy put a pleading hand on her skirts. *"Bueno, bebita.* You hide here." Then, without another word, she sat down and closed her mouth tight, ignoring them all grimly.

"Hal, what in the name of heavenly glory are you doing, wandering around? Didn't I tell you it's dangerous?" Burns glanced briefly at Hai Chan and Yi Xiao. "Didn't I see you two... oh, wait. You don't speak a civilized tongue, why bother asking?"

To Hai Chan's surprise, Yi Xiao just smiled, the broad, friendly expression of a fool unaware he'd been insulted. Nor did he speak, leaving Kraft to say, "Jo was hungry for something asides from flatbread and dried meat. I thought I'd see if anyone here would sell me some fruit."

"Damnit, man, what did I say about letting me handle the natives? You're too trusting and they'll steal the shirt off your back, soon as look at you." Burns scanned the area. "Where is that... boy... of yours anyways?"

Kraft didn't miss a beat. "You said it was dangerous to wander around, so I left him back at the inn. Figured Joel and Cletis could keep an eye out for him for a little."

There was doubt in Reverend Burns' eyes but he didn't see Jo where the boy hid behind the old lady. He didn't argue, simply told Kraft. "Well I guess it's okay to get some fruit. Just make sure to wash it real good before we eat any. Can't tell where them as picked it have been. Come back to the inn as soon as you're done. That Yankee captain was being difficult and we gotta make plans like I said we would. Understand?"

"Right, sir. I understand you perfect."

"Good."

Burns didn't bother looking at Yi Xiao or Hai Chan again, just turned around and went the way he'd come. Hai Chan waited for him to be out of sight before saying, "You don't trust him much, do you, Mr. Kraft."

Yi Xiao leaned over to call Jo out from under the cart. "You especially don't trust him with your daughter." When Hai Chan, Kraft and Jo all stared at him, he continued, "I said I don't speak Spanish, but I do know enough to be sure *bebita* can't possibly refer to a boy."

"Pa?" Jo sounded a bit scared and Hai Chan couldn't blame her. She wouldn't be pretending to be a boy if she didn't have good reason.

Kraft took his daughter's hand. "Her ma died last year. Used up most of our spare cash, taking care of her. So I thought I could make our fortune, here in California. Or at least find work, where there weren't none back home. I couldn't leave Jo back there, though, so I thought if she pretended to be a boy, we'd be all right."

From Burns' way of talking earlier, Hai Chan had a feeling the disguise hadn't worked.

"And the Reverend noticed?"

"I thought he was a man of God, he acts like a man of God. But he keeps trying to get her alone and keeps hinting that he knows." Kraft swallowed hard at the thought. "I don't like the way he talks, neither. Like he's offering to keep our secret if she goes with him. It ain't right. She shouldn't oughta be made to go with no man she don't want to."

Yi Xiao inclined his head. "I cannot possibly promise to protect her from every danger, but if you'll trust me as a traveling companion, I'll do my best to make sure she isn't harmed."

After a moment of hesitation, Kraft agreed. "Just don't get any ideas of your own, mister."

"That I can promise." Yi Xiao turned to look at the old woman, "You speak a little English. Enough to tell us where we can hire horses, and perhaps a mule or so?"

For a moment Hai Chan thought the woman would remain obstinately silent. Then she asked, "You have money?"

"I do. I think it's enough."

She considered him. Nodded approvingly. "You go out of town, up that hill just a little away and you find ranch. Tell them, Mama Imelda sent you. Tell them I say they sell you three horses, one mule." Before Yi Xiao could ask how she could be so sure they'd obey, she added, "Owner my grandson, Arturo Martinez. He do as he's told."

With a laugh, Yi Xiao bent over the lady's hand in a gesture he had to have learned from his father's second wife. "Mama Imelda, I do believe you're right."

○○○

Arturo Martinez proved to be as obedient to Madam Imelda's will as Yi Xiao was to his own grandmother's. Of course, Yi Xiao's payment, a hundred-tael silver boat, proved more than sufficient to convince him. Chinese money, in and of itself, wasn't useful in America, but silver was silver no matter where one went. Yi Xiao had had Burton go over American currencies, just to be sure, and knew enough to avoid being cheated too badly.

It was late afternoon by the time they finished negotiations. Arturo was an honest man and he insisted on giving them packs of food and equipment along with their mounts. It was just as well. Yi Xiao had his bedroll and Hai Chan had borrowed a blanket off the *Henrietta Marie*, but all Kraft and his daughter had was a bag of clothes. "I didn't want Burns to realize I was leaving," he explained, when Yi Xiao commented on his lack. "As it is, I'm afraid he'll notice what I did take and get suspicious."

It was an understandable concern. "Well, with luck, he'll be too busy trying to figure out how to convince Burton to let him aboard the *Henrietta Marie*."

"That's the boat you came on, right Yi Xiao?" Jo had climbed up behind her father and was peering back the way they'd come. San Diego's port was in sight from here and Yi Xiao had pointed out the *Henrietta Marie* where she'd docked. "Oh, she's moved."

The news surprised Yi Xiao only a little. Burton hadn't trusted Burns much more than he had. Scanning the port, he spotted the *Henrietta Marie* anchored in the middle of the bay, where it'd be even harder than before to approach her unnoticed. When he pointed her out, Hai Chan asked, "He's finished unloading already? That was fast."

"I think he wants to head for Panama as quickly as he can." Yi Xiao mounted his horse, a pleasant mare just a little bigger than the Mongolian pony he'd owned as a child. "The less time he stays, the less likely he'll have Burns trying to convince him to go to San Francisco."

Kraft coughed in an embarrassed way. "I think Reverend Burns might be just about done with convincing," he admitted. "He was making noises about using stronger means to persuade the next boat, earlier."

It sounded as if Yi Xiao and Burton had been right to worry about Burns. Hopefully Burton would make every effort to keep that man off his ship. According to Nana Grace, western clergy were supposed to be kind and gentle men. According to what Yi Xiao had seen in Burns' eyes, he was neither. Even worse if he really was trying to seduce young Jo.

Making their farewells of Arturo, and refusing to impose on him to start fresh and early the next day, Yi Xiao and his companions started up the El Camino Real. It was a dusty path that reminded Yi Xiao of some of the trails in the mountains of his homeland, albeit a bit wider and a great deal smoother.

The trees alongside the road were mostly odd looking oaks; all twisted and gnarled by the wind. There were scrubby little pines and a great deal of bushes whose species he didn't recognize. There was also a familiar feeling, a sense of being watched by something old and curious. Heng Shan had similar spirits, creatures bound to the elements, holding apart from the world of men.

Aside from that faint sense, the road was quiet, though Yi Xiao suspected it could be quite busy at the right time of day. He could see other ranches, similar to the sprawling ranchero of their recent host. A few cattle browsed along the roadway, disinterested in the presence of humans. Somewhere high above, a huge bird circled and every so often Yi Xiao thought he heard it call.

They traveled for several hours, to near dusk, before Kraft finally begged a halt. "You two are used to riding, I can see that, but my legs feel like they been pounded to ground meat. Besides, it's getting dark and Jo's tummy's growling like a mad wildcat."

Alone, Yi Xiao could and would have walked a great deal further before stopping. They'd barely gone fifteen miles, after all. Still, he wasn't alone or on foot. The horses couldn't travel in near darkness like he could and his companions did seem to be getting tired. He found a place to camp off to the side of the trail and pointed it out.

It only took a little while to set up camp. Even with Arturo's generous help they didn't have much to work with. A blanket and a bedroll each, a little pan for cooking and some provisions; dried meats and fruits, an odd flour Arturo called maize, and a bag of beans. Arturo had made sure they knew how to cook what they'd been given before they left, another kindness Yi Xiao appreciated. He'd have to remember to find a way to thank both Arturo and Mama Imelda for their help.

Setting up a watch between the three adults—despite Jo's assurances that she could help too—they settled in for the night.

ooo

Sleeping on land was never an easy thing for Hai Chan. He had no trouble changing his walk to deal with solid ground but his body was accustomed to shifting waves. Bed for him was a constantly moving bunk in a stuffy dark room that smelled of fish and human sweat. No matter how tightly he shut his eyes or how much he shifted and moved to find a comfortable position, he simply couldn't fall asleep. The constant breeze flowing over him didn't help.

Thus he heard the faint sound in the darkness before Kraft did, even with Jo's soft snoring. Something moved in the trees, a broken twig that could have been cracked by an animal or a man. Either way, Hai Chan didn't want to be snuck up on and he shifted again, moving as if he were simply sleeping restlessly, and muttered nonsense under his breath.

Another sound, just as faint but a little closer, told Hai Chan he'd failed to scare the stranger off. He shifted again, this time so he was facing away from the fire. Eyes slitted just enough to see, he spotted a slim shadow amid the trees, moving slowly and cautiously towards them.

Something about the shape was familiar and Hai Chan flopped an arm out to poke Yi Xiao's foot. Or, rather, intending to poke Yi Xiao's foot. All he felt beneath his hand was the priest's bedding, rumpled and empty. Had he noticed Gan Han's approach and gone to surprise her? Or was he wandering around the woods in the dark? Knowing him, it was probably the latter.

Hai Chan's movement caused Gan Han to slow her steps. So she was sneaking up on them, perhaps intending to surprise Yi Xiao by being there when morning came, perhaps for less innocent purposes. Hai Chan didn't care which, because he had no intention of letting her do either. "Kraft, there's someone in the trees over there."

"Eh? What?" Kraft started upright and Hai Chan realized the man had been half-asleep. "Who? Where?"

Hai Chan sat up and glared in Gan Han's direction. She was just starting to back away when Yi Xiao came up behind her. "Oh, hello, Gan Han. Whatever are you doing here? I thought you were headed back to China."

The young woman slammed her elbow into Yi Xiao's chest, or where Yi Xiao's chest had been a second before. As usual, the priest's talent for worming his way out of trouble—physical or otherwise—meant the blow slid past him. "Damn you, Yi Xiao. Don't sneak up on me like that!"

"You were sneaking up on us," Hai Chan pointed out dryly, which earned him a sharp look. He was about to ask why Gan Han was there, instead of back aboard the *Henrietta Marie*, but movement behind Yi Xiao drew his attention and made him stop and stare wildly.

It wasn't human, for all it had a human form. No human stood so tall. No human was so utterly black as to reflect no light. No human had arms so long and thin. Jo squeaked at the sight and when Gan Han turned to see what they were staring at, she shrieked as well. She leapt backwards, practically falling over her feet to get away.

The shadow figure cocked its head, bending towards Yi Xiao. Hai Chan was about to leap forward and grab the idiot priest before he was eaten, but Yi Xiao simply reached up and touched the shadowy face with his customary lack of fear. In English, he told them all, "It's all right, everyone. He... she... I'm not sure which, is just a shadow."

"That isn't just shadows!" Hai Chan protested, watching the thing as it floated awkwardly around the camp. It didn't come properly into the light, but it seemed fascinated by the fire. "That's a monster!"

"It might be," Yi Xiao admitted. "Back home it'd be a kind of forest spirit, but I can't understand it well enough to tell if that's true here in America. I get the impression the folk around here call it a dark watcher."

"Is... is it going to eat us?" Jo asked, pressing close to her father for protection.

"I don't think so. Shadows follow the light, at least the ones back home do. It doesn't want to hurt us. They're usually harmless."

Usually harmless meant there was a chance of the opposite. Hai Chan didn't say so, not wanting to frighten the child. "Can you get it to go away?"

It already was. Having satisfied its curiosity about them, the shadowy figure stretched out an arm like a tree branch and patted Yi Xiao's cheek. The touch left a slight silvery mark against his skin, like the skeleton of a leaf. Then it was gone, leaving them all staring at Yi Xiao wildly.

"*DON'T SNEAK UP ON ME LIKE THAT.*"

"Well now, it being late and we having a long trip ahead of us, may I suggest we go back to sleep? Gan Han, you've obviously been walking all night. I won't ask you to take watch this time." Somehow they all fell in with Yi Xiao's plans without argument, a fact Hai Chan found almost as marvelous as the dark watcher itself.

○○○

It didn't surprise Yi Xiao to learn Gan Han hadn't bothered taking much in the way of supplies. When he pointed out her mistake she simply said, haughtily, "As soon as I defeat your blade I'm going to the nearest port and heading home. You brought water and food. What more do I need?"

They both knew she was overconfident. Not only was he not going to fight her, but her English was almost non-existent. Even if she did, by some stroke of fortune, defeat him, she'd little hope of finding a trustworthy captain to take her back to China. At least she'd managed to find suitable clothing. Like Yi Xiao and Hai Chan she was dressed in trousers and a loose shirt, a broad-rimmed hat covering her long hair and protecting her skull from the hot sun.

Still, she shouldn't have followed them. "Why in Lao Tzu's name didn't you just stay on the *Henrietta Marie*? And how did you find me, anyway?"

The questions made Gan Han turn away, staring at the road ahead. Softly, against her will, she muttered, "I was sent to fight you, to prove myself against you. I can't go home until I do."

This was the sort of nonsense citizens of the martial world insisted on making part of their lives. Yi Xiao understood filial piety. After all, he wouldn't be walking a long and winding trail along the Californian coast if he didn't. Yet filial piety that required a child to chase after a grown man so she could face his sabre in a meaningless duel? Surely no God would approve of it.

"You couldn't beat Tsang."

"He cheated with his magic. You may be a sorcerer like Hai Chan says, but…"

"I'm not a sorcerer and neither was Tsang. I saw you fight. You're good, excellent in fact. But you. Are. Not. My. Match." Her lips went tight and he tried another tack. "You have to duel me. Does it have to be with weapons? How about a nice game of mahjong?"

"Why can't it be weapons? Did you swear an oath? From what Burton told me, you already broke it, fighting Tsang."

The accusation was fair. "I didn't swear it, no. But I no longer seek the *dao*, but the *Dao*." She glared at him for the pun but he ignored her irritation, adding, "I'm a priest now. I've left the martial world…"

"There are monks and priests in the martial world and you know that as well as I."

She was right, too, though such men and women were often more interested in battle than they were in their faith. "True though that is, my master is not, and thus, neither am I."

"If you didn't swear an oath…"

"My sword is no longer the most powerful. Even if you did defeat me, you'd still have to defeat whomever took my place."

"I'm your closest rival, you damned fool! Just fight me, let me prove my worth, and I'll leave." She tried wheedling, "You refused aboard ship because I was still sick from Tsang's poison. I'm well enough now."

Yi Xiao refused to consider the possibility. "You still haven't told me how you found me."

"Your sabre led me to you."

"What?" The very idea was nonsense. "My sabre isn't magic. It has no mind or spirit to guide it to its rightful owner."

Sniffing disdainfully, Gan Han tapped the cloth hiding their weapons. "All blades grow attached to the one who wields them. I followed that attachment. Just like I followed you from Heng Shan."

Her certainty stunned Yi Xiao. If she were a trained sorcerer, or gifted with the kind of mind magic his mother's people often possessed, he'd have believed her right away. But she'd shown no signs of such skills before. Was she mad? Confused? Or did she really have such a talent?

"Well you can just stop following me. Take the sabre back to my grandmother. She'll know what to do with it."

"I. Will. Not."

It was likely the argument would have continued for some time if Kraft hadn't interrupted. "I'm not sure what all you folk are talking 'bout, nor why that girl's got such a mad on at you, but I've been trying to get your attention these last five minutes."

Yi Xiao apologized. "What's wrong?"

Both Kraft and his daughter pointed towards a cloud of dust off to the east. "There's someone, a whole lot of someones, coming down that road over yonder. I thought you'd like to know, cause they're moving pretty fast and they'll be here soon."

Even in the relatively peaceful countryside of his father's duchy, it wasn't a good idea to ignore strangers on the road. Yi Xiao grasped the reins of Gan Han's horse, and those of the mule. "Get to the side," he ordered. "Let's see who's coming. Gan Han, keep those weapons sheathed. I'd rather not get into a fight here."

The newcomers were all westerners, six white men and one black, all led by a lean older man who looked like he had all the patience in the world. They were dressed in leather boots, scuffed jeans, loose cotton shirts, and broad-rimmed hats. Pistols gleamed from their holsters, though Hai Chan wasn't sure what sort.

As soon as the new group reached the road the leader held up a hand to slow them down. If there'd been any sign of trouble, or aggression, there'd be a fight. Fortunately, despite Gan Han's yearning to prove herself, they all kept their hands to their sides.

The only one who remotely succeeded in appearing innocent was Yi Xiao. He gazed up at the newcomers with the wide eyed wonder of a child. The men's leader dismissed him immediately, obviously deciding Kraft was in charge. "You there. What's your name?"

It took Kraft a nervous second to respond, which worried Hai Chan. These men had the look of the local authorities. In his experience such men didn't like an apparent reluctance to cooperate. "Hal Kraft." With uncharacteristic spirit, Kraft added, "And yourself?"

The man eyed Kraft. "Jim Trendle," he finally said, sounding grim. "And before you ask, I'm the law around here, so don't think about lying to me."

Kraft spread his hands, which caused his horse to shift uneasily. If Yi Xiao hadn't caught the reins from where he stood and whispered in the animal's ear, there would have been trouble. "S.. sorry. No. I'm no liar, Mister Trendle."

Hai Chan reflected the man had been lying about Jo earlier, but that was a different matter altogether. Seeing Gan Han about to say something, he reached over and caught her hand. "This isn't our business yet," he said urgently. "Don't interfere."

"That man is rude." She stared grimly at Trendle with a hard expression none of the men in his group liked.

"What's that little China girl mad about?"

Again Kraft stammered. "I'm not sure. I don't speak her language. She probably wants to keep moving. We do have a long trip ahead of us."

It would have been useful if Gan Han could put on the same sort of sweet, empty-headed, expression Yi Xiao was expert at. Useful for Hai Chan to do so as well, for that matter. Having no such ability, he contented himself with saying, in deliberately broken English, "We have long long way to go. Is trouble? We continue now, maybe?"

Trendle eyed Hai Chan, dismissing him without a word. "You're obviously not the ones we're looking for, but that doesn't mean you can't be helpful. Where did you come from and where are you headed?"

"San Diego to San Francisco." Before Trendle could ask why they hadn't taken a boat, Kraft added, "We tried to hire a ride, but the captains don't want to lose their crews to the gold fields."

One of the men behind Trendle laughed, "I heard the dock up San Francisco way is full up. They're having to ship supplies in by land from Los Angeles."

"What I want to know is why that little China girl is carrying a couple of great big pig stickers. She a butcher?" That was the large black man towards the back of the group. He was observant, Hai Chan would give him that much. The pig-stickers in question were covered in dark green silk and slung over Gan Han's back. Their shape was obvious, but only to one who knew weapons.

Trendle turned to Hai Chan. "Well, Chinaman?"

Cursing his luck, because he didn't want to be the center of attention, Hai Chan said, "She go meet husband to be. They gift. Male, female, blade. For wedding ceremony." There wasn't any traditional ceremony in China that used such props but he was sure Trendle and his companions couldn't know that.

After a moment, Trendle relaxed, returning his attention to Kraft. Hai Chan could see his disdain for the man's apparent cowardice. "Right. You're obviously not the ones we're looking for. But you be on the lookout, understood? There's a gang out here, been robbing the locals. You see anything, hear anything, you send word to me, got it?"

"Ah, yes, of course sir." Kraft hesitated. "Though it'd help if I knew what they were looking like?"

"Well, that's true," Trendle admitted. "There's about ten white men, led by a tall rangy fellow with a nose like a hatchet and a bad temper. One looks a bit like you, so be careful no one mistakes you for him."

"Yeah, like that'd happen," muttered one of Trendle's men. "This guy's got about as much much spine as a worm. No way he's Ginger Pete."

After a sharp look at his man for interrupting, Trendle added, "They're a nasty bunch. Murdered a whole family, all the way to the baby, over near El Cajon. Word is they've been heading north. So be careful and don't do anything stupid."

Kraft hurriedly and repeatedly assured Trendle that they wouldn't, leaving Hai Chan to wonder if anyone could make such a promise for a man like Yi Xiao.

ooo

Travel became easier further north. There were small ranches along the way, places to stop and buy food, and water the horses. They made good time, traveling around twenty-five to thirty miles a day. Yi Xiao had to walk alongside to allow Gan Han to ride, but he didn't mind. He enjoyed the extra effort. The air was fresh and clean, and if it smelled of strange plants and dust, it was warm and pleasant as well.

Gan Han continued trying to persuade him to duel her, but Yi Xiao ignored her efforts, knowing the rules required him to respond in kind. As long as he refused to face her she'd could do nothing but talk.

Walking through the scrubby little coastal forest, Yi Xiao let most of his mind drift, listening to the life in the woods as he'd been taught. He still wasn't good at it, not at all like his master. She could not only hear the spirits of the land, she could understand them. The closest he'd come had been the shadowy being he'd met earlier, and that only because it understood him better than he understood it.

Whatever it was, spirit, Immortal, forgotten God or even monster, it knew humans well enough to communicate its emotions. It'd liked him for some reason. Enough that it was somewhere out in the woods following him, its curiosity palpable despite the distance.

Several days after they'd met Trendle, Yi Xiao and his companions came upon a little ranch hidden among the scrubby trees. Like Arturo Martinez' place, it was a pleasant sprawling complex of buildings, all covered in that clay called adobe. Unlike Arturo's home, the building and yard were quiet and empty.

Yi Xiao could tell how wrong the silence was. A place like this ought to be bustling with activity, especially at mid-day. When he slowed to a halt, Hai Chan said, "Don't just stand there. We need water."

They needed to be safe and Yi Xiao was sure they weren't. He stopped the others, saying, "Let me go see if the owners mind our coming inside."

At least that was what he'd planned to say. Before he'd half-finished his sentence, a tall man came hurrying out the door, calling out cheerfully, "Welcome! Come on in!"

Hesitant, because he still didn't like the situation, Yi Xiao told him, "I think perhaps you've mistaken us for someone else. We're just travelers hoping to get some water before continuing on our way."

The man grinned, tobacco stained teeth jagged beneath a steel-grey mustache. "Now don't you worry none. We're not expecting nobody. It's just good hospitality and the fact we ain't seen another soul for a week. People don't usually stop in here, with that big old mission just up the road."

Most of the mission houses they'd passed on the way from San Diego had been shut tight or in use for other things. "I hadn't realized there were any still in operation. I'd been told they were closed down some years ago."

"That one's been turned to an inn. It's a nice place if you're looking to stop for the night. But why go walking another five miles when you can get water and food right here."

Kraft said, "It wouldn't hurt nothing to stop a little early, now would it?"

Seeing his companions didn't share his instinctive sense for trouble and willing to admit he might be wrong, Yi Xiao agreed, letting the man lead them inside, once their horses were settled with some hay and water out in the yard.

The central room of the ranch was big, a tall open space with comfortable looking furnishings and decorations of a sort Yi Xiao had never seen. Attractive hangings, a carved wooden jar, a shield with a heavy saber thrust behind it. It hung oddly, as if it were missing a blade. Their host coughed, gesturing towards an opening in the far wall. "If you'd like to come eat?"

Yi Xiao bowed politely but refused to be distracted. "Are you by yourself right now?" he asked, looking around for a servant or at least the man's family. There were signs everywhere that he had children, a few wooden toys dropped on the ground, a child-sized poncho woven of bright wool. "Did your children go visiting?"

The man blinked and Yi Xiao thought a flash of annoyance crossed his face. "My grandkids, you mean? Yeah, they went back to their ma just this morning. Still haven't had a chance to pick up after 'em. Rowdy lot they are, always making trouble." He grinned at Kraft, adding, "With hair like that, bet your boy's just as bad, right?"

Kraft chuckled, unaware of, or ignoring, Yi Xiao's suspicions. "I'm afraid so, Mr..." he left the sentence hanging, letting their host finish.

"I'm Montgomery Jones. Just got this place recent. Haven't had a chance to get it started up proper." Jones explained. "Furnishing came with it, so don't bother asking me about it. Now come and make yourselves comfortable."

Guessing he'd get no more from Jones right then, Yi Xiao followed the man to the dining area. "A meal would be most welcome."

"We've got that covered, I promise." Jones paused to lean through a doorway, "Pete, get that food on the table quick. These people been on the road for quite a while."

They all sat down, Jones at the head of the table, smiling genially. Yet despite his friendly behavior and kindly manner, something about him still seemed strange. It took Yi Xiao several minutes before he realized the westerner wasn't reacting to him, or his fellow countrymen, the way most Americans had so far.

Admittedly, Burton had been equally polite but he'd been a stranger in a strange land at the time. Whereas it was Yi Xiao, Hai Chan and Gan Han who were the outsiders now. At the very least Jones ought to have remarked on the oddity of three Chinese on a trek through southern California. So far he hadn't turned a hair.

A man wearing a bandana came in carrying a bowl of some sort of soup. It smelled hot and spicy, though in an unfamiliar way that almost distracted Yi Xiao from his concerns. His sense of danger was growing, however, and he examined the man carefully as he served the food.

The cook, if cook he was, was thin and fine-boned. His skin was light, with a generous dusting of freckles to rival Jo's. His eyes were light brown, with a scar across one lid from a wound that must have come a hairsbreadth from blinding him. His hair was hidden beneath the bandana but it almost had to be bright red, given the color of his brows.

As Yi Xiao tasted the stew, or soup, or whatever it was, he recalled the name one of Trendle's men had mentioned a few days earlier. Pete. Ginger Pete. What was it about the name that reminded him of his second mother? Barely noticing the raw heat of the spices, or the way the others gasped, he searched his memory. "Oh!" he said. "Ginger means red haired!" Immediately, he could have cursed his fool mouth.

The announcement puzzled his companions but Jones and the man who had to be Ginger Pete glanced sharply at each other. A moment later they had guns out and had grabbed hold of both Jo and Gan Han. "Don't move or they get it!"

Yi Xiao wasn't surprised when Gan Han slammed her head back into Jones' face. An elbow to the chest was quickly followed by a stamp of a heavily booted foot that scraped straight down the man's shin. Jones screeched, trying to get his gun into position to fire. Before he could, Gan Han slid her sword from its sheathe. She was about to cut the man's throat for him when a glance at Yi Xiao made her stop.

"Damn you for being so soft," she muttered, slamming the hilt into Jones' temple. The man slid to the floor, unconscious.

Everything had happened so fast Ginger Pete didn't have a chance to react. By the time he opened his mouth to demand Gan Han stop it was too late. He stared at his compatriot, then turned a hot glare on Gan Han. "Nice moves, missy. But you can't stop me from shooting this boy. So just put that pigsticker of yours down and be quiet."

"Do as he says, Gan Han," Yi Xiao said in English, knowing she'd understand even if she didn't know all the words. When the girl glared at him, he gave her a pleading look. To his relief, she sighed and set the blade down on the table. She did not, he noticed, do the same with his sabre. It remained in its sheathe on her back, hidden by green silk.

"Now then," Pete said calmly. "I want you lot to go through that door, one at a time. You with the pretty talk, go first."

The man forced them through a hallway and Yi Xiao smelled something other than the spicy dish they'd been offered earlier. Blood and the stink of fear. He and Hai Chan glanced at each other, steeling themselves for what they were about to find.

They came to a door at the far end of the hall, where the smell was worse. There was a noise, too, a frightened little sound that might have crying. When Yi Xiao opened the door and stepped in, someone shrieked.

The room was a pantry, though most of the food had been thrown to the floor. It was full of children and young women; the real house-servants, working for whomever really lived here. Yi Xiao didn't like to think why they'd been spared.

"Get in there, all of you." Pete ordered and they obeyed unwillingly, crowding into the room. As the bandit dragged Jo back with him, her father tried to snatch at her arm. "Oh, no you don't," Pete snapped. "I'm keeping the boy with me. Just so you lot don't try anything stupid."

The door slammed shut, leaving them in darkness.

ооо

Hai Chan gave the bandit several minutes before he smashed the door open, letting a little light into the room. When Kraft protested, he pointed out, "That man's trying to get away. We probably trapped them inside, showing up when we did, and they meant to fool us long enough to escape. Besides, it's too damn close in here. I like cuddling, but not when the poor things are terrified out of their minds."

By this time Yi Xiao had slipped through the doorway. "What are you going to do?" Gan Han demanded. "I'm sure that man will injure the child if you show your face."

"I am going to sit down here in the hall," Yi Xiao announced calmly. "And we are all going to be quiet for a little while."

"More of your sorcery?" Hai Chan demanded.

"It's not sorcery." Yi Xiao slid into the cross-legged position he used when he was meditating. At the same time Kraft leapt past the man, tearing down the hall in a headlong rush. Sounding resigned, Yi Xiao added, "Keep an eye on him. Don't let him get his daughter killed."

Hai Chan set off running, with Gan Han close behind. "What is he up to?" the girl demanded as Hai Chan tried to figure out which way Kraft had gone. The house was a maze of hallways and he was thoroughly lost. An odd noise drew his attention and he cautiously opened the door to the room it came from.

"Gods."

What lay beyond had been a bedroom, once. Now it was an abattoir, filled with the fly covered remains of a half-dozen bodies. The ranch's menfolk, some hardly more than children, their throats slit and their fly-covered eyes wide and empty. An old man leaned against the wall, a sabre—twin to the one in the living room—thrust through his belly. He raised his head, staring blankly, and said something in Spanish that Hai Chan didn't understand.

"We can't help you," Hai Chan said gently, hoping the man understood English. "And there's someone else who needs us."

"Go," the man whispered. "Kill them."

"With pleasure," Gan Han growled from beside Hai Chan. "Let's go. I want my sword."

A sword was a poor weapon against a gun, but Hai Chan knew better than to argue. They continued searching and when they found the dining room, they both cursed. The sword was gone. Had the bandits taken it?

Gan Han closed her eyes. "It isn't far." Surprised, she added, "I think Kraft has it."

The girl had claimed she could follow a weapon's owner. Apparently the reverse was true as well. "Never mind, then. Unless your sorcery extends to stopping bullets, a sword isn't much use right now." Hai Chan could see how the accusation of magic infuriated her, but ignored her in favor of heading into the central room.

The sound of an argument drifted through the open windows and Hai Chan dropped to his knees, gesturing for Gan Han to do the same. To her credit and despite her annoyance, she obeyed. They crawled closer, listening intently.

"Telling you, we gotta get moving. That damned Trendle's onto us."

The voice was Montgomery Jones' and Gan Han growled a curse. "I should have killed him," she muttered.

"He can't know where we are," Ginger Pete said and more voices agreed with him. "Besides, I got this cute little hostage… OW!"

At a guess, Jo had bit Pete as hard as she could. There were a few wild moments of shouts and bangs, ending with, "And stay there, you little brat!" The child had tried, but she hadn't managed to escape.

Hai Chan tried to decide what to do. Jo needed help but if he stuck so much as a hair into view those men would surely do him or her some damage. Gan Han looked equally helpless, her fists clenched tight at her sides.

A moment later something crashed through a door on the other side of the courtyard. "You let my kid go!" Kraft screamed furiously. As predicted, he was armed with Gan Han's sword; though it was obvious he'd no idea what he was doing. It was stupid, pointless and useless, but it was about the bravest thing the man had ever done. It gave Hai Chan the distraction he needed and he leapt through the wide open window, getting his bearings rapidly.

There were several men there, all turned to look at Kraft as he used Gan Han's sword to cut at the man holding his daughter captive. Pete had been startled just long enough to give Kraft a chance to stab him in the back of his hand, forcing him to drop his gun.

Catching hold of Pete by the back of the neck, Hai Chan flung him to the ground and grabbed Jo, tossing her back towards Gan Han. "Get inside," he ordered. "Gan Han, help me keep them out."

At the same time a shot rang out, setting Jo screaming. Hai Chan turned to see Kraft drop Gan Han's sword, hand going to his belly as he stared wildly at Montgomery Jones. He'd been so busy attacking his daughter's captor he hadn't noticed the man who'd shot him.

Hai Chan was strong. Strong enough to take injuries that would incapacitate most men. He was not stronger than a bullet. Instead of attempting to help a man beyond help, he dodged back inside, helping Gan Han drag Jo along.

"He killed my father! Let me at him. Give me a gun! I'll kill him!"

Hai Chan shook her. "This isn't the time for vengeance. We have to get out of here!"

With Gan Han's help, he dragged the screaming and crying girl back the way they'd come.

ooo

Yi Xiao didn't consider what he'd learned from the Hermit sorcery but he wondered if it was close. Gathering his *qi* and using it to command wind and water was one thing. Even using it to sense everything around him was part of that same skill.

This, however, was an extension of his abilities that pushed the definition almost out of shape. Connected to world around him, he could feel the movement of life as it ebbed and flowed. There, the terrified lives of the survivors. Here, the rapidly ebbing life-force of an old soldier who'd lost his final battle. There, his companions, searching for their quarry. Here, that quarry, too focused on his daughter's safety to protect himself.

And there, just outside, were twisted lives, glorying in bloodshed and the pain and fear they caused. Yi Xiao knew some of what they'd done had been for money, but a great deal of it had been love of cruelty. Their current victim, Jo, struggled against her terror, trying to find a chance to escape.

That moment came alongside something so terrible it almost shattered Jo's heart. Yi Xiao didn't need sight or sound to understand. He felt Kraft's movements, the way he'd closed with the twisted ones. Felt the moment of his death.

Jo's rescue was equally obvious and Yi Xiao thought they were safe enough now. They just had to escape the house and hide, at least until the men gave up. Given, of course, they would. Yi Xiao was about to put freshly cultivated *qi* energy to use protecting his companions when he felt the twisted ones turn gleeful.

A moment later there was an explosion and Yi Xiao realized the enemy's solution to their problem. They were going to burn everyone inside the building alive. There'd be no witnesses, no victims seeking vengeance. Just a pile of ash, smoking in the rubble.

If this were Heng Shan, whose elements Yi Xiao had long practiced connecting to, he could have drawn down a storm to douse the fire. Here, however, he'd barely begun to scratch the surface of this land's elements. He'd no hope of commanding air so dry and still.

Something moved at the edge of Yi Xiao's thoughts. The dark watcher, observing what he did and curious as always. Could it help? Would it help? Calling it took all Yi Xiao's attention, so he was only dimly aware of his companions returning and babbling about the fire.

"Master says, when in danger, panic leads to self-destruction," he said without opening his eyes. "Be quiet. I'm asking for help." Neither Hai Chan nor Gan Han understood but they didn't argue, letting him focus all his attention on the dark watcher.

They connected; a deeper and more intimate connection than before. The dark watcher, or watchers, were ancient. So old the ones who'd called them into being were long gone. Now the forest, the great huge trees that had been their homes, were gone, leaving them to wander alone and lonely, through a changed landscape.

Yi Xiao dared not offer hope. He didn't even know what would help these ancient beings. He did offer friendship, even a kind of companionship, should they desire it. At the same time he pleaded, showing the beings what was happening, showing them the killers and their victims. Showing them the fiery death awaiting him and his companions if nothing were done.

Wood moved. The trees around the ranch shifted, twisting their way free of the dry and rocky dirt. Drawn along with the spirits, Yi Xiao sensed the killers and hungered for their end.

Someone screamed, then another, as his new allies tangled their roots and branches around the murderers.

Yi Xiao focused his attention on one in particular. Montgomery Jones. If he had let Gan Han kill him, Kraft might still be alive. Without hesitation, without so much as a qualm, he set his allies on the man, twisting their branches around his neck in a grotesque and appropriate hangman's noose. Jones screamed and went silent a moment later.

"Now, make an exit," Yi Xiao whispered. "Quickly."

The nearest wall buckled and crumbled away as hundreds of tendrils tore the clay apart. Then they pulled back from the flames, and Yi Xiao opened his eyes. "Out of the house. Now."

ooo

Escaping the burning ranch required Hai Chan and Gan Han to chivy the terrified servants from the 'safety' of the pantry and through a shattered wall. To Hai Chan's surprise, what calmed the frightened women wasn't the fresh air and sunlight. Rather it was the sight of the bandits who'd attacked them, trapped within within the branches of the same trees that had torn up the courtyard and the building's wall.

They seemed particularly pleased by the corpse dangling above them. Nor did Hai Chan blame them. He'd seen Jones' victims. Hanging had been the least of what he'd deserved.

"It's going to be quite a time getting them out," Hai Chan commented.

"I'm just glad only Jones died." Yi Xiao's sentiment wasn't shared by anyone else, but Hai Chan knew how hard the young priest yearned to break with his upbringing. Right then he was holding Jo in his lap, letting the girl cry, his eyes distant as he watched Gan Han gather their things so they could go on. "Spirits like the dark watchers don't have the same morality we humans do. But it was I who asked it of them."

Hai Chan wasn't one to judge. His own morality was barely better than the dark watchers'. It certainly wasn't as noble as Yi Xiao was trying to become. The survivors weren't the only ones viciously pleased by Jones' fate. "What do we do now?" He didn't think they could just walk away.

"We'll send someone to find Trendle. Once he's here, he and his men can have their quarry." Yi Xiao patted Jo on the head, adding, "Not to mention finding a family to take our young lady here in. Once that's done, we can continue to San Francisco. I'm in no rush, but I'm sure you want to get back to sea again."

It was a truth Hai Chan didn't need to confirm. He enjoyed Yi Xiao's company. Was even beginning to appreciate the man's sorcery, or whatever he insisted on calling it. But he was a sailor, first and foremost.

And a sailor belonged on the sea.

Chapter 4: Fire –
The Goal in Sight brings Progress

They buried Jo's father in the same churchyard as the rest of Pete Grubb's victims, on a hillside overlooking the Pacific. She thought he'd like that. He'd liked watching the sun setting over the ocean. Said it put him in mind of the way her Ma would shell peas, sitting on the stoop in the evening.

Once her Pa was properly settled, Jo made it clear she wanted to stay with Yi Xiao and his companions. "Everyone around here talks Spanish," she pointed out when Yi

"...TANGLED THEIR ROOTS AROUND THE MURDERERS."

Xiao tried to persuade her otherwise. "And that Trendle fellow don't need a kid hanging round him."

Yi Xiao might act like a damnfool, but he had a sharp way about him that saw through Jo's excuses. There were a few English speaking families in the little town nearby. She could have stayed with them if she'd wanted and they both knew it.

To her relief, all he said was, "I'm not a good choice for a father, but I am expert at being a big brother." That made Gan Han snort, proving the girl understood English better than she pretended. "Still, you should know I have a way of running into trouble whether or not I try to avoid it. Will you allow me to teach you to defend yourself?"

Jo understood. She'd gotten herself used as a hostage back at that ranch. If she could have fought back, or at least done a better job of escaping, her Pa might still be alive. "Will you teach me how to use a sword? I already know how to handle a gun."

"I will not." His refusal irritated Gan Han but she didn't say a word, just drew her sword, raising it towards Yi Xiao's throat. He pushed it aside without effort, adding, "Nor will I fight you."

For Jo's sake Gan Han answered in heavily accented English. "You will. Sooner. Later. You will."

Somehow, Jo had a feeling Yi Xiao had more stubborn in his little finger than Gan Han had in her whole body. She didn't understand the pair's relationship at all; it seemed obvious to her Gan Han must be in love with Yi Xiao. But they played the same sort of game some of the older kids did back home, pretending to hate each other. Or, at least, Gan Han did. It was hard to imagine Yi Xiao hating anyone.

After the burial they were on their way again, wending their way through dry, brush covered hills and scrubby pine forests. Every morning Yi Xiao practiced that odd dance he called a fighting style, trained Jo to defend herself, then continued towards San Francisco.

It didn't take long before Jo noticed Yi Xiao going distant every so often. Sometimes he said he was communing with the land. Sometimes he said he was cultivating—whatever that meant—his *qi*. But other times he just looked sad, like there was something eating at him.

Jo did ask why he looked that way, but the only answer he had was, "Master says, the heart's fire can be harnessed, but never doused."

It meant nothing to Jo, but Gan Han muttered something in Chinese Jo was pretty near sure wasn't complementary. Jo was trying to learn the language, but there were things her companions wouldn't teach her. The best she could guess was that Yi Xiao's mood had something to do with the reason why Gan Han kept trying to fight him. She didn't understand what they meant by a martial world but she didn't have to know to realize it ate at Yi Xiao something fierce.

Whenever Jo saw that look on Yi Xiao's face, she tried to distract him with questions about his home and family. He didn't talk much about his parents but he had a great deal of fun telling her all about the troubles he'd get into with his brothers and sisters.

"How'd you avoid getting beaten?" Jo asked, after one elaborate tale about how he, his half-sister and his older brother had climbed the supporting pillars of some temple and gotten stuck.

"Oh, we didn't avoid it. We weren't sitting for a week after they got us down. But that was nothing, compared to the time my cousin and I switched places. I was nearly killed."

That made Jo's eyes go wide. "How'd you manage that?"

Ruefully, Yi Xiao scrubbed his hand through his thick hair, the short locks sticking up all over, "Someone thought I was him." Embarrassed, he muttered to himself, "Master says, a patched wine-jar doesn't leak. I shouldn't have brought up the subject."

"Now that you have, you may as well finish," Hai Chan pointed out. "You have me curious. Gan Han, too."

"Not include me in nonsense." Gan Han pretended to look away, as if she didn't care. But Jo could tell she was interested, despite herself. Interested enough to speak in English so Jo could understand.

"Well, yes. I suppose." Yi Xiao considered his words carefully. "My cousin and I look a great deal alike. Some people even think we're twins. We're not, of course, for all we were born on the same day and in the same place."

A cold snort escaped Gan Han's lips. "Given who cousin is, see why that problem." She paused, adding, "That why they exile you?"

"I'm not exiled," Yi Xiao denied. "But it is why I've been sent away." He looked west, like he thought he could see all the way to China. "Maybe someday, when things settle down, I can go home. Right now all I can do is hope my cousin's all right. Him and all my family."

ooo

It was mid-morning, over three weeks after they'd left San Diego, when Yi Xiao spotted the tip of what had to be San Francisco Bay. By this time they'd begun seeing more and more people using the same road they were on. Californios, Mexicans, the occasional native, white men and black and a few other Chinese.

"Why won't they smile at you," Jo asked suddenly as the third group of Chinese prospectors passed. As bright and sharp-eyed as she was, she couldn't fail to notice the way they avoided Yi Xiao's gaze.

"They probably don't like my face." At Gan Han's dour chuckle, Yi Xiao added in Chinese, "Oh, you do have a sense of humor after all?"

"It's not your face they don't like, you know."

"I know. But do you really want me to give the young lady a history lesson?" The trouble wasn't Yi Xiao's face, but his ancestry. Most of the Chinese immigrants to America were Han, with some enclaves of other Chinese minorities. Yi Xiao might lack his people's traditional shaved forehead, but his Manchurian ancestry was obvious.

"She's bright. You don't need to hide truths from her."

Gan Han might be obsessed and stubborn as their pack mule on one subject but she was right about Jo's intelligence. The girl had sharp eyes and learned quickly. In English again, he told her, "China has a long history of dynasties rising and falling. It also has dozens of different peoples. Miao, Han, Mongolian, Manchu… the list is huge, especially if you go further west. Right now the ruling family—the Qing—are from the Manchu people. But prior to that, the Ming ruled, and they—like most of the immigrants here—were Han."

Jo caught on quickly. "So they don't like you because you're Manchurian?"

To be honest, Yi Xiao thought some of them had better reason than that. "Ruling classes are seldom well-loved by those they rule," he noted. "I'm not really all that important... be quiet, Gan Han... just a priest searching for understanding. But they can't know that." It'd be different if he were Buddhist. Their shaved skulls were easily recognized and mostly respected.

They continued riding along a hillside that grew taller and taller as they went. More hills rose around them, hiding the bay. Buildings started to appear, square temporary structures more like tents than anything else. If they were tents, they seemed odd to Yi

Xiao's eyes. He'd visited his grandfather's clan in Manchuria once, when he was young, and had fond memories of the lovely round yurts dotting the grassland.

As they rounded a bend, Yi Xiao scanned the scene ahead of them. The hillside was covered in more buildings overlooking a bay so full of boats it was almost impossible to see the water beneath. It was an amazing sight, leaving him wondering if one could just walk across by leaping from boat to boat.

Even as Yi Xiao contemplated the possibilities, Hai Chan grinned and clapped his hands together. "You see?" he told them. "All I have to do is find a crew."

ooo

San Francisco was a cacophony; shouts, things banging into other things, metal ringing on metal. It was a bewildering mix of odors; meat, burning wood, tar, coal and other things far less savory. It was a blur of colors and people; all moving to and fro about their business. Jo wanted to run wild, to explore every nook and cranny of the place. If her father had been alive she'd have tried, knowing he'd trust her not to wander far. Yi Xiao might not, seeing himself as her guardian as he did.

The road ahead grew steep, leading to a series of larger and better constructed buildings. They were nothing compared to the brick and glass houses back home in Shanksville, but they were a sight better than the rough tent structures covering the hillside.

Just like on the road, there were all sorts of people in San Francisco. Most looked like prospectors taking a break from their work. Others seemed to be shopkeepers or the like, all going about their business with barely a curious glance at the strangers wandering their town. Newcomers like Jo and her companions were likely common as weeds and just as interesting.

There was one fellow caught Jo's eye, but before she could point him out to Yi Xiao the man disappeared around a corner. It had nothing to do with them, but it was funny to see someone wearing that haircut Yi Xiao'd mentioned, the one Manchurians preferred back in China. He was oddly dressed, too, in a long dark robe with shiny embroidery, big sleeves and a high collar. There being other Chinese wandering around San Francisco, Jo guessed it didn't matter. He was probably just stopping in town for supplies or a rest.

By then they were close to what looked like a main street. There was a greengrocer of sorts, a dry-goods place, a land office, a bank and—about halfways down—an inn. She pointed it out. "Should we get rooms?"

"It's only mid-afternoon," Yi Xiao answered. "Are you really that tired?"

"There are people arriving all the time, least that's what my uncle Caleb said when he wrote Pa. If we're going to be staying, we gotta strike while the iron is hot."

Blinking, Yi Xiao considered her words. "I understood that one. All right, if you think it'd be better, I can't see a good reason to refuse." He said a few words to Gan Han, who shrugged without argument. They left the horses tied with a half-dozen others and set Hai Chan to keep an eye on their things.

Inside, the inn was dark but clean. The man behind the desk was neatly dressed and looked pleasant enough, but his expression changed as Yi Xiao walked closer. "No havee roomee for you. You go, find Chinee place. Stay there."

It hadn't occurred to Jo that there'd be a problem. Of course, back home she'd never seen a Chinese, anymore than most of her people had. No one would have known what to make of Yi Xiao, but they would have been polite. Well, most of them would be.

Yi Xiao stopped at the desk and smiled broadly at the innkeeper. "I'm sorry. I'm not familiar with that dialect." he said in that crisp sharp English of his. "Or is it a speech impediment?" At the same time he set one of those oddly shaped silver lumps his people called money on the desk between him and the man. It was one of the bigger ones, its surface glittering in the lamplight, the shape of a Chinese word stamped at its center.

The innkeeper stared at the money. "I do apologize sir. I mistook you for..." Flustered, he fell silent. They all knew he'd done nothing of the sort. "What sort of rooms are you looking for? And for how long?"

"Two, for a few days—until we get settled. Preferably next door to each other. You may put us towards the back of the inn, if need be, but not right over the kitchen please."

Having determined that real money was involved, the innkeeper bowed. "They aren't very large, but I have two such rooms on the third floor." He hesitated, "It's an attic, but I promise it's clean and kept proper."

"Excellent. Is a bath included?"

"Yes, sir," the man answered quickly. "Only space for one in each room, but I'll have them refilled as soon as need be, if you like?"

"I would be most appreciative." Yi Xiao bowed. "And, while I have your attention, would you happen to know where I can find a Mr. Chang in this city?"

The question set the innkeeper staring. "Near as I can tell, there are dozens. They all live over in the Chinese district, up the way some." He pointed off to the west, towards the hillside.

"Then that is where I shall start. Just as soon as we've settled in." Yi Xiao paused to ask Hai Chan to stable the horses, then led the way upstairs.

The rooms turned out to be small and dimly lit. Servants' quarters, no doubt, and hardly worth the amount of silver Yi Xiao had paid for them. If it'd been Jo's Pa, or Reverend Burns, there'd have been an argument on the subject. Yi Xiao just smiled ruefully, when she told him so, saying, "I expected his reaction."

"Why didn't you argue none with him, then? That was a lot of money you paid."

"Master says, money is a fine tool but a poor paving material."

Gan Han muttered something under her breath as she examined the bed for bugs. "Why ask Chang? Common name."

Yi Xiao moved out of the way of the servants bringing the baths and buckets of hot water to their rooms. "I know. But I wanted to know where the local Chinese are living. Without being told to go stay with them again."

It still bothered Jo, the way that man reacted to her guardian. "Why would he? Your money's good."

"And I'm a stranger in a strange land." By now Hai Chan was thumping up the stairs to join them. "You grew up in a remote town out in the country. No one taught you to think Chinese are barbarians. Our host, on the other hand, likely believes that very thing. That's why, despite paying enough to get us into the best room in the best hotel in San Francisco, we are here in these tiny rooms and grateful they're at least well-kept."

Hai Chan looked into the room he'd be sharing with Yi Xiao. "They're better than my bunk aboard the *Southern Cross*, at least." He tossed his bag in a corner and headed back outside. "I'll go check out the ships. Gods know what condition some of them are in." Before Jo could ask what he was going to use to pay for a whole ship, he was gone. With a shrug for their companion's abrupt disappearance, Yi Xiao went into his room and closed the door.

"Child, bathe first." Gan Han ordered.

"I'm all right," Jo told her roommate, though she knew she didn't smell too good. "I've got to go look for someone myself." Then, like Hai Chan before her, she hurried downstairs, hoping Gan Han wouldn't go all maternal on her, trying to keep her out of trouble.

○○○

A hot—or relatively hot—bath was a rare luxury and Yi Xiao took gleeful advantage of an even rarer moment of solitude to soak in its heat. This was the first time he'd been properly alone since he'd left Heng Shan and he reveled in the quiet. Well, mostly quiet. The noise of the streets outside was a faint rumble of bangs, clangs and curses. Distant and muffled as they were, he barely noticed.

It was almost half an hour later when Yi Xiao realized his charge was missing. He'd finished his bath, dressed and tapped on Gan Han and Jo's door, intending to tell them he was going out.

Gan Han answered, wrapped in a sheet from her bed and annoyed at the interruption. "I've no clue where she went. She said something about finding someone and ran off. She's a big girl. I'm sure she's fine."

Yi Xiao wasn't so sure. Gan Han had grown up in the martial world. She'd been defending herself from bullies and the like for most of her life. She could have walked through the worst districts of Shanghai or Hong Kong without much risk.

Jo, on the other hand, had only two weeks of limited self-defense training to protect her. She was smart, hopefully smart enough to run from what she couldn't fight, but she was also impetuous and hot-tempered. Yi Xiao could imagine her saying or doing the wrong thing in the wrong place all too readily. "I'll go look for her." He hurried outside, pausing only long enough to ask the innkeeper which way the child had gone.

Gan Han was dressed and following Yi Xiao before he got more than a dozen steps away from the inn. "Why are you so worried?"

"She's a child."

"She's a year younger than I am."

"You're a child too."

"I. Am. Not."

Yi Xiao ignored her in favor of asking a man fixing a wooden sign, "Did you see a red-haired boy come through?"

"That I did. Asked where the post office was." The fellow pointed down the street. "The building with the flag up top. Can't miss it."

Yi Xiao hoped that was true and tossed the man one of the coins he'd gotten from Arturo back in San Diego. He was about to continue when something caught hold of his shoulder and spun him around. "Where's the girl?" Reverend Burns hissed into his face furiously. "And don't play dumb, Chinaman. I already know you speak English."

○○○

The post office wasn't much of a place, but Jo figured it didn't need to be. It was also almost empty, with just three men working behind the desk packing up boxes of envelopes. The oldest of them looked up at her sharp, "Ain't been no mail yet, boy. That new ship just come in from China, of all places. They got nothing for the likes of you."

Jo smiled, imitating Yi Xiao at his most engaging. "Naw sir, I ain't here for mail." At the same time she wondered why a boat had come from China. For that matter, why hadn't Yi Xiao and the others taken a straight trip to San Francisco if one was available?

"Got a letter to send, then? Where's it going? Further away, more it costs."

Jo walked on up to the desk. "Not a letter, neither," she admitted. "I was told you got post boxes here?"

The man agreed on that. "You better have your pa take care of renting one, though. I can't be doing business like that with a kid."

"Ain't renting. Picking up. Here, I got a letter saying I can." Jo pulled out the envelope she'd been carrying all the way from Shanksville. Pa had thought it'd be safer with her. She could move fast and hide better than him, if anyone tried to take it. Besides, who'd think a kid like her would have anything valuable?

The clerk took the letter and read it careful. Then he took the little key at the bottom of the envelope. "Well, I guess it's in order," he allowed. "Give me a moment. That box is way in the back and it's a tight squeeze."

"I'll just wait over there," Jo told him, pointing to a corner where she could look out the window. "Out of the way."

The street outside was as fascinating as ever and Jo tried to imagine what sort of people were passing by. Some looked like they'd been soldiers, once upon a time. They walked straighter, with a confident air. Some had been around for a while, ambling along without a care in their world. And, of course, the newcomers were obvious. They stared wide-eyed at everything, taking it all in.

A familiar figure walked past the building. The same Chinese man she'd seen earlier. He strode along confidently, ignoring the way passersby stared at his odd clothes. Now she saw him up close, she could see he was clean-shaven, a little older than middle-aged, and sternly handsome. He had the look of a man used to being obeyed, like a soldier or something. Jo wondered who he was and why he'd seemed to recognize their group. Was he from that ship the clerk had mentioned?

To Jo's surprise, the man turned and walked straight into the post office, dark eyes scanning the room until they found her. "Well, hello there. Was that you I noticed with my countryman earlier?" His English wasn't as polished as Yi Xiao's, but it was excellent, nonetheless.

He seemed nice and polite and Jo relaxed. "Yes, sir, that was me."

"It's terribly rude of me, of course, but could you tell me your companions' names? I've a feeling I know them and would like to be sure. It's been some time since I saw them last, after all."

Jo didn't see any reason to stay silent. "The tall one is Hai Chan. The short one is Yi Xiao and the lady is Gan Han. I'm just finishing my business here, I could take a message to them, if you'd like." By this time the clerk had come out from the back room with her package.

The man smiled in a genial way. "You could take me back to meet them, instead. I'd like that even better." He waited for her to sign the clerk's log book and put her package in her bag. "If it wouldn't be too much of an imposition?"

There didn't seem to be a reason why she shouldn't. She'd taken longer than she'd meant to and she needed to hurry back anyway. "All right, mister. I suppose that's fine. It's not far, just about five minutes away. Maybe a bit more, with that hill out there."

They walked up the steep street, the man apparently oblivious to the noise and fuss surrounding them. He was more interested in Jo's relationship to Yi Xiao. "You're obviously not blood kin to him. How is it you're with him? Surely you have family?"

Jo didn't want to explain too much about herself and wasn't sure what her companion wanted to know. Her Pa once said if there was a hinge on her tongue she'd rattle on both ends. It got worse when she was anxious and this tall, powerfully built, man was just the sort to make her nervous. "I got separated. He's helping me out 'til I find my family."

They weren't far from the inn when Jo spotted the first sign of trouble. Reverend Burns' assistant, Joel—the one who never bathed and seldom brushed his teeth—was just heading into alleyway. And if he was there, surely that meant Burns was as well.

"Is something wrong?"

Jo spotted Yi Xiao and Gan Han talking to a man working on a sign. Yi Xiao tossed the man a coin and was about to move on when Burns appeared from between two buildings. As the man caught hold of Yi Xiao's shoulder, more of Burns' men came out quietly to surround the pair. It was done so smooth no one around Yi Xiao and Gan Han noticed. Or if they did, they made nothing of it and left the group alone.

Jo stepped behind her companion and watched as Burns spoke sharply to her friend. He towered over Yi Xiao, glaring down intimidatingly and Jo waited for Yi Xiao to use his skills to break free. To her surprise, he didn't. Instead he cocked his head in that annoyingly foolish way of his and went with Burns, letting the man drag him off to God knew where.

"Come on, mister," she gasped to her new companion. "I don't know what's going on but I know that fellow's trouble. Yi Xiao needs help."

ooo

"Why are you letting this man drag us off where he likes?"

"Tell that girl to stop talking Chinee and speak like a real person," Reverend Burns snapped, glaring down at Gan Han as he dragged them both by the elbow through the streets.

"Her English isn't very good," Yi Xiao explained, giving Gan Han a warning look. "She wants to know why I'm cooperating."

"You're cooperating 'cause I'm gonna beat your yellow hide black and blue if you don't, you little bastard."

"Oh, I sincerely doubt that." Yi Xiao gave Burns the sweetest smile he could muster. "I don't think you could afford it, anyway."

One of the other men, the one with the bad teeth and worse breath, asked, "Afford? What's there to afford?"

"I charge for damage," Yi Xiao explained. "If you hit me and the blow lands, you pay me." He considered the matter thoughtfully while their captors stared at him. "Though I must admit, I haven't worked out the going rates here in America."

Gan Han kicked at his ankle but he slid his foot out of the way before she connected. "Idiot! Turtle's Egg!" she growled. "Must you?"

"Well, yes, I must. After all, if they manage to hurt me I'm going to need medical aid." Yi Xiao spoke in English so he couldn't be accused of conspiring.

"If you don't shut your damned mouth you'll be needing an undertaker," Reverend Burns snapped. "Now be quiet until we're someplace private."

They continued to the edge of the bay, where dozens of warehouses stood alongside the docks. Rounding the north end, Yi Xiao could see an island with a few buildings, and a spit of land rising into a densely wooded hillside. One of the men shoved at him to get his attention and he shifted his shoulder just enough to send his attacker stumbling forward when he missed.

"Stand still!"

"Not until I've worked out how much to charge. For that matter, even if I did know how much I was going to charge I wouldn't stand still. There's no reason to make it easy for you." Yi Xiao let Burns lead them into an old and crumbling warehouse at the very edge of the pier. "How charming. Is this where you gentlemen are staying? And however did you get here ahead of us? I do hope you didn't manage to capture the *Henrietta Marie* after all."

"We didn't get here before you, you stupid bastard. We've been just behind you the whole way." Something about the way Burns spoke suggested the delay wasn't according to plan. The only reason they'd taken so long was because they'd only just caught up. "Now where's Kraft and his girl? Did you lose 'em somewhere? Maybe steal that letter of theirs?"

Yi Xiao was puzzled. "Letter?" he asked. "What letter?"

Jo's voice came from the darkness at the other side of the warehouse. "The one my uncle sent us before he died, giving Pa a share in his mine up in Heavenly Valley."

∞

Two weeks training wasn't good enough to go up against Burns and his friends and Jo knew it. She was glad she had someone backing her up. Belatedly, she realized she didn't know anything about the fellow, much less if he'd help. But he'd followed along readily when she'd said Yi Xiao was in trouble, so he couldn't be anyone bad.

They all stared on each other, taking everyone's measure. Jo could tell Burns wasn't bothered by her sudden appearance, or her companion. He didn't think much of anyone who wasn't a white man, of course, so likely figured the Chinese man to be nothing more than a nosey local prying where he wasn't wanted.

"Mine, Jo? You never mentioned any mine?" Typical of Yi Xiao, he might have been asking the time.

Two could play Yi Xiao's game. Jo answered as lightly as he, "I'm sorry. I shoulda told you back when Pa got killed. My Ma's brother was working for Mr. Sutter when they found gold. He was one of the ones earned enough to do something with, so him and his partner got a bit of property somewhere north of here, out in the hills. He willed my Pa his share in the profits."

"Profits your father promised... Wait... he's dead?" Burns stared.

"Mr. Kraft was killed by bandits somewhere near... Los Angeles, I think it was?" Yi Xiao explained.

"That means..."

"That means the share belongs to me, Reverend Burns." Jo looked firm on the man, not at all willing to give an inch. He was a bully, always insisting on his own way and Jo was tired of him.

"You're a child. A little girl," Burns sneered, adding, "Oh, I'm sorry. Did I reveal something you didn't want known?"

Since even the fellow behind Jo wasn't surprised, she just said, "It don't matter. I'm the only one left in my family. I'll fight you for it..."

Yi Xiao interrupted. "Child, I haven't taught you nearly enough to duel with."

"I mean in court. Reverend Burns and I got no blood tie. He's just one of the group we were traveling with. He got no say in what happens to my Pa's property." Jo wasn't experienced in the world but she knew her rights.

If Burns could have set Jo alight right then and there, he'd have done it. She knew he didn't like being thwarted and a girl thinking she could say 'no' to him was about the worst thing ever. She wondered how many people had to have let him have his way for him to get like this. Too many, that was sure.

Somehow, despite his fury, Burns kept his temper. "Your father owed me for helping you two get as far as you did. Or are you forgetting I'm the one had the quinine that saved your life?"

That was as maybe and Jo said as much. "Pa's gone, though."

"Dead or no, he promised me a share of what was waiting for him here in California. So if you're the one owns that bit of property of your uncle's—and until there's a deed put in your name, you ain't—you owe me what he did."

"You forced him to make that deal while I was sick. When he didn't have no choice." Jo still felt guilty over that. It was her fault her Pa had agreed at all.

"But he did make it, girl. You know it, just as well as I. And I'm not being greedy and asking for the whole thing." Burns spread his hands, smiling beatifically. "I promise, I wasn't cheating him none and I'm not cheating you."

It didn't seem right and it didn't seem fair. It especially didn't seem right when Yi Xiao said softly, "Master says, a debt forgotten hangs on the soul." He slipped past Burns and his men before any of them could notice and walked up to Jo.

"I don't care if he says he's a man of God. I been watching him this whole way and he's a dirty, no good, scoundrel."

Yi Xiao set a light hand on her shoulder. "He may not be a good man. He may frighten you. But he hasn't wronged you. If your father owed him, you shouldn't refuse the debt for those reasons."

Jo wanted to argue but she couldn't find an adequate defense. Helplessly, she told Burns. "What did Pa promise, for that quinine?"

"There's a box up on that property of your uncle's, hid in a cave. It's got something special in it, meant for your father. You give us that, we're even."

"From the sound of things, we need to go to the property and find whatever it is Jo's uncle left." When Burns opened his mouth to object, Yi Xiao raised a finger to stop him. "Do you know what's in the box? No, I see you don't."

Burns didn't look at all pleased at the argument. "Don't test me!"

"I most assuredly am not," Yi Xiao answered. "But it'd be disappointing if all the box contained were a few family mementos, of no value to anyone but Jo." Seeing Burns wilt, he added, "If I may suggest, find a place to stay for the night. Tomorrow we will replenish our supplies and head to Mr. Kraft's…"

"Uncle Caleb was a Yancey, Yi Xiao."

"…Mr. Yancey's property and discover what was left for Jo's father."

There being nothing more Burns could say on the matter without starting a fight, the man accepted the suggestion.

ooo

Yi Xiao sent Jo and Gan Han back to the inn. "You might see where we can eat. I'll be along in a little while."

Neither girl liked the suggestion, especially since Yi Xiao deliberately phrased it like an order. But they didn't argue the point, either. Once they were gone, Yi Xiao turned his attention on the man who'd been silently hovering behind Jo like a large carrion bird. Given, of course, carrion birds dressed in the heavily embroidered silk robe of an Imperial court official.

"Your Highness," the man said, going to one knee, despite the dirt and rust on the warehouse floor. "I hoped I would reach here before you."

The honorific was one Yi Xiao had no right to. "I'm no prince. There's no need to stand—or kneel—on ceremony with me. I'm not even sure who you are?"

"I'LL FIGHT YOU FOR IT . . ."

"Your Highness is pleased to jest with me."

It wasn't hard to work out what was going on. This man, whomever he was, was an official of the Imperial Court. No doubt he'd been sent to find and bring Prince Yi Zhu back home, only to be fooled by the same trick Grandmother Lang had used on General Hwei.

Yi Xiao could play along, let this strange man take him home as he obviously intended. But that would mean pretending to be his cousin. It'd be fatal, because—if the rumors of the Daoguang Emperor's dying were true—by now Yi Zhu had either taken his rightful place as Emperor or had fallen in the attempt. Impersonating him would be treason either way. Whomever sat upon the Dragon Throne could not afford to have Yi Zhu's 'twin' cousin roaming free.

"What is your name?"

"I am Wang Tsun Hsin, your Highness." Wang refused to raise his head or unclasp his hands. "Please, accept my humble service and allow me to assist you in returning home. Your father needs you desperately."

"When did you leave China?"

"But a few hours after you, your Highness. We followed your ship, but a storm forced us off course. I had our Captain head for San Francisco, in hopes that we'd find you here. Thank the Gods, we have!"

The man's sincerity was heart-warming. It was also damned inconvenient. "Whatever and whomever I may be in China," Yi Xiao said finally, "I am Lang Yi Xiao here."

If Wang hadn't been an official at court and therefore trained from an early age to submit to the will of the Emperor, he might have questioned Yi Xiao's statement. Instead he bowed deeply. "Your Highness has but to will it."

"And so I do. I am also not ready to return to China."

"But your Highness…"

"Don't call me that." Yi Xiao pulled the man to his feet with little effort. "And no more bowing."

Wang nearly bowed to acknowledge the order. He stopped himself, saying, "I will try to remember. But, Mr. Lang, what of the Emperor? You must return home!"

Bleak though he felt, Yi Xiao managed a smile, "Whatever happens in China is beyond our control. It has been more than three months since I left. It will take at least that long to return. By then, the Emperor's illness will have passed one way or another. A week, at most, will hardly affect matters. I have promised that child protection and I must and will keep that promise."

"I… yes… a Prince must keep his word. I see that."

Having won the argument, Yi Xiao continued. "I will remain at the inn with my companions. It would look strange for me to leave them. You may accompany me, if you must, but be careful to treat me as you would any other man." He'd make sure Jo was safely settled, preferably with some family who would love and care for her, then evade this man somewhere in America's mountains.

And, with luck, evade Gan Han as well.

ooo

It took two days to prepare for the trip to the mine. In that time Jo barely said more than a few words to Yi Xiao. He didn't seem to notice but he was expert at keeping his feelings to himself. Better at it than she was, certainly. But how was she supposed to feel, with him letting Burns walk all over her like that?

It was Hai Chan, who was getting ready to leave them for his newly acquired ship, who took her aside to talk. "I've been sailing long enough to know when something's brewing. What is it?"

"I have no idea what you mean."

"Yes, you do."

Hai Chan was one of those straightforward, no-nonsense sorts one couldn't lie to. Came to that, Jo doubted she could lie to Yi Xiao, but that was because the man would see through her. "I don't want to be doing this. Burns is a nasty, dirty, old scoundrel who doesn't deserve whatever my uncle left us."

"I can't blame you for not liking it," Hai Chan admitted. "But that's not why you're acting like Yi Xiao cut your anchor and sliced your sails for you."

Somewhere below them, Yi Xiao was practicing his dance again, performing for a half-dozen young women from the saloon down the street. They were applauding wildly and someone was playing a harmonica in time with his movements. That was part of the problem. She wanted him to ask why she was upset, so she could tell him off. But he either hadn't noticed or wouldn't admit it.

"He didn't have to treat me like a little kid."

That made Hai Chan laugh, which almost offended her all over again. "You are a child. So is Gan Han, for all she refuses to admit it."

"Still, that was my property he bargained with. He didn't ought to have lectured me on what's right and wrong. Not right in front of Burns like that."

Hai Chan leaned out the window and shouted to Yi Xiao, "Hey. Apologize to Jo!"

"All right." Yi Xiao clambered up the back wall of the inn and clung to the window sill. "Apologize for what?"

"Treating her like a baby and making her feel bad about not wanting to keep her father's bargain."

It startled Jo to realize just how precisely Hai Chan pinned down why she was angry. "You could at least have talked to me private-like. Made me feel stuck in a corner."

Yi Xiao thought on that a moment. "I too felt 'stuck in a corner'," he admitted. "Which, when you think about it, we were. Do you think Burns and his men would give up without a fight?"

"No." She'd expected a brawl and had been quite ready to give them what they asked for.

"Do you really, truly, believe we'd have won?"

"You could beat them. I've seen you fight." Admittedly, it'd mostly been him evading and blocking Gan Han whenever she tried to force him to draw his weapon. It was still obvious he knew what he was doing.

"Maybe. But why fight when you don't have to?" Jo's mother would have agreed. She was always on Jo to stop brawling with the neighbor boys. Seeing her begin to falter, Yi Xiao pressed his point. "Master says, violence is what happens when we forget the *Dao*."

"Your master sure did have a saying for everything," Jo muttered. She didn't understand Yi Xiao's *Dao* and didn't want to. Still, "I don't want to fight just to fight. It's just that Burns isn't…"

"Isn't a good man. I know. I don't like him or how he behaves either. But not liking a person doesn't give you carte blanche to break your word. Would you have changed your mind if I'd told you so in private?"

Jo thought on that a moment and sighed. She probably would have. The biggest reason she'd been annoyed had been looking at that smug smirk on Burns' face when Yi Xiao sided with him. "Yes."

"Then if there is another time when I must persuade you of a thing, I will try to do it without an audience."

She managed a smile. "All right. Now will you get back down from here before you break your neck?"

With a laugh, he flung himself backwards, putting her heart straight up her throat as he spun around and landed lightly on the pavement below. She didn't know if he could fight much, but he'd make some circus one heck of an acrobat.

Or, more likely, a clown.

ooo

They left Hai Chan behind in San Francisco, gathering a crew of disappointed prospectors. As he'd predicted, the Gold Rush had proved less than profitable for the vast majority of its fortune-hunters. Gold didn't pave the riverbeds nor glitter in every rock. Some more stubborn prospectors were sure they just had to find the right stream, explore the right mountain, and they'd be rich beyond their wildest dreams. Others just wanted to go home with enough profit to make the trip worth it.

Once they'd gathered supplies they headed north from San Francisco, crossing the bay by ferry and following a narrow, difficult, roadway into the hills. To Burns' disgust, they were forced to leave the horses and mule behind in Sausalito, carrying the heavy equipment themselves. He was equally disgusted when Gan Han insisted on coming along. "Girls don't belong on trips like this!"

Yi Xiao pointed out, "You don't object to Jo coming along."

"That's only 'cause she won't give me the map."

It was also because Yi Xiao wouldn't let him take the map, but neither man mentioned the point. "The camp we're headed for is only ten or so miles away. Master says, a little walk never hurt anybody."

Caleb Yancey's property might be only ten miles away from San Francisco, but it was ten miles of twists and turns and ups and downs, to the annoyance of everyone but Yi Xiao. It wasn't exactly the same as Heng Shan—the plants and wildlife were too different—but it still felt pleasantly familiar. He looked forward to exploring it further, once he was alone.

They were nearing their destination when shouts, clangs, and thuds echoed down the narrow valley. A fight, from the sound of it, and one with oddly familiar words. Yi Xiao couldn't be sure, but he thought he heard someone yelling in Hunanese about restoring something.

"Your Highness, I believe those are rebels. You should let me and my men go ahead."

"What's that friend of yours talking about, Chinaman? Tell him to talk English, stead of that gobbledygook."

"Should we hurry? That sounds like it's right near my Uncle's place!"

"It sounds like a fight. Would you like your sabre?"

Yi Xiao gazed through the trees, spotting smoke around the bend of the trail. "Master says, where there's smoke, there's fire." He returned his attention to his companions. "Wang, this is America. Chinese laws don't apply. Burns, not everything he says is about you. Jo, don't run straight into trouble. Gan Han. No. Just no."

Having made his position clear, Yi Xiao strode up the trail as quickly as his legs could carry him. The others followed, arguing with him and with each other, but he ignored their fuss in favor of the one ahead.

Rounding the corner, Yi Xiao took in the situation. A village of sorts had grown up beside the narrow stream leading down from the steep hillside. Composed mostly of small tents and a few wooden structures, it had a temporary air, made the more so by the fact that it was being torn apart by a large group of white men. This in spite of the dozen or so Chinese trying to stop them.

The central structure was the source of the smoke and Yi Xiao recognized a smithy in the midst of being burned down by a group of the attackers, to the fury of its obvious owner; a tall black man wielding a bar of iron as if it were bamboo. Already three of his attackers had gone down and he was working on the fourth. Not that his efforts were enough to protect his property. There were just too many enemies.

Not liking the odds, Yi Xiao started forward, only to find Wang holding him back. "I cannot allow you to endanger yourself."

"You don't have a choice," Yi Xiao told him, slipping his grip before the man had a chance to react. Wang's men tried to catch hold of him next, but by then Yi Xiao had rolled past them and was running up the path. Gan Han came up beside him, saying, "You don't even know why they're fighting."

She was right, of course, but from the look of the place, the white men were the intruders. While they might have the law behind them, he saw nothing suggesting it. "Don't kill anyone," he ordered her, catching hold of one of the men breaking down the smithy and tossing him into the nearby stream.

"I'm a swordswoman. I'm not trained to fight without killing."

"Start learning." Yi Xiao elbowed the next man in the chest, ducked beneath the smith's staff and kicked another man in the ear. "Or you'll be the next one I knock out."

"You will not." She swung around, knocking an attacker unconscious with a carefully controlled blow. Yi Xiao focused his attention on the men still trying to burn down the smithy. A pinpoint strike here, a kick there, an arm twist and a knee lock; all while trying to put out the fire with water from the dousing tank.

Wang and his men rushed into camp a minute later, forcing Yi Xiao to shout, "Don't kill anyone!" The order clearly confused his would-be defenders. Unlike Gan Han, they didn't argue, knocking men out as they spread through camp.

Within minutes the battle was over, with men lying on the ground groaning, or simply breathing heavily, staring at the sky. Yi Xiao set the last of his opponents down on the ground, patted his cheek, then turned to the smith. "Are you hurt?"

"Only a little… you speak good English, mister. Who are you?"

"Your Highness, you are unhurt?" Wang demanded, rushing up to Yi Xiao.

"Don't call me that. Someone will understand you here," Yi Xiao told the man in Chinese, then turned his attention back to the smith, once again speaking in English. "My name is…"

"Your Highness?" The man's Chinese was as startlingly good as Yi Xiao knew his English was to most westerners. "You're a prince?"

"That's what he says," Yi Xiao sighed, supposing it only made sense for a man working with so many Chinese speakers to have learned the language. "I beg you not to mention it."

"I'm in your debt. I'll hold my tongue. Though I'm afraid your friend here might not."

As if to prove the point, Wang was busy scolding him, "You can't rush off into danger like that, your Highness! It's our job to defend you." His voice was loud and angry, loud enough to attract the unwelcome attention of the Chinese miners. They gathered close, their unfriendly expressions causing Wang's men to circle around Yi Xiao, guarding him from attack. A moment later Gan Han joined them, sword ready.

"Depose the Qing! Restore the Ming!" someone shouted angrily. As if to make things worse, Burns and his men hurried up the path, yelling something about claim-jumpers and squatters.

ооо

Jo had watched the fight from a safe spot on the hillside above, excitement setting her blood racing. Gan Han in particular, left her in awe. The Chinese woman's movements flowed from one position to the next, a rapid series of blows and kicks, combined with strikes with the flat of her blade that knocked her opponents out easily. Jo itched to join in, but knew she wasn't up to it.

Compared to Gan Han, Yi Xiao didn't seem nearly as good. He barely ever raised a fist, contenting himself with finger poking, swooping movements and foot sweeps. He didn't even take the offensive, staying close to the forge and occasionally throwing a bucket of water on the burning wall. Admittedly, the fire was important but Jo felt more admiration for Gan Han—who was all over the place with her attacks—than for Yi Xiao's cautious defense.

When the fight ended and the miners surrounded Yi Xiao, Jo thought they were going to thank him. Except someone was shouting in an unfriendly way, his voice drowned out a moment later by Burns and his men adding fuel to the fire by accusing the Chinese of claim jumping.

Jo should have stayed put but her impetuous nature set her running into the camp, pushing her way through to Yi Xiao and Gan Han. "Stop it!" she yelled, "He just helped you!" Belatedly it occurred to her that these men had no reason to listen to her. Worse, all she'd done was make herself a target. Another fight was brewing and she and her companions were at the center.

A clang loud as thunder broke through the noise. "ENOUGH!" As the crowd returned to shouting, the big blacksmith slammed his staff against his anvil again. "I SAID ENOUGH!"

The voice was familiar, even if the man's face hadn't been. It'd been six years since Jo's uncle had left home, with his best friend Zak for company. Caleb had planned on settling in Ohio but somehow wound up all the way out in California, working for Sutter. Zak must have stayed with him, though he'd obviously done some growing since then. He'd been a skinny fellow of fifteen the last time she'd seen him. His voice was the same, though, deep and resonant and able to shout the cows home from across the field.

That shout silenced everyone in the little settlement, too. Jo looked up at Zak, barely able to see the scrawny nervous youth she remembered in those broad shoulders and confident features. "Now then. I'm not sure what's going on, and I don't know who you lot are, but we've had enough fighting." He said something in Chinese that made the obvious leader of the miners frown. He was an older man, with a pinched up face and pursed lips that tightened every time he glanced at Yi Xiao.

"Zak? What's going on here?" Jo asked, eliciting a well-remembered smile. Zak used to carry her on his shoulders when she'd been little and she guessed he remembered her fondly enough.

"Little girl, you shouldn't be out here in the wild on your own. Where's your Pa?" Zak's voice faltered when he saw her face. "Oh. I see. We'll talk about it later, when things are quieter."

The miners' leader interrupted, speaking in English out of deference for Jo. "The child is safe but we will not allow a Prince of the Qing to stay among us."

Wang stepped towards the miner but Yi Xiao was in front of him and bowing politely before his self-appointed guard could say a word. Like the miner, he spoke in English. "Sir, I have no intent of interfering with you and your fellows. By the Mother of Lightning, I swear it."

"You dare swear by Her?"

Once again Zak put his staff down, the sound echoing up and down the valley. "We don't have much time. It's almost night and we have to get everyone in the shelter before it gets dark."

"Leave those thieves and these Manchu scum to the voice that calls in the night. You may bring the girls inside, if you want."

Zak snapped, "I don't know what your problem is with these people, but there's no way I'm agreeing to leaving anyone to that thing."

"He's one of our oppressors!"

"He isn't wrong," Yi Xiao admitted. "I am a Manchu, after all."

The statement didn't help at all and Jo snapped, "Why you gotta be so much trouble? Can't you keep your mouth shut for nothing?" She didn't know what it was made Zak so nervous but he had a cool head on his shoulders. If he thought there was something bad coming, he was probably right.

Off to the side and sulking because he was being ignored, Burns suddenly snapped, "Where's that box your uncle left you, girl? The sooner I have what I came for, the sooner we can part ways."

Zak frowned on the man. "What are you talking about, mister?" He stopped himself, gesturing towards a solid barn. "No. Tell me later. Everyone, we have got to get inside. If you can walk, you grab someone who can't. And for your lives sake, don't call anyone by their name!" He turned a worried look on the sky. "Getting dark. Not much time left."

"How dare you tell me what to do?" Burns might have said more but Zak's commanding voice did its job. People were dragging the unconscious into the barn without argument.

Yi Xiao said something incomprehensible to Wang, who bristled. Except Yi Xiao's voice, usually soft and unassuming, held a note of command just like Zak's. Wang bowed, giving orders to the others and helping clear the campsite of the unconscious and injured.

Zak grinned at Yi Xiao. "Come on, your Highness. Get inside to safety. We can talk about it later."

ᴑᴑᴑ

They'd barely gotten a few feet into the surprisingly well-lit barn when Yi Xiao realized Burns and his men weren't coming. "Damn him, anyway," he muttered. He had no idea why Zak wanted everyone inside but he could tell the man was afraid. Zak didn't look the type to scare easily.

When Yi Xiao started back for the others, Zak put a hand on his shoulder. "Stay here. I know how to keep it off. You don't."

"It?"

"Yeah." The man glanced back outside. "I don't know what it is. Some hoodoo a fellow from the next mine camp over sent us. I've been fighting it off every dark moon for months now."

"Can you keep them safe as well as yourself?" Yi Xiao asked, pointing. Burns' men were following him towards an opening in the rocks on the other side of the settlement. He could hear Burns giving querulous orders as he went. "I don't believe they're going to cooperate."

Zak had the look of a man with a severe headache. "Where the hell do they think they're going?"

"Jo's father promised Burns something before he died. The Reverend is nothing if not persistent." Yi Xiao went outside, to Zak's obvious annoyance. "You said we have until nightfall? Perhaps we can persuade them to come inside before it gets dark."

"Doubt it, but we better try." Zak headed for the cave.

Yi Xiao followed behind. "What is this thing you fear?"

"I wish I knew. Wish we could leave. It's got our names, though, and it follows us wherever we go. Ah Sen made it all the way down to San Francisco before it found him." Zak stopped in his smithy to get a lantern. "It doesn't like fire, or light, so as long as the one it calls doesn't answer, it can't hurt anyone. Trouble is, it won't stop calling until morning. So I have to keep it distracted."

At a guess 'it' was some kind of monster, created by an unfortunate combination of human fears and the presence of strong magic. "What does it do to its victims?"

"We don't know. Them it takes, it takes away. All we ever find are bones, their marrow sucked dry." Zak clambered up the last rocks to the cave entrance. "It attacks with the ones it killed, but they're not strong. Just empty skin, mostly. And it doesn't know my real name cause I don't, so it can't call me proper."

That would be why Zak was the best one at the camp to fight the thing. "It doesn't know my name, either,"

"I hope you're right about that. If it does, you'll have a hard time ignoring it."

"Master says, don't borrow trouble when you're neck deep already," Yi Xiao answered, to Zak's great amusement. "Let's find those others and get out of here."

The inside of the cave was dry and dark. Its walls echoed every sound, a soft susurration that reminded Yi Xiao of the sort of voices one might hear falling asleep, when one's dreams tried to start too soon. Zak handed him the lantern. "Don't talk. The less attention you draw, the better."

The whispering became more like a voice, though still incomprehensible. Yi Xiao followed Zak as silently as he'd been ordered, scanning the dark grey stones and spotting tool marks and other signs of mining. The prospectors must have searched for gold here before. He yearned to ask questions but knew Zak was right.

Burns and his men weren't as sensible. They searched around somewhere ahead, muttering and talking to each other. Calling each other by name and entirely unaware of the whispers in the dark. Yi Xiao could hear the word 'hungry' in them, oddly enough in the Hunan dialect. Then Burns' name echoed and the man himself bleated like a terrified goat. Arriving just in time, Yi Xiao grabbed him by the shoulder, "All of you. Out of here!"

They ran willingly, the voice in the darkness more than they could take. Burns was the only one who didn't move, requiring both Zak and Yi Xiao to pull him along as fast as they could. They ran back outside, into the twilight, back across the stream and finally into the barn. All while something fluttered after them. What was it? Cloth? A swirl of dust covered cobwebs? An empty bag of human skin?

Burns struggled, trying to go back, screaming that he was being called. Yi Xiao struck Burns behind the ear, paralyzing him, then shoved the stiff body through the door to the barn. He turned and joined Zak in staring the monster down.

When it began chanting a new name, ice crawled straight up Yi Xiao's spine.

"Jo. Jo. Jo."

ooo

The miners tried to hold Jo back but she was fast and slippery, escaping outside before anyone could stop her. She knew the thing meant to eat her but she couldn't fight the urge to do what it wanted. She moved towards it, feeling its empty flesh grasp her outstretched arms. It was a filthy touch, dry and desiccated, like old and dusty parchment. She'd have screamed if it didn't have its claws in her head already.

Zak caught hold of her, dragging her backwards and trying to push her into the barn. She struggled to slip free, yearning to answer the call. Visions of her father, of her mother, of her little brother, all rose in her mind. She'd never have to grieve again. Oblivion would claim her and she'd be one with it. Just as the others were.

Something bright red fluttered into view. One of Yi Xiao's scarves, distracting Jo from her trance. "Your name's not Jo," he said. "You don't have to listen."

Jo was short for Josephine, but it was what everyone had called her for years. Of course it was her name. She struggled to break free of Zak's grip, to embrace nothing and forget everything. Except Yi Xiao wouldn't let her. He yelled something in Chinese and someone in the barn began striking the wall. It almost sounded like a heart beat and she felt her own heart pound to its rhythm.

At the same time Yi Xiao began spinning and dancing around the thing trying to consume her. A chill wind blew down the valley, damp and tingling like the air after a stroke of lightning. The emptied skin tried to slash at Yi Xiao, its substance catching at him. "Prince of Qing," it whispered and sounded desperate.

With the thing no longer focused on Jo, she found herself freed. She and Zak sprawled in the dirt. Realizing it'd turned its attention on Yi Xiao and knowing how hard it was to fight; Jo searched for a weapon and found it in the weapon Gan Han kept trying to give Yi Xiao. She yanked it from the dirt and tried to swing it, nearly cutting off her toes in the process.

At the same time Yi Xiao kept dancing, showing amazing focus given what the thing could do. Still, it was only a matter of time before its will overwhelmed his. Jo couldn't let that happen and she swung the blade again, cutting into the non-fabric and once again drawing its attention. It stretched an 'arm' out towards her, the shapeless mass becoming more real as it said her name.

Jo fought the urge to listen as Zak slammed his staff into the thing and flung it several yards away. It was up again a moment later, calling out, "Zak."

"Sorry. Not here."

The wind was getting stronger and now it was beginning to spark, as if a small thunderstorm was forming. It followed Yi Xiao, who spun around and around as if he were at the center of a twister. The wind dragged the thing along, catching hold of its 'substance' and spinning it.

Yi Xiao dropped to one knee below the whirlwind. Jo caught sight of his face and almost dropped his blade. The kindly, humorous, man she was so fond of had disappeared, lost behind a demonic mask of bloodlust and killing intent. She fell backwards, staring wildly at her friend. "...no..."

Something flickered in Yi Xiao's eyes and was gone. As the thing reached for him, he wrapped his scarf around its outstretched wrist. Once again it whispered, desperately. "Prince of Qing!"

"No," Yi Xiao said firmly. "I am not." Then he gestured and the wind dove straight into the flames of Zak's smithy, until the storm was terrifying mixture of mist, dead branches and fire. Something screamed at its center as the whole mess shrank in on itself and disappeared.

For a moment Jo couldn't find a single word to say. She stared at Yi Xiao as his

"ALL OF YOU. OUT OF HERE!"

expression softened, returning to the old, gentle, one Jo was accustomed to. Slowly, she stammered, "What are you? What kind of hoodoo are you?"

"I don't even know what that is," he complained, spreading his hands as if that would prove he was harmless. "But I can guess. It wasn't magic. Not quite."

The fear in Jo's eyes must have been obvious, for he sighed. "I see. Well, I'll be on my way then." When she didn't argue, he turned away, adding, "For what it's worth, I'm glad you're safe. Zak, don't let that Burns fellow walk all over her."

"I won't. I don't understand what's going on, but I won't."

"Jo, be careful with that sabre. Make Gan Han show you how to use it, if you insist on swinging it around." Jo's silence made him sigh. He walked away into the shadows but his voice echoed back to them. "I'm so tired of killing. I'm glad nothing died, this time."

Then he was gone.

Chapter 5: Earth –
An Encouraging Resolution

The next few days were occupied in cleaning up the mess from the fight. As the settlement's owner, Zak Striker spent most of it getting the claim-jumpers down to Sausalito. He held little hope his prisoners would be punished for attacking his mine camp. Chinese miners were mostly admired for their hard-working ethos and sober ways, but they weren't citizens and they weren't white. The law didn't favor them any more than it favored a free man of color like Zak.

Jo came along on the trip and she talked his ear off the whole way. By the time they reached Sausalito, Zak knew all there was to know about her journeys and how her Pa had died trying to protect her. The only thing she didn't talk about was the odd Chinese man who'd brought her to camp; nor even how she'd come to travel with him.

Zak wasn't sure who she was madder at; her friend or herself. She always did have a short temper, though, and Yi Xiao had scared her badly. After years of traveling with Caleb and running into the occasional odd occurrence, Zak was less bothered. He knew enough about magic to understand that it was the user who decided how to wield it.

The miners who helped him with the prisoners were more vocal about the stranger. The young man was obviously one of the Emperor of China's many sons. A soldier of Wang's high rank would never be assigned to protect anyone less important. And that, in turn, made him an enemy to any right thinking Han like themselves.

Zak didn't argue the point. He'd listened to his leasees' long and bitter discussions of the cruelties of the Manchu for months now. He even sympathized with them. But if Yi Xiao really was an Imperial Prince he seemed a harmless, kind, and sensible sort; hardly the tyrant his rebellious subjects claimed. Besides, if Yi Xiao were the prince then why hadn't that thing been able to call him? Zak had the advantage of having forgotten his real name years ago. Yi Xiao surely knew whether or not the title Prince belonged to him.

Admittedly, a title alone might not be enough, but that thing only needed part of a person's name to work. Yi Xiao hadn't even flinched when it'd called him. That hoodoo of his might have protected him, but Zak doubted it. It made him curious to know just who and what Yi Xiao was. Not that he was likely to find out anytime soon, given Yi Xiao had run off.

When they returned to the camp it was to find Reverend Burns and his men guarding the safe Zak and Caleb kept in the storage cave. The rest of the miners were guarding them, keeping them from getting into the rusty old thing. Near as Zak could tell, it was a stand-off that'd been going on a while. Burns and his men looked like they hadn't slept a wink for days.

"Jo told me what you're here for," Zak told Burns before the man could open his mouth. "So I understand you got some right to what's in that safe. But you don't got right to all of it."

Burns didn't like a black man telling him what to do but at least he didn't argue the point. Maybe he was too tired. "I didn't plan on taking everything. Just what was promised me."

"That'd be the agreement Hal had with you for helping Jo out, right?" Behind Zak, Jo muttered angrily, still hot over the whole thing.

"Exactly."

"Well now, I can't argue with that." Zak opened the safe and pulled out the two folders sitting inside. "See, back when Caleb sent that letter to Hal, he'd used his share of our profits to buy the valley over that ridge there. He figured Hal could come out, run it like he and I were running this one. These are the deeds to that valley and this."

Greed glittered in Burns' eyes. "What's this valley worth?"

Zak grinned. "Oh, nothing to you, cause when Caleb died, he willed his share to me. I was his partner after all. And before you ask how a slave can own a damned thing, I'll point out I'm a free man and a born citizen of these United States. So the law's on my side."

Burns might have argued the point but he remembered the miners surrounding them and he backed down quick. "And the other?"

"Like I said, it's right next door, so likely it's got as good a source of gold as we have. You'll have to go downhill a piece to get over to it, but it'd be yours all free and clear." Jo bristled a little at the suggestion but Zak ignored her. He and his miners could have got rid of Burns and his men easy, but he didn't want the sort of trouble killing someone could bring. Not to mention it just wasn't right.

It only took Burns a moment to make up his mind. "Fine. I'll take that valley." He snatched the folder and had his men packing to head out before anyone could say another word.

Given how annoyed she was, it was a miracle Jo kept her mouth shut until her nemesis had gone. "I hate this. He took advantage of my Pa, saving my life. He don't deserve no fortune."

Zak was tempted to correct her grammar but knew from experience she wouldn't listen. "You're right. He doesn't deserve it. But maybe he deserves what he's going to get." He jerked his thumb over his shoulder towards the hillside. "Those men we just dropped off at the Sausalito jail? They were claim jumpers who took over that valley after your uncle died. I've been trying to pry them out ever since." Jo stared and smiled broadly. "Reverend Burns and his friends can have the joy of trying, now, and you can have half this valley instead. Just like Caleb would have wanted."

Now Jo looked really pleased as she flung her arms around Zak and crowed. "Thank you! I'm going to go tell Gan Han!"

Ma Yun, the miner's headman and spokesperson, interrupted. "The young lady's gone, just like those other bastards. I think they went after that Prince of theirs. Good riddance."

Somehow Zak had a feeling Yi Xiao wouldn't be nearly so pleased.

ooo

For the first time since he'd left Heng Shan, Yi Xiao was alone and surrounded by nothing but trees, bushes, rocks and water. Everything was different, but in essence, everything was the same. It wasn't home, but he could make a life here and be content. Or he could, if he weren't so disquieted by everything that had led him to this place.

Thinking about it, he'd let himself get too attached to the girl. Back on Heng Shan he'd always known he could see his family any time. It'd given him a solid base, a feeling of connection to the world. Here in America, with no way to tell if his family was safe and no way to return to them quickly, he'd felt lost. Jo, so like his young half-sister, had been an anchor in this strange land. Even her annoyance with him, when he'd made her angry for scolding her in public, had felt familiar, normal and right.

The fight with nothingness had changed their relationship. Yi Jin would never be terrified of him. She'd seen him at his worst, when the killing urge was on him and only their father's restraint could hold him back. Jo, having never seen such powers in her life, having never seen the light of violence in his eyes before, had wanted him gone and out of sight. It hurt in a way he hadn't expected. Even understanding the reason for her fear didn't help him feel better. He needed time and quiet to think.

The remarkably huge trees of California's coast provided Yi Xiao with a place to hide. His woodcraft provided him with nourishment. His training provided him with the beginnings of emotional replenishment. What none of those things could do was keep him from being bothered.

One problem was Gan Han. The young lady was obstinate and despite her complete lack of woodcraft, somehow able to follow him. It took him several days of constantly having to change his campsite before he realized it was his sabre—once more in her hands—that betrayed him.

It was mere metal, a particularly fine blade handed down through the Lang family's line from an illustrious ancestress. Yet in Gan Han's hands, it was a tie to him that let her search him out. He wondered if she knew she possessed such a talent and guessed she'd never believe him if he tried to tell her.

Then there was Wang, who didn't need Yi Xiao's sabre to follow him. Instead the soldier trailed after Gan Han, despite her attempts to lose him. Yi Xiao could hide his presence and cover his tracks all he wanted but he couldn't hide hers.

On leaving the mining camp, Yi Xiao climbed up and down the hills surrounding the area. He wasn't sure why, but something held him there, a sense of unfinished business with Jo and the others. Yet at the same time he had no reason to approach and plenty of reason to avoid.

About a week later, Yi Xiao climbed to the top of the tallest mountain in the area. It was steep and difficult for someone unaccustomed to such things like Gan Han and Wang. It also afforded him both a grand view and a place to seek focus until his pursuit caught up again. He didn't doubt they would, but it'd take them some time to get there. He'd led them on a merry chase some miles north before heading south again. Besides, while the mountain was no steeper than Heng Shan, it lacked steps. They'd have to crawl their way up the rocks.

Like Heng Shan, the mountain was one of those places with deep roots into the world; a holy place, sacred to those who knew such things. It was a good place, a balanced place, and one where Yi Xiao could cultivate his *qi* and replenish his Self. A place where he could come to terms with what disturbed him and why. As he understood why Jo's reaction had hurt, he also understood it didn't matter. Not really.

Yi Xiao had been so caught up in his childish reaction to Jo's fear he hadn't recognized his real accomplishments. He'd mastered his inner strength, so that his *qi* attack barely tired him. He'd mastered his killing desire against the men he'd fought. He'd mastered his Self, maintaining balance against a force that meant to obliterate him.

Even better, Yi Xiao had done all this without killing. The thing he'd fought had been a mental construct, a *tulpa* formed from a dead man's life force. What little remained of the soul used to create it could only be freed, not saved. As for its master, well they'd have a headache for awhile but nothing worse.

By late afternoon, something roused Yi Xiao. Gan Han? Wang and his men? No, it couldn't be. They'd be coming after him from the mountain's northern side. This movement came from the south, a sound of rustling in the bushes below.

Lying on his belly, Yi Xiao peered over the edge. Two men were climbing towards him. They were too busy to look up, but Yi Xiao thought they were familiar. That was right, he'd knocked the one on the left unconscious at Zak's smithy a week ago.

Under other circumstances Yi Xiao might have hailed the strangers and asked them what they were doing. Not wanting attention, however, he slid backwards to hide in the nearest bushes. Unlike the approaching pair, he could be as silent as a breeze.

The men weren't trying to hide. They grumbled under their breath, complaining about the steep hill, the loose rocks and the fact that they were there at all. "Don't know why we both had to come."

"To keep the other honest," the second man suggested.

"Hah!"

"All right, honest ain't the word. But if one of us has to piss, the other can keep watching." The man cursed as he stuck his hand in some thorns. "Won't be long, anyway. Just gotta wait until it starts getting dark. Soon as those Chinee and that black bastard settle down for the night, we'll give the signal."

Yi Xiao realized these men planned another attack on Zak's mine camp. Though he wasn't sure he wanted to deal with Jo's fears, or his countrymen's hatred, he also didn't want anyone hurt. No one had died in the last attack but that had been sheer good fortune. They might not be so lucky next time.

Silently, Yi Xiao headed back to the camp. It was only a mile or so away, but steep and difficult as the mountains were, it would still take him at least an hour or so to get there.

ooo

It was late afternoon when Zak heard angry curses outside his smithy. Sighing, because sometimes it seemed like the bunch he'd leased the mine to were incapable of going a day without an argument, he set his hammer down and stepped outside.

This time the men had reason, though he still wasn't sure it was a good one. The young man sauntering up the trail towards camp might be hoodoo and might be their oppressors' prince, but he'd done nothing to harm anyone in camp and quite a bit to help. Besides, Zak found it hard to dislike that friendly smile and easy-going personality. "Stop yelling," he ordered the men, knowing they wouldn't. At the same time he put himself between Yi Xiao and the others. "Afternoon, Yi Xiao. Or should I say, your Highness?"

"Yi Xiao is just fine, Zak. Despite Wang's insistence to the contrary, I'm not a Prince of any sort." Yi Xiao craned his neck so he could look past Zak, adding in Chinese, "I'm the Duke of Jin's youngest son and I promise, I don't care at all that you're members of the Heaven and Earth Society."

Zak was usually glad he'd taken the time to learn Chinese, but he would have felt more comfortable not understanding the threats and jeers the young man's assurance received. "I have no problem with you myself," he told Yi Xiao. "But they do. I'm not sure it's a good idea for you to stay."

The sound of something breaking interrupted the argument. Looking over, Zak saw Jo standing at her cabin door, the bowl she'd been drying smashed at her feet. She stared wild-eyed at Yi Xiao, then stepped back and slammed the door shut behind her, the faint sound of sobbing just audible.

"Was it something I said?" Before Zak could react to the man's idiocy, Yi Xiao added, "Tell her I'm sorry I scare her, would you? That was never my intent, but I know that doesn't change her feelings. Master says, apologies don't fix broken statues."

Somehow Zak suspected Yi Xiao had earned that particular lecture. He didn't say so, returning his attention to the men surrounding them. "Will the lot of you please stop shouting?" To his surprise, they did, though their muttered imprecations weren't much better. "I hate to be inhospitable, but…"

"But you don't want another fight." Yi Xiao pointed off towards the peak of Mount Tam. "I wasn't hoping to stay. But I was just up there and overheard a couple of men spying on your camp. I have reason to believe they intend to attack you tonight."

"Liar!" That was Chao, youngest son of the miners' headman, Ma. Impetuous, thoughtless and given to getting into fights at the least opportunity, he was—naturally— the one most willing to go after a man who'd amply demonstrated an ability to command the wind. "You're just here to spy on us yourself!"

"I promise you that isn't true. I realize you have little reason to believe me, but I did see those men and hear their plan. When night falls and you settle in for bed, I fear they'll invade the camp and cut your throats in your sleep."

Chao swung his fist, striking Yi Xiao in the chin and knocking his head sideways, splitting the man's lip.

Instead of fighting back, Yi Xiao wiped the blood away. "I usually charge for any blow that lands." he told the other boy. "But in this case, I think I'll waive the fee. Besides, I have a proposal."

Chao's father grabbed his son's arm, holding him tight where he stood. "What?"

"I am the Storm Hermit's best—all right, her only—pupil. I will fight anyone you choose to a knockdown. If I win, you listen to what I've said and prepare yourself for your attackers. If I lose, I leave quietly and without argument."

Zak couldn't help interrupting. "I know these men pretty well. None of them have any hoodoo like yours."

Yi Xiao smiled, spreading his hands apologetically. "Despite appearances, *qi* is not magic. It is, however, an unfair advantage that I will not use as long as no one else here does."

The implication that one of the miners might have such a skill was obvious. If so, no one admitted it. Seeing Ma Yun appeared amenable, Zak sighed. "I won't argue then. But one knockdown and no serious injuries, understood?"

Both men bowed in agreement.

○○○

Yi Xiao borrowed a strip of cloth from one of the miners and tied it round his head. "I was required to cut my hair recently," he told Ma when the headman raised a curious brow. "It bothers me when I fight."

"Cut? Or grew it out?" Ma went to the center of the ring, swinging his queue around his neck to get it out of the way.

"I told you, I'm a disciple of the Storm Hermit and a follower of the *Dao*. Thus, I don't shave my forehead."

Although Ma snorted irritably at the claim, all he did was bow. Yi Xiao followed suit, then took up stance; left heel raised, right foot flat and turned sideways, hands spread in the wind dancing posture. "Any time you're ready."

Ma eyed Yi Xiao's stance critically. "Who taught you how to do that?"

"I told you, the Storm Hermit."

"That's not the right position for crane style."

"It's not crane style."

"Then what is it? Because you're off balance."

"I'm not supposed to be balanced."

"Who was the idiot taught you that?"

"If you want to call the Storm Hermit an idiot, go ahead. I, personally, wouldn't suggest it."

"You are such a liar. The Storm Hermit doesn't take pupils. And if she did, why the hell would she teach you such an unbalanced stance?"

"Master says, balance is in the mind. Achieve it there, and all else will follow."

From somewhere towards the back of the crowd, someone shouted, "Would you finish him already!"

"I just want to know what this young idiot is thinking. Manchus aren't usually this stupid and that stance..." Ma's sentence, suggesting he was entirely focused on the argument, broke off suddenly as he swung into action, taking two long steps forward, aiming his fist for Yi Xiao's chest.

Yi Xiao didn't give Ma time to reach him. He spun around, movement forcing his opponent to step further in than he would have otherwise. Before Ma recovered, Yi Xiao flung himself upwards and forward, somersaulting through the air, using the force of the motion to kick Ma in the ear and send him flying.

It almost worked. Ma hadn't expected the attack and barely managed to recover. He stumbled and forced himself upright. Then he launched a series of attacks—leopard style—that Yi Xiao countered with falling blossoms, blocking and redirecting the strikes.

Still, Ma managed to get a good solid hit in, sending Yi Xiao stumbling backwards. This time it was he who had to recover, dropping into a long, lightning strike, stance. They stared at each other for what seemed forever but really couldn't be more than a second or so. "Fast," Ma said. "Faster than I expected. You had good teachers, Prince."

"I have an excellent teacher and I'm not a prince," Yi Xiao answered, dodging beneath the man's next attack. Ma caught him by the shirt; fingers crooked in eagle claw, then shoved him between the shoulder blades, forcing him into a forward roll. He rose to his feet and turned to face the man, once more in wind dancing posture.

"The Americans have a saying. Fool me once, shame on you. Fool me twice, shame on me." Ma rushed him again, but this time spun into a position to block Yi Xiao's flying kick. When Yi Xiao landed and repeated the stance, the man shook his head. "Is that all you have? Don't keep doing the same..."

This time it was Yi Xiao who took advantage of the distraction, flinging himself forward in a roll that brought him right in front of Ma and kicking the man in the gut. It wasn't enough. Ma had a solid stance and Yi Xiao wasn't in the right position to put him off balance. Still, it was enough to make the man cough, which felt like an accomplishment.

Once more on his feet, Yi Xiao noticed a draft. Ma's eagle claw had done more than he'd realized. His cotton shirt was torn, the shoulder ripped down his back all the way to his belt. "I hope someone has a spare," he said. "Because I don't."

Ma didn't pay attention. He frowned at something behind Yi Xiao. "Turn around."

"Eh?"

"I said, turn around."

Ordinarily, Yi Xiao would never have obeyed such a command from an opponent but some instinct told him to do so now. He turned and saw the wide eyes of the audience behind him, their fingers jabbing and pointing as if he'd grown wings.

"Who are you?" Ma demanded suddenly. "The Mother of Lightning would never bless a Prince of the Qing."

Yi Xiao returned his attention to Ma. "I'm not a Prince."

"You're a Manchu of the royal house, yet you wear Her mark. Who. Are. You."

Yi Xiao glanced at his shoulder at the tiny lines—like dozens of lightning bolts—engraved on his flesh from wrist to shoulder and down his back. Inflicted by the Storm Hermit during his training, they were proof of his mastery of grounding. No one could survive her lightning without it.

The headman was waiting for Yi Xiao's answer impatiently. "I told you I'm the Storm Hermit's disciple."

"And I told you…" Ma stopped himself. "You're not who we thought. Please, sir. Tell us who you really are?"

"Lang Yi Xiao, the Wanderer. Least worthy and youngest son of the House of the White Wolf. And," he added more brightly, "not at all interested in fighting rebels, if they aren't interested in fighting me."

OOO

While the miners checked the borders of the camp and set up traps for the would-be claim jumpers, Zak went to find Jo. He'd been so caught up in dealing with Yi Xiao he'd half-forgotten how upset she was by the young man's presence. Fortunately, despite having gone to hide, she was easily found. She'd always liked caves and the one right near the campsite was a favorite place for her.

"I'm glad you didn't go deeper," Zak remarked, shining his lantern around. The cave had been his and Caleb's first dig, a straight tunnel going through the southwestern ridge of the valley wall. They'd found a little gold before a fault in the stone made it too dangerous to mine. In the end, they'd blocked the far end and made the cave a storage room.

Jo sat in a corner with a candle, knees pulled to her chest and arms wrapped round tight like she was still the little girl who got picked on by the bigger kids. She'd always given as good as she got, but her ma's scolding would have her sulking for days. "Is he gone?"

"No, and he's not going to leave." Zak sat beside her. "He's not a bad sort."

To his surprise, she burst into tears. "I KNOW!"

Now Zak really didn't understand. "If you know, why are you hiding from him?"

"I was scared of him. I was traveling with him for weeks. I knew he was dangerous, but I knew he was trying hard not to be. How can I be looking him in the eyes now?"

"He said to tell you he's sorry about that." Zak didn't know what qi was, nor if Yi Xiao was right about it not being magic, but he did know it was powerful. "You had good reason to be. The sort of thing he did isn't natural."

"You're not scared of it," Jo pointed out, wiping tears from her face and smearing dust all over.

"I've seen enough hoodoo, traveling with Caleb to know it's not the power you should be scared of, it's the person using it."

Jo shuddered suddenly. "You didn't see his eyes that night. He had the killing urge on him something fierce."

"I saw it when he was fighting those bastards earlier," Zak pointed out. "Not a single one died, even though some of them gave him cause." It'd been a terrifying sight, the fierce, joyful, expression of glee, combined with near perfect control. The same look had flickered in Yi Xiao's eyes during the duel. Zak didn't know how Ma—seeing that expression—had managed to keep from running in terror.

A thought occurred to Jo and she looked sad. "That's what he's been dealing with, this whole time, I bet. He told Gan Han he doesn't want to kill anymore, a while back. Didn't occur to me that meant he had to have, at least once." She smiled, a little weakly. "I trusted him to get me this far and the only one got hurt was the one killed Pa. So I guess I can trust him not to hurt me now."

"Then let's go…" Zak rose, about to offer her his hand, when an explosion rocked the cave. "The hell was that? It's too late to be mining right now!" Besides, the miners had just found a nice little vein further into the valley. They didn't need to break any more rock yet.

Something cracked above them and Zak realized their danger just barely in time. "The roof's collapsing," he shouted, grabbing Jo's hand. "Run!"

ooo

The camp was just pretending to settle for the night when the explosion struck somewhere further up the valley. Startled voices began babbling immediately and Yi Xiao caught a whiff of gunpowder on the breeze. Stones rolled down the valley's southern ridge and a sound, like ice cracking, filled the air. As a cloud of dust and dirt spurted from the storage cave, Yi Xiao set off running.

Two figures stumbled out from amid the flying dust, coughing and choking. "Zak? Jo?" Relief was almost painful. "Are you hurt?"

"Naw," Jo managed. "Got out in time. What happened?"

It was Ma, coming up to join them, who answered. "Some fool set off an explosive further up the valley. I wouldn't be surprised if it were in the new mine shaft."

Yi Xiao didn't understand. "Why would you blow up your mine shaft?" Realizing they were staring at him like a fool, he thought harder. "You mean sabotage, don't you?"

"Exactly." Zak wiped dirt from his face and glared up the valley. "I should have thought of it. Those men haven't been able to beat us up into going. That thing couldn't chase us out. The only way left is destroying our mine so we can't work."

Whomever was behind the attacks wouldn't be able to work a destroyed mine either, but Yi Xiao suspected the attacker hadn't thought of that. "Should we investigate?" Belatedly he realized he was including himself in the situation, despite not being involved.

Zak didn't comment on Yi Xiao's self-invitation. "We should. Jo, you stay here. If there's trouble I want you out of it."

"But…"

"You aren't big enough to do much damage. And before you point out that you shoot pretty good, I remind you that you've never had to kill a man. Besides, I'd like to avoid killing anyone. There's too much risk the law won't side with us." He squeezed her shoulder to comfort her. "You stay here and keep an eye on the camp in case those bastards come over for another round."

" HE SHOUTED, RUN!"

Jo sulked but accepted Zak's order. "All right. I won't let any of those yellow-bellied sapsuckers get in." She hesitated, looking shyly at Yi Xiao. "Sorry I was scared of you. Thanks for helping us now."

"I was frightening," Yi Xiao told her as Zak gathered a few men together. "I am frightening. I walked away from the martial world because I didn't want to be frightening."

She grinned at him and if her smile wasn't quite as full as it was before she'd seen his inner beast, it was bright enough to make him feel better.

ooo

The mine was at the far end of the valley, almost to the top of the long north-south ridge it descended from. They'd have built the camp closer, but the surrounding hillsides were too steep. Zak wondered if he should have had a guard staying up there anyway. It wasn't easy to reach, but a sufficiently determined climber could get anywhere.

It was almost dark by the time they neared the mine entrance. Their lanterns shone on freshly shattered rock and fallen trees, revealing someone had, indeed, set off an explosive. It was going to be one hell of a time clearing. Weeks, possibly months, depending on how deep the explosives had been when they'd gone off.

Zak's curses cut off when another, smaller, explosion split the air. Someone was shooting at them. "Cover your lanterns!" he shouted, concealing himself among the rocks. He scanned the cliffs above them but it was too dark to see anything but shadows.

Chao shouted, "I see them!" The impetuous young idiot immediately began scrambling up the side of the hill, making so much noise that—if there'd been a gunman on the other side—he'd have made a perfect target.

"Damnit, boy! Get back down here!" That was Ma, hiding near Zak. "Don't be a fool!"

Something shifted above Zak. Yi Xiao, using the cover of Chao's noise to climb the cliff-face. He was good, sure and steady. Zak just hoped he was also fast because he was certain the gunman wasn't alone. He'd heard more than one shot at one time.

With little else to do, Zak began herding his people back down the valley. Ma continued shouting at his son. Chao continued ignoring him. The others continued escaping, knowing better than to hang around. One by one, they ran from rock to rock as more bullets zinged past them. Until the only ones left were Ma, Chao, Zak and Yi Xiao.

"Damned if I'm going to leave it all up to those two," Zak muttered to Ma. "You keep yelling; it'll help distract those bastards. I'm going to try something."

Ma had no trouble shouting at his son. He'd spent most of the boy's life doing so, after all. Not that it did any good. Chao was and remained stubborner than the camp mule and just as hard headed. Of course, he came by it honestly, because Ma was just as bad if not worse.

Leaving Ma to entertain himself, Zak slipped further forward, closer to the shattered mine entrance. In the near total darkness, lit only by the waxing moon's light, he could barely see how the rocks had fallen in, creating a dangerously steep path. It'd be risky, but easier than the ways Chao and Yi Xiao had taken.

Zak soon discovered the flaw in his plan. The rocks weren't just steep, they were unstable. Not impossibly so, but he pinched his fingers and trapped his toes several times as he struggled to get up the slope. If Ma weren't shouting, the noise Zak made would have been easily noticed. Worse, he'd have been a sitting target for whoever it was up there.

By the time Zak reached the top, Chao was already there, crashing through the bushes and trees, searching for the gunmen. Not that he was having much success. It was too dark for such nonsense. Of course, Chao, convinced of his immortality, didn't seem to care.

Something flickered in Zak's vision. A crackle of lightning? Was a storm coming? Then he remembered Yi Xiao's strange hoodoo and realized the man had his own solution to the darkness. It was a dim light, hardly more than static electricity, but it was enough to draw a gunman's attention and make him fire in that direction.

Another flare—several feet away from the first—followed and another shot rang out. Again and again the gunmen tried to hit their constantly moving target and again and again they missed. Between Chao's noise and Yi Xiao's trickery, the enemy was running out of bullets. Even better, every time the men fired they revealed their positions. There were three of them, spread out among the trees.

Zak grinned, creeping through the darkness until he was just behind the closest of the three. He tapped the man on the shoulder, startling him into turning, then hit him in the jaw as hard as possible. Another thud followed soon after, as Yi Xiao knocked out the second man. As for the third, quieter and less given to firing blindly, sheer dumb luck turned in Chao's favor. The boy tripped over him and managed to knock him out after a brief struggle.

Once he'd tied the men with their own belts, Zak leaned over the cliff and called out, "Hey, Mr. Ma. Could you tell cook we'll have three for dinner?"

Ma went silent a moment. Then, "How would you prefer them? Stewed or fried?"

ooo

The men they'd captured were familiar yet unexpected. Yi Xiao had thought they'd be more claim jumpers. He hadn't anticipated their being Burns' men. When he commented on the fact, Zak coughed in an embarrassed way. "That Burns fellow wanted what Jo's Pa promised him; the deed to the valley over that ridge. I figured he and those claim-jumpers would fight over it and maybe solve our problems for us. Guess I figured wrong."

"Guess you did," Yi Xiao agreed wryly. "Though I'd have done the same. Burns is the sort who wants to be in charge. I have a feeling your claim-jumpers' leader is probably just as bad."

"I've never met him," Zak admitted. "Though I've tried. I'm told he doesn't like the color of my skin."

Yi Xiao had known Manchu like that, all too willing to abuse their Han subjects and all too sure of their superiority. He didn't say as much. He didn't know enough about the situation to comment. Besides, the man he was carrying was trying to talk. "Yes? Hello? Did you have something to say?"

The man's words were muffled, but he managed to make himself clear. "Burns is dead. Doc Jeffreys is in charge now."

"That'd be the boss of those claim-jumpers," Zak explained. "Sounds like he won the argument. I suppose I should have expected this sooner or later. So he killed your boss and you just fell over and joined him?"

Yi Xiao's captive growled under his breath. "That Doc Jeffreys is a hoodoo man. He didn't just kill Burns, he turned him into a ghost. We don't do as he says; he'll do the same to us."

Hoodoo was the term Zak had used for magic. "A sorcerer? A necromancer?" It made a chilling sort of sense. The thing Yi Xiao had fought the other day had clearly been a necromantic summoning. "That... isn't good."

"Now that's an understatement if ever I heard one. I should have expected something like this." Zak sounded exhausted and small blame to him. He and his fellow miners had no idea how to deal with a man like Jeffreys. "I don't suppose you…"

"I'm not a sorcerer," Yi Xiao pointed out. "What I do uses *qi*, not magic."

"From where I'm sitting, I don't see much difference."

Thinking on it, Yi Xiao supposed it would seem that way to an outsider. "Magic draws on energies from outside the world. *qi* on the energies from within. A really good, really powerful, sorcerer can stretch their influence for miles. I'm told the best a *qi* master can manage is an acre or so." There were other sources of power, some less influential, some so vast only the Gods could handle them. None of which mattered right then.

"Point is, can you do something to stop Jeffreys?"

"I don't know. I can destroy his creations, the same way I did the other, but stopping him? That probably means killing and I'm done with that. At least I want to be."

By this time they were getting close to the campsite and Yi Xiao slowed to a halt. "Didn't you post a guard?"

"I did."

Someone hissed at them from the trees. Jo. "Douse your lantern. Quick."

They didn't argue with her, though Chao might have. Fortunately, Ma put a hand over the boy's mouth and muttered, "For once in your life be quiet." To Yi Xiao's amazement, Chao obeyed, albeit sulkily.

In the meantime Jo slipped down the hillside quietly and told Zak, "We got trouble."

She didn't have to say more because they were close enough to the camp for Yi Xiao to hear raised voices. Some were yelling in Chinese, others in English, still others in Manchurian. He sighed. He'd expected Jeffreys. He'd expected Wang. He'd expected Gan Han. He hadn't expected them all at the same time.

ooo

Leaving their captives tied up behind them, with Ma and Chao to keep guard, Zak, Yi Xiao and Jo climbed up the slope of the valley. Zak wanted to leave Jo behind but could see by her expression that she wasn't going to cooperate. They didn't have time to argue the point, forcing him to agree.

"Don't expect me to rescue you if you get caught." Yi Xiao's callous statement made Zak bristle, until he added, "You're too smart to be a hostage, Jo. Find a way to get out of any trouble yourself."

The compliment was surprisingly effective. Zak supposed Jo must have been feeling useless for a while now. He hadn't helped, leaving her behind. But it was a good thing he had. She was the only one small and fast enough to slip off and warn them of the trouble ahead.

By now they'd reached a spot overlooking the campsite, where they could see everything going on clearly. Zak's understanding of Chinese was being tested, though some of what the miners were saying didn't need translation. Their meaning, vulgar and unrepeatable in polite company, was clear. Their sentiment was shared by the other two groups, creating an incomprehensible and slowly loudening babble of rage.

"Blood's gonna spill any minute," Zak muttered. "Can you do anything about your men, Yi Xiao?"

"Strictly speaking, they aren't mine. But since they think they are, maybe?" Yi Xiao scanned the scene and pointed, "The real problem's right there."

The man Yi Xiao pointed to was a tall, thin and elegantly dressed white man. He was watching the argument without expression, one hand clenched on a cane of what looked like carved bones. It was impossible to tell much about him but Zak guessed he was probably that Doc Jeffreys their captive had mentioned. He didn't look like much, but if he really had summoned the bone marrow eater he wasn't one Zak wanted to cross. Not that they had much choice.

Yi Xiao was already heading for the camp, sidling down the hillside in that slippery way of his. Zak stumbled after, with Jo a little bit behind. She was showing sense for once, understanding that she'd be putting him and Yi Xiao at risk if she got herself caught.

Zak got to the bottom of the hill just as Yi Xiao reached the soldiers who'd accompanied him earlier. As if to prove they considered themselves his, whether or not he agreed, they fell silent at his touch. Parting like the Red Sea, they let the young man pass without argument. Zak, arriving a moment or so later, hurried after, not wanting to get left behind.

The center of the argument was Yi Xiao's follower, the girl called Gan Han. Jo had told Zak she thought the girl was in love with Yi Xiao but the look she now turned on the young man held nothing but anger and distaste. Love could blossom in the strangest places but Zak doubted Jo's judgment. Such emotions weren't good soil for a long and happy relationship.

Jo came up behind Zak, staying close and keeping an eye behind them. "Gan Han? Why are they all yelling at her?"

"I don't think it's her they're mad at," Zak answered. "She's just put herself at the center of attention." Near as he could make out from the noise, Gan Han had decided to defend the miners against both Wang and Jeffreys. The latter's men didn't want to raise a hand to her because she was a girl. As for the former, he wasn't ready to risk her sword.

When Wang saw Yi Xiao he bowed and said something in a language Zak didn't know at all. Fortunately, Yi Xiao ordered, "Speak English. We're guests in this land and I don't want to have to translate for you."

"Lord, this girl defends the rebels. We meant to take them prisoner and return them to China with us for trial…"

"No."

Wang's eyes narrowed. "No? They rebel against your father. They rebel against the Dragon Throne. In time, perhaps soon, they will rebel against you."

Yi Xiao dismissed the suggestion with a negligent wave of his hand. "Oh, I sincerely doubt that. But we can discuss that question later, once these other men have been dealt with." He turned his attention on Jeffreys, adding, "Unless I'm seriously mistaken, you are the leader of these men?"

Jeffreys picked thoughtfully at his teeth with a delicate white splinter that put Zak in mind of bone. Silently, he looked Yi Xiao up and down before finally saying, "I see no one here worthy of my attention." His thick drawl was pure deep south and his arrogant sneer was pure plantation master. "Where is the white man who commands this camp?"

Zak realized Jeffreys didn't know Caleb had died. Or, perhaps, he'd thought the camp, like the valley he'd been trying to steal, belonged to Hal Kraft now? "I own this land, mister," he said quietly.

That resulted in a snort as cold as ice. "A black man pretends to own land? I think not. Where is the real owner?"

Now it was Jo's turn to talk and she took it. "I'm the only white person here, mister. And I own half this camp, so if you can't bear to put your words to my partner, you can be telling them to me."

The man's eyes seemed to glow from inside and it wasn't a reflection. Fire didn't have a sick yellow-green tint like corpse-lights. Zak moved forward to set himself between Jo and Jeffreys and found Yi Xiao doing the same.

Slowly Jeffreys recovered himself. "Where's your Pa, little girl. I'll do business with him if you don't mind."

"You can't. Pa died on the way here and I'm his only heir. So I say again, you tell me what you want or you go away."

Another flare, this one bright enough to send most of the miners, and Jeffreys' men, huddling backwards. Wang's men were soldiers and apparently had seen such things before. All they did was set themselves, prepared to dodge or attack as ordered. Zak stayed where he was as well, saying, "There's no point in getting angry, sir. We don't even know who you are, much less why you think you have business here."

Before Jeffreys could insult Zak again, Jo added, "You're the uninvited guest here. Ain't right for you to waltz in making trouble without so much as an introduction."

Stiff as a board, Jeffreys snapped, "I am Doctor Tyrone P. Jeffreys, late of Atlanta. That's all you need know." He bowed mockingly, adding, "Now then, little miss. I know your name's Jo, but I don't know the rest of it."

She was about to answer, but Zak realized in time what a mistake it'd be. "No. Don't say a thing," he said quickly. At the same time, Yi Xiao added, "He has a new tool to replace the one I destroyed. Don't give it a weapon against you."

As Jo fell silent Jeffreys turned blazing eyes on Yi Xiao. "You destroyed? You're an ignorant savage. What do you know of power and magic?"

"Master says, those who seek power over others should first master themselves." Yi Xiao's hands sparked as he raised them. "This ignorant savage has not yet achieved that goal, but he is more than a match for a dead thing forced to exist beyond its time."

Almost everyone, including Wang and his men, backed away. Not from Yi Xiao's power but from the bone chilling energy emanating from Jeffreys. The man pointed at the fire with his cane and it suddenly went dark, so that the only light came from him. Zak grabbed Jo and dragged her back, knowing he couldn't help. The man's skeleton seemed to be burning from within, the same sickening corpse-fire that shone from his eyes.

Something fluttered in the air between Jeffreys and Yi Xiao. "I know your name," Jeffreys said calmly. "Lang Yi Xiao, the Wanderer. Least worthy and youngest son of the House of the White Wolf."

The thing's substance darkened as what little remained of Burns took shape. More shadows thickened into human shapes; some unfamiliar, others the men the Bone Marrow Eater had killed. All drew close, crying out in pain but forced by Jeffreys' will to act.

Yi Xiao smiled. "True," he agreed. "But I'm also the best and only disciple of the Storm Hermit." As he spoke a bolt of lightning rose from around his feet to pierce the sky above.

ooo

The energies flowing through Yi Xiao weren't just his *qi* this time. Close as he was to one of the roots of the world, he'd automatically and without thinking about it, reached deep. If he'd been closer to its source it would have burned him to a crisp. This far away it jolted through his body and shuddered through every nerve. He let it, balancing atop the power as if he was perched atop Heng Shan's highest peak.

"Lang Yi Xiao, the Wanderer. Least worthy and youngest son of the House of the

White Wolf." The souls his enemy had stolen shrieked his name over and over, trying to worm their way into his thoughts. They could not. The force of the world raged through him, overwhelming all else.

No mortal could take such power for long and Yi Xiao was as mortal as any man. He knew he had to act quickly, before what was human in him was burned away. He spread his hands, centering himself, maintaining his position despite the energies trying to transform him.

It was the hardest thing he'd ever done. By nature he was active, a constantly moving force upon the world. Making himself the center of so much power, making himself its focus, was not his natural state at all. He corrected himself, remembering his teachings. "Master says, it is not the world that centers on you, but you upon the world."

Time slowed. Time stopped. He found himself hanging between seconds, face to face with the men Jeffreys had killed and bound. Their torment was obvious, for they were trapped in this timeless state, unable to die and unable to return to life. They sought other lives, hoping to find their way out of their bondage, but could not be free.

Or could they? "His name is Doctor Tyrone P. Jeffreys, late of Atlanta."

Time sped forward. Jeffreys' victims howled triumphantly. The earth shook. The wind wailed. The others cowered in terror. Only Jeffreys didn't move, too certain of his control to react. The paper-thin remnants of the lives he'd stolen and enslaved spun round him, a whirlwind of rage and desolation.

"Use my strength," Yi Xiao said, offering it freely. "Save yourselves."

By the time Jeffreys realized he was no longer their master it was too late. They tore the clothes from his flesh, his flesh from his bones and shattered his bones to dust. Until all that was left was a mewling yellow-green worm that somehow managed to dig into the dirt and escape, his victims following behind, howling.

Yi Xiao released his hold on the power he'd summoned, letting it sink back into the roots of the world. Standing in near darkness, all he could do was take deep, slow, breaths. Somehow, he stayed upright, though his knees and legs trembled from the effort.

Light flared as someone relit the fire. Others were babbling prayers, still others curses. Then someone said in Manchurian, "Commander, that thing called him…" The voice broke off suddenly, accompanied by a sound Yi Xiao knew only too well. He raised his head, tried to turn and crumpled to the ground, staring at Wang as the man drew his sword from his own soldier's throat.

"What… why are you…"

Wang ignored Yi Xiao's weak protests, gesturing to his lieutenants. "Kill them."

As the two men drew their swords, walking slowly towards their former compatriots, Yi Xiao struggled to stand. "Help them," he called to the miners. "Don't let them do this."

Once again Gan Han tossed Yi Xiao's sabre to his feet. "You stop them. They're your responsibility." Despite what she said, she drew her own weapon, blocking the pair from attacking their own cowering men.

Yi Xiao ignored his weapon where it lay. He didn't have the strength to fight, no matter how much he wanted to. "Wang! Stop your men. Now."

"They've heard the truth. All these men have heard the truth. They can't be allowed to live, your Highness. The Xianfeng Emperor—your twin—sits upon the Dragon Throne now, but when we bring you home we will make you Emperor in his stead."

Yi Xiao stared at the man. "You knew I wasn't Yi Zhu. Wait… Xianfeng Emperor? My twin?"

"Your father, your true father, died three months ago, your Highness. Despite my commander, General Hwei's best efforts, that hag Madam Lang snuck your brother into the Summer Palace just in time for him to be declared heir. Hwei sent me to find you, so you can take your brother's place unnoticed."

The very idea was laughable. Even more laughable than Wang believing he was Yi Zhu, gallivanting off to America while his father, the Emperor, died. "You're an idiot."

Wang's expression darkened. "What?"

"Were you listening just then? Did you hear those things call my name, my true name?"

"But…"

"But I was born in the Summer Palace, on the very same day as my cousin Yi Zhu. I know the rumors saying I'm his twin and a threat to his inheritance. Saying Madam Lang took me into her family to protect the lineage…"

"You are those things. You're the only one to save us from that fool on the throne's stupidities."

"No. The rumors are wrong. You're wrong. I'm not Yi Zhu's twin. I'm the youngest son of Lang Mianzhen, grandson of the Imperial Princess He Xiao. Great grandson of the Qianglong Emperor and of the traitor, Lang Heshen. My father is the Duke of Jin and my mother a Princess of Tu. And I will not be used as a pawn to give General Hwei a puppet on the throne."

Wang drew his sword. "I don't have to kill you to defeat you," he growled. "You can barely…" He didn't finish the sentence. He'd been so focused on Yi Xiao he hadn't noticed Zak moving slowly up behind him, iron staff in hand. The thump to the back of his head wasn't hard, but it was enough.

"That… was an unfair and effective solution," Yi Xiao told the man.

"Would you like me to wake him up so you can go back to fighting?"

"No. No, not really." Yi Xiao grinned wryly, his arms giving way now that they were no longer needed to prop him up. "In fact, I'd much prefer taking a nap for a while." Without bothering to wait for an answer he did just that.

ooo

When he woke the next day, Wang raved and cursed, fighting the ropes holding him down and frothing at the mouth like a madman. His men, having realized he and his two lieutenants were traitors, ignored his demands to be freed, willingly assisting the miners in their work.

As for Jeffreys' men; without the sorcerer and his terrible magic to keep them in line, most drifted off. Some remained, hiring on with the Chinese miners in the hopes of earning enough to buy a share along with the others. Jeffreys' sabotage had turned out serendipitous, for it'd revealed a vein of gold in the rock that Ma and his men might have missed otherwise. It might not be enough to make them rich, but it was a start.

Zak spent most of his spare time working on a special project for Yi Xiao, one the young man insisted he keep secret from everyone. Jo practiced the exercises Yi Xiao had taught her and helped keep the camp running. Her arguments with Chao often resulted in chases that had those watching laying bets as to who would win the latest fight. Zak could tell from the way both children laughed that it was just a game. One that might turn to something else, if he read their characters rightly.

Aside from overseeing Zak's work, Yi Xiao spent a great deal of his time just sitting in one place, completely ignoring the chaos around him, including Gan Han's continuous attempts to get him to draw his blade. Zak had a feeling it'd take some truly remarkable circumstances to force Yi Xiao into action but he didn't bother trying to persuade the young lady. He could tell she wouldn't listen.

At last, almost a full week after Jeffrey's final attack on the camp, Yi Xiao looked up from his meditations to say. "I believe it's time for me to go."

"Where are we going?" Gan Han demanded. "Your grandmother may have sent you to America, but that doesn't mean you have to wander all over the place."

Zak wasn't surprised at Yi Xiao's bland answer. "Second question first. She also didn't say I had to stay in one place. I don't have to wander. I want to." He rose to his feet, fending off the girl's attack with ease. "First question last. You're not coming with me."

"Nonsense. I will follow you wherever you go until we duel."

The girl's response was no more surprising than Yi Xiao's. Yet Zak couldn't help asking, "What did he do to you to make you so determined to fight him?"

It was Yi Xiao who explained, "Her family demands it of her. Her family is mad. If I were still the person I was before I joined the Wind and Rain sect, I'd probably have killed her." At Zak's shocked stare, he added, "She's not my match. She knows it, yet still tries to fight me. No one in the martial world would blame me at all if I stabbed her to the heart."

"But she's a girl..."

"The rules of the martial world are harsh, Zak. Gan Han knows it." The girl inclined her head gravely, agreeing, and Yi Xiao continued, "Women can and do take high positions within it, but they cannot expect to be exempt from the danger simply because they're women. Not and retain the right to take those positions."

The very idea disgusted and shook Zak to his core. He'd seen Yi Xiao at his most ferocious and the thought of him cutting pretty little Gan Han down was terrifying. "Is that why you left the martial world, then?"

"Part of it." Yi Xiao's expression went distant. "I killed my first man when I was fourteen. To be fair, he was trying to kill me, so I didn't really have a choice. But I liked it. I wanted to do it again. Yet at the same time it sickened me. I didn't want to be the person I was becoming. I sought out the most dangerous, most difficult to persuade, teacher. If she killed me, I'd be done with the killing. If she accepted me, I'd learn to master my violence. I haven't, yet, but I've learned to harness it."

Gan Han looked away and Zak guessed she didn't want to admit she was asking too much of the man. "Then all you have to do is fight me and I will prove my skill against yours, as I was commanded."

"You are not my match. We both know it."

"I do not know anything of the sort." Gan Han's voice trembled and Zak knew she was lying.

"I could prove it, here and now, but I will make a deal with you instead." Yi Xiao pointed to Wang's men. "Take them, and the traitors, to my grandmother in China. Tell her what Wang and Hwei meant to do and give her this letter." He took an envelope from his shirt pocket and held it out.

"And you'll come home to fight me?"

"I won't come home until grandmother sends for me. But you may return to America, if that's still your wish."

"And then you'll fight me."

"Again, no." Before Gan Han could argue more, Yi Xiao added, "When you find me, given you can, I will teach you my blade techniques. I will make you at least the weapons master I was before I became the Storm Hermit's disciple. You may even become my better. That's what your family wants, after all, for you to take my place in the ranks of the martial world."

Gan Han hesitated. Took the envelope. "I will find you. I have your sabre and it will call to you."

Zak almost opened his mouth to protest, then realized what Yi Xiao was doing in time. Only when Gan Han had gone off to gather her things and talk to Wang's men did he say, "That's why you had me copy your weapon."

"It was."

"You switched it."

"I did."

"So even if she could use your sabre to find you, she won't have it."

"That's right." Yi Xiao smiled wryly. "She's a stubborn child. I'm sure she'll still try to find me. She may even succeed. But I don't see any reason to make it easier for her."

Zak chuckled. "So you're leaving now? Before she notices?"

"Of course." Yi Xiao bowed. "I appreciate you letting me stay in camp for as long as I have. But I'm not called The Wanderer for nothing and it's time for me to live up to my name."

As the young man disappeared into the trees, as slippery and impossible to hold onto as ever, Zak reflected that he had more than enough adventure ahead of him, given the way things were in California right then.

Of course, that was probably exactly the way Yi Xiao wanted it.

Epilogue –
Advancing to one's Potential

TO: The Imperial Princess Qing He Xiao. Last daughter of the beloved Emperor Qianlong. Head of the White Wolf Clan
FROM: The wandering priest Yi Xiao. Second son of Lang Mingzhen, the Duke of Jin and Lady Tu, Princess of Tu in Khaitan

Beloved Grandmother,

I stand atop Mount Tam and clasp my hands to the center of the world.

When last we met, you commanded I travel to the American territory of California. At the time, I believed you meant me to act as decoy while my cousin Yi Zhu escaped to meet his father, the honored and honorable Daoguang Emperor. Indeed, I am sure that was your primary purpose at the time.

Yet circumstances here in America, a chance meeting with General Hwei's cohort, Commander Wang, has revealed a deeper purpose to my exile. And exile it must be. As long as my illustrious—and now Imperial—cousin sits upon the Dragon throne I, as his apparent twin, shall always be a threat to him. He may or may not realize it, but others will, and will seek to use me. Just as Commander Wang intended to.

The young lady who brings you this message will tell you how I came to meet with this Commander Wang and the full nature of the treachery he planned. Aside from his two lieutenants, Huan and Fu, his men are innocent. He would have killed them when they learned I was not who Wang pretended I was. Please see to it they are fairly treated. They could not know his intentions.

Regarding the young lady... She is Gan Han, a daughter of the Xihua clan and their finest swords-master. She was ordered to seek me out in battle, even brought my sabre to me from where I left it on Heng Shan. I'm sure she believes her purpose was to raise her position in the martial world, since defeating my blade—at the risk of arrogance— is no easy thing.

I also suspect, or fear, an ulterior purpose, one I cannot help but decry. Neither she, nor I, are breeding stock nor tools of political maneuvering. You, yourself, taught me that. Yet her family likely believe that I will become attracted to a woman of her skill and inevitably fall in love. Be kind to her. Protect her, if you will, from their machinations. I do not love her, nor do I think I ever will, but she has been a comrade in arms and I would not have her mistreated.

I have learned much and have much more to learn. Yet I miss and love you all. Give my love to all the family. Tell them that my body may walk these strange lands until the end of my days, but my heart will walk with all of you for eternity.

I shall clasp my hands to the center of the world.

Be safe. Be well. May our people prosper, our crops grow fertile and the train I know my father would have us build fly on its rails with great speed and greater safety. May your years be long and may we meet again.

With love and profound respect,
Lang Yi Xiao
Priest and Wanderer.

Chapter 1
Air - An Ill Wind Blows No Good

Shouts echoed through the valley, accompanied by dull thuds and sharp snaps. A fight of some sort? The traveler paused, cocking his head to listen. Muffled as they were, the words were hard to make out, but some were in English, others in some foreign talk. Hunanese, he thought it'd be called.

Based on what little he could hear, the fight was more a contest. The sort of thing bored and restless men did when there wasn't anything else to occupy their time. Well enough, it meant they might welcome his arrival with pleasure, instead of distrust.

Of course, distrust would be natural. The traveler knew the place's background, knew how things were in California. Knew, too, what kind of troubles a mine camp run by a black man and a young white girl would run into. Already they'd faced claim jumpers and bandits. Soon enough, they'd face legal difficulties. That was always the way of it.

He kept walking, strolling easily up the rocky path, ears perked. There were guards ahead; he could tell they were there, bored and not really paying attention. He hoped he looked presentable enough. Not too much, though. He let his hair grow long, down past his collar, straggly and greying. Clean shaven, only because he could, and wearing a pair of blue-grey spectacles to hide his eyes. Not much could be done about his face; weathered skin stretched tight over high cheekbones, thin lips, jagged teeth, jutting nose and brows like scruffy black caterpillars.

His clothes shouldn't be too bad. Jeans, scruffy but well-kempt. A loose blue flannel shirt. A leather jacket—it got cold this late in the year—and a black hat with a big old coyote tail hanging off the side. He shifted his pack, made sure his boots were on the right feet and continued forward.

"Hey! You! Stop right there."

The speaker was Chinese, not quite old enough for a man, too old for a child. Lean-built, muscular, with a broad nose and lips that looked like they ought to be constantly smiling. They weren't that moment, but the traveler couldn't blame him. "Well now," he said, choosing English because the kid had, "What's this?"

The boy jumped down from the top of a big wooden sign arched over the pathway. "Strike It Rich Mine", it said. "Proprietors: Zak Striker and Jo Kraft. Established: 1849."

"Who are you?"

"Just a traveler, carrying mail. They call me Deathshead." He grinned broad. "Would there be a fellow name of Lang Yi Xiao round about? I've got a letter for him, all the way from China."

⇒)(⇐

"I really hate that stance of yours."

"So you've said before."

"It's ridiculous looking."

"Take that up with my master. I'm sure she'll correct it for your benefit."

They had this discussion every time they sparred, with the same result each time. Yi Xiao's stance, loose, slightly twisted and entirely off-balance, remained the same. Yi Xiao grinned as he slid beneath boss Ma's fist, knee coming down into the back of the other man's leg. At the same time he caught Ma Yun's wrist and torqued the older man's arm backwards.

The maneuver would have taken some men down. Ma Yun just flipped around along with Yi Xiao's motion. He even took advantage of his momentum to kick Yi Xiao in the belly, almost knocking him out of the ring. Almost, but not quite. Yi Xiao dropped, rolled, flung himself sideways and came up in Rising Bolt Strikes Flower, a position that didn't make Ma Yun any happier.

"That one's worse." As usual, Ma Yun tried to use words to distract Yi Xiao. Swinging around in Plum Blossom technique, he almost nailed Yi Xiao in the eye.

Yi Xiao was ready. He gauged Ma Yun's speed. Shifted his weight. Leapt straight up over the man's head, kicking backwards as he went. The blow landed solidly, sending Ma Yun flailing, one step over the edge of the ring.

Immediately the older man dropped stance, turned and bowed. "Well done."

Bowing in turn, Yi Xiao was about to speak when he noticed Ma Yun's boy, young Chao, running up the road from his post. "Brother, brother, brother!" he shouted. More words poured from his mouth, mostly incomprehensible.

Ordinarily, Yi Xiao's Hunanese was more than sufficient to let him understand Zak's Chinese miners. Young Chao, however, was talking fast and slurring his words so badly that even his father was having trouble. Ma Yun rapped his boy on the forehead with a knuckle to get his attention. "Stop blathering and speak clearly."

"There's a stranger coming up. Says he has a letter for brother Xiao. Says it's from China!"

Yi Xiao did some mental calculations. It'd been five months since he'd arrived in California, four since he'd reported his status to his grandmother. More than enough time for his letter to reach home. More than enough time for its bearer to head back, given his grandmother let her leave. "Is Miss Gan Han with him?" That was the risk of coming back to Zak's camp. Sihua Gan Han might find him if he stayed too long.

"I'd have said," young Chao started to protest, then faltered at Yi Xiao's raised brow.

"No, you wouldn't." Young Chao thought the situation romantic and was certain Yi Xiao and Miss Gan Han should just admit their attraction and be married.

"No," Chao admitted. "I wouldn't. But she isn't. I promise you. And the stranger's not Chinese. Looks Indian to me, says he's called Deathshead!"

Yi Xiao knew the youngster was mostly worried about his safety. They all knew why he'd had to leave China in the first place. Why visitors from their homeland could bring trouble. Long rumored to be the new Emperor's twin brother, Yi Xiao was target for assassinations or abductors, all seeking to use him as a pawn in an Imperial game of chess.

Seeing a tall lean figure approaching, Yi Xiao sighed for young Chao's foolishness. He might as well have flung fireworks in the air and planted a banner saying young Lord Lang was here and ready for murder.

⇒)(⇐

Deathshead grinned broad and wide at the miners gathered round the man who had to be Lang Yi Xiao. Protective lot, they were. Like the boy were a prince or something.

Which, from what Deathshead had heard, he was. Still, it made no sense, really. Near as he could tell, most Chinese workers belonged to a group of folk didn't like their rulers at all. What were they called again? Oh, yes. Han. While their rulers were Manchu.

The boy who'd blocked Deathshead's path started forward, about to point, but an older man grabbed his arm and shoved him off to the side with a curse. Then he stepped in Deathshead's way instead. "Sir. Can this old man be of assistance?"

From the looks of the fellow he was related to the boy. A helluvalot uglier, of course, with broad flat features and heavy lips. Deathshead paused, a few feet away, hands up and away from his sides. He wasn't armed, at least not visibly, but anyone fool enough to believe he was safe deserved to.

"Well, now. Not unless you're Lang Yi Xiao or Zak Striker." Deathshead cocked his head slightly, adding, "And I know Striker's no Chinese, so...."

"I could be Lang Yi Xiao."

"Stop." Behind the speaker, the man the others protected spoke up finally. To Deathshead's surprise, his English was perfect, with a crisp and refined British accent. "Don't pretend to be me, Mister Ma. I appreciate your concern, but, please, allow me to handle my own affairs."

Deathshead eyed the young man thoughtfully. Short and slight, with dark eyes and tanned skin, he didn't look impressive. He was dressed similarly to Deathshead, blue jeans and a flannel shirt, instead of the looser clothing the miners favored. His hair was collar length, hanging loose around lean features. "Mr. Lang, then. Got a letter for you." He took the envelope from his pack and held it out.

Yi Xiao examined the letter thoughtfully. To Deathshead's surprise, he shoved it into a shirt pocket with a careless air. Curiosity piqued, wanting to know just why the man would treat a letter from home so casually, Deathshead asked, "Aren't you gonna open it?"

The others were watching Yi Xiao as well, expressions showing their interest. He just smiled. "It's from my grandmother. If it were urgent, she'd find a better way to reach me than trusting the mail." He patted the letter protectively. "And, really, I don't want you seeing me crying over news from home."

A new voice said, "It's his business, gentlemen. Why don't y'all go along and do something useful. More useful than beating each other up because you're bored." The newcomer was a big, muscular, black man. Dressed in a leather apron, smelling of iron, smoke and fire, it was obvious he'd just come from the forge off to the side of the little valley. Based on what Deathshead had been told, he almost had to be, "Mr. Striker?"

The mine's co-owner eyed Deathshead thoughtfully, towering over him in a way not quite intended to intimidate. It would have failed anyway. "I am that," he agreed. "And I heard you say you needed me as well?"

Deathshead agreed. "Good to meet you, Mister Striker. I got another letter for you. Serious official by the looks of it. Wouldn't waste time getting on with it." He held the envelope out without blinking an eye and Striker took it with a sharp frown. "I'll just wait around here, if you'd like, if you maybe have something you want to send back. Fact, if any of you lot have letters to send, just you give 'em here and I'll take good care of 'em."

As Deathshead found himself a perch on a nearby rock, Striker opened his letter carefully. From the look on his face, it was obvious he wasn't happy. Not happy at all.

"Jo and I have to go to San Francisco," he told Ma grimly. "It looks like someone wants to challenge our claim."

⇒)(⇐

Yi Xiao was concerned for his friends, but as a foreigner, one with no experience in property law, he knew he'd be useless for anything other than moral support. He'd been planning on moving on as soon as he received his grandmother's letter, however, so he offered to come along. He wasn't sure where he'd go, once they reached San Francisco, but California was a very big place indeed. Plenty of places for a young man inclined to wander to go.

It being late in the afternoon, Zak decided to wait until morning to set off, giving him time to gather his notes and discuss their plans with his young partner. Jo had been helping out in the storeroom when the letter arrived and didn't yet know their troubles. Just as well for Zak to tell her privately. She took her red hair for license and was likely to—what was the term?—blow her stack.

Having little to do until dinner, Yi Xiao found a quiet corner overlooking the camp. One where no one could sneak up on him unawares and he could read privately. He hadn't been entirely joking when he'd said he might end up crying over his grandmother's letter. He'd barely seen his family the last time he'd been home and now he wasn't sure when they'd meet again.

The letter appeared to be exactly what a dignified Imperial Princess would send her reprobate grandson. Chill encouragement, reminders to work hard and to keep the family honor. A few side notes mentioning his brother and his brother's wife expecting another child. Another mentioning his half-sister becoming affianced to a Khaitanese nobleman. A precise and elaborate description of his cousin, the Xianfeng Emperor's, coronation. No mention of the Imperial Predecessor's death, but then there wouldn't be.

All of which hid more important messages. Miss Gan Han had gone back to her family with a message from Madam Lang. They were to keep her home and stop throwing her life away for the sake of their family pride. Colonel Wang had been summarily executed for treason, but his master, General Wei, had managed to avoid blame. Most importantly, however, Grandmother's contacts had heard rumors that the *Nian* rebels were looking for the Emperor's twin 'brother'. They'd yet to learn where Yi Xiao had gone, but it was just a matter of time.

Yi Xiao carefully folded his letter and put it away. The *Nian* were a loose coalition of rebels who mostly just protested government unfairness. Yi Xiao had never had any dealings with them, but at a guess that was going to change. His cousin didn't have much patience with such people and had probably offended them already.

Perhaps he should acquire a facial scar or so? Something bold and dashing in an X on his cheek, perhaps? Just as quickly as he considered the possibility, he discarded it. For one thing, both mother and grandmother would be furious with him. For another, he really didn't want an infection.

"I've heard you're a Prince."

Deathshead's voice coming from the nearby trees startled Yi Xiao. If he weren't long accustomed to controlling his reactions he might have fallen straight off his boulder. "Not really," he denied. "My grandmother's a princess, but my father is just a duke, and a minor one at that. As his second son, I hardly have any rank at all." He looked sideways, then tilted his head so he could see the man better. Not many adults hung by their knees from trees while talking. "Good trick keeping your hat on, by the way."

The man dropped to the ground and brushed himself off. Ignoring Yi Xiao's jibe, he continued, "So not valuable at all?"

"Not in the way you're thinking, no." It was an odd conversation to be having with a total stranger. One most people would likely balk at. Accustomed as he was to strange situations, Yi Xiao didn't bother commenting. Just added, "And Grandmother wouldn't allow a ransom, so you might forget such ideas. Given, of course, you were having them in the first place."

With a laugh, Deathshead approached, only to stop when Yi Xiao drew on his inner *qi*. Sensing danger, the man backed off. "Ah. I hadn't realized. You do have some defenses." He smiled. "I wonder if the fellow who'd tried to follow me up here knows that."

Yi Xiao blinked. Considered the question. "Hard to say," he admitted. "Might, might not. I have so many enemies it gets hard to count."

The question was, was Deathshead warning him so he'd be ready? Or so he'd run?

⇒)(⇐

Getting up at dawn was not, at all, something Deathshead enjoyed. Given the choice, he'd sleep in till way past noon, wander around looking for something to eat or trouble to get into, then maybe do some hunting in the late evening hours. Still, he wanted to keep an eye on Yi Xiao. The boy probably didn't realize it yet, but his little display of power a few months earlier had drawn attention and not just Deathshead's.

Not many humans these days had the mental fortitude to draw on Old Lady Mountain's power. If Yi Xiao had been a bit closer, he wouldn't have any mental fortitude left at all. Old Lady Mountain would've snatched him up, chewed him flat and spit him out empty. Still, there was talent there and Deathshead was always interested in talent.

All of which meant that when Striker, his young partner Jo, and Yi Xiao packed up to go to San Francisco, Deathshead tagged along with them. He didn't bother hiding, either. Why would he? He was a traveler who just happened to be going the same way. There was safety in numbers, after all.

"You don't carry a gun?" That was little Jo Kraft, her bright red hair cut short, her cheeks covered in freckles and her blue eyes sharp as needles. She dressed like a boy, but Deathshead could tell she wouldn't be able to hide herself much longer. "That don't seem safe, out here."

"I have other ways of dealing with problems." Deathshead gave a significant glance towards Yi Xiao, whose only weapon appeared to be the cloth wrapped object stuck under his backpack. It smelled of iron, whatever it was. Iron and, oddly enough, wolf. "Like your friend here."

The youngster inclined his head. "My favorite way is avoiding them," he admitted honestly. "So much safer to walk around a fight than straight through."

To his great amusement, Jo continued her effort to find out more about Deathshead. "Where you from, mister? You sorta look like you might be Indian, but...."

"I've no tribe to speak of, really. I like to think of myself as a man of the world." Deathshead grinned, knowing how unnerving the expression was on his face. "Belonging nowhere, I can be anywhere."

That set Striker laughing. "You sound just like Yi Xiao here." The mine boss eyed Deathshead, adding, "Y'know, I was wondering. What happened to the usual carrier? He strike it rich somewhere and move on?"

The big mine boss's eyes were watchful. Not that Deathshead blamed him for his distrust. Not in the slightest. He was a chancy looking fellow, no two ways about it. Besides, he had shown up unexpected, bringing a message neither Striker nor his little partner liked. "Tell the truth, I've no idea. I needed a bit of spare change and a reason to leave town for a few days. So I just asked at the post office if there were any jobs would take me out of sight and out of mind for a bit. You know how it is."

"Lucky thing for you, Zak," Yi Xiao pointed out genially. "If I understood that letter correctly, you need to get things sorted out quickly. We weren't expecting the next post for another two weeks."

Striker admitted that was true, then turned his attention back to Deathshead. "Well, since you've been out and about traveling, have you heard anything folk like me and Jo should know?"

"You heard California's a state now?"

"Heard rumors that was coming."

"And there was another big fire in San Francisco, just a bit ago."

"That I didn't know about. Bad?"

"Not too bad, near as I can tell. There weren't many places built since the last fire." Deathshead grinned, more to himself than Striker. Someone took offense to that place and it wasn't him, for once. "Heard tell there's were some con-tre-temps month or so back, down near Los Angeles. Some bandits went and tangled with the local wildlife. Round about two three months ago, I think."

Yi Xiao didn't react to the story but Deathshead knew he was paying attention. As well he might, because he was the one who'd instigated the watchers, set them stalking those bandits. Deathshead hadn't seen their sort get so excited in a long while and now, like others, he wanted to know just what they were dealing with.

Looking at the kid now, he had to wonder. Yi Xiao was human. Purely human, with just the speck of something small and weak. The sort of critter who lived fast and died faster. A short sharp squeak in the night and barely a mouthful for a hungry predator. Something like that shouldn't have power.

And yet he did. And Deathshead, being who and what he was, wanted to know why.

꒓꒤꒐

Yi Xiao felt stalked. Stalked and intently scrutinized. Was it Deathshead? Someone else? Both?

Movement drew his attention up the slope of the hill beside the narrow path. Something lurked in the shadows. Something familiar. No killing intent, as far as he could tell, but definitely not friendly. Whomever it was, he was the center of their attention.

In a way it reminded him of Miss Gan Han. That same intent desire to have something from him. That same inability to let go of a thing, once decided. Yet it couldn't be her. He'd traveled with the young swordswoman for too long not to know the sense of her. Constantly dissatisfied. Frequently irritable. Occasionally sad and vulnerable. None of these things could describe this sense. Whomever his new watcher was, they were far better centered than she'd been.

A sound in the bushes below the path made him look that way, next. Once again, no killing intent, but he sensed disinterested malice. Someone meant someone ill. Not from hate or greed, but just because they were there. He corrected himself. There was greed involved, but nothing immediate. He didn't think this watcher meant to rob them, recognizing there'd be nothing to gain from doing so.

Deathshead was still blathering on but Yi Xiao was sure he sensed the danger, too. The man shifted his position, setting himself so he could run or fight as the situation required. Yi Xiao followed suit, preparing himself for whatever hunted them. As they moved, they glanced at each other, acknowledging the danger.

Trouble wasn't long coming, but it came from an unexpected direction. A group of men climbed the narrow path towards them, coming around the corner as it bent round the mountainside. As far as Yi Xiao could tell, there wasn't a care in their world. At least there wasn't until they spotted the group coming towards them. Then their gazes focused and their expressions changed. Sharpened.

"Well, well, well," one man murmured to another, just barely audible at this distance. "Look for the devil and there he is."

The newcomers were familiar. At least their leader was. Trendle. Yi Xiao had met him just a month or so back, when Jo's father had been killed by those bandits. To Yi Xiao's surprise, he wasn't the center of attention. Trendle had been suspicious of him back then. If anyone was likely to try and bring him in for questioning, Trendle was the man.

The man's gaze reminded Yi Xiao of his mother, when he and his brother were children looking for and finding trouble. It was Yi Xiao's fault because it always was. Trendle's expression was exactly like hers. Honed, sharp and filled with the weary knowledge that someone had done something wrong. Again.

If that gaze were turned on Yi Xiao, he wouldn't have been surprised. Trendle hadn't been happy about their story, back when Jo's father had been killed. If he could have proved Yi Xiao had caused the trouble at the old Vega ranch, he'd have dragged Yi Xiao straight to the nearest court.

This time, though, it wasn't Yi Xiao he wanted. Wasn't Yi Xiao in trouble.

It was Zak.

⇒)(⇐

Trendle and his men looking for Zak wasn't at all what Deathshead expected. If anyone ought to be their target, it'd be himself. He'd run afoul of this merry band of trouble-seekers before, in fact. Quickly he tried to think if he had any recent wanted notices to his name. Then, satisfied he should be safe, he asked, "What'd I do this time? Sheep rustling? Seduction? Setting fires?"

Trendle hadn't noticed Deathshead until then. He'd been so focused on Zak. "You. What are you doing here? Warning an accomplice?"

Little Jo took up a position between the men and her partner. "What you fellows talkin' on? Accomplice? And why you lookin' so hard on Zak here?"

A child Jo's size and cuteness could get away with things a grown man like Deathshead couldn't. Trendle actually managed a smile. "You're that boy lost his father back then, ain't you? Joe, wasn't it?"

It hadn't occurred to Deathshead that Jo dressed the way she did—trousers, loose shirt, short hair—to keep her gender secret. Of course, he'd smelled the truth, soon as he'd met her. He could start some trouble with this. What was it white men called it? Setting the cat among the pigeons?

To Deathshead's annoyance, Zak interrupted before he could, taking up the attention. "I'm admitting puzzlement, here," he told Trendle. "Y'all're looking on me like I'm some criminal and talkin' like this fellow I just met yesterday were involved. So could you tell me what it is I'm supposed to have done?"

By this time some of Trendle's men, the newer ones he hadn't had time to train, were shifting position. From the looks of it, they wanted to block escape. They weren't doing a good job, though. One slipped on the slick grass on the upper slope, the other tripped right over his own two feet and nearly went rolling downhill.

Before the man could actually fall, Yi Xiao caught hold of his arm and set him straight. If nothing else, it proved the outlander was nicer than Deathshead. He'd have let the idiot roll down, straight into the arms of the little monsters watching them pass. They were mostly harmless, anyway. At worst, the man would have had a few bites taken out of him.

Returning his attention to Trendle, who was cursing his men under his breath, Deathshead added, "I am the most innocent of men, Mr. Trendle." That got roundly ignored, so he tried again. "At least, I'm innocent of anything this fellow might have done. Though I'm finding me hard put to think he'd do anything even a teensy bit against the law."

Trendle sighed. "We got a job posting from some Easterner to look for a runaway slave who'd gone and stole his little girl, a red-head named Josephine. According to him, the fellow was calling himself Striker and got hisself a mine camp up this way."

Setting a hand on Jo's shoulder to stop her from blowing steam straight out the top of her head, Zak said. "Well, my name is Striker and I do run a mine camp. But everything else about that story's a bald-faced lie and I have the papers to prove it."

Deathshead didn't have a high opinion of most of Trendle's men, but Trendle himself wasn't a fool by any means. He eyed Zak. Eyed Jo. Took a second, more careful, look at the red-faced, furious, ready to pop any moment, girl. Another, more careful look towards her chest. All her panting made the truth easier to see. Trendle looked away just as fast as he could.

Recovering himself, Trendle said, "Well, Mr. Striker, I'm not going to say you're lying. But maybe it'd be a good thing if you came to Corte Madera with us, even so?"

Zak sighed. "Mr. Trendle, I don't mind proving myself in a proper court of law, but right now I've a legal issue to deal with, down in San Francisco. One I can't ignore for any length of time. I'll come with you, if you insist, but only after I've done my business with Land Services."

Another moment of hesitation. Then, to Deathshead's complete surprise, because he'd dealt with people after his hide before and never talked them down this easily, Trendle said, "If it weren't for the fact I know that young'un alongside with you lost her father in Los Angeles, I'd argue the point more. All right. We'll escort you to San Francisco, first."

That set the others arguing. It was a waste of time. They'd be losing money. They had work to do. If Yi Xiao hadn't coughed and quietly said, "The road is long. Bandits lurk. Wolves prowl. A paid escort might be welcome." He raised a trio of oddly shaped, bright silver coins. "I promise there's more than enough for all of you."

⇒)(⇐

The offer of money had the hoped-for effect of turning enemies to allies. Trendle would have waited without it, of course, but Yi Xiao knew it'd save the poor man some face if he could justify the change in plan with silver. The only trouble he could see was that his Chinese coins' only value in America was the metal they were poured from.

"My contact in San Francisco will cheerfully pay you for your services, should my coins be undesirable," he assured Trendle as they continued down the roadway. "His name is Mr. Chang, owner of Jeen Loon dry goods. If you give him this and tell him the Wanderer asks he pay you and your men fifty American dollars, he will do so." 'This' was a bamboo slip with his seal, marked with the amount Yi Xiao offered.

Trendle eyed him. "Your English is a great deal better than I remember, Mr. Lang."

With a smile, Yi Xiao spread his hands. "I am a quick learner. And my father's second wife is English."

"Why'd you play dumb back in Los Angeles, then?"

Truth was playing dumb made people underestimate him. He thought Trendle could guess that much and chose only to say, "It amused me to do so. That and I didn't have much to offer to the conversation. We were traveling from one place to another and simply ran into a bit of trouble."

Admittedly, Jo couldn't have thought it just a bit of trouble, but she'd just lost her father. Yi Xiao was glad she'd found a place with Zak and his miners. He'd be leaving soon and he liked knowing she was safe and sound with friends. Of course, that could change.

The thought reminded him, "Did you meet the person claiming Zak was his slave?"

"No," Trendle admitted, not at all surprised by the shift in subject. "The job was posted with our contact in San Francisco. We were told to bring them two to El Rancho Corte Madera, over near Sausalito. And it could be he's looking for someone completely different."

The man wasn't a fool and Yi Xiao looked sideways at him, raising a dubious brow. "You don't really think that, do you?"

"No. No, I suppose not. Striker's lucky it was me took the job, though. A lot of bounty hunters wouldn't listen to a black man claiming innocent."

Truth be told, Yi Xiao thought Trendle would have doubted Zak's story himself. If he hadn't known for a fact that Jo's father was dead, if he hadn't worked out she had to be the red-head named Josephine, he'd have insisted Zak accompany him no matter what. "About when did you get hired?"

Trendle thought about it. "Around a week ago."

Yi Xiao turned his attention on Deathshead where he ambled alongside the road, keeping watch on whatever it was trailing them. That was another thing Yi Xiao wanted answers on, but those were questions he couldn't ask in front of someone like Trendle. "When did you pick up that package for Zak?"

"Well, now, I'm not so good at time, but the moon just about dark, if that helps."

It did. The moon was a little over half-full now, so it'd been a bit over a week since Deathshead had left San Francisco. A dedicated postal worker could make the trip in less than that, but Deathshead seemed the lazy type. Possibly lazy and distractible. One couldn't guess at how long it'd take him to finish a job.

Of course, the main thing was that, within days of Deathshead having accepted the job of bringing Zak that letter, someone had set up a trap for the miner. One that would have delayed his visit to the Land Office. Yi Xiao didn't understand American land laws very well, but he could guess from Zak's behavior just how bad it'd be for him to be delayed.

He thought on the subject the rest of the afternoon, all the while prattling on to whoever was fool enough to listen about whatever came into his head to talk about. He couldn't hide his English anymore, not if he wanted to get anywhere. That didn't mean he couldn't seem too light-headed and distracted to be dangerous.

After all, he'd no idea when some member of Trendle's posse might decide to wander off with whatever he could get.

⇒)(⇐

They stopped to camp about halfway to San Francisco, choosing a clearing off to the side of the road amid some pines. Deathshead picked up some sticks here, a handful of leaves and needles there for tinder. He didn't really like working much but knew the others would be on him if he didn't at least look like he was busy.

When Yi Xiao beckoned him to help check the edges of the campsite, he wasn't sure he was relieved. The young man was entirely too noticing and he'd been holding back questions all day. Questions he obviously couldn't ask in front of the others. Not without revealing things about himself and Deathshead neither really wanted known.

"Who or what's been following us?" the youngster asked without preamble.

Taking a moment to make sure they were out of earshot, even though he was sure Yi Xiao had already, Deathshead decided to be honest. For once. "Little 'uns. Ground spirits, mostly. Wouldn't surprise me if they got you in their sights."

Yi Xiao considered that thoughtfully. "I'm not a sorcerer and I don't think I've done anything recently to draw supernatural attention. Are you sure it isn't you they want?"

Tell the truth, Deathshead wasn't. "It might be." All this honesty was beginning to hurt, so he added, "But I'm just an old man looking for peace and quiet."

As expected, Yi Xiao scoffed. He didn't argue, though. "Will they attack?"

Deathshead felt around thoughtfully. "That's a good question. They're not too bright. Not too brave. Long as you don't go poking them, they probably won't poke back. Not so sure about that other one out there." He was pretty sure the lone presence sneaking around the hillside above them was the same one who'd followed him before, once he'd taken that letter to Yi Xiao. The one he thought he'd lost in the woods.

"We'll have to see." Not said, implied, they were both in the same situation. Stalked, potentially in danger, betrayal would be foolhardy, right that moment.

Admittedly, foolhardy betrayal was a way of life for Deathshead, but only when it might profit him. He didn't see profit here. Not even amusement. Besides, he wanted to see what Yi Xiao was. He'd have to stay nearby for that, which meant he had to keep the trust for the moment. Only for the moment, though.

"We could go looking," he offered. "Why involve them lot, when they don't know a thing about how the world works?"

"Master says, if you go looking for trouble, it will find you," Yi Xiao answered calmly. "Neither your friends, nor mine, seem to want violence just yet. I'd like to see what they'll do, first."

The youngster had too much sense for his age. And who was this master he mentioned, anyway? Deathshead was about to ask, but Jo called them to dinner before he could.

꒰꒱

If Yi Xiao were a sorcerer he could have set up a proper ward around the campsite. Lacking that, he made sure to put out a few extra branches and traps. Long experienced with traveling the woods on his own, he knew how easy it was for someone to sneak up on the unwary.

Trendle's men set up watch, insisting it was their job to keep an eye on their charges. After all, that was what they were being paid for. Of course, given the circumstances, they weren't going to let someone they needed to bring to Corte Madera later have a chance to get away. And they certainly weren't going to leave chancy fellows like Yi Xiao and Deathshead in charge of security.

Yi Xiao chose to spend his night in contemplation. He could go days without proper sleep this way and he wanted to be ready the instant trouble began. He could sense their watchers circling closer, testing their limits and—in the case of Deathshead's 'little 'uns'—bolstering their courage. The other one backed off after a time, though Yi Xiao was sure they weren't gone for good.

One of Trendle's men went out into the dark to relieve himself. Came back shaking and muttering to himself. "Eyes," he told his friends. "Red eyes. Watching."

That'd be the little 'uns, unless Yi Xiao missed his guess. Had they reached the point where they'd make their move? Or had the man just gone far enough to notice? And what about the other watcher?

As he refocused his attention, listening intently for movement, sudden howls rose from somewhere south of their campsite. Distant though it was, he thought he recognized someone shouting in the Shanghai dialect.

Trouble, as always, drew him forward. He was on his feet and diving into the woods before anyone could speak or stop him. Trendle would keep an eye on Zak and Jo, he was sure. As for Deathshead, what that man did was his own business.

California's forests weren't a great deal different from those Yi Xiao was accustomed to. He had no difficulty navigating the darkness, though vines, rocks and the occasional little 'un tried to trip him up. The latter weren't really interested in him but they apparently regarded making difficulties part of their purpose in life. A few even nipped at his spirit, but they weren't big enough to do more than sting.

Something moved in the shadows alongside him. Deathshead, just as curious as he and in no mood to wait. Just as well. Better to keep an eye on that man than leave him behind with Zak and Jo. Besides, Yi Xiao was just as curious about him. This was a chance for clues.

The source of the yelling lay on the hillside above the roadway. Not a proper campsite at all. So why were men fighting here, this late at night? And, for that matter, why was one of them speaking Shanghai dialect? All in all, this was beginning to look like his problem.

Two men, shadow against shadow, dodged and struck in the darkness. Loose dark fabric whipped around, swirled with the one's motion. The other was more simply dressed; a coolie's outfit, grey trousers, grey tunic, braid wrapped round his neck for battle.

The robed man was tall and slim, the other hefty and a bit shorter. It was the latter cursing, Yi Xiao noted quickly. The tall one remained dead silent, dodging blows by a huge mace with ease, blocking and slicing with two slender sabers. One blade was bright silver, its surface flashing in the moonlight. The other was dark, barely visible in the night. Both moved fast, almost too fast for Yi Xiao to see.

The fighting style was familiar. Gan Han preferred a single sword, but this man's movements were very like hers, swirling slashes and dodges that relied on speed over strength. Was this, then, Yi Xiao's stalker? If so, he'd gathered his thoughts better now. Yi Xiao could only tell where he was by his movements. The other was too angry and startled to hide himself. Already he was on the defensive.

"Who you think's gonna win? My money's on the thin one, myself."

Yi Xiao didn't bet on fights. He most definitely didn't bet on fights where the outcome was all too obvious. "Is there a point to gambling when we agree?" he asked Deathshead quietly.

"I could be wrong. You could give it a try."

"I could. I won't. Besides, I'm stopping this." Yi Xiao might not know who these people were, but he could guess he was their target. That made him somewhat responsible for what they did here. He grabbed a fallen tree branch, launched himself forward and redirected the thin man's nearest blade.

⇒)(⇐

Deathshead had watched Chinese immigrants fight before, but never quite like this. Even his brief glimpse of Yi Xiao's sparring match back at camp hadn't prepared him. The youngster was fast, lightning fast, body dodging below and leaping above his opponent's strikes with ease.

The third fighter, the one the thin man had been attacking, scrambled to his feet. Tried to find an opening. Failed. Failed again. Took a punch to the face when he got too close. Deathshead wondered why. The thin man could have driven one of his swords straight into the man's heart from that position.

Yi Xiao used his branch to twist one of his opponent's swords free of his grip. It flew, straight as if aimed, to bury itself into a nearby tree. That made his opponent cut once, sharply, breaking several twigs free of the branch's main body. Without missing a beat, Yi Xiao slid forward, his shadow and the other man's merging briefly.

A moment later the two shadows separated again. Once again the third man tried to grab someone, either of the others. Once again he took a blow to the face. An elbow this time, gifted him by Yi Xiao along with a few sharp words in Chinese. The order had no effect. The damned fool seemed determined to get himself killed. If either man actually wanted him dead, he would be. He struggled to get close again.

Simultaneously, as if of one mind on the matter, both Yi Xiao and his opponent turned and slammed their fists into the third man's face and belly. He stopped in his tracks. Swayed. Fell.

Seeing the pair weren't ready to continue their hostilities, Deathshead lit a cigar and approached cautiously. As he expected, the thin fellow took a step back, remaining sword coming up defensively. Deathshead grinned. "Hey now, handsome. No need to get all het up over nothing. I'm a lover, not a fighter."

The man's face was limned by moonlight, revealing his face. Chinese, yes, but of a different sort from Yi Xiao. This one almost looked like a woman, what with his soft features, long black braid, ice pale skin, long lashes and delicate brows. If his robe hadn't got pulled open in the fight, making the truth obvious, Deathshead would've been fooled. "I can think of few things I would want in my bed less than you," the man said scornfully in excellent but accented English.

Deathshead grinned about to say more, but by this time the thin man had turned to go on one knee before Yi Xiao. "Lord Lang. I greet you. Had I recognized you, I would have ceased fighting immediately."

They all knew that wasn't true. There was something about his tone showed his real regret was not being able to finish their match. Yi Xiao didn't comment on it, though, so Deathshead didn't either. Instead, he just said, "It's rather late and dark for sparring, don't you think? And who are you, anyway? Aside from trouble, that is?"

The man answered in Chinese. Fortunately, Deathshead could understand far more than anyone realized. "I was following that fool from the *Nian* rebels there. Seeing my chance to capture him for you, I took it. As for who I am, I am Sihua Wu Chang, acting on the orders of your honored Grandmother in payment for my cousin's life." He raised his hands respectfully, holding out an odd little stone carving.

⇒)(⇐

Yi Xiao controlled the urge to curse. He should have expected this, or something like. He took his grandmother's jade seal, verifying it was real. Then he looked at the man kneeling before him. Strangely pale, he wore his hair in a tight braid. Like some more rebellious Han, his forehead went unshaven, a minor defiance against Qing rules.

"Your cousin? Sihua Gan Han?"

"TOOK A PUNCH TO THE FACE..."

"Yes. We are distant kin, my family but a small and unimportant sept of the clan. When your grandmother demanded recompense for the trouble my cousin caused you, I offered myself."

It hadn't occurred to Yi Xiao that his grandmother would take quite so much offense at Gan Han's attempt to force a duel. Or, for that matter, her family's attempt to set the girl up as a potential wife. Thinking about it, he ought to have expected that very thing. His grandmother was an Imperial Princess, the Emperor's distant aunt and much favored by her father during his reign. Both attempts could be seen as skirting treason. He hoped she hadn't been too hard on the girl. It hadn't been Miss Gan Han's fault.

"And your purpose here?"

"To protect you, Lord Lang."

"I don't need a protector."

"You are still at the center of a dozen plots, Lord Lang. Exiled to America or no, there are those who will seek you out to use against your Imperial cousin."

The trouble was, Wu Chang was right. "I'm safer traveling alone."

"A second pair of eyes are useful, my Lord. Especially if you persist in traveling with someone as obviously untrustworthy as this man here." Wu Chang glanced at Deathshead in an unfriendly way. "He understands our speech and pretends he does not."

That made Deathshead snort. "Damn. You're good, kid. Too good." He spoke the same dialect Wu Chang did, with exactly the same accent.

"I have met another like you. I erred and trusted him once. I will never trust your sort again." Once again Wu Chang turned to Yi Xiao, his serene expression belying the pleading in his eyes. "Lord Lang, if you tell me to stay away, I will still follow you. I am sworn to do so and cannot disobey."

Yi Xiao sighed. "I'll tell you the same thing I told Miss Gan Han, then. I don't kill. If you travel with me, neither do you."

Surprise suffused Wu Chang's face. "But of course not, Lord Lang. Your Grandmother already informed me of your desire. My blades are dulled to that purpose, and will remain so as long as I am your guard."

⇒)(⇐

That Wu Chang fellow was as close mouthed as they came. Deathshead spent the entire walk back trying to get a word out of him. "I know rocks that talk more than you do," he said finally. "Got no conversation at all."

Yi Xiao was obviously and irritatingly amused. "He did say he doesn't trust you." He paused, adding, "Your cousin was a great deal more talkative. Is that because she's First House or...."

"She's a woman."

There were some women would take complete offense at that sort of comment and Deathshead didn't hesitate to say so. "Don't look down on womenfolk, boy. They bite."

A slight quirk to the man's lips was accompanied by, "Sihua women take precedence."

Now that, Deathshead didn't understand at all. Nor did he get a chance to ask because that was when they reached the campsite. He'd been wondering how they were going to explain their prisoner, and their new companion to Trendle, but it looked like they wouldn't have to. Not any time soon. The site was empty.

Deathshead would give Yi Xiao credit. He was dismayed. Angry. Scared. He showed none of these things. Simply said, "I'm an idiot."

"Lord Lang?"

"Wu Chang, my name is Yi Xiao. Call me that." Before the bodyguard could respond, Yi Xiao turned to Deathshead. "Lie to me and there will be consequences. Do you know what happened to our companions?"

Ordinarily, Deathshead would be inclined to play games. After all, Trendle, Striker, even little Jo, weren't important to him. Their existence or failure to exist, were of no consequence. However, he didn't like being blamed for something he didn't do and he wasn't sure he could handle both Yi Xiao and Wu Chang. The one had abilities he'd yet to identify. The other? Well there was something not at all canny about the tall bodyguard.

"Got no idea at all."

"Those little 'uns?"

"If it were just little Jo missing? I'd think them likely. Even a couple of Trendle's men?" Deathshead spread his hands helplessly. "But all that lot? That's why I figured we could leave 'em behind to go gawkin'." Admittedly, he hadn't been worrying over the regular human folk when he'd left 'em, but he shouldn't have needed to.

Helplessly, Yi Xiao examined the ground. "I'm no tracker...."

"I am," both Deathshead and Wu Chang said at the same time. They glanced each other, Deathshead humorously, Wu Chang darkly. "And I know the area," Deathshead added primly.

"That's true," Wu Chang admitted, though it was obvious he had to force the words from his throat.

"Then," Yi Xiao said calmly. "What price?"

The youngster's quick acknowledgement that Deathshead owed him and the others nothing was only a little surprising. Yi Xiao's skills didn't come from nowhere. He surely had enough experience to understand bargains and costs. "Tell me the source of your power."

That surprised the boy. "The source of my power?"

Deathshead jerked a thumb north towards Mount Tam, though they couldn't see her from where they stood. "You drew on the Old Lady back there, a month or so back. You're full of something...."

Wu Chang scoffed. "No less than you are. Why does it matter to you?"

"Knowledge. Knowledge is power. Depending on how much danger they're in, I may ask for more later. There's some I won't fight. Some won't fight me."

Ignoring Deathshead, Wu Chang told his master, "I don't trust him."

"So you've pointed out frequently. Do you think you can find my friends on your own?"

"I tracked that one there."

They all looked at the unconscious man on the ground. "He's not much at hiding, though," Deathshead pointed out. "He's the one followed me here, earlier. So tracking him isn't all that hard."

Yi Xiao examined Deathshead thoughtfully. "I don't really trust you any more than Wu Chang does. And he will, I think, notice if you try leading us astray. So, fine. If you help me find the others, I will tell you the source of my power."

It might not be the best bargain but it'd have to do. "Then first things first. Let me call in a few favors from those little 'uns." It wasn't so much as they owed him right that minute. But let him hunt them down and shake them up a few times and they'd change their minds on that subject.

Yi Xiao probably wouldn't mind a few magic kind sent on their way. They weren't human, after all, and all humans ever really cared about were themselves.

⇒)(⇐

Yi Xiao sat down and focused his attention on Wu Chang. "I don't actually want you following me," he pointed out, once Deathshead had gone off to, as he put it, 'acquire some informants.'"

"Understood."

"I certainly don't need you around to help me cultivate."

Equably, the young man told him, "Naturally not. Cultivating is generally a solitary exercise."

"The only reason I'm allowing you to follow me, for now, is because my Grandmother sent you. I got rid of your cousin. If I can, I'll get rid of you."

"As your Grandmother warned me. She said if you send me back without good reason, she'll have my hide." Deadpan, Wu Chang added, "I'm attached to it and would much prefer it remain attached to me."

And that, in the end, meant Yi Xiao couldn't sneak off casually. Cursing his grandmother's overprotectiveness would be unfilial. Sending this young fool back by trickery would get him hurt. He didn't like the situation but he supposed he'd have to accept it.

"Very well. Then tell me something. I knew this idiot here was around because I could sense him following. How did you hide yourself so well? And don't tell me it's part of your training. Your cousin would have had the skill too and I know for a fact she doesn't. You're so good I can't even hear your heart beat."

Wu Chang's expression didn't change. "My Lord...." At Yi Xiao's raised brow he corrected himself. "Yi Xiao, I owe you my protection. I do not owe you my secrets. I beg of you. Do not ask."

"As long as your secrets don't put me in danger...."

"I will tell you if they do."

"I suppose I'll have to accept that, then. I won't ask again." Yi Xiao turned his attention to another question. "Has my Grandmother actually threatened your cousin? It wasn't her fault, after all."

"Your Grandmother has taken my cousin into her household. Hostage, if you will, to our family's good behavior." The slightest of smiles quirked Wu Chang's lips. "Or, perhaps, protected from our family's manipulations. I will leave it to you to decide which."

Relieved, because he couldn't blame Miss Gan Han for obeying her family's wishes, Yi Xiao accepted the reassurance. He might have continued the discussion, but Deathshead was coming back to join them, a couple of child-sized figures swinging in his big hands. They squirmed and shrieked, almost human in appearance but for the odd fur covering their cheeks and big fluffy tails like squirrels. They also had more than a few cuts and bruises. "Informants? Or victims?" he asked, rising to his feet, not bothering to hide his anger.

Deathshead had the nerve to look surprised. "They're just little 'uns. Barely anything to them but spite and tricks." Seeing Yi Xiao's expression, he set the pair down. "Try to run. Just see what happens."

"There's no need to hurt them." Ignoring Deathshead's puzzled expression, Yi Xiao crouched in front of the terrified pair. "You've been watching us. Do you speak English?"

It took one, the braver one, a moment to answer. "Understand. Little. Little."

"Were you stalking us, or just curious?"

Another moment while the being worked out the question. "No. Yes. Curious. No hurt."

That wasn't entirely true. Yi Xiao remembered the way they'd nipped at him earlier, when he'd been running towards Wu Chang's fight. "Did you see what happened to the others?"

"Big 'un. Grab. Grab." The little 'un's body shifted, formed a much larger version of itself. No, not exactly a larger version. This was darker, its head longer. Straggly teeth jutted from its mouth. Its eyes glowed dark red and its fur was longer and wiry.

The monstrous shape was translucent, suggesting it was only an image; a bit of illusion created by the little 'un. Yi Xiao touched the closest paw carefully, verifying the fact. "Was this some people's god?" he asked Deathshead. "Or just a monster?"

"You've some education on the subject," Deathshead said appreciatively. "Not a god, that sort, no. Just fear of the dark given fur and fangs." He eyed the illusion thoughtfully. "Not very good fur and fangs, either, if I do say so myself."

Yi Xiao sensed some underlying joke and chose to ignore it. He returned his attention to the little 'un, "Does this being have a name?"

"Called wolves like men. No name. No people. Just hunger."

There were creatures like that in China, too. Old monsters, born of belief and seeking to survive, forgotten by the ones who'd thought them up. Forgotten, but still dangerous. "One of these beings alone couldn't take everyone without making a noise. How many?"

Nervous now, the little 'un admitted. "Many many. Hunt us. We lead here."

So that was what'd happened. The little 'uns couldn't be blamed for wanting to live, but Yi Xiao wished desperately they'd found another way to distract their enemies. "All right. Do you know where they went?"

"Sun down."

At Yi Xiao's puzzlement, Wu Chang offered, "Perhaps they mean west? There are hidden places in those hills. I ran across them, following our captive here." He set a hand on their still unconscious prisoner. "He left some friends behind in one."

"You didn't mention friends," Yi Xiao muttered. "No. Tell me later. Do you mean that way, little one?" He pointed further down the road.

"Yes. Yes." The braver little 'un set a paw-like hand on his. "Go now? Free? No hurt?"

"You can help us find those...." At Yi Xiao's look, Deathshead trailed off. "They're just tools to you, right?"

Yi Xiao sighed. "To you, perhaps. Not to me. Let them loose. They're small. Weak. All they can do is get hurt and maybe die."

It was obvious Deathshead didn't understand. Nor was there time to make him, even if it were possible. Still, with a shrug, the man released his prisoners, muttering something in a language Yi Xiao didn't recognize. "Well, now we've given up that little advantage, what foolish sentiment would you like to follow next?"

⋧⟩⟨⋦

To Deathshead's annoyance, the youngster took him seriously. "I intend to find my friends. What you do is up to you." It felt like a dismissal. A young chieftain releasing a poorly behaved vassal from his service. The boy might not admit to royalty, but he damned well acted the part. Deathshead hadn't felt so shunned since that one tribe had enough of him and kicked him out.

"I haven't gotten what I want from you."

"And do you consider beating up two weak little spirit beasts and scaring them out of their little heads sufficient payment?"

Oh. Now Deathshead understood. The youngster was angry. Furious. Without turning a hair, without so much as showing a flicker of how he actually felt, he was still one step away from drawing the sword he hid with his pack and cutting off Deathshead's head for him.

The risk was exciting. Deathshead was confident the boy couldn't kill him, but he probably could do him some hurt. It made him even more interesting. How far could Deathshead push the child before that calm demeanor failed. Before the white hot sparks inside escaped and seared everything and everyone in reach?

Then there was another question. The boy was human. He had no reason to give creatures like the little 'uns protection. No reason to be angry when Deathshead had been, maybe, a little rough on the nuisances. In all his years, Deathshead had never known more than a handful of humans who sided with spirits and monsters over their own kind.

Shrugging, seeing Yi Xiao was waiting for an answer, Deathshead said, "They're hard to kill. Harder to persuade. I wanted to save time. Shall we wait for daylight, boss, or do you want to start hunting now, in the darkness? When the wolves like men are strongest?"

"No time like the present," Yi Xiao answered. "Besides, I don't want to risk their getting too familiar with their dinner. Not when I plan on stealing it away."

They gathered a few things. Hid the rest beneath the brush to keep it safe. Then with Deathshead at the lead, they continued along the road, searching for signs of their quarry. Now he knew what to look for, it was easy. Greasy black fur here. A bit of spoor there from things so strong they never had to hide their tracks.

"You okay, dressed so light?" Deathshead asked Wu Chang as they went. "Gets awful cold out here at night. Might freeze your jewelry right off."

Wu Chang eyed him. "I wear no jewelry, westerner."

That set Deathshead laughing while Yi Xiao quietly explained his real meaning. Wu Chang's reaction, a mild, "I hardly feel the cold anyway," only made Deathshead laugh harder. He forced himself to keep the noise down. No point in warning the enemy he was coming.

If there were time and safety, Deathshead would have pressed his luck further. Wu Chang seemed the perfect target for his particular sense of humor. Grim, the dark and silent type, utterly humorless and completely dedicated to his duty. Whatever that might be. His claim to be loyally serving Yi Xiao's grandmother seemed fishy. No doubt there was more to the story. Once Deathshead was done figuring Yi Xiao out, he'd have to turn his sights on Wu Chang.

Something shifted in the bushes ahead, just where the road bent south again. Deathshead scented the air. Smiled. "We have company."

Before Yi Xiao could move, Wu Chang was ahead of him, weapons out and readied. To Deathshead's annoyance, the man didn't attack. Just held his ground and let his master do the talking. Which, because Yi Xiao was just the sort to talk first, shoot later, was exactly what the youngster did.

"Hello? Is someone there?"

His calm voice drew the scurrying shadow out. Red hair, turned dark by the moonlight, ruffled in the wind. "Yi Xiao? That you? You're all right?" Without a moment's hesitation Jo raced at them and slammed into Yi Xiao, wrapping her arms around him tight.

꒰ ꒱

"Jo. Can't. Breathe."

"Oh! I'm sorry!" She backed off and Yi Xiao took a deep breath. "I was so scared!"

Yi Xiao checked her over quickly. A few scratches. An ugly smell, rancid and bitter, all over her. Nothing fatal, as far as he could tell. "Tell me what happened."

"I'm not sure. I was asleep. Got woke up by that yelling.... what was that yelling, anyway?"

"Later." They'd left the *Nian* rebel behind, knowing he was likely to escape and be after Yi Xiao again. But he wasn't important right then. "What next. And try not to breathe so fast. You'll make yourself sick."

Jo fought her panic down, her eyes closed as she struggled with herself. Then, "Something picked me up. Just wrapped my blanket round my head and carted me off. I couldn't move. Couldn't even shout. I'da shouted if I could."

"And then?"

"Got tossed in some cave." Jo shuddered. "It stank. Stank worse'n I'm stinking now. Like dead things."

"Their previous victims," Deathshead said cheerfully. "That lot ain't neat eaters."

Staring at Deathshead, Jo almost went into another panic. "There was a gate. Old. Wood. I squeaked through, just barely. Came out looking for help. Didn't realize you weren't one of them caught." Relief flooded her voice. "Thank God it was you. You'll save Zak, right? Please?"

Yi Xiao agreed. "I'll try." He was about to say more, but noticed Deathshead eyeing the girl thoughtfully. "What?"

"You sure got yourself out easy, girl."

There was fear in Jo's eyes. Understandable fear, no matter what. "Leave her be, Deathshead." This could be a trap, this could be Deathshead trying to play games. Either way, his friends needed help.

"Your funeral."

"Yes, it is." Yi Xiao squeezed Jo's shoulder. "Don't worry. Just show us the way to go and I'll handle things from there."

Once again they set off. Quieter now, because they were getting close. "Deathshead has a point, Master... Yi Xiao," Wu Chang murmured. "Those walking wolves surely know they missed you. She could be a trap."

The trouble was, there was no way of telling until they got where they were going. "We'll see."

"Who you talkin' to, Yi Xiao?" Jo turned and looked up at him, eyes wide in the moonlight. "See what?"

He squeezed her shoulder. "Who's who and what's what. Don't worry. I'll do my best. So will Deathshead."

That elicited a short bark of laughter. "I'm a lazy bum, Yi Xiao. Don't expect my best for something this simple." Deathshead grinned at her. "Probably don't need my best right now anyway."

By now they'd left the road, making their slow and careful way through grass and rocks. The moon was dropping towards the horizon, making walking harder for those without a talent for seeing in darkness. Luckily, that appeared to be none of them. Indeed, Wu Chang seemed to glide through the meadow soundlessly, his dark figure dimly visible in the shadows.

"You never said what that noise was," Jo asked suddenly.

"Some old friends from China wanted my attention." Once again Yi Xiao squeezed her shoulder. "Don't worry about it. They won't be causing trouble. Let's focus on getting Zak and the others safe." Her chattiness in such a tense moment was inconvenient, to say the least. This simply wasn't the time for explanations.

There were trees ahead, rising along another ridge to their west. Deathshead sniffed the air. "Too bad we don't have a way to wash little Jo here. She's so covered in stank I can't tell what's her and what's some others."

"You might go ahead," Yi Xiao suggested, looking at Wu Chang quickly. Deathshead knew the landscape, yes, but his unwanted bodyguard had been navigating California's hills long enough now to know what he was doing, too.

Wu Chang inclined his head obediently, gliding forward without hesitation. At the same time Jo asked, "I thought you were gonna go first, Yi Xiao. Thought Mr. Deathshead weren't interested."

The question created new questions, but Yi Xiao didn't ask them. "I don't know. Would you like to take the lead, Deathshead?"

Scoffing, Deathshead waved off the question. "Said I'd help. Never said I'd do all the work."

"True. You didn't. In any event, I think you're better off right here. Why don't you keep an eye on little Jo, instead?" Before either Deathshead or Jo could object, Yi Xiao followed Wu Chang into the woods.

⇒)(⇐

The boy was either an idiot or a genius and Deathshead wasn't sure which. Did he leave Jo with Deathshead for her protection, or Yi Xiao's? If the former, leaving a little girl with someone like Deathshead showed a naïve trust that went far beyond anything he'd seen since that silly Unhcegila crawled out of the ocean to play. Foolish little black snake still hadn't forgiven him for that, either.

If the latter, though, that meant Yi Xiao had realized the girl's story stank as much as she did. The question was should Deathshead play along, pretending to assume this really was Jo, or let the little sneak know her trap failed? "Them two got guts, I'll be giving 'em that much."

Jo stared at Deathshead. "Two?" She turned to search for Yi Xiao in the darkness, but the youngster was already lost to the shadows.

"Yeah. Don't tell me you didn't see the tall one. Or hear him, for that matter. He was right next to Yi Xiao just now, talking to him."

"Tall one?" The girl's eyes widened. "Talking?"

There were few things Deathshead liked better than turning someone's trap into a playground. Few expressions he liked better than that moment when his target realized they'd been had. Fear. Anger. Disappointment. All three flashed across Jo's face before she tried to pretend she wasn't fooled. "You're just having me on, aintcha, Mr. Deathshead?"

Sometimes the truth could be more enjoyable than a lie. Especially right now. "Nope. Funny thing is, he followed that other human up this way; the one was watching that young princeling earlier. He followed along and went completely unnoticed. He's good. He's really good. If I weren't looking straight at him, I wouldn't even know he was there. Can't smell him. Can't hear his heart. Can't feel his breath. Don't know how he does it. Must be some Chinese magic I ain't heard of yet."

"I don't getcha, Mr. Deathshead."

"Plenty of folk don't, baby girl."

The girl tried another tack. "Chinese got magic? Yi Xiao's a sorcerer?"

A human girl like Jo shouldn't know anything about magic at all. Near as Deathshead could tell, Zak and Jo were about as unmagical as they came. Of course, he supposed it was possible Yi Xiao had taught her more about the world than what she'd known growing up. He wasn't a sorcerer of course; Deathshead could feel the difference in his power, even if he couldn't identify it. But the boy had already proved he knew about magic. How else would he know about Gods and monsters, anyway?

"Tell the truth—which I hate, by the way—I've no idea what that boy is. Anymore than I do his pretty bodyguard." Deathshead took Jo's hand. "Never mind, kiddo. We'd better catch up. Just in case them two run into trouble."

The hand in his was cold, rough skinned, and her nails could do with some work. He debated telling her so. Decided to prolong the game a little while longer. She was nervous enough already, now he'd set her on edge.

The interesting question was how would Yi Xiao react when he got to the wolves like men and found a second Jo waiting there? The very thought set him salivating and hurrying forward, anxious to see the fun.

And fun there'd certainly be, between himself, a batch of walking wolves, and a Chinese princeling with unknown powers and a most peculiar bodyguard.

ꞏ)(ꞏ

Following Wu Chang into the trees, Yi Xiao had to admit the man was far better at woodcraft than he. This despite his years training with the Storm Hermit. Once he was in the shadows, Wu Chang was impossible to spot, his presence hidden even to a well-trained cultivator's perception.

As he continued into the darkness, expanding his senses so the dim light from the stars was just enough to see by, Yi Xiao wondered if he'd done the right thing, leaving Jo with Deathshead. Was her inability to notice Wu Chang because he was deliberately obscuring himself from her? Or did she fail to notice him because she perceived things differently than humans? Was she, in fact, some sort of illusionist who depended on other senses to navigate?

Yi Xiao didn't like distrusting his friends. Training with the Storm Hermit, though, meant learning the tricks and sneaky ways of the supernatural world. There were places in China still deeply haunted by ghosts, goblins, ogres and undead spirits. California's otherworldly creatures were different in form, but not—he suspected—in function. All of which meant there were probably monsters with the ability to take another's shape and fool the unwary.

From their brief interaction, it seemed likely the Jo that'd found them wasn't truly her. It could be possession, of course, but his training should have warned him if some other spirit had imposed itself on the girl's. Which meant Jo was likely still with the others, hopefully alive, but captive.

"Master, respect."

Wu Chang's ability to sneak up on people meant Yi Xiao nearly jumped out of his skin. "I don't suppose you could find some way to warn me you're approaching? And what did I say about calling me master?"

"I really do apologize. I can't help the first and will try as best I can to remember the second." Wu Chang sounded slightly dejected. "I wanted to tell you, I've found the cave. The captives are alive, but I fear the one they call Sims cannot survive his treatment."

The news made Yi Xiao tighten his lips. Why was it he kept running into situations like this? He just wanted to cultivate. Just wanted to find his *Dao* and seek peace. Circumstances, fate, some twisted karma kept drawing him straight back to the martial world, where the only thing one could do was kill or be killed.

"How many are there?"

"I counted ten."

It might be he, or his bodyguard, could knock them out. They'd have to do it one at a time, though. "Can you draw their attention?"

"Regret to say I cannot. The same thing that makes it difficult for you to notice me coming prevents them from seeing me at all. They rely on senses other than sight."

As Yi Xiao'd suspected, then. "And the Jo I left back there?"

"I can't be sure, not having met her before, but I don't believe that person to be human. It seemed obvious you already guessed, or I'd have said so."

If nothing else, Yi Xiao had to appreciate a follower who didn't underestimate him. "All right. You said the captives are alive. How are they being restrained?"

"As the one calling herself Jo said, they are locked inside a cave, secured by a wooden gate."

That was good. It might make things easier. "Are they in any condition to run?"

"I believe so."

"Then I'll distract the wolves. You free the captives. Once they're clear, help me knock the enemy out." At Wu Chang's dubious expression, he added, "I know. I may not be able to avoid killing them. I'd like to at least try."

⇒)(⇐

The one thing that puzzled Deathshead was the nature of the enemy. Wolves like men types didn't have much in the way of brains. They were mostly just appetites on legs. Grabbing people up, tossing them into a cage and saving them for later wasn't their way. It was like someone had given them extra smarts, to help 'em out.

"Mr. Deathshead, what you gonna do?"

"Observe, child. Observe. You don't think I got any stake in this fight, do you?" He'd help, he supposed, but only if he had to. He wouldn't see what those two were capable of if he didn't let them handle the fighting themselves.

They reached the wolves like men's campsite just a few minutes after Yi Xiao and Wu Chang. Deathshead hadn't bothered running too fast, not wanting to get forced into a fight, which gave them two plenty of time to get themselves a plan and get started.

The campsite was fairly small. Just a clearing outside a crack in the rock that might have been someone's attempt at a mine once. A small stream dripped down the cliff-face behind the campsite, but its water stank of rust. As for the site itself, it stank of blood and viscera. A body lay at the center, stripped down to its skin. In some places it didn't even have that much. The wolves like men had started the usual way, ripping open the belly and pulling the guts out to feast.

"Oh no," Jo whispered behind Deathshead. "Oh, that poor man!"

"Yeah. Don't look too comfortable. But that's the way them sort are," Deathshead agreed amiably. "Not much on sharing, either, are they? Or did you tell 'em to go ahead while you caught us?"

She stared at him, freckles standing out against her pale face. There wasn't much light here, of course, but Deathshead didn't need any to see. Neither did she, a fact she must've forgotten in her anxiety to fool him. Slowly her expression changed, her features shifted. "Damn you. You knew?"

"You'll need a few more centuries to fool this old man, brat. Don't know why you're smarter than them lot, but you're not smart enough."

The fake Jo turned, opened a fanged mouth to scream, "I'll kill you!" Just like he'd expected. Then the little brat leapt at Deathshead, knocking him backwards into the dirt. They tussled wildly, him holding the monster's jaws open, ignoring the critter's rancid breath and digging claws.

A normal human would've stood no chance. This particular specimen was weak for its kind, but still a sight stronger than most men. Deathshead wasn't most men. He tightened his grip. Saw panic in his attacker's eyes. Panic, then pain, as he dragged its jaws apart and ripped its head in half.

Their fight drew the other monsters' attention, but that lot weren't near as bright as the one pretending to be Jo. Too, at least half were chasing something in the other direction. Lightning crackled in a cloudless sky, quickly followed by yelps and the smell of scorched fur.

The other half of the monsters were distracted before they could head for Deathshead. Someone had released the prisoners and rearmed them. Already Trendle and Zak had accounted for two of the monsters, one with a well-aimed bullet, the other with the hammer he always carried.

Rather than watch what little was left of the fight, Deathshead loped into the woods to find Yi Xiao. It was high time he got a good look at what the odd little Chinaman could do.

$$\Rightarrow)(\Leftarrow$$

Yi Xiao had hoped to avoid killing but these wolves like men monsters were making it difficult. He'd seen what they'd done to that man. Knew they'd do it to anyone they got their claws and jaws into. "Master says, when killing is inevitable, don't prolong it," he muttered to himself.

The monsters gathered round him, snapping and snarling, trying to get past the branch he was using as a weapon. It was hard to see them properly in the dim light, but he scented human blood on them and knew he'd be next if they got hold of him. No choice then. Regrettable. Infuriating. Necessary.

Even now, he daren't draw his saber. He could feel his own bloodlust trying to rise. Until he had it under control he shouldn't touch the blade again. He didn't need it anyway. He drew on his *qi*, drew on the energy of the world. The power Deathshead had called The Old Lady wasn't close but he wasn't trying to call her. She was far too dangerous to draw on casually. She'd only allowed it the one time out of pity.

Lightning crackled around his feet, drawn from the earth and the surrounding air. The scent of ozone rose around him as his *qi* gathered. It'd be easier if there was a storm. His master could draw full bolts out of a clear blue sky. He wasn't that good, yet, but all he needed was one quick strike.

Slamming his hand to the ground, Yi Xiao sent the lightning he'd gathered flowing across the dirt. If the monsters had been smarter, or faster, they'd have dodged backwards. Instead, thinking his motion a sign of weakness, they leapt forward, straight into a field of lightning that jolted through them, sending every nerve in their bodies spasming. They were dead before they touched the ground.

Exhausted, Yi Xiao stayed where he was. He'd had to do this, he reassured himself. He hadn't been taught not to kill at all, but to avoid it as much as possible. To not take pleasure in it. Well, at least he was that far along the path. Maybe someday he'd be strong enough and wise enough to find ways to make killing unnecessary.

Someone was clapping. Deathshead, his lean figure approaching through the trees. "Well now. That was quite a show."

Yi Xiao looked at him. "I'm not a street performer."

"You'd make a fortune."

"I don't need a fortune." Yi Xiao managed to stand. He didn't know what Deathshead was, but it was obvious he wasn't merely human. Likely he wasn't human at all. A sorcerer? A monster? An immortal? The old man could be anything. Whatever he was, though, Yi Xiao simply didn't have the strength to fight him. Not now.

"So. You gonna explain all those pretty fireworks? Like you promised?"

He had, too. "It really isn't a secret. Not at all. I'm a cultivator and a student of the Storm Hermit back in China. My training allows me to use my *qi*—my inner energies—to manipulate lightning." He shrugged. "It takes years of practice and I'm not especially good at it. Yet."

Deathshead pondered that. "An inner skill? Magic? No, I'd sense if it were magic. Not mind magic, neither. Something new?" He approached, expression thoughtful, eyes glowing from behind his spectacles. "Power. Definitely power."

It was obvious Deathshead meant him no good. Equally obvious he couldn't fight back. Yi Xiao shifted his weight, prepared to do the only thing he could do when he noticed something. "I've kept my side of the bargain. And, frankly, I've no desire for anything more. I think it's time you went on your way Deathshead. The two of us have nothing to do with each other."

A derisive cackle echoed through the woods. "You're spent. Exhausted. And you're too far from The Old Lady to call on her, even if she'd answer an outlander like you again. What are you going to do to stop... AHHHH!"

Behind Deathshead, hand clutching his hair and pulling him backwards, Wu Chang said calmly, "I mentioned I didn't trust you, right?"

⇒)(⇐

As busy as he'd been dealing with that brat monster and chasing Yi Xiao down, Deathshead had completely forgotten Wu Chang. It was an embarrassing slip. "Let go. We're all friends here!"

"Liar."

Well, yes. Of course he was a liar. It went with the job description. "Your boss don't want you hurtin' or killin' anyone."

"I don't recall saying anything about not hurting anyone... within reason," Yi Xiao noted. "And given you were thinking of doing me some harm, I'm not going to tell him 'no'. Not that he'd listen."

"I'd give your words some weight, Yi Xiao," Wu Chang assured the man. "But my duty is to protect you."

Things might have progressed to a dangerous situation if Jo's voice hadn't echoed through the trees behind them. A dozen men and one little girl, all rushing in like the fools they were. Still, it saved Deathshead some trouble. "Might want to let me go, now. I promise, I ain't gonna do anything to your little master. Not tonight, anyways."

Wu Chang glanced behind him. Released Deathshead's hair. "Not ever," he said calmly, in a way that would have made Deathshead nervous if he were the sort to take things that way.

The others ran up to Yi Xiao, Zak carrying a lantern and the others looking scared and mad. Jo grabbed Yi Xiao around the waist, half strangling him the way the other Jo had. Then, to prove she wasn't that fake Jo, she looked at Wu Chang. "Who's that fellow, Yi Xiao? Was it him yelling, earlier?"

"A cousin of Miss Gan Han's," Yi Xiao explained, expression peaceful, as if they were sitting around in a saloon having a chat, instead of the middle of a forest just after being attacked by monsters. "Are all of you all right?"

Trendle came up. Glanced at around the charred remains of the monsters that'd attacked them. "All right," he agreed. "But why is it weird things keep happening around you, Mr. Lang?"

"It's my fate," Yi Xiao managed a smile. "We'd best get back to our campsite. There's another countryman of mine I need to check up on. And we really should get some rest before we go on. This hasn't been a good night for any of us."

"We'll have to take care of Sim's body, first, but yeah. You're right, Mr. Lang. We'd best do those very things."

The group headed back through the woods, Deathshead trailing along behind grumpily. Things had not gone his way at all and he was out of sorts.

A voice spoke in his ear. Wu Chang, sneaking up on him again. "Mr. Deathshead. A word of warning. I'm sure you'll be following behind my master, trying to steal his power."

"Now what makes you say that?"

"Because it's how you're made. Because it's what you are." Wu Chang's cold fingers wrapped round Deathshead's wrist. "But keep this in mind. I am guarding him and I will not allow you to harm him in any way."

"Think you can stop me? I'm harder to kill than I look."

"So am I." Quite suddenly, before Deathshead could do anything, Wu Chang buried his teeth in Deathshead's wrist.

"The hell? Why'd you bite me? What're you trying to prove?"

Wu Chang smiled. Licked his lips. "I had to bite you. How else was I going to taste your blood?" Ruby light flickered in the back of his eyes. Then, with a bow, he added, "Remember what I said, old man."

Watching the tall skinny Chinaman seem to glide away, Deathshead felt a sense of unease like he hadn't felt since before white men started wandering his lands and chasing his people out.

Healing the injury on his arm with barely a thought, Deathshead followed behind. He'd have to be a great deal more careful than before, but now his curiosity was truly piqued. Trouble like those two wasn't common. It might also be useful.

They most certainly would be entertaining.

Chapter 2
Void – Heartless but not Empty

The one calling himself Deathshead was a fool.

There was no doubt in Wu Chang's mind on that count. No doubt, either, that Deathshead was dangerous, troublesome and a risk to Wu Chang's master. The creature was following them, stalking them, just at the edge of Wu Chang's perception. A constant reminder to be wary.

"Are you sure you don't mind this?"

'This' was his master's wise choice to have him change his appearance. Back home, he'd been remarkable, but not outright strange. Americans seemed confused, even bothered, by the sight of a man in robes. Wu Chang didn't mind being stared at, but it drew unwanted attention to his master.

Wu Chang corrected himself. Unwanted attention to Yi Xiao. Wu Chang really did need to remember to use the young Lord's name. It was just so difficult. Wu Chang's traditionalist upbringing demanded he respect the one he'd been bound to serve. Using one's master's personal name without so much as a proper honorific went against everything he'd been taught. Nor did the profound respect he was beginning to form for this particular master help.

Realizing he'd allowed himself to become distracted, Wu Chang answered, "No. I don't mind." He eyed his pale reflection thoughtfully. Local styles were plain and simple, yet oddly uncomfortable. Jeans, boots, a light cotton shirt and a denim vest. All too tight, even on someone as thin as he. At least the hat would keep the sun off. He didn't burn like some, but he didn't care for its brightness.

"And the haircut?"

Wu Chang understood Yi Xiao's concern. His braid had to be trimmed because it, too, drew attention. Yet most Han Chinese considered it an insult to cut their hair. Some more rebellious types even refused the frontal shave. Wu Chang had never bothered with the latter because he wasn't interested in any sort of governmental position. He had quite enough to do as a member of the martial world.

Turning his attention back to Yi Xiao, Wu Chang continued, "I'm your vassal. It's my duty to present myself appropriately. Since you've cut your hair and wear Western clothes, I shall as well."

It was obvious Yi Xiao didn't like being anyone's master. Accustomed to solitary and wandering ways, having someone following in his footsteps rankled. To his credit, he didn't argue what couldn't be changed. "Let's go see how Jo and Zak are doing, then."

"Do you plan on going back to the mines after this?"

"I wasn't. I'd been waiting for word from Grandmother. Now I know things are settled back home, all I need to do is keep myself occupied until she sends for me." Yi Xiao paused. Looked wryly at Wu Chang. "Keep us occupied, that is."

Wu Chang inclined his head, acknowledging the problems his presence caused. Near as he could tell, though, the young lord attracted trouble. That Deathshead creature was just one of many difficulties. And because Yi Xiao's cultivation was growing, more and more of that trouble would involve the spiritual world. Which, though he couldn't tell Yi Xiao so, was why the Princess had sent Wu Chang in particular.

They strolled down the street past miners looking for ways to spend their gold. Past would-be miners hoping to find more gold. Past those who'd strip either of all they possessed. And, somewhere behind them, a distant and irritating presence. Wu Chang could taste his blood even now. Not human, certainly. Immortal, demon, monster? Wu Chang neither knew nor cared. As long as Deathshead kept his distance, watching Yi Xiao, Wu Chang would ignore him.

After a brief walk they came to the land offices, where the man called Trendle and his men were waiting not at all patiently for Yi Xiao's friends. "Still no word, Mr. Trendle?"

"He had to cool his heels for an hour," Trendle said, ignoring his companions' mutters. He, at least, was sure there was nothing to the story apparently told about Zak. "Did you get that... friend... of yours dealt with?"

"I did. He was quite lost, so far up into the mountains. But I set him straight." The 'friend' was a member of the *Nian* rebels, a group of outlaws who'd caused trouble back home for some time now. As far as Wu Chang could tell, he'd been sent to abduct the

Emperor's twin cousin and bring him back to China. Whether the *Nian* meant to hold Yi Xiao hostage, trick folk into believing he was the real Xianfeng Emperor, or switch him with his cousin didn't matter.

Wu Chang made a mental note to send a letter to the Princess. She surely knew about the plot but she'd likely want names and further information. In the meantime, all he could do was make sure none of the rebels succeeded in capturing Yi Xiao.

The land office door opened and Zak stepped out, tipping his hat to someone inside. "Many thanks, Mister Tuttle. I knew if I got here quick I could get this problem settled proper. Awful sorry for not taking care of it sooner. Just didn't realize adding Jo here on the title meant I needed her to sign things."

A voice spoke from inside. "Well, it's all taken care of now, Mr. Striker. It's been a pleasure doing business with you."

As soon as the door closed, Zak muttered, in a voice not meant to carry, "An expensive pleasure. First time I had to pay to get... ah... taken to the cleaners."

It was obvious that wasn't what he'd meant to say. Fortunately, young Jo ignored him, coming over to join Yi Xiao. "We got it all took care of, Yi Xiao. You gonna come back with us?"

"I'm afraid not, Jo. I'll stop in to visit, later, but I've got an itch in the soles of my feet and a great big state to scratch it with." Yi Xiao patted her on the shoulder as she looked disappointed. "I'll be around, little sister. Don't you worry about that."

Zak coughed. "About that, Yi Xiao. Before you go scratching those itchy feet of yours, I don't suppose you'd mind coming with us to Corte Madera? You and that bodyguard of yours, I mean?"

One of Trendle's men stiffened, clearly insulted. "You sayin' we can't take care of you?"

From what Wu Chang understood, Trendle and his men were supposed to be bringing Zak in as an escaped slave. That implied they'd have no real care for him while doing so. They'd protect Jo, of course, but that was because she was young and a girl. She'd be safe until she was in the hands of the one claiming she was his daughter, at least. Afterwards? Not so much.

Yi Xiao ignored the argument. "Wu Chang, what do you think?"

Knowing the answer he ought to give and the one Yi Xiao wanted were entirely different, Wu Chang inclined his head. "Your itchy soles can be scratched whatever direction you choose. It may as well be with these men."

⇒)(⇐

The way between San Francisco and Strike It Rich Mine Camp had been more of a trail most of the way, which was why no one had bothered with horses thus far. Now they were headed to Corte Madera on a much better road, Trendle and his men retrieved their mounts from the local stable and let Zak and Jo ride their pack mules.

Not wanting yet another thing to take care of, Yi Xiao chose to walk. Which, in turn, meant Wu Chang did as well. "At least you don't scare the poor things," Yi Xiao muttered to his companion once they were on their way and at a point no one would hear him.

"I don't believe they notice my presence. At the moment." Not said but implied was the animals might be terrified if they did become aware of him. "They'd be more disturbed by our stalker if he came near, however."

Their stalker was Deathshead, following behind Yi Xiao with trouble on his mind. Yi Xiao wasn't entirely sure why the man was so interested in him. Likely it was the novelty.

Whatever else Deathshead was, he clearly belonged to this land. Yi Xiao's foreign ways had apparently piqued his interest. Well enough. As long as Deathshead didn't cause too much trouble, Yi Xiao would put up with him.

Corte Madera was just a ferry crossing and about half a day's ride from San Francisco. An easy trip and one that reminded Yi Xiao of his travels from San Diego to San Francisco when he'd first arrived in California. There were even some of those same shadowy spirits he'd met in Los Angeles. Word about him must have gotten around, though, for they took his presence for granted. One, a giant of its kind, did pause in the trees alongside the road, but only to briefly acknowledge his presence.

"Master has made friends," Wu Chang murmured. "I mean, you've made friends." His expression didn't change, but his tone revealed embarrassment. "I apologize."

"You're trying not to. That'll have to do." At least the man was speaking Chinese. It'd draw less attention. In the same language, fairly sure only Jo and Zak would understand, he added, "They're called watchers. I think they're nature spirits. Strong, but mostly forgotten."

Wu Chang eyed the forest, a distant look on his face. "Sad," he said softly. "And perhaps a little lonely."

From the man's expression, he wouldn't explain more and Yi Xiao knew better than to press. Besides, they were coming into town, and that meant he had to be on his guard for other dangers. He hadn't discussed it with Zak, not when Trendle was there to hear every word, but he really didn't like the story that'd dragged his friends here. He'd seen similar situations back home, where someone with money and power used his influence to rob lesser folk of their possessions.

If Zak were white, Yi Xiao would have worried a little less. In the month or so since his coming, though, he'd come to understand the sort of danger a black man stood in this country. Zak was a free man but he had to carry papers to prove it. And there was no guarantee an official would accept them. If he weren't careful, someone could drag him off east to be sold as a slave.

Then there was the question of protecting Jo. She'd been pretending to be a boy, but couldn't do so anymore. Not when the paperwork naming her part-owner in that mine called her by her full name. A child her age didn't have any rights, as far as Yi Xiao could tell. There'd be those looking askance at her being Zak's ward, despite her father's will naming him such.

No, there was clearly going to be trouble. "I can't just walk away from this," he muttered to himself.

"Naturally not," Wu Chang murmured, surprising him. When Yi Xiao glanced his way, his unwanted bodyguard added, "They're your friends. If they need help, you should help them."

"My bodyguard is encouraging me to act dangerously? Master says do you ever not get into trouble?"

The slightest of smiles quirked Wu Chang's lips. "Lord Lang, it was never my duty to prevent you from seeking danger. Merely to be there to carry you back out, should it become necessary."

Which, given the way things seemed to go for Yi Xiao, was all too likely.

⇒)(⇐

Corte Madera reminded Wu Chang of some of the small villages of his youth. Dirt street, wooden buildings, poorly dressed people going about their business. The clothing and the architecture were different, but the general air of poverty and self-sufficiency was much the same.

"The one thing I don't get," Zak was saying. "Why Corte Madera? I mean this isn't really a proper town. Most of the folk here are squatters, way I heard it."

Trendle shrugged. "I'm not the one to ask. The job posting just said the fellow was staying with the Reed family and to bring you and his daughter there."

As usual when someone mentioned her supposed father, Jo sniffed. "Getting a bit tired of some stranger saying I'm his daughter when I ain't."

"As you've mentioned frequently, Jo," Zak answered equably. "I don't know what's going on, nor why. But if we don't get this cleared up right quick, we're going to have more folk coming up to the mine causing trouble. Best to find out what's up and do sommat about it."

Yi Xiao had privately explained the situation to Wu Chang while they traveled. He would admit some of the nuances were lost to him but he could understand Zak's desire to keep this matter from spiraling out of control. "The hope being, of course, that you can."

"Yeah, that's true." Zak sighed. "But I gotta try."

The Reed family's house was what Trendle called a hacienda. Two storied, with a veranda around the main building, at the center of a tree covered park. A wooden fence surrounded the property, protected by six men carrying rifles and a bad attitude.

Shown inside after a long wait, a maidservant led them to an attractive sitting room. Colorful woven hangings and rugs covered the walls and floors and there was a beautiful little fountain in the middle. A huge fireplace lay on the other side of the room, several small logs blazing away inside.

"Nice," Trendle muttered. "I heard this place was fancy."

"My thanks. I am quite proud of it." The speaker was an attractive older woman. Her dark hair was streaked with grey and she had what Wu Chang thought of as a motherly air. One with an iron spine to back it up. "Welcome, gentlemen. Young lady. I am Hilaria Reed."

"Missus Reed." Trendle took her hand. Kissed her fingers for reasons Wu Chang didn't understand. "I'm Jim Trendle. I was hired by Smith and Jones detective agency down in San Francisco to fetch someone for a guest of yours. Richard Bly, I believe his name is?"

"Mr. Bly was indeed my guest, though he has wandered into the hills lately and not yet returned. Have you, then, brought the people he was searching for?"

Something in her tone didn't sound at all pleased. Wu Chang and Yi Xiao eyed each other. Moved to stand beside Zak and Jo. Now Wu Chang was sure something was wrong. He just couldn't guess what.

"I brought the only two remotely resembles the ones he's lookin' for," Trendle agreed. "But, honestly, I don't think they're the right ones."

While Wu Chang wondered why Trendle was being so forthright, the woman scanned the group. Eyed Zak and Jo. "You do not bring them as prisoners?"

"Like I said, this fellow matches the physical description. 'Cept he's a free man. I've seen his papers. So've my men."

"And the girl?"

"That's me," Jo interrupted bravely. "And my Pa's dead these two months. Killed and buried down in Los Angeles."

"Which I, in turn, can attest to," Yi Xiao added. "So either someone is lying or deeply mistaken."

The woman eyed Yi Xiao. "And this is?"

Yi Xiao bowed, hands clasped before him respectfully. "Ma'am, I am Yi Xiao Lang. A visitor from China who happened to accompany Miss Kraft and her father from San Diego. I was with them when Mr. Kraft died. After which, I brought her to her father's friend and partner, Mr. Striker, here."

Again, it seemed odd that everyone was telling this woman, who was only hostess to Trendle's client, so much. Perhaps it was an American custom? One which required total strangers to divulge information casually?

The woman examined Yi Xiao's face thoughtfully. "It seems there's been a great deal of confusion here. Yet without Mr. Bly, we cannot possibly untangle this knot. I have space here for you to stay while I send someone to find him, if you'd like."

"It is getting late," Trendle admitted. "But there's that little village...."

The woman sniffed. "That is not a village. Those are squatters. Land thieves who think to take what my husband and I built. Stay with them and your reward is most likely to be a blade to the throat and shallow grave."

It was obvious Trendle was taken aback. "I didn't know. Well, then, if you don't mind the lot of us imposing on you, I suppose I can't argue it. Thank you kindly, ma'am. We sure do appreciate it."

⋟)(⋞

The Widow Reed was an excellent hostess. Having taken on the task of entertaining a dozen or so unexpected visitors, she set to the job with a will that reminded Yi Xiao of his grandmother. She fed them. Made sure they were well supplied with drink. Made space in the servants' quarters for the menfolk and put Jo in one of her children's rooms. Apparently the lady's family was down in San Francisco with her second husband.

"Keep an eye on Jo," Yi Xiao ordered Wu Chang, once they had a quiet moment. He didn't know what was going on here and but he didn't dare trust Mrs. Reed to protect the girl. "And don't argue. You know where I am."

Serenely, Wu Chang bowed. "Master... Yi Xiao... I can protect the both of you if need be." A slight flicker of worry crossed his face. "Given, of course, you don't run off without me if there's trouble. Will you at least take this with you?"

'This' was a delicately carved carnelian pendant of a phoenix with a ruby eye. Yi Xiao didn't sense anything odd about it, but then he wasn't a sorcerer. "What is this?"

"A way for me to follow you, should you become lost. I promise, I will only use it if it becomes absolutely necessary. Even if it's lost or broken, I will be able to find you."

Reflecting that sorcery never made any sense to him, Yi Xiao sighed and agreed. "If you insist." He pulled the pendant's cord over his head and waved his bodyguard off. "Be careful."

"I would say the same to you, mas... Yi Xiao. But I know the very idea is preposterous." Wu Chang was about to leave when a thought occurred to him. "One question, before I go. Why are you trusting me to protect her?"

It was a good question. Yi Xiao made no claim to a special talent for reading personalities. All he had was instinct and a general sense for knowing who meant him ill and who didn't. Of course, a good assassin could present themselves without any killing intent at all. Yi Xiao could tell nothing about Wu Chang because his presence seemed so separate from the world.

"To tell the truth, I don't. Not entirely. But I also haven't seen a good reason not to." Yi Xiao pointed in the direction of Jo's room. "Now, if any harm comes to her at all? That changes entirely."

With a bow of respect, Wu Chang told him, "Then I shall make her life and safety my priority. Wanted or unwanted, a vassal's first duty is to earn their master's trust."

Before Yi Xiao could find an answer to that, Wu Chang was gone.

⇒)(⇐

To tell the truth, Wu Chang wasn't sure why he'd asked Yi Xiao about trust. It wasn't wise, putting ideas in one's master's head. Bringing up such matters without cause like that could have the exact opposite effect. Admittedly, he didn't need to stay with Yi Xiao to keep an eye on him, but it simplified his duty.

It was probably Deathshead's fault he'd even thought about it. Yi Xiao was smart but often seemed terribly naïve about the world and people. He'd let Deathshead travel with them. Even believed a total stranger like Wu Chang without proof beyond a carved seal. Wu Chang knew how dangerous it could be to trust someone too readily.

Settling himself in a shadowy corner overlooking Jo's room, Wu Chang let his thoughts spread out. Most cultivators couldn't stretch their awareness very far, but he had advantages most cultivators didn't have. He could feel the lives around him, some young, some older. Some powerless, some so full of life it seemed they ought to glow.

One of those sources was Yi Xiao, of course. He might not have found his *Dao* yet, but he was getting closer and closer to gathering his Self into a proper core. Not many cultivators managed that, these days. The martial world just wasn't what it used to be when Wu Chang was young.

Yi Xiao wasn't the only bright source, either. There was someone downstairs, their life energy glowing intensely enough to be perceived straight through the floorboards. Whoever it was, they'd appeared in that spot out of nowhere. Wu Chang might have investigated if he weren't set to guard Jo. Not for the first time he wished he had some sort of familiar spirit to fetch and carry for him. His nature made that impossible. Besides, the last thing he needed was a pet.

None of which helped with the question of that new source of power. If they moved, Wu Chang would have considered it his duty to rouse Jo and go find Yi Xiao. Since they didn't, he kept them in mind but remained where he was.

Focused as he was on the two stronger life sources, Wu Chang didn't initially notice something cold and dark creeping close. Its presence was overpowered by the others and would have been partially hidden even without them. If it'd left the other lives alone entirely, it probably would have gotten through unobserved.

Instead, Wu Chang was alerted when he sensed one of the lives at the edge of his perception go cold and disappear. It hadn't moved—he'd have recognized that—just faded to nothing in a few seconds.

Wu Chang rose to his feet immediately and went to the nearest window. There wasn't much light. The moon wasn't nearly full yet, but he didn't need it to be. He quickly spotted the slumped figure against the fence post.

"Mr. Wu Chang?" Jo said sleepily. "Why're you in my room?"

She was another who trusted too easily. Most girls would have screamed the house down, finding a man in their room. Smart girls would have kept their silence and tried to find a way to escape. Jo, being Jo, just casually asked him what he was doing.

"Keeping an eye on you," he told her calmly. "Master... I mean, Yi Xiao, was worried."

She thought about that. "Kay. Next question. I didn't notice you cuz you looked like part of the furniture. So, why'd you get up and look out the window?"

All right, so she was smarter than he'd thought. "Something's out there," he admitted.

"Something dangerous. I'd like you to be ready to run."

"That's fine." She pulled her shoes on. Gathered her things. "Hope it's goes away fast," she admitted. "I'm tired. I just want to sleep."

"Go ahead and rest, then. I'll wake you. Or carry you if need be."

As she did as he told her, he reflected that she was quite like Miss Gan Han, and so many other Sihua daughters. Smart, innocent, and a little too sure of her own immortality. He hoped he could keep her safe, and not just because Yi Xiao wanted him to.

⇒)(⇐

"Where's the spook?"

The question puzzled Yi Xiao. He and the others had been given the rooms originally meant for the house servants which meant everyone had congregated in what must be the servants' common room towards the back of the house. As soon as he'd walked in one of Trendle's men, Jimmy, wasn't it? had called out to him.

"Spook?" It was a reminder that Second Mother's English lessons might have given him an excellent understanding of formal British English but was useless for American slang. "What would that be?"

"The stiff. Pretty boy."

The only thing in there that made sense was the last. "Wu Chang, you mean? He's decided to keep watch elsewhere." Yi Xiao paused, adding, "I don't suppose you could explain those other terms? I'm quite confused."

It was Trendle who explained, ignoring the others' laughter. "Spook means a ghost, Mr. Lang. Sort of thing you run across in cemeteries. Stiff is a dead man. Given Mr. Sheewah's appearance and behavior, I think you can understand why my men call him that."

Yi Xiao didn't bother correcting the pronunciation. He'd leave it to Wu Chang to decide if he minded before making a fuss over something that, really, couldn't be helped. Most Americans just weren't used to Chinese. Zak, and now Jo, were exceptions and only because they dealt with Ma Chao and his men all day. Come to think of it, the pair's Mandarin wasn't good. Their miners spoke Hunanese most of the time, and that was a language unto itself.

"I see. Thank you, then. I always appreciate having my knowledge expanded. And American English often seems another language entirely to me."

Zak laughed, about to offer some joke, when something drew his attention. "I heard a noise outside," he said. "Might be the wind. Might be someone wandering around on the veranda." The shutters on the high windows were closed, though, meaning no one could see which.

Though he hadn't heard anything himself, Yi Xiao didn't doubt his friend. He crossed the room and climbed up on a stool, peeking through the cracks of the shutters. As he did so, he regretted that American architects didn't use rice paper for their window covers. It would have been easy to peek through them then. One wet finger, one poke, and instant spy hole.

One of Trendle's men said, "Whatcha see?" His voice was a little loud, though, causing Trendle to shush him furiously. They shouldn't be in any danger, here in someone's home with guards on every fence and at every door. Yet their experience the other night with those wolves-like-men creatures had made them skittish. Yi Xiao didn't blame them in the slightest.

Ignoring the others, Yi Xiao slid the shutter open a bit, moving slowly so it wouldn't get attention. Now that was interesting. Why was Mrs. Reed out there, sitting on the veranda in the dark? She was fully dressed, so she wasn't sleep-walking, but it was getting late.

Mrs. Reed sat quiet. Quiet enough, Yi Xiao was sure she wasn't the source of the sound Zak had heard. There was a still calmness to her that reminded him of his master in repose. Such a person would have taken her seat unnoticed.

Spreading his awareness, Yi Xiao ignored the weaker human lives surrounding him. He knew his companions well enough to easily filter them from his senses. There were other humans, Mrs. Reed's servants, no doubt. And there was Mrs. Reed herself. Human, he was almost sure, but a great deal stronger and more centered than most. A cultivator, this far from China? No. Something else. Something similar.

She was focused outward, which was why she hadn't noticed him yet. Yi Xiao debated letting her become aware of his presence. Decided against it. Her resemblance to his master was superficial and uncertain. As much as he'd like to trust it, and her, he daren't.

He did, however, turn his attention the same direction she had. Ah. There. That was what she was watching. Small blame to her, either. Whatever it was, it was cold and dark. Nothing innately wrong with that, but worrisome, given it seemed to be coming closer to the house.

"I said, what's out there?"

Trendle's voice, right in his ear and accompanied by a hand on his arm, startled him out of his trance. Absorbed in seeking, he'd forgotten those around him. He jerked back into awareness and nearly fell over. "Nothing but darkness and a few guards," he told the man, embarrassed by his inattention. "Don't worry."

Trendle eyed him. "I wish I could believe you. You're white as a sheet."

That was an exaggeration, Yi Xiao was sure. "I'm just tired," he lied. "I've been quite busy lately. We all have. You should get some rest and trust our guards."

"Even so...."

"Mr. Trendle, if by now you don't realize there are things you aren't equipped to deal with in this land, then you're in the wrong business." Hoping the man would take the hint, even if his companions didn't, Yi Xiao headed for the door. He was going to have to have a few words with Mrs. Reed, it seemed. And, possibly, confront whomever it was had breached the lady's defenses.

⋗⋉⋖

The cold spot moved slowly across the yard, aimed directly for the house. Or it did until it'd crossed halfway. Then it sidled sideways, evading the bright spot that Wu Chang had perceived earlier. Whatever it was, it didn't seem interested in directly facing that power. Too weak? Or just saving its strength?

So intent was Wu Chang on keeping watch on the coldness, he didn't quite notice someone at the door until Jo hissed sharply at him. "Someone's coming!"

Wu Chang turned, just as the door opened to reveal a woman standing there. Most wouldn't have been able to see anything in the dim light, but he had no difficulty. Medium build, with light, attractive features and dark red hair. Like Jo, her face was a constellation of freckles, though her features were softer and rounder. She was the maidservant who'd led them inside, though she'd changed to pants and boots since he'd last seen her.

As Jo sat up, staring, the woman said, "Miss Kraft. You're in danger. Please come with... what are you doing here?"

The last was because she'd just noticed Wu Chang standing at the window. Her expression darkened and she set her hand to the weapon at her belt. A pistol of some sort. He could have disarmed her quickly and easily as slowly as she reacted. He remained where he was, not looking for a fight. "I'm here to guard Miss Kraft," he told the young woman. "I could ask the same of you. However, you speak of danger?"

She hesitated. "We don't have time to talk, Mister. There's someone out there wants Miss Jo's power. I have to get her safe. He's got past our defenses before we could stop him."

Wu Chang wasn't impressed with the story. The situation was already questionable. Especially when it came to claims of Jo having power. He didn't argue. Just asked, "Your name?"

"Jenny Walks Far. I don't have time to explain more, though. Please, will you trust me? Trust us?"

Wu Chang took Jo's hand. "I've been asked to protect Miss Kraft. Nor do I know you or the one who sent you." It was obvious this woman wasn't in charge. At a guess, that'd be the source of the spiritual energy downstairs. "Jo. Stay close to me. If I draw my swords, stay low and within three feet of me." He didn't want to accidentally hit her. Like any bodyguard, he was trained to keep a protected circle around himself.

The woman at the door stared at them. "Please," she repeated. "He's coming. He'll eat her up."

"Why would he do that, Miss?" Jo asked. "You said he wants my power? I got no power to speak of. I'm just a kid." The girl sounded sorry to admit it, too. No surprise. From what Wu Chang had been told, she'd had been the helpless victim of circumstance for most of her life. She must hate it and he couldn't blame her in the slightest.

A puzzled look crossed Jenny's face. "No power? But you called the Old Watchers. Called them to help you, down south. They've been following you ever since. And the Mother of the Mountain gave you her strength. We felt that. Everyone with even a touch of power felt that for miles around."

"The... Mother of the Mountain? Old Watchers?" Jo stared at Jenny with utter confusion. "You're talkin' out your hat, lady? I don't even know what you're goin' on 'bout."

Wu Chang had a feeling he knew. "Is it possible you've mistaken who the one was who called that power?"

With a sniff of disdain, Jenny told him, "The Mother wouldn't answer any but a woman. The only other girl's gone back to China. If it were her, the watchers would've quieted down by now."

"Are you sure it was a woman? Perhaps a man asked politely, in a moment of desperate need?"

Now doubt crossed Jenny's face. "But...."

The cold spot was moving again. Shifting position further away from the bright spirit. Drawing itself in tight. "I don't think we have time to argue the point. Would the one you say hunts her believe what you do?"

"Of course. He's been our enemy for so long. He found out our plan to bring her to safety. He's after her too."

Wu Chang had a feeling he understood how the situation drawing Zak and Jo to this place had come about. He didn't bother discussing it. Not because he didn't want to know more, but because that coldness was shifting position further away and getting ready to do something.

As it flung itself forward, speeding towards the house and rising in the air, Wu Chang grabbed Jo and raced for the door, pulling Jenny out along with them. "RUN!"

Behind them, glass shattered and something dark and hungry filled the room.

⇒)(⇐

The crash of glass above them came just as Yi Xiao slipped outside to confront Mrs. Reed. She was on her feet in an instant, her appearance shifting as she moved. The much older woman who'd greeted them earlier was gone, replaced by a handsome middle-aged lady. Her appearance was still Hispanic, though, dark-haired and brown skinned.

A word Yi Xiao didn't recognize escaped the woman's lips. He doubted he needed to understand because the sentiment was obvious.

"What is it?" Yi Xiao asked, deciding to trust the one guarding them over the one apparently attacking. "Or who?"

The woman turned, startled, as if she hadn't realized he was there. "You!"

"I'd rather not waste time with explaining myself. That was Jo's room, wasn't it? What or who is it and what does it want with Jo?"

She hesitated. "You snuck up on me. *Brujo?*"

The word was unfamiliar. "I don't know what that is." He listened to the noise above them, the sound of something crashing against something else. Something hammering on a door. "You were obviously protecting us. Will you keep doing so? Or waste time with meaningless definitions?"

"You're the one wasting time asking what attacks!" By now the lady was gathering herself, rushing inside.

"I'd like to know what I have to fight," Yi Xiao answered reasonably as he followed.

"If you aren't a *brujo*, you've no hope of fighting him, or his tools."

"Him?"

"Bly."

Bly was the name Mrs. Reed had mentioned earlier. The name of the man who'd supposedly claimed to be Jo's father and Zak's owner. Things were getting terribly confused here, though. Yi Xiao trailed behind the lady. "And you?"

"Call me Dona."

That had a sense of a title, not a name. It was good enough. "I'll ask how this came about later. What can this Bly do? Aside from send a giant shadow able to leap through a second story window?"

She faltered. "To be honest, I'm not sure what he can do. Just that he collects people like the young lady for their powers."

Jo's power? If they had time, Yi Xiao would have made Dona stop and explain. "Human?"

"Mostly. I'm not sure if he's properly alive, though. We keep thinking he's dead and he keeps coming back."

They were inside and up the stairs by now, just as Jo, the young maidservant who'd let them in, and Wu Chang were hurrying towards them. "Jenny. Are you all right?" Dona demanded. "And why is that man here?"

"He was guarding Jo," the girl, Jenny, explained.

"At my request," Yi Xiao added. "Wu Chang, what did you see?"

"Shadows given solid form. An old power, bound by another's will. I only caught a whiff, but I think it's kin to the ones who like you."

That made Dona turn and stare at Yi Xiao. "Shadows that like you?"

Yi Xiao shrugged off the question. "This isn't the time. Can you fight him?" He aimed the question at both Dona and Wu Chang. Jenny looked too young to know what to do, but between the three of them he hoped to stave off disaster. Preferably without anyone dying this time.

"Do you think he would have tried to evade me if I couldn't?"

She had a point. Yi Xiao gestured back the way the others had come. "I'll back you up. Wu Chang, protect Jo and the young lady, please. No hostage situations if you can help it."

Wu Chang inclined his head. "Both of you stay close," he ordered. "Jenny, is there a safe room?"

If Dona hadn't nodded agreement, the girl probably wouldn't have listened. Instead, she gestured towards the stairs. "This way."

As the three hurried off to safety, Yi Xiao turned back to the problem at hand. Now he looked at it, he couldn't work out why the enemy hadn't followed his prey by now. "What's holding him in?"

"Jenny set a ward on the door."

The term meant nothing to Yi Xiao. "Ward? Is that like a seal?"

"It... may be." She eyed him. "I don't know what magic you use, if you're not a true *brujo*. You are a Chinese sorcerer?"

Strictly speaking, most of what Yi Xiao used wasn't magic. Just a direct application of his spiritual energy. The effect, however, was similar enough that he wouldn't waste time arguing the difference. "Of a sort. How strong is this ward?"

"Not strong enough. Jenny's young. Inexperienced. The ward won't hold longer than a minute more."

From the way the door was shaking, Yi Xiao thought it might not last that long. "Then I think we're about to find out if my type of... magic... is effective against whatever creature it is on the other side."

The door slammed open before Dona could answer, revealing thousands upon thousands of black shadowy strands, all stretching out towards them.

⇒)(⇐

The safe room Jenny led them to was the main room of the house. One dimly lit lamp glowed against the wall, setting shadows flickering. It seemed empty, but Wu Chang knew differently. As they entered he made his companions stop. "Wait."

"What is it? This room's protected. Nothing could get in."

Wu Chang stepped forward, putting himself between his charges and the one he'd sensed. "He's too solid and human to be just nothing."

"Can't say the same about you," a man's voice said from across the room. Light flared as the stranger lit a cigar, revealing a weathered face and collar-length white-blond hair. "You're an odd one, aintcha. I can hardly tell you're there."

"Bly? How?" Jenny's despair was obvious. Whomever this man was, she was likely not his match.

"Now that would be telling, missy." The man grinned. "No need to be upset. I just wanted to pay you three young ladies my respects. Not very hospitable of you to run off like this."

Three young ladies? It took Wu Chang a moment to realize his features, often considered womanly, had fooled the man into thinking he faced only women. Coughing lightly, deliberately softening his voice, he said, "I'm a man."

That got the reaction he'd hoped for. "You? A man? You lot might let men work for you when it comes to muscle and brawn, but you wouldn't go running around with one.

Next you'll be telling me you're not a *bruja*."

Wu Chang almost did but thought better of it. "How did you get inside?"

"The trouble with you silly womenfolk is that you look down on men's magic." That set Jenny growling, but the man called Bly continued, "Likely you didn't let a single man jack inside until them men of Trendle's came in."

"Then you bought their services? Gave them some tool to help you get past? Or perhaps you hid among them?" The man's face wasn't familiar. If he was part of Trendle's group, he'd been disguised. "No. I'd have sensed you before now." This Bly was new to Wu Chang. Human, with an interesting addition. A familiar of some sort, bound to him and furious. Wu Chang could almost hear its growls within the man's shadow.

"Didn't need to go that far. Just had a friend help me get through another way." The stranger shrugged. "That lot just made it easier, cuz you had to let up your guard a bit."

Being part of a matriarchal clan like the Sihua, Wu Chang doubted the *bruja*—whatever they were—were quite so naïve as suggested. More likely the man's tool upstairs, busy fighting Yi Xiao and his companion, had forced them to focus their attention elsewhere. "And what do you plan now you're here?"

"I came for the girl. The one I was promised."

Promised? Who had promised Jo to this man? No one with any right to do so, that much Wu Chang was sure. Behind him, Jo made a frightened noise and he felt her step away from Jenny. "No."

"We didn't promise you to him. I swear it. None of us did. He hired this house from its real owner. Wanted to use it to catch you. But we drove him out."

Somehow, Wu Chang was sure there was more to the story than that. There wasn't time to discuss the matter. "Jo. Don't move. Remember what I said. Stay within three feet of me."

"Three feet?" the man repeated. "You can't even protect three inches!" He flung something at Wu Chang, a card like the ones he'd seen Americans use for gambling. It cut his cheek as it flew past him, drawing a thin trail of blood.

"Wu Chang!"

"Don't worry, Jo. Stay where you are. Jenny, do you have any skills to fight this man?"

"I'm trying to raise a ward. He's got something blocking me."

That something was likely the familiar spirit that'd gotten the man into the house in the first place. Wu Chang expanded his senses, feeling for the thing. Not shadows as he understood them. True shadows were spawned from the outer chaos and required a physical focus to exist in the human world. This was similar, but older and more part of reality. It might have been a true shadow once, but now it was... Ah, that was it. "You've bound a watcher?"

The man grinned. "You're the first of your lot figgered that out. Bright girl." He gestured and a being formed from the darkness. Spindly limbs, too many of them, reached out towards Wu Chang, only to be forced back by Wu Chang's sabers. "Oh, so those pig stickers of yours got a use, after all."

"Butchers' weapons have many uses," Wu Chang countered. He'd dulled his blades for Yi Xiao's sake, but their protective seals would block most supernatural beings. The watcher was no exception.

Again and again the watcher tried to get past. Again and again Wu Chang's blades forced it back. He could have continued all night, undisturbed by the effort, but it was obvious Bly didn't have the patience. He called his familiar back to him. "If they won't cooperate, we'll just have to put a little umph into it." He pointed at the floor. "You know what to do."

Before Wu Chang could react, the watcher sank into the wooden floor, becoming part of it. As the floorboards warped and twisted, reshaping themselves to a giant fist surround the three of them, Wu Chang flung one of his sabers into the wall.

The world shifted and faded to black, as the watcher surrounded them, dragging them off through the roots of the world.

⇒)(⇐

Tangled in a tentacles of black energy, Yi Xiao ceased struggling and let himself be dragged towards their owner. At the same time he drew his *qi* together, sensing the source of the tentacles and slamming it with the tips of his fingers as it pulled him close.

Lightning flared around his hand. Drove deep into his attacker's substance. It wasn't a watcher after all, just a watcher's creation, a watcher's power flooded through shadows and attached to something long dead, its entire purpose to grab what it could. No doubt it was intended to kill what it caught, too.

The woman who'd been disguised as Mrs. Reed chanted in a language similar to Spanish. Yi Xiao could only make out a few words, but he caught the gist of it. Some sort of verbal command, followed by the rapid application of herbs and ashes. The smell of burning pine filled the air, accompanied by a few sharp stings when the cinders struck Yi Xiao's hand where it was pressed against the thing's 'skull'.

Immediately the thing jerked to a halt and began crumbling. Left standing in the middle of the room, Yi Xiao bowed to the lady. "Good timing."

"You were a fool to let it take you. You'd have been its next meal if I hadn't destroyed its maker's binding."

Yi Xiao wasn't sure that was true but he didn't argue. "I thank you." He examined what was left of the thing, a human shaped skull covered in a thin layer of gold and silver. The art on the top was unfamiliar, full of odd shapes he could only guess at. "What is this?"

"You are a sorcerer and don't recognize a bound soul?"

"I am a cultivator and what you speak of sounds like necromantic magic to me. There are cultivators who use such skills, but I am not one of them." Yi Xiao sent a small bit of *qi* through the thing, feeling for signs of life. Nothing. Not even a regretful soul. Of course, he couldn't be sure what it'd had been before its power was broken.

"Cultivator. *Brujo*. Sorcerer. I wonder if there's a difference?"

To some extent there was. In other ways, Yi Xiao supposed there wasn't. He also didn't want to argue the point. "We should go find Jo and the others." Without bothering to wait, he headed downstairs after the trio. "Is Dona your name, or a title?" he asked as they went.

"My title. Properly, I am Dona Estrella." The woman sounded out of sorts with him, but apparently not so out of sorts as to scold. Just as well. If years of maternal and grand-maternal efforts hadn't changed his fundamental nature, a total stranger's wouldn't to do any good either. "I'm sure you want to know what's going on."

"I would," he admitted. "But first I want to be sure my friends are safe...." He broke off, standing at the door to the central room and staring blankly at the floor. Half its boards were missing. A great many others curved upwards around the edges. And there was one of Wu Chang's sabers buried in the wall, its hilt quivering as if it'd just been thrown there. "Which they quite obviously are not."

Dona Estrella stared at the floor. "This... isn't possible. He couldn't have gotten in."

"He?"

Furiously, the woman answered, "Bly. The magic thieving bastard who started all this."

Bly was the name of the man who'd claimed to be Jo's father. The one who—

supposedly—had gone hunting and had to return before the problem could be resolved. "I think you'd better explain yourself. But, before that, why is it my other companions haven't noticed all the noise and come out?"

There was an embarrassed expression on Dona Estrella's face. "I didn't want them to interfere. They've been sent to sleep. You should be too, but apparently you failed to drink the wine I gave you."

"I don't drink wine. It gives me a headache." Yi Xiao shrugged off the complaint. "And Bly?"

"Bly is a self-proclaimed *brujo* who uses the darkest kinds of magic for his work. He binds the spirits of the land to his will and makes them follow his command. When he realized someone had the power to call the Mother of the Mountain, he decided to capture her and steal her power."

Yi Xiao didn't recognize the title but he had a sneaking suspicion who the 'Mother of the Mountain' was. "Her?" he repeated. "Do you mean Jo?"

"There were only two girls within miles of the mountain when the power was called. The one has left America, but the watchers still watch. Who else would it be? You?" The last was said derisively.

If they'd time, Yi Xiao might have argued the point. He decided proving his skill was less important than finding Jo and the other two. Wu Chang was surely doing his best to protect them, but Wu Chang was no more a sorcerer than he was. "So he laid a trap to capture Jo. That doesn't explain where you come in."

"I lead a women's community on the coast, not far from your friend's mine. We sensed the use of the Mother's power a few months ago. When we realized Bly was involving himself, we thought to kill two birds with but one stone. We hoped to capture Bly and strip his magic from him. At the same time, we wanted to persuade the girl to join us. The ability to call the Mother is a fine one, but it needs training to use effectively."

"Did you have something to do with the attempt to interfere with Zak's mine?"

"We have no use for something like that. All we had to do was wait until word came that Mr. Trendle was bringing Jo here. We took over the ranch for the time being, intending to wait for Bly." A grim expression crossed the woman's face. "I underestimated his magic. He must have added more familiars since the last time we'd fought."

The explanation didn't make Yi Xiao happy at all. If arguing with Dona Estrella would do any good, he'd have set to it with a will. Right that moment, however, he needed the woman's help. "Do you know where Bly will have taken them?"

"If I knew where Bly's hideout was, I would simply hunt him down, not set a trap for him."

It was a good point. "Then do you have any ability to trace a person by their possessions?" At her stare, Yi Xiao pulled Wu Chang's saber from the wall. "Such as this?" He pulled the pendant Wu Chang had given him out of his shirt, adding, "Or this?"

A slow smile crossed the woman's face as she understood his point. "The sword is mere metal and thus of no use, but I can follow the blood within that gem to the ends of the earth if need be."

That the gem held blood was a surprise, but Yi Xiao's suspicions about the man had been growing for some time now. "It's almost certainly Wu Chang's blood." He handed the thing to Dona Estrella. "I set him to guard Jo and I know he won't leave her for an instant. Find him, we find her."

He could only hope they'd find Dona Estrella's young companion as well.

꒜)(꒜

They were trapped on a peak, sheer cliffs all around them. To top it off, gold light as bright as day formed a sphere over the peak, blocking sight of whatever lay beyond. A lone pine grew at the center of their prison, its branches twisted, its needles brown and dry. It was alive, Wu Chang could tell that much, but barely. The being who'd dragged them there hid inside, its strength used up.

Jenny, apparently terrified of heights, grabbed hold of the tree and buried her face against its badly damaged bark. "Nononononono. Let me down. Please let me down!" Meanwhile, Jo, whose experiences traveling with Yi Xiao had taught her to expect all sorts of difficult situations, simply grasped hold of a rock, tested it to be sure it was steady and peered over the edge of the cliff.

"Miss Jo, if you injure yourself, or—Gods forbid—kill yourself, my master will be most unhappy with me."

"Sorry, Mr. Wu Chang. I'm being careful, though. There's a bit of a ledge below. Maybe we could get down that way?"

Wu Chang joined her. "It might be a path," he told her dubiously. "But that array surrounding us doesn't look safe for you or Jenny."

"Not sure what an array is, but if it ain't safe for us, it ain't safe for you, neither, Mr. Wu Chang."

Forbearing to correct her grammar, or her assumption, Wu Chang said, "Perhaps not. Let's see." He dropped a pebble down into the golden fire and watched it fall through. The sound of it striking another rock echoed a moment later, then again.

"We could get through, then?"

"I doubt it will be that easy." Wu Chang tried again with a beetle he found hiding beneath a rock. This time it disappeared, only to reappear back where he'd found it. "Ah. I see. Living things on the peak stay on the peak."

Jo scanned their surroundings. "No food. No water. Just that one tree looks like the thing what brought us here. Is it the thing what brought us here?"

At a guess the girl was probably right. Wu Chang focused his attention on the tree. Yes. It was definitely more than what it seemed. Back home, he'd have called it a plant spirit, one of the self-aware beings that formed when there was sufficient magic to give it life. Here? He had no idea.

Whatever else, the being inside the tree seemed too exhausted by its efforts to communicate with. Given, of course, it could communicate at all. Even if it was possible to persuade it to help them, it was obviously in no state to do so. Noting Jenny was still clinging to its branches, terrified by their situation, Wu Chang said, "Can you feel its nature, Miss Jenny?"

The girl started. Stared at him. "I... what? Nature?" She paused. Looked at the tree. "I'm not fully trained. I might pick up a little, if I try. I think it's got some old watcher inside."

"If you can, would you try communicating with them? It's possible we can learn where we are and how to get back." Wu Chang would attempt it himself, but certain types of beings couldn't perceive his presence at all. A tree spirit, especially one as weak as this one was now, wouldn't even know he was there.

Luckily, it didn't occur to Jenny to wonder why a man able to recognize a spirit's existence couldn't talk to it. If nothing else, focusing on doing so herself meant she didn't have to look around. As scared as she obviously was of the height, that was for the best.

Now the question was, why had Bly dropped them there and why wasn't he somewhere nearby, gloating over his captives? As if in answer, Bly's voice came through the fire, the sound echoing all around them. "Even if you could communicate, little witch, you won't persuade it to help you. It belongs to me, just like all of you do now."

Wu Chang scanned the boulders and jagged rocks of the cliff. There wasn't much space. A dozen or so feet side to side, about twice that lengthwise. The tree at one end, a high point at the other. Something about the place didn't seem right. Now he looked at it, it had a false air, as if it were just the idea of a peak, not a peak itself.

Expanding his senses, he felt the lives of those around him. Jo and Jenny, the latter brighter and more defined. Hadn't anyone bothered to examine the girl's spirit before deciding she had power? Jo was young, intelligent, better disciplined than most girls her age. Nothing more.

A bit more searching identified a chill spot hanging ahead of them. So that was where Bly was. "Why don't you show yourself?"

"Well, missy, if you insist. I suppose it'd make negotiations easier." An image formed on the rocks ahead of Wu Chang. The same blond-haired man from before. It wasn't really him, of course. Just an image intended to hide Bly's real presence. Choosing to accept the pretense, Wu Chang stepped forward to block the image's path. Coincidentally, he set himself in the way of the man's real location. "Satisfied?"

"Not until my charges are safely out of this place and back with their families." Strictly speaking, Jenny wasn't Wu Chang's charge. But knowing Yi Xiao, he'd have wanted her protected so that was what Wu Chang would do. "By the way, would you happen to be related to someone called Deathshead?"

That set Bly fuming. "That lying, cheating, faker? Not a chance in hell!"

To keep Bly on his toes, Wu Chang simply said, "My mistake, then. All you westerners look alike to me."

The insult had the desired effect. Bly pulled out a wand of pale ivory. A human thighbone, unless Wu Chang missed his guess. Aiming it at Wu Chang's feet, he set the rock Wu Chang stood on rising into the air, stone fingers stretching out to grasp at him.

Without missing a beat, Wu Chang somersaulted from the rocky palm, striking Bly's wand with his remaining sword and sending it flying from Bly's hand. No surprise it didn't shatter. Wu Chang felt the energies running through it course up his arm. The backlash tossed him backwards.

Backwards and off the edge of the cliff through the array.

϶)(ϵ

Carrying the lantern Dona Estrella had given him, Yi Xiao rode easily alongside the lady. He could have walked, could even have run to keep up, but she'd insisted he save his strength. She was probably right, especially since he could tell these mounts were enhanced. They looked like donkeys, but moved too smoothly to be real. Given they were currently climbing a cliff-face too steep for any normal beast, they couldn't be mere animals.

They'd moved fast, too, racing silently into the hills overlooking Corte Madera, up and down the valleys, until they'd reached a familiar mountain. The same one whose power Yi Xiao had borrowed a few months earlier. Now he'd have to be careful, because in Her favor or not, his mind just wasn't up to so much energy.

The fact that they were headed towards Her mountain worried Yi Xiao for more reasons than just that. "You said this Bly wants to use the mountain's power?"

"He's learned to bind spirits to his will. He's fool enough to think he can bind Her."

Anyone stupid enough to try and command an elemental force like Her deserved to. "And he thinks he can use Jo for this." It wasn't a question. "Even if she had power, even if the mountain did answer her, she'd be burned mindless. I nearly was, and I was over a mile away."

Dona Estrella looked up from her examination of Wu Chang's pendant. "You nearly were? As if She'd give any power whatsoever to a man?"

With a shrug, Yi Xiao said, "I was desperate. People were in danger. I asked nicely. Master says proper manners overcome many obstacles."

An expression of doubt crossed Dona Estrella's face. "Are you claiming you're the one who called Her power three months ago? The one we should have been looking for?"

"I don't know if I'm the one you should be looking for. I'm just a wanderer, a cultivator seeking the *Dao*. Nothing more." The mountain's slope grew steeper, the closer they came to the peak. "And, honestly, I'm not sure why you need someone who can summon Her power. It isn't the sort of thing anyone should play with."

"Boy, are you trying to teach your grandmother?"

Yi Xiao smiled ruefully. "I'd never tell my grandmother what to do. But you're the one convinced a little girl barely halfway through her second decade is able to...." He paused, noticing a tremble in the rocks above them. The cliff-face shook and for the first time since they'd set off, his mount shuddered and startled. "Look out."

Already Dona Estrella was exerting her own power, chanting and casting more herbs into the air. Warmth washed over them, giving Yi Xiao a sense of safety. Not much of one, though. The ground still shook beneath them. Luckily, whatever she'd done calmed their mounts. One mistake at this height would be fatal for all involved.

Something flew into the air over their heads, a human silhouette, passing through the moonlight so fast Yi Xiao barely caught sight of it before it'd disappeared into the trees below. A crash followed. Then silence. "That... that was Wu Chang."

"If it was, he is certainly dead. We have to hurry."

Yi Xiao agreed. Even if Wu Chang were alive but horribly injured, he wouldn't want Yi Xiao to worry about him. Not, at least, when the girl in his charge needed help. Angrily, Yi Xiao leapt off his mount, catching hold of the cliffside. He'd spent the last few years following his master through far worse terrain. This was a walk through Beijing comparatively.

Dona Estrella's donkey followed behind, the lady remonstrating with him as he went. He was being rash. Foolish. Impulsive. He didn't even know what lay ahead.

"Be quiet," Yi Xiao ordered calmly. "You're the one who'll get us noticed." By now he was close to the top, just another dozen yards and he'd be over the side. He paused here, listening, and heard Jo's voice over the wind. "You bastard! What'd you do to him?"

A man's voice answered. "Don't worry. She'll be back. Nothing living escapes my wards." The voice faltered. Strengthened. "Unless I accidentally killed her, throwing her off the mountain. Ah well. She would have been useful. I'll just have to do without whatever magic she wields."

Softly, Dona Estrella spoke from behind Yi Xiao. "Bly."

Yi Xiao had guessed that much. Guessed, too, that Wu Chang's softer than usual features had given Bly the idea he was a woman. "Can you fight him?"

"He mentioned a ward. If I can get through, I can face him."

Yi Xiao spotted a trail to the top of the peak. "We'll have to try." Something wavered in the air ahead of them. He touched it. Was repelled. Pushed harder. Drew his *qi* together and pressed it against the invisible wall. Lightning flickered around his fingers. Failed to break past.

"Master, if you'd allow me, I believe I can get us through."

⇒)(⇐

Both Yi Xiao and his companion turned startled looks on Wu Chang. He smiled, tilting his head a little at their expressions. It was Yi Xiao who broke the silence. "Yes. If you can, do so." Later, Wu Chang knew, his master would be demanding answers. Right now, lives were in danger.

Drawing his *qi* together, expanding his Self so it enveloped both Yi Xiao and the lady, Wu Chang ignored the way they both gasped and shuddered. Another thing to explain. Later. He gestured forward, indicating they should keep moving.

Though the lady gave him a distrustful look, she set her suddenly nervous mount walking forward. Yi Xiao was already past Bly's array, climbing the path to the peak as quietly as he could. Once the lady had moved on, Wu Chang followed suit, stepping from the cold darkness of night to the false day of Bly's little prison.

As expected, Jo was yelling at Bly, cursing him in Hunanese. "She has quite a command of the language," Wu Chang murmured to Yi Xiao.

"That'd be her friend Ma Chao's fault."

Wu Chang hadn't met this Ma Chao person, but he didn't need to. Besides, Bly was just noticing their presence. When he spotted Wu Chang, his eyes widened and he swore sharply. "How the hell'd you get past my ward so easy?"

"I had help." Wu Chang lied. "That old acquaintance of ours." He pointed behind Bly, to where a lean figure was taking shape. "All I had to do was call."

Deathshead faded completely into view, grinning broadly. He hadn't been pleased to discover Wu Chang could summon him through his blood. Happier to learn it was only the one time, but not pleased at all. He was the sort who manipulated, not the sort to be bound. Still, to Wu Chang's relief, Bly and he were old enemies and the prospect of causing trouble for the man set him salivating.

Rocks rose from the ground again, but this time they were hindered by the lady's magic. At the same time Yi Xiao launched himself at Bly, dodging around the watcher infested stones. A twist here, a slide there. A moment later he was right on top of Bly, driving his fist into the man's belly, lightning trailing through the air as he moved.

Deathshead grabbed hold of the boulder rolling towards him. Reached into it. Dragged the watcher inside free and flung the spirit towards Wu Chang. Catching it gently, Wu Chang pushed it out of the array, using his *qi* to hold the way open again. One after another they repeated the effort, until the only one left was the watcher hiding inside the tree.

By this time Jenny and the lady were setting up their own array, guarding Jo—despite their obvious wish to join the fight—and protecting the badly weakened watcher from its so-called master. Seeing darkness stretch out from Bly's feet, Wu Chang called out, "Master. His shadow!"

Yi Xiao wasted no time. Drawing his lightning together, he flung it straight into the dirt, shattering Bly's attack and sending the man flying. Bly regained his feet, stepping towards Yi Xiao, hands twisted as he grasped hold of his attacker's *qi* and tried to absorb it.

Before he could, the peak itself shuddered and cracked, sending him flying off the other side of the peak. That would be the mountain, expressing her displeasure. A moment later the array disappeared. It wasn't clear if Bly was dead or badly injured, but at least they could escape now. Wu Chang called out to the others, "Quick. Get out fast!"

"Help Dona Estrella, Wu Chang. I've got Jo."

Dona Estrella had to be the older lady who'd been accompanying Yi Xiao. She was busy breaking the watcher free of their trap, forcing Wu Chang to wait for her.

"You done with me?"

Wu Chang turned to look at Deathshead, the man's greying hair wild in the moonlight, his lips drawn back from straggly fangs. His sort didn't like being forced to do anything, even when it was something they wanted to do. "Done," he agreed. "Make trouble for my master and you'll see what I do next." He gestured around them. "You'll follow. I know you'll follow. Just stay back and I won't have to bite you again."

With a sniff that almost had Wu Chang believing he didn't care, Deathshead set his hat on his head and turned away. The last Wu Chang saw of him was the coyote tail, tip white in the moonlight, bouncing along as he headed down the other side of the peak.

Seeing Dona Estrella had finished her work, Wu Chang offered her a hand up. "We'd better go. I don't think the mountain is in a good mood for visitors right now."

⇒)(⇐

Scrambling down the slope, Yi Xiao's main concern was getting Jo safely to solid ground. She'd been climbing around the mine area often enough, but this path was a great deal steeper than what she was used to. She muttered curses under her breath as they went, reminding Yi Xiao to have some words with young Chao about the sort of language he taught the girl.

The bottom of the hill came quickly enough. Spent, Yi Xiao leaned against a tree and felt the mountain's spirit quiet down. She really didn't like that Bly fellow. He could feel her aggravation even now. She certainly would have done the *brujo* a mischief a great deal earlier if She'd spotted him among all the small lives wandering around the area. It was only when She'd realized who Yi Xiao was fighting that she'd attacked. The small connection that'd formed between them, back when he'd borrowed Her power had given her a sense of what he was doing and why.

He'd been lucky, though. She hadn't used him as a focus for her power. Just targeted what he'd targeted. He wasn't sure if Bly survived his fall. The trees were thick enough it was possible. Still, Yi Xiao wasn't going to go hunt him. With luck, the man would realize he was outmatched and look for easier prey. Or, at the very least, be too badly injured to come after them anytime soon.

A donkey's excited bray split the night as Dona Estrella led her animals back down the hillside after them, Jenny mounted on the one. She inclined her head at Jo. "You should come with us."

"I'm not what you and that fellow were thinking," Jo pointed out warily. "Just so you know."

Resignedly, the lady glanced Yi Xiao's way. "No. You're not. But it's late, the road difficult, and I should get you back to your guardian before he wakes to find you gone."

Jo agreed, clambering exhaustedly onto the donkey. "You gonna be okay, Yi Xiao?"

"I'll be along. There's something I need to do, first. Don't worry about me."

Once the three had moved on, Yi Xiao said quietly to thin air, "Wu Chang."

He was at Yi Xiao's side in a flash. "Master... ah... Yi Xiao is unhurt?"

Wu Chang's ability to appear out of nowhere was becoming something Yi Xiao simply expected. "A few bruises and a headache from one of Bly's rocks. Aside from that, I'm fine." He eyed his companion. "And you have something to tell me."

The man had the grace to flinch. "It has nothing to do with my duty as your bodyguard."

"Yes, it does." If, as it appeared, they were going to be running into more and more supernatural troubles, knowing what kind of being Wu Chang was would be vital. "I need to know what you are and what you can survive. Otherwise I'll worry about you. I might even try coming to your rescue when I don't have to."

Wu Chang gave up. "You never asked the reading of my name."

"I'd assumed it was probably the same as the city. Martial light."

A slight quirk to the lips as Wu Chang wrote in the air between them. "Impermanence," he said. "I'm named for the ghosts who guide the dead. Appropriately so, I might add."

"You mean...."

"Yes, master. I'm dead. I've been dead for a good five hundred years now. Ever since my best friend stole my heart and turned me into a walking corpse."

They stared at each other for a long moment. Then, with a sigh, Yi Xiao asked, "Does my grandmother know?"

"The Princess knows the darkest secrets of all the clans, master. Of course she knows. That's why she sent me. I might be the only bodyguard capable of surviving the kind of trouble you get into." He tilted his head inquiringly, adding, "Please don't send me back, Yi Xiao. You really do need my help right now."

Yi Xiao considered his options. Some priests would mind having a walking corpse around. Would regard it as a form of demonic cultivation and a sin. Fortunately, he wasn't that kind of priest. At least Wu Chang was an amusing companion and an excellent watchdog. "I suppose I'll have to let you stay," he agreed at last. "For now. Until I find a reason to send you home my grandmother would approve of. I don't really want her flaying you for disobedience after all."

"Nor I." A smile quirked Wu Chang's lips. "Skin takes years to grow back and everyone runs from you until it does."

Chapter 3
Water - A Woman's Place

Ordinarily, Estrella would never invite strangers to her little enclave. There'd been visitors, of course, but up until now, none of those outsiders had been men. Majeure Community was intended for women only, a safe haven for the non-religious to find peace and comfort away from the secular world. Educated in Spain and France, she'd founded the place in imitation of the old European tradition of the Beguine.

That Majeure had become a haven for young women with magic was known only to those in the community. The missionaries who'd once ruled California had driven those they called witches out of their lands, forcing them to gather together for safety.

These days, with the missions closed and California under American rule, their only dangers were the usual mundane sort. Bandits, greedy government agents and would-be gold miners. Luckily, no one had found gold in the valley. Estrella was sure they'd have to move on if that ever happened.

If Estrella ruled the valley entirely, she could have taken Jenny back home and simply explained that they'd been wrong to think young Jo Kraft an infant *bruja*. As things stood, she couldn't. She was senior among the sisterhood, but she was not supreme. She had to bring Yi Xiao Lang back with her to prove he was the one the Mother of the Mountain had favored. And bringing Yi Xiao back meant bringing the man calling himself Yi Xiao's bodyguard and vassal: Wu Chang Sihua.

Having garnered a promise from Jo to at least visit her later, Estrella set off for Majeure Community, on the west side of the peninsula. It wasn't far; a bit over ten miles. She and Jenny could have made it in half a day on their mules. Enhanced by Estrella's magic, the creatures could have taken them straight across the mountains between Corte Madera and Majeure without turning a hair.

That, however, would garner notice Estrella wanted to avoid. Her enclave was safe because it was tucked away in an area most people didn't have a reason to visit. The last thing she needed was for someone to see their beasts clambering up near vertical surfaces. She couldn't depend on an accidental witness mistaking what they saw as a mirage or hallucination.

Thus, they traveled the rocky paths between the mountains, climbing winding roads and trying not to breathe too much dust. The sun beat down on them, with only the chill mountain air to stave off heatstroke.

Of the three of them, Wu Chang seemed to suffer the most. He covered himself in his sleeping blanket and was wearing a broad rimmed hat. It gave Estrella an oddly reminiscent feeling; her brothers would sit like that, guarding the sheep for the mission. All he needed was a sombrero and a staff and he'd be a proper match.

As pale as Wu Chang was, he was probably just sensitive to sunlight. Still, Estrella couldn't help asking, "You're not ill, are you?"

The man's soft voice held a humorous note. "I don't tend to get sick anymore. It's just a bit bright for me today."

"We've found it's good to get a little sun. Not too much, of course, but enough to toughen your skin," Jenny offered kindly.

A chuckle. "I don't tan."

Some people didn't and Estrella pointed that out to her student. Admittedly, there was something quite odd about the boy. His dislike of sunlight alone didn't make her suspicious, but the fight with Bly and the things he'd done to help them did. Was he even human?

If her magic was the sort that let her probe a being's life-force, she'd have turned it on the child already. As it was, all she could do was trust Yi Xiao's judgment and Wu Chang's commitment to his master.

Still, he was a mystery and she didn't like mysteries at all, especially when they were going to be visiting her safe haven. Estrella was about to shift the conversation to last night again when movement drew her attention. A black mare clopped along lazily ahead of them, her rider swaying back and forth as she went.

Before Estrella could point or even react, the man dropped out of his saddle and landed in the road, a cloud of yellow dust rising around him as he fell.

⇒)(⇐

They hadn't seen anyone on the road since they'd left Jo and Zak heading back to Strike It Rich Mine Camp. As far as Yi Xiao could tell, this wasn't a well-traveled area. It was, however, near the place where they'd met up with those wolves like men creatures. So was this a trap, or simply a lost traveler who'd pushed themself too hard?

Stopping beside Dona Estrella's donkey, Yi Xiao looked up at her. "Do you want to approach? Or shall I?"

She handed him a canteen. "You're afoot. You may as well check him out."

With a quick bow, Yi Xiao did as she bade him. He felt a little like he was back with his master, traveling up and down the mountains. Being naturally friendly and garrulous, he generally handled the task of communicating with strangers or shopkeepers. Not that they often met either, but even the Storm Hermit couldn't avoid human contact entirely.

This time was slightly different. Back then he'd have had to approach a stranger alone, leaving his master to wait just out of sight. Now he had Wu Chang with him, staying just close enough to be seen, not so close as to look like an overprotective mother. Of course, right now he'd look like an overprotective pile of bedding, but the point remained the same.

Spreading his senses, Yi Xiao could tell there was no one else nearby. Not unless they were like Wu Chang, that was. If so, he doubted his unasked-for vassal would miss them. A five hundred year old walking corpse capable of pretending he was alive had to have talents along that line. "What do you think?" he asked his companion.

"I think the person is dying and could do with some water."

That was what it looked like to Yi Xiao, but it was good to get confirmation. He knelt beside the man, telling Wu Chang, "Catch his horse. No point in letting the poor animal wander off to get eaten."

As Wu Chang obeyed, Yi Xiao turned the man over and carefully lifted his head so he could put the canteen to his lips. "Careful," he warned, when the man gasped, tried to drink quickly and choked. "There's plenty. Drink slow."

While the man sipped, eyes closed against the sun, parched lips working thirstily, Yi Xiao eyed him more carefully. Middle aged. White. Dressed in black with a white collar, he looked a bit like the Christian preacher who'd once come to bother Second Mother. Of course, her marrying a heathen Chinese had been scandalous to her British kinfolk, which was why they kept trying to dissuade her.

This man had nothing to do with that, though. Likely he was just as much a wanderer as Yi Xiao. "Can you sit up?"

Shuddering, the man struggled to do so, only to fall over into Yi Xiao's arms. Yi Xiao took the canteen from him before he spilled it and turned his attention on Dona Estrella. She didn't look at all happy. "Perhaps it would be for the best if I took him to San Francisco before our visit?" She'd warned him her community didn't welcome men, after all.

Dona Estrella gestured west, "We're within two miles of home. As badly injured as this man is, he's sure to die before you could get him to San Francisco. Unless your interesting talents include flying?"

It'd be nice if they did. There were legends of cultivators who could ride their swords, using their *qi* to control their weapons and carry them rapidly across the sky. "Unfortunately, this humble student of the Storm Hermit has not progressed nearly far enough to accomplish such a deed. Wu Chang?"

"This servant's cultivation is not the sort to permit flight," Wu Chang answered, voice trembling slightly with amusement. "Unless, of course, he is aided by being thrown."

"Master says, being thrown is falling, not flying."

"I bow to the Storm Hermit's greater wisdom, master." Wu Chang suited action to word.

The look on Dona Estrella's face was a familiar one. From both mothers, from his grandmother, from his master. From Gan Han. "Do you ever stop?" she demanded. Then, before he could answer, she raised a hand. "I don't want to hear it. Just bring that man with us. Keep an eye on him, though. I won't have him disturbing my family."

Grinning, because the one thing he loved most was getting a rise out of people, Yi Xiao carefully helped the man back onto his horse. "Wu Chang and I will help you stay seated, sir. Sip your water and we'll get you safely settled as soon as we can."

The man muttered weakly, "Thank you... thank... you...." Then he leaned forward on his horse and sprawled there, leaving Yi Xiao and Wu Chang to keep him from falling off.

⇒)(⇐

They reached Majeure just as the sun was about to set, its warm light limning what had once been an old mission house and its outbuildings. The adobe bricks gleamed red-gold in the sunlight, with only a few cracks here and there showing the places they hadn't been able to repair. Estrella smiled at the sight, glad to be home again.

Jenny was outright grinning, with an expression that said she'd race her donkey straight into the main courtyard if she were on her own. Instead she asked politely, "Should I go ahead? Tell them to get ready for guests?"

It'd be just as well. "Don't gallop. Trot politely in and give your donkey to Sister Imelda before you announce our return."

As Jenny happily hurried off, Yi Xiao said, "An attractive home. If I ever decide to settle down, I think I wouldn't mind a place with such a view." He gestured towards the ocean, its waters gleaming bright gold in the sunset.

Somehow Estrella doubted the boy would be doing anything resembling settling down for a long time to come. There was something like a wild animal about him, the sort that never sat still. Even so, she told him, "There are plenty of places on the coast like this. Some more difficult to reach than others. All beautiful."

They continued down the road, reaching the walls of the community just as a dozen youngsters came running out to greet them. The children crowded around Estrella, chattering loudly, while she smiled and patted heads as they passed. Then she was face to face with the senior sisters and sighing inwardly at their unwelcoming expressions.

Before Sister Sophia could open her mouth, Estrella told her, "Men are discouraged. They are not forbidden. And the one is ill. Sister Susanna, take him to the hospital right away. I'll have someone carry word of our meeting to you later."

Susanna might not like having men in the community but she wasn't the sort to let anyone lie ill and injured for long. She called for help from some of the younger sisters and did as she was bade.

Dismounting, Estrella handed off her donkey and the stranger's horse to the children. "Bring our things inside, please and thank you." Then she turned her attention on the other sisters. "Come to the meeting hall."

They followed her, discontented and unhappy, especially when Yi Xiao and Wu Chang came along after them. Sister Margarita voiced all their objections as they went. "Why are these men here? Why are you allowing them in our sacred place?"

"I'll explain when we're in the meeting hall. This is for your ears only." Estrella led them into what had once been the mission's church. In a way it still was, but the old symbols had been removed, leaving only white walls, dark brown pews and an altar on which a jagged grey stone sat.

To prevent an argument, Estrella called Yi Xiao over to the stone. "Do you feel Her power?"

He hesitated, even as the Sisters muttered irritably to each other. "I feel something familiar. This comes from Her mountain?"

"It does. A gift to the tribe who once climbed her slopes. They're long forgotten, lost to the missions, but I and my sisters try to keep some small part of the memory alive." Estrella took his hand, set it on the rock. "Show them the thing you call your *qi*, boy. Show them why you're the one She answered and why I've brought you here to prove it."

This was the first time Estrella had ever watched the boy summon his power. Up until now they'd been too busy fighting for her to focus on what he did. He was right. It wasn't magic. The difference was subtle, but the power he summoned came from inside him. Not from his mind, either. It seemed to envelop his whole body, a spiritual force that gathered within him and focused through his flesh.

Lightning crackled around his body, delicate little bolts no bigger than a static shock. They gathered along his fingers and she hurriedly added, "Just a little. Don't break the stone."

"I did rather think you'd want to keep it," he reassured her, setting his fingers to the stone's surface. His lightning flickered down into the rock and set it glowing softly in the late afternoon light.

A moment later the rock answered, a pulse of Her energy filling the room and everyone in it.

⇒)(⇐

It'd be a lie to say Yi Xiao's proof that he could call on these people's Mountain Mother changed their attitude towards him. Dona Estrella and Jenny had both made it clear that their community was women-only for a reason. Nor, given what he knew of some men, did he blame them.

Still, at least the senior sisters were impressed enough to relent a little. Enough to allow Yi Xiao and Wu Chang to stay the night in their garden shed. It was a tight fit but once they were alone, Wu Chang pointed out, "Being dead, I don't need to sleep."

"Can you if you want to?" Yi Xiao unrolled his bedding and spread it out in the middle of the floor.

"Not really, though I've learned to pretend." Wu Chang looked amused. "You'll have plenty of time to learn my few talents and many limitations, Yi Xiao. But I'm sure you're tired by now. We can talk privately later, when you're ready to scratch those itchy feet of yours again. Given you're allowed to."

Something in his tone made Yi Xiao ask, "You think I'm going to stay here? Where I'm not exactly wanted?"

"I think your life is one long bounce from trouble to trouble. You may not plan to stay, but I'll wager three coins that something will delay our departure tomorrow."

Yi Xiao grinned. "Done." He didn't know that Wu Chang was wrong. Indeed, it was true he tended to fall into trouble's lap on a regular basis. But he couldn't resist playing along with the game, even so. "A thought does occur to me. Deathshead?"

"I can't sense him anywhere close. I think he doesn't like this place."

Somehow, Yi Xiao suspected the ladies of this place wouldn't care much for Deathshead, either. "He's surely still out there, keeping an eye on us. On me, rather."

"After what I did to him, I suspect he's keeping an eye on me as well." At Yi Xiao's raised brow, Wu Chang explained, "I bit him. Not hard, but enough to draw blood. It allowed me to control him briefly."

A little appalled, because he was fairly sure Deathshead was quite a bit more than just a mortal, or monster for that matter, Yi Xiao repeated. "You controlled him."

"It wasn't easy. If he didn't hate Bly even more than he hated being controlled, though, I doubt I could have done it." Wu Chang looked thoughtful, "It's possible he could turn the tables if he figured out what I was. And, of course, found my heart. But that, I fear, is still somewhere in China."

The kind of sorcery required to remove a heart and have its owner still walk around like a living creature was far beyond Yi Xiao's knowledge. Nor did he wish to know. "One day I'd like to just be allowed to cultivate quietly and alone."

"An admirable goal," Wu Chang agreed. "But even when I was alive, there always seem to be interruptions." He waved at Yi Xiao's bedding. "You should sleep now. If trouble is coming, it's coming. Until it does, nothing to be done."

Yi Xiao grinned. "Master says, the best thing to do about trouble is avoid it," he murmured, sliding into his bedding and closing his eyes.

"She also says 'Stop chattering and go to sleep'." At Yi Xiao's startled glance, Wu Chang smiled. "Five hundred years, remember? I was never her disciple, but we've met a few times."

Before Yi Xiao could ask another question, Wu Chang went to the door. "Rest well, master.... Yi Xiao. I'll see you in the morning." With that, he was gone, leaving Yi Xiao to settle himself down like a good boy.

⇒)(⇐

It seemed whenever Estrella left her community she came back to twice as much work as she'd have faced if she'd stayed. There was always something. The older girls picking on the younger. The senior sisters disagreeing on exactly how to handle a minor matter. Someone forgetting to order supplies. The community was mostly self-sufficient but there were some things they couldn't produce for themselves. Not yet, at least.

And, of course, there was the question of Yi Xiao. When they'd sensed the Mountain Mother's response to a call for help, they'd been sure it'd been a woman. An inexperienced sorcerer of some kind, ignorantly calling on power she didn't understand.

Instead it'd been a strange, flighty yet oddly centered boy-child whose power was something other than magic. Estrella hadn't believed him at first, but the more she watched him work, the more obvious it became. It wasn't a priest's power, either, for all he claimed to be something of the sort. Whatever it was, it came from inside him, a brilliant spark of lightning; fierce and untamable, yet somehow controlled.

Admittedly, lightning, or rather electricity, could be mastered. Estrella remembered watching her father's experiments, based off Franklin's and Faraday's. She'd even shocked herself on his toy, accidentally brushing the metal with her fingers. The thought of somehow generating that power through some inner force was both fascinating and terrifying.

If Yi Xiao had been a woman, Estrella could have asked him to stay. Asked him to teach her charges a little of what he did. He'd claimed anyone could seek that *Dao* of his, after all. Asking her community to accept him as a teacher, however, was more than she could hope for. The Senior Sisters would never agree.

Estrella was just in the midst of going over the community's plans for winter when one of the novices—the new, nervous one called Henrietta—came to her door. "Mother?"

"Ave, daughter. What is it?" She was up past bedtime, but Estrella refused to dismiss her concerns simply because of that.

"The man you brought. I'm afraid of him."

Estrella had brought three men. "Which man?"

"The cold one."

The cold one almost had to be Wu Chang. But why would Henrietta be afraid of him? The children had barely seen either boy. "The Chinese boy?"

To her surprise, Henrietta shook her head. "No. The other. The one who was in the hospital."

Was? Estrella considered shaking the girl for not just telling her outright what she feared. "Where is he now?"

"In the courtyard, staring at the meeting hall."

Now Estrella was truly irritated. Not just at Henrietta for her almost deliberately obtuse way of explaining the situation. At Susanna, for not keeping her patient properly in check. At herself for not having someone guard the stranger properly. He'd seemed so weak and helpless, though, and she'd been distracted by her other guests.

"See me tomorrow to discuss your priorities, daughter. For now, it's past curfew and you should be in bed."

Henrietta flushed. Looked ready to fuss. Saw Estrella's expression and sulkily curtseyed. "Yes, Dona Estrella."

Once the girl was gone, Estrella headed for Sister Margarita's chambers and scratched at her door. Without preamble, she ordered, "Have our stronger sisters go to the courtyard and persuade our patient to return to his bed." The community's security was under Margarita's command and she'd know the best choices for the purpose.

"Immediately, Dona."

As Margarita went to do just that, Estrella headed for the courtyard, gathering magic together in case she had to fight.

ʒ)(ɀ

It was past midnight when something woke Yi Xiao. Immediately alert, he didn't sit up, just listened cautiously for the source of his concern. His instinct for trouble was well honed and he knew better than to dismiss it as mere unfamiliar circumstances.

The sounds outside the shed didn't seem any different than before. A faint breeze, a frog, a few insects. The waves against the shore, distant but distinct. He paused. Listened closer. He was wrong. The sound of the waves had changed after all. Something moved in the water. A soft plunk, followed by faint drips. A hollow thump here and there.

More accustomed to mountains than oceans, it took Yi Xiao a few minutes to recognize the sound. The last time he'd heard anything similar had been aboard Burton's dinghy, coming in to San Diego. This was softer, slower and far more stealthy; a sign that those aboard were trying to sneak their way onto the beach.

Yi Xiao slid out of his bedding and left the shed. "Wu Chang?"

"Yes. I hear them." As usual, his companion seemed to melt out of the shadows to appear silently beside him. Fortunately, by now Yi Xiao was not only used to it, but expected it. "Your orders?"

"Can you tell anything about them?" The beach was a little too far away for Yi Xiao to sense the boat's occupants. It was only because of the way the mountains came together around the valley heard anything at all.

"They're beyond my reach. Would you like me to investigate?"

"I would. While you do so, I'll go warn Dona Estrella, or at least whoever's on guard. They may be expecting these people, but I suspect not."

Wu Chang inclined his head and was gone in an instant. Envious of the man's speed, Yi Xiao headed for the wall surrounding the old mission, climbing it with ease and peering into the courtyard.

To his surprise, a half-dozen of the sisters were up and about, gathered around a figure at the center. The man from earlier, clad in a long nightshirt, his legs bared, his greying blond hair disheveled. Dona Estrella was there, speaking kindly and firmly, her voice just audible. "Sir, you're ill. Too ill to be wandering. Please return to your bed."

"No. No. Sanctuary. Sanctuary. He's looking. Looking for me. Looking for us." He tried to catch her hands, voice quivering with fear. "Please!"

One of the sisters stepped forward. She was tall, brawny, with the expression of one who didn't take nonsense from anyone. "Stop that."

Yi Xiao could tell the woman should have no problem dealing with the man. Rather than leap to her aid, he slid down the wall and came up to the group. "Dona Estrella, might I interrupt?"

All but the tall woman and the old man stared at him and at least two tried to grab him. He slid past easily, adding, "It's urgent. I promise. I'd wait for you to finish otherwise."

Before the rest of the sisters could react, Dona Estrella said calmly, "What is it, Yi Xiao?"

"I just heard a boat being pulled into your bay." He gestured towards the beach. "I apologize if you're expecting them, but you may want to prepare for intruders."

She considered the news while one of the sisters snapped, "You're lying."

"I won't pretend to always be truthful," Yi Xiao admitted. "But I'm not lying this time."

At the same time, the sick man wailed, "HELP ME!" He flailed wildly, sudden stronger than any normal human had a right to be. "HE'S LOOKING FOR ME!" He shoved the tall sister aside, racing for the meeting hall as fast as his skinny legs could carry him.

Yi Xiao moved faster, setting himself between the man and his target. Rather than simply standing in the stranger's way, he twisted sideways, moving with the man's movements, shifting his weight to trip the man and send them both falling. The man sprawled, while Yi Xiao flipped and dropped, just in time to catch hold of a flailing arm and twist it behind a skinny back.

"Sanctuary. Please. Please. Mother's sanctuary. Please!"

Yi Xiao held the man in place. "Whatever is he trying to say?"

"I'm not sure," Dona Estrella came up to join them. She paused, turning her attention on her sisters. "Half of you to your posts. Watch for the intruders Yi Xiao mentioned. The rest of you, rouse the children and get them to safety."

"You can't believe this... man...."

"I've seen what he can do. I've taken his measure. Not all men are users, Triona. Now do as you're told."

Beneath Yi Xiao, his prisoner flailed weakly. "Please. Mother. Please!" Something was happening to him. His bones didn't feel right. Yi Xiao looked down. Saw thin objects sliding free of the man's skin, as if his skeleton was turning into branches. "Please."

Yi Xiao suddenly realized what the man wanted. "That stone of yours." He dragged the man upright. "He's looking for the Mother of the Mountain."

"What?" Dona Estrella reached out, about to stop Yi Xiao. "Wait. You can't...."

"He's a watcher, stuck in a human body." Yi Xiao couldn't be certain he was right, but he thought he was. "He's trying to reach Her for help."

More branches were forming around the man's body, blood trickling from torn flesh as they broke free. The man was crying, tears of sap and blood. Needle-like leaves burst forth, turned brown in seconds. Began to fall. "Your choice, Dona Estrella. But I think he'll die soon if you don't let him in."

$$\Rightarrow)(\Leftarrow$$

The decision wasn't easy. But it was obvious the man wasn't human anymore. Might never have been. Estrella had dealt with the spirits of this land, but she didn't properly know them. So many had been lost when the people who'd lived here had been taken. Estrella was descended from one such tribe, but she knew nothing, absolutely nothing, of their beliefs.

"Dona Estrella," Margarita protested. "You can't!"

"I can. I must." Estrella gestured to Yi Xiao, who hoisted the man over his shoulder easily, despite being a foot shorter and at least half his weight. "If his warning is true, we need him to be coherent. We'll give him a chance."

They entered the meeting hall and Yi Xiao carried the man to the altar. He was half buried in branches by now, redwood by the look of them. Yet another sign this being, whatever it was, had ties to the Mother. Such trees grew in the folds of her skirts, rising tall and proud in the misty valleys.

He stretched his hands towards the stone. Broke free of Yi Xiao's grasp. Stumbled. Gasped. "Mother!" Then fell, human flesh absorbed into a sapling spreading its roots across the floor. A voice creaked, the groan of wood against wood. "He's looking for me. Looking for us. Help us. Please help us!"

Then it fell silent, a slender tree struggling to remain upright without a proper tap-root.

Someone shrieked behind Estrella. "Henrietta. Why aren't you with the other novices?" Estrella asked, not bothering to look at the hysterical child. Honestly, she never seemed to know how to behave. Undisciplined from the first day she'd come to them, she was a constant trial.

"I was curious." The girl sniffed wetly, especially when Margarita muttered an imprecation. "I'm the one saw him first. I just wanted to know what he was doing."

"The question I have is what that boy is doing?" Margarita grumbled, returning Estrella's attention to Yi Xiao. Having dragged the man into the church to be transformed to a tree, he was now trying to drag that tree back outside. He'd managed the first, but it was obvious the tree was too much for him. It wasn't terribly big, not yet, but it was too long and bulky for his slight weight.

"Indoors is not healthy for trees," Yi Xiao pointed out breathlessly. "Master says a place for everything and everything in its place."

Estrella had a feeling she'd highly approve of this master Yi Xiao kept quoting. Approve and sympathize, if they'd had the boy under their care for any length of time. Yi Xiao could try the patience of a saint. He certainly tried the patience of the *bruja* leader of the Majeure community. To say nothing of the other sisters.

Still, some of the others came to his aid, guiding the tree back through the door and out into the courtyard. To Estrella's relief, it didn't argue the point. Just kept crying that 'he' was coming. That and automatically burying its taproot into the dirt as soon as it was given the opportunity.

"Could 'he' be with the ones Wu Chang and I heard?"

Estrella decided not to take the chance. "Would you go check the situation?"

That made Margarita bristle. "The security of this community is my job."

With a polite little bow, Yi Xiao told them both, "I would gladly go with comrades. We don't know who's there or what they want."

Once Yi Xiao, Margarita and three of her strongest guards had gone, Estrella turned her attention on the others. "Double the guards in the towers. I don't want anyone coming onto our grounds without express permission. Henrietta, go back to the safe room with the others."

"But...."

"No buts, child. You shouldn't be here in the first place. Go. Now."

Silently. Sulkily. Utterly unwillingly, the girl turned and left the courtyard, pausing once in a while to look pleadingly back at Estrella.

"Honestly, I don't know what's wrong with that child," Estrella muttered to herself.

One of the sisters turned. Stared at her. "What child?"

᠄)(᠄

The beach was white in the moonlight, the ocean's water glittering brightly. Under other circumstances, Yi Xiao would have taken the time to pause and admire the view. Instead he stuck to the shadows, scanning the secluded cove.

It was no wonder the strangers had come in by boat. The only other approach to Dona Estrella's little community was by one of two steep and difficult valley paths that met just east of the cove. The former mission had been built right at the crossroads, with farmland to the east and a twisted road leading north into the mountains.

Everything seemed peaceful, but Yi Xiao didn't trust it at all. Something lurked in the darkness and it wasn't Wu Chang. Or, rather, it wasn't just Wu Chang. "Master, respect. May I report?"

Yi Xiao glanced at the man who'd appeared behind him out of the shadows. Immediately Wu Chang bowed his head with an embarrassed expression. "Ah. Sorry. Yi Xiao, may I report?"

"Go ahead." Reflecting that he was fighting what was likely a five-hundred year old habit, Yi Xiao decided he wasn't going to bother scolding. At least Wu Chang tried not to do it, even if he failed most of the time.

"The intruders landed their longboat at the north end of the cove. There's a steep trail into the hills there."

"Can you catch up?"

"It might be for the best if I didn't. One of them nearly noticed me. I'm not sure I can remain hidden."

Yi Xiao stared. "Noticed you?" No one noticed Wu Chang if he didn't want to be noticed. At least, no one had noticed Wu Chang up until now.

"Yes. I think he may be a necromancer."

Well, that'd explain matters. There were some types of sorcery a dead man like Wu Chang couldn't hide from. Necromancy was, for obvious reasons, one of them. So was Gods' magic, but they hadn't run across that so far. "All right. Did you examine their boat, once they were out of earshot?"

"I did. There are few markings. A ship's name, written in English. *The Calico Cat.*"

The name meant nothing to Yi Xiao, but then it wouldn't. From Wu Chang's tone, however, his companion obviously did. "And?"

"Do you recall the pirate you met on the way to California? Kramer?"

"I do." Kramer was dead, one of Yi Xiao's unfortunate victims, killed when the sorcerer had given him no option that didn't end in death for someone. "Why?"

"*The Calico Cat* was Kramer's own ship, or so your Grandmother's sources say. It was damaged earlier and he sent his second-in-command, a woman called Brigid, to get it to port and repaired."

The news was a surprise and not a good one. "Is she hunting me, then?"

"I've no idea, to be honest. Pirates aren't known for their loyalty. But it's possible their relationship was closer than some."

Yi Xiao sighed. "Let's go back to the community and report, then. I'd rather not confront this woman if I don't have to."

Wu Chang bowed. "An understandable desire, master... I mean, Yi Xiao."

They turned back and a thought occurred to Yi Xiao. "Can you be controlled by a necromancer?"

"I've only known one able to do so and that was almost three-hundred years ago." Wu Chang looked thoughtful. "That doesn't mean it's impossible. Necromancy is as individual as any other magic."

"Be on your guard, then. I'd rather not have to hurt you because you couldn't resist the lady's charms."

Wu Chang chuckled. "Being dead, it's hard to injure me. Even harder to keep me injured. If you reach a point where you have a choice between someone else dying and beheading me, please, do what's necessary. Just, when it's over, please put my head back on straight. It's quite difficult to walk when you're looking at your backside."

It was probably better not to ask just how Wu Chang knew that.

⋧⟩⟨⋦

"A necromancer? So?"

From Yi Xiao's expression, Estrella's reaction had been entirely unexpected. "Every Senior Sister of this community knows how to protect it from sorcery. A necromancer would need to be quite powerful to get past our walls. And if they're that powerful, we're not going to be strong enough to fight them anyway. Panicking won't help."

Tell the truth, Estrella was worried. If it weren't for her other concern, that tree and the mysteriously missing Henrietta, she'd likely be more focused on this new problem. The tree had fallen quiet once it'd rooted itself, so she wasn't quite as worried about it. Henrietta, whatever she was, was a different question altogether.

There were spells that could confuse their victim, concealing the caster behind a sense of rightness. Used carefully, they fooled a person into believing a thing belonged where it were. This one had even been clever enough to make Estrella feel irritated and out of sorts with the caster, adding to the distraction.

"Why didn't you follow them?" Margarita asked suddenly. She'd listened to Yi Xiao's story with barely concealed impatience. Like Estrella, she was more concerned by the sorcerer who'd managed to wangle her way into the community unnoticed. A group of strangers pirates or not, didn't matter unless they were targeting Majeure community.

"I didn't see a good reason to." Yi Xiao spread his hands. "Since they went a different way, they either plan to come around to surprise us from the north, or have no interest in this place at all."

Before the two could argue further, for Margarita had certain strong opinions about how intruders should be handled, Estrella raised a hand. "Tell the guards to be on the lookout for those strangers. In the meantime, Yi Xiao, could you assist me with something else?"

The question made Margarita bristle angrily. "You can't possibly intend to involve them with our private business."

"Do you have any idea how long Henrietta's been here? Where she came from? Who she is?" As Margarita faltered, Estrella returned her attention to Yi Xiao. "You're not a sorcerer. Neither of you are, as far as I can tell?"

They both answered 'no', but Wu Chang added, "I've had occasion to deal with sorcerers. I may not be able to cast spells, but I have some understanding of the subject."

That'd have to be good enough. "Then this is the situation. Last night a girl I thought was named Henrietta involved herself with the situation with that tree."

"By the way you put that, I'm guessing you mean she'd used some spell to conceal her identity? To make you think she belonged here when she didn't?"

The boy was smart, that much was obvious. Estrella agreed. "I didn't notice until just recently that the only ones she spoke to, the only ones who spoke to her, was myself and Sister Margarita."

"Has anyone else remembered this child's existence aside from the two of you?" Wu Chang paused, corrected himself. "Believed the child exists, that is?"

A good question and one Estrella had failed to ask. "Margarita? Could you please ask around?"

It was obvious Margarita would much prefer to put her energies towards guarding the community from physical attack. Still, she agreed without argument, leaving Estrella to turn her attention back on Yi Xiao. "For that matter, do you remember a little girl in the meeting house when you carried that man inside?"

"The one who pretended to be terrified? Yes. I remember her."

"Pretended?" Estrella was about to ask for clarification, then realized there wasn't a point. "I suppose she would be pretending, given her behavior." Henrietta had to be a spy of some sort. Possibly she was connected with the tree now growing in their courtyard. The question was, what exactly was she looking for?

A thought occurred to Estrella, one that ought to have come to her a great deal earlier. "The stone. What if she's after the stone?" Without hesitation she headed outside again, not caring whether or not the two men followed her.

⇒)(⇐

By now the first hints of sunrise were glimmering over the mountain ridge, casting purple and gold color into the sky. The tree quivered in its place, branches reaching out as if it were stretching sleep away. It creaked softly, a sad noise that made Wu Chang stop and eye it thoughtfully. "You said the man we rescued became this?"

"I did."

"I didn't feel anything strange about him earlier." Before Yi Xiao could point out that he hadn't been expected to, he added, "I ought to have sensed if the man were possessed."

Dona Estrella was already at the doors to her meeting hall and pushing them open. "We'll look into it later," Yi Xiao decided as the lady moaned in dismay. "I think the stone may be more important."

Inside, the meeting hall didn't look any different from before, except for one notable exception. The stone was gone. Which, when Yi Xiao thought about it, really shouldn't have been a surprise. "Dona Estrella, I fear this may be my fault. It never occurred to me someone was here trying to get at your treasure."

She stood silently, staring at the empty altar. "It isn't gone."

"Ma'am."

"I can feel its presence. If it was gone, entirely gone, I'd have felt it leave." She shook herself. "It's here, but it's too powerful for me to figure out where."

Yi Xiao stretched out his own senses. He'd felt the stone's power earlier, but he'd had to be right on top of it to do so. If it was here, it was out of his range. "Wu Chang?"

"It's a thing of life, master." Not said but implied; a walking corpse like Wu Chang couldn't have sensed something like that.

Yi Xiao pondered the situation. "It's obvious this Henrietta has something to do with its going missing. We need to figure out who remembers her presence, so we can trace her path."

Dona Estrella agreed. "And we need to work out if the tree's warning was real, or part of her trick to get access to the stone."

They headed into the main hall of the community, where the novices were snuggled safely in a protected corner. A protective array—what Dona Estrella called a ward—glimmered around them and a half dozen of the Senior sisters were gathered close, guarding its borders.

"Children. I want you to consider the name Henrietta. If you know it, stand up." Dona

Estrella gestured at the sisters guarding the array, adding, "The same to you. Raise your hands."

Two or three little girls did so immediately and Yi Xiao thought they were the same little girls who'd stabled the horse and donkeys when they'd arrived the night before. One of the women did as well. The one in charge of the hospital, Susanna, he thought her name was.

Something occurred to Yi Xiao. "Dona Estrella, I have an idea. If you'd go ahead and question the young ladies, I'll go investigate it."

She eyed him. "What is it?"

"I'd rather be sure first. Master says, better safe than sorry."

Wu Chang muttered, "Now you're just making things up."

"Hush, you."

With a sigh, Dona Estrella gestured. "Fine. Go. Don't waste too much time. If you're right about those others, we've got more trouble coming."

Yi Xiao hurried outside, Wu Chang close behind. When they reached the stable, his companion murmured, "I think I've guessed your thoughts."

It was a crazy idea, though. One Yi Xiao didn't want to share until he was certain. He entered the building, ignoring the complaints of the donkeys. They had water and were obviously well-fed. They could wait for their breakfast. Instead, he headed for the back of the building and came to a halt at the last stall.

The mare the man from earlier had ridden raised her head, staring blankly at them, chewing casually on a mouthful of oats. Yi Xiao smiled at it. "Now that's interesting," he told Wu Chang.

"Yes, master?"

"The donkeys are claiming they haven't been fed for ages. Decades, even. And, indeed, their troughs are quite empty."

"Indeed, master."

"Now it's possible they ate faster than this pretty young lady here. She does seem to be eating more slowly, after all."

"True, master."

"But," Yi Xiao grinned, stepping into the stall and stroking the mare's pale neck, "for the last few hours everyone has been too busy to consider feeding the livestock. Which means the last time anyone gave them grain would have been last night, before bedtime. Given that man's state, I doubt his mare had been fed recently before then. Can you imagine a horse ignoring food that long?"

Wu Chang chuckled, stepping back from the gate. "Master, I cannot."

"Neither can I. Isn't that right, Henrietta?" Before the mare could react, Yi Xiao leapt onto her back, tightening his legs around her torso as she bucked and whinnied, slamming her way through the gate and out into the courtyard.

⇒)(⇐

That nuisance boy was causing trouble again. No real surprise, but was this really the time to be playing cowboy? Odd, though. The mare he was struggling with was surely tame. She'd been meek and biddable from the moment they'd found her and her master.

Yet right now she was bucking and neighing furiously, struggling to get the man off her back. Having broken a few horses in her time, Estrella had to admit he was good. Knees tight to the animal's sides, one hand wrapped in her mane, the other stroking her neck as he leaned forward towards her head.

He was talking gently to the animal, his tone reassuring, even if his words were incomprehensible. It was obvious he wanted her to calm down, to relax. It didn't seem to be working. When the mare made a break for the gate, Estrella was sure the pair would be lost in the mountains in minutes.

Instead, Wu Chang seemed to appear from nowhere, a shadowy figure blocking the mare's path. Something about him spooked the animal. Sent her running back into the courtyard to shriek and whinny some more. Until, at last, she gave up.

"There you go, Henrietta. No need to be upset. No one wants to hurt you."

Estrella approached slowly. Henrietta? That young fool thought the mare was Henrietta? Was he out of his mind or had he worked out the truth? "How can you be sure?"

"Aside from the fact that she threw a fit as soon as I called her that? I can't." Yi Xiao gestured at Wu Chang. "Take her halter, would you?"

The other youngster did as he was ordered, both hands clinging to the straps, eyes intent on the mare's. "I don't suggest escaping." There was an odd echo to his voice that hadn't been there before. One Estrella felt she should recognize.

A vague inkling came to her. A memory of dealing with something similar in her younger days. But this man stood in the bright morning sunlight, undamaged and unafraid. No, she had to be imagining it. She returned her attention to Yi Xiao. "I'm not sure that's good enough. You startled her. Any animal reacts badly to being startled."

He didn't argue. "It's possible I've misjudged her," he admitted. "But I'd point out that the only ones who've actually seen Henrietta are the ones who've touched this horse."

Surely that wasn't right. "Margarita?"

"Ask her if she'd gone to the stable for anything." Yi Xiao gestured around them. "She and her people are in charge of protecting the community. Is it possible she came in to make sure everything was properly closed up?"

The boy was, unfortunately, right. Sister Margarita was a Senior and therefore not required to do anything of the sort. She also didn't trust anyone else with what she regarded as her responsibility. "That's true." She returned her attention to the horse shifting nervously under Wu Chang's apparently negligent grip.

As far as Estrella could tell, the animal seemed perfectly normal. Light brown hide, dark eyes, alert ears. Young and in excellent shape. She'd make an excellent mount for any rider, if not for a tendency to twitch and jerk around like a frightened child.

It was the movements that confirmed Yi Xiao's suspicions. Henrietta had behaved similarly, the few times Estrella had interacted with her. It wasn't proof, but right then they didn't have time to play games. "If you're Henrietta, tell me what happened to the stone."

The horse flinched. Tried to jerk out of Wu Chang's powerful grip. Whinnied again. Above them, the tree that'd been a man groaned. It'd gotten bigger, Estrella realized. It was easily twice the height it'd been in the night. She stared from it to the horse, unsure what to do or how to protect her community.

Then, the northern warning bell chimed.

⋗〉〈⋖

It was obvious from Dona Estrella's expression that the sound was bad news. It was oddly sweet for a warning signal, a delicate *gong* that reminded Yi Xiao of a temple celebration. It was followed by other chimes, some short, some long. His father—obsessed with railways and telegraphs— had tried and failed to teach him Morse Code when he'd been little. This sounded like that. He even thought he picked up a letter, here or there.

"Put... Henrietta... back in the stable and get ready for trouble," Dona Estrella ordered. "That's a warning people are coming from the north."

Based on what he'd seen, Yi Xiao was almost certain the strangers were the ones who'd landed their boat in the cove. As he'd feared, they'd climbed up the other path and were coming back from the north trail. "Wu Chang?"

"I'll take care of her." Wu Chang had no difficulty persuading the horse to come with him. Whether due to his nature or his strength, she seemed utterly cowed. "Please do not seek a fight until I've returned."

Yi Xiao waved him off, refusing to make promises. Circumstances were what they were and would fall as they might. It was possible the strangers were just wanderers, looking for shelter. It was also possible they were enemies. If so, if the name on that longboat meant anything, it was likely Yi Xiao that was wanted.

Joining Dona Estrella in the northeastern watchtower, Yi Xiao peered through the trees and spotted the movement of a dozen or so men. They were gathered close, guarding each other's backs and walking down the road as if they didn't have a care in the world. They might be right, too.

A woman strode ahead of the group. Bright red hair gleamed against her vest, shining in the morning sunlight. Another man walked beside her, holding a sack in his left hand, a rifle of some kind in the right. "They look friendly."

Sister Margarita, who'd joined them within minutes of hearing the alarm, glared at him. Turned to Dona Estrella. "Why do we have to include a bird child like this in our business?"

Bird child? Yi Xiao was puzzled by the term and guessed she meant he was flighty and thoughtless. A common misconception, one he cultivated almost as assiduously as he cultivated the *Dao*. Fortunately, Dona Estrella, who saw through such things with disconcerting ease, simply said, "He has skills that might be useful. However, Yi Xiao, it'd be good if you could hide for now. I can hardly tell these people we don't allow men inside, with you around."

He didn't argue. Just headed down to the next floor, where a narrow window allowed him to see the intruders approach. It wasn't long before Dona Estrella called, "My friends, may I ask where it is you are headed?"

The group stopped. Gazed levelly up at the tower. No surprise the man with the rifle started and almost raised his weapon towards Dona Estrella. The red-haired woman set a hand on his arm, quieting him, then raised a friendly face. "Hello there. I didn't expect to find anyone here, so far from civilization."

"We're a non-religious community," Dona Estrella explained. "A woman's community, or I'd let you in."

The man with the rifle muttered angrily in the red-head's ear. She hushed him. "Would you allow me in alone? And, if you have water, allow us to take some? We've been on the road for quite some time now and our supply is low."

No self-respecting community like Majeure would allow travelers to go without water or food. No traveler would fail to take advantage of that, especially if they'd really been on the road for a while. Yi Xiao knew Dona Estrella wouldn't let the woman realize their doubts. Thus, he wasn't surprised when she said, "I'll allow you and only you inside. If your men send their canteens in with you, we will fill them."

Behind Yi Xiao, Wu Chang murmured, "The necromancer is the one with the sack."

Accustomed to his companion's sudden appearances, all Yi Xiao said was, "Keep away from him, if you can. How's Henrietta?"

"Displeased. Fractious. Inclined to bite. At least until I bit back." Wu Chang smiled. "You were right to think her something more than a horse. I couldn't identify her nature, but I could taste the power in her."

"You didn't hurt her?"

"One nip on the ear. A trick I learned from some steppe riders." Wu Chang returned his attention to the group working their way around the community's walls to the front gate. "She'll behave for the moment. I'm more concerned about these strangers."

"I am too." Yi Xiao eyed his companion. "I can't afford to be seen. People keep mistaking you for a woman. Can you hide yourself among the sisters?"

A soft laugh. "I think I should be able to do so, yes. It won't be the first time."

"Then I'll stay out of sight in the stable and keep an eye out for trouble." Given, of course, that it didn't come looking for him.

∌)(∌

Estrella noticed the addition to her flock before they reached the gate. Wu Chang, dressed in Sister Susanna's long skirt, his dark hair allowed to fall around his face. One of Susanna's shawls was wrapped around his shoulders, tied in front in such a way as to conceal his lack of cleavage.

If he moved normally, his disguise would have been obvious. If he'd tried too hard to look feminine he'd have broken the illusion. He did neither, walking like a quiet young woman intent on doing her duty. She eyed him. Raised a brow. Received a slight nod in return. Well enough. With that many men outside, the chances Margarita's trainees could stop them were a great deal lower. They were good, strong, young women. They weren't bulletproof.

There was a small door in the larger gate, allowing the community to better control the number of people entering and exiting. With a half-dozen of Margarita's trainees settled on either side of the entrance, Estrella opened the door and allowed the young woman through, then closed it in the face of the man with the bag and rifle.

"I really am grateful to you. I don't suppose you have someone who could help an injured man? One of my companions broke his leg, coming down from our mine camp. We had to leave him further up the road."

There were several mine camps that could be reached by the north road. The young woman's story seemed true. If it weren't for Yi Xiao and Wu Chang's warning, Estrella would have accepted it at face value.

Thankful Wu Chang had chosen to disguise himself as a woman, Estrella turned to the young man. "Sister Jane. Would you be willing to assist that poor man?"

There was an odd look on Wu Chang's face. He almost looked afraid. Still, he said, "May I be accompanied?" He glanced significantly at Margarita, adding, "And make use of your horse?"

The first was something Estrella didn't want to agree to. They needed Margarita to help protect the community. At the same time, the look in Wu Chang's eyes worried her. There was some reason he wanted someone with him. "I suppose so. Margarita, please?"

With a grumble for the interruption, Margarita inclined her head and agreed.

∌)(∌

"Master, respect. It may not be a good idea for me to approach these people. Their necromancer is unexpectedly strong."

Yi Xiao, who'd been busy brushing Henrietta and talking nonsense to her while he waited for the strangers to leave, raised a brow at his companion. It was a good thing Sister Margarita didn't understand Chinese. "You're afraid he can control you?" he said in the same language.

"This one is deeply embarrassed to admit it. But, yes."

"What are you two discussing?" Sister Margarita sounded out of sorts. "And why did you insist I accompany you, youngster?"

Yi Xiao hesitated. Decided limited honesty was the best choice. "Sister, Wu Chang senses someone in their group whose magic could force obedience from him. He's particularly sensitive to...."

"The necromancer you mentioned? Why didn't you just say so?" At both Yi Xiao and Wu Chang's stare, Sister Margarita added, "I'm the only one who's noticed, of course, but you don't have a proper heartbeat. I'm not sure what sort of undead you are, but you've been behaving yourself a great deal better than some living souls, so I've no objection to you."

Somehow, Yi Xiao thought Wu Chang would be blushing bright red if his body allowed it. He ducked his head in an embarrassed fashion. "Then you understand, if I go out there, that necromancer could make things difficult for us. I think I could stop myself from obeying, but I'd rather not take the chance."

"You planning on letting Yi Xiao here go instead? He doesn't look much like you. Someone's liable to notice."

Wu Chang smiled. Took off his skirts, shirt and the shawl. "If master... Yi Xiao... rides, our height difference won't be obvious. If he wears this shawl and a hat, he can keep his face hidden."

Sister Margarita considered that. "All right. And I can help keep their attention on me. Get dressed, boy. And, please, remember you're pretending to be a sister of this community."

Dignity wasn't one of Yi Xiao's strong suits but he attempted it. "I do know how to dress and act like a woman, Sister Margarita. This isn't the first time I've had to disguise myself."

The older woman scoffed. "I've no doubt. Just try not to sashay around like a dance-hall girl looking for a partner."

It took a few minutes to get ready, by which time Dona Estrella sent someone over to check on them. "Dona's worried you're having problems," the girl said, eyes wide at the sight of Wu Chang with his shirt off.

She was obviously about to ask about the huge scar across his chest, but Sister Margarita stopped her. "Leave it, girl. Run back and tell Dona Estrella her horse was being difficult and we'll be out in a moment." She glared at Henrietta, adding, "It won't take long to get her mare in line."

Recognizing a prompt when he heard one, Yi Xiao set to work saddling the mare and preparing to leave. "Just do as you're told, little one," he told the beast. "We'll discuss your situation later, when our current problems are dealt with."

Given, of course, they managed to deal with them.

⇒)(⇐

Estrella wasn't sure why Yi Xiao had taken Wu Chang's place. She was just glad the fool boy was taking precautions. Riding that strange horse, his head bent, his face half-hidden by both shawl and a broad-rimmed hat, he looked the model of maidenly humility. As he and Margarita left the community, following two of Brigid's men back the way they'd come, she could only hope he knew what he was doing.

In the meantime, there was Brigid to deal with. "I'll have some of the novices draw water for you."

"Oh, but I hate to make trouble. Please, allow me to handle this task."

Arguing the matter would only create suspicion. Estrella accepted the young lady's request. "Then, if you don't mind.... What in the world is that?"

That was a sudden wooden groan from the new tree in the center of the courtyard. It was taller now than it'd been earlier. Just how big was it planning on growing? And why was it making that noise? It almost sounded like a warning.

"What a wonderful tree! You know how valuable its wood is in San Francisco?" Brigid stepped closer. Put her hand on the wood and immediately pulled back as if stung. "Oh, splinters."

"You should get that seen to. Here. Let my novices fill your canteens for you and we'll have our hospitaller look at it."

"But...."

"I insist. Really, you don't want an infection. I've known folk to lose their fingers." Estrella shamelessly began describing some of the worst effects of such injuries while drawing Brigid towards the hospital. "Let's just have Sister Susanna take a look at it."

When Estrella chose, she could be a force of nature. When one added Susanna to the mix, there were few who could stand in their path. Susanna would never, ever, let a patient escape without being fully and properly cared for.

While Susanna did her work, carefully examining their visitor's hand and making sure every last splinter was properly removed, Estrella asked, "I thought you said you were miners."

"I am. Some of my brothers are loggers."

"I admit, I'm impressed you managed to join them. Most of the mine camps around here only have men."

A fierce grin revealed slightly twisted teeth. "I'm not the sort men argue with." The young lady shrugged. Spread her hands. "And you, of all people, should appreciate a woman's need to choose her path without a man's guidance."

Well, truth to tell, Estrella did. "I agree. A woman should be able to do what they can, as honestly as any man."

Dourly, Brigid told her, "If a woman acts as a man, we're expected to do better."

Another frustrating truth. "I can't deny that." Estrella rose as Susanna finished bandaging Brigid's injured hand. "But you didn't come here to discuss such things. Would you care to join me for tea before you leave?"

"Oh, I couldn't possibly impose. I've already interrupted your busy day for too long. Besides, I should get back to my men and see about poor Henry up the way."

Having no justifiable reason to keep the woman occupied, Estrella led her back downstairs to the well. Already the canteens had been filled, as had been the one small barrel Brigid's men had brought with them.

Gathering her things, Brigid paused at the well, sniffing the water appreciatively. "It's good to know this is here. We've passed before, but never had reason to come this far towards the beach before. I'll have to stop in again when the opportunity presents itself."

Estrella led the woman back outside, where most of her men still waited with barely concealed impatience. Only when she'd sent Brigid on her way and firmly closed the door to keep anyone from peering in after her, did she go back to the well.

Under other circumstances, Estrella wouldn't have worried nearly as much. Under other circumstances she wouldn't have wasted her limited resources on something like this. She certainly didn't have any reason to act as she did.

Yet suspicion and worry made her pour every last grain of her purification powder into the well. Just in case.

⇒)(⇐

The mid-afternoon sunlight beat hot on Yi Xiao's head, making him glad of the hat. Not only did it protect him from the heat, but its broad rim concealed his face from the two men walking with them. He kept his head bent, maidenly modesty shining around him. What man would even consider touching a little sister like him?

Truthfully, there were plenty who would. But for the moment these two were pretending to chivalry, the one kindly guiding Henrietta so Yi Xiao didn't have to. The other staying off to the side, weapon ready should there be trouble. They weren't even bothering to talk to her, regarding her as shy.

What actually worried Yi Xiao was the small group of men who'd followed them. Only to be expected, of course. Their leader's story had been an obvious lie. Well, obvious to him at least. Aside from the fact that he knew all the mines and farms nearby, he was sure these were the men climbing the hill from the shore the night before.

Thus, he wasn't at all surprised when a voice called out behind them, "That's him, right there."

He didn't hesitate. Just leaned forward and caught hold of Sister Margarita's hand. "Up." To his relief, she understood immediately, tightening her grip and letting him tug her onto Henrietta's back. Immediately, he leaned forward and whispered into the horse's ear. "Run."

She was a small horse, barely big enough to carry two. Yet she set off at a speed few beasts could match, racing up the road kicking up dust behind them. Shots fired over their head, accompanied by angry shouts. Neither stopped her, though she flinched every time a bullet passed.

"Good girl."

"They're after you, then?" Sister Margarita clung to his back, voice calm. She could be out for a morning ride, not on the run with a distrusted man.

"I'd say so, yes."

"We shouldn't have let you stay."

She was likely right. "If I'd known they were hunting me, I wouldn't have." He sensed danger, shifted Henrietta's path, just as another bullet flew past. "Life's like that."

"True." She did something behind him, a motion not unlike a cultivationist's sealing gesture. Magic, though. Whatever it was, it caused the next bullet to go wide. "I can't keep this up for long. I'm better at close-in combat."

No surprise she was a sorceress of some sort. Dona Estrella was. Quite likely a number of the community's members were. "Faster, Henrietta. They're on foot. They can't match your speed."

"The road ahead gets too rough for horses," Sister Margarita warned.

"I know. That's why I'm going to get off in a minute and let you ride on."

Both the Sister and Henrietta made startled noises. He continued, "They have a way to trace me. It's not fast or certain, but I'm sure they'll figure out I'm in the trees. Once you have a clear path, turn around and get back home."

That didn't make Sister Margarita happy. She didn't like Yi Xiao, didn't like having a man anywhere near her community. She most definitely didn't like that he'd brought this trouble down on them just by existing. "I'm not abandoning you."

"If you're captured, I'll be forced to give myself up."

"Do you think I can't defend myself?"

"Of course not." Yi Xiao peered over his shoulder at her. Shifted Henrietta sideways again as another bullet flew past. "You're still a potential hostage."

"And if I come up on them from behind?"

"You'll be a less obvious target, but still a danger." He thought about it. "Of course, they're going to focus on me. Not on a weak woman escaping on a horse."

Her hands stiffened on his waist. Clenched into fists. "I'm not a weak woman."

"I'm certain you aren't, but do you think they'll believe it." Just because that lot was led by someone like Brigid didn't mean they'd consider a small, slender, young lady like Sister Margarita a danger. They weren't the sort to see past such superficialities.

After a moment, Sister Margarita agreed. "As soon as we're out of their sight, you get off. But I'm not leaving you behind. That *draugr* of yours might not catch up fast enough."

"I don't even know what that is," Yi Xiao protested. "And he isn't mine."

"Tell that to him." They rounded the corner, Henrietta putting on a burst of speed that increased the distance from Yi Xiao's hunters. She slowed enough to let him slide free, then set off running as fast as she could, Sister Margarita clutching her reins and clinging tight to her saddle.

Yi Xiao headed straight into the woods, tossing off his skirts and climbing the most likely tree as fast as he possibly could. His pursuit ran on up the road, determined not to let him escape, their curses and shouts echoing through the mountains. They'd turn around soon enough, he was sure.

"And now it's just the two of us," Deathshead said from above Yi Xiao.

⋺)(⋵

With the strangers locked outside and whatever mischief Brigid might have attempted on the well hopefully taken care of, Estrella turned her attention on Wu Chang. "Why did you send Yi Xiao, instead of going yourself?"

"I was afraid," the man admitted. "They have a sorcerer who might turn me against my master. I'm susceptible to that sort of thing."

Estrella wasn't sure what sort of magic that might be. "You should learn to shield yourself, child."

He laughed. "There are some magics I can't shield myself from, Dona Estrella. And, really, I think I'm much older than you." With a shrug, he added, "What was it you put in the water?"

"A purifying herb. I didn't like that woman's insistence that she get near our well." Estrella was about to say more, but the tree groaned again, another warning that set her worrying. "I wish I understood you," she told it.

"Do any of your sisters have an affinity with plants?"

Wu Chang had a good point and Estrella called for Susanna. "Could you see if you can communicate with our new guest?" Ordinarily, she'd be worried, given how the tree had managed to plant itself in their courtyard. Right then, they had too many other problems to worry about. Namely Brigid and each and every one of the men the woman brought with her.

Returning her attention to Wu Chang, Estrella noticed a flicker of concern in his eyes. He kept glancing north, as if expecting trouble. "What is it?"

"Am I failing my duty, letting my master go because I fear to be misused?" He smiled wryly. "Yet if my will fails me, I will fail my duty even more certainly; turned into a weapon against him."

"I've seen him at work, Wu Chang. I think he can handle whatever trouble is headed his way." To take the youngster's mind off his worries, she asked, "Do you think you could guard the gate, in case those outside try to break in?"

"I think they wouldn't come through the gate, even under the cover of night. It's too obvious." Wu Chang was about to say more, but Susanna suddenly stepped away from the tree. "Dona Estrella! They're attacking!" She wasn't pointing at the door, either, but back behind the dormitory.

Stunned, Estrella followed the young hospitaller's gesture. She saw nothing, but the long two story building hid the wall behind it. "Come," she ordered Wu Chang, never doubting he'd follow. "Sister Kenica, you too!" Kenica was Margarita's personal trainee, a big girl with little magic but both the brains and brawn to make up for it. "All guards, come!"

They ran around the back of the building, just as a big man in rough clothes dropped down from the wall. More like him were coming and Estrella wondered how her guards had failed to spot them. This wasn't the time to find out, but she hoped her charges weren't injured.

Wu Chang was on the first intruder before he'd properly gotten his bearings. A single blow to the chest sent the bigger man flying into the wall. He slumped there, stunned, while Wu Chang continued to the next.

There were too many by now for one man. Luckily, Kenica and the other guards were there to catch them. Wielding clubs and staves, they set on the intruders without hesitation. Only the sound of a bullet striking the wall forced them to back off.

"Can someone other than you use your herbs?" Wu Chang asked suddenly, as they cowered behind the wall of the dormitory, trapped by the rifleman's bullets. They were at a stalemate. The enemy couldn't jump down or come around the corner without losing their sniper's protection. They couldn't go after the attackers as long as that sniper was there.

"Yes. But...."

"Give me something to knock him out. I'll take care of that man."

"You can't." Even as she protested, Estrella brought out one of her most potent knockout powders.

"You'd be amazed at what I can do." Wu Chang took the bag from her. Headed away from the fight. "Don't worry. Just keep them from getting out."

Estrella had no idea what the man intended. The watch towers weren't connected to the wall and there was no easy way to get up there. Not to mention the wall was narrow and covered in sharp stones. She didn't know how the rifleman was staying in place. Sheer stubborn determination, it looked like.

Shadowy movement drew Estrella's attention. Wu Chang, dropping from the watchtower's shadows to the wall below. The rifleman hadn't noticed him but it was only a matter of time. She shifted forwards, as if trying to peer around the corner, causing the man to fire in her direction.

At the same time, Wu Chang ran lightly along the wall, seemingly unconcerned by the sharp edges and narrow surface. He was fast, a blur in the sunlight. Even so, the rifleman noticed him and fired, weapon raised just barely in time. Estrella gasped, seeing Wu

Chang's shirt billow and blacken, sure he'd been killed.

Instead, the man flung the powder she'd given him into his attacker's face. The two stared at each other for a moment, motionless. Then the rifleman tumbled forward to the ground. Wu Chang paused, waved a gloved hand at Estrella, and disappeared down the other side of the wall. Shouts followed, accompanied by the sounds of someone being punched and punched hard.

Estrella hesitated. Decided to fix what had to be fixed first. "Children, we have uninvited guests. Please assist me in properly welcoming them."

⋺)(⋵

Yi Xiao didn't bother being startled by Deathshead's sudden appearance. "Why so it is. At least until those gentlemen come back looking for me." He'd expected Deathshead to show up at a time convenient to him and him alone. Naturally, that wouldn't be the case for the one he wanted to meet. "At which point, given I'm still in a position to do so, my attention will be occupied."

Deathshead flipped down to crouch on one of the other branches. "Now did I say I was going to hurt you?"

"You haven't said what you plan, Deathshead. A man like yourself is liable to do anything." Yi Xiao smiled brightly.

"So you have my attention. What is it you want?"

"Where's that ghost of yours?"

"Not here, so you don't need to worry about him biting you again. No promises what he'll do later. What do you want?"

Deathshead wasn't convinced. He searched around, leaping from tree to tree, sniffing the air. At last he came back. "You're sure he's not around?"

Amused despite himself, Yi Xiao said, "Not yet. Once again I ask, what do you want?"

The man landed on a branch in front of Yi Xiao, one that ought not have supported his weight at all. "That man Bly."

"An unpleasant individual."

"A thief." Before Yi Xiao could point out the irony of that accusation, Deathshead continued, "You've seen all the little broken ones."

"If you mean the spirits of this land, the ones without people to remember them, then yes."

"You like them. You approve of them. Will you help them?"

Yi Xiao frowned. "How?"

"Bly has more like the ones you freed. Many more. Break his hold. Free the others." A sly look crossed Deathshead's face. "I know your type, hero who thinks. You're kin but not kin to me, and you'll do, little rabbit. You won't leave those poor broken ones to be used."

Trouble was, Deathshead was right. He couldn't. "Once I'm done here, I'll do what I can. You know where he's got them?"

"I don't. The pretty horse and her tree, though? They might."

Yi Xiao agreed. "Then yes. Can't promise success...."

"No one can promise success."

"But I'll try."

By this time the sound of men shouting and arguing came from the road below Yi Xiao. Hidden among the branches, all Yi Xiao could see were small flashes of color. Then one man stepped into a clear spot, clutching a large, slightly bloodied, sack.

A man's voice came from the bag. "...here... ...here... he's... here. Let me go. Let me go. Found him. Let me go."

"Well that's not something you see everyday," Deathshead murmured. "Wonder what's in there. Looks sorta wet to me. Smells like death. Tasty."

Yi Xiao would be hard put to call death tasty. He also wasn't going to draw attention to himself by discussing the subject. Instead he waited, watching the men step cautiously into the woods. A half dozen of them, one armed with a rifle, the rest with pistols. He grabbed a pinecone from the tree. Tossed it.

The noise had the desired effect. The men headed that way, moving slow and cautious. Or they did until the bag said, "Up. Up. Let me go."

"Damn." Whatever was in the bag was what these men were using to hunt him. Yi Xiao tumbled down the tree branches, flipping and spinning from one to the next, ignoring needles, bugs and splinters as he came down just beside the man holding the bag.

Pausing only long enough to check his surroundings, Yi Xiao grabbed the bag from the man, tossing it further into the woods. Its contents said, "Ow. Ow. Let me go. Ow."

"My apologies. We'll discuss freeing you later, sir. Just as soon as I'm finished here." Without hesitation, Yi Xiao kicked the bag's former holder in the chest. As the man fell, Yi Xiao dropped to a crouch and grabbed a fallen branch, sending it flying between the next man's legs. The man tripped, stumbling forward, and Yi Xiao slammed his fist into the man's jaw.

Two were down; the other four were just coming round with their weapons. They fired, but Yi Xiao flipped backwards into the bushes, narrowly avoiding being shot. He drew his lightning together. Sent a ball of it spinning into the one with the rifle and dropping him.

Three down. Before Yi Xiao could move again, the last three fired. Except this time their bullets went astray, flattening as if the air itself had hardened. Sister Margarita was back, coming up behind the three and hitting the nearest with a fist covered in what looked like solid cloud.

Four down. Yi Xiao leapt for one man, even as Sister Margarita, tiny and fragile though she looked, broke the jaw of the other. They straightened, taking deep breaths, and grinned at each other while Deathshead, who'd dropped down to watch, applauded.

The noise made Sister Margarita turn. Glower. "You. What are you doing here?"

"Nothing Maggie milove! Not a thing. Not even helping, right?" Deathshead grinned, rising to his feet and brushing leaves from his trousers. "And now I'm gone. Don't forget your promise, little prince." He faded, disappearing little by little until all that was left was the fuzzy tail on his hat. Then that, too, was gone.

⋧⋉⋦

Accompanied by her guards, Estrella came out of the community's gate and walked round the wall to the other side. Everything had quieted down by now and there'd been no more sign of the intruders. All she could do was hope Wu Chang hadn't been hurt, protecting them from their attackers.

They found unconscious bodies scattered for yards. Broken guns lay wrecked, bent in half by some powerful force. What was Wu Chang? Estrella wondered, suddenly glad he was on their side. Spotting him sitting atop the unconscious Brigid, she hurried over to him. "Are you all right?"

He tilted his head, smiling wryly. "As all right as I can ever be," he promised, though his shirt was filled with bullet holes and his pale chest equally marked. If there'd been blood she'd have been terrified for him. Instead, she was terrified of him. "I'm sorry. I would have kept you from seeing this if I could."

"You're... not alive."

"No. I am not." Rising, he stepped back. "I have no wish to harm you or your community," he promised. "Even if I weren't bound to serve my master's wishes, I wouldn't want to harm you."

"What are you? Vampire? Ghoul?" Was this what he'd meant when he'd said he was older than her?

"I'm afraid I don't know those terms. I have no heart, but no desire to harm." He sighed, seeing her continued fear. "I will remain outside the community until my master is ready to leave. It won't be long."

He turned away, looking so dejected that she couldn't help herself. "No. Wait. You haven't hurt anyone. Besides, you'd both be sleeping outside anyway. I'm scared but I trust you." Seeing his expression lighten, she added, "I don't suppose you can help us get these people locked up until we work out what to do with them?"

"Of course I will." He looked ruefully at his clothes. "Also, I don't suppose you have something I can wear in the meantime?"

They were half-way done with the task when Yi Xiao, Sister Margarita and Henrietta came back to fetch a cart. "Oh, good to see you've handled your side of things. Good job, Wu Chang. Not too much damage, I hope?"

"I'm rattling a little from all the bullets, but it shouldn't be long before I rid myself of them," Wu Chang answered, bowing. "Do you need my assistance?"

"No, finish up here. Dona Estrella, I do apologize. This lot is my responsibility. They've been hunting me for a little while, it seems." Yi Xiao held up a sack, opening it enough to show a wild-eyed human head that kept muttering to be let go. "I don't suppose you have someone who can lay a dead man's head to rest properly?"

Estrella sighed. She should have expected there'd be problems, dragging a young troubler like Yi Xiao into her community. Still, "I'm sure I can find someone to set any dead who wants to be to rest. Afterwards, there's still the question of what I'm going to do about that tree and Henrietta over there."

Both horse and tree made squeaky little noises as if begging for mercy, while Wu Chang carefully stepped behind Yi Xiao. "I can't speak for those two," he said, "But until I find my heart and the thief who stole it, I'd much rather stay above ground, thank you."

With a laugh, Yi Xiao murmured, "Besides, I've gone and accepted a new commission and I'm going to need to discuss it with those two." When Estrella eyed him, he added, "I don't think it has anything to do with you, fortunately."

He might be right, but Estrella had a feeling she wasn't going to be rid of the problem entirely for quite some time to come.

Chapter 4
Fire – Seeking Freedom

By the time night fell, they'd gathered the intruders together and settled them in the closest thing to a jail the community had. As many guards as possible were placed on the wine cellar and the intruders had been given sleeping drugs to keep them from causing trouble.

That handled, Dona Estrella ordered the novices and younger sisters to see to their supper, while she, Sister Margarita and Sister Susanna saw to the adults' food. While they ate, Sister Susanna dragged Wu Chang to the side to help remove the bullets embedded in his torso, while Henrietta snuck in to join them in a form better suited to eating bread and highly spiced beef stew. Apparently whatever kind of horse she was, she wasn't a vegetarian.

"We need to decide what to do with these people," Dona Estrella said, once she'd finished scolding Henrietta for trying to eat by sticking her face straight into the bowl.

Back home a village attacked by bandits like this would have been well in its rights to execute them. According to Dona Estrella, they could have done so as well. To Yi Xiao's relief, however, she added, "But that's not our way. We'll have to take the men to the authorities."

"Only the men?"

Dona Estrella smiled. "I'd like to see if this Brigid woman can be rehabilitated. If nothing else, it wouldn't be appropriate to put her in jail with the rest."

Yi Xiao wasn't sure the idea was feasible, but he approved of rehabilitation over execution. That still left over a dozen prisoners they'd have to drag to the authorities. It wouldn't be easy to manage, either; especially given the community would have to use their only cart. They'd also need to keep the prisoners sedated. "Is there no better road than the mountain trail?" Yi Xiao asked. The sooner they got them dealt with, the better.

"None. The only other way would be by boat and we don't have anything like that."

Wu Chang lifted a hand, only to be scolded by Sister Susanna for moving. She was cutting into his chest and didn't want the distraction. "Just talk," she ordered. "Quietly, and don't move around too much. Just because it'll heal doesn't mean you have to ruin yourself."

"Yes, Sister." Meekly, Wu Chang continued, "Our prisoners came here by longboat. Perhaps it would be quickest and easiest to take them along the coast to San Francisco."

Looking a little annoyed that she hadn't thought of that, Margarita said, "If they came by longboat that implies a ship. What if its crew notices?"

Yi Xiao had scanned the ocean for *The Calico Cat* once they'd gotten Brigid and her men properly restrained. He'd seen no sign of a ship on the horizon. That didn't mean it wasn't somewhere out there, of course, but he'd a feeling it was a good distance away.

"If their ship is out there and still has crew, they're likely to be trying to find out what happened soon. We're better off moving before they do," he pointed out. "It would help if we make it look like our uninvited guests are simply moving on." Too, if they left the longboat where it was, it'd make Brigid's crew think she was still at the community. Better by far to avoid that possibility.

Dona Estrella considered the suggestion. "It'd need fewer guards and we'd be finished faster. I agree. Margarita, choose four of your students, preferably ones with sailing experience, and have them go with Yi Xiao and Wu Chang tomorrow morning."

With a bow, Sister Margarita said, "It's not my favorite solution, but short of killing them out of hand, it's the only one that works quickly. The sooner we're rid of them, the better. I'll go along to explain things to the authorities."

"Then that leaves us with our other problem. Or problems." Dona Estrella gestured towards the tree in the middle of their courtyard. It'd grown again, though not quite as much, nor quite as fast, as before. "The tree and Henrietta."

Henrietta, currently in her human child form, curled tight and stared wide-eyed at Dona Estrella. "Sorry."

"Sorry isn't quite good enough. You still haven't told us where the Mother's stone is.

Much less why you came here and what you intend."

"Haven't had a chance to tell you," Henrietta protested. Her coloring shifted as she talked, so what had been a dark brown-haired child of about seven became a blond-haired girl in her teens. She didn't seem to notice the change, however. "Mother's stone is with Woody." She gestured at the tree for emphasis.

"That's the tree's name?" Yi Xiao guessed. It seemed a bit too obvious.

"That's what the master called him." Henrietta shuddered suddenly and Yi Xiao remembered what Deathshead had said about her and the tree. "He'd like a better, but...."

Wu Chang offered, "Oren, perhaps? It means pine tree in Hebrew." When everyone looked at him, a little surprised that he'd know such a thing, he shrugged. "I'm five-hundred years old. It'd be more surprising if I hadn't learned any odd and mostly useless facts."

"Lie still, unless you want me to cut your lung open."

"It'll go back together when you're done. And, frankly, you're being too gentle. It tickles."

While Wu Chang and Sister Susanna argued genially on the subject of bullet removal, Yi Xiao returned to the question at hand. "Whatever name your friend chooses is up to him, I think. But what do you mean, the stone is with him?"

Henrietta pointed down below the tree. "He took it in his roots for safekeeping. To keep that bastard from getting at it."

Dona Estrella set a hand on Henrietta's shoulder. "We try to avoid such language here, child. But based on what I've been told, I understand the sentiment. Bly?"

The little girl, now looking no more than three and sporting bright red hair, agreed. "He stole us. Bound us. We got away when you fought him."

Reminded of the fight, Yi Xiao asked, "Was your friend the tree who helped capture my friends back at Corte Madera?" At her scared expression, he told her, "Don't worry. We don't hold any grudges. I'd just like to verify."

"Yes," she told him finally. "And he rode me to get there. So when he got knocked out, we took a chance and ran. We didn't dare go home to the Mother, though. He'd know to chase us that way. So we went west and when we felt the stone... well we had to go to it."

Thoughtfully, Dona Estrella said, "Do you think he can trace you here?"

"I don't know," Henrietta admitted. "The only thing we could think was to get the Mother's power so we could protect ourselves. Woody...," she stopped, glanced ruefully at the tree, "I mean, Oren, took as much as he could so he could protect this place."

There was no doubt the tree spirit had done so for his own sake, but his presence would benefit the community as well. Yi Xiao didn't say so. It wasn't his place to tell Dona Estrella how to run things. "Will he act in our benefit as well as his own?" the woman asked finally.

"Yes." Henrietta stamped one foot and nodded her head bravely. "He promises."

"And you. Will you be of use to us? No more attempts to trick us with false knowledge?"

"I promise." Henrietta looked at Dona Estrella with wide and sincere eyes. "And I'll try not to change so much. It isn't easy, though."

"We can deal with it, as long as you don't try to pretend you're not yourself." Dona Estrella returned her attention to Yi Xiao. "You said something about a promise to Deathshead."

"I did," Yi Xiao agreed. "These two aren't the only ones to suffer at Bly's hands. I've promised to try and free the others. Given I can find them and figure out how."

Quite suddenly, Henrietta grasped his arm. "Please. Let me help."

He frowned at her. "Are you sure?" To his eyes she was just a child, despite her apparent ability to appear adult on occasion. "It'll be dangerous."

"He has my friends. And you need someone who knows how to find him."

Yi Xiao turned a helpless gaze on Dona Estrella. "She knows the danger," the woman pointed out. "And you do need a guide. Bly doesn't stay in one spot for long. He's got too many enemies for that."

With a sigh, because this meant he now had two extra people to worry about, Yi Xiao agreed. "After we get Brigid and her men taken care of, then."

The girl grinned. "I can travel with you, no worries. I'm a water horse, after all."

⇌⟩⟨⇋

Henrietta pranced on the shore. She wasn't a foal anymore, but she wasn't terribly old, either. Just big enough to carry a rider without strain. Still young enough to enjoy the fresh ocean air and the feel of the water around her hooves.

"We'll be ready soon, Henrietta," Yi Xiao called. "If you want to start swimming now, go ahead."

Swimming wasn't what she'd be doing, but Yi Xiao didn't know her kind at all. Given permission to do so, she leapt into the ocean, letting her body become one with the water. Then she rose up, several times bigger than before, and whinnied, sending a wave splashing over her new companions. Well, splashing over the dead one. Yi Xiao flipped backwards too fast to be hit.

Wu Chang brushed bits of sand off himself while Yi Xiao laughed. "I know you're in high spirits, but we really can't play right now." He didn't seem awed by her size, either. Of course, it seemed like he was incapable of being intimidated.

Neither was Sister Margarita. Henrietta had been careful not to let her get splashed. If anyone was intimidating around here, it was the sister. She was small but she was mighty. Her magic, affecting fluid things like air and water, could drop Henrietta's current shape like a stone or send her flying into the sky.

"Child, control your behavior." Sister Margarita approached the water. "Are you sure you'll be able to pull the longboat without capsizing it?"

Henrietta bowed her head. She wasn't skilled enough yet to talk in this form, so the best she could do was gesture. That and use the foam to spell out words. 'Certain am I yes.'

"I make note that while your handwriting, or whatever we should call it, is excellent, your grammar could do with some work. We'll discuss that more, later." The sister turned her attention back on the others. "Are our guests properly tied down and sedated?"

One of her guards, the one called Kenica, answered. "Yes, Sister Margarita. And I've made sure the necromancer's hands are tied and his mouth covered. Just in case."

Necromancers weren't the sort of sorcerer Henrietta knew much about. But since Wu Chang, being dead, would be in danger if this one were able to use his powers, it made sense for Kenica to make doubly sure of him.

"Thank you, Sister Kenica. I appreciate your consideration."

To Henrietta's surprise, Kenica blushed at Wu Chang's response. It was a strange sight on someone as big and imposing as she. Humans usually saw women Kenica's size as tough and no-nonsense. Of course, humans didn't always get things right when it came to how people behaved.

The other two guards Sister Margarita had chosen joined them, each carrying a bludgeon and wearing daggers. The latter made Henrietta nervous. Iron wasn't her friend and she wanted to be as far from the blades as possible. 'I go water', she told them.

'Tie rope bridle.'

That was how they were going to move the longboat down to San Francisco quickly. All she had to do was swim ahead and swim fast. All they had to do was keep the boat properly balanced and warn her if she went too quickly. She'd be good, though. Yi Xiao had promised to rescue her friends if he could and that was more than enough reason to do her best.

At last they were ready. Yi Xiao at the front, calling out directions. Wu Chang at the rudder, keeping the boat aimed the right way. Towards the center, hidden among the unconscious bodies of their prisoners, sat Sister Margarita and her four assistants.

With luck, they'd get to San Francisco unnoticed. With luck, their prisoners' allies wouldn't follow them. Admittedly, luck wasn't the sort of thing Henrietta had much faith in. Yi Xiao, on the other hand, she felt like she could trust entirely, mere human though he was.

⇒)(⇐

Yi Xiao had to admit Henrietta's water horse form was impressive. Several yards long, her lower body melded with the water so it could hardly be seen. He thought it'd resemble a fish's tail, though he wasn't certain. Her upper half rose and shifted with the waves, sometimes resembling sea foam, sometimes a huge and elegant horse's head and fine boned forelegs.

Attached to Henrietta's impressive form, the longboat moved fast. Not quite as fast as Burton's *Henrietta Marie*, but quickly enough that it took barely half-an-hour to reach the north end of the entrance to San Francisco Bay. They planned to land just past the southern arm of the bay, right near the tip of the southern peninsula, so as to make it easier to get their prisoners to the local jail. There was a small army base there and hopefully someone available to help.

It amused Yi Xiao to realize that he was, once more, crossing the water with a Henrietta. He doubted Burton would appreciate the comparison. The captain was fond of his ship and likening her to a water horse would probably not go over well. For that matter, he doubted Henrietta would appreciate it either.

He'd spent some time the night before remembering Second Mother's fairy tales. If any of them were true, he'd found himself some true danger to walk with. Some breeds of water horses could be as perilous as certain types of *yaoguai* in China. Of course, he'd long since learned that demons, monsters and spirits were all individuals, just like humans. How they treated one depended on their personal perspective.

As far as he could tell, Henrietta wouldn't go out of her way to hurt anyone. She might cause trouble, but it'd be out of ignorance, not malice. All he could do was keep an eye on her and make sure she learned what things should and shouldn't be done.

Seeing they were getting close to shore and not wanting to draw attention, Yi Xiao told Henrietta, "I'm cutting your bridle now. Stay hidden until I find a safe place for you to come ashore."

Henrietta obeyed without argument, though she whinnied mischievously, slapping the water with her tail so a spurt of it almost hit him in the face. Then she faded away, melting down to seeming nothingness. Yi Xiao glimpsed a ripple that might have been her, but it was gone before he could be sure.

Now they had to row to shore, no easy task for a longboat as full as this one. It was difficult, but they couldn't let Henrietta help them all the way in. Someone would surely notice how impossibly fast they were going. They'd been lucky so far, avoiding curious eyes. They couldn't depend on that luck all the way.

Passing Fort Point Rock, they landed on a marshy beach, where a half-dozen men in uniform were exercising. One, a big fellow with cropped brown hair, walked towards them with a stern expression. "This is a military facility, not a dock. Take that thing and get out of here."

Sister Margarita climbed out of the longboat, smiling sweetly at the big man. "We do apologize. But it's been quite a strain getting here and we have some people who attacked our community over on Majeure beach."

Faced with a tiny, pale, elegant young woman like Sister Margarita, the soldier's tone shifted. "Majeure beach? Where's that?"

"On the north peninsula. We didn't have a big enough cart, so we used the same longboat these people came to us in." She smiled, unashamedly taking advantage of her small size and gender. "Even if you and your men can't help us, would you be willing to guard these people until we can get help?"

"Now young lady, I can't ask you to wait that long. We have a nice big cart and more than enough strong arms to help out."

With a little curtsey, Sister Margarita told him, "Sir, I can't tell you how much I appreciate it."

⇒)(⇐

Henrietta waited until almost nightfall before sneaking out of the water to join Yi Xiao and Wu Chang. By this time the prisoners had been carted away and Sister Margarita and her companions had gone with them. "We're to meet at my local contact's place," Yi Xiao told her, once she'd chosen a human form. "Best not to get too much attention."

That meant she needed to keep to a single shape rather than let her mood shift her. Though she wasn't fond of it, she chose a shape at random. Slight, dark-haired, with emerald eyes and light skin, hidden in a costume of blue and green colored taffeta.

"Sister Margarita might object to a perfect twin," Yi Xiao suggested. "And you might want to change the clothes to something less noticeable?"

She liked both shape and clothing and wanted to argue. Except Wu Chang added, "Unless you'd be mistaken for a saloon barmaid, you'll want something less flashy."

The dead one was right, Henrietta supposed. She shifted her clothing, but not her basic form, so she was dressed more like Sister Margarita. Out of respect for the sister, she reluctantly changed her hair to a muddy brownish gold and her eyes to a dark blue.

"Good. Good." Yi Xiao patted her on the head and she found herself reflecting that the same gesture from Bly had once made her step as hard as she could on the man's foot. Odd how she didn't feel like hurting Yi Xiao for it. Quite the opposite, in fact.

Unaware of her confusion, Yi Xiao gestured towards the town. "We'd best get moving. Sister Margarita will be wondering where we are."

The last time Henrietta had been in San Francisco, she'd been saddled, bridled and carefully bound to Bly's service. If he hadn't lost his grip on her back at the Mother's mountain, she probably still would be. Now, freed of all constraint, she looked around the lamplit streets with wide-eyed fascination.

"I seem to be surrounded by children," Yi Xiao murmured, sounding amused. It took a moment for her to realize that Wu Chang was gawking as well. "You've been here before, right?"

"Of course," Wu Chang told him. "But we're being followed and it might be for the best if I don't look too intimidating. Not that I do that at all well, I fear."

Henrietta didn't think anyone could fail to be intimidated by a dead man walking. Wu Chang's true nature would have been terrifying if he weren't carefully controlling his undead aura. "What follows?" she couldn't help asking softly.

"Deathshead, for one. He's staying back, though, so I think he just wishes to be entertained by our doings."

The name was unfamiliar to Henrietta, but she supposed Yi Xiao and Wu Chang must know a lot of different people. "For two?"

"Some men. Human. Normal as normal can be. They may just be bandits."

Bandits? Why would bandits be looking for them? When Henrietta tried to look around, tried to spot these people, Yi Xiao caught her hand, whispering, "No, little one. Don't let them realize we've noticed." As she quieted, he added, "We may have attracted attention just from our involvement with those pirates. Or they could just be wanderers who think we look an easy target."

Henrietta couldn't think how anyone would believe that. Oh, her current form wasn't impressive, but Sister Margarita wasn't the sort you crossed thoughtlessly. As for Yi Xiao and Wu Chang, they were far too strong for any common thief to harm. Only idiots would go after men like her companions, surely.

⇒)(⇐

Yi Xiao noted Henrietta's confident look with a mix of appreciation and chagrin. For some reason, she appeared certain the three of them could handle any sort of trouble sent their way. She was wrong, of course. He and his companion were excellent fighters, but they weren't perfect.

Admittedly, the men following them didn't seem all that skilled. After all, they'd been noticed. The question was, were they being deliberately obvious or just really bad at their 'jobs'? "I don't know about you, Wu Chang, but I need a drink." He spoke loud enough to be overheard.

"I too could do with something." Wu Chang scanned the street. "Nothing too extensive. Just a sip or so."

"Well, shall we see what we can find? I'm sure there's a place on Du Pont that'll serve us properly."

"I believe you're correct, Master. Where is it you suggest?"

"Old Mr. Chang's place sounds absolutely capital."

Wu Chang tilted his head thoughtfully. "Capitol? I don't believe the Jin Long has anything to do with heads of government. Unless, of course, you believe their claim to be descended from a real gold dragon."

Yi Xiao wasn't sure if Wu Chang were pulling his leg or if it were simply his English not being up to British slang. He set to teasing his companion as they walked, maintaining the pretense that they were completely unaware of their surroundings. Deliberately, he didn't include Henrietta in the argument, though he squeezed her fingers reassuringly. With luck, she'd understand why he ignored her.

From previous experience, Yi Xiao knew he couldn't expect much help from the town's tiny police department. Unless things had changed a great deal, they remained a half-step up from hired thugs, as likely to rob you and leave you stripped of everything except—if you were lucky—your life.

They could wait until they reached Chang's place, of course. The old man's hired thugs were better equipped and better trained than the local police. They were also fiercely loyal to their master. And since Chang was reasonably loyal to Yi Xiao's grandmother, he would certainly provide some protection.

If the walk from Henrietta's landing point to Old Chang's place didn't take quite so long, Yi Xiao likely would have chosen to wait. The roads were too steep and there was enough of crowd to make for slow going. There were plenty of dark alleys and hidden corners for mischief as well. If he didn't make a move quickly, he suspected their followers would make one first.

Choosing one of those dark alleys, Yi Xiao quietly ordered Wu Chang to wait and let their pursuers pass. "Henrietta, stay with me and do exactly as I tell you." He didn't have high hopes for her obedience but he was fairly sure she couldn't be easily hurt.

Since his arrival in the area, Yi Xiao had spent a great deal of time exploring. He preferred wilderness over cities and towns, of course, but he always liked knowing where he was. This particular alley came to a dead-end among a group of two-story wooden buildings, making it a perfect trap.

The alley was dark, a good sign that no one was likely to walk in on them. "Corner, Henrietta. Stay there unless I ask for help."

To his relief, the little water-horse obeyed. He didn't know her abilities yet and right that moment wasn't the time to find out. Once she was settled, Yi Xiao turned to face the entrance to the little cul-de-sac, waiting for the half-dozen men to enter.

The moon was closer to full by now but hidden by the buildings. Yi Xiao didn't need its light, nor the starlight shining dim on the garbage strewn ground, to know when the others came. He stood quietly, listening to their breath as they walked.

Their dim silhouettes weren't tall but they were burly. They were mostly silent, but Yi Xiao caught a familiar word or two as one tripped over a bottle and nearly crashed into the one ahead of him. He hadn't heard that language since he'd visited his grassland cousins.

"I presume the one who came seeking me last week was with you?" he asked in that same language. "You are with the *Nian* rebels?"

The men came to a halt. One, the obvious leader, spoke calmly. "Prince. You have led us a merry chase. But it's time to come home."

"First, I am not a Prince. Second, if there was a game, it was one I was not informed of. Third, your home is not my home."

A light flared as one of the men brought out a lantern. As expected, the men were all northern Chinese. Several different tribes, but the only one Yi Xiao knew for certain was the man sporting a medallion with a familiar symbol. "Cousin," the man told him, "You are descended from the White Wolf, just as I. Of course my home is your home."

Giving the man a polite bow, Yi Xiao told him, "Cousin, I acknowledge our kinship. But I am my grandmother's loyal servant. Until she and she alone gives me permission, I shall not be returning to China, much less to the grasslands."

"Regrets, cousin, but I must insist. There are but three of you and you are trapped."

Yi Xiao smiled. "Regrets, cousin, but I stand alone and it's you who are trapped." As he spoke, a shadow moved behind the group and tossed the last man to the ground.

ﮯ)(ﮯ

Henrietta fought her instinctive urge to run. A natural coward, she really didn't like fighting. If it weren't for her admiration for Sister Margarita and her respect for Yi Xiao and Wu Chang, she'd be gone in an instant. It'd be easy, too. Just shift to water and she could easily slip past the fight.

Instead, she forced herself to stay where she was, to watch the fight and try to learn. She couldn't manage Yi Xiao's particular skill, of course. His strange talent for summoning his inner energies and transforming them to lightning was a magic she didn't understand.

She understood Wu Chang's fighting style better. Fast movements and immense strength; both within her abilities. He dodged below one big fist, catching it and twisting it around. It couldn't have been as effortless as it seemed but walking dead like him were stronger than they looked. She moved her hands, trying to visualize how he'd caught the man.

"Drop your weight, too," Wu Chang told her as he passed. "You'll find it works better. Like this." He stepped in, dropped down several inches. Slammed the next man in the chest hard enough to send him flying.

"Try not to hurt them too badly, please," Yi Xiao reminded. "There aren't many good doctors around."

"Respect, Master, I shall try to be careful.... Apologies. Yi Xiao, that is."

Yi Xiao laughed, catching his own attacker by the wrist and flinging him over his shoulder. "At this point I'm just glad you remember I have a name."

The only man left standing growled in a language Henrietta didn't understand at all. It was likely a curse, however, based on its tone. He drew a huge sword, speaking commandingly if incomprehensibly.

For Henrietta's benefit, Yi Xiao answered in English. "My saber remains sheathed, cousin. If you'd like to cross blades with someone, do so with Wu Chang here."

Wu Chang obligingly drew his weapons, one shining bright silver, the other a dull blue-black in the light from the fallen lantern. He bowed. "This humble bodyguard has been called The Hollowed Blade. May I know the name of the one I am about to knock unconscious?"

The name caused the man's eyes to widen. He stared at the swords, sweat dripping down the sides of his face. Then, without a word, he turned and ran.

As he sheathed his weapons, Wu Chang murmured, "My reputation precedes me, I see."

⇒)(⇐

Yi Xiao was highly amused by his bodyguard's mild embarrassment. "The Hollowed Blade? Not much better than your given name, is it?"

"An undead bodyguard assassin cannot hope to have an auspicious epithet, Wanderer." Wu Chang helped settle the men in more comfortable positions before joining him. "Shall we continue?

"One moment." Yi Xiao paused, noticing their attacker's lantern had fallen and broken in the fight. "Henrietta, would you mind washing that oil away?"

She agreed in a puzzled way. "Why?"

"The town's mostly built of wood. I don't want to risk burning it down." There'd been several fires in the area already. Yi Xiao didn't want to be responsible for the next.

"Oh." Henrietta shifted her form, becoming a flood of water that soaked their boots as it cleaned the cul-de-sac. "That good?"

"Excellent." Yi Xiao turned his attention on Wu Chang. "Now then, we need to find Sister Margarita and make sure everything is well with her." Not to mention talk to Chang about all these visitors from China who seemed to think he was a precious bauble to be captured. It was nice to be wanted, but not that much.

"Why were they after you, Yi Xiao," Henrietta asked as they headed back out the alley.

It was such a long story, but Yi Xiao attempted as simple explanation as possible as they walked. Even so, Henrietta just looked more confused when they reached the corner of Grant and Washington. "But how would they think you'd do what they want just because they tell you to? You're stubborn as a mule, as far as I can tell."

"Everyone has leverages," Yi Xiao told her. "There are those I'd protect if I were in such a position. Though, honestly, I wouldn't suggest anyone put my family in danger. We may appear to be frightened rabbits, but we bite and we bite hard."

She obviously still didn't understand, but she didn't press. "Is this the place?" she asked dubiously as they approached a single story building on the corner. "It doesn't look like much." Nor was she wrong. The building was plain wood, painted yellow and red, with a single entrance. There were no markings and no sign of lights or life. "Not like any of the taverns Bly goes to."

"I'm sure," Yi Xiao admitted, leading them through the door and into the darkened hall. Stopping there, he spoke in Chinese, "Ching Shi's blood rocks the world."

"The Gold Dragon welcomes you," a voice said in response. "Enter."

Instead of a door opening, the floor slid back, revealing a stairway down into a softly lit passage. Without hesitation, Yi Xiao went down, his companions close behind. Within minutes they were in a larger room with several dozens tables, a stage where a lovely young woman was singing something from home and a number of diners and drinkers going about their business.

Sister Margarita was sitting in a corner with her companions and a simply dressed old man whose queue had seen better days. Clean shaven, with narrow, patrician, features, he might have been a retired scholar or bureaucrat enjoying the atmosphere of home.

At Yi Xiao's approach, however, he rose and bowed, far too low for Yi Xiao's tastes. "This humble servant is honored to serve the young master, Wanderer. Please, inform this one of how else he may be of assistance?"

Discomfited by the formal language and knowing it'd be rude to say so, Yi Xiao bowed in return. "This humble priest is honored by the recognition of his grandmother's rank and offers his thanks for all Master Chang has done for us." It was a tricky judgment call in etiquette. Mr. Chang was head of a large and powerful triad back in China. He'd take offense if Yi Xiao offered him greater respects than a great-grandson of the Emperor ought. Even if that great-grandson had no title and was nothing more than a wandering priest.

A glint in Mr. Chang's eyes told Yi Xiao the old man was amused. Quite suddenly his posture shifted and he stood straight. "We are, of course, in America. Our positions back home hardly matter, now do they, youngster?"

Relieved of the need to maintain just exactly the right level of haughty majesty, Yi Xiao grinned in return. "I agree." Speaking in English, he asked Sister Margarita, "Did everything go well?"

"Mostly. Chief Fallon didn't spare much time for me." Sister Margarita sniffed. "Apparently there was a riot on Jackson street earlier and his jail was almost full already."

Mr. Chang coughed. "To be fair, our chief of police lacks men and resources. The proprietor of the Philadelphia Follies saw fit to offer free shots of whiskey to his first hundred customers. This, in turn, led to his rival at the Red Wolf to double the offer."

At a guess, the result was a street full of drunks and two bar-owners perfectly happy to push their problem drinkers at the other. With, of course, an eye towards shutting their rival down entirely. "By which I expect there's a few more prisoners in Chief Fallon's hands than he knows what to do with?"

"Exactly." Sister Margarita smiled wryly. "Fortunately, though the Chief's faults are many, he's dealt fairly with us in the past. I convinced him our bunch was dangerous and liable to come back to the community if they weren't kept under guard."

More likely they'd be after Yi Xiao if they worked out where he was again. He wasn't sure why that lot wanted him so badly, but he didn't plan on relaxing about them anytime soon. "Good enough for now, then." He turned his attention on Mr. Chang. "Sir, could I make a request of you outside the usual?"

The usual request was, of course, for the money his grandmother had supplied him. This surely went beyond the bargain, however. When Mr. Chang inclined his head, Yi Xiao continued, "I've been requested to find some people held captive by a man calling himself Bly. Would you have any idea where to find him?"

Mr. Chang smiled thoughtfully. "I know the name, yes. Thus far he's been sensible enough to stay out of my business." He tapped his teeth with his knuckle. "I do know that he's dangerous. That he's one I'd prefer not to cross as long as he continues to stay out of my territory. As for finding him, he has his fingers in a number of different enterprises here in San Francisco. No doubt one or the other will have the information you seek. I'll have someone look into it."

"I knew you could help," Yi Xiao bowed slightly from his seat. "He's dangerous and has *yaoguai* slaves. Please be sure they're careful."

The man smirked. "My dear youngster. Please tell your grandmother how to hunt deer."

Grandmother He Xiao was a bit too old for that kind of thing these days, but Yi Xiao took his meaning. "Apologies, sir. I forget who I speak to and what deity you've taken as your patron." Those who served the mad god of delirium probably knew better than most just how dangerous *yaoguai* could be.

"Accepted, youngster. I admit, I was unaware of the nature of the man's allies, or even that he was a sorcerer, so it is good to know." Mr. Chang inclined his head with princely condescension and added, "Is there any other way I might serve you in the meantime?"

The only thing they needed right then, after several days of hiking and strenuous exercise was rest. "Would you mind terribly finding us a place to stay the night? It's been a long couple of days."

The old man agreed without hesitation.

⋝⟩⟨⋜

Henrietta didn't sleep the way humans did. As long as she could get in the water, her spirit at one with the waves, she could replenish herself. That meant she spent the night sitting on the roof of the building, basking in the moonlight and contemplating her situation.

Sister Margarita had asked her what she planned when she was done helping Yi Xiao. From her manner, it'd been obvious what the sister expected from her. What the sister thought she should do. Yi Xiao was powerful and kind and a gentleman. He was also a skilled rider, more skilled than any of the sisters at Majeure. A water horse without home or friends could do far worse than accept him as a master.

Yet it was just as obvious to her that Yi Xiao didn't want to be anyone's master. The dead one's habit of calling him that aside, the young man clearly would have been just as happy on his own. He'd let her come with him, certainly, seeing as how she had no one. But he wouldn't ask it.

Then there was the fact that, though she liked Yi Xiao, she liked the sisterhood better.

Dona Estrella had scolded her for her poor behavior, of course, but she'd been just as kind as Yi Xiao. The little sisters all wanted to ride her. And her best friend while they'd been Bly's captives was there now. Oren would be fine where he was, but he might get lonely without her.

She'd have to make a choice sooner or later. But first they had to deal with Bly. She had every confidence Yi Xiao would find the bastard. Every confidence he'd free each and every one of Bly's prisoners. But she could make the whole thing easier, simply because she knew how Bly worked and could smell him out. Well, she could smell him out if he left the city that was. The human stink of this town was too strong to distinguish one person from another.

Speaking of stinks, wasn't that smoke she smelled? Of course, human towns always smelled of smoke but this stench was stronger. More acrid. As if it came from something other than a mere woodfire. Where had she smelled it before?

The answer came to her a moment later. "Blackie." One of Bly's most recent and more difficult acquisitions. A fire elemental who'd hidden in the Mother's western skirts for generations, there hadn't been much left of him by the time Bly found him. Bad tempered and defiant, Bly had been keeping him carefully under wraps for the time being. How did he get free?

Remembering what Yi Xiao had said back in the alleyway about fires, Henrietta quickly raced inside. It wasn't dawn yet. If she moved quickly, she could wake Yi Xiao and warn him of the danger before she had to take her horse shape again.

She slammed into Yi Xiao's room and found herself faced with Wu Chang's strange weapons a moment later. Recognizing her, he stepped back, saying, "Yi Xiao, emergency."

Yi Xiao was seated on the bed, wearing light trousers and nothing else, his legs crossed and his hands set on his knees. He opened his eyes at Wu Chang's voice and calmly told Henrietta, "Master says, panic never helped stop a stampede."

Ignoring Yi Xiao's strange comment, Henrietta quickly reported what she'd smelled and why it was a problem. "I'm not sure if Blackie got free or if Bly sent him, but he'll set the whole town on fire! We have to get out of here."

"We have to warn the firemen, given they don't already know. Wu Chang, how are you with fire?"

"It can't destroy me, but I will be weeks recovering," Wu Chang answered. "Shall I be the one to handle that step?"

As Yi Xiao agreed and Wu Chang left the room, Henrietta danced around nervously. She didn't like fire either. "Can't we just run?"

"There are people involved. I won't ask you to stay, but I should do my best to help." He stood up. Sniffed the air. Grabbed his shirt and pulled it on. "Not enough clouds for a storm, I'm afraid. We'll have to do this the old-fashioned way." With that, he hurried out the door, calling "Fire! Fire!"

⋛⟩⟨⋚

Reflecting he'd be in deep trouble if Henrietta turned out to be wrong or, worse, lying, Yi Xiao pounded on doors as he passed. Chang's hostel stood towards the middle of the Chinese district, among the many carefully constructed buildings his countrymen had claimed since they'd immigrated to America. They'd begun building with brick and stone since the last big fire, but there were still more than enough wooden structures to be at risk.

Once on the street, the smell of smoke was strong and pervasive. Behind him,

Henrietta clung to his side, shivering wildly. "Run if you have to," he told her gently. "Head for the water." The fire was a block north of them and though its light glowed bright against billowing clouds of smoke, it was far enough away that she'd have time.

"No."

"Brave girl." That was Sister Margarita, who'd joined them just that moment, wearing only a long night shirt and a pair of hastily pulled on pants. Like Yi Xiao she was barefoot, but didn't seem bothered. "You'll be going horse soon. Stay close and we'll figure out what to do."

Accepting Sister Margarita knew what she was doing, dealing with a spirit like Henrietta, Yi Xiao quietly murmured, "There may be a monster involved. A fire elemental Bly calls Blackie."

"Then you and I may be the only ones who can deal with him. There aren't any real sorcerers in San Francisco. None I'd trust, anyway."

Yi Xiao hadn't run across any sorcerers in San Francisco so far either. Of course they tended to stay hidden, so that proved nothing. "We'll do what we can when we can. First thing we get people out. Second thing, get water to that fire." It wasn't as far away as he wanted it to be. The third thing, finding the spirit whose flames had started this mess, would be easy. Stopping the being called Blackie might well be beyond his power, however. "Henrietta, will you help us with the rescue?"

"I'll try." She shuddered. "Not much time. Let's go."

Others were already heading for the fire, some carrying buckets of water, others hatchets. Yi Xiao chose a different direction, further east to the next block. There were enough people going straight for the fire as it was. They needed to get around to warn the people in the other buildings.

When they reached the next street, Yi Xiao spotted a familiar name. What was it Chang had said the night before? Two rival saloons that'd caused a huge fight? The one's name was the Red Wolf Bar? Just like the one right there? Was all this just the result of a business war? By the looks of things, the fire had started in the other bar, the one called Philadelphia Follies.

Deciding to worry about that later, Yi Xiao focused his attention on getting as many people as he could out of the place. He shouted, deepening his voice as if he were a general commanding an army, or his grandmother dealing with the more wild elements of the martial world. He wasn't her match, but it was good enough for now.

It was early in the morning and the flames pouring out the windows of the Philadelphia Follies provided the only light. It was enough for people to run by, and that was all Yi Xiao cared about. At least until he found himself face to face with a huge pillar of smoke that seemed to have grown eyes.

⇟)(⇟

It was him. Blackie. Worse, it was Blackie in his natural form, a huge black snake formed of smoke and crackling fire. The stink of him nearly sent Henrietta screaming off to the bay, but Sister Margarita's calm presence stopped her. Instead, she shifted to her water form, though she knew she'd no hope of putting a creature like him out. He was hotter than any normal fire, a thing spawned from the depths of the earth.

"Can you talk sense to him?" Sister Margarita asked. "If he's a prisoner like you were?"

"I don't know." Pulling water from the air, Henrietta flung it against the nearest building. It wouldn't stop the fire, but it'd give people time to escape. Blackie wasn't chasing anyone, after all, just focusing all his power on that one building. The rest was collateral damage. "Maybe if we can break the control on him?"

While Yi Xiao dodged and rolled, catching Blackie's attention, Sister Margarita scanned the area. "If he's being controlled there has to be a controller. Any idea what distance?"

Bly had always kept near her when he used her. Henrietta thought about the size of the circus. Her former master wouldn't have insisted everyone stay within the boundary if he could reach further. She wrote on the ground with her water, 'Block, maybe two.'

"Yi Xiao," Sister Margarita called. "If you can keep the elemental's attention, we'll try finding his controller and breaking his bonds."

The fact that Sister Margarita had included Henrietta in the plan ought to have terrified her. Instead, the sense of trust filled her with determination. She'd do anything to earn Sister Margarita's regard.

"Master says, fight fire with water," Yi Xiao answered. "Soak me, first, please."

Realizing he needed protection, Henrietta gathered herself together and hurriedly splashed over him before galloping back for Sister Margarita. Behind her, Blackie hissed furiously, barely missing her tail hairs as she passed.

"Quick. Inside there."

Henrietta wasn't sure why Sister Margarita thought the one controlling Blackie was inside the saloon, but she followed without hesitation. The main room was empty, but Sister Margarita spread her hands, sending a wave of air flowing past. "There!" she said suddenly, pointing towards the back of the building.

The saloon's offices were empty too, but the back door swung wildly as if someone had just run through. Sister Margarita followed, in time to slam into a burly older man. "The hell, woman? What kind a goldarn stupid thing are you up to, running round back here?"

Henrietta recognized the man suddenly. She'd never seen him like this before, but he was Kohl, one of the humans who assisted Bly with keeping his many pets, both natural and supernatural, under control. Immediately, she dropped to the ground, spreading her water so as to avoid notice. At the same time she hurriedly set her water swirling on the ground between him and Sister Margarita, writing the words, "He with circus."

With a smile, Sister Margarita said, "I'm terribly sorry, sir. I'm trying to make sure no one's trapped. You really should get out of here. Let me help."

"Y'don't need to do that, gel. I got this."

"I insist."

"I insist y'get yer pretty hiney outta here 'fore I toss ya out on it!" Seeing Sister Margarita showing no signs of obeying, Kohl reached out to grab her.

A staff of pure air formed in Sister Margarita's hands. She slammed it into the man's skull, but he barely seemed to notice. "Gel, you got some guts. Be nice to take a good look at 'em."

As Kohl drew a knife from his belt, stabbing, Henrietta slammed into him, soaking him to the skin. She couldn't fight him properly, not without a source of water, but she could hinder him. He slashed and splashed, breaking free of her influence easily.

"Oh, it's you. Boss was hot you'd gone and done a runner." Something grasped at her thoughts, tried to bend her to its will. If Kohl had been Bly, instead of using one of Bly's tools, it might have worked. But Henrietta had been free long enough, had seen real strength at work, and was stubbornly unwilling to give way.

Margarita came in for a sucker punch, a blast of solidified air breaking Kohl's dagger. At the same time Henrietta flung part of herself into the man's nostrils. He coughed and choked, flinging her away again. "I'll kill the both of yah!"

"I don't think so. Henrietta, cover the floor. And don't be afraid." Sister Margarita beckoned and though Henrietta had no idea what she planned, she obeyed. Then she felt her substance harden as Sister Margarita exerted her magic, transforming her water to solid ice.

Kohl skidded. Fell. And just as he was trying to get back to his feet, Sister Margarita slammed the top of his head with the nearest barstool.

Immediately, Sister Margarita released Henrietta, letting her take her horse form again. Then she knelt, searching the man for whatever it was he'd used to control Blackie.

They found it a moment later, a strangely carved piece of stone that still glowed faintly with whatever power Bly had put in it. Without hesitation, Sister Margarita smashed it, sending the pieces skittering across the floor.

Outside, something screamed and howled, the sound of rocks scraping against rocks, of hot wind rushing from a smoking vent. "I WILL KILL YOU AND EAT YOUR BONES!"

⋛⟩⟨⋚

By this time Yi Xiao was all too accustomed to threats to his health and safety. He wasn't quite used to them coming from a huge snake formed of pure black smoke and fire, but that didn't matter.

His main concern was keeping the snake from carrying his fire into the rest of the town. By now the Philadelphia Follies was a charred cinder, as were most of the buildings on that block. Blackie couldn't do much more harm here than he'd already done.

Thus, Yi Xiao leapt and rolled, holding his breath as much as possible, dodging as best he could. There wasn't anything else he could do. He might have to draw his sword for this one after all, but he wanted to avoid that if at all possible. It wasn't the fire elemental's fault he'd been bound and commanded.

Attempting communication was probably useless. He still tried. "Now, Blackie, there's no need to be so angry."

To his surprise, the elemental answered. "Don't call me Blackie!" His English was as good as Yi Xiao's, though the accent was pure American.

"What would you like me to call you instead?"

"Just die, you obnoxious bug! You're that bastard's tool. I can smell him on you!"

Bastard? Tool? "I'm afraid I really have no idea what you mean." Yi Xiao dropped backwards with a lightning flash step. He was getting better at it. A move like that would have worn him out a month or so earlier. Seeing he was too close to the Red Wolf Saloon, he flung himself sideways. Sister Margarita and Henrietta were still inside.

The snake spat fire laced stone at Yi Xiao, forcing him to flash step again. This time forward, though the creature's heat worried him. To his surprise, it wasn't as hot next to the snake as he'd have expected. Could he control those flames of his? Or was he tiring?

"I'll call you dead, insect!"

Noticing the other saloon's roof had caught fire, Yi Xiao yelled, "Sister Margarita. Henrietta! Get out of there!"

"Never mind them! You're my dinner now!"

Two figures were stumbling out the Red Wolf Saloon's door. Relieved, Yi Xiao passed the snake, forcing it to twist painfully around. At the same time, a third person came out of the saloon, grabbing wildly for Sister Margarita and coming up with a handful of water horse instead. Henrietta bucked and kicked, knocking the man to the ground.

Spotting the man, the snake reared upwards, fire spilling from his mouth, clouds of black smoke swirling around him. Unwilling to let the creature kill someone, even if that someone was his controller, Yi Xiao leapt forward, spun around and smacked the snake on the nose as hard as he could. For emphasis, he summoned a solid dose of *qi*, a bolt of lightning slamming the snake's head into the ground.

Yi Xiao had no doubt the fire elemental was painfully weak already. He looked huge and impressive, but had barely burned anything beyond the one saloon. At full, even half, strength, he would have had the entire town alight by now and Yi Xiao would be nothing but a badly roasted lump of meat.

Instead the elemental collapsed, howling painfully, struggling wildly to get back up. His flames were dying down, sign he couldn't do much more. So when Henrietta slammed into him with all her spare water, all he could do was scream and shrink down to a mere handful of black coils.

Quickly, Yi Xiao pulled his robe off and wrapped it around the squirming body. Still warm, but not hot enough now to burn anything, all the snake could do was howl and threaten. "Quick," Yi Xiao ordered his companions. "Let's get him where he can't cause more trouble. Fast."

He just hoped such a place existed.

⋧⟩⟨⋦

The best solution they had was to take Blackie to one of the islands in the bay. That, in turn, required Henrietta to carry both Yi Xiao and Sister Margarita on her back again. Luckily, neither were terribly heavy; Henrietta's horse shape was still fairly young and she couldn't handle much more than the two of them.

In the water, of course, she had more than enough strength to swim straight north to one of the smaller of islands. Alcatraz, Sister Margarita called it. There wasn't much there, just the remnants of a lighthouse. It didn't really have a beach, either, but Henrietta didn't need one. All they had to do was toss Blackie onto the rocky shore and stay back while he regained what little temper he had.

It took a while. If he'd been stronger he probably would have set the island alight, as furious as he was with his treatment. As it was, he charred the sand and stone beneath his body. Nothing was melted or badly damaged, but not for the lack of trying.

"Bastards. Bastards all of you! Let me go! Don't you dare leave me here! Don't you dare!"

Henrietta snorted, spraying seawater to warn him back. He shrieked, swirling away from her and tossing a ring of black smoke her way. It was gone before it reached her.

"Don't tease him, Henrietta," Sister Margarita ordered.

"Yes, Sister."

Yi Xiao, who was standing in the water, far enough back to keep Blackie from reaching him, not so far Blackie didn't know he was there, added, "I don't want to leave you here. But at the moment you're liable to kill someone."

"So?"

Even Henrietta knew that answer. "Because they didn't do anything to you and killing's wrong." She pawed the sand beneath her forehooves happily when Sister Margarita patted her on the shoulder. "So you shouldn't do it."

Before the two of them could start arguing, Yi Xiao said, "Sir, earlier you said your name wasn't Blackie. Is there something you'd prefer I call you?"

The snake stopped slithering back and forth. Stared at Yi Xiao. "I," he said proudly, "Am the Unhcegila, the Black Snake. The fire at the heart of the world."

Once again Henrietta snorted, though she was more careful not to let the spray hit him again. "I'm just a baby and I know that's pretentious."

Suddenly the monster curled up into a sad little ball. "Everyone's gone. Everyone who knew me. Everyone who feared me. I was power and terror and fire. Now I'm nothing. Don't even bother with a name. I'll be gone soon enough."

Monsters didn't just go away because the people who believed in them were gone, even Henrietta knew that much. All they needed was to change. "There are other people around."

"Useless. They're useless. They don't even notice me. That bastard's fault." Again he reared up. Hissed into the air and sent a stream of delicate black smoke rising.

"You mentioned that before, Unhcegila," Yi Xiao said. "Bastard?"

"He's the one got me lost. We had a race. I won. I swear I won. But he left me there. All alone. No one to think of me. No one to remember. No one to believe."

That sounded like the sort of thing Deathshead would do and Henrietta said so. "The old man of the hills? Trickster breaks the world?"

Yi Xiao paused. Looked at her. "Does he sometimes call himself Sun Wu Kong?"

"I believe he sometimes calls himself Coyote. Though I'm quite certain he's not the only one," Sister Margarita noted. "I doubt it matters at the moment. Deathshead isn't all that strong, either."

He was strong enough to cause trouble, Henrietta wanted to say. But she could tell both Sister Margarita and Yi Xiao already knew that. Yi Xiao returned his attention to Unhcegila. "I can't do much about Deathshead. And you were right that he's got his scent on me. But for a cause I think you might approve of. Stopping Bly and freeing his captives."

Bly's name had its effect. Unhcegila snarled, though he also twisted himself into a frightened knot. "Bly. I'll kill him."

"Killing's terribly permanent, though. Would you settle for freeing his captives and breaking his power?"

The black head shifted closer, peered nearsightedly at Yi Xiao, then at Henrietta. "You trust him, nag?"

Though she wanted to take offense at the insult, Henrietta decided to be magnanimous. "I trust him."

"I'll help you," Unhcegila told Yi Xiao. "I want him stopped."

Giving the fire elemental a long, thoughtful, look, Yi Xiao asked, "Will you refrain from killing? I'd like to avoid that as much as possible."

"I'm a monster."

"True. But monsters don't have to walk the low road."

"I'm not fit for the high road, human."

"That's up to you. But for now, you could hold your power and try not to kill." Yi Xiao spread his hands questioningly. "I know of no way to be sure you'll keep your word. All I can do is trust you. So? Will you help and try not to kill? Or do I take you somewhere away from people so you can't cause trouble?"

"Why not just leave him here?" Henrietta demanded. "He can't hurt anyone here."

"Sooner or later this island's going to be wanted, I'm sure. I'd rather not leave a dangerous gift for those who come after us."

Unhcegila eyed Yi Xiao for a long, silent, moment. Then he shifted, becoming a brown-skinned human youth, just barely taller than Sister Margarita. "All right. I won't kill anyone unless you tell me to," he said, human voice not much less rough and gravelly than his snake one. "I'll behave. At least until Bly's stopped and the others are free."

Nothing was said about what he'd do after but Henrietta was sure Yi Xiao knew it likely wouldn't be good.

⇒)(⇐

By the time they returned to town the fire was mostly under control. Yi Xiao couldn't help noticing Unhcegila's smug expression as he surveyed the damage. "Best not look too pleased," he noted to the apparent boy. "Unless you want someone thinking you started it."

Before Unhcegila could respond that he had, after all, started it, Sister Margarita set a light hand on his shoulder. One covered in a solid layer of chilled air, Yi Xiao noticed. "Don't say it, boy."

"I'm not a boy. I'm a monster."

"Right now you're a boy and a very irritating one at that."

Henrietta whinnied her agreement and Yi Xiao found himself sympathizing with the little monster. It had to rankle, to go from a dangerous and powerful force of nature to a little kid getting picked on by those around him. He was about to say something when he felt as if someone was watching them. "We'd best get over to Chang's," he murmured, not liking the sensation. It wasn't quite killing intent, but it wasn't pleasant, either.

Wu Chang was waiting for them at the entrance to Chang's place. "Master, respect. Someone has been nosing around looking for a stolen horse." He spoke in Chinese, warning Yi Xiao that there might be listeners. "It would, I think, be for the best if we didn't bring our troubles on Mr. Chang."

"Agreed." Yi Xiao turned to Sister Margarita and Henrietta. "You should go now. Quickly. The sooner you're safely back with your community, the better."

To his surprise, Sister Margarita disagreed. "I'll send my fellow sisters home, yes, but I'm staying as long as Henrietta does."

An odd look crossed Wu Chang's face. As if he couldn't quite help it, the man murmured, "Master says, when destiny follows, don't bother hiding."

Yi Xiao didn't need an explanation. He seemed cursed, or blessed, with a tendency to be drawn into situations and gather others around to help him. Apparently, right now, those others were Sister Margarita, Henrietta and Unhcegila. "Never mind that. Sister Margarita, if that's the case, I suggest you get your sisters headed to Majeure Community now. The fewer targets we give Bly, the better. Henrietta, can you carry me and Unhcegila?"

"I'm not riding a water horse!" Unhcegila protested, though he was smart enough to keep his voice down. "Are you trying to kill me?"

"Then can you walk as fast as she can run? Because I'm almost certain someone's going to be coming after us and soon."

"Master, if he can control his flames, I can carry him on my back. I don't think we can waste any more time."

Wu Chang's sense of danger was likely better than Yi Xiao's. If he said they had to hurry, they had to hurry. "Sister Margarita, I'll send word to Mr. Chang when it's safe. Get your sisters to safety first." He turned to the others. "As for the rest of you, we go south, as fast as our various limbs can take us."

⇒)(⇐

If it were night, Henrietta could have taken a human form. As it was, her horse shape was putting Yi Xiao at risk. She knew horse thieves were considered among the lowest of criminals. If someone accused him of stealing her he wouldn't be able to prove otherwise.

"What's got your tail down, nag?"

She glared at the snake curled up around Wu Chang's arm, resting his head on the dead man's shoulder. "Don't call me that. And I'm worried about them crooks coming after us." They were probably part of Bly's crew, hunting her and Unhcegila down. She didn't want to think about what they'd do to her new friends. "What happens if someone thinks Yi Xiao stole me?"

"I'm likely to have more troubles if someone notices the two of you talking," Yi Xiao pointed out, patting her shoulder. "As far as I know, horses and snakes aren't known for conversation around here."

Unhcegila snorted. "They'll just think they're mad. That's what most humans do."

"Even so...."

"If you're that worried about being noticed, try being a horse of a different color." The snake mouth opened in what passed for a grin. "Or just be yourself. All wet."

Though she knew he'd meant the advice for mockery, the first idea wasn't that bad. Ordinarily she liked a trim long-limbed shape for her horse form. But she didn't have to. She waited until they reached a quiet street and adjusted herself. Short, round and poorly groomed should work. No one would think of stealing such a beast.

"You look like my cousin's best mare," Yi Xiao murmured. "Good choice." He settled comfortably in her saddle, weight shifting along with her gait without hesitation.

Henrietta yearned to compliment him on his riding, but they were coming on more people, now they were getting to the edge of town. Miners heading out to their camps, with a few traders and assorted others. To her eyes they all looked similar. Mostly men, mostly dressed in rough denims. Nothing remarkable.

No. Wait. There was a smell in the air. Not the stink of smoke from the fire. Not the stink of people and animals. Something else. A faint whiff of animal musk. "Deathshead."

"He's following us," Wu Chang confirmed. "Closer than before."

As if the words alone summoned the old man, he was there beside them, appearing out of nowhere to walk alongside Henrietta. "You're going the wrong way."

Shying, Henrietta kicked out at the old man, missing him by less than an inch. He'd chosen his position well, just barely out of reach of her hooves. She tried biting, but Yi Xiao tugged on her mane. "Manners, little one."

"I'll kill him!" That was Unhcegila, raising up on Wu Chang's shoulder, smoke trickling from his mouth and nostrils.

"Save your fire for when it's needed." Wu Chang stepped between Yi Xiao and Deathshead, adding, "What is it you want, old one?"

Yi Xiao ignored the argument, interrupting to say, "The wrong way? Do you know where Bly is right now?"

"Nope. Not a clue."

Henrietta couldn't help trying to snap at him again. Neither could Unhcegila, twisting round on Wu Chang's arm to blow smoke in Deathshead's face. All that did was make the old man laugh. "Oh, it's you! Got bored hanging round Mama's skirts?"

"You bastard. You got me lost in there!"

Reaching out to tickle Unhcegila's chin got the response it deserved, a sharp fiery bite on the index finger. Not that Deathshead seemed to care. He returned his attention to Yi Xiao, adding, "I don't have to know where Bly is to know you're going the wrong way."

"Master says, if you have something to say, then say it."

A sharp laugh. "I don't know where Bly is, but I know you want to be getting at his power source. And that ain't here."

Power source? It'd never occurred to Henrietta that Bly had a power source. Much less that it'd be something he couldn't just carry around with him. She tried to think if she'd seen such a thing. Failed. "Don't trust him, Yi Xiao," she whispered.

"Oh, trust, don't trust. Doesn't matter to me. But you'd best not forget your promise, boy. Bly's a blight on the land and I want him gone."

"Now I was just thinking the same about you, you mangey old beast."

This time Henrietta really did shy, as the shadows suddenly filled with human figures. And, there, right at the center, was one all too familiar person. Tall, thin, dry blond hair falling loose around a bony face just visible in the late afternoon light.

Bly.

⇒)(⇐

Yi Xiao wasn't surprised. He'd sensed they were being followed and knew Henrietta's attempt to conceal herself wouldn't work on her old master. His main hope had been to get Unhcegila as far from the town as possible. Preferably to some place where his fires couldn't create another disaster. That was why he'd chosen to head for one of the rocky mountain paths south of town.

He dismounted. "Henrietta, Unhcegila, protect each other, please. Wu Chang, you know what I want done."

"Master, respect, I will do my best." There was a faint hint of doubt in the man's voice, explained by his next words. "I may not be able to avoid killing entirely."

It wasn't necessary to tell Wu Chang to try. Yi Xiao knew his bodyguard—his friend—understood Yi Xiao's desire. Tell the truth, he wasn't sure he was going to get out of this one without at least one or two deaths. He let Henrietta back away. Glared at Unhcegila to do the same. To his surprise, the fire elemental obeyed, though he was beginning to smoke more furiously, his body growing a little with his anger.

As for Deathshead, the man also stepped back. "Ain't my fight, now is it?" he asked.

"That's up to you," Bly growled. "I gave as good as I got, last time we clashed."

Yi Xiao coughed to get their attention, which caused the men surrounding Bly to raise their guns. "Now, now. I'm not looking to fight if I don't have to."

"You have my horse. My snake. You're conspiring with my enemy against me. You think you don't have to?"

Yi Xiao spread his hands, ignoring the way Bly's men shifted nervously. "I'd like to avoid violence. I'd hate to have any of you hurt."

That set Bly laughing. "Any of us? You out of your mind, Chinaman? Or you think you're bulletproof?"

The Storm Hermit's teachings weren't the sort that allowed a cultivator that sort of protection. "No," Yi Xiao admitted, drawing his *qi* together. This'd be easier if it was raining. Even easier if he were closer to the Mother and dared ask her for help. Since neither were available, all he had were his own skills and the hope they were up to the challenge.

The wind rose around them, circled them, drawn in by Yi Xiao's *qi*. The air, cool and rather dry, began to crackle, sparks flickering along Yi Xiao's body as he summoned the power inside him. Bly's men raised their guns higher. Started to pull the triggers, just as Yi Xiao released his *qi* into the crowd.

Lightning struck from gun to gun to gun, forcing the men to release their weapons. At the same time, Wu Chang leapt forward, a flash of shadow against shadows. His blades flickered as he moved, striking and cutting almost too fast to see.

"I want to fight!" Unhcegila growled.

"Do you think you can beat Bly right now?" Yi Xiao asked calmly. "Master says, know yourself, know the other."

That made the little black snake quiet down. He grumbled, but remained with Henrietta, the two of them staying back and out of the way. Good. Unhcegila had fought hard earlier. He needed time and rest to recover his power. Keeping him out of the fight was for the best.

Meanwhile, Wu Chang was picking off gunman after gunman, dodging blows and disarming those Yi Xiao's lightning hadn't already dealt with. Those still armed fired, but without effect. Yi Xiao just hoped the men didn't notice that their bullets were hitting their target.

"So," Bly murmured. "Deathshead told the truth for once. That little girl wasn't the one called the mountain's power down. You were."

Though the fact that Deathshead had told Bly any such thing shook him, Yi Xiao refused to show his reaction. He bowed slightly. Bly wasn't armed and wasn't strong enough to fight hand to hand. Nor did he seem to have any magical beings at his command. Had Deathshead been telling the truth about Bly's power source? "This wanderer was briefly favored by the Mother, yes. But it was her choice, not mine."

"Still. You're a sorcerer of some power and I can use men like you." Bly turned a sharp gaze on the pair behind Yi Xiao. Whistled.

"No." Two voices gasped. "Won't."

Bly whistled again and suddenly the pair were locked in battle, steam and smoke rising as water and fire struggled against each other. Another whistle followed close on the last, transforming Bly's men to creatures similar to the ones Yi Xiao had fought a few days earlier. Some leapt for Deathshead. Others gathered round Yi Xiao, growling furiously. Still others trapped Wu Chang.

"Unhcegila! Henrietta! Stop!" They were killing each other and Yi Xiao was powerless to help them. Even if he could summon enough *qi* to deal with Bly, it wouldn't be fast enough.

"I'll stop them, if you like," Bly offered, looking pleased with himself. "As long as you come with me."

Yi Xiao eyed him, well aware of his danger. "Free them and I'll agree."

"Those two are practically useless to me. You, however, will make a fine addition to my stable, little sorcerer. Very well." Bly whistled again and the pair broke off from each other, falling to the ground and whimpering in pain. "I don't need the other one," he added, with a negligent wave at Wu Chang. "Get rid of her."

Before Yi Xiao could open his mouth to protest, the biggest of the wolves like men launched himself at Wu Chang. His bodyguard dodged backwards a bit further, leaping to the edge of the cliff. "Master says, sometimes we have to fall to rise." Suiting action to word, he flung himself off the edge of the cliff.

"WU CHANG!" Yi Xiao rushed forward, ignoring Bly's monsters. Landing on his knees at the edge of the cliff he peered down into the shadows. "No.... no...."

Bly came up beside him, grabbed him by the arm and pulled him to his feet. With a fierce grin, the man glanced down the cliffside at the twisted body lying crushed on the rocks. "Sorry, Chinaman. Your gel's dead and gone. Guess she didn't like her odds."

With that, he dragged Yi Xiao off into the night.

Chapter 5
Earth – Finding the Center

The first thing Bly did was take everything Yi Xiao had on him, including his saber. "Nice." He frowned at the bared tang. "But where's the hilt?"

Yi Xiao gestured west. "This one believes it to be in China." He'd had to sacrifice the hilt when he'd had Zak make a double for Gan Han to carry. She'd have noticed a fake immediately and he'd wanted her to be as far from him as possible before she realized what he'd done. Her strange ability to trace a sword's owner made the subterfuge necessary.

They were inside a stage-coach by now, its windows covered, its interior lit by a single lantern attached to the side. Yi Xiao thought Bly hoped to keep him from seeing where they were going. Not that it'd work. Yi Xiao recognized the smells and night noises. South of San Francisco and just about to the far end of the bay. Based on Deathshead's comments earlier, he suspected they'd be turning east as soon as possible.

"So, Chinaman, what brings you to our fair and lovely country?"

"I had some problems at home. Ones that forced me to make a hurried and unplanned departure for parts unknown."

That made Bly smile viciously. "Haven't we all?" he murmured. "What sort of problems?"

After a moment's consideration, Yi Xiao smiled, the most blazingly innocent smile he could possibly offer. "I used that saber you're holding so poorly to remove a man's head for him. His family was... displeased."

Every word of it was the truth, though that same family hadn't been able to claim judgement on him for it. The man in question had attacked his cousin and Yi Xiao had had to act in Yi Zhu's defense. Attempting to murder an Imperial Prince carried a high price and they'd had no choice but to disown their kinsman. Otherwise their heads would have been joining the assassin's on the execution grounds.

Now Bly laughed, a clear, clarion, laugh of pure joy. "I like the way you think, Chinaman. Shall I get a new hilt for this thing, so you can remove the heads of my enemies for me?"

Yi Xiao didn't lose his smile, but something in his eyes must have shown his opinion of that idea. Bly almost flinched at his expression. "I am not a killer for hire," he murmured. "Indeed, I would be most grateful to destiny if I could avoid killing ever again." It was unfortunate that he kept running into situations where he was given no good choice in the matter.

Recovering himself, Bly shrugged. "You may change your mind on the subject in the future. For now, I can see other uses for you. Once I have you properly convinced of my control."

Raising an eyebrow, Yi Xiao repeated the word. "Control?"

"You'll have noticed I have a special skill," Bly told him. "One that allows me to force monsters to follow my will. Those two little brats you had with you surely told you about it."

"They did. But despite my particular talents, I am mortal born and no monster."

Another laugh. "Oh, I'm certain you are, Chinaman. Speaking of those particular talents, why don't you show me a bit of what you can do. Right here and now."

Bly's expression was bland, but Yi Xiao suspected it immediately. Bly had seen him use his *qi*. He had to know Yi Xiao could blast him unconscious at this close range. He held out his hand. Closed his eyes. Opened them sharply and stared blankly at the man sitting across from him.

"Can't use your magic, can you?" Bly reached up and stroked something hiding in his collar. A rat? The little black face raised up to stare at Yi Xiao wildly. "I can, as you've guessed, only control monsters and force them to my will. But this little fellow here can keep sorcerers from accessing their power."

Yi Xiao kept his face blank as blank could be, gazing at the rat intently. After a moment it blinked. Curled up against Bly's neck and went back to sleep. He tilted his head at his captor. "And what will you do with me, having bound my magic so?"

"I have other tools when we return home, Chinaman. Not least of which is a way to bind you to my will and make you use your magic to help me." Bly leaned back in his seat and smiled expansively. "Whether or not I persuade you to kill, I believe I'll find you quite... useful."

Yi Xiao had no doubt he meant every word he said.

⇒)(⇐

Sister Margarita found what was left of Yi Xiao's expedition some hours after midnight. She'd left her sisters at the ferry and headed straight south along the only road Yi Xiao was likely to take. It still took her far longer than she liked to reach them.

The first sign of trouble was a pair of wolves torn apart in the roadway. There weren't many beasts could rip wolves to shreds like that. Seeing an arm with a human hand and wolf's fur, she knew its killer had to be impressively strong. Whether the victims were wolves like men or were-beings imported from Europe didn't matter. Only a true power could do that much damage to such beings.

The sound of something whimpering in the darkness drew Margarita's attention. She hurried forward and wasn't surprised to find Henrietta in her watery shape, puddled into the rock and trying to hide. A black snake, its eyes and throat barely glowing within, lay on the other side of the road, curled up into the tiniest ball it could manage.

Something moved a bit further on, over the edge of the cliff beside the road. A moment later a gloved hand grasped at the rock. Struggled to find a grip. Struggled to pull its owner further up. "Wu Chang," she gasped, as a pale face rose above the edge of the cliff. She caught his arm and helped pull him up.

Only when she'd gotten the man onto the road did Margarita realize his head was twisted around. He'd been crawling up the cliff on his back. A mere week ago the sight of a dead man struggling to walk again would have had her running for Sister Clarence to lay the poor being to rest. Now all she did was ask, "Can I help?"

Wu Chang's lips moved and he struggled to whisper, "Twist head back.... Please."

Even now the man remembered his manners. She managed a smile and checked his neck for the direction of the twist. Then, carefully, but not too gently, she turned his head back the way it belonged. He choked. Made a peculiar wheezing noise. "Thank you. Wait. Heal soon."

"Do you need anything?"

"Could... use.. blood...."

Well, he would. And, really, there should be plenty from the bodies of their attackers. Margarita dragged one of the corpses close and dripped its blood into Wu Chang's mouth. "Enough," he said after a minute. "Rest... up to me. Others?"

"I've found Henrietta and Unhcegila. I don't see Yi Xiao anywhere."

"You wouldn't. Yi Xiao let Bly capture him. His choice."

"How'd you get down that cliff?"

A sweet beatific smile. "I jumped." At her expression he added, "Bly doesn't know what I am. It seemed the best way to keep him from figuring it out."

It was the sort of logic a dead man would have. Throw yourself entirely off a cliff. Break every bone in your body and twist your head backwards. All to keep from being captured or having your true nature discovered. It made sense, though. Yi Xiao wouldn't worry about him and it'd give Wu Chang a chance to tell Margarita what'd happened.

"Tell me the details when you're better. In the meantime, I'm going to see if I can get Henrietta and Unhcegila moving. We don't have time to waste."

"Agreed." Wu Chang pulled himself to a sitting position and dragged himself to a rock to lean quietly. "Don't worry. I promise I'll be all right."

She hoped so. She didn't know enough about undead to be sure how much a being like Wu Chang could take. Still, if he was in pain he wasn't admitting it. She moved back to Henrietta. Touched the puddle the girl'd become. "Little one. Can you get up? Are you all right?"

"Don't wanna."

"I know. You hurt and you're scared and you're probably angry too. But right now I need you to be brave and strong. Please try."

Eyes formed in the water. Stared up at her. Slowly rose within a narrow horse's face. "Sister. I tried. I really tried. Bly made me fight."

"Made us both fight. Bastard," Unhcegila gasped from behind Margarita. He uncurled. Shifted to his boyish human form. "I'm gonna char him to cinder and eat everything but his bones."

She couldn't help asking. "Why not his bones?"

"To provide an example for others."

Margarita sighed. She did ask, after all. And why should she expect a reasonable humane answer from a monster? Especially one who'd been abused the way this one had. "I won't say don't. But I will say it'd be better if you didn't get too bloodthirsty."

"Fine. I'll leave his blood too."

Wu Chang laughed. "Unhcegila, I don't think that's what she means."

"I know what she means. I still want to kill that bastard."

Truth to tell, they might have to. Bly's particular magic wasn't the problem, but his use of it was. Sooner or later he was going to bite off a bigger monster than he could chew. And if he did, that monster might be roused to do far more damage than one tiny fire elemental. Though, to be fair, there were several blocks of San Francisco that might disagree about how little damage a tiny fire elemental was capable of.

Henrietta took the human form she'd been using last and glared at Unhcegila. "You make too much trouble; I'll turn you to steam."

"You think you can, girly?"

Before the pair could resume their argument, Margarita raised her voice. "Both of you, enough. I don't insist on you helping me rescue Yi Xiao. But if you intend to, if you want to do something about Bly, then you're going to have to learn to cooperate. Understood?"

Two young voices answered sulkily. "Yes, ma'am."

ꝫ)(ꝯ

"Wake up."

Yi Xiao had been meditating, not asleep, but he wasn't going to tell Bly that. The less Bly understood about him the better. "I take it we've arrived." The fact that the coach was slowing down was enough to warn him. A vaguely familiar trumpet startled him. "Elephant? And is that a camel I smell?"

"I do run a circus, you realize?"

Unfolding his legs, Yi Xiao waited until the coach came to a stop. Waited, too, for Bly to gesture for him to get out. No point in being too obliging. It'd create suspicion. More suspicion, that was. Bly couldn't be naïve enough to think he wasn't plotting escape.

It was just past sunrise and the sky was a clear deep blue. Sunlight gleamed over the mountains to their east, much closer than Yi Xiao was accustomed to seeing them. "So we're on the other side of the bay."

"And miles more to go before we're done," Bly told him. "What do you think of my circus?"

He considered the scene surrounding him. Men hurrying back and forth, packing tents, loading carts. Moving horses, mules, an elephant and a camel. The last didn't look at all happy or cooperative. But then, unhappy and uncooperative was a way of life for camels. The elephant, a youngster just barely three foot taller than its huge handler, bounced along joyfully; the world one large playground.

Someone was making beans and salt pork and those not busy packing up the circus stood in line waiting for their food. At the same time a dozen or so men shouted curses at an uncooperative cat the size of a small tiger. Its coat was black, though, with faint discolorations mottled throughout. It roared angrily, struggling against the ropes binding it.

Bly growled under his breath. "Wait here, boy. Don't get in the way."

Yi Xiao leaned against the coach and watched Bly approach the beast. "You know what happens if you argue, brat. Get in that cage or take the consequences."

The beast roared. Twisted. Snagged a rope and dragged one of its captors towards it. Before it could sink its claws into the man, Bly whistled. One sharp note, then another. It set the beast howling, rolling on the ground as if in pain. Immediately the men dragged and dragged, pulling the beast into a cage barely big enough and slamming the door shut.

Bly returned to Yi Xiao. "She'll rip you to pieces soon as look at you," he said.

"What type of being is she?"

"Y'know, I'm not really sure. Found her down in South America, poking around some old ruins." Bly shrugged. "She's just a monster. Easy to subdue, if you have the trick of it."

To Yi Xiao's mind, nothing, not even monsters, were 'just' anything. He could tell Bly wasn't the sort to listen to that kind of argument, so he didn't bother making it. "You seem to be moving camp. Afraid my friends will catch up?"

"Your friends? All you got left are them two brats who couldn't get along if they were tied together in a barrel. Oh, and that idiot Deathshead. If you're waiting on him, you'd best not hold your breath. That one worries about his own skin before he thinks about anyone else's."

"A not uncommon behavior," Yi Xiao demurred. "How do you know I don't have more friends than just the youngsters?"

"Well it for sure ain't that pretty gel of yours. She knew which way the wind was blowing, jumping like she did. Them lot of my wolvers would've dragged her down and done a few things fore they finished."

Yi Xiao didn't doubt they would have tried, but he knew that wasn't why Wu Chang had leapt from the cliff. Recognizing and acknowledging Yi Xiao's right to exchange himself as a prisoner, his bodyguard had chosen that path to conceal the fact that he couldn't be killed. He'd be along, just as soon as he put himself back together.

"You assume Wu Chang was a woman."

"With a face like that? What else?" Bly waved off the question. "Don't bother trying to confuse me, boy. Man or woman, that one's dead now and no use to you at all."

"You also assume I don't have other friends." Yi Xiao smiled. "Ah, but never mind. I'm more interested in what you intend to do next. It's obvious your people didn't expect to move so quickly."

Bly grinned. "Well now, you have yourself a gift and I plan on making good use of it."

That gift would be Yi Xiao's ability to ask for power from the Mother of the Mountain. "Are you sure you want to get anywhere near that lady?" he asked. "She doesn't suffer fools gladly and you've been stirring up a great deal of trouble at her skirts lately."

The grin broadened. "Well, now, I won't say you're wrong about that. But it ain't Mount Tam we're headed to." He gestured east, adding, "You can't see it from here, of course, but past them mountains is another place just as big, just as old and just as powerful. Except he's quiet right now, holding his Self to his Self. I've gotten a bit of power off him. I want more."

Another mountain like the Mother? Yi Xiao didn't doubt it. Any more than he doubted this other mountain and the Mother's were closely related. He might, indeed, be able to contact that power. Might even summon it.

The question was, would he still be sane if he tried?

꒳꒷꒦

Once Wu Chang was recovered enough to walk they returned to San Francisco and Mr. Chang. Bly might have taken Yi Xiao anywhere and Wu Chang thought they needed to do something to protect the children first. "Mr. Chang, himself, may not be able to help, but he can surely lay hands on someone who can."

Margarita had to bow to Wu Chang's greater experience in such matters. Thus they soon found themselves back at Mr. Chang's place and waiting for someone to fetch their master. It didn't take long, though from Mr. Chang's expression, he would've been happier if they hadn't dropped themselves in his lap.

He spoke in Chinese to Wu Chang, who gently said, "I come on behalf of the Wanderer, not myself, Mr. Chang. And if you will, please speak English for Sister Margarita's sake."

"I have a water horse and a fire snake sitting in my courtyard arguing. A number of properties to repair, thanks to that same fire snake. A band of *Nian* rebels threatening my business and demanding your master be handed over to them. Oh, and the police and the fire chiefs both asking searching questions about the fire yesterday and your master's involvement. Please explain to me why I should prioritize your master's needs over my own?"

Margarita didn't blame Mr. Chang for his annoyance. The situation would set anyone's teeth on edge. "The children will be coming with us as soon as we're done here," she promised. "And Unhcegila won't be starting any more fires if I have anything to say about it."

The old man eyed her dourly. Then, suddenly, laughed. "Some might call your words bravado, but I think you mean what you say. Whether you can follow through is, of course, another question." Before she could answer, he returned his attention to Wu Chang. "What can you offer me for my help? Young Yi Xiao's grandmother pays me to provide him monetary aid and advice. Nothing more."

Wu Chang bowed. "I can promise that once my master is returned safely to his family I will be free to offer my services to the Jin Long. With, of course, the usual restrictions."

A sharp toothed smile. "You value the boy highly, Hollowed Blade. I hope he is worth your effort."

"I value the boy and his master the Storm Hermit, Mr. Chang. Both are more than worthy."

Margarita added, "Besides, do you want it said that Bly can walk off with one of your people like that?"

Now Mr. Chang really did laugh. "One could say the boy entered Bly's trap of his own free will, but your point is well taken. It is my duty to protect those under my care and that includes our young wanderer. So what is it you would have of me?"

"We think Bly took Yi Xiao to his circus. We need to know where that is. We also need some way to protect those two elementals from his magic," Margarita explained. "Oh, and transport across the bay if it turns out we need it?" Wu Chang had mentioned Deathshead's conviction that Bly was somewhere east of San Francisco.

The old man smiled broadly. "She doesn't want much, does she?"

"To be fair, she hasn't asked for people to help us," Wu Chang pointed out. "And, thinking about it, I may have a solution to those *Nian* rebels who keep bothering you."

"Hohhh?"

"They want to find Yi Xiao too. Perhaps it would be useful if we let them lead the hunt?"

⋝⟩⟨⋜

The caravan set off soon after Yi Xiao and Bly's arrival. Several dozen horses, twice that many mules, the elephant and the camel, and various carts full of animals, all jostling their way east along a narrow dirt road between the mountains.

Bly attached a handcuff to Yi Xiao, one he claimed would negate magic just as surely as the black rat the man carried along with him. Perhaps it could, but Yi Xiao already knew it couldn't negate *qi*. Not that he'd admit any such thing to his captor.

Wandering alongside the caravan on foot, Yi Xiao reflected that Bly probably would have done better to get them to that mountain of his with just Yi Xiao. All those animals and carts simply couldn't move much faster than a man walking. He could have reached the other side of the mountains by himself long before the rest arrived.

"Shut those damned critters up!" someone grumbled when the beasts complained. The road was rocky and uneven and they clearly didn't like being jostled. One, the creature Bly called a jaguar, roared mournfully, calling for help that couldn't come.

Yi Xiao wended through the group, mostly ignored. Bly was too busy keeping his monsters under control to worry about him and the others too busy forcing the equipment up the trail. He'd stumble here and there, resting his hand against a rock or a tree as he walked, leaving a single character behind as he went. *Dian*. Lightning.

One such stumble did get noticed, but not by his captors. He'd slid a little further than usual, testing how far Bly would let him go, and found himself being glared at hatefully by something in the woods. He seldom felt such strong killing intent and he couldn't help stopping in his tracks, peering between the trees until he spotted a pair of green eyes glowing among familiarly shaped shadows.

"Hey! Don't think you'll get away that easy," Bly shouted suddenly. "Get over here."

Yi Xiao obeyed, calmly backing away and rejoining the others. "So sorry. I slipped."

"You're awful clumsy today, boy. Maybe I should make you ride."

Offering his brightest and most innocent smile, Yi Xiao said, "Oh, could I? I've been on the road for a long time and could do with a rest."

Distrustfully, Bly eyed him. "Sure," he said. "If you don't mind riding with Jacqueline." He pointed at the cage holding the jaguar. "In fact, you can make yourself useful and drive her cart. Her usual handler's busy and she's scaring old Jones something fierce."

Small blame to the jaguar's driver if he was terrified. The animal kept sticking her paw through the bars of her cage and trying to grab the man by the shirt. It was obvious the only thing stopping her from doing so was her leg being too big to reach through. Her blue eyes were narrow with effort, determination at war with reality.

"All right. I will then." Yi Xiao sauntered over to the cart and gestured at its driver to trade places. Seeing he was being replaced, the driver was off the cart so fast he nearly did get snagged when he got too close. Calmly, Yi Xiao climbed up, took the reins and clicked his tongue at the mules. Behind him, the claw kept trying to catch him, but he set himself just out of its reach.

Only when they'd been driving awhile longer, long enough for Bly to be satisfied he wasn't up to anything, did Yi Xiao say softly, "Your kinsman's out there following."

The jaguar roared and struggled to reach him.

"You'll only hurt yourself. Stay strong so you can be helped. Do you need food or water?"

The growl this time actually had a word in it. One Yi Xiao didn't recognize. He suspected he didn't need to. "Don't be that way. I'd like to help if I can. Master says, those who stick together, hit harder."

Silence. The claw stopped moving and hurriedly, Yi Xiao added, "Best make it look like you're trying to catch me, even so."

That made the jaguar resume her efforts, though with less force, as if she was too tired to fight. Yi Xiao kept his face quiet, not wanting anyone to notice his satisfaction. "No guarantees. But I promise, if I can get us all out of this situation, I will."

The only question was, when would he get the chance?

⋺)(⋵

Mr. Chang supplied them with two rather large pills. Ones he said would protect the children from control magic. "It won't block anything else," he warned. "But it should keep Bly from getting his claws into them again."

"That bastard doesn't have claws," Unhcegila grumbled. "Just that damned whistle."

"Which is more than enough," Margarita pointed out to the boy. "Take one."

By this time Henrietta had been a good girl and swallowed hers. "Ugh! That's huge!"

"You're a horse. You telling me you can't handle a horse pill?" Unhcegila mocked. "It's easy peasy." To prove himself right, he shifted to his snake form, dislocated his jaws and proceeded to swallow his pill without effort. The shape of it slid down his body and slowly disappeared.

By this time Wu Chang had gathered a half-dozen heavy set men in rough fur-trimmed clothes. To Margarita's eyes they looked like they might be some native tribe, but Wu Chang spoke to them in Chinese, calmly ordering them around as if they were a troop of soldiers. From the way they reacted, it was obvious they were terrified of him.

Shifting to English when he noticed Margarita approach, Wu Chang said, "I won't tell you your business, but understand that you aren't going to change Yi Xiao's mind on the subject of helping you."

The one man looked grim. "We have to do something. His cousin...."

"All Emperors have their problems, Harachul. Put Yi Xiao on the throne in his cousin's place and those problems will change. They won't go away."

Grumbling, Harachul waved his hands angrily. "If you say he won't help, why should we bother helping him?"

"Because assisting the favored grandson of the Head of the White Wolf Clan will be beneficial to you and your kin."

Whomever the Head of the White Wolf Clan was, it seemed they held some respect. Harachul sighed. "Very well. We'll do what we can." He and his companions went off, leaving Margarita with Wu Chang and the children.

"We shouldn't just sit here doing nothing," Margarita pointed out, once they were alone.

"Agreed. Since Bly is likely on the other side of the bay we should get a boat to cross."

Margarita smiled wryly. "Mr. Chang was already ahead of us. He just told me the circus had been in Fremont this morning."

"That is where?"

Realizing Wu Chang didn't have the area memorized, Margarita pointed southeast. "It's a town just around the far end of the bay. But before we get too excited, Mr. Chang also said the circus packed up and headed into the mountains early this morning."

The news startled Wu Chang. "I can understand moving, but why into the mountains?"

Unhcegila offered an answer. "Bet he's heading for the Old Man."

The Old Man? Margarita frowned at the young fire elemental. "Who do you mean?"

"The Old Man of the Mountain. Bly keeps going there, trying to get a rouse out of him. Good thing he never has, though. You think Mother's bad? Wait 'til you see Father in a snit." Behind Unhcegila, Henrietta shifted nervously, suddenly frightened.

The fact that both elementals seemed to know and fear whatever it was Bly hunted worried Margarita. She visualized a map of the area, trying to guess who or what the Old Man was. Then it hit her. The Mother of Mountains was Mount Tam, rising strong and proud to their north. The same mountain their holy stone got its power from. But there was another mountain to the east. Just as big, just as strong and just as proud.

"Mount Diablo?"

Unhcegila thought about it. "That's what Bly calls it. Don't think the Old Man would like being called a devil, though. My people used to call him *Tuyshtak*." A sneer. "That's Dawn of Time for you English speakers."

Whatever name it was the mountain bore, Margarita was sure of one thing. Bly must think Yi Xiao's ability to borrow the Mother's power would let him borrow the Old Man's as well. She said as much, adding, "I think we'd better get there before he tries."

Because it was one thing to call on the Mother to save lives. Calling the Father to give a greedy man power was sure to be disastrous. Not to mention fatal.

⇒)(⇐

They reached the other side of the mountain range in the late afternoon, coming to a halt near a town of sorts called El Alisal. A sprawling community, its buildings were rough and its inhabitants rougher. As soon as they arrived, Bly's men began setting up a tent and organizing for a show.

Noticing Yi Xiao's surprise, Bly grinned, "Gotta make a living somehow and them in town need entertainment," he explained. "It'd look strange if we didn't run a show. Don't want that lot thinking we've gone and struck it big somehow."

By which Yi Xiao guessed the inhabitants of El Alisal weren't the most law-abiding citizens in the state. He generally tried not to make assumptions based off appearances, but something about these people's manners suggested Bly was probably right to avoid drawing attention to himself. Unwelcome attention, that was.

Once his men were set to work, Bly made Yi Xiao come with him to the local saloon, "So I can get the word out that we're doing a show tonight."

"I'm not sure I'll be much assistance in that," Yi Xiao pointed out.

"You're the sort could talk the hind end off a donkey and make it thank you for the favor. I don't want you out of my sight."

The latter was Bly's priority, certainly, but Yi Xiao cheerfully added his voice to the invitation as they walked through the town. No point in being unmannerly, after all. Besides, the more he kept Bly's attention on him, the less attention the man would give to the brown-skinned gentleman stalking them through town. The one with the impossibly green eyes.

They reached the saloon just as it was filling up with the evening crowd. The noise of a poorly tuned piano could just be heard over the grumble and rumble of men's voices. The stink of tobacco, sweat and alcohol was thick in the air and the dim light was made dimmer by the cloud of smoke swirling above them.

"Bly, you old bastard! Ain't seen you in a month of Sundays!" One of the men slapped Bly on the shoulder, a gesture that got a sharp stare, followed by a false grin. "You got those pretty girls still working your circus?"

"I do indeed. Going to have a show tonight. Just around sundown. Thought I'd come out and let everyone know."

Another voice asked, "You in a rush? You don't usually have a show first day you get here like that."

"You're right, Eb. I don't usually. But I got me an appointment with the Old Man of the Mountain and no time to stay." Bly waved a negligent hand. Spoke louder. "So I'm running a show tonight. Half-off and you know how much it hurts me to say that."

General laughter followed. "That Old Man you're talking about must be some big spender!" someone shouted. "He hit a lucky strike or something; he can afford to be paying you to drop your price?"

"Dunno about a strike or nothing. But it's worth my while and that's all I'll say on the matter."

A heavily bearded white man walked out of the crowd to look down at Yi Xiao. "This Chinaman one of your clowns, Bly? He's a skinny bit of nothing, ain't he?"

Yi Xiao just smiled sweetly and said nothing, sizing the man up. Big, seemed to move slow, but faster than he looked. Hopefully he wasn't looking for a fight. The less attention Yi Xiao drew to himself the better.

"He's got some skills, near as I can tell, Bear. We'll have to see if they're any good, later."

The big man leaned close. Breathed whiskey fumes straight into Yi Xiao's face. "You talkee Englee Chinaman?"

"I've been known to." The expression on people's faces at his accent never failed to amuse him. "Is there something you need?"

A startled look crossed the man's face. Then he laughed. "Don't suppose you play cards?"

"I'm afraid not." Yi Xiao tilted his head thoughtfully. "I do play a vicious game of *mah-tiae* however." The tile game was a favorite in his household, in fact.

Before anyone could ask what *mah-tiae* was, Bly interrupted. "Gentlemen, this young man does have some acrobatic skills and I believe he might be persuaded to show them off tonight. But I am a busy man and I'm trying to be efficient here. Yi Xiao, come along.

We have things to do."

Yi Xiao bowed, to Bly and the others. "I hear and obey, Mr. Bly. Hoping to see all of you tonight." As he straightened he made sure to look directly into the intensely green eyes of the big man standing at the edge of the crowd. "We have so many wonderful things to show you."

And, if he was lucky, he'd be able to get the young jaguar back to her kinsman before the creature went on a rampage.

⇒)(⇐

They reached the Freemont area not long after the men Wu Chang had hired to help them. Not because they were moving slowly but because Harachul and his men had a greater head start. Mr. Chang had gotten them a boat, but San Francisco's harbor was difficult to maneuver in, even with the help of a water horse. There were just too many ships left empty by sailors turned miners.

It was late afternoon by the time they found the place where Bly's circus had been camped and long past dark by the time they reached the trail crossing over the mountains. Margarite could tell a large group had passed that way, though she wasn't at all certain what'd left the huge spoor right in the middle of the road.

"Elephant," Wu Chang offered when she asked. "An unusual beast to find here in California. Though I wouldn't be surprised if it's another monster."

"All the animals Bly owns are monsters," Henrietta told them, stamping her foot and shivering her mane. "That's how he works."

Margarita had heard bits and pieces of Bly's history over the years. She hadn't liked what she'd heard, but this was the first she'd truly understood how much trouble he'd caused. "What are the chances of getting them to cooperate?"

"While he has his magic? While he can imbue it into objects so others can use it?" Unhcegila scoffed. "None."

At a bet, Yi Xiao would want to help all the monsters Bly had captured. He was that sort of person. Wu Chang, without needing Margarita to say so, murmured, "Then we'll have to find a way to break his control. Preferably without killing him."

They continued up the trail and Wu Chang paused suddenly. "Young master has been this way." He touched a peculiar mark, half hidden among the rocks. A square with two lines through it, one struck through and curving like a fishhook. "Part of the word for lightning."

"Any sign of those friends of yours?"

"I've seen some, yes. Familiar boot marks, of a sort our people's nomads wear. At a guess, they're not far behind our quarry."

Margarita kept moving, letting Unhcegila walk ahead, lighting the way with a handful of molten rock. Well, he did say his fire came from the depths of the Earth. "They know not to blindly attack, right?"

"I believe so. Harachul is impetuous, but I don't believe he's a fool. I warned him that we have to find out what Master... Yi Xiao... wants us to do."

It was quite dark by now. Not so dark they couldn't see. The moon alone was still bright enough to light their path. Unhcegila's fire made sure of it. Unfortunately, it also attracted attention.

The first sign they were being followed was a faint unexpected echo. The next a scrape of wood against wood. Nothing loud. Nothing obvious. It could be a bear, or a wolf, or some other nocturnal beast. Whatever it was, Margarita was sure it was following them.

Leaning forward to whisper in Henrietta's ear, Margarita told the water horse, "Move slower. Act like you're going lame."

To her relief, Henrietta did so without argument or discussion. It was Wu Chang who spoke up, asking, "Is everything all right?" At the same time he gestured slightly behind them, warning her they were being hunted.

"My horse must have a rock or something in her shoe. I'm going to check. You and Unhcegila rest." She dismounted, pretended to raise Henrietta's foot while peering back the way they'd come.

A shadow moved. Merged with the darkness. Not an animal. Human-looking. Was it just a bandit, noticing a small group of wanderers and deciding to be brave? Or was it some sort of monster, hoping for a late-night snack?

"I shall take advantage of the moment for a proper break, then," Wu Chang told her. "Youngster, you should too."

"Youngster? I'm old...." Whatever Unhcegila wanted to say was quickly squashed by Wu Chang's hand on his shoulder. "Oh. All right."

The pair went into the woods, ostensibly to do what men did in forests while traveling. Margarita kept examining Henrietta's foot, watching for the shadow, listening for the noise. Thankfully, Henrietta understood they were in trouble, for she didn't ask any questions. Just stood there, occasionally making a little snoring noise.

A voice spoke from the darkness. "Well now, looks like you done been left all by yerself, missy."

Missy? Margarita was in her late twenties, no child to be called such a thing. She set Henrietta's foot down and watched two men approach from the path below. Neither were familiar. Just average looking men. Big and burly, certainly. Not the sort anyone would want to meet on a dark road at night. Especially not alone.

"My friends will be back soon enough," she told the men. "No need to worry about me."

One chuckled. "Wouldn't be too sure about that." A shout and a yell up in the trees seemed to prove him right. "Hope our buddies aren't too rough with that pretty gel you're traveling with." Shots followed. Then silence.

Margarita set her hand on Henrietta's flank. "Why is it everyone thinks Wu Chang is a woman?" she asked. "I realize he's quite pretty for a man, but he's flat as a board. Doesn't have much in the way of hips, either."

The man stared at her. Sneered. "Pretending you aren't scared?" He raised his gun. Fired it past her. Or, rather, tried to fire it past her. By now she'd exerted her magic and hardened the air between them. The bullet struck, embedding itself, then fell to the ground when she released it. "The hell?"

"Henrietta, would you mind assisting?"

"Got it, Margarita." The water horse shifted form, streamed down the path to gather around the other man's ankles. At the same time Margarita launched herself at the first man, wrapping solidified air around his weapon and hitting the man in the jaw with a fist covered in more of the same.

The men just weren't ready for the kind of assault Margarita and her companion could offer. They tried to break free. Tried to run. But Henrietta half-drowned her opponent while Margarita half-suffocated hers. By the time Wu Chang and Unhcegila came back, two more bandits slung over their shoulders, the pair who'd accosted Margarita were down and out for the count.

"Ah, good. I was sure you'd manage." Wu Chang set his victim down beside the others. A huge bruise crossed the man's face, a long narrow mark, as if he'd been struck by a bar.

Or a blunted sword. Unhcegila's opponent's face looked as if he'd stuck it in a chimney and he smelled like sulfur. He was coughing softly, though deeply unconscious.

"I'm glad you didn't kill him, Unhcegila," she told the boy. He sneered, turning away as if unimpressed. Except she caught a glimpse of a faint smirk as he hid his face from her.

"I reminded him the young master would prefer it if we avoid killing. Fortunately, he seems willing to cooperate for the moment."

"It's Bly I want," Unhcegila growled. "The rest don't matter."

Even so, it was good to see the monster trying to be less monstrous. Margarita had a sneaking liking for him, despite his grumpy ways and foul temper. She'd be quite happy to see him choose to change his nature.

"What do we do with them?" Henrietta asked. "We don't have time to take them to jail."

They didn't. But, of course, they didn't have to. These four might, just might, be useful. "I think we persuade them to help us search for Yi Xiao. Given we can scare them enough."

⇒)(⇐

Yi Xiao allowed Bly to convince him to perform. Not out of fear, or any special desire to entertain, but because it'd give him a chance to properly investigate the circus and its captives. He was almost certain each and every one of the beasts under Bly's command were some form of monster. The question was, could they be freed and if so, should they be?

The elephant and camel had been stolen from their homelands. They had no human forms and almost no power, this far from their origins. There were several more monsters among the horses; a creature calling himself a nightmare, another belonging to this land. Neither were truly dangerous. Nor were the various rats, cats and dogs and one fox that wandered the camp stealing scraps.

Many of Bly's men were monsters as well, or a close kin. Some were descendants of human sorcerers who'd transformed themselves. There were more wolves like men, more intelligent than the ones Yi Xiao had met on the way south from Zak's mine. They were obviously cooperating with Bly and not his problem at all.

The jaguar felt like something more than a monster, not quite a God. Old power surged inside her, weakened by time and loss. "Your kin seeks you. Wait for him and I'll help. Master says, patience is a virtue. Try it some time."

She managed a purr, though it was obvious she didn't like waiting any more than he did. He was about to say more, but sensed someone headed their way. Not wanting anyone to see him so close to her, he stepped several feet back and watched her watch him, her tail twitching slow danger inside her cage.

"There you are. Boss wants you out soon. You got what you need?"

Yi Xiao smiled at the older man. "I do." Bly had given him the run of the costume cart earlier and he was now dressed in loose and brightly colored clothing, his hands full of handkerchiefs. "Please, lead the way."

The circus's performance area was surrounded by a temporary rope fence, from which the young man in charge of the horses was just leaving, the nightmare on his left shifting nervously around, as if he'd caught scent of something dangerous.

Spotting the green-eyed man among the crowd, Yi Xiao knew the nightmare had. He hoped the jaguar's friend would be sensible and wait for the right moment. There were too many people and too many weapons to impetuously leap into action. Spirits and Immortals were tougher than human but they weren't invulnerable.

As Yi Xiao walked to the center of the arena the audience howled with laughter. Bly, who'd been busy introducing him, turned, a little startled. Chagrinned, he gave Yi Xiao a sharp glare. He couldn't say anything about Yi Xiao's decision to play clown without losing face himself. All he could do was shout, "And so I present, the master of flying fabric, Xing Lu the Wanderer!"

Someone played a trumpet, the noise of it rising above the crowd. Happily, Yi Xiao shouted in Mandarin, "Is everybody happy?"

The audience had no idea what he was saying, of course, but the less they understood, the better. Yi Xiao flung insults at Bly in every dialect and language he knew, tossing handkerchiefs in the air in a wild dance that sent him careening around the arena. At the same time he made sure to get close to the jaguar's kinsman and once again met his eyes. "Wait," he mouthed, before dancing off and yelling in Chinese again. "What belongs to you but others use it more?"

Somewhere in the crowd, someone answered his shouted riddle. "Your name!" The language wasn't Chinese, but he recognized it immediately. Grassland speech. The *Nian?* He scanned the crowd. Spotted one of the men who'd attacked them two nights earlier. Now what were they doing, still following him around?

Knowing better than to draw attention to his countryfolk, Yi Xiao continued leaping and jumping, watching the rebel's behavior. It was just the one man, the same one who'd been scared off by Wu Chang. He ought to be angry, but instead he grinned and made gestures Yi Xiao recognized from his visits to the grasslands. Affirmative gestures from one ally to another.

At last Yi Xiao finished his performance, carefully avoiding letting the *Nian* rebel try to talk to him. Bly was sure to get suspicious. From his expression, he was already. "Who's that fellow talked back to you?"

"This humble clown doesn't know. Does not know. Really doesn't know." Yi Xiao spread his hands helplessly. "I'm not sure what he said, either. He looked a bit like a nomad to me."

Suspicion remained in Bly's eyes, but he shrugged it off. "You're good at what you do, Chinaman. Could have warned me you'd be doing a clown act. I thought you'd at least do some knife throwing."

"This one prefers gentler play, Mr. Bly. If you allowed me my magic, of course, I could really have shown you something."

That made Bly sneer. "No doubt. But since I don't want you running off on me, I think we'll just keep things as they are."

A bow. "As Mr. Bly wishes, so it shall be. Now, if you don't mind, I think I could do with a bit of water. It may not look it, but throwing handkerchiefs around is thirsty work."

A little disgusted, Bly waved him off without another word.

⋺)(⋵

It wasn't difficult to frighten their would-be attackers into cooperation. Keeping them moving in the right direction was a bit harder, but Wu Chang's cold presence proved an effective encouragement, despite their plain desire to run as far and as fast as they could.

Margarita knew from her map of the area that the pass over the ridge was only about eight miles. Eight miles of difficult, rocky, terrain just barely suitable for a caravan. Still, Bly had had a head start, so she wasn't surprised to find them reaching the other side a little after midnight.

"What's the nearest settlement?" she asked one of their captives, the oldest one, called Burt. "The most likely place for Bly's circus to go next?" They'd already discussed who they were chasing and gotten past the 'who are you more afraid of' stage of the conversation.

"Probably El Alisal. It's just his sorta place."

It was indeed. Margarita liked to know the lay of the land and while El Alisal was at the edge of her knowledge, she had heard of it. The town was more of a bandit hideout than anything else. Oh, it pretended to respectability but word was there was a shoot-out on its streets at least once if not twice a day. Bly would certainly love the place.

Of course, the fact that it was right along the path to El Diablo probably didn't hurt. Margarita was fairly sure they'd guessed right about Bly's plans for Yi Xiao. He meant to drag the young man all the way to that mountain and try and force him to draw on its power. To what purpose aside from curiosity? That, Margarita wasn't as sure of.

It only took another hour to reach El Alisal and barely half that to find the circus outside town. From the looks of things, the show was just closing down. "Why would he put on a show when he knows he's being hunted?" she wondered.

"Hubris comes to mind. That or he doesn't realize we're following." Wu Chang indicated himself and the children. "He never saw you. He might not know you were around. He thinks the children wouldn't dare. He thinks I'm dead. Which, granted, I am, but not the way he believes."

That last made one of their captives shudder. He'd shot Wu Chang straight between the eyes earlier and watched the man walk over and calmly shatter his gun with one blow of his black sword. The others hadn't seen what he had, but Margarita could tell the man would never, ever, go after a pallid skinned stranger in the dark again.

Margarita turned to their captives. "This is all we need for you to do. Approach the circus. Find a Chinese man called Yi Xiao. He is about my height, with collar length hair. If you find him and he answers to his name, give him this."

'This' was a solidified rectangle of air, marked with a few words in Chinese. Margarita and Wu Chang had prepared the message together and all Yi Xiao needed to do was trace the characters to read it. The spell wouldn't last past morning, but with luck, the men would find him before that.

"We're done with you after?"

"Yes. As long as you stay out of our way."

The four men ran into the circus grounds with admirable diligence. Margarita grimaced, hoping they wouldn't accidentally reveal their purpose, and scanned the landscape. Between the moonlight and the torches across the field it was possible to see a dozen carts, a single stagecoach, a number of cages and a bulky shape at the far side that almost had to be that elephant.

"Any sign of Harachul and his people?" she asked Wu Chang.

"I believe they may be setting up camp on the other side of the circus." Wu Chang paused. Added, "Except for Harachul, who thinks he can sneak up on the Hollowed Blade for some reason."

A chuckle above them. "I should have known you'd notice." The man slid down a low rockface and leaned beside them, teeth white in the moonlight. "Yi Xiao's in there. Don't know why you sent those men in to check."

"We weren't sure where you were, yet," Margarita explained. "Does Yi Xiao know you're here to help?"

The man shrugged. "Doubt it. Probably thinks we're still trying to get him to come home with us. Which we would if we could."

"Can't we just go in and burn the place down?" Unhcegila asked suddenly. "You wouldn't have to worry too much about the landscape. Henrietta can put stuff out before it spreads."

"Henrietta is not your personal water bucket," Henrietta grumbled.

"Both of you hush." As the pair fell silent, glaring at each other, Margarita put her fingers to the bridge of her nose. They were good kids, really, but so difficult at the same time. "While burning the circus down would be satisfying, there are other people involved."

"Fair number of monsters, too," Harachul told her. "Never seen so many in one place, all dancing to one man's orders."

Wu Chang inclined his head. "That whistle spell of his is powerful and not to be underestimated."

"Can he do anything to you?" Harachul asked suddenly. "I've heard you're a monster."

A slight smile crossed Wu Chang's face. "I am dead and alive because I have no heart, Harachul. Not a monster as such." He considered the caravan thoughtfully. "I suppose it isn't impossible, if Bly's magic extends to transformed humans. Fortunately, I have a supply of that pill Mr. Chang gave us. If need be, I will take one."

Margarita wasn't surprised Wu Chang had made sure to bring those pills along. "Good. Knowing Yi Xiao, he won't be satisfied as long as Bly can hold even one captive."

A new voice spoke, rough and harsh, like a wildcat's growl. The words it spoke weren't in English but Margarita understood them even so. "You have pills to block the evil one's call? I'll have one of those. Now."

The voice didn't sound human and when Margarita turned to face it, she wasn't surprised to find herself face to face with a huge black jaguar, eyes glowing bright red in the darkness.

⇒)(⇐

The sound of a wild animal howling drew everyone's attention southwest. Yi Xiao sighed, recognizing a cat's yowls, magnified by rage and fury. What had that other jaguar found to set him off? If he weren't supposed to be a prisoner, he'd have gone out immediately to find out.

Bly growled a curse. "That damned thing again?" They were sitting in his coach, eating a late meal after all the efforts of the afternoon.

"Again?"

"It keeps following. It's probably related to our pretty Jacqueline, but it's too damned clever and too damned quick for me to get at." Bly sneered. "I'll capture it sooner or later. Maybe once you've gotten me more of the Old Man's power."

Yi Xiao kept his face blank, but the idea that an old and still powerful existence like that one would give even a bit of their power to someone like Bly seemed nonsensical. Not to mention Bly had yet to persuade Yi Xiao to try. "Speaking of whom, is it my understanding that you plan to take me directly to this Old Man. How close do you expect to go?"

"Close as possible, boy. That thing's been lying dormant for ages. It'll need a good solid yell in its ear to get its attention."

A good solid yell in the ear of an ancient power, especially one being woken from a sound nap didn't seem like the height of sanity. "What," Yi Xiao said slowly, "Makes you think I want to be turned to charred embers?"

"Eh?"

"You say that Old Man is connected to the Mother of Mountains. The same Mother of Mountains whose power I borrowed a month or so back, right?"

Bly shrugged. "Yeah. So? You were right on top of her then. Or near enough."

"The Mother was also awake, favorable to my cause, and willing to share. I've no such guarantees with this Old Man you want to poke. Do you stick your hands down snake holes to find out if you'll be bitten too?"

It was obvious from Bly's cold eyes that he was furious. He kept his voice calm as he said, "Do you think I don't take proper precautions?"

"True. I'm sure you have someone else put their hand down the snake hole instead." Yi Xiao tilted his head. Smiled. "But I've no death wish and if you actually want a positive result from this, you may want to reconsider your plans. Because I promise you, if you force me to summon this power where he's strongest, I'll make sure to let him know just who asked me to do so."

Bly was about to respond furiously when one of his men opened the coach door and poked his head in. "Boss. That damned cat's fighting someone just outside the circus grounds. You want we should try and get him while he's distracted?"

"An excellent proposal." Bly gave Yi Xiao a sharp look. "I'll be back to talk to you later, boy. We're not through here. Not by a long shot."

Once Bly had gone, Yi Xiao leaned back in his seat. He needed to see if he could reach that Old Man from a greater distance. Not for help, but because he might be able to rouse the old being without putting himself at risk. He was about to close his eyes and reach out mentally when someone tapped on the coach door.

"Yes?" With a sigh, Yi Xiao pushed the door open.

A complete stranger peeked inside. "You.. ah... are you Mr. Yi Xiao?"

"I have the honor to be called that, yes."

The man thrust what seemed like an empty hand at Yi Xiao. "Message. Take it."

Confused, Yi Xiao automatically reached out and bumped his fingers into a solid surface, one that seemed formed from the air itself. Remembering Margarita's magic, he took it, asking, "Sister Margarita?"

"If she's a nun, I'm the goddamned Pope," the man snapped. "I'm done here. Good luck. Near as I can tell, you're gonna need it." Before Yi Xiao could open his mouth to ask another question, the man ran off into the darkness.

Yi Xiao had no idea what Sister Margarita had done to scare the man so and decided this wasn't the time to try and figure it out. He examined the solid square with his fingers. Found writing on it in Chinese. A simple message. "We are here. We will rescue you at your signal."

Well, at least those two knew better than to come running straight into camp and try dragging him out. Aside from the dangers of dealing with Bly's people and monsters, there was the fact that Yi Xiao wasn't leaving until he'd broken Bly's hold on his slaves.

Once again he sat back. He wasn't sure what was going on with that fight outside, though he suspected his friends had something to do with it. He did know he had to figure out what he was going to do about that Old Man of the Mountain.

Before he really did wind up a charred lump of overcooked flesh on the mountainside.

⇒)(⇐

Margarita's magic was too weak to completely stop the jaguar from reaching them. It wasn't just his physical strength but his spiritual. His body slammed into her shield of thickened air at the same time his magic did. He yowled fury, clawing wildly. Before she could do anything he was through and leaping for her.

Swords flashed in moonlight, striking the jaguar out of the air. The beast leapt on their owner, ripping at his throat, only to gag and spit a moment later. "Dead man. You're mine. Get up!"

Wu Chang rose to his feet. Gazed levelly at the jaguar. "Respect, old one. Regret to inform you I belong to another. Also, tasting my blood is a mistake." The jaguar howled, forced backwards somehow.

"He's right, old fellow, old pal. He's still got someone's faith on him. All we got are the dregs." Deathshead's laughter echoed across the valley, a yipping cry like a coyote hunting. "And now we got company because you just had to go making a fuss."

The jaguar growled. Shifted form to a human man with long jet black hair and dark brown skin. Mexican? Or something else? Margarita couldn't tell. He glanced towards the camp. People were running their way and she was sure it was their fight that'd attracted them. "I'll kill them all."

"Pardon, old one, but perhaps discretion would be better?"

Margarita seconded the idea. "We have a friend we'd like to save. And if I know him, he wants to save everyone Bly's captured. I'm guessing you've kin over there. Could we, perhaps, find a hiding place and make plans?"

Deathshead joined them. "Put up that pretty air wall of yours. Right there."

"What?"

"I'll cover us, but I need something solid to work on." Deathshead's grin broadened. "Or don't you trust me, Maggie milove?"

Of course she didn't trust him. She'd learned a long time ago not to trust him. Still, they didn't have time to waste. She drew on her magic to build a new shield of thickened air between them and the others. A moment later the men from Bly's camp came to a halt.

"The hell? Where are they?"

"I was sure...."

A noise off to the side drew the men's attention. Unhcegila had suddenly taken off running, Henrietta close behind. The pair raced away, so fast nothing could have caught up. Margarita forced herself not to react, not to call out. At a guess, those two young fools were creating a distraction. She'd talk to them about such impetuous stunts later. She hoped.

The men all ran after the escaping pair, until they were once more alone and quiet. Margarita removed her shield and turned her attention on Deathshead. "What are you doing here?"

"I hired that boy to do some work for me. I wanted to make sure it got done, uninterrupted."

"Trickster, your interference comes at a high cost. If it endangers my daughter...."

Margarita interrupted the two Old Ones. She didn't know what arguments lay between the pair and didn't' want to. "Gentlemen. We all have reason to want something from Bly and his camp. Can we please discuss our plans elsewhere, before someone notices us again?"

"Don't worry, Maggie milove. I've made sure that won't happen. We can talk here." Deathshead turned to Wu Chang. "Yer boss know what he's doing?"

"Old one, respect, but I'm not even sure you know what you're doing." Wu Chang sat on a rock, holding his torn throat with one hand so the skin would heal back properly. He turned his attention on the other man. "Pardon, but could we know a name to call you?"

"No."

Margarita sighed. "All right, then, sir. You were asking...."

"Demanding."

"Demanding one of the pills we were given to help protect Bly's victims from his magic."

"You will give them."

"Not all. I'll give you one."

Deathshead's mouth worked. "Hey, you're never near this cooperative with me, Maggie milove."

"Think about why that might be and be quiet, Deathshead," she retorted. "I'm giving him one because Yi Xiao wants those monsters down there freed too. Since this gentleman wants to save his daughter, it doesn't matter who gives it to her. In fact, if he'd like one for himself I think we can spare two."

"No need. That bastard cannot touch me with his magic. Try though he might."

Which meant this one wasn't a monster. Possibly neither was the one he wanted to save. But both he and Deathshead were of a higher order than the creatures Bly commanded. "Then have this and go. But please, if you would, don't hurt our friend."

"Given what he attempts this moment, the strange one is more a danger to himself than the world is. I go now." Taking the pill Margarita proffered, the old one ran off silently. Just as the ground beneath them began to rock.

Wu Chang was gazing down towards the campsite with a resigned expression. "I'd hoped to avoid this. We can only pray we're out of range."

"What?"

With a barking laugh, Deathshead answered, "That boy's contacted Father Mountain, just like Bly wanted."

⋺)(⋶

Yi Xiao really hadn't expected to connect with that power Bly wanted immediately. But other things were happening close by to disturb the Old Man's rest. Nothing strong, but even the deepest sleeper can be woken if someone started yowling outside their door. When another being added yipping laughter and two small and aggravating children chased each other at the edge of the Old Man's robes? Well it'd be a miracle if he didn't start waking.

Add Yi Xiao's light touch, at just the right moment, and the Old Man rousing and turning his full attention on the latest irritant was no surprise at all. Yi Xiao tried to pull back and almost succeeded. He wasn't close by, after all. But the Old Man was awake and curious and wanted to see what was going on.

Opening Yi Xiao's eyes, the Old Man gazed inquisitively at the things humans had made. Different. So very different from the world He'd known before He'd gone to sleep. What a strange box this was. Nothing like His people's houses. It bounced a little beneath him, twisted metal rising and falling with every movement.

The Old Man pushed on a wall. Felt one piece give way. Punched. Wood splintered and crashed to the ground, revealing a darkened sky. He stepped out, ignoring the little humans coming to see the source of the noise. Someone shouted. "Hey! You stay where boss put yah!"

The words weren't the language of His people either, but He had no difficulty understanding them. If He wanted, He could even respond. He chose not to, gazing up at an unfamiliar night sky. How far was He from His own place and land, for the stars to be so changed?

He corrected Himself. He wasn't at all far from His place. The Old Man could sense His mountain, not terribly far away. Feel His Lady Wife in the distance. It wasn't His place that'd changed, but the time. He'd watched the stars change for thousands up on thousands of years in the past. He'd just slept so long that the difference was more noticeable.

"I said, get back in that coach!"

The human was being annoying. Not annoying enough to kill, much to the relief of His host, but annoying enough to silence. He reached out. Touched the pale-skinned human in the middle of his forehead. "No. You." Without hesitation, eyes blank, the human turned and climbed into the boxy thing. A coach, His host verified. A vehicle on wheels, pulled by beasts.

His own people hadn't used such tools. But then, it was obvious by the feel of the land that His own people were no more. His host corrected Him. Not gone, as such, but diminished, their memories of the past and their faith in Him long since passed.

Well, that was the way of the world. All His kind faded or split or became new things. He persisted only because He, like His Lady Wife, were part of a very old power. Stoppers, his host suggested. Protectors? Yes. That. The Old Man began walking, examining His surroundings with interest. A circus? Imprisoned monsters, forced to dance for their supper?

Other monsters gathered. Some with human ancestry, others purely created beings. Some were familiar, old beasts who'd haunted and hunted this land for generations. Others were newer, imported beings with no proper connection. They came at Him, tried to catch Him. He brushed them off easily, refraining from killing only because the thought distressed His host.

Something came at Him from the dark. Human in form, but with hands half-transformed to claws. Power slashed at Him, raging fury from the depths of the underworld. Ah, yes. That was right. This one had come to His mountain years back. Had tried to steal His place, him and his daughter. Been rebuffed.

His host was strong for a human. Not strong enough to take the power the Old Man could draw on. Fortunately, His host's natural skill, the one he called *qi*, was more than enough. He summoned lightning out of the clear night sky. Sent the southerner flying. To His surprise the idiot was back on his feet, hungry for more. That one had had sense, once. How much had he lost?

People were running towards them as they fought. Claws caught at His host's clothes, tore the shirt from His shoulders. Lightning crackled around them both, setting the southerner yowling. Another voice answered, a child screaming for her father.

He took a chance. Tossed the southerner as far from him as possible. Raced for the source of the noise. Ah. There. A little baby monster, just fallen from the high road. She was trying to break out of her cage. Failing, of course, because a spell twisted around her spirit. A human's magic, binding her in place and keeping her under his control.

A voice shouted. "The HELL is going on around here?" Something exploded past his host's ear and he automatically shattered it with his lightning. "How'd you slip your lead, boy?"

The speaker was another human. Pale-skinned like so many of the others. The men from earlier were behind him, their rage bright orange. They waved sticks that smelled of sulfur, setting more explosions off as they yelled. What strange weapons were these? Like but not like the spear-throwers he remembered.

Guns. Rifles. That was the name the humans called the things. His host's explanation didn't help much, but made it clear the weapons were even more dangerous than spear-throwers. The Old Man's host could destroy the bullets they fired with his lightning, but he was tiring. It wouldn't be long before his strength would fail.

The southerner was back, trying to get at the one His host called Bly. Trying and failing because those bullets were doing him some damage. At the same time, men were shouting in yet another language, calling, "We'll help you, Prince! Don't worry!"

Men were fighting all around him now. Bly was whistling, his magic twining itself through the monsters' thoughts and trying to force obedience. The jaguar baby screamed in terror. And to top it off, two small elemental monsters were trying to help.

He recognized Unhcegila, a being who'd dragged himself from the depths of the earth and become a thing of both fear and awe. The fire-snake was weaker now. Shattered into separate pieces, with this one speck existing as a lonely cut-off part on His Lady Wife's skirts. The other was strange, a creature of waters quite far from her origin.

At His host's request he called out to the children. "Protect the cage." All those bullets flying might hurt the baby monster. She hadn't done anything wrong.

Unhcegila shot Him a sharp look of recognition but He ignored it, focusing on keeping those bullets from hurting His host. At the same time Bly's whistle grew louder. More insistent. It called the other monsters around them closer; demanded they fight.

A figure flung itself out of the darkness. One His host recognized. An undead called Wu Chang, a monster of sorts, but one already under a geas. Bly's magic couldn't touch him. He tackled Bly, flinging him to the ground and blocking his mouth with one hand. "Call them off."

The monsters were getting closer but without a whistle to control them, they were losing direction. The less violent ones were escaping, but that left a good dozen or so still willing to fight. They growled, ignoring the bullets aimed their way.

Someone laughed delightedly in the darkness. "Now, when I said break up Bly's little operation, I didn't mean wake the Old Man and start a riot. But what an excellent comedy this is, even so!"

⇒)(⇐

Margarita yearned to punch Deathshead in the gut, just for being himself. If she didn't need her magic to keep Bly trapped she might well have. Instead, she said calmly, "Bly, call them off. Unless you'd like Wu Chang to break your neck."

"Got... to... whistle... for that." Bly's voice was muffled by Wu Chang's hand, his body pressed into the dirt beneath the undead swordsman.

He was right. But letting him do so was a fool's game. They couldn't trust him at all. She drew on her magic. Built a sphere of solid air around him and Wu Chang. She had to find another way. Turning to Bly's human followers, she said, "Stop fighting. Your boss isn't going anywhere. I'll let him smother first."

One, smarter than the others, could tell what she'd done and scoffed. "That gel's in there with him. You won't let her suffocate."

"Three things," Margarita told the man. "First, Wu Chang is a man. Second, he isn't mine. Third, he doesn't need to breathe." She let the sound of her voice pass through her spell, so Bly could hear too. "Bly, you tell them. Surrender. Now."

Bly tried whistling, but Wu Chang wasn't interested. He just pulled the man to his feet and spoke in the man's ear. At last, angrily but clearly helpless, Bly gestured at his men. As unwillingly as their boss, they set their weapons down and let the *Nian* rebels tie them up.

Margarita turned her attention on Yi Xiao, who'd been watching the entire thing with a look of wide-eyed wonder. "You good?"

"Good? Evil? Such things don't apply to me." The man's voice sounded strange. As if there were a multitude speaking. "But the host is unharmed, which I think is your concern?"

Host? Oh no. "Yi Xiao. What have you done?"

"Ah, something stupid." This time it was one voice speaking and clearly Yi Xiao's. "I think I'll be all right, once this gentleman has finished his business."

"What business would that be?" Margarita asked, trying to stay calm despite her terror. She could feel the power inside Yi Xiao. Could tell it was nothing any mortal should contain. Not with any expectation of surviving.

The being possessing Yi Xiao took over again. "Really. All of you are so noisy." He turned his attention on the man who'd attacked her and Wu Chang earlier. "And I was sleeping so soundly, too."

"You should have just given up and left it to me. I've better uses for your power than you."

"I'm sure. But would the lives around us agree?" A smile; chill and dangerous. As the other man snarled, the Old Man continued. "I thought not. And see what poking your nose where it doesn't belong bought you? Half your power stripped away, your daughter lost. Go home, southerner. You don't belong here."

Another growl. "Not without my daughter."

"Oh, her?" A negligent wave of the hand shattered the cage bars. "Take her."

"Sir? If you don't mind being a little more careful? I think you've broken my wrist." That was Yi Xiao, reminding the Old Man that the body he wore was all too human and fragile.

At the same time, the young jaguar leaped out and into the big man's arms, snuffling at him wildly. Margarita caught the man's eye. Mouthed, 'Go'. To her surprise, he actually listened, turning jaguar himself and running off into the darkness, his daughter close behind.

Yi Xiao, or rather the one possessing him, turned to look at Margarita. Smiled. "Maybe you can tell me just why it is everyone's been making a fuss? It's like an Old Man can't get any sleep around here."

"You've been sleeping too much... ahgha ehaiial...." Deathshead, whose love of attention had overwhelmed what little good sense he had, choked as the Old Man gestured, a lackadaisical brush through the air that simultaneously silenced the trickster and dropped him into the dirt.

"Quiet, you. I was talking to the young lady. I smell my Lady Wife on her, and that means she's got more sense than anyone else here."

Margarita doubted that was nearly true. Politely, she told the Old Man, "I'm not sure about everything, but I believe that man there is the one who most wanted your attention." She pointed at Bly. "He wanted to ask you for power."

"Oho? Power? And is he worthy?"

"I don't think so. I don't think any of us here are worthy of your power." She bowed, "Old One, truly, unless there is something you would do here, it would be better for all if you returned to your rest."

"But I haven't seen my Lady Wife in.... oh... a thousand heartbeats." Yi Xiao tapped his chest. "My sort of heartbeats, of course. Not yours."

That might be true, but Margarita didn't think it would be at all good for anyone if he tried. Yi Xiao's face was getting pale, sweat soaking his hair, his hands trembling. "You'll kill your host before you can reach her."

A smile. "Well, true. And I don't actually want to do that." He turned his attention on Bly. "But this one did call me and it would be terribly impolite not to hear him out. Release him from your spell, if you would?"

Again Yi Xiao interrupted. "Could I ask you not kill him?"

"Kill? Why would I kill him just for coming to me as a supplicant?" The Old Man gestured towards Bly. "If you would?" he repeated.

Something told Margarita that the Old Man was capable of far worse than killing. He didn't seem too angry, though. And, really, Bly had been asking for his attention. She sighed. Released Bly and Wu Chang from her sphere.

By now Bly had been breathing stale, stuffy, air. He took a single deep breath, pursing his lips to whistle, but Yi Xiao moved faster. Three steps carried him to stand right in front of Bly, his finger pressed against the man's lips. Their eyes met and Bly froze like a frightened rat.

"You were the one called me?"

"I... yes."

"And you wanted?"

Greed made some men foolhardy. Bly was one of them. "This land is empty of its people," he said. "Your people. Your power fades. I'd like to do something about that. I'll bring you followers. Bring you monsters. Make you a God again. Just give me the power to do so and I'll be your willing servant."

The Old Man eyed him. "If my power fades, why do you seek it? If I'm not a God, why would you worship me? If I have little power of my own, why should I give it to another?"

Bly stared. Stammered. Didn't find the words he needed to find. The Old Man smiled. Patted his cheek. "I can't blame you. It's in the human heart to reach for what you do not have. To quench your thirst at all the wrong streams."

"Sir... I...."

"It's all right. You did rouse me at a time when my place might be endangered by the new ones coming. So, yes. I'll give you power." The Old Man's smile broadened and Margarita felt a chill run down her spine. "Just remember, the price of a God's gift is the gift itself. Do you still want it?"

Margarita wouldn't have touched such a bargain with a ten foot pole. Bly was made of different cloth and he grinned. "Sure thing. I truly would."

The Old Man set Yi Xiao's hand on Bly's chest. "Then have it."

Light flared. The ground shook. Something howled. Margarita covered her ears, aware everyone around her was doing the same. And somewhere amid the noise and ruckus, she heard Bly cry out, "Wait. No. That's not...." Then, silence.

Everyone had fallen to the ground except Bly. He stared up at the sky. Turned his gaze down at his hands. Smiled. A terribly familiar smile. The same smile that'd been on Yi Xiao's lips a moment earlier. He took a deep breath. "Well, now. That's settled."

Yi Xiao looked up at Bly. "Did you kill him, after all?"

"Now that'd be a cruel thing to do. I just sent him to take my place for a while. Long enough for me to get things settled proper." Bly... the Old Man... Tuyshtak... grinned. Turned his attention on Bly's men. "What are you idjits doin', staring around like that. Go clean up the mess. Oh, and make sure you get them monsters fed proper. I'm gonna need to have a talk with 'em soon."

Such was Bly's power over his men that they obeyed. At the same time the Old Man helped Margarita to stand. "Could you tell my Lady Wife I'll stop in for a visit sometime in the near future? Seems to me I've got a lot of work to do, right 'round here."

She could hardly refuse. "What are you going to do?"

"That mountain of mine needs protecting, little girl. Gotta check out the lay of the land and work out what I can do about it." He turned his attention on Yi Xiao. "Thanks for the loan, boy. You handle yourself well. Hope I didn't break nothing. Aside from that wrist, I mean."

Yi Xiao was checking himself for injuries. "Beyond that, all I need is a long rest. I'll be fine, thank you for asking, sir."

"You give my regards to that Lightning Master of yours when you get the chance. She done taught you good."

"Master says, a teacher for a day is a father for life." Yi Xiao paused. "Well, mother, in her case. Also, my thanks, Old One."

"Ah, call me Bly. It'll confuse everyone if y'all use another name." Bly picked Henrietta and Unhcegila up and set them both on their feet. "You kids find yourself a safe place, 'kay? I don't want you causing trouble."

"Don't trouble trouble if it don't trouble you, Tuyshtak," Unhcegila snapped. Margarita was only mildly surprised when Henrietta echoed the sentiment. "We got homes and we're going to 'em."

One last person wanted the Old Man's attention. Deathshead. The trickster pointed at his mouth significantly and once Bly removed the spell silencing him, said, "You got any work for me?"

"Trickster, you find your own work where you want. I appreciate you getting me roused, but I'd rather not risk your kind of help for too long." The Old man smiled. "Run along for a while. And be careful out there."

Deathshead harrumphed. "Don't tell me how to steal chickens, Old Man. I know what I'm doing." He was gone, having had what he thought was the last word, before Tuyshtak could open his mouth.

"Of course you do. Which is why someone is always pulling you out of the clay pot you've stuck your pointed nose into," the Old Man muttered. "Very well. It's late, I'm sure the lot of you are plumb tuckered out. Better get some sleep 'fore you head yourselves back to San Francisco. I'll have my men set up a place for you lot, don't worry."

For a moment Margarita wasn't sure she liked the idea of staying the night in a circus full of monsters, run by an old God who'd incarnated on a whim. Then she remembered what she'd been told about El Alisal and decided they were probably safer with the monsters.

>)(<

It took a couple of days to get back to Majeure Community. They'd shed companions along the way: Bly and his circus to Santa Clara; the *Nian* rebels—under protest—in San Francisco to be returned to China. Well, Harachul stayed, but he'd decided to become a miner. Yi Xiao tried to convince Wu Chang to escort the *Nian* home, but his unwanted bodyguard would have nothing to do with the idea.

"Master says, when trouble is always behind you, it's best to have a friend there, too."

"Now who's making things up?" Yi Xiao demanded. Though, admittedly, he was a little relieved, too. If Gan Han had been more like Wu Chang—quiet, thoughtful and unaggressive—she would have made a fine traveling companion. He wasn't lonely, but there was something to be said for having someone around to talk to, if talking was needed. No one said seeking the *Dao* had to mean abandoning all human contact.

They left Henrietta with the community and her friend Oren. Dona Estrella even offered to let them stay. When Yi Xiao pointed out he was a man, she said, "One of the few I think I can trust not to molest my girls. And I'm fairly sure Wu Chang couldn't, even if he were interested."

The fact that he'd no desire to molest anything was so basically true Yi Xiao chose not discuss it. "I'm still a distraction you don't need. Best if I keep moving. Besides, I promised Unhcegila I'd help him find his hidey hole near Mount Tam." The fire snake mostly wanted to be left alone and Yi Xiao figured he wasn't ready to be socialized enough to do otherwise.

Dona Estrella smiled. "True. And if that one stays here we'd be rebuilding every time he and Henrietta fight. Which is entirely too often, I fear. Then I will bid you farewell and hope you return once in a while. You will always be welcome here."

Once he'd paid proper respects to the sisters, Yi Xiao left the community to head north, Unhcegila a warm ember curled on his shoulder. Wu Chang walked beside him, head covered by a broad rimmed hat, body by a handsome serape given to him by the sisters.

Sunlight gleamed on ocean to their left. Wind sang through the trees alongside their path. And somewhere in the distance, Yi Xiao felt the Mother of Mountains watching, keeping a close eye on the wandering fools who'd stumbled their way into her land and along her skirts.

Watching and keeping them safe.

THE END

Chapter 1
White Tiger Hunts the Mountains

"Get the little bastard!"

"Damnit, he's too slippery!"

"He's headed your way...don't let him...DAMNIT!"

Huge hands grabbed. Booted feet stomped. Knives flashed. All missed their target, increasing their owners' fury. They weren't used to being thwarted, especially by what locals called a little bit of nothing.

Jigme watched with professional interest, recognizing the youngster's style and puzzled by it. How had he persuaded the Storm Hermit to accept him as a pupil? The last time Jigme had seen that venerable, she was old, crotchety and not at all interested in taking disciples.

Yet there could be no doubt. Accused of cheating, Lang Yixiao had stripped to his underclothes, unembarrassed to stand practically naked in the middle of a crowded saloon. It'd proved he'd no cards hidden anywhere in his clothing. It'd also revealed a peculiar set of scars running along his arms and back.

Most of the crowd knew nothing about those scars. Jigme, on the other hand, knew they marked the boy as the Storm Hermit's student. Enemies might bear the scars of her attack, but only a true disciple could survive so many blows. Young Lang's back was covered in them.

For that matter, how had a disciple of the Storm Hermit wound up so far from home? The last place in the world Jigme would expect to find such a person would be a saloon in California's gold fields. Surely he wasn't a miner like so many of their fellow countrymen? The Storm Hermit practiced a restrained sort of style, cultivating self-control and moderation. Her disciples had no need of wealth.

No matter why the boy was here in Wildcat Gulch, he'd more purpose than brawling for the sake of it. He'd instigated the fight for a reason; playing an ignorant foreign youngster wandering far from home and falling into the hands of card-sharps.

Within minutes of meeting his would-be fleecers, the boy had shown off the fruits of his efforts in the gold fields and drunk far more than he ought to. At least Billy and Joey Royd thought so, offering to deal him into their game of poker. He'd gleefully accepted and gleefully played a brash and reckless game. A game he'd gleefully won and won and won and won. If he'd been what he'd seemed, that would have been his second mistake. Billy Royd did not like losing at anything.

Oh, Billy Royd absolutely let the first few hands go to the boy, but that was just to tempt him into increasing his risk. It was obvious when he planned to shift the balance of fortune his way. A glance at Joey, a half-dozen hands in, told Jigme the time had come.

Somehow that hand didn't go the way Billy Royd intended. Young Lang won again. And won the next. And the next. And each time he won, his opponents' expressions grew tighter and tighter, because the odds ought to have been in their favor.

Not that the Royd brothers would cheat here. Wildcat Gulch's saloon was their favorite watering hole. They wouldn't muddy the waters by obvious cheating. The locals drew the line at fraud; it'd give the saloon a bad reputation.

Cheating wasn't necessary. Anything Joey Royd won was Billy Royd's as well. Even playing fair, the brothers had the advantage here. If young Lang hadn't been so damned good at poker, they'd have wiped the table clean with him.

At last they'd reached the point of raw fury, of pointing fingers, of laying blame. They'd accused the boy of chicanery and demanded he strip to prove he wasn't hiding anything. To everyone's surprise and a great deal of cat-calling from the audience, young Lang had cheerfully removed everything except his underdrawers.

He'd still won that last hand, to the Royds' complete and utter fury. What sent them over the edge, however, wasn't young Lang winning, but the boy's offer to accept a certain bag instead of the money. A bag whose contents, according to the boy, included the mail-bag belonging to the carrier who'd been found that morning, throat cut, body still warm, tossed to the side of the road.

Realizing the young cultivator's purpose, Jigme considered helping out. That mail-bag held something important, something he'd sensed coming for a while now. He'd no wish to leave matters to chance. For all Jigme knew, the boy could be his enemies' spy. If so, letting young Lang get his hands on the thing would be dangerous.

In the end, Jigme decided to wait. There were others watching the fight with interest and he didn't want to draw attention to himself. His enemy might come from the homeland but that was no reason he'd limit himself to using fellow countrymen against Jigme.

Besides, from the looks of things, the boy didn't need help. Not at all.

⇒)(⇐

Yixiao freely admitted to enjoying himself. Even if he didn't want to kill anyone, he didn't mind the occasional free-for-all. That this particular fight had more purpose than relieving tension only made it more important. These two might be responsible for the death of a fellow mail-carrier and he meant to see justice done for young Tony Johnson. The kid might not have been bright, but he'd been dedicated and honest and good-natured.

The thought almost made him loose a full-on attack, complete with Lightning Smashes the Boulder and Thunder Splinters the Tree. But, no. These men weren't worth it. He'd take them down, retrieve the mail-bag they'd stolen and hand all three off to the local authorities. The mail-bag alone would be proof enough of their involvement. At least he hoped so.

Letting his body drop loosely below Billy Royd's grasping hand, he came up to catch the man's wrist, twisting effortlessly, flinging him head first to the floor. Knocked cold, Billy Royd lay still while his younger brother stopped to decide whether this was worth sticking around for.

Discretion was the better part of valor and the man clearly chose survival. If he'd simply made a run for it, abandoning everything in favor of escape, he might have made it. Instead he foolishly grabbed his stolen goods first.

Before the man could get out the door, Wuchang was on him, lifting the heavier and taller man off his feet by his throat. Yixiao's best friend and would-be protector had been waiting and watching for this, staying close to the door as backup.

As Joey Royd gasped and struggled, Yixiao winced for the victim. Wuchang might appear slim and soft, but he was immensely strong. A peculiar being, neither dead nor truly alive, he had powers most humans couldn't match. That was why Yixiao generally didn't ask him to fight; it simply wasn't fair.

"LET ME GO, YOU BASTARD!"

"Apologies, but this one cannot agree to your request," Wuchang told the man. "Unless, of course, you release that bag?"

That did the trick. Half-choked and flailing, Joey Royd obeyed the order and was instantly dropped to the ground a foot or so away. Yixiao grabbed the bag himself, just as one of the saloon's patrons, a tall and rangy white man with longish grey hair and an amused expression, came up.

Before Joey Royd could run, before Yixiao could react, the newcomer dropped a booted foot on the thief's chest. "Now kiddo, this fellow's nice and I guess he'd let you go, since you've been mostly smart enough not to push your luck. But I know you and even if you weren't the one cut that poor boy Johnson's throat for him, I'm sure you know something. So you're not going anywhere."

Yixiao eyed the man. "And you would be?" He dropped the false accent, speaking English correctly, just like Second Mother taught him.

"Preston Pierce, Mr. Shoe. You might call me a local lawman of sorts. At a guess, you thought you'd collect on the reward for the one stole the mail-packet young Johnson was carrying? Not that I'm doubting you, but you sure it was Royd and his gang?"

Yixiao cupped his hands. Bowed. Opened the sack Joey Royd had tried to abscond with. Inside was a mailbag, its ties still closed. "Is this proof enough, Mr. Pierce? And it's Mr. Lang. Yixiao is my personal name." He didn't bother trying to correct the pronunciation. There was only so much one could hope for this far from home.

Pierce frowned. "Lahng?" Yixiao must have flinched slightly, because he tried again. "Lang?"

"Yes, Mr. Pierce. Lang Yixiao...," he paused, realizing he'd inverted the order again. "Apologies. Yixiao Lang."

Ignoring the apology, Pierce looked into the bag. "They didn't have a chance to open it, I see." He took it, or tried to.

"Mr. Pierce," Yixiao murmured, "I've no proof aside from your say-so that you're a lawman. As a registered mail-carrier, I regard this as my responsibility. Master says, 'Finish what you start.'"

Giving him a long, thoughtful, look, Pierce finally said, "Then accompany me to the Sheriff's office and we'll handle this thing together." He looked over Yixiao's shoulder at Wuchang. "Him too, I guess. If nothing else, I could use help carrying those two."

Yixiao was about to agree when Pierce added, "You, ah, might want to get dressed first. It'll do wonders for Sheriff Lane's attitude if you don't show up at his door in your skivvies and a chuckleheaded smile."

᠍ ⇒)(⇐

Jigme gave young Lang and his companions a few minutes before following. He trusted neither American law nor cocky youngsters who might or might not be working for his enemy. Until he'd a better idea of the situation he'd stay back and await his chance.

It was dark outside, with a peculiar rusty tang to the dry air that worried at him. He was used to odd smells, this far into the gold fields, but this one was familiar. Had his enemy found him? He hoped not. He wasn't strong enough to fight. Not alone.

A shadow flickered and faded off to the side. Automatically, he spread his senses. With his spirit connected to every piece of metal in range he could 'feel' those around him easily. There were the saloon patrons, rowdy and unconcerned by the fight they'd just witnessed. Here were a horse and a mule, waiting patiently for their masters. There was old lady Stark, the only woman miner in the camp. And there, a faint and icy presence. One that faded almost as soon as he noticed it.

Jigme focused his cultivation on that presence, feeling it closer and faster than he liked. He evaded barely in time, bending flexibly as a hand reached out to touch his shoulder. Catching the other's wrist, he used their weight and motion to send them flying.

The stranger flipped and twisted, as if they were well-accustomed to being tossed around. The dim light of a nearby lantern limned attractive, almost feminine, features. This was the man who'd helped capture Joey Royd. Han Chinese, but unusual in that he wore his hair in the western style like young Lang. Not many of the Chinese miners who'd come to work the gold fields had broken tradition so thoroughly. Certainly Jigme had not.

"Respect, sir. But if you take interest in my Master's business, I must take interest in yours." The voice was quiet and gentle, unmarked by anger or even disdain. He spoke in Mandarin, faintly tinted with a Cantonese accent.

Jigme looked the man over, spotting the signs of long experience. Young Lang wasn't Jigme's match in a fight yet. This man might be. "You are?" Like the stranger, he used Mandarin. That, at least, he spoke well enough.

"Heibai Wuchang is the name I've been given." A slight smile at Jigme's expression. "Not, of course, the ones who serve the King of the Dead."

Taken aback, Jigme couldn't help asking, "Just who is Young Master Lang, that the Hollowed Blade serves as his guard?" Heibai Wuchang was a well-known assassin and bodyguard back in China. One with a reputation for being unkillable and possibly immortal. Now he faced the man, Jigme knew the rumors were true. As far as he could tell, the man's heart did not beat.

A slight smile curved the other man's lips and he dropped the formality. "That's not your business unless my master allows it. Why are you following him?"

If young Lang had ignored the law-man who'd shown up at the end of his fight, or run off with the mail-bag, Jigme would have refused to answer. The youngster's willingness to obey the rule of law said he might, possibly, be an ally instead of an enemy. "There's a package in that mailbag addressed to me."

Heibai Wuchang considered the explanation. Seemed to accept it. "You may as well come along, then. I can't speak for Mr. Pierce, nor for Sheriff Lane, but you have a right to whatever belongs to you."

The assassin led the way to the little building that served as the Sheriff's office. They arrived just as Pierce and Young Lang were setting their captives down on Sheriff Lane's rough wood floor.

"Pierce, I told you, unless you got proof...." That was Sheriff Lane, looking groggy and out of sorts. Apparently they'd woken him up for this. His red hair was a wild mess and his watery blue eyes blinked as he struggled to rouse himself.

"I have proof right here," Pierce told the Sheriff, handing him the sack the Royds had been carrying. "Take a look. You'll find the mail-bag with Tommy Johnson's name on it inside."

The sheriff looked towards the door then. "Oh, it's you, 'Brother' Jigme. What's wrong? Somebody try to dip your pigtail in ink?"

Jigme ignored the jibe. "This Jigme has mail." He pointed at the mail-bag. "Asks to retrieve."

Sneering, the sheriff looked about to send Jigme on his way but the man called Pierce interrupted. "There might be. You are?"

"Brother Jigme. Can describe package, if helps."

Young Lang was about to undo the bag's strings when Sheriff Lane grabbed his hand. "Hey. You can't be poking through U.S. Mail."

"I beg to differ, Sheriff Lane." Young Lang's English was oddly accented, leaving Jigme wondering where the boy had learned it. Not from an American, certainly. As Sheriff Lane opened his mouth to argue, young Lang held out a well-worn card. "I'm a mail-carrier myself, as I'm certain I informed you when I reported young Tommy's death this morning."

At a loss for words, the sheriff fell silent while the boy opened the mail-bag and poked around for a moment. Then he looked up, holding something hidden inside. "You said you could describe it?"

In English, to avoid problems, Jigme told him, "A blue package with metal dragon seal. A book of exercises."

"Blue?" Pierce repeated disbelievingly as he looked into the bag from the other side. "Don't try pulling the wool over our eyes, boy."

The reaction puzzled Jigme. "It should be blue, though. Sender's color."

Before Pierce could react, young Lang asked, "*Qing?*" At Jigme's agreement, the boy added in English, "It's a translation error, Mr. Pierce. *Qing* can mean either blue or green, and this is right between." He took a package wrapped in blue paper from the mail bag, adding, "We'll have to see about distributing the rest of this mail tomorrow, but I don't see a reason to hold this."

Neither Pierce nor Sheriff Lane were entirely happy with the idea but they clearly didn't have a reason to argue. "He knows to expect it. How about he opens it here, just to prove it's what he says it is."

By this time Jigme had already taken the package. He paused, worried. "Regret to say cannot be sure." He pointed at the seal, ever so slightly bent at one corner. "This one believes it's been opened already."

⇒)(⇐

Yixiao examined the package. "It looks to have been," he agreed. "Exercises, you said? What sort?" He eyed the newcomer curiously. At first glance he looked like most Chinese miners. Black hair braided tightly down his back, bangs thick and smooth, proving him the sort who refused to conform entirely to Manchurian laws. His features were broad, with sharp dark brows and startlingly white teeth in his well-tanned face. He was also surprisingly tall and rangy, with features suggesting a western Chinese origin.

Brother Jigme had an unwilling expression, suggesting there was more to the book than mere exercises. In Chinese, Yixiao told the man, "Trust is hard to gain, I know, but I am no agent for the Emperor."

That didn't entirely change the man's expression but Brother Jigme still said, in Chinese, "You won't be able to read it, but the title is Claw of the Tiger. It should be bound in white cloth."

That was an entirely unfamiliar form, but that meant nothing. There were hundreds of different martial styles in China. It wasn't possible to know of each and every one. In English, because he could tell his American companions weren't pleased to be left out of the conversation, he said, "Then let me open it and see if there's any reason to worry."

It was clear Brother Jigme would prefer not to allow it. He didn't have a choice, however, because neither Mr. Pierce, nor Sheriff Lane would let him take his package without knowing what was in it. That much was obvious.

Really, the package's contents ought not matter to either man. Yixiao wondered if there was a reason for the pair's suspicion, or if it was simply their distrust of foreigners. California might have become a state just the year before but it'd yet to become civilized. Foreigners were always an uncertain factor. Foreigners who competed for the same resources even more so.

Yixiao slid the wrapper off the package, revealing a small book bound in red cloth, its front marked with words in a familiar language. Not Chinese but one Yixiao knew even so. "Voice of the Vermillion Bird."

Brother Jigme started. Stared at him. "You read Khaitanese?" he asked in that language.

"My mother is from the Tu clan." Yixiao forbore mentioning just how closely she was related to Khaitan's king. No need to boast. Besides, there was no telling why Brother Jigme was so far from home. If he'd come from far distant Khaitan, he might have done so to avoid trouble with Yixiao's royal kinswoman.

Brother Jigme considered that. Came to a conclusion. "I wronged you."

Mr. Pierce interrupted. "You two talk so we can understand you. What's up with the book? Is it what he said?"

"No." They both spoke together, and Brother Jigme continued, once more in broken English, "It one of five books but not one expected."

Yixiao offered the book to Brother Jigme, but Sheriff Lane grabbed it before the man could take it. "Why you getting the book anyway, 'Brother' Jigme?"

"Eldest brother borrowed and returns."

Somehow Yixiao suspected there was more to it than that. He also doubted it had anything to do with the problem at hand. "Unless you think the Royd gang have some connection with Brother Jigme's kinfolk back in China, I don't see why it matters. Master says, 'Focus on what's important, before it focuses on you.'"

A dour expression crossed Sheriff Lane's face. Grudgingly, with a sneer of disdain, he handed the book to Brother Jigme. "You better not be up to something round here," he warned. "Run along. You got what you came for."

Brother Jigme bowed. Looked hesitantly at Yixiao. "Would like to discuss further. Have space in cabin for you, if willing to squeeze."

At a guess, Brother Jigme wanted more information. Since neither Mr. Pierce, nor Sheriff Lane would let Yixiao hang around while they interrogated their prisoners, Yixiao decided he'd be more useful accepting the offer.

"My partner and I would be delighted, Brother Jigme." Yixiao turned his attention on the two lawmen. "As a mail-carrier, the contents of that bag are my responsibility. When you're done with it, I'll be glad to take it on to the next stop."

The sheriff didn't look terribly pleased but Mr. Pierce agreed, much to Yixiao's relief. He wouldn't be able to grab the mail-bag by force, after all, but he hated the idea of leaving it to rot away in the law's hands while they decided what to do with it.

After all, there were people out there who expected news from their family. No reason to make them wait for it.

꒦)(꒷

Jigme's cabin wasn't quite big enough for three men, but Heibai Wuchang was perfectly willing to leave the inside to Jigme and young Lang. "I've an odd feeling trouble's brewing," he told them. "I'll be happier keeping an eye out for it."

Young Lang waved his companion on and settled comfortably on the floor of the cabin while Jigme made a small pot of tea. "I didn't think you'd want me to say anything in front of Mr. Pierce or Sheriff Lane, but I noticed the book titles both mention the beasts of the directions."

"En. That's right." Jigme poured two cups of tea and sat down across from Yixiao.

"And the book that was supposed to go to you is associated with the White Tiger of the West."

Again Jigme agreed.

"My mother told me tales as a child of a group of warriors called the Five Elemental Masters. Are you, by any chance, associated with them?"

Brother Jigme sipped his tea, trying to decide exactly how far he could trust young Lang. "You said you're a Tu? Could I ask who your mother is?"

A wry smile. "Tu Leilan."

That startled Jigme, almost enough to make him drop his cup. He choked on his tea and finally managed to recover enough to say, "Your mother is the King's sister."

"Yes," young Lang agreed ruefully.

"Which means your father is the Duke of Jin."

"If you know that, you know his mother is the Imperial Gurun Princess, Lang Hexiao." Young Lang sighed. "Not a single bit of which matters to me because I've become a follower of the Storm Hermit and have no interest in inheritance nor politics of any sort."

Jigme yearned to ask just how someone of young Lang's background had found his way so far from home. He held his tongue. He ought not pry when there were things he wasn't willing to share. Instead, he sipped his tea thoughtfully before finally saying, "You're the one who found young Tommy's body?"

A flicker of anger shone in the other man's eyes. "My friend and I were traveling to Blue Ridge Town with another delivery when we discovered him; tossed into the ravine beside the road for the vultures."

The anger was understandable, yet unexpected. Up until now young Lang had appeared cheerful and carefree. Now Jigme realized there was something beneath the surface, a bloodthirst unbecoming to a student of the Storm Hermit. Then it was gone. "Apologies. I've not yet learned to hold it in." Young Lang gave him a regretful smile, "Master says, 'Rage unmastered is not the way.'"

That the youngster realized his anger was noticeable was remarkable in itself. Jigme just smiled. "You've yet to complete your training."

"I can control my actions. I can control the desire. I can't seem to make it go away entirely." Young Lang waved off the discussion. "You offered me a place to stay for more than just small-talk, Brother Jigme. Was there something you wanted from me?"

"The book in that bag should have gone to another. Yet it was addressed to me, in a package that'd clearly been opened." Working out exactly how to ask what he needed was difficult. There were so many things he wasn't supposed to share. "As a mail carrier, is there any chance you would know where she might be? Her name is Lin Bianhua, if that helps any."

A startled look crossed young Lang's face. "I know the name Lilly Lin. Which, of course, could translate to Lin Bianhua." He frowned thoughtfully. "Is she the sort to run a brothel?"

That set Jigme chuckling. "Yes, I'm afraid she is." As fiery tempered as his elder sister was, she'd prefer hiding in plain sight over sneaking off into the mountains. "Where is she?"

"Oddly enough, not far. Leggetsville. Which happens to be part of my rounds."

No surprise. Young Lang wouldn't know of Sister Bianhua otherwise. "Would you happen to be going there soon?"

Young Lang tapped his mail-bag. "The book sent to you should be hers, right? In which case it's my duty to take it to her."

"Would you mind, terribly, if I accompanied you?"

Another thoughtful glance. "Thinking she might have received your package by mistake?"

"She might have. But I suspect there's more to the story than that. It's bait to lure me out and make me look for her." Before the young man could ask why he'd do such a thing, Jigme added, "Sometimes you have to put yourself in the open to find your enemy."

Young Lang tilted his head thoughtfully. "Master says, 'Walking into the bear's den finds the bear, but you have to be able to fight it, too.'"

That sounded very like the Storm Hermit and Jigme smiled. "I'm the White Tiger of the West, young Lang. If I can't fight my enemies then a century of cultivation has been pointless."

Besides, he was damned tired of hiding. It was time and past to deal with their enemy and end this game.

⋛⟩⟨⋚

Having agreed to let Brother Jigme accompany him to Leggetsville, Yixiao settled in a corner of the man's small hut to meditate. There wasn't any bedding for either of them but they didn't need it. Like Yixiao, Brother Jigme preferred contemplation over sleep.

Neither got much time to do so. Barely an hour after they'd quieted for the night, a low call from outside the hut drew their attention. "Yixiao. Enemies."

Wuchang's warning forced Yixiao to his feet. "All I want is a quiet place to cultivate," he grumbled.

"Your master has a saying for that," Brother Jigme noted as he joined Yixiao.

Well, yes. She did. "If you can't maintain your balance when the world is spinning around you, you've not found the true *Dao*."

"Ah. You do pay attention. Some of her students have not."

Any student who failed to pay attention to the Storm Hermit didn't survive their training. Yixiao didn't need to say as much. Not to a cultivator as old as Brother Jigme. Instead he murmured, "What sort of enemy, Wuchang?"

His best friend said quietly. "By their feel, human and mortal. By their language, members of the Niohuru clan."

That meant these enemies were Yixiao's specifically. Meant, too, that they might not be enemies so much as badly misguided distant kin, wanting to drag him back to the martial world of the *jianghu*. Some of his kinfolk thought he should return to his old life as a warrior of the White Wolf. The fact that he didn't want to, the fact that his grandmother had freed him from it, didn't matter to them.

"Given it's a fight at all, it isn't yours, Brother Jigme." Yixiao told his companion. "I'll deal with them."

"You've accepted my hospitality and drunk my tea, young Lang. Your troubles are mine." To Yixiao's amusement, Brother Jigme added, "My Master said, 'A good host guards his guests.'"

Outside, the quarter-moon was almost useless as a light source. Nor did the lamps on the other huts help. Most were too dim to be useful. If Yixiao's training hadn't increased his night vision he might not have noticed the half-dozen or so people approaching the hut.

As Yixiao stepped out, a faint whisper of sound warned him to dodge. Cartwheeling sideways, he landed lightly, narrowly missing a drunken miner who'd chosen an unfortunate place to sleep. At the same time Wuchang caught a handful of fine needles between his fingers and drove them into the dirt with a flick of his hand.

"That answers one question. Not friendly. Not at all."

"Kill the traitor," someone whispered behind Yixiao. He ducked below a heavy curved saber and slammed his elbow into his attacker's sternum. She dropped to the ground, stunned, and Yixiao sighed. Now he was a traitor? It was getting terribly hard working out who wanted what from him and why.

Closer to the door, Brother Jigme's hands were a blur in the dim light. Not so blurred Yixiao didn't recognize a style similar to Shaolin's Tiger Claw. It was harder and rougher, with movements resembling a tiger stalking their prey. He handled his opponents easily, dodging missiles and catching limbs with fingers twisted into claws.

Wuchang did his part as well, swords flickering as he forced his opponent backwards and into a water trough. Another grabbed at him, but he shifted sideways and came up again as the man stumbled. An elbow strike to the back of the man's neck dropped him to the ground.

Something flew through the air at Yixiao and he flicked it aside with his borrowed saber. Metal clanged on metal, but the sound wasn't followed by the dagger hitting the wall of the hut beside him. Instead, something creaked and scraped, corroded iron squealing as it moved.

Yixiao glanced over his shoulder. Backed into the main street. "Careful. This one isn't human." A shadowy thing moved towards them, stalking them. Was it yet another of the many supernatural beings he'd met here in America? It certainly wasn't anything he'd seen before.

It moved like a human, was shaped like a human, even had human eyes, but that was all. Its body seemed formed of some dark misty substance. It stank of rust, a sharp, bitter, odor. Every move was accompanied by that scraping sound. Blades formed of rusty metal rose and sank into the mist surrounding them, the noise climbing straight up Yixiao's spine.

"Rust-born," Brother Jigme whispered and Yixiao heard a faint echo of fear. "I can't fight it."

Suddenly, screaming furiously, one of Yixiao's would-be assassins attacked the thing, only to be torn to pieces by the rusty blades within its mist. Another assassin tried throwing daggers, but it just absorbed the things into itself.

"You're making it stronger," Yixiao told the assassin. "Suggest you run. I don't believe you're its target."

For a wonder, the assassins decided they were better off listening than standing and fighting. He'd have to keep an eye out for them later, but for now the rust-born was his main concern. "Is it vulnerable to anything?"

"I'm not sure. I almost died the last time I fought one."

That explained why Brother Jigme was frightened. Yixiao turned to Wuchang. "Hitting it directly gets you sliced to pieces. Throwing weapons makes it stronger. My lightning does nothing."

"Steel weapons," Wuchang pointed out. "It consumes them. Makes them part of itself. My blades don't corrode, but I don't think I can harm it, either."

Of course. Given the name it made perfect sense, too. "What, exactly, is it made of?"

" ... TORN TO PIECES BY RUSTY BLADES. "

"Negative *qi*. Their kind exist in antithesis to the elements." Brother Jigme's voice was tight.

The White Tiger of the West's element was metal and Brother Jigme had called it 'rust-born'. No wonder he couldn't defend himself against it. "It has to have a weakness."

They backed up, being forced further and further into town. Not good. Not good at all. They had to stop this thing before some innocent noticed the fuss and got caught in it. Yixiao searched his memory. "Water generates wood, generates fire, generates earth, generates metal."

"Water overcomes fire, overcomes metal, overcomes wood, overcomes earth," Brother Jigme countered. "But I don't know what the equivalents are for the demonic elements. Given there are any. And even if there were, none of us can control negative *qi*. Not even the Hollowed Blade."

True. Then there had to be some other means. Nothing was invulnerable, not even rust. Sooner or later it would fall apart, or at least become so solid nothing could move it.

A thought occurred to Yixiao. "Brother Jigme, can you bait it towards the water trough?"

"Surely water just makes more rust," the older man pointed out.

"Mm. Yes. But the trough's a hollowed out log. There's no metal to feed the thing."

Suddenly understanding, Brother Jigme moved, the rust-born following behind with slow inevitability, its body screeching metal on metal as it went.

⇒)(⇐

Though Jigme understood young Lang's theory, he wasn't entirely sure the plan would work. He'd needed elder sister Bianhua's help the last time he'd fought the Demonic Master of Rust's creation. Fire couldn't melt rust but it could burn it away. What could water do but make more?

As the rust-born moved towards him, Jigme braced himself, prepared to run for it. If this failed he'd have to move fast. People were waking up and noticing the fight. The last thing he wanted was for some poor innocent to be caught in his troubles.

The rust-born followed him, focused entirely on consuming him. Jigme knew from experience that the thing only attacked its target or those who got in its way. Right that moment, he was the only one it saw. As long as no one interfered, things should be well. At least he hoped they would be.

Jigme couldn't help wondering what young Lang planned to do, given he and his friend couldn't touch the thing or use a normal weapon on it. Heibai Wuchang might survive contact with the creature but he'd be badly injured even so.

To Jigme's relief, the two men took proper precautions. Instead of striking the rust-born directly or using a sword on the creature, the pair detached a wooden rail from the walkway. They moved silently, holding the rail up between them, and when the rust-born came close to the water trough, used it to push the thing in.

The splash was surprisingly quiet. The rust-born wasn't dense enough to cause anything larger. Wasn't large enough to displace the water much, either. And wasn't bright enough to climb out quickly. It tried to rise but young Lang and Heibai Wuchang pushed it down again with the help of the railing.

As young Lang had planned and hoped, the water soaked into the rust-born's form, turning what metal it had left to rust as well. Without a structure to keep it in one cohesive form, it abruptly melted away, until all that was left was slag and sediment, fallen to the bottom of the trough.

"I'm not sure we deserved to have that work," Heibai Wuchang muttered, sounding relieved. "Almost too easy."

"Master says, 'Don't borrow trouble. It might want to stay,'" young Lang countered, as a half dozen men came out of their cabins, shining lanterns on the scene. At the same time the Sheriff, furious at having been woken, rushed towards them shouting. "Or call in friends, as the case may be."

Jigme was almost sure the boy had made that up. Almost, because it did sound a bit like something the Storm Hermit would say. Instead of arguing the point he turned his attention on Sheriff Lane. "Sheriff. A small difficulty, already taken care of."

The sheriff glared at him. Glared at his two companions. Glared at the water trough. "A small difficulty. What were you doing? Trying to poison our horses?"

"Oh, no, Sheriff," young Lang countered glibly. "A piece of canvas caught fire. We didn't have a better place to put it. Wuchang and I will clean it up right away."

Jigme had to admire the boy's fast thinking lies. Even if his English were better, he'd have trouble coming up with a reasonable excuse. Not that the sheriff would accept even reasonable excuses. "You lot are just causing trouble every other hour. I want you out of town and fast."

Bowing, young Lang smiled. "Sheriff, I'll be glad to. Would you like me to take that bag of Tony's back to Leggetsville while I'm at it?"

Marshall Pierce, who'd joined them just a little after Sheriff Lane, interrupted. "No need. I'll be taking it myself, along with those two Royd brothers." He considered young Lang a long moment before adding, "Though if you're headed the same way I am, maybe it'd be good if we all went together. For safety's sake, of course."

Jigme had a feeling there was more to it than that. At a guess, so did young Lang. Not that that wiped the smile from his face or slowed his tongue for him. "If my companions don't mind, I don't." He eyed both Jigme and his friend inquiringly.

"This Jigme has no objections."

"It's fine with me," Jigme and Heibai Wuchang said in near unison.

Young Lang returned his attention to Mister Pierce. "There, that's settled. I was thinking of leaving bright and early tomorrow morning, all right?" As the man agreed, he continued, "I'll be looking forward to it. It's always nice to have traveling companions, this far from civilization. It can get lonely, when it's just the two of us. Master says, 'The more the merrier.'"

Now Jigme was sure his new friend was making things up.

⇒)(⇐

"Where'd you learn to talk like a Limey?"

Yixiao grinned. Sooner or later every new acquaintance here in California asked that question, or at least the English speaking ones did. The answer ought to be obvious, of course, but most Americans were accustomed to dealing with Chinese miners. His countrymen weren't stupid by any means, but they used pidgin English more often than not, giving the impression of ignorance.

"My second mother was from Great Britain. I learned it from her."

Pierce frowned. "You speak it pretty damned good."

"I will convey your approval to her, the next time I see her. Sadly, I doubt that will be soon."

By this time they were traveling the main road, twisting its way down from the Sierra Nevadas to the Central Valley. Warmed by the early spring weather, the air was sweet and a little damp. It wouldn't last, of course, but that just made it all the more enjoyable.

Or it would be if not for some of the company. The Royd brothers had been cursing them all the way, grunting and grumbling at their captor. Cursing was about all they could do, chained up as they were. Pierce and Sheriff Lane hadn't taken any chances with them. Cuffs on their wrists and ankles, with a short chain between. All locked down to the base of the cart by a huge padlock, with a half-dozen miners to help keep an eye on them.

"You better be watching out, Pierce. Our brother ain't gonna stand for you dragging us off."

"Yeah, bastard."

"He'll be doing for you, just you wait."

"That's right, bastard."

"And he'll do you too, Chinaman. String you up by your heels and take what's left of your...eep...."

That last was because Wuchang had guided his horse closer and leaned over to gaze straight into the man's eyes. He didn't even have to say anything because his nature gave him an edge when it came to intimidation. It took more confidence than a loudmouth like Billy Royd possessed to come face to face with a predator like Wuchang.

Ignoring the by-play, Pierce asked, "You found Tommy's body around here, didn't you?"

Ah. Now Yixiao understood why the man had wanted him along. He was hoping to catch Yixiao out in a lie. "I did. Though I'd say it was about a mile or so further back." He scanned the trees surrounding them and pointed. "There's a ravine running alongside us. He was down at the bottom and not long dead."

"Now I'm puzzled. How'd you know he was there?"

Yixiao indicated a lone buzzard circling high above them. "Some not so little birds told me."

A sharp frown. "Them buzzards find dead things all the time. Why'd you go looking for trouble?"

"That is a question we all ask him," Wuchang noted dryly. "He never does have a reasonable answer."

"Unfair," Yixiao countered. "I had a perfectly good reason. I was curious."

"You see?" Wuchang added, sounding a little helpless. "Although I admit, I too was concerned." He didn't add that he'd smelled human blood. No way Pierce would believe him.

Pierce clearly decided to give up that trail. Instead, he asked, "What made you think them two had anything to do with the matter?"

"Wuchang and I passed them just ten minutes earlier. Tommy fought back hard. I found blood under his nails." Yixiao tapped his own fingers. "No way those two could have passed a fight like that and not noticed."

That set the Royd brothers off again. They'd been caught with stolen goods, yes, but they weren't the one who'd done it. They'd just found Tommy and tossed him into the ravine so no one would know the mail-carrier was dead. The one killed him was probably the skinny stranger with the long red hair and the weird eyes. Neither of them were even scratched, so it couldn't've been them, anyway.

Listening to the pair's attempts to justify themselves, Yixiao couldn't help noticing a slight frown on Brother Jigme's face. The description of the third stranger, Tommy's probable murderer, was obviously familiar. He didn't comment on his new companion's concern, saying instead, "So you're claiming this man just killed Tommy and left him there without stealing anything?"

If Tommy had been the sort to make enemies his death would be understandable. Wrong, absolutely wrong, but understandable. But Tommy had been an innocent, unable to comprehend - or even recognize - unkindness. Most of the bandits in the area let him be. Mail-carriers seldom had anything valuable in their bags, after all. He wasn't worth their time or energy.

Perhaps the Royds hadn't killed the boy after all? Their story made sense, though it meant the real murderer was still out there. "Maybe the killer meant the body to be found? Maybe he hoped to draw someone out."

"Yeah, but who? You? Me? Brother Jigme?" Pierce shrugged. "All we can do is drag these two to Leggetsville and keep our ears open."

As far as Yixiao could tell, that really was their only option.

⋧)(⋦

Jigme was absolutely certain he knew who the killer was now. He couldn't understand what that enemy intended, killing a mail-carrier, but he recognized the Demonic Elemental Master of Rust by the description. Had he switched the books? Or was he following the one to find both Jigme and his elder sister? And did that mean Sister Bianhua was in danger already?

Young Lang clearly had ideas. But Jigme didn't dare discuss the matter in front of Marshall Pierce. Speak in Khaitanese and he'd think they were plotting against him. Speak in English and he'd think they were crazy.

They continued down the road, passing one or two travelers along the way. Most were miners headed for Wildcat Gulch and its saloon. A few were headed back into the hills to their claims, having used up all the gold they'd found on food, drink and other luxuries. None gave them more than a passing glance, even though the Royd brothers made a fuss just because they could.

When night fell they were three-quarters of the way to Leggetsville and just clear of the foothills. There being no town or wayside inn, their only recourse was to set up camp by the side of the road, using the same cleared area other travelers had stopped at for some time now.

After feeding and cleaning up their prisoners, Marshall Pierce set a watch, staggering their times so no one would be watching alone. Jigme wasn't surprised when the schedule ensured that he, young Lang and Heibai Wuchang were never together. It was obvious Marshall Pierce still had his doubts about them.

As for Jigme, he mostly wondered when someone would attack. The Royds' older brother surely wouldn't stand for them being captured; young Lang had those northerners from back home; and, of course, Jigme's enemy might regard this as his best moment to act.

The attack came late at night, when a gunshot interrupted the sound of crickets and toads. It was quickly followed by a shout from the woods to their south. One of Pierce's men gestured for them all to get under cover of the wagon, while he and his fellow guards took position behind some rocks.

"Preston Pierce, you let my brothers go this instant, I may let you live." The voice came from deep in the woods, far enough back that no one could have shot him if they were foolish enough to try.

"You come try and take 'em, Tom Royd. You just try!"

Something rustled in the woods north of them, a faint soft sound that faded quickly.

An animal? Jigme stretched his senses, then touched young Lang's hand. A slight tilt to the young man's head, barely visible in the light from the banked fire, told Jigme he too knew there were others out there. Ten of them spread out among the trees, using the noise of the fight to sneak closer.

Soft insect noises sounded between the gunfire. Signals. Their quarry making sure everyone stayed in formation as they approached the camp. Yes. Definitely a well-trained group.

Jigme looked for Heibai Wuchang. Gone. Not surprising, really. He was probably slipping around behind the second group to catch them unawares. Carefully, so he wouldn't be overheard, Jigme leaned close to Marshall Pierce. "Others coming. Young Lang and I will handle."

Pierce's expression was impossible to make out, but his exasperated tone was enough. "Don't get yourselves killed."

"This Jigme will do his best." Not waiting for an answer, Jigme slithered across the campsite and into the forest, Young Lang not far behind.

Their quarry were well-trained but they knew nothing about *qi* or cultivation. Their movements were smooth and stealthy, however, and Jigme had no intention of underestimating them. He stalked through the woods, using the shadows and moonlight to guard his motions. Then, coming on the first of their would-be attackers, he caught the man by the throat and slammed him into the ground.

The noise drew the others' attention, but Jigme leapt into the trees. By the time the others gathered to find their unconscious comrade, he was out of sight, crouched silent in the branches above them.

They spoke in the same language as the men and women who'd attacked young Lang the night before. Jigme hadn't learned more than a few words of the northern tribes' tongue, however, so he couldn't guess what they said. Whatever it was, it wasn't 'retreat'.

Jigme waited as their quarry spread out and chose his next target. This time he swung his knees around the tree branch and grabbed the man from above. This time he blocked the man's mouth, so he barely made a noise and didn't attract attention again.

Dropping his latest victim atop the first, Jigme used a particularly noisy moment of gunfire to take to the trees again. A faint sound off to the side told Jigme that young Lang had taken out one, then another of the enemy. He was quieter about it than Jigme, though, so the others didn't notice immediately. Only when no one answered their signals did they realize they were losing comrades.

By this time Heibai Wuchang had also taken a hand in the fight, knocking the enemy out with barely any effort. It surprised Jigme that the assassin was being careful not to kill. Apparently young Lang had impressed his guard enough that he willingly controlled himself.

Together the three of them made short work of the enemy. The gunfight still blazed on the other side of the campsite, but at least this danger was over. Jigme went to help his companions with gathering and tying up the enemy, only to find a tall figure in dark robes confronting young Lang.

"This Master is impressed. But it is one thing to incapacitate such low-lives as these. Quite another to face your true antithesis."

Xiu. The Demonic Elemental Master of Rust. Jigme's sworn enemy.

⇒)(⇐

Yixiao blinked at the newcomer. Half-hidden by shadows, the man's features were impossible to make out. The moonlight was enough to suggest light hair, but not its shade. Somehow he suspected it was red. It'd fit with what the Royd brothers had claimed.

"Should I know you?" he asked. Was this the one behind these assassins? If so, he was doing nothing to protect his allies.

"I am Xiu, as you well know, White Tiger." The man's voice was harsh, sounding a bit like the rust he apparently named himself for. "Don't pretend. Your cultivation betrays you."

"My cultivation is nothing to speak of, sir. And I truly have no idea what you mean."

"These northerners were no easy target. There are none in this land capable of what you did tonight except the White Tiger and myself."

Yixiao raised a brow, "You're saying no other cultivators have come to America? I find that hard to believe. Master says, 'Cultivators are like cockroaches. Always popping up out of nowhere.'" Admittedly, he hadn't expected to find any others, but he hadn't met every immigrant to California yet.

Spotting Wuchang moving closer, Yixiao knew his friend would act at the best possible moment. In the meantime, he needed to keep this Xiu's attention. He shifted backwards, keeping his eyes on the enemy, his hands loose and readied.

"Why do you not draw your saber White Tiger?"

The saber in question was the weapon handed down to him from his noble ancestress. He'd removed its hilt almost a year earlier, using it on a copy of his blade to fob off the young woman who'd insisted on following him to America for a duel. He'd no intention of using it.

"If I take your name correctly, the only metal you can't harm is gold," Yixiao pointed out. "I'd be a fool to use it against you. Master says, 'Don't pick a fight with a fire when you're made of straw.'"

The man chuckled. "Then you have no defense at all, White Tiger." He stopped wasting time, rushing forward at a speed Yixiao knew he couldn't match.

All Yixiao could do was twist and evade, using a wind-tossing gesture to send his attacker flying over his shoulder. Now there was a relief. The man was fast but he wasn't nearly as flexible as Yixiao. His cultivation was certainly stronger but his body had limitations. It moved oddly, too, reflexes just a touch off.

Xiu came back at him, hand seeming swathed in shadowy mist. The sharp tang of rust filled the air and Yixiao had a feeling it'd do him no good. He flipped backwards, grasping a fallen branch as he flung himself out of the way. Xiu was on him then, and he used the branch to redirect his attacker's grasp. He wasn't quite fast enough.

Pain shuddered through Yixiao's arm. "Do you forget?" Xiu murmured, "Flesh and blood carries metal within."

Iron in human blood shouldn't actually rust but Yixiao didn't argue the point. He gathered his strength, sending lightning qi down his arm and exploding through Xiu's hand. To his surprise, it actually worked, at least enough to force Xiu's grip to loosen.

Wuchang flash-stepped into Xiu's path, striking the man's chest with his open palm. As Xiu went flying, Wuchang drew his sabers and moved between Yixiao and his attacker. "This one's weapons do not corrode, Master of Rust. Suggest you withdraw and find another target. My master is not your prey."

A moment of silence followed as Xiu recovered from the blow. He raised his head, eyes glittering faintly in the moonlight, long hair tangled around his narrow face. "Your master? The White Tiger needs a bodyguard?"

"This one must contradict you again, Master of Rust, but he is not the White Tiger and has no idea why you persist in assuming it." Yixiao shook his wrist, adding wryly, "I do wish you wouldn't call me that, Wuchang."

"Apologies, Yixiao. I will endeavor to remember."

"Not the White Tiger? Not? You lie!"

Before the man could get another word out, Jigme dropped down behind Xiu, slamming a heavy log down onto his enemy's head. As the man fell, he added, "Young Lang is not the White Tiger. I am."

⋟)(⋞

It felt wrong that a single blow would take Xiu down so easily. Yet a quick check confirmed Jigme had succeeded. Did that mean rust's weakness was wood as well as water? Jigme wished his Eldest brother was around. Brother Zhengfeng understood metaphysical matters best.

"Why'd he think I was you, when we look nothing alike?" young Lang asked as he and Jigme tied their captives up and Heibai Wuchang went to check on the others. "And... thank you for not killing him."

The last was said with a slight plaintive note and Jigme guessed the youngster had to spend a great deal of his time persuading those around him to be less blood-thirsty. He inclined his head. "My sect, like your master's, frowns on indiscriminate killing." Besides, if he did kill this Xiu, a new one would come looking for him sooner or later. They'd learned that much back in Khaitan.

"As to the other question: though they often wear the same face, they don't always remember previous meetings. This particular Xiu was sent to find me, but had to use our master's call to seek me out." Now Jigme understood why his book and Sister Bianhua's had been switched. Xiu must have hoped to draw Jigme from his hiding place and make him seek his sister. He said as much, adding, "Which means her antithesis must be seeking her as well."

Young Lang frowned. "Since yours was rust, I presume hers is ash?"

The boy was smart. "Yes. Your master would be proud of you." At young Lang's snort, Jigme continued, "I'm torn, now. Should I seek her out or not?"

"The books were switched. That means she might have already received yours and searches for you."

True. And if they were called back with the Demonic Elemental Masters still out there hunting them, then Brother Zhengfeng had reason to believe they should come home. Jigme finished tying the last of the assassins up. "You might not wish to continue helping me, however."

"Nonsense," young Lang retorted. "I'm already involved. And who's to say this Xiu won't decide I'm you again. Besides, I know a bit about the area, having spent so much time wandering. I can't go back to China with you, but I can at least help you find your way while you're here."

Another truth. Jigme had gone straight for the hills and hid there all this time. His English was barely passable, whereas young Lang's was excellent. And the boy was cultivated enough to have built a proper foundation. He might not be able to fight a Demonic Elemental Master head on, but he could protect himself. "I shall have to trouble you, then," he murmured, accepting the offer.

Heibai Wuchang returned from his mission, a lantern in hand. "Mr. Pierce and his men have prevailed," he told them. "Some are coming to assist with our captives." He didn't need to mention the last. The noise as Mr. Pierce's men tramped through the underbrush would have warned Jigme.

Quietly, young Lang told his friend. "We're going to do what we can to help Brother Jigme. I'll send word to the post office that I won't be available for a little while."

Unsurprised, Heibai Wuchang inclined his head. "Of course, Yixiao." From the sound of it, he was long accustomed to his master…his friend's…tendency to get caught up in troubles not his own.

Jigme just hoped this wouldn't be the time the young man bit off more than he could easily chew.

Chapter 2
Vermillion Bird Rises From the Ashes

"Don't you come in here with all your dirt and looking like you'd just had a shoot-out!"

"Respect, Miss Brigid, but we did just come from a shoot-out."

"Well y'all can take yourselves right out again and go clean up proper."

"We've only come to find Judge Jones, Miss Brigid. A little thing about having someone open up the jail for us. If you'd tell him we're here?"

"I ain't doin' nothing of th' sort. Th' judge is busy and ain't t'be disturbed."

The argument grew louder, at least on Brigid's side. She took her responsibilities as Senior Hostess seriously and she allowed - what was the word? - guff from no one. It wouldn't be long before she sent for the guards.

Ordinarily, Lin Bianhua, currently known as Lilly Lin, would ignore such situations. She was comfortable, having an enjoyable conversation with her companion and in no mood to deal with obstreperous guests. This guest, however, was one she knew her men couldn't handle. Gods knew how a disciple of the Storm Hermit had found his way so far from China, but there Lang Yixiao was.

Knowing things would get out of hand in the most foolish way possible, Bianhua set her tea cup down and looked at her dinner companion. "I think we'd best stop this."

Judge Lawrence Jones didn't shift an inch. He didn't like being pushed around and he didn't know just how aggravatingly stubborn young Lang could get. "Dunno. Sounds to me like Brigid's got this one covered. They can wait for regular business hours if they want me."

She eyed him grimly. "Don't argue, Law. Come."

A startled look flickered in her lover's eyes as he realized she meant it. Realized, too, that she wouldn't be so firm if it wasn't important. He rose unwillingly, following Bianhua out of her private saloon to the grand entrance of The Scarlet Chamber; Leggetsville's biggest and most expensive dining hall and whorehouse.

They found Brigid faced off with Lang Yixiao at the door, the young man's clothes all ripped up, blood on his sleeves, his boots covered in mud. To his credit, he wasn't trying to come inside, but he wasn't leaving either.

Noticing another familiar face behind young Lang's, Bianhua came to a dead stop on the stairway. Law almost bumped into her, grabbing the rail just in time. "Lilly, hun? Something wrong?"

Brother Jigme inclined his head slightly at the sight of her. No words passed between them but they didn't need to. It was obvious something dangerous was afoot. She returned her gaze to young Lang and Brigid. "Children, people are attempting to have a pleasant evening. Let us not disturb them." Too little, too late, but one must say something.

"But Mistress Lilly!"

She stopped Brigid's protest before it properly began. Turning a calm gaze on the youngster waiting at the door, she continued, "Young Master Lang. Dare I ask what it is that brings you here, so anxious to find the judge at this late hour?"

To his credit, young Lang knew how to behave. He cupped his hands. Bowed. Looked properly embarrassed when a large tangle of leaves fell out of his hair and landed on Brigid's skirt. While the girl sputtered, he said, "Sorry, Miss Brigid. Respect, Mistress Lilly, but Judge Jones' presence is required at the courthouse. The guards won't allow us to bring in some prisoners and Marshall Pierce sent me to fetch him."

That startled Law. "That's odd. Johnson usually isn't a stickler for rules." He turned to Lilly. "My dear, I'd best run along and take care of this little thing."

"Of course. I'm sure it's nothing." Bianhua was lying through her teeth and they both knew it. Knew, too, that she couldn't come along and help.

Not publicly, at least.

⇒)(⇐

As they returned to the courthouse, their way lit by flickering streetlamps, Yixiao reflected that he wouldn't have recognized Lilly Lin - Lin Bianhua - as a cultivator. She appeared young, with a gravitas that had allowed her to build and run the most popular whorehouse in Leggetsville. But she'd never shown any sign of any martial skills.

Watching her reaction to Brother Jigme, however, confirmed that she was the fourth of the Five Elemental Masters. She hadn't acknowledged her martial brother, but he'd sensed their rapport as soon as their eyes met. As they headed back for the courthouse, walking behind Judge Jones, Yixiao thought he sensed someone trailing behind them.

Certain they'd found Jigme's compatriot, Yixiao asked in Khaitanese, "Do you want to stay and speak with her?"

"I will do so before the night's over," Brother Jigme told him. "For now, I'd rather be sure our captives are properly accounted for."

To his surprise, Judge Jones glanced back at them. "You friend of Bianhua's?" he asked, speaking in the same language. It was stilted, but his accent was excellent. At their identical expressions of surprise, he grinned, adding, "She teach me. Not good, yet. Working on it."

Brother Jigme relaxed. "It's hard to gain Sister Bianhua's trust. If she's teaching you our native language, you've done so."

"Hope you not think I show off."

Far from it. The judge could have hidden his knowledge and let them blithely talk on unaware. "Actually, it's good of you to let us know you understand. Master says, 'If you want honesty, be honest yourself.'"

As Brother Jigme agreed, Yixiao noted they were just about to the courthouse. He shifted to English, not wanting to draw attention to the judge's knowledge. "Our companions took the prisoners around back," he told Judge Jones. "On your door guard's order."

"I'm still puzzled over why they didn't let you bring the prisoners inside. They know Marshall Pierce. They shouldn't be giving him trouble."

The guard they'd spoken to hadn't recognized Pierce and Pierce hadn't recognized him. Yixiao told the judge as much as he described the man. "Average looking, with grey

"DO YOU WANT TO STAY AND SPEAK WITH HER?"

hair and grey eyes. He had a scar across his forehead, here." He slid a finger from left temple to hairline.

"That doesn't make sense. Sheriff Thomas doesn't have any men like that and neither do I." Judge Jones paused. Looked worried. "We'd better get over there fast." Without bothering to make sure they followed, he set off running.

A glance at Brother Jigme showed the other man's confusion. "Something's wrong at the courthouse," Yixiao told him. "The man we spoke to may be an imposter."

They hurried after Judge Jones, rounding the corner behind the courthouse to find the cart empty and the back door wide open. "I thought you said the guard wouldn't let you in," the judge said, rightfully suspicious.

"I did. He didn't." Yixiao tilted his head, listening for voices, and heard nothing. "The fact they let our companions in after I left is…worrisome."

From the judge's expression he wasn't sure what to think. "Why wouldn't they want you around?"

"I really don't know. But I'd suggest playing along for the moment. At least until we've a better idea of what's going on."

They entered the building quietly, walking down a short hallway towards an open door. Someone was inside, a shadow cast on the wall showed that much. Impossible to tell who it was, or what they were doing. Bending over something, it seemed. As they approached, the shadow lifted its head, clearly watching the door and waiting for them.

There was an odd scent in the air, one that grew stronger the closer they came. It took Yixiao a moment to recognize it and when he did, he turned and stopped his companions from taking another step forward. "Out. Now."

"What?"

He wasted no time. "Out!"

Though the judge looked like he wanted to argue, Brother Jigme accepted the order without question. He grasped Judge Jones' wrist and ran, Yixiao close behind.

Once outside, they leapt sideways; Yixiao to the left, Brother Jigme and Judge Jones to the right. They were barely in time, as a cloud of ash poured through the open doorway, smashing the cart and shattering the wall of the stables behind the courthouse. Horses screamed, their cries cut short moments later.

Curled up against the hot ash, using his *qi* to redirect the energy as best he could, all Yixiao could do was hope his friends were all right.

⸫⟩⟨⸪

Knowing her younger martial brother wouldn't show up without good reason, Bianhua ordered her head assistant to take over. "I've a sick headache and don't wish to be disturbed."

"Yes'm."

Bianhua changed to dark clothes quickly, slipping outside to follow the three men. She kept to the shadows, not wanting Law to realize she was there. Young Yixiao and Brother Jigme would notice, of course, but neither would speak until she chose to show herself.

Overhearing Law demonstrating his Khaitanese, Bianhua smiled. Her lover was smart and considerate. Smart in that Khaitanese was a difficult language for a westerner. Considerate in that he made sure his companions knew he understood at least some of what they were saying. Someday she hoped to bring him and his little girl back to Khaitan with her. They'd do well there, she was sure.

Of course, going back to Khaitan required dealing with those damned Demonic Elementalists. Bianhua still wasn't sure they'd done right, spreading themselves out like this. Eldest brother Yang Zhengfeng had thought it'd force their enemies out into the open, but so far nothing had happened.

Still, Brother Jigme wouldn't be here if he didn't have good reason. Most likely Rust or Ash had finally shown themselves and he needed her help to fight back. She just wished she knew how.

The biggest trouble fighting their enemy was lack of information. The bastards had shown up out of nowhere, striking from the shadows and disappearing before anyone realized they were there. Their so-called elements made no sense, seemed to have no weakness, and kept creeping back no matter how many times they were beaten. Like the decay they represented, they could never be destroyed, only staved off.

When Law set off running, Bianhua sighed for her lover's impetuous ways. He was a judge, for the Gods' sake. He ought to have more sense than to go rushing straight into danger thoughtlessly. At least young Lang and Brother Jigme moved more cautiously.

Bianhua had just reached the corner to the back of the courthouse when the three men rushed outside. A moment later a cloud of ash poured out of the doorway, forcing her back. Ash's attack struck her weak point, smothering her flames before they could properly form. All she could do was hide and hope the others would be all right.

Something moved behind her and she spun, just in time to avoid two glowing bars of superheated air, wielded by a figure formed of ash and clouds. Forced backwards and backwards again, she stepped into a pile of warm ash and tripped. Damnit, this was just like last time she'd fought that bastard and she still had no way of dealing with him.

"Bianhua!" Law was beside her a moment later, firing his gun uselessly into the thing trying strike her. He was a mess, with black marks all over his face and hands. Thankfully, Brother Jigme had protected him from the worst, shielding them with his *qi*.

As relief flooded her, Bianhua set her hand on Law's. "Don't waste your bullets. You can't hurt it that way."

Brother Jigme was up and at her side a moment later, just as messy as her lover. "Sister Bianhua, are you hurt?" he asked, pulling his *qi* together to block the ash-born's attack.

"I've been better." The ash's heat didn't bother her but like last time, it smothered her *qi*, weakening her. "I still can't fight it, though." This one was especially troublesome. She'd never seen an ash-born fight so well before. She'd especially never seen one with two weapons.

Law holstered his gun, accepting its uselessness. "Bianhua, milove, is there anything I can do? Aside from staying out of the way?"

"Keep an eye out for more of these things." Back in Khaitan, each of Demonic Elementalist had been able to summon several dozen slaves to their service.

"Rust only managed one," Brother Jigme told her. "I don't know if that means anything."

"Still, keep watch."

As Law turned to do just that, Bianhua focused her attention on the ash cloud masquerading as a human being. Its heat was tangible even through Brother Jigme's *qi*. Its weapons charred whatever it touched, turning wood to charcoal in seconds.

The heat might not bother Bianhua but it exhausted Brother Jigme. His element was metal and could only take so much before melting. "If only Sister Xuan was here," Bianhua grumbled as she drew her *qi* together.

Behind her, Law growled a sharp curse. "Another!"

She glanced over her shoulder as a grey cloud rose from the pile of ash beside the doorway. Another human figure faded into view, dimly lit by the lantern hanging above them. She tightened her lips, flames chasing their way along her fingertips, and knew she'd little hope.

As she stepped towards the enemy she spotted something that made her withdraw her flames and stare. Up until now, the ash-born had used weapons formed of superheated parts of their own self. This one flickered from inside its body, a coruscating storm of lightning playing through the grey powder.

Wait. Lightning? Storm? She grabbed Law and Brother Jigme, pulling them out of the way, creating an opening. "It's young Lang!" she said, even as the Storm Hermit's disciple released a flood of electricity that scattered the ash surrounding him in a swirling cloud.

He glared at the first ash-born. "That's my best friend you've possessed," he growled. Storm clouds gathered above them, thick and threatening. "Let him go. Now!" He rolled forward, one hand grasping the ash-born's wrist, the other raised to the sky.

As lightning struck that hand, going through young Lang and into the ash-born, all Bianhua could do was hope the boy knew what he was doing. No untrained human could possibly survive that attack.

⇒)(⇐

Ash tumbled to the ground around Wuchang and Yixiao held his breath. Not just to avoid breathing the stuff but because he wasn't sure he'd done enough. Wuchang's wrist relaxed in his grip and he met Yixiao's eyes with a relieved smile. "Thank you, Yixiao. That thing was more than I could handle."

"What the hell just happened?" That was Judge Jones, staring at the two of them wildly. Brother Jigme and Madam Bianhua were calmer. Clearly they understood the situation better.

"The ash tried to possess us," Yixiao explained, not caring if he sounded insane. "I was able to fight it off with my lightning."

"I saw it. I don't believe it. What are you!?"

Yixiao sighed. "A disciple of the Storm Hermit. Summoning lightning is just one of the many skills I've learned." He brushed ash off himself, adding, "I'm lucky I was able to break free of that stuff."

"I believe it has to work harder against cultivators," Wuchang noted. "That and it needs its creator's full attention."

Judge Law didn't look like he understood any better than he had before. "Could someone explain what just happened from the beginning?"

As he cleaned his face, Wuchang explained. "Marshall Pierce continued arguing with the guard after you left and convinced him to bring the prisoners inside. We were in the midst of doing so when the Marshall overheard something in the Sheriff's office and went to check. A minute or so later, the entire building was filled with that ash."

"Did the others get...possessed...was it?" Judge Jones asked.

"As far as I know, no. Not being privy to the sorcerer's powers, I've no idea why he focused on me."

The ash had tried to control Yixiao as well but the effort had felt weak. "Perhaps he wasn't strong enough?"

"He created a great deal more back home," Madam Bianhua noted. "But Khaitan has more magic and spiritual energy to draw on. Brother Jigme and I have to work a great deal harder to use our skills. Perhaps the same is true for the Master of Ash."

No surprise Judge Jones understood. If Sister Bianhua had been teaching him Khaitanese, she was likely teaching him other things as well. Which meant by now he knew enough about cultivation and magic not to question their word.

Deciding they'd stood around talking long enough, Yixiao suggested, "Let's get inside and see about the others." He'd a bad feeling about them. It hadn't been just ash he'd scented earlier, before they'd run out of the building.

The judge agreed, leading the way back inside. "Gods. What a mess," he muttered as they walked through the charred hallway. "How can ash do so much damage?"

"It's hot, Law. Hot as a volcano's cloud during an eruption." Sister Bianhua smiled ruefully. "You…should be ready for unpleasantness."

She wasn't wrong. The room at the end of the hallway was the courthouse jail. A large chamber, there were several prison cells attached to each side and a blown open door on the other wall. The sole lantern was dusty grey, casting strange shadows across the piles of ash covering the floor.

Those piles were suspiciously placed and even more suspiciously shaped. Yixiao had little doubt what lay beneath. Covering his mouth with his handkerchief, he knelt beside one and brushed the ash away.

"God!"

Judge Jones' exclamation was justified. Beneath the ash lay charred and greasy remains, ruined flesh and shattered bone. Yixiao brushed a bit more, revealing the rounded shape of a skull, the bones shattered, a fatty substance leaking through the cracks.

"This was one of Pierce's men," Yixiao said finally, brushing a bit more away to find the melted remains of a pair of glasses. "The one they called Doc."

"Law, this is your place and your people. What would you have done?" Sister Bianhua turned to her lover, her expression calm but sympathetic.

"Do? I want to find the one did this and boil him in a stewpot." Judge Jones hit the wall, knocking more ash into the air and shattering the charred wood. "Damnit!"

"Respect, Judge Jones, but first we must capture him." Yixiao scanned the room, spreading his senses. They were the only ones nearby. "He seems to have escaped."

Another curse followed, but Judge Jones had the sense not to hit anything again. "Yeah. You're probably right, Mr. Lang. Whoever did this meant to kill us. He'd still be trying if he were here."

"It is always their way," Brother Jigme said in Khaitanese. "A quick strike from nowhere, then escape."

That was probably why Brother Jigme and Sister Bianhua had been sent so far from Khaitan. Not to escape, but to draw their would-be killers out. Both looked stricken and deeply regretful. They hadn't expected or intended this collateral damage.

Sister Bianhua confirmed Yixiao's suspicion. "Up until now we'd been able to sense them coming and evade. We'd hoped to avoid pulling innocent victims into our trouble. We failed. I'm sorry, Law."

"Sorry won't bring these people back, Lil. All we can do is make that bastard pay for it." As Sister Bianhua flinched, Judge Jones managed a little smile. "First things first. Let's get these people properly cared for. Can't figure out what happened here if we don't clean up this mess."

Truth to tell, Yixiao wasn't sure they'd figure things out even if they did clean up. Still, the judge was right. They couldn't leave the dead like this. They could search for the Master of Ash later, after they'd done right by his victims.

⇒)(⇐

Cleaning up the courthouse took the rest of the night and a good deal of the next day. All in all, there were around twenty victims. The six deputies who'd accompanied a man named Pierce. The two men who'd stolen a mail bag from a murdered carrier's body. Seven men and women who'd attacked young Lang for reasons yet to be determined. The person they believed to be the Master of Rust. The sheriff, the courthouse's night guard and the old man who did the cleaning up.

That last was the most pitiful. The poor man had been working towards the front of the building and the walls between had partially shielded him from the Master of Ash's attack. Instead of being killed instantly like the others he'd had time and just enough energy to try and crawl to safety. Not that it would have done any good. Over half his body had been burned.

"Is it just me, or are we missing someone?" Young Lang scanned the remains lain out on the courtroom floor with a tight expression. "Where's Pierce?"

It was almost impossible to be sure which body was whose. They'd had to guess based on what little remained of their possessions. Still, whether or not Marshall Pierce was one of the victims, that still meant there weren't enough corpses.

"For that matter, who got into my safe?" Law said, coming out of his office with a grim expression. He'd gone in to get some paper to make notes.

Bianhua glanced through the office door to the big wall safe where Law kept evidence and other important documents. "It's wide open. Got ash all over inside."

That said the thing was opened before the Master of Ash had attacked. "You don't mention a body, so I'm assuming there's none. The thief obviously got in before the attack and escaped barely in time."

Brother Jigme, who had been carefully examining each body, looked up at them. "May this one speak Khaitanese?"

"If it'll make things easier for you, sure. Lil can translate if I don't get it."

"You said the one who refused us entry wasn't your man?"

"Eh?" Law came closer. "Yeah, that's right. You described someone different."

"But this man is your guard?" Brother Jigme pointed at the man they'd found in the corner of the jail's office. "And this is the sheriff?"

"As far as I can tell through all the burns. Why?"

Bianhua had an inkling what her younger brother meant. "How did they die?"

Carefully, gently, Brother Jigme tilted the head and pointed. "Blade work, here. Not hot ash." The man's throat had been cut. "The one you said was the sheriff was shot."

Bianhua joined them, examining the bodies more carefully. "Killed before the attack, then."

"But why? And who?"

"You did say your safe was robbed?"

The question made Law go back into his office for some reason. He came out a minute later, saying, "I didn't check what was missing," he admitted. "Should have. But things are all cattywumpus right now."

Cattywumpus was one of those odd sayings Law had that never made sense to Bianhua. She ignored it, staying focused. "What was stolen?"

"You remember that coach robbery just a day or so back?" At Bianhua's agreement, Law continued, "We caught the robbers, at least a few of them...." His voice trailed off.

"What is it, sir?" Yixiao asked.

"I just realized. We don't have enough bodies for another reason. There should have been three men from the Royd gang already in the jail cells. They're gone." Law flung his hand towards the three barred cells at the far end of the room. Covered in ash, yes, but with no sign of occupancy.

"The missing items were from the robbery, then?"

"Yep." Law counted on his fingers. "A silk purse with a dozen silver dollars. A man's watch. A diamond ring. A red glass paperweight. A box of food and clothing supplies from San Francisco. A mail-bag....is something wrong, Mr. Lang?"

Young Lang had straightened and stared at Law at that last. "Another stolen mail-bag. And the Royds again," he muttered. "Coincidence?"

Brother Jigme said, "I think, possibly, there are too many hands slicing the meat. The book sent to me should have gone to you, Sister."

Wuchang agreed. "The Royds are bandits. Stealing mail-bags would be expected. But I wonder, if the enemy switched the books to draw you out, they may entangled the thieves in his plans."

Ordinarily, Bianhua would have considered the Royds' problems self-inflicted and been inclined to leave matters be. But the Master of Ash was out there and they had to find a way to stop him. She turned her attention on the body Brother Jigme claimed to be the Master of Rust.

The remains were still covered in ash. Not that it mattered. All the other bodies they'd uncovered had been charred beyond recognition. No doubt this one was too.

Even as she thought so, she noticed something odd about the victim's profile. Aside from the thick layer of ash covering it, it seemed undamaged, as if the ash's heat had had no effect on it. She wiped its forehead with her handkerchief. "What in tarnation?"

"Sister has been listening to American slang too long," Brother Jigme said, even as he looked at the result of her investigation. "But you're right. What in tarnation?"

The skin beneath the ash was undamaged. She touched it cautiously. Cold. Smooth. Impossibly smooth. Like stroking polished wood or stone. She wiped more ash off, revealing his features, and lifted an eyelid. A Pamir native by the looks of him, with the reddish hair and hazel eyes common among the people of Khaitan's western quarter.

He appeared to be dead. Certainly he wasn't breathing. He could be faking it, of course, but she didn't think so. She continued her examination, undoing his shirt buttons, intending to listen to his heart. Even cultivators skilled in deep trances had to let their hearts beat once in a while.

Except when she pulled the man's shirt open, she found herself staring at something not at all right. Someone had sliced open the chest, revealing black metal beneath. And when she poked at it she realized the metal was a lid of sorts. She pried it off with her belt knife.

Inside was empty except for five long bars of black metal, all coming together where the heart would be. One bar had been bent, suggesting someone had twisted it to free some object. Behind her, Wuchang made a startled noise. "Unliving metal," he said softly. "Like my left blade."

Bianhua touched the bar, feeling the cold *yin* energy within. "I've heard of such devices before," she murmured. "A human puppet, transformed by dark magic, controlled by the will of its creator."

"Which means the true Master of Rust is still out there somewhere," Brother Jigme said. "Lying in wait."

It didn't matter. They had to find their enemies and stop them. Hopefully before they killed again.

⇒)(⇐

Rather than risk either of the Demonic Elemental Masters showing up and attacking innocent townsfolk, Sister Bianhua asked Yixiao and Wuchang to help her and Brother Jigme hide in the nearby mountains. She had to argue the point firmly with her lover, but when she reminded him her presence risked his daughter's life he gave in.

Yixiao, who'd spent the last year riding back and forth through the Sierra Nevadas, had no difficulty finding a defensible cave. One far enough into the hills that the enemy couldn't make any bystanders into hostages. One close enough they could see if there was trouble in Leggetsville.

"How much has your mother told you of Khaitan?" Sister Bianhua asked, once they'd settled in.

"She mostly talks about Tu Marsh, where her family lives. But she's told me about the Four great Gods and the Four minor. She's mentioned your sect as well, though only in passing."

"You know Khaitan law forbids the clans and sects from forming martial alliances, like the *jianghu*?"

"I do." The *jianghu* was the term for the dozens of Chinese groups associated with martial arts and cultivation. They often acted as a law unto themselves, the government ignoring their constant infighting unless it interfered with the Emperor's power. Sometimes even the Emperor became involved. Certainly Yixiao's family was, thanks to Grandmother Lang being considered the leader of the White Wolf Clan.

Khaitan, however, was a smaller country and its rulers didn't want the sort of trouble the *jianghu* caused. So while there were martial and cultivational families and sects, any sign of a feud was quickly controlled. "I'm guessing the Demonic Elementalists disagree with that idea?"

"The one who disagreed was the Demonic Elementalists' master, a man calling himself Fall of Time." Sister Bianhua sounded disgusted, "He tried forcing different families to ally with him. And when those families refused, he wiped them out. Two families died in one night. Only one child escaped, saved by the family's head-servant. It was…ugly."

Yixiao believed that. There'd been far too many such massacres in the *jianghu*, after all. "What happened next?"

"The King called the Five Elemental Masters in to deal with the problem. Just as the five Itinerant Magistrates uphold common law, the five of us uphold cultivational ones. We stopped the bastard from harming a third family but that meant he turned on us instead."

At a guess, Fall of Time had realized he'd never get what he wanted as long as the Elemental Masters stood in his way. Yixiao considered the matter thoughtfully. "The man's title is suggestive. He trained the demonic elementalists, then?"

"Yes," Sister Bianhua replied.

"We're not sure," her brother said.

The pair glanced at each other and Sister Bianhua sighed at her brother's uncertainty. "Brother Jigme and Sister Xuan both think there's more to those five than just training. Sister Yuren and I can't think what else it could be and Eldest Brother Yang isn't sure of anything. The point is, within a year of our thwarting Fall of Time, those five showed up and tried to destroy us. And it was always at least three of them on one of us."

Given how hard one of the Demonic Elementalists were to fight, Yixiao could see how that'd been a problem. "So you spread out to force them to separate. What would you have done if they'd cooperated and all come at once? Master says, 'villains can team-up too.'"

"I asked that myself," Sister Bianhua admitted. "Eldest brother Yang thought they'd have no choice but to spread out as well, simply so they could find us."

That still left the question of why the Demonic Elementalists bothered to give chase.

Once the Elemental Masters had left Khaitan, they wouldn't be in a position to interfere with Fall of Time, after all. When Yixiao asked, Brother Jigme explained, "The plan was to spread out and come back if there were any signs of Fall of Time attacking again. It's been two years now and nothing. Brother Yang must have decided to call us back so we can try a different tactic."

"They must have been waiting for him to do so," Sister Bianhua added. "It's just the two of them, though. Brother Jigme and I may have a chance."

Something in her tone told Yixiao she was concerned. Yixiao and Wuchang weren't part of this mess. Nor was Yixiao's cultivation strong enough to defeat even one Demonic Elementalist. She was clearly working her way around to persuading Yixiao to stay out of the matter.

Before she could, he said, "I realize I can't be much help, but I can protect myself from the enemy's tools; those rust and ash-born. If nothing else, Wuchang and I can provide distraction while you two fight. Master says, 'even a rabbit can trip a swordsman.'"

Besides, those Demonic Elementalists had already murdered too many. It was high time someone stopped them.

⇉⟩⟨⇇

To tell the truth, Bianhua was torn between sending Yixiao off and letting him be involved. His cultivation was strong but it wasn't strong enough to take a Demonic Elemental Master on directly. On the other hand he was quick-witted and aware of his limitations. Too, they could use the help.

She was less concerned for Heibai Wuchang. The Hollowed Blade didn't visit Khaitan often, but his reputation stretched both miles and centuries. Not alive, not properly dead, he'd be difficult to destroy. The Master of Ash had managed to possess him, admittedly, but he knew to protect himself now.

Which reminded Bianhua, "Master Heibai," she asked the man standing at the entrance to the cave. "You said the guard changed his mind and let you into the jail after young Lang left you?"

"I did."

"And it was while you were dealing with the prisoners that the Master of Ash attacked. Did you see him?"

"I did not. Though I believe the attack originated from the center of the jail. Which, I admit, puzzles me because the only ones there were Marshall Pierce and two of his men."

Bianhua considered the information, visualizing the jail and the path of destruction. All the bodies had been laid out in a near perfect circle from the center of the room. The fallen door to the back hall had no ash under it, suggesting it'd been damaged by the first blast. The second blast, which had partially covered the damage from the first, had been aimed down the hallway.

"Is it possible the ash burnt the Marshall entirely?" Brother Jigme asked.

"Surely the other two would have been equally damaged."

Yixiao's suggestion was true and Bianhua admitted it. "The fact that there's no sign of this Marshall Pierce is suggestive. Could he be the Master of Ash himself?"

That made Brother Jigme scoff. "The man is a westerner. He knew no Khaitanese nor Chinese."

"Perhaps his tool, instead?" Heibai Wuchang offered. "I thought he wished to accompany us out of suspicion. What if he meant to keep an eye on Brother Jigme?"

"There's also the question of the mail-bags," young Lang added. "I don't like how they, and the Royd gang, keep becoming involved in this mess."

"What happened to the book Brother Jigme received?" Heibai Wuchang asked suddenly. "The one intended for Sister Bianhua?"

"I have it here."

Taking the book her junior brother offered her, Bianhua scanned through the pages. It all seemed in order. This was her old copy of her style's manual, its pages well-read and torn in places. It even had the soup stain her Master had left on it and never managed to clean.

She frowned. She'd stared at that stain for years while she was training. Its color and placement was correct but something seemed off, as if it were imperfectly shaped. Examining it more carefully, she realized there was a thin line scoring the page from top to bottom.

Fiddling with the edge of that line Bianhua realized someone had somehow cut the paper halfway through and unfolded it. It was an impressive feat. The paper was thick, but not thick enough to casually divide it in half this way. She picked at the score, pulling the paper up slowly, revealing a pattern drawn on the inside.

"That...." Brother Jigme stared. "What is that?"

Curious, Young Lang leaned close and frowned at the pattern. "I've never seen such a thing. It's written in seal script, yes?"

"As far as I can tell." Bianhua had never learned the arts of magical arrays, but she thought this looked like the work of a talisman cultivator. "And before you ask, it wasn't in this book when I had it last."

Young Lang frowned. "You may be best off ridding yourself of the thing."

He was likely right. Except, "You think it might be used to find me?" At his agreement, she suggested, "Perhaps we should let him. We've no idea where he's gone to."

"And no idea how many allies he has," Brother Jigme pointed out. "It'd be better to find him before he finds us."

Bianhua was just about to ask exactly how they could do so when a thought occurred to her. "That other mail-bag. The one stolen by the Royds. I think it might have had your book, Junior Brother. I thought I sensed Eldest Brother Yang's metal seal approaching just last week, just before the stagecoach was robbed."

"How would that help us?"

"Ash or Rust must have swapped the books intentionally. The seal is supposed to search us out. Perhaps he has your fire seal still, sister?"

It was possible, even probable. "If so, I can follow it, as long as he doesn't take it too far away." Bianhua could only hope that - once they found him - they could stop the bastard before he murdered more innocents.

ᗒ)(ᗕ

For once they had a quiet night. Yixiao had half-expected the Master of Ash, or more ash-born, or some of the Royds to show up. "We didn't even get a stray nightwalker," he commented to Wuchang as they cleaned up their camp.

"Do you wish trouble that badly, Yixiao?" Wuchang gave him an amused look.

"No. I've just gotten too used to it. It feels wrong when we have a peaceful night. Master says, 'Anticipation makes a thing take longer.'"

"We will be having far less peace soon enough, young Lang," Sister Bianhua told him, folding her blanket and putting it in her pack. "I spent some time searching for the seal's aura last night. I believe it's southwest of us."

"I HAVE IT HERE."

That led down to the foothills and the gold fields. There were mining camps all over the place and dozens upon dozens of twisted little valleys where people could hide. "We'll need to be careful, then. Best let me take the lead." At Sister Bianhua's raised brow, Yixiao patted his mail-bag. "I have a legitimate reason to be wandering around the area. Mail-carriers are like cockroaches. You never know where we might turn up."

That made Sister Bianhua chuckle. "How will you explain the three of us?"

He thought about it. "Training. I'm teaching you and Brother Jigme how to navigate the area so you can carry mail yourselves. Wuchang's already known to be my partner."

They gathered their things together and headed down the trail, following Sister Bianhua's guidance as best they could. It wasn't easy. The foothills of the Sierra Nevadas were steep and full of twisting trails leading nowhere. Full of miners hoping for a strike as well, which complicated matters.

Over and over again they had to change direction. Not just because the trail shifted but because it'd lead into a miner's territory. Yixiao did his best to keep the peace but some miners were born of distrust and hatred for all humanity. They weren't there just for gold but for the sake of being alone.

They were screamed at. Shot at. Had rocks thrown at them. On one memorable occasion, they even had a puma sicced on them, one Brother Jigme scared off through sheer force of will. It seemed the White Tiger of the West was too much for the beast.

Despite the interruptions and diversions they slowly came closer and closer to the seal Sister Bianhua sensed. It wasn't moving, fortunately, though that warned Yixiao of another problem. "We may be about to stumble onto the thieves' lair," he told his companions. "I doubt it's in a legitimate miner's possession."

"Shall I investigate, Yixiao?" Wuchang asked, only to stop and sniff the air. A familiar and terrifying scent drifted past them on the breeze. Ash and burned meat.

Sister Bianhua tightened her lips. "It seems we're too late."

"Change of plan, then. Wuchang, you still go first. Signal what you see. Brother Jigme, Sister Bianhua, we should separate and approach carefully."

His companions, who likely had as much or more experience in situations like this, accepted Yixiao's suggestion. Really, he didn't mean to be so commanding but he kept finding himself ordering people around like he was still the Second Young Master of the Lang clan.

Yixiao took the trail, leaving Brother Jigme and Sister Bianhua to slip through the woods on either side. Wuchang would go all the way around and come in from above whatever camp lay ahead. From there he could warn them of danger.

They gave Wuchang a good several minutes before taking their chosen paths. As Yixiao expected, both Sister Bianhua and Brother Jigme were as stealthy as Wuchang. Within moments they were out of sight and sound, their movements just barely visible to Yixiao.

Once he was alone, Yixiao headed up the path, expecting to run across someone long before he reached its end. Instead, he approached a fenced-in area of land at the far end of the ravine. The gate was wide open, letting him see a rocky plateau and a cave opening into the mountainside.

He also spotted a stand-off between a dozen apparent miners, gathered around a tall and familiar figure. Marshall Pierce, it looked like, his expression grim and hard. No sign of damage to him, either, which Yixiao thought was significant.

A bird whistled somewhere in the trees above the campsite, the notes clear and concise. Wuchang's message wasn't complex; it couldn't be without drawing attention, but it was enough to warn Yixiao. Six corpses on the outskirts. A dozen or so inside.

Another dozen still alive

One of the men in the group, a Royd by his looks, noticed Yixiao's approach. "You! You with this idiot?"

Yixiao smiled. "Don't mind me, folks. I'm just a local mail-carrier. Seems I took a wrong turn at Helltown. Don't suppose one of you could help me out? Master says, 'You scratch my back, I'll scratch yours.'"

⋛⟩⟨⋚

The man questioning young Lang looked disgusted and Bianhua could hardly blame him. Bandits, especially ones accosted by a Federal Marshall, would have little patience for the boy's antics. Likely that was why young Lang behaved the way he did. That lighthearted and naïve-seeming attitude of his surely fooled most people. It'd fooled Bianhua for months, at least until she'd noticed the tell-tale marks of a disciple of the Storm Hermit.

Kneeling among the trees, she scanned the Royd Gang's hideaway. The sloped area in front of the cave entrance was open and defended by a heavy wooden fence that curved round the lower edge of the slope. The bandits had cut down the trees on the outer edge of the fence, creating an open area covered in sharp-edged rocks.

Ordinarily, the hideout would have been protected by guards stationed atop makeshift towers leaning against the inside of the fence. Six of them, two on either side of the gate, four more evenly spaced around the fence line. The guards still stood at their posts, rifles in hands as they leaned against the fence looking over. They'd never fire another shot. Each and every one was dead, their faces covered in a thick layer of ash whose heat must have killed them long before they'd had a chance to smother.

Bianhua climbed up a tall tree so she could see what was happening inside the compound. Nothing good, as far as she could tell. The man at the center was unfamiliar, but she knew several of the bandits from their occasional visits to Leggetsville. They'd gotten themselves banned from town after one barfight too many.

As far as she was from the argument, Bianhua couldn't quite hear what was happening. She caught a word here and there, however, and guessed the man in the middle was the one who'd gone missing. Marshall Pierce, wasn't it? If so, how had he survived the Master of Ash's attack unscathed?

Sensing Brother Jigme sneaking closer to the fence on the other side of the compound, Bianhua followed suit, leaving young Lang to do his part. It looked to her like the bandits weren't going to put up with his presence much longer. She slithered down the tree and made for the fence, climbing up just enough to let her see inside and hear the argument better.

"I promise, Marshall Pierce and I aren't working together," young Lang was saying. "I'm just a mail-carrier looking for Mister John Reid. If he isn't here, I'll have to look for him elsewhere."

"You wander in just when this bastard shows up and you expect us to believe a fool story like that?"

"When you put it that way," young Lang admitted, "It does seem a bit of a stretch. And I admit, I have traveled with Marshall Pierce before. Isn't that right, Marshall?"

"I've nothing to do with you," the marshall said in an oddly stilted way. "You're interfering."

"And you're in over your head. Or did you bring anyone with you on this little adventure? Master says, 'it's dangerous to go alone.'"

The marshall chuckled. "Of course I did. Haven't you noticed them yet? They've spotted your friends, hanging around outside the fence."

Bianhua dropped to the ground quickly, intending to make a run for the trees. Except a sound behind her made her look over her shoulder, just in time to spot three ash-covered figures slither over the fence. The guards, the ones the Master of Ash had killed, transformed to ash-born to take her down.

She spun around and slammed a fire-claw strike into the fence, shattering it so she could break into the compound. A moment later Brother Jigme did the same.

It wouldn't make them much safer, Bianhua knew, but at least she'd have young Lang and her younger brother at her back.

⇒)(⇐

Yixiao spotted Marshall Pierce's smug grin. He looked nothing like a Khaitanese - not even like the red-haired Pamir - but there was only one person he could be. "Master of Ash, I presume?" he asked in Khaitanese.

A smile. "You know more than I expected, boy." The answer had a faint accent, but Yixiao didn't know enough about his mother's native land to tell where it came from. "I'd like to know how you broke my ash-born last night."

Spreading his hands and stepping back, ignoring the Royd gang's mutters and grumbles as they tried to figure out what was going on, Yixiao said, "Try me and see." He dropped into stance, the clumsy looking pose that never failed to annoy other fighters.

This one was more knowledgeable. "Ah. A follower of the Storm Hermit. Do you think that will protect you from me?"

Yixiao controlled the urge to say it already had. If the Master of Ash didn't realize Yixiao's cultivation had thwarted that last attack, he wouldn't disabuse him of the notion. "It isn't much," he admitted, watching the man's hands. They were thinner than he remembered, with a greyish tint just below the nails that he hadn't noticed before. "So, when exactly did you take Marshall Pierce over?"

Before the Master of Ash could respond, one of the Royd Gang stepped in. "The hell is going on here? Mike, what happened to you?" The last was shouted at one of the six 'men' lumbering towards them, their bodies covered in a thick layer of ash, with only staring eyes and the smoking remnants of their clothes to show there was once a human being inside.

No surprise the man clung to normality in the face of what'd just happened. With two strangers ripping the hell out of their fence and six of their own men transformed to some fireside horror story, the only thing they could do was either fight or flee. Lacking knowledge, they chose to fight.

One man grabbed at his former compatriot. He screamed, leaping back, hands charred black, blood seeping from the cracks. Yixiao winced inwardly for the damage and made note to avoid the ash-borns' touch.

The rest of the Royd Gang reacted predictably. Lacking better weapons they fired on their former compatriots. Fired and failed entirely to damage the ash-born. If the creatures weren't focused on Sister Bianhua and Brother Jigme, their attackers would have been their next victims.

Wisely, the Elemental Masters evaded their attackers and stood back to back. They might not be strong enough to deal with the things directly but at least they could support each other. They moved rapidly, dodging in and out as the six ash-born struck, neither giving way nor able to bring the things down.

The Royd Gang, more interested in self-preservation than anything else, made a run for it, escaping out the front gate, leaving half their number dead or dying behind. Apparently they weren't important. The Master of Ash let them go.

Yixiao focused on his opponent. Thus far the man had remained where he was, as if he didn't regard Yixiao worth fighting. Most of his attention was on the two Elemental Masters. Yixiao moved to block him. "You've yet to answer my question."

"Why would it matter, little would-be cultivationist?"

"Curiosity is my besetting sin," Yixiao admitted. "But if you've no answer, I can at least guess."

The Master of Ash's smile revealed nothing. To Yixiao's surprise, though, he still didn't move. Did he disdain Yixiao's skills, or was there more to it than that? Yixiao stepped sideways, forcing his enemy to turn and turn again when Yixiao moved a bit further to the side. "Go bother someone else, boy. I'm busy."

"You don't want me dead?"

"You're useless to me. Why would I bother ending your life?"

"Useless?" Yixiao repeated. "Then why not dispose of me like the trash you think I am?" He moved further, backing towards the cave entrance.

"Do you think you can escape me in that hole?"

Likely he could. The Royd Gang almost certainly had a hidden escape route, somewhere in their base. However, "Why not fight me and find out?" At the Master of Ash's sneer, Yixiao continued, "Could it be that you can't? Could it be that controlling those ash-born of yours is too much of a strain? You're playing with more than last time."

The sneer faded. "Clever boy. Don't think it'll do you, or that undead pet of yours, any good."

So, he did know Wuchang was somewhere nearby. Not good, not bad. Wuchang was nothing if not circumspect. He wouldn't blindly attack without some advantage. It was Yixiao's job to distract their opponent enough to give his partner that very thing.

Quietly, he drew his lightning to him, fingers and arms crackling with blue fire. Smiling with a confidence he didn't feel, he said, "He's not my pet and I don't need his help."

Without another word, he struck.

⇒)(⇐

The ash-born were much weaker than the one that'd used Wuchang's body the other night. Was it because Wuchang was undead and a great deal stronger than most men? Or was young Lang right, thinking the Master of Ash was straining to maintain so many tools?

Possibly it was both, but either way, it made Bianhua and Brother Jigme's efforts easier. Brother Jigme couldn't touch their enemies without being burned, but he could use whatever metal came to hand to block and cut back.

Bianhua was in more trouble. She could take the heat, but the fine ash their opponents flung at her made her choke and cough, struggling to see and to breathe. Keeping her bearings became difficult, especially when the fight forced her and Brother Jigme apart.

She ducked and dodged blows she barely saw coming and would have been severely injured if the ash-born had been a bit stronger or a bit faster. They were neither and she managed to roll out of the way, landing next to a broken down gold sluice.

Once again she was on her feet, wiping ash from her face, preparing to attack again. She'd fought and defeated ash-born before, though she'd needed Elder Sister Xuan's help. She'd have to do it alone this time.

If only it would rain. But this wasn't the right time of year. Nor could young Lang do anything. There wasn't enough water in the air for a storm cultivationist to use. No water in this dried up gully, either. If only the bandits hadn't blocked the stream that once flowed down the mountainside.

A thought occurred to her. What if the stream was still there, just diverted? She wiped more ash from her eyes, ducking and dodging her attackers as she raced for the bandits' cave. From the looks of things, it'd been the stream's source. Likely the bandits had enlarged the hole and dug a lair into the mountainside.

"Keep them occupied," she called out to Brother Jigme. It wouldn't be easy for him, she knew, but she couldn't waste time explaining. Fortunately, her martial sibling didn't argue, just set to distracting all six ash-born while young Lang kept their master busy.

The cave was lit by a few guttering lanterns. As she'd thought, it was man-made, carved from the rock by a combination of pickaxe and dynamite. She looked around, spotting a heavy stone wall covered in cement. There. That had to be it.

If she were Second Sister she could have broken the rock easily. Even Jigme might have been a better choice. All Bianhua had was the intense heat of her element. It'd have to be enough.

She set her hands to the cement, feeling something vibrate behind. Calling on her cultivation, she set her flames burning, focusing them as tight as she could on the wall. Something moved behind her, three ash-born had followed her in, refusing to be distracted by Brother Jigme.

More heat. More and more until she almost thought she'd burn herself to a crisp. She might be the Elemental Master of Fire, but she was comparatively young and inexperienced. There was only so much she could take. Only so much she could do.

An ash covered hand grabbed at her and she kicked its owner backwards, hands flat on the cement surface. Another kick for the next ash-born sent it rolling. Both rose to their feet, clearly intending to try again, while the third was already on her.

A loud noise drew her attention. Yes. It was working. Her heat, combined with the chill of the water behind the wall, was doing the job. The cement cracked further, dampness seeping through, turning to steam as it hit the hot cement. A moment later the whole thing shattered, the flooding stream slamming into Bianhua and sending her flying.

Fortunately, the water that carried her out of the cave took out the three ash-born as well.

⇒)(⇐

The sudden flow of water coming from the cave mouth startled Yixiao and almost gave his enemy a chance to get a hand on him. If the Master of Ash hadn't been equally startled, he might well have caught Yixiao and seared a hole through him. Instead he fumbled and almost fell into the water.

When he pulled back, expression momentarily panicked, Yixiao understood why Sister Bianhua had gone into the cave. She'd put herself at risk, given her element. Seeing her struggle to her feet at the far end of the compound, soaking wet and barely able to stand, he knew she couldn't help any more.

Fortunately, Brother Jigme came to his sister's defense, kicking one of the ash-born into the stream. Steam hissed and billowed around the thing and the ash covering the body it'd possessed washed away.

If it were in Yixiao's power he'd have pulled the water into a cloud and surrounded the Master of Ash with it. Storm cultivation didn't work that way. Instead he shouted, "Wuchang, cover me!"

A moment later, Wuchang leapt down from a high point above the fight, silver and black blades gleaming in the afternoon light as they cut into the Master of Ash's clothes. No blood, Yixiao noted. The man must have dodged backwards just in time.

Yixiao searched around the compound. Spotting an old bucket stuck under the remains of the gold sluice he grabbed it, dodging around Brother Jigme as the man kicked water into the face of the second ash-born. It flailed and slowly fell apart, leaving the charred corpse of the man it'd possessed crumpled.

Yixiao filled the bucket, water dripping from dozens of rusted out holes. He cursed the bandits for not keeping the thing in good condition. So what if they weren't using the sluice? Buckets were useful, damnit! At the same time he turned it over the head of the third ash-born.

Not waiting to see the thing fall, Yixiao caught more water in the bucket and flung it at the Master of Ash. It missed, but Brother Jigme splashed the man a moment later, startling him and giving Yixiao time to refill his bucket. About to attack again, he noticed their enemy pull a dark red stone from one pocket. The thing pulsed in his hand, looking oddly like a human heart, despite its glossy sheen.

A memory flickered. That puppet's empty chest, with the five bars of metal that might once have held some power source. Some instinct told Yixiao the thing was dangerous. "Wuchang, get back!"

Wuchang obeyed, just as the Master of Ash flung the stone to the ground, shattering it. Instinctively, Yixiao dove to the side, flinging himself behind the broken sluice. He was barely in time to avoid the resulting explosion.

The noise was deafening. A strange, almost sulfurous, stench overwhelmed the nostrils. As for sight, it was impossible through the cloud of rust particles. Yixiao crouched, waiting for the air to clear, eyes closed and face pressed against his knees to avoid breathing the stuff.

At last he looked up and, seeing blue sky again, managed to stand and look around. The others were slowly getting to their feet, their faces just as covered as Yixiao's. As for the Master of Ash, his body lay flat on its back, one hand stuck in the air as if paralyzed.

Yixiao stumbled over. Poked the body. Prodded. Then, barely able to hear himself talk, he said, "It's another puppet." He opened its chest, revealing yet another red-tinted stone.

Sister Bianhua, who'd been furthest from the blast and least injured, came closer. Examining the puppet, she muttered, "Then where is the real Master of Ash? For that matter, where's the real Master of Rust?"

Brother Jigme coughed. "I don't know how to answer that."

A damp handkerchief appeared in front of Yixiao's face. Wuchang being helpful again. "We should look for the mail-bag," he suggested. "It won't have answers, but we shouldn't risk its contents going wandering again, spell or no."

Yixiao agreed. "Sister Bianhua, Brother Jigme, if you would make sure this puppet can't come back to attack us, I'd appreciate it. I'll go check the cave for the mail-bag."

They agreed and Yixiao sloshed through the stream, slower now the pressure had been released. Wuchang accompanied him, helping search through the bandits' meager treasures. "Here," he said at last, pulling the bag out from beneath a pile of clothes and other goods.

Taking the thing outside, Yixiao opened it and soon found a package like the one in poor young Tony's bag, this one with a fire-opal seal. He handed it to Sister Bianhua and went through the envelopes, only to slow to a halt as he recognized the name on one. Fingers shaking, he opened it carefully and drew in a long, slow, breath.

"Brother Jigme, Sister Bianhua, am I right in thinking you're called to return home?"

"We are," Sister Bianhua agreed.

"If you've no objections, I'd like to join you on the trip back to Shanghai." They and Wuchang all gazed at him with startled eyes. "My father writes to tell me my Grandmother is sick and not expected to survive the year. I have to go home, too."

And hopefully, if the Gods were with him, he'd make it back before Grandmother Lang left them forever.

Chapter 3
Black Turtle Crosses the Ocean

"You lot are the sorriest bunch of would-be sailors I've seen in a long time!"

Shen Lenghai ignored the Captain's grumbles. He wasn't their target anyway, being peacefully engaged in repairing the damage done to the *Jeen Loon*'s hull. Someone, no longer a crewman, had steered the ship towards a reef on the way from San Diego. Fortunately, Captain Hai Chan had turned the ship in time, but there was a long scrape along the side he wanted sealed.

"No muscles! No legs! No stomach! Half of you can barely stand. Some of you can't speak anything but English!"

Having seen the latest would-be recruits, Lenghai had to agree with his captain. Most were failed miners looking for a new line of work. Some had never set foot on a ship before now. The ones who had, had spent their entire time below decks trying not to be sick.

"You! You're not ready at all!"

"I can...be...."

"You're green." Captain Hai Chan's voice softened. More kindly, he added, "Spend some time on the docks and get used to the water. You can try again when I come back from China."

"I...I...oh...."

The sound of the recruit's voice warned Lenghai. So did the rapid pounding of feet as the damned fool rushed for the side. Two sides and over forty foot of rail to choose from and he naturally aimed himself straight for where Lenghai was working.

Dodging the stream, drawing on the water below him, he redirected the vomit away from the ship. The idiot was too busy getting his stomach under control to notice. At least Lenghai hoped the idiot wouldn't notice. The last thing he needed was to be noticed.

It's all right. His eyes are closed. Master Xi's voice in his head was a soft ache, her breeze a poor substitute for her presence. She fluttered around him, a butterfly formed of air.

Rather than acknowledge her, Lenghai raised his head. Shouted, "HEY! Warn a person next time!" He clambered up the rope and glared at the kid.

"Things go over the side all the time, boy. Just be glad you're not mending the back end." Captain Hai's grin was obnoxious but it didn't last. More seriously, he gestured at the skinny blond youth still leaning on the railing. "You go back to land. I'm not hiring someone who gets sick on an anchored ship. You'd have your head over the rail all day long."

Lenghai was relieved to see resignation in the young man's eyes. As the kid turned away and the Captain returned to his task of choosing new recruits, Lenghai turned back to his work, only to pause when he noticed one of the new men sticking to the shadows beside the *Jeen Loon's* cabin.

The man had a vaguely shifty air to him. He also seemed familiar. He indicated the stranger, knowing Master Xi's natural curiosity would send her over to check the man out.

Although no one but Lenghai could see his master, the breeze she haunted could be felt. Aimed at the right place and in the right way, and it could startle even the most stoic of people. This man wasn't nearly self-disciplined enough to stay silent when Master Xi goosed him.

"YAH!"

The sudden shout drew Captain Hai's attention, just as Lenghai had hoped. He spun round and for what had to be the first time, took notice of the burly figure doing his best to pretend to be a part of the scenery. "Eddy Long! The hell you doing back on my ship?"

The man's lips tightened. In an obsequious way, he pleaded, "Captain, y'gotta take me back."

Lenghai had been about to go back to work, but this was far too entertaining to ignore. Eddy Long was the crewman who'd steered the *Jeen Loon* into that reef. There was no way Captain Hai would rehire him. Lenghai would be lying if he pretended not to be interested in watching an idiot get what was coming to him. He leaned his arms over the railing and wished he had some melon seeds.

"Like hell I will! You broke my ship!"

"Cap...."

"Do not Cap me! You get off now."

"Captain, I gotta go back to Taiwan! I got no money. Don't strand me here! I'll work, I promise I'll work." Eddy Long turned to the crew, clasping his hands together pleadingly. "My old mum's back there. She needs me to come home!"

Lenghai might have sympathized but for the calculating look in Eddy Long's eyes. He was playing for sympathy, knowing how protective his targets would be towards their own parents. He was tempted to say something but Captain Hai spoke first. "Didn't you tell me she was dead before we left Taiwan?"

A look of raw fury suffused Eddy Long's heavy features. "YOU...You let me go home! I'll work for free! I...I'll pay you!"

"NO! NOW GET OFF MY SHIP BEFORE I THROW YOU OFF!"

Eddy Long was a good foot taller than the Captain. Taller and broader shouldered and just as mad. He swore loudly, adding, "I'D LIKE TO SEE YOU TRY!"

Before the Captain could retort or his men stand up for him, a new voice spoke from the other side of the ship. "Master says, 'A subordinate who refuses to obey a simple command can't be trusted with more important ones.'"

The captain turned towards the newcomer and shouted happily, "LANG YIXIAO!" To Lenghai's surprise, he followed it up by grabbing the speaker in a huge embrace, lifting the smaller and lighter man up off the deck. "HOW'VE YOU BEEN YOU LITTLE IDIOT!?"

⇒)(⇐

Coughing, grinning, Yixiao pulled free. "This idiot is glad to see you're well and delighted to be so happily welcomed." He turned his attention back to the man his old friend had been yelling at. "He is also disappointed to see your crew treating you so poorly."

The man glared. "Who the hell are you and what're you doing talking so big when you're so small?"

"Shall I make space for you, Yixiao?" Wuchang asked, obviously knowing what was coming without having to ask. Of course, he'd long experience with situations like this.

"Mm. Yes. I believe this is going to be one of those occasions," Yixiao agreed. He glanced at Hai Chan inquiringly, adding, "Given you're all right with it?"

"None of that damned lightning of yours. We've got enough to fix thanks to this idiot here. But, yeah." Hai Chan waved at his men, ordering them back as far as possible. Wisely so, too. Yixiao was liable to throw his opponent a fair distance, given the chance.

Someone shouted "It's a fight!" which inevitably drew more of the crew out to watch. It could get boring aboard ship and a fight broke up the monotony. One swarthy young man, thin and light boned, hair tightly braided down his scalp, perched on the railing with a dour smile. Was Yixiao imagining it, or did he spot pale mist flutter past the young man's head?

Focusing, Yixiao turned to his opponent. "We don't have to fight," he said calmly. "But I'm willing if you are."

A sneer. "You're half the Captain's size. If I'm not scared of him, why be afraid of you?"

Admitting the man had a point, Yixiao cupped his hands and bowed. "This one is Lang Yixiao, sometimes called The Wanderer. Might he know the name of the one he faces?"

"Long. Eddy Long. Sometimes called the guy who's gonna pound your face in."

Yixiao kicked off his shoes. Smiled. "Well then, Mr. Long. Shall we?"

For a moment it seemed the man would back off. Then his lips tightened and he stomped towards Yixiao, growling. "I'll rip that smile off your lips, boy."

"What was it you just told Captain Hai? Ah, yes. I'd like to see you try." Yixiao dropped into fighting stance, reflecting that he was working under a handicap this time. It'd been over a year and a half since he'd been aboard a ship and his footing was still a bit off. "Master says, 'talk is cheap'."

From Long's movements, he was used to the swaying deck. Used to brawling, too, no doubt. He'd need some finessing to keep up with. Those big hands were a danger. They looked like they might snap bone.

Letting Long grab for him, Yixiao ducked and flipped. A sharp blow to the sternum set the man gasping and choking. Another - aimed for a nerve point - missed, giving Long the chance to catch his wrist. Using the momentum of the man's grab, Yixiao slammed his foot into the side of Long's knee, sending him sprawling.

A flailing hand nearly struck Yixiao in the face but he caught it instead, twisting the man's pinky at an angle it was not supposed to go. Long shouted furiously, swinging his free fist for Yixiao's throat. A quick bend backwards, followed by an equally quick adjustment and Yixiao tugged sharply, pulling Long off to the side. Drawn forward by the momentum of his attack, Long couldn't stop himself from being slammed face down onto the deck.

Quite suddenly the boy on the railing jumped forwards, setting a bare foot on Long's shoulder. "Want to die?" he asked casually, forcing the man to stay flat. "The young master is being polite."

At first Yixiao didn't understand why the boy had interfered. Then the youngster nudged Long over, revealing the short dagger Long grasped in one hand. Before Long could recover, the boy slammed his foot down on the fallen man's wrist.

"SHALL I MAKE SPACE FOR YOU, YIXIAO?"

Hai Chan growled a curse. "That's quite enough," he ordered, grabbing the blade and tossing it overboard. "Throw him off my ship. No need to offer him a ride back to shore."

As his men gleefully obeyed, Hai Chan returned his attention to Yixiao. "Come to my office. You can tell me why you're here." He glanced behind Yixiao, apparently just noticing his companions. "While you're at it, introduce me to your friends."

Behind them, Long yelled furious curses that terminated in a huge splash.

⇒)(⇐

You should present yourself....

There was no way in hell Lenghai would do anything of the sort. Those two were Master Xi's martial siblings, not his. He might have the power and knowledge of the Master of Water but he'd no real connection to the Five Elemental Masters. Worse, given how he'd gained that power and knowledge, the other four would likely regard him an enemy.

I'm here to tell them not.

Master Xi was dead though, or the next thing to. Those two might not listen. Might not hear her words. No. Lenghai would keep an eye on the situation and do his best to avoid notice.

Brother Jigme and Sister Bianhua's two companions were interesting and dangerous. Lang Yixiao was a mere human, though his foundations were good and he seemed close to stepping onto the true path of cultivation. He was also powerful, despite his mortality.

The other man was even more unnerving. Dead but not dead, he breathed only to speak. His heart did not beat, or at least Lenghai couldn't hear it. Master Xi thought the man might be literally heartless, but Lenghai found that hard to believe. Only true undead could exist without a heart. Perhaps that was why he called himself Heibai Wuchang; the Yama Kings' guide to the Underworld?

Fortunately, Heibai Wuchang stayed below decks. Apparently he couldn't swim and preferred not to risk falling overboard. Lenghai felt some sympathy there. Before his transformation he would have sunk straight to the bottom of the sea. Even now the only thing protecting him was his power over water.

Avoiding most of the newcomers was easy. All Lenghai had to do was keep working on the repairs to the hull. Captain Hai didn't want to put the *Jeen Loon* in dry dock to replace the reef-damaged boards. He'd promised to deliver important goods to Shanghai and couldn't wait the week or so it'd take. Fortunately, the damage was superficial. All they needed was sealant to keep the scraped boards from soaking up sea water.

Lenghai spent most of the next two days hanging on a rope slung over the railing, sanding and smoothing and resealing the scrape. He'd already repaired the damage below the waterline, using his mastery of water to let him get at it. Now he finished the bits left over, no longer needing his power to assist. A good thing, too, because half-way through the next day Lang Yixiao dropped down another rope and came to assist him.

"You're a passenger, Young Master Lang. You don't have to."

"Will my help speed things up?"

Lenghai eyed the other man. "That depends on how well you do. I'll kick you straight off if you make more work for me."

Unoffended, the young man set to work on the nearest part of the scrape. "Fair enough. I'd expect nothing else, really."

They worked side by side, surprisingly quiet. Lenghai would have thought Lang Yixiao the sort to talk one's ear off, just like Master Xi. Instead he did his work peacefully, only speaking when he wanted Lenghai to check his work. It startled Lenghai just how much it pleased him to be listened to.

Look out. Master Xi's voice in his ear caused Lang Yixiao to look his way. Had he heard her? He shouldn't have been able to. Up until now, Lenghai was the only one who could hear her voice.

Rather than explain, Lenghai turned to look, spotting the reason for Master Xi's warning. A water elemental, its body shaped like a horse, galloped beneath the waves of San Francisco Bay, racing straight for the *Jeen Loon*.

Water elementals could be damned dangerous. Lenghai drew on his power and set it flowing downwards, redirecting the creature away from the ship. To his surprise, it tried again, calling out Lang Yixiao's name in an excited way.

"Stop that," Lenghai snapped at the elemental. "You'll swamp the boat."

"Shut it, sorcerer. I'm not looking for you!" The elemental rose above the water, flailing its forelegs as if it thought it could harm him.

"Henrietta, you settle down right this minute!" Lang Yixiao called out, dropping into the water and swimming towards the elemental. Apparently he knew the creature. Equally apparently, it listened to him where it wouldn't listen to Lenghai.

"I'm not a sorcerer," Lenghai grumbled. "Young Master Lang, you get that monster to go away, it likes you so much."

"Her name is Henrietta," Lang Yixiao told him quietly. "And she's an old friend. An overly excitable old friend who's too young to know her manners, Master of Water."

Realizing he'd revealed far too much of himself, Lenghai flinched. "I don't know what you're talking about," he lied.

"If you wish to pretend otherwise, it's not for me to tell you your business. Give me a moment here, if you will."

Lenghai returned to work. "Whatever you want. It has nothing to do with me."

⋺⟩⟨⋸

Henrietta swam around and around Yixiao, swamping him momentarily before she remembered he needed to breathe. "Sorry, Yixiao!"

"It's all right. I expected it. You do it every time." Yixiao set his hand on her forehead, stroking the cold wet surface. "I didn't expect to find you here, though."

"Sister Marguerite is shopping. I'm supposed to help move the boat when we go home."

"She'll be terribly pleased that you've come to pay me a visit, instead of staying with the boat." As Henrietta drooped, he added, "I'm sure she'll understand. Is there a reason you came looking for me aside from just wanting to say 'hello'?"

The clear horse-like shape leapt out of the water excitedly and splashed him. "Isn't that enough of a reason?" She paused. "Oh, but wait, there was something. What was it? What was it?" She dove deep into the water, embarrassed by her forgetfulness.

He waited, knowing it was impossible to pry answers out of his young friend when she was in this sort of mood. It took her several minutes before she finally surfaced and said, "I remember, I remember! That lady pirate, Brigid. The one who wanted to catch you. She escaped."

Captain Brigid Kramer was the wife of another pirate, one Yixiao had been forced to kill on his way from China. She was bold and clever and determined, not to mention vengeful. He really wasn't surprised she might still be after him. "I see. Well, I'll keep an eye out for her, then."

Henrietta shifted to a human-like form, though still clear as the water she inhabited.

"Why are you here? Did you lose your job? Did you get bored? Are you going to be a sailor?"

Chuckling, Yixiao waited again for her to calm, then told her, "I've been called home to China."

It was hard to read Henrietta's expression, clear as her shape was, but her voice revealed her sadness. "You're leaving? Without saying goodbye?"

Gently, he stroked her soaking wet 'hair'. "If I stopped to say goodbye to every friend I have here in America, I wouldn't make it home in time. My grandmother's dying."

As huge tears flowed down her cheeks, Henrietta wrapped her arms around Yixiao and hugged him tight. "Oh. Oh, I'm sorry. I'm sorry!"

So was Yixiao, but he wouldn't say so. "I can't promise I'll be coming back," he murmured. "But I hope to. Until then, you take care of yourself and the Sisterhood. And pass my farewell on to those who know me, all right?"

She sighed. Nodded. Then hugged him one last time before hurriedly swimming away. No surprise she faded off so quickly. She was young for her kind and the emotions of the moment had to be hard on her.

"Where'd you meet that one?" the sailor called Shen Lenghai asked.

"Along my travels. A sorcerer with power over spirit beasts had her in his thrall. I freed her." It'd been a difficult time, with him chasing all over the countryside, fighting wolves like men, being abducted by the same sorcerer who'd enthralled Henrietta. He'd barely come out of that adventure sane.

"I see." The water beneath Yixiao lifted him up so he could reach the rope swing again. When he thanked young Lenghai, the boy muttered, "Don't mention it."

Yixiao had a feeling young Lenghai meant that as a broad statement. "I won't," he promised. "I'm not sure why you're hiding yourself from your fellows, but I won't tell them."

Young Lenghai remained silent for several minutes, focused on finishing his work. At last, grudgingly, he said, "Thank you for your silence."

From the fact that young Lenghai held the power of water when Brother Jigme and Sister Bianhua had mentioned an older woman, Yixiao guessed something had gone amiss. He didn't ask what, not wanting to frighten the boy. "I should warn you, the other two are being hunted. I think it likely you will be too. If that's a problem, you may not want to travel with us."

Dourly, young Lenghai muttered, "It won't matter. Wherever I go, I'll be in trouble sooner or later."

That was a feeling Yixiao understood only too well. "Then we may as well be in trouble together. At least for now."

⇒)(⇐

To be honest, Lenghai wasn't sure he wanted to risk befriending Lang Yixiao. Not because the man was unlikeable; far from it. But befriending anyone wasn't Lenghai's way. There was so much about the world, about people, he didn't understand. There were too many ways for him to misstep and reveal his ignorance.

Lang Yixiao's friendship with Brother Jigme and Sister Bianhua didn't help. Oh, Lenghai was almost sure the man wouldn't reveal what he knew. Almost wasn't enough. Lang Yixiao was smart and quick with his words but that didn't mean he'd make no misstep at all.

As the *Jeen Loon* sailed for China, Lenghai kept to his usual duties. Not being a true sailor, those mostly involved helping out in the galley, swabbing the decks and, when he was lucky, keeping watch from the crow's nest. The last was his favorite because it meant he could be alone with himself.

Well, mostly alone. Every so often Lang Yixiao would come up to join him. Not to be companionable, thank all the Gods, but because he too liked the relative solitude. They'd sit back to back, silent and watchful, eyes on the horizon.

At least they remained silent and watchful until three weeks into their journey. The skies were clear, the wind constant and the ship's movements even. Yet Lenghai couldn't help feeling on edge, as if something lay waiting for them.

That thing appeared over the horizon around mid-afternoon, a dark shadowy silhouette that should not have been there at all. A storm? An island? Neither should be possible, here in the middle of the Pacific. His breath caught in his throat as he peered through his spyglass. "Damn."

To Lang Yixiao's credit he didn't ask questions, just gazed out at the shadowy mountain forming in the distance. Only then did he murmur, "Not a storm. I'd feel it."

"An uncharted island?" Lenghai offered hopefully.

"I don't think it's the right shape. The edge is too straight."

They considered the sight for a moment or so longer. Then Lang Yixiao sighed. "I'll tell the Captain. He's not going to like this."

True. Captain Hai Chan had no great fondness for peculiar events and this was damned peculiar, even to Lenghai's understanding. It gave him a sick feeling, as if he were being hunted by a great beast. Maybe he was.

You should tell the others.

He didn't want to tell the others. Didn't want the trouble that would bring. And had to admit he had no choice. He waited, though, unable to leave his post until Lang Yixiao returned with the Captain.

From Captain Hai Chan's expression, he half-blamed his friend for whatever was headed their way. An unfair reaction, Lenghai felt. Surely not everything that went wrong around the Storm Hermit's disciple was his fault?

"I've been crossing the Pacific for years now and never seen such a thing," the Captain grumbled. "Why does trouble always follow you?"

Lang Yixiao tilted his head and smiled, "Wasn't it just last night you told me about meeting the queen of all octopuses? Or was that and your other stories all tall tales?"

An embarrassed expression crossed Captain Hai Chan's face. "Some of them were. That one wasn't." He glared out at the darkness ahead of them. Still distant but crossing their path in a threatening way. "Whatever it is, storm or something worse, we don't want to head into it. Much as I hate to, I'll shift our course."

Before the Captain could head down to do just that, Lenghai asked, "Permission to descend, sir?"

A sharp look. "You're on duty until dusk, Shen Lenghai. Unless you've good reason to leave it early?"

That made Lenghai bite his lip. He didn't really want to go down and didn't want to do what he had to do. Waiting wouldn't hurt anything and maybe he could use the time to think of a way to avoid the issue without putting everyone in danger. He didn't even know if that thing had anything to do with him, after all.

"No," he admitted. "I don't. It can wait."

As Master Xi whispered disappointedly in his ears, he turned his gaze forward and returned to duty.

ᗱ)(ᗣ

"You might want to go speak with the young man up top," Yixiao told Sister Bianhua. He was interfering again and pretty sure he wouldn't be thanked. But he'd a sense the thing they faced had something to do with the Elemental Masters and young Lenghai specifically. The boy's name alone, meaning cold ocean, was suggestive.

"If he wants to talk to us, he'll talk to us," she said firmly. "I've better things to do than chase him down."

At a guess, that meant Sister Bianhua knew young Lenghai was the Elemental Master of Water, or at least somehow related to her. What was the name they'd told him? Ah, yes. Master Xi Xuan. Sister Xuan.

"Do you have any thoughts on what we're headed into, then? Because I have a feeling that young man knows."

Brother Jigme considered that, leaning against the railing to watch the horizon ahead of them. "At a guess, it's the Demonic Elemental Master of Mist."

Mist didn't seem to be nearly as dangerous as Rust and Ash had been. When Yixiao said as much, however, Sister Bianhua sniffed. "They can put my fires out, for one thing."

"Can they possess someone, the way Ash did?"

"Quite probably. They can smother anything that breathes."

Yixiao could do without air for quite some time if he had to. Wuchang didn't need it at all. But the rest of the crew was definitely in danger. He watched the shadowy wall draw nearer and scanned its motion. "Oh, that's not good."

Both his companions saw his meaning immediately. Hai Chan had shifted the *Jeen Loon's* course to evade the wall of mist and it looked like they'd pass it easily. Except the far end of the wall was curving and extending itself, slowly working its way around, as if were a giant snake encircling its prey.

A glance further back drew Yixiao's attention. There was something in the distance, sails on the horizon following behind. He sighed, "Wait here," he told his companions before hurrying to speak to Hai Chan. "Check to the…I think you call it aft? The wall's getting longer and there's a ship that looks like it might be following."

To Hai Chan's credit, he didn't argue, though Yixiao could tell he wanted to. Instead he handed the wheel over to the nearest sailor and hurried to the aft railing. When he lifted his telescope to look, he muttered, "The ship isn't necessarily an enemy." From his tone he didn't believe it himself.

"Remember what I told you about Captain Brigid? It might be her."

"Is that water elemental you mentioned trustworthy, though?"

"Not entirely, but she's honest and earnest enough. And that Captain did have a strong desire to do me harm. Likely she's none too fond of you, either." After all, Hai Chan had helped defend the *Henrietta Marie* from her husband and his crew.

A discontented sigh. "You keep an eye on that vessel, then. I'll keep working on getting us away from this other mess." Hai Chan gestured at the wall of mist, then frowned. "It is getting longer, too. Damnit!"

Yixiao accepted the telescope, scanning for the other ship's flag and sails. At the same time, Hai Chan hurried back to his post, shouting orders at his sailors that Yixiao didn't understand at all. No doubt they were intended to move the *Jeen Loon* faster, since a minute later the ship put on speed.

Steadying himself against the rail, Yixiao kept searching, spotting and losing sight of the other ship with every jolt and bounce. Really, he'd no idea how sailors managed in these circumstances.

As he gazed backwards, a soft voice whispered in his ear. *Up and to your right.*

That was the same voice Yixiao kept hearing near young Lenghai. Whatever it was, it was being helpful and he followed its instructions, then followed them again. Ah, there the ship was.

Not being a sailor, Yixiao had no idea what sort of ship followed them, but he couldn't help noticing a faint white cloud rising from its rear. "Is it on fire?"

Not smoke. Steam.

Steam? "Like a train?" Yixiao dimly remembered his brother and his parents - all three of them - discussing steam engines excitedly at the dining table. "Can steam power a boat?"

I think it can, yes.

Not good. Not good at all. That meant the other ship wasn't limited by the wind the way the *Jeen Loon* was. If it were a pirate ship attempting to catch up with them, it could do so easily. He was about to ask the voice if it could help them move faster when a wave made him lose track of the other ship, shifting his view sideways.

For a moment he thought the telescope had broken because all he saw was a blur. Then he lifted his gaze from the device and realized the wall of mist had extended further, curving around yet again, drawing closer and closer to the other ship.

Steam rose faster as the other ship increased its speed, clearly trying to escape the mist, racing towards the *Jeen Loon*. Yixiao held his breath, not wanting the others to reach them but not wanting them caught either.

The wall of mist slammed into the other ship's rear, setting it spinning in the water behind them. A moment later the ship foundered, half-sunk into the water, its crew yelling and shouting desperately. Helpless, Yixiao could only hope they'd survive until rescue could come.

It wouldn't be soon. Not when the *Jeen Loon* was desperately trying to evade disaster as well.

⋧⟩⟨⋦

The wall of black mist drew closer. Close enough that Lenghai could see the way it swirled and shuddered with resentful energy. Its presence sent a chill through him, a faint urge to join the dance. He would not, he could not. Its creator had no power over him. Not anymore.

Seeing the wall close in behind them, curving round to trap them inside the circle, Lenghai tightened his lips. The damned thing was after him, he knew that much. Knew, too, that he could escape easily. The ocean depths were too deep for the Elemental Master of Mist.

But escape meant abandoning the *Jeen Loon* and its crew to his enemy. He'd no doubt Master Xi's fellow disciples could fight them off, but someone was likely to be hurt.

"First thing, get the ship out of danger," he muttered to himself. The wind wasn't blowing fast enough to get them past the trap. Nor was there any natural current to carry the ship faster. They didn't need either, not with Lenghai aboard.

He turned his attention on the water, reaching deep, commanding its movement. Master Xi couldn't have done this. Her mastery was over the shallows, the waters that could be stirred by the wind and warmed by the sun. Lenghai, born of the darkest and deepest depths, his heart pure black ice, was another story altogether.

Cold water rose from below. Caught the *Jeen Loon* in its path. Carried it fast. Faster. As fast as Lenghai could manage. Somewhere below him, someone shouted "MAGIC!" and he sneered. This wasn't magic, not the sort human sorcerers drew on to work their will on the world. This was a thing of the spirit. A thing of his spirit.

Men panicked below him but he ignored their shouts. This took too much concentration to risk breaking his focus. Besides, Captain Hai Chan was calling for calm. He'd noticed the current carrying them faster towards safety. Since that was exactly what the Captain wanted, he wouldn't argue with the result.

Careful, Master Xi murmured in Lenghai's ear. *You're not practiced enough.*

There wasn't any choice but to push and push. The black mist drew closer, speeding up, its creator realizing they were escaping. They only had a hundred or so yards to spare. Then fifty. Then only a dozen. Master Xi whose power was limited to the wind alone, added her limited strength by filling the sails.

They shot through the narrow pass, mist roiling and shifting within the chill black fog on either side. Then they were out, the wall slamming shut behind them, stretching out to grasp them as they passed.

Lenghai didn't relax. If anything, he pushed harder, wanting to get the ship as far from that mist as he could. That proved a mistake. He was a great deal stronger than any human would be. He was not omnipotent. He'd reached too deep, pushed too hard. Dizzied, exhausted, he struggled desperately to keep them moving and slowly lost the fight.

At last, unable to hold on another moment, he released his grip on the water. The sound of fighting below told him the Elemental Master of Mist had sent her tools aboard, but he was in no condition to help.

Not that he could have done much even if he'd been.

⇒)(⇐

As the *Jeen Loon* raced through the narrowing passage, barely missing the closing walls of black mist, Yixiao didn't relax. He didn't dare. The Demonic Elemental Masters had already proved themselves obstinately unwilling to give up. The one controlling this wall surely wouldn't, either.

He was quickly proved right. They'd just cleared the wall when parts of the thing twisted and tore away, dropping onto the deck rapidly. It was a startling move, in part because the mist-born landed so quietly. They looked solid, even if their substance roiled and twisted within their human shapes. They should have made some noise, not landed like cottonwood fluff.

Sister Bianhua leapt onto the aft deck a moment later, closely followed by Brother Jigme. Each blocked a mist-born from advancing, trading rapid blows as the invaders tried to reach Hai Chan. "Stay back," Sister Bianhua shouted when some of Hai Chan's sailors came to help. "They'll possess you!"

"Never mind the fight. The current's dying down," Hai Chan ordered. "Just get this ship moving faster!"

Yixiao set himself between Hai Chan and the mist-born, drawing his cultivation together. As lightning crackled around his fingers, Hai Chan snapped, "Stay away from the sails with that!"

No need to acknowledge the obvious. Hai Chan was just shouting to keep his spirits up. Focusing on the mist-born, Yixiao blocked its first blow, then the next. That almost proved a mistake. Like its close kin, the rust-born and ash-born, the thing was malleable and stretchable. Its 'arm' coiled around his, taking on a tentacle shape that attached itself to him and tried to pull him in.

The ash-born had acted the same way. These beings seemed to need a physical form to attach to and this one meant to use Yixiao. Before it could, he loosed a flow of lightning down his arm and into its 'body'. It pulsed inside the mist, rumbling and roaring through its shape. Storm scent filled the air, followed by a clap of thunder that carried his lightning across to the mist-born Sister Bianhua fought. "Get back," he yelled, just barely in time.

Sister Bianhua's fire was invisible - she was being careful to avoid notice - but it was hot. Hot enough to burn her attackers' substance away and force them to condense to protect themselves. That was their downfall. The change did something to their structure that made it attract the lightning Yixiao had blasted into its fellow mist-born.

One after another the mist-born exploded in a spray of black droplets, disappearing entirely. Even the one Brother Jigme fought shattered, leaving the three of them with nothing to fight.

Help Lenghai. The whispered voice fluttered in Yixiao's ear. He turned his attention to the crows nest and saw young Lenghai clutching at a rope, clearly struggling to stay upright. Realizing he was about to fall, Yixiao rushed to the mast and clambered up as fast as he could.

He was barely in time to catch the boy as he tumbled over the edge.

⇒)(⇐

Lenghai was only dimly aware of being lain on the deck. He'd exhausted himself, summoning so much water to his will. This was the price he paid for not cultivating his powers. The price he paid for pretending he could be a mere human when he hadn't been to start with.

"Is he going to be all right?"

That was Lang Yixiao, bending over him solicitously, clearly worried about his health. Not that Lenghai wanted him to be. It made him feel strange, setting an odd hard lump in his throat. His kind didn't cry and didn't know how. What business was it of Lang Yixiao's, making him feel this way? Who told him to care about a near stranger so easily?

Lenghai forced his eyes open. Pushing Lang Yixiao's hand away took more strength than he had, but he tried even so. "Don't…bother…."

"Don't try to move. You used too much strength, you foolish child." Sister Bianhua sounded particularly out of sorts. No surprise. Master Xi had told him everything about her siblings in the year or so after his so-called ascension. The Elemental Master of Fire had a temper to suit her element and a tongue as sharp as Brother Jigme's blades.

Struggling to sit up despite Sister Bianhua's orders, Lenghai blinked at the faces surrounding him. Captain Hai Chan and Lang Yixiao of course, plus both Master Xi's martial siblings. He didn't expect practically everyone on deck as well. "I'm…fine. I should…go back…to my…post."

"You are not fine and you are not going anywhere," Captain Hai Chan growled. "You'll stay right where you are until Masters Bianhua and Jigme decide you're well enough to move."

There was no way he was going to let those two have anything to do with his care. They'd figure out the truth about him. Figure it out and try to destroy him, the way he'd destroyed Master Xi. He pulled free of Lang Yixiao's grasp, forcing himself to his feet and rushing towards the rail.

He'd intended to throw himself over. He'd be safe there. No one could follow him, not even those two Elemental Masters. Except as he reached the rail a chill sensation washed over him and he stopped, staring wildly, paying no mind to the one trying to hold him back.

"... AND TRIED TO PULL HIM IN."

"Young Lenghai, whatever it is, we'll try to resolve it," Lang Yixiao said, hands on his shoulders. "Running won't help."

Running wasn't possible. Not anymore. Lenghai pointed. "Never mind me," he gasped, trying not to fall to his knees in terror. "She's coming for me. For all of us."

By this time the Elemental Masters had joined them. Sister Bianhua glared furiously at him. "It's just that damned cloud we already escaped. It can't move fast enough to catch up, now."

"No," he gasped. "Look more closely."

They all gazed at the blackness behind them and Lang Yixiao murmured, "I'm not sure why you're worried. It's shrinking."

It was, but that didn't make it any less dangerous. If anything, that made things worse. "She's found a new focus."

As Lang Yixiao frowned, not understanding, Sister Bianhua and Brother Jigme glanced at each other. Then Brother Jigme said, "There's only one person he could mean. Wusuo. The Demonic Elemental Master of Mist."

Sister Bianhua added grimly, "It's obvious what she's focusing through. That ship you spotted. The one you thought might be following us. The one powered by steam and more than capable of catching up, even without wind."

All of which meant the fight wasn't over and couldn't be avoided. Because run though they tried, they couldn't possibly evade the enemy forever.

Not when she meant to have Lenghai and the power he'd taken from Master Xi.

⋨⋊⋉⋩

It was obvious Hai Chan was angry. Fortunately, he reserved his fury for the thing behind them. "Why is it I can't ever cross this ocean without running into something supernatural?"

"Just lucky?" Yixiao couldn't help asking, and ducked the light blow Hai Chan aimed at the top of his head. "There's some folk who seem drawn to such things, or to whom such things are drawn to. Master says, 'Sometimes, all you can do is weather the storm and hope to make it through.'"

That made Hai Chan grumble, "Don't we have enough trouble without you bringing your master, and storms, into it?"

Knowing it'd just aggravate the situation more, Yixiao didn't bother pointing out that he was the Storm Hermit's disciple after all. Instead he returned his attention on the blackness behind them. Young Lenghai had been right. The mist wall had trapped and captured the other ship instead of them.

"Is there some way we can find out what's going on over there?" he asked.

I can find out for you, the voice that'd helped him earlier whispered in his ear.

"Could you, please? Given you're not putting yourself in danger?"

Everyone except for young Lenghai stared at Yixiao. "Ah, Young Master Lang, who are you talking to?" Sister Bianhua asked in a concerned way.

Now that was interesting. The voice he and young Lenghai could hear was inaudible to everyone else? He raised a hand, stopping further questions and walked away from the group. To his relief, no one followed him. He didn't want to look too much a fool but he needed to question the voice.

"I'm sorry to be rude, but could you tell me who you are?"

Xi Xuan.

That was the name of Sister Bianhua and Brother Jigme's Third Sister, the original

Elemental Master of Water. "Forgive me, Water Master, but are you a spirit?" It was a risky question. Those dead who remained in the world could turn violent when reminded of their condition.

Dead, not dead. Power lives on in Ah-Hai. There was a fond note in Sister Xuan's voice as she spoke of young Lenghai. Which in turn told Yixiao a great deal. He'd noticed signs of guilt and self-disgust in the boy's behavior and while his reasons were unclear, his feelings of unwillingness were obvious. *Help him. I cannot. Can only guide water if it's willing to flow.*

In other words young Lenghai was a stubborn piece of work who didn't want to be involved. Yixiao had been there and understood the feeling only too well. "I'll do what I can. In the meantime, if you can investigate that other ship without endangering yourself, please do."

The voice was gone almost before he'd finished his sentence and Yi Xiao returned to the others, still staring at him as if he'd grown a tail or a new set of ears. When he said as much, Hai Chan grumbled, "With you I expect almost anything. You turning out to be a fox spirit would only confirm my suspicions of you."

Grinning, Yixiao went to young Lenghai and knelt beside him. "Do you want to tell, or shall I? Because you can't keep this secret anymore."

Young Lenghai's lips went tight but he turned his gaze aft to look at the thing coming after them. "I was a slave of Wusuo's, sent to capture Master Xi. Except she - Master Xi - captured me instead. Cared for me. Treated me kindly. When Wusuo realized I wouldn't cooperate, she tried to steal my heart back."

"Steal? Your heart?" Hai Chan demanded. "Don't you mean kill you?"

"You can't kill what isn't alive," the boy whispered. "Wusuo created me. She had every right to end me when I refused to obey her."

Remembering the things they'd fought before, Yixiao asked, "You're a puppet?"

"Yes. Or I was. Master Xi transferred her power to me." Desperately, young Lenghai stared up at Brother Jigme and Sister Bianhua. "I didn't want it. I didn't ask for it. But I couldn't stop her, either."

The two Elemental Masters looked at each other. Then Sister Bianhua sighed, sounding particularly out of sorts. "The trouble with water is it goes where it wants. You can try to block it, try to control it, but in the end it wears you down."

"Our sister means you couldn't have stopped Sister Xuan from doing what she wanted no matter how hard you tried, little brother," Brother Jigme added.

A stunned expression crossed young Lenghai's face. "Little brother?"

"Well I'm not calling you elder brother when you're...what...all of fifteen years old?"

"Three months."

"Even worse! You're a baby and...Wait...three months?"

Young Lenghai shrugged. "That's when Wusuo made me."

The statement made Brother Jigme stare blankly, while Sister Bianhua said, "It doesn't matter. You've been granted our Sister's power. She wouldn't have done that if she didn't think you worthy."

"You're accepting me as one of you? When I practically stole..."

"Not as one of us, not when our master hasn't confirmed you." Sister Bianhua set a hand on the youngster's shoulder. "You had your powers given to you. It's not the way we usually do things and you're ill-trained because of it, but you're our sister's disciple and very much one of us."

As Lenghai...Disciple Lenghai's...expression shifted from confusion to stunned gratitude, Yixiao noted, "Right now we're going to need your help to avoid becoming

Wusuo's next victims."

The boy wasn't stupid. He picked up on Yixiao's meaning without needing it written out for him. He looked at his fellow Elemental Cultivators. "Master Xi has been helping but she's not strong enough. Will you instruct this poorly trained disciple in the proper use of his power?"

As the two agreed, Yixiao turned to Hai Chan. "All the speed you can manage won't be enough. We'll have to fight."

Lenghai let the other two help him to his feet. "We should wait until Master Xi comes back," he told them. "She went to investigate our pursuit."

That made Brother Jigme frown. "Is she putting herself in danger, doing so?"

Master Xi had become a wisp on the wind, a disembodied voice neither water nor mist could touch. "She's safe enough. But she can't help either. All she can do is talk."

Sister Bianhua sniffed. "In other words nothing's really changed with her."

An unfair statement but one coming from the heart. Master Xi had told Lenghai all about her siblings over the months since he'd ascended. There was love there. Real love of a sort he didn't fully understand but yearned for, even so. Knowing he didn't need to defend his predecessor, he just murmured, "Perhaps."

They moved to the aft railing, keeping close eye on the black blot in the distance. It was definitely growing closer. "Maybe I could...."

"That water you used came from the deeps, right?"

"Yes. Is...is that a problem?"

"Not a problem. But you're not strong enough to keep it moving for long. You already used a great deal of your spirit getting us out of that trap. You need to save what you have left until it's needed." Sister Bianhua eyed the water. "I don't suppose you can communicate with sea creatures?"

Well, he could, but, "The biggest and strongest of that sort is practically a Goddess in these waters. She'll listen to me but she won't fight unless it benefits her. This won't." Herself was ancient, powerful and mostly concerned with her worshippers. All of whom were of her own eight-limbed kind. Getting her to cooperate required careful handling and persuasion. They didn't have time for that.

"Actually, I was wondering if you could persuade all the sea life to stay away from us." At Lenghai's confused look, Sister Bianhua gestured at their pursuit. "Wusuo's mists can possess living creatures. I'd rather our only enemies be ones who can't come at us from below."

Ah. That made sense. "I'll do what I can, then." Lenghai set to vibrating the water, sending a warning to every sea creature within miles. It took several minutes and felt a great deal longer. It was certainly long enough for Master Xi to return to him.

The ship is similar to the Jeen Loon, she told him. *But there's something odd about it. A metal tank in its hold. I couldn't get near. The heat blew me off.*

"That's probably the steam engine," Lang Yixiao murmured. "Just like a train."

"What's a steam engine?" Lenghai asked.

"A device that uses steam to move ships and trains." As they all three looked puzzled, Lang Yixiao added, "I only understand a bit because my parents and brother are obsessed with the things. The main point is that ship doesn't need wind to move."

Lenghai thought about it. "Master Xi says the tank is hot. It holds this steam?" At Lang Yixiao's agreement, Lenghai continued, "My waters are cold, almost freezing."

"You already...."

Lenghai interrupted Sister Bianhua's protest. "It wouldn't take nearly as much. I've strength enough to pull a few dozen gallons up from the depths."

Lang Yixiao frowned thoughtfully. "What would you do with it, though?"

Wasn't that obvious? "Hot and cold things don't mix. Won't it damage this...engine... you mention?"

The man looked uncertain. "It might? It might not. I never really paid much attention to such things." From his tone, Lang Yixiao was clearly embarrassed. "I wouldn't depend on it. Could you control the steam and increase its pressure? That much I do know is bad."

"Steam is practically mist. Even if I'd cultivated to Master Xi's level I doubt I could do much." Tell the truth, he'd hardly cultivated at all. "Isn't there some way? Could your lightning do something? Or Brother Jigme or Sister Bianhua? And we have to hurry because they'll be on us soon."

Clearly cudgeling his memory, Lang Yixiao leaned on the railing and watched the enemy's approach. "We need to break their boiler somehow. If the steam inside over-pressurizes, or the tank is damaged, it'd explode. But that could kill dozens...."

"They're possessed. They may already be dead."

"Some might survive. I'd rather not kill anyone."

They all fell silent, each admitting they felt the same. Whether or not the sailors aboard that other ship had been enemies to start with, they still shouldn't be killed out of hand just for convenience's sake. Then Lenghai had a thought. "What if the tank could be damaged without blowing up?"

"How do we do that?"

"Brother Jigme, you can control metal. If you weaken the tank in just the right way, and if Sister Bianhua heats it with her fire, I could use my water to keep the escaping steam from injuring anyone." He turned to Lang Yixiao. "Would that work?"

"It might," Lang Yixiao agreed. "I'm willing to try, if you three are."

Really, there weren't many choices. With only a moment or so of hesitation, they agreed.

⇒)(⇐

Intense regret was a hard lump at the back of Yixiao's throat. Why hadn't he paid better attention? Why hadn't he valued what his parents and brother valued, at least enough to understand more than steam made trains go fast?

They sat in the *Jeen Loon's* dinghy, Disciple Lenghai using his control over water to carry them faster than rowing, or even wind and sail. It wasn't as fast as the steamship coming up behind, but it didn't need to be since they were headed straight for the thing.

Don't overextend yourself.

Yixiao couldn't help smiling a little at Disciple Lenghai's sulky, "I know." It sounded so much like he, himself, had when his parents had tried to keep him from getting himself in trouble. It hadn't worked for them and he'd a feeling it wouldn't work for Master Xi.

"You know, but still you persist," Sister Bianhua murmured. "You nearly fainted, using your powers to move the *Jeen Loon.* There's no need to rush here."

With a sigh, Disciple Lenghai let the boat slow a bit. "I just want this over with."

"I think Wusuo may as well," Brother Jigme pointed out, gesturing ahead. "Their ship moves more quickly towards us, as eager to meet as we."

Brother Jigme was right. The other vessel, wood for the most part, with two huge water wheels attached to her side, had noticed their approach and turned slightly towards them. No doubt the one controlling it - whoever they were - knew their quarry was aboard the dinghy.

The other ship drew closer and closer, until the word, "Misfortune" became visible. Just the sort of name a pirate's vessel would be given. His suspicion that Captain Brigid was involved grew.

Spotting movement on deck, Yixiao peered closely and tightened his lips. "They've cannon."

"Now's the time to use your powers," Sister Bianhua told Disciple Lenghai. "Can you lift us so we can board?"

Without bothering to answer, Lenghai drew the water beneath them together, balancing the dinghy easily. "Can't fight cannonballs," he said tensely, as it became clear they were about to be fired on.

"That's our job." Brother Jigme and Sister Bianhua turned their attentions on the weapons, eyes intent as they focused their talents and simultaneously bent the cannons' metal and burned their gunpowder. As the cannons exploded, the mist-covered crew dodged backwards, flowing along the decks as if they possessed neither bone nor flesh.

Some of the crew tangled up with each other, forming a towering shape resembling a human arm. It struck at Yixiao and his companions, only missing the dinghy because Disciple Lenghai shifted them sideways just barely in time. Reacting quickly, Yixiao gathered his lightning, flinging it across the gap and into the misty shape. Just as in the last fight, it darted through the black fog, destroying whatever it touched.

Disciple Lenghai moved them closer to the deck, giving them a chance to leap to the *Misfortune* and move to surround him, protecting him from the enemy. He was the most vulnerable here, just as Brother Jigme had been to rust and Sister Bianhua to ash.

"Get to the engine," Yixiao ordered, scanning the deck and pointing towards the boiler house. The noise of the steam engine sounded off to him, reminding him of an incident in his youth. An explosion barely averted by his father's quick thinking. "Be careful. Something's wrong."

"What?" Sister Bianhua asked.

"I don't know." The trouble was, though he remembered the accident, he didn't remember the details. "Dad, I swear, I'm going to pay better attention to what you say when I get home."

"A filial, but useless, intention. We need to know now." Sister Bianhua struck down a mist-born, her fire burning it away easily. At the same time Brother Jigme blocked an outstretched tendril, his element protecting him from its touch.

It's hotter than before.

Heat. Why was that important? As he dodged and struck, exploding mist-born with his electricity, Yixiao struggled to remember. Then it hit him. "Brother Jigme, can you check the boiler's metal? Find any weak spots?"

"En. Cover me."

As Brother Jigme focused his attention on the boiler, Yixiao and Sister Bianhua worked to keep the mist-born away. Disciple Lenghai, lacking the ability to fight the things properly, stayed between them, drawing his water up the side of the ship to swirl around in his hands. He might not be able to damage the boiler but he was prepared to try.

Quite suddenly Brother Jigme gasped, "The tank is cracking inside."

"Can you keep it from shattering?" They'd intended to sabotage the thing. Letting it explode uncontrolled would count, but they wouldn't survive to reap the benefits.

"I can hold it. I can't fight the heat inside."

"Do your best," Yixiao ordered. "If that thing blows, we'll all go."

"Then we will all go together!" That was a new voice, a familiar woman's voice. Captain Brigid, her skin glistening and her clothes damp from the mist roiling around her.

"I'd a feeling you were involved," Yixiao answered. He turned to his companions. "See? She's involved. Didn't I say she'd be involved?"

"You did, Young Lang," Sister Bianhua murmured, eyeing the woman. "The question is how much of her is left in there. I think she's a puppet, just like the other two. We need a way to tell."

Now that was an excellent point indeed. "It depends on how much she's willing to sacrifice." Yixiao tilted his head questioningly. "Your engine is about to blow, Captain. Your ship will sink, along with what remains of its crew. Is that your intent?"

She sneered. Drew her sword. Stepped forward. "If it will take my enemies down with it, what care I?" Leaping over the rail, she thrust at Brother Jigme, no doubt intending to distract him. He dodged the attack easily and Sister Bianhua smacked Captain Brigid with a red-hot hand.

The woman barely reacted to the heat. She just glared, beckoning more mist-born to gather close and smother Sister Bianhua's flames, proving her true nature beyond a doubt. Wusuo must have disguised her puppet as the Captain to control the *Misfortune's* crew.

Lightning sparking around his hands, Yixiao blocked the mist-born. Some snuck past narrowly avoiding his attack, but Master Xi blew them back. At the same time, Disciple Lenghai gathered his water, a bubble of clear liquid taking human form. Sometimes it blocked Wusuo's blows; other times it let the sword slice straight through, reshaping itself around the cut.

"The tank," Yixiao gasped urgently. "Take care of that first." He dodged past the fight, rushing for the boiler, a swirling mass of mist-born right behind him.

Somehow he managed to stay just ahead, tossing bolt after bolt of lightning into his enemies. Not a single body left to them. Did that mean there was no one left to save except themselves? Using the momentary respite, Yixiao studied the controls, struggling to remember his father's words.

Oh. That was right. The tank would blow because of the pressure. A release valve had failed, overheated perhaps, so the boiler's contents just kept pushing and pushing at its metal prison. He searched the panel. Found the words "Pressure Release". There. That had to be it.

Without hesitation, he pulled the lever and hoped he'd gotten it right.

⇒)(⇐

Lenghai couldn't see the steam escaping from the vent, but he sensed it. Intensely hot, incredibly fast and impossibly dense, he feared it'd kill any living thing fool enough to get in its way. He backed up, momentarily unsure of what to do.

Wusuo called more mist-born to her side, sending them against Sister Bianhua and Brother Jigme. She avoided Lang Yixiao, considering his lightning too great a threat. Not that the man could help. The lever he'd pulled was trying to flip back, forcing him to cling to it tightly.

"Little traitor. Think you're human now?"

"I don't. I'm not. But I'm not a traitor." Traitor implied loyalty and a puppet had nothing of the sort. That he'd gained a mind and a soul and been given his savior's cultivation didn't make him any less a puppet.

Wusuo sneered. "You belong to me. You will always belong to me. And you will give me what I demand!"

As Lenghai edged sideways, trying to think what to do, Master Xi swirled around him, whispering, *You belong to yourself and yourself alone. The only one who pulls your strings is yourself.*

Master Xi had said those same words, the day she'd saved him from his creator's control and let him live. For that alone he owed her. That she'd sacrificed herself in the doing meant he owed her kin, her fellow Elementalists. Owed them and would not fail to repay.

"I don't think so," he told Wusuo. "Not now. Not ever. Now scram. Because I'm sick and tired of you." He scanned the deck and noticed something about Wusuo's movements. Every time she tried to reach him she shied sideways, avoiding the narrow band of steam venting from the boiler.

So that was it. Wusuo represented mist, the breakdown of water, but she couldn't exist without real water to feed on. She could be burned away by fire or blocked by metal. Her power was similar to steam, but couldn't bear such intense heat and pressure. He gathered his water and set the icy liquid spinning, flinging Wusuo straight into the vented steam.

The heat and pressure had lessened in the few minutes since the fight had started. It still slammed Wusuo across the deck and into the mast. There was a wail and a shattering sound, then she dropped to the ground, black mist rising from the body she'd possessed and dissipating. A moment later the mist-born disappeared as well.

Brother Jigme approached the body cautiously. Nudged it over. Said quietly, "Another puppet. As we thought."

Lang Yixiao finally released the lever now the boiler pressure had been relieved. He joined them around the body, kneeling beside it and examining it carefully. "Yes. The question is, how?"

Thoughtfully, Sister Bianhua offered, "The Master of Ash used Marshal Pierce. Obviously they all have some skill that lets them turn humans into puppets." She looked at Lenghai curiously but didn't ask the obvious question.

"If…If there was someone before I was shaped…I don't know who they were." Lenghai rubbed at his joints, unsure how to respond. "I only know from the moment I was freed of Wusuo's control."

And I have no idea of your past, either. You came to me as you are.

Lang Yixiao repeated Master Xi's words for the others, adding, "I really am not liking these people. Captain Brigid was a murderess, but Marshall Pierce was a good man. He didn't deserve being used that way." The man sighed. "We'd best return to the *Jeen Loon*. I don't think there's much more we can do here."

There wasn't. Not really. Wusuo would surely find a way to come after Lenghai again, of course. He'd no hope of escaping her alone and unaided and it was high time he recognized it. High time, too, he accepted that his only chance of surviving was allying himself with the sect siblings of the one who'd sacrificed herself for him.

He'd hidden long enough. It was time to rise from the depths and act.

Chapter 4
Yellow Kirin Guards the Earth

Doctor Song Yuren sensed her kinfolk long before they arrived. As second eldest Sister of her sect, her strength was a hair short of their Eldest's and her connection to the earth extended far beneath the ocean.

Not only could she tell her siblings were returning as planned, but that one of them was not the same sibling who'd left her behind. It gnawed and worried at her, but there was little to be done about it until she met this new child.

The day she felt them draw close, she went to Shanghai's docks to wait. No point in making them hunt around for her. Their enemy was still out there somewhere but there was no need for secrecy anymore. She could tell he and his tools had been weakened. He wouldn't attack until he thought he had the advantage.

"Judge Lang! You shouldn't be wandering around alone."

"Nonsense. I'm not on a case right now. Just an ordinary citizen."

The argument came from two familiar voices. Judge Lang Yide and his chief guard, Captain Chen. Yuren had heard variations of this discussion frequently over the last few months, ever since she'd taken on the task of keeping Guren Princess Hexiao alive until her grandson came home.

Lang Yide was in his late twenties, an elegant gentleman dressed in a simple dark-grey *chang pao*. His carefully shaven forehead gleamed in the morning sunlight and his gentle manners spoke of an excellent education. Which, given his post as Old City's Magistrate, was only to be expected.

The others were a little too obviously military men. Oh, they were dressed similarly to Judge Lang, but they stood and moved like warriors. Their leader, Captain Chen, was tall, bony, and dour-faced. As far as Doctor Yuren could tell, he spent much of his time trying to keep Judge Lang safe despite his charge's preferences.

The judge looked around, clearly trying to find a way to escape the argument. When he noticed Yuren, she smiled, willing to be a distraction for him. No surprise he took up her offer, approaching her with a slight bow. "Doctor Song so unexpected to find you here. Wishing you well."

Bowing just a bit deeper in return, Yuren smiled. "I've kinfolk coming home today. You may have heard me mention them to your grandmother."

"Ah, yes. Two sisters and a brother, yes?"

From the feel of it, that count had changed. "Not quite. Two brothers and a sister." At the judge's frown, she smiled faintly. "It's complicated. Perhaps later I can explain. Now is not the time." Her glance at his guards made it clear why. This wasn't their business. Wasn't really Judge Lang's business, for that matter.

The sound of someone shouting "Yide-ge, Yide-ge!" interrupted the discussion, much to Yuren's relief. The complicated relationships of her sect weren't something she wanted to explain.

Judge Lang turned his attention to the shouter, a young man leaning over the railing of a ship just coming into Shanghai's harbor. His hair was shockingly short, cut just above his collar, and he wore a sailor's light top over hemp pants. Yet his face bore a marked resemblance to Judge Lang's, making it clear who he had to be.

Lang Yixiao, the anxiously awaited prodigal grandson.

ᗘ)(ᗘ

Yixiao dropped to the dock beside the *Jeen Loon* and helped tie the moorings. Then he turned to grin brightly at his brother. "The Wanderer, Yixiao, greets his elder brother!" he said, cupping his hands and bowing deeply.

No surprise when Yide-ge's first response was to cuff him. "Brat. Idiot. Trying to die?"

He laughed. "Of course not, Yide-ge. A little drop like that isn't going to kill me." His cultivation had improved, after all. He'd have to fall off a mountain to actually hurt himself and even that might not do it if he was fast and clever enough.

"You're still an idiot."

Well, that was a given. Yixiao just bowed. "Younger Brother knows he's wrong. Begs Elder Brother's forgiveness."

A sniff. "I suppose I shouldn't expect you to have learned much responsibility, wandering around America among all those barbaric westerners."

"I promise, I sought out very little of the trouble I landed in."

"This doesn't make me feel at all better, brother." Yide-ge paused. Stared him up and down and added, distastefully, "And what did you do to your hair? You look like a convict."

Yixiao ran his fingers through his hair. He'd cut it down to a western style when he'd reached America and it was only just reaching his collar. "It was more suitable for California. Master says, 'When in Rome, do as the Romans do.'"

"She does not and it looks awful." Yide-ge cuffed him again, clearly prepared to take up their relationship where they'd left off, despite his position as a magistrate.

A woman around the same age as their mother coughed softly from where she stood behind Yide-ge, clearly reminding him of his manners. "Ah. Yes. Apologies, Doctor." Yide-ge bowed to the lady, then gestured to Yixiao. "Younger Brother, this is Doctor Song She's in charge of our grandmother's care."

Mentioning Grandmother Lang turned Yixiao's mood from humorous to worried in seconds. "Greetings to you, Doctor Song This incompetent child is grateful to you for all the care you've given our grandmother." He paused, asking hesitantly, "Is…is she…."

"Greetings, Young Master Lang." A gentle smile curved the woman's lips. "She is not well but she is cognizant. She has also been looking forward to seeing you again."

That made Yixiao wince. "I apologize for taking so long. I came as soon as I heard but the message went astray towards the end."

The gentle smile grew kinder. "Child, you were across the ocean. No one could expect you to return any faster than you did." She bowed. "Judge Lang, Young Master Lang, if there's no objection, I will accompany you to your family home. I'd like to be available to provide support for my patient when her grandson presents herself."

By which Yixiao guessed his grandmother was close to the end and in need of all the assistance she could get. He bowed. "This foolish grandson will be grateful." Noticing Wuchang approaching diffidently and remembering that he'd made an offer to his companions earlier, he turned to his brother. "Is there space for guests? I have four friends who will be needing a place to stay for a little while."

Yide-ge gave him a look. One that said he should have expected Yixiao to bring home strays. He just smiled back innocently, waiting for his brother's answer.

At the same time he noticed Doctor Song glancing at his extra companions with interest. Did that mean she knew them? If so, she didn't speak, letting Yide-ge do the talking. "I can't speak for Father, you know that. But if there isn't, they can stay at my side of the house. Given they don't mind lodging with a local magistrate?"

That was his brother acknowledging that some of Yixiao's friends might not want to accept rooms from someone like him. As far as Yixiao knew, though, not even Disciple

" YOU'RE STILL AN IDIOT. "

Lenghai was likely to have a problem. "Let's have them follow us and I'll find out once I've seen Grandmother."

"Mm. Good enough."

Yixiao turned to Wuchang. "My brother's guards won't let anything happen to me. Would you escort our friends?"

Wuchang bowed. "This one obeys and asks you pass his respects to her Highness."

Having settled what to do about Wuchang and the others, Yixiao hurried along with his brother and the doctor. Typical of Yide-ge, he hadn't bothered with transportation; even though Yixiao was sure his brother had every right to a carriage, or even a palanquin.

Walking through the streets of Shanghai towards the Old City, Yixiao had dozens of moments of sharp memory. There was the dock where he'd boarded the *Henrietta Marie*. There the guard post they'd passed with the unconscious Sihua Clanswoman, Gan Han. And there the place where he'd fought and killed the traitorous colonel seeking to murder the Emperor's heir.

The voices around him were both familiar and startling. It'd been so long since he'd walked through a crowd speaking the languages he'd grown up on. Street vendors shouted their wares. Servants hurried back and forth. Europeans wandered up and down, struggling to ask questions and understand what was being sold. He breathed in the familiar scents; fried foods, sugar, salt, sweat and blood.

"Have things been well here?" he asked his brother.

"They've been well enough for the most part." Yide-ge frowned, gazing ahead thoughtfully. "The usual troubles. Our cousin has barely taken the throne and still seeks a balance between rules and lenience."

Unsurprising. Yizhu - no, the Xianfeng Emperor - wasn't good at bending. He wasn't a cruel man, or even mildly unkind, but he knew his rights and his position and expected the world to acknowledge them. That he seldom received the honor he felt due was a thorn in his side.

Yide-ge couldn't say as much. His guards were surely loyal to him, but one didn't criticize the Emperor. Not publicly. Not even the descendants of the much loved and favored daughter of the Qianlong Emperor dared to be that shameless.

"Wishing our cousin the best," Yixiao murmured.

"Indeed." Yide-ge shifted the subject. "There've been the usual troubles here in Shanghai. Clashes between our foreign guests and our own people. Of course, British law takes precedence for the most part." He smiled ruefully. "But that doesn't mean I've no work. There's always something for a magistrate to address, no matter what."

Remembering the people who'd attacked Brother Jigme back in America, Yixiao asked, "Have any of our clan been causing trouble? I ran into a small group of assassins from our ancestral lands." He never did figure out what they wanted with him, either.

"Eh? How odd. We've had a great deal of trouble from the south. There's a madman claiming he's the son of the Western God. Whole towns have been turning to following him."

Someone had mentioned that situation to Yixiao already. "Hong Xiuquan?"

"That's right. We're not directly involved, yet, but his forces have been gaining ground." Yide-ge sounded deeply concerned, and rightly so. Rebellions of the sort Hong Xiuquan led were usually more destructive than successful. No matter which side you joined, you were dragged along in a wild ride that destroyed property, possessions and, worse, people.

"Master says, 'win or lose, you lose'," Yixiao murmured, eliciting a sharp glance from the quiet Doctor Song.

"Master?" she repeated. "You have a master?"

Yide-ge chuckled. "It's not something we make generally known, but when Xiao-di ran away from home, he went to study martial arts with the Storm Hermit."

"Elder Brother is mistaken. Younger Brother did not run away from home. He had Grandmother's permission."

"I don't think 'do what you want and go to hell' counts as permission, Xiao-di."

Truth to tell, Yixiao hadn't been completely sure of it either. But his Grandmother had sent him a stipend later. He hadn't bothered to use it, much, but he'd understood its purpose. Grandmother Lang had wanted him to know that - even though she disapproved of his choice - she stood by it. It'd been a relief at the time.

As they came to the round entryway into the Lang family's Shanghai home, all Yixiao could do was hope his grandmother still felt that way. He'd hate to find himself torn between his own needs and her dying wish.

Because, filial grandson though he was, he wasn't at all sure he could obey if she ordered him onto a new path.

⇒)(⇐

Visiting Madam Lang was always troublesome. She was old, sick and all too aware of her mortality. Her temper, already sharp and demanding, had deteriorated, making her difficult to deal with. She'd become particularly fretful waiting for her grandson to return.

By all accounts, young Yixiao was a trial and a tribulation. Stubborn and head-strong, he'd been unwilling to take the path a younger son of a martial family was supposed to follow. Rather than remain at home, cultivating his skills and protecting the family's interests, he'd chosen to run off to train on his own.

The fact that the boy had gone to train with the Storm Hermit, of all people, surprised Yuren a great deal. Not just because the Storm Hermit was a sharp-tempered woman who'd long since turned her back on the mundane world, but because of who the boy was. The grandson of the Imperial Princess who'd taken over the Lang clan and practically ruled the *jianghu* for decades was not the sort of person she'd have expected to turn to the Storm Hermit's pacifistic teachings.

Still, over a century of experience had taught Yuren not to make assumptions. Whatever it was that drove the young man to change his heart, it had to be sincerely meant. The Storm Hermit was no fool. She would have recognized an attempt to steal her knowledge without commitment to her ideals.

Another surprise, this one more personal, was the fact that young Yixiao had befriended her younger siblings. Befriended and been allowed to help, even though - by rights - he ought have nothing to do with the cultivational politics of Khaitan. The fact that he was the King's nephew wasn't enough to justify involving an outsider.

Yet there her siblings were. All three, or should she say four? She could sense Xi Xuan's spirit, clinging close and protectively around her chosen replacement. From that youngster's behavior, he'd come into her power in a questionable way. He was too skittish for it to be otherwise. He certainly hadn't been Xi Xuan's disciple; not officially at least. That would have required their Eldest's agreement.

They entered Madam Lang's room, or rather her yurt. When the old lady became too sick to leave her bed it'd been necessary to soothe her spirit by recalling her younger, more exciting and happier days. That meant setting up a tent in the style of her clan, out in the middle of the gardens. They'd even brought in some ponies, so the sound of their snorts and whinnies could lull her to sleep.

The tent's interior decorations were true northern clan in style. Fur hangings. Carved bone frames. Small boxes of heavy wood. And, of course, sheep and goatskin bedding. All of which practically engulfed the frail old woman they surrounded.

She was asleep when they entered, snoring softly, her pet cat curled up under her fingers. Her white hair was carefully bound up and she wore a voluminous dark robe, hiding just how thin she'd become. Yuren eyed the woman professionally and knew it wouldn't be long. It certainly wasn't her own work that'd kept Madam Lang with them so far past her time. That'd been the sheer obstinacy of an old woman determined to see her favorite grandson before she passed.

Young Yixiao approached the bed alone, leaving Yuren and Magistrate Lang to wait at the entrance of the yurt. Neither spoke. This was between young Yixiao and his grandmother. No need to interfere.

Rheumy eyes opened when the cat raised his head and meowed in a rusty voice. For a moment Yuren wondered if Madam Lang would even recognize her grandson, or if she'd reached the point where she no longer knew anyone.

Then the old woman said, "It's about time you turned your feet back home."

"This foolish grandchild has been remiss. No excuse is possible."

Madam Lang smacked young Yixiao's hand, then grasped it tight. Well, as tight as she could. Yuren knew how little strength she had left. "Don't you go all formal on me, boy. What word do you have?" Before he could answer, she set to coughing, causing the boy to turn a worried look at the doctor.

Moving quickly, Yuren brought Madam Lang some of her medicinal tea. She might hate it and avoid taking it most of the time, but she needed it if she intended to be at all coherent. They glared at each other and it was Madam Lang who surrendered, accepting the medicine with eyes full of grievance.

Once she'd finished, she shoved the cup back into Yuren's hands and snapped imperiously, "Go. Leave the two of us."

Magistrate Lang didn't hesitate and neither did Yuren. Bowing silently, they left the yurt. Whatever it was between young Yixiao and his grandmother, it was clearly not their business.

"I'm sorry she's like that, Doctor."

"No need for apologies. I've dealt with worse patients." *Not many, thank the Gods.* "And, actually, I'd welcome a chance to speak with your brother's friends."

Surprise flickered across Magistrate Lang's face. "I've no reason to object, but...."

"Because somehow your brother has managed to befriend the very same kinsfolk I was waiting to meet." Yuren smiled wistfully. "Based on that, I can only guess they have quite a tale to tell."

And it was high time she learned it.

ﰗﰗﰗ

"I'm sorry I sent you so far away."

It was so rare for Grandmother Lang to apologize that Yixiao just stared at her, mouth agape. That got him swatted and he pretended the light blow hurt, cowering before the old lady's hand like a small child.

She laughed. "Oh, I have missed you, boy."

"I've missed you as well, Grandmother." He kept his eyes on hers, not wanting to pay attention to how wasted she was. Not wanting to notice how light her strike had been.

The tumor had been removed months ago but from what he'd been told, it was returning, eating away at what little remained of her healthy flesh, slowly taking over. "Isn't there anything to be done?"

Regret crossed Grandmother Lang's face. She was just about seventy-five years old. Not young but certainly not so old that she couldn't have lived to see her eldest great-grandchild married. Before Yixiao could say as much, she smiled. "I've seen four Emperors on the throne. The fifth is too much to ask for, no matter how soon it comes."

Something about the way she said that sent a chill up Yixiao's spine. "Grandmother?"

"How do you like America?"

The sudden change of subject added to Yixiao's fears. "It's a nice enough place. Like anywhere, there are good people and bad. Good spirits and bad, as well."

"Could the family thrive there?"

That was the question he'd feared she'd ask. He thought about it. "We could. There's no railroad yet, but I'm sure they'll be building something sooner or later. Father would like that. But...."

"But?"

"There's prejudice. It wasn't too bad at first, but I've seen some miners and farmers wanting to drive the Chinese workers out. It could get worse."

She sniffed. "It will almost certainly get worse. But things will be worse here in China, too."

There could be no doubt Grandmother Lang knew what she was talking about. She'd spent her entire life keeping her eyes and ears on the doings of her Imperial kinfolk. She'd always been expert at keeping the Lang clan out of trouble. If she thought there was something coming, there probably was.

"I have watched my brother, my nephew and now my grand-nephew, rise and fall in their people's eyes. I've watched our military strength wasted in fruitless battles against the West. I've watched our country be riddled by rot from within. I've watched our people destroyed by western greed and our own government's unwillingness to change its ways."

From anyone but the Gurun Princess Hexiao, those words could be considered treasonous. Even from her, they were risky. Yixiao was desperately glad they were alone. "Grandmother...."

"We can't do anything. The flaws go too deep, the damage is too widespread. All I can do is send you away. All of you."

Yixiao wasn't at all sure America was the right place for that. Not yet. He said so and she agreed. "There needs to be a place for you, first. I've talked to Mister Chang. He is investigating the possibilities, but it may be years before he can find a way."

Yixiao had a feeling he knew his Grandmother's greatest concern. The Emperor feared and respected his great-aunt. He didn't dare act against her family while she lived. Once she died, that protection would be gone.

Sooner or later some enemy of the family would lay some blame at their door. Defenseless, lacking the position and personality necessary, Yixiao's father would never be able to stand against such a thing. He wouldn't even see it coming.

"What would you have us do?"

"I want you to go to Khaitan once I'm gone. My physician comes from that land and is willing to assist you in passing the border. Ask the King, your aunt, for refuge for your family until there's a safe place for you somewhere in the outer world; should such a safe place ever come to be."

Father didn't like Khaitan much. Not because it was unpleasant but because it didn't interest him. He wanted to build trains and Khaitan's people didn't care for machines. Not when they had sorcery and other skills to make such technology unnecessary. Before Yixiao could say as much, Grandmother Lang smiled ruefully. "I've ordered your father to go once I've died. He doesn't like it but he'll obey."

That was true. The entire family obeyed Grandmother Lang. Speaking of which, "What would you have me do?"

She stroked his cheek. "It won't be safe for you to go back to the Storm Hermit. I'll leave it to you to decide if you wish to go to Khaitan as well."

To tell the truth, Yixiao didn't. Khaitan was gorgeous and full of power but it'd never felt like home to him. He'd been happier in the mountains of California than he'd ever been visiting his mother's family in Khaitan. He said as much, adding, "I may see if the Storm Hermit would be interested in going to America when I return. There's some places there I think she'd like very much."

Grandmother Lang stroked his cheek lightly. "Then do so and do so with my blessing, boy. Just make sure your family is safe."

He laughed. "As if I would do anything else." Because the one thing Yixiao valued as much or more than his cultivation was his family.

⇒)(⇐

The boy called Lenghai was not at all human. That much was obvious now Yuren stood in front of him. "So what, exactly, are you?"

He flushed like a human. Muttered, "A puppet."

At the same time a soft wind fluttered protectively around young Lenghai. The spirit it belonged to wasn't audible to Yuren, but the boy added, "She says 'not anymore'."

Brother Jigme added, "If he were still a puppet, his master would have turned him against us."

Sister Bianhua disagreed. "It isn't impossible his master's playing a long game. He might be waiting until we get back to Khaitan with him. It's Eldest Brother they want."

Young Lenghai turned hurt and startled eyes on Sister Bianhua. At the same time Sister Xi Xuan's spirit swirled away from her charge and flipped Sister Bianhua's hair for her, eliciting a sharp, "HEY!"

Yuren sighed inwardly. It was good to see her fellow Elementalists again. Good to be back together. It was also a trial, because the one thing none of them were good at was getting along. These three in particular always liked to argue. She turned her attention back to young Lenghai. "I can't confirm you as Master of Water," she began.

That drew Xi Xuan's attention and she was back, spinning pleadingly around Yuren. It was clear she believed in her replacement and wanted to have him recognized. Clear too that she would protect him with all she had and was. Not that there was enough left of her to do much.

"Sister. It's not my place to accept or deny him. He has your power and I won't interfere with that. But it's Eldest Brother who must make that choice. I can, and do, accept him as your disciple."

"Haven't we discussed this a dozen times already?" Disciple Lenghai added. "Masters Jigme and Bianhua already said it can't be their decision."

The wind curled up on Disciple Lenghai's shoulder like a small and sulky ferret. Yuren, who knew Sister Xuan best of all of them, could almost see her little pout. She'd just have to deal with it.

Not long afterwards they were served food and drinks and waited for young Yixiao's return. Apparently he'd agreed to assist them as much as possible with their problem. "Though now we're back in China, I'm not sure how much he can do. His family has precedence," Sister Bianhua pointed out.

Yuren knew from Madam Lang that the boy's next task would be taking him to Khaitan. Knowing Yuren was a native, the old lady had asked dozens of searching questions about the hidden kingdom, ones strongly suggesting she hoped to send her kinfolk there for safety's sake.

They ate and discussed their recent adventures, all three doing their best to include their possible fourth. Disciple Lenghai was young and scared and whatever he'd been before he'd been given Xi Xuan's powers, he was closer to human now. Close enough to need reassurance and support. Close enough to be wary of both.

"Why are you willing to help me?" he asked suddenly.

Sister Bianhua eyed him. "Didn't we already go through this?"

"You just said...."

"I said it isn't impossible your creator still has some control on you. I didn't say she does or that we should turn you away."

That was the trouble with Sister Bianhua. She tended to say exactly as she thought without bothering to soften it for others. One might think, based on her earlier comments, that she didn't like or want Disciple Lenghai around. Nothing could be further from the truth, of course. Sister Bianhua clearly liked the youngster, even if it wasn't obvious to him.

Gently, Yuren set her hand on the boy's. "Disciple, our sister entrusted her power to you. We believe you have no desire to cause us harm. Your creator might still have power over you but we won't let him win. We'll work out a way to keep you safe."

Because whether or not the boy became one of their number; he was someone their sister had sacrificed her life for. And that made him family.

⇒)(⇐

Once he'd confirmed plans with Doctor Song and the others, Yixiao spent the rest of the day with his family. He'd missed them terribly on his travels and was glad to spend time listening to his kinfolk as they rushed around being themselves.

His only regret was that his parents and little sister were still at their farm, testing a new engine. He'd go see them the next day. In the meantime, he'd rest and hope not to be woken by news of his grandmother's death. She'd held to life for months longer than she ought to have, simply to see him safely home. Now she had, she'd no reason left to cling to pain and exhaustion.

Instead, while he woke to quiet panic, it wasn't for the reason he'd expected. Servants whispering in the hall drew his attention. A sense of worry and dread filled the air. This was not grief for their deceased matriarch. This was fear.

Tapping lightly on the door to the room across from his, Yixiao murmured, "I'm going to find out what's wrong. Follow if you would." He didn't think the problem required Wuchang's skills but he wanted his friend available, just in case he was wrong.

Spotting the oldest of his four nieces rushing past, crying, Yixiao caught her gently. "Hey there, little bee. What's wrong?"

"Unka!" she gasped, burying her face in his shoulder. "Gampa'n'Gamma in twouble!"

Rather than stress his niece out further, Yixiao kissed her forehead and patted her on the back. "I'll see what I can do, all right? You go back to Nursey and let me and Wuchang take care of things."

She nodded and he set her down to run back towards the children's quarters. He looked up at Wuchang, who'd come out by then and clearly heard enough. "It could be anything," he said. "Let's find my brother."

Yide-ge was in their father's office, talking to a tall man in uniform. "I understand. There's only so much you can do. Try to keep them contained so they don't cause problems for the neighboring farms."

The man saluted. Turned. Glanced at Yixiao dismissively and came to a sharp halt when he saw Wuchang. "Magistrate...this man...."

"Is my friend," Yixiao interrupted before Yide-ge could speak. "Do you have any objections to that, Captain?" He'd never met this particular member of the military before, but he didn't need to. He could tell by his attitude what he thought of Wuchang.

Truth to tell, he couldn't be blamed. Wuchang was a notorious member of the *jianghu*, whose association with the Sihua Clan made him a most suspicious character. But he was also Yixiao's best friend and compatriot. Yixiao wouldn't put up with any nonsense regarding his past.

For a moment it looked as if that nonsense wouldn't go away quietly. But Yide-ge coughed softly and gestured to the officer to leave. Obedient soldier that he was, the man did so, though not without one last hard glance at Wuchang.

"You've obviously heard. We're doing everything we can. You needn't worry."

Yixiao turned to his brother. "I've heard there's trouble. I've heard it has to do with our parents. I can guess it has something to do with our farm near Lake Tai. I can even guess it's a military affair; which implies rebels, given the current situation with the Taiping."

A sigh. "Almost correct, di-di. But...."

"But what I've yet to hear is exactly how our parents are involved. I trust you plan on telling me. I also expect you to tell me to stay out of it; an order I doubt I'll obey."

Yet another sigh. "It isn't the Taiping Rebels, di-di. These are renegades from the Niuhuru clan. They've been trying to persuade father to commit treason."

That explained a great deal. "Those clans-folk who came after me in California."

"I believe so, yes. I didn't connect it before, but they've been sending representatives for over a year now." Yide-ge tapped his desk thoughtfully, adding, "I wouldn't be surprised if they're trying to take advantage of the Taiping Rebellion distracting our cousin."

"And what is it they've done?"

"I told you yesterday that our parents and baby sister were all at the farm testing a new engine. The Niuhuru have found an ally with some sorcerous skill and have trapped them inside with a dust storm." Before Yixiao could open his mouth to say anything, Yide-ge added, "As for telling you to stay out? You're the only member of the family with any skill in this sort of thing, now grandmother's so sick. I was just telling Captain Tan that I'd be sending you in to try and deal with the problem."

Yixiao smiled. Sometimes his elder brother could be surprisingly reasonable. "Yide-ge, I will be glad to do whatever I can."

Before Yixiao could begin making plans, Wuchang interrupted. "Respect, Yixiao. Respect, Magistrate Lang. But you mentioned dust?"

"Eh? I did, Master Heibai. Is there a problem?"

"No. But it seems to me we've been running into much the same sort of problem our whole trip here. Your grandmother's physician is the Elemental Master of Earth. Which means the enemy attacking your parents may also be hers."

ᗘ)(ᘓ

"You may well be right," Yuren murmured, once her patient's grandsons explained the situation. "I'm not sure why Shachen would target your family, but a dust storm is his trademark."

Young Yixiao considered the answer thoughtfully, clearly the one in charge of the situation despite being the younger brother. "Can the Demonic Elementalists communicate with each other across distances?"

That was something Yuren had never considered. "We know so little about them. I hate to admit it, but we haven't done a good job fighting them. Otherwise we wouldn't have had to hide from them for so long."

Brother Jigme added, "I think they must communicate. They've never been surprised to find us together."

Turning his attention on Disciple Lenghai, Yixiao asked, "I realize it isn't something you want to remember, but whatever you know about your creator would help us."

Up until now the boy had been struggling with his identity. Yuren and her fellows had deliberately let him be, not wanting to press too hard, too fast. She opened her mouth, wanting to speak up for him, but Disciple Lenghai stopped her. "I've tried very hard not to think about that time. Tried very hard not to remember anything before I awoke to being myself. But...I know you need to know."

Setting a hand on his, Yuren told him, "Don't force yourself."

"It's all right, ma'am, I need to. I just haven't wanted to." The boy took several deep calming breaths. "I...I've dreamt of being built. Bones of unliving metal, bound within stolen flesh and blood. Heart and brains...I'm not sure whose they were. I wasn't aware of anything when that was made."

Xi Xuan's wind whispered around the boy, telling him something. He repeated it, sounding confused. "Heart and brain stolen from a grave, made shadowed stone? I don't understand."

Heibai Wuchang offered, "I believe that to be a necromantic art. The sorcerer preserves the organs with condensed *yin* energy."

"Like that stone the Master of Ash's puppet shattered?" young Yixiao asked.

"I think so, yes." Regret flickered. "The method is similar to the sorcery that changed me, but not similar enough for me to know more."

Returning her attention to Disciple Lenghai, Yuren asked, "The one who created you was Wusuo, correct? She sent you to harm Xi Xuan...."

Again Xi Xuan whispered and this time it was young Yixiao who answered, clearly recognizing how hard this was for the boy. "She says Wusuo's control was incomplete. That she sensed the soul of the life Wusuo used to create Disciple Lenghai still existed. She gave him her power so he could live."

All of this they'd guessed at already. "Do you recall if Wusuo ever contacted any of her fellow Demonic Elementalists?"

Lenghai thought about it. "Not really. But I do remember hearing her cursing, just a bit before Xi Xuan saved me. Something about losing contact. And about an emptied one ruining her puppet."

Yuren frowned. Her siblings had told her all about their adventures already. "How long ago was that?"

"Xi Xuan gave me her power a month or so ago...just a bit before I signed on with Captain Hai Chan in San Diego."

"And we took passage with him two weeks later?" young Yixiao asked.

"Yes. That's right."

Young Yixiao turned his attention on Heibai Wuchang. "That was just about when we

" SHE SENT YOU TO HARM XI XUAN... "

fought the Master of Ash's puppet, isn't it?"

"I believe so, yes."

"I think that proves they do communicate, then. I wonder why they only use puppets? Is it that they're afraid to face us directly? Or because they can't?"

That was a question they'd have to investigate further. But right that moment they had something more important to concern themselves with. "More importantly, Young Master Yixiao, your parents are obviously in danger because you helped us. We owe you our help in turn."

"I admit, I was hoping you'd say that." Young Yixiao considered them all thoughtfully. "The trick is going to be finding your enemy and stopping him. As well as dealing with the Niuhuru renegades who may, or may not, have allied themselves with him."

And that was going to be quite a task, given how little they knew of what was happening inside the Demonic Master of Dust's whirlwind.

⇒)(⇐

The sky was a peculiar reddish-brown, one more commonly seen in the dry and dusty lands of California. The grassy plains surrounding Lake Tai were not the sort of place one expected such skies, especially so early in the day.

The cause of the strange light was obvious. A towering yellow cloud sitting at the edge of the lake, casting dust into the air, spreading it far and wide. It crouched in place, resembling a huge and threatening lizard circling its nest.

"This is not going to be easy," Yixiao muttered. "I hope the locals got away before Shachen could get his claws into them. How does one fight dust-kin, anyway?"

"I don't," Doctor Song might be trying to sound unbothered, but it was obvious she was afraid. As well she might be. It seemed each of the Demonic Elementalists' skills were too strong for a single Elemental Master to handle. They struck at their enemy's weakest point.

Which begged the question, "The enemy each have their own weak points. Why didn't you team up to deal with them?"

A dour glance. "Do you think we didn't try? Bianhua and Jigme's predecessors died before we realized what was happening. And when we tried to gather together, they kept getting in our way. In the end, our Eldest ordered us to scatter east, hoping to spread the enemy out."

There was surely more to it than that and Yixiao said so. Doctor Song's expression tightened. "Our Eldest was trapped by the enemy's leader. As long as the Demonic Elementalists were together, they could maintain the trap. If we forced them to separate, trying to reach us, we hoped to give our Eldest a chance to break free."

A dangerous plan but a necessary one. Three of the Demonic Elementalists' puppets had been defeated. It was possible the enemy could create more to take the old ones' place, but they hadn't yet.

"For now we need to find a way inside that mess. Preferably without being turned to dust-kin ourselves."

"The only one of us with any chance is young Lenghai here," Sister Bianhua pointed out. "Fire won't burn dust and the best metal can do is block it."

"I said I'm willing." Disciple Lenghai didn't sound willing. He sounded scared and unhappy and ready to flee back to the depths of the ocean if given half a chance. That was his way, though. Unaccustomed to concealing his opinions, he showed everything he felt. Right then what he felt had to be sheer raw terror.

You aren't alone. I'm with you.

"I can't tell you how much safer that makes me feel, Xi Xuan. You're a ghost. A voice on the wind. Your breeze means nothing to a thing like that."

Turning his gaze on Lake Tai, glittering bloodily beneath the red-tinted sky, Yixiao pointed. "The wind can carry water for miles. And water can transform dust to mud. Xi Xuan's body may be gone, but her spirit is strong. If the two of you gather a water spout and spin it around Shachen's dust cloud, it'd give us a way past."

Disciple Lenghai considered that. Turned to Doctor Song. "Master?"

"It's worth a try, child. It might even give me a chance to help. I can't affect dust, but mud is within my power."

"All right. I'll do it. Just hope the two of us are strong enough."

⇁)(⇐

As Disciple Lenghai and Sister Xuan went off to gather water from Lake Tai, Young Yixiao tried to convince Yuren to remain back. "You're weakest to Shachen. If we take out his dust-storm he's likely to target you."

She waved off the suggestion. "I may not be able to fight, but I can support those who do." After all, that was Earth's purpose; support. "Brother Jigme and Sister Bianhua can guard me until we've a chance to fight."

Young Yixiao didn't look at all happy. Not because he disdained her abilities, or saw her as an older woman in need of protection. He was, however, the Second Young Master of the Lang and the danger they were headed for involved his family. There was no doubt he felt a need to keep those uninvolved with his troubles from being injured by them.

Except this was Yuren's trouble and her siblings' as well. She pointed it out, "Shachen is my enemy. The fact that he's working with yours doesn't make that any true."

"Doctor Song is correct, Yixiao. You cannot ask her to stand back in this matter." At least Heibai Wuchang understood. But then, he would, as old and experienced as he was.

At last Young Yixiao shrugged off his instincts. "At least let me take point. Wuchang and I, that is."

"I did say support, did I not?"

By this time Disciple Lenghai and Sister Xuan had done their part. Already a slender tower of water rose above the surface of Lake Tai. To Yuren's surprise a blizzard surrounded the waterspout, spreading out faster and further as the water swirled.

"His water is cold," Sister Bianhua told Yuren, noticing her puzzlement. "Combined with Sister Xuan's wind, it must be freezing."

Yuren wondered if that would interfere with the attempt to take down Shachen's dust storm. Snow might not be heavy enough to capture the dust and bring it down. She was about to ask when the waterspout slammed into its target and set to whirling even more wildly.

Balls of hail spun out of the mess, forcing Brother Jigme to create a wall between them and the icy missiles. For several minutes the noise made it impossible to hear anything. Small dents appeared in the metal shielding them, dents that had to come from some huge hailstones, given how much damage they did to Brother Jigme's wall.

At last things quieted, though it took a minute or so before Yuren could hear anything after all that banging. Brother Jigme waited a bit, only lowering his wall when he felt things were safe.

"My family's going to have to pay recompense," Young Yixiao murmured, looking at the ruined crops in the nearby field. Then he turned his attention forward. "I think this is our chance."

It was. The dust storm had cleared and the hail and sleet covering the land around them made it unlikely Shachen could manage another. At least not quickly. "He likely has dust-kin under his control," she warned. "Be ready."

They moved forward, Brother Jigme ready to raise another wall if need be, Sister Bianhua warming the frigid air as they approached. Meanwhile, both young Yixiao and Heibai Wuchang took the lead, the one sauntering blithely, a young master on an early morning walk, the other with his sabers drawn, posture ready for battle.

No surprise that meant the enemy aimed straight for young Yixiao. No surprise, either, that the boy was ready for them. As they entered the mansion's courtyard, a half-dozen northerners in ill-fitting farmers' clothes rushed at him, yelling incomprehensibly.

At the same time human shaped things raced at Yuren. Dust-kin, targeting their creator's primary enemy. She slammed them backwards with a wall of mud, while Sister Bianhua and Brother Jigme combined their skills to create a wall of heated metal that melted the dust-kin to bits of blackened glass.

"There you are at last, Master Yuren." The voice was familiar. A man stood at the far end of the large courtyard. His face was hidden behind a demon mask but Yuren didn't need to see it to know it was Shachen. He gestured, sending more of his dust-kin out, possessing the bodies of the northerners young Yixiao and Heibai Wuchang fought.

Fortunately, Yixiao's training meant he could keep the dust-kin from getting at him. He used his lightning to scatter the things before they could catch hold of either him or his partner.

Keeping most of her attention on Shachen, Yuren searched their surroundings for ways to fight the Demonic Elementalist. The dirt around them was too dry, too easily subverted by her enemy. Nor were there any obvious weapons, except perhaps the paired metal bars lain out around them. Railings for that strange experiment Duke Jin was obsessed with?

A peculiar wheeled device sat on the rails and there were other odd objects throughout the courtyard. Blocks of wood. A lever, sticking out of a piece of wood. A large structure overhead, with a cylinder of oilcloth hanging from below. As she watched, a drop of water fell from the tip.

"What can you do, Master Song?" Shachen mocked, small clouds of dust rising taller around him with every step. "You have no power over me."

To be honest, Yuren had only the vaguest of ideas and little certainty of success. But she was damned well going to try.

⇒)(⇐

The fight forced Yixiao into the main hall of the mansion, where he'd long since been forbidden to cause trouble. The rule didn't matter anymore. Someone had already torn down the decorations and broken every piece of furniture in the room.

"My Mamas aren't going to be happy with you lot," he told his opponents. "You'll be cleaning the outhouses for months."

A growl from one, "Who cares what your outlander mothers want, Wanderer?"

Wuchang kicked the man across the room, using the flat of his black saber to knock another out. "This Heibai Wuchang cares," he said calmly. "Madam Lang and Madam Jones are owed respect."

That got a sneer from one of the other Niuhuru clansmen. A sneer and an insult to both mothers that could not be allowed. Yixiao snapped lightning through the air like a whip, striking the man across the mouth and dropping him to the ground.

A moment later Yixiao dodged out of another attacker's path and struck him in the solar plexus with just enough force to knock him down. "I do wish I were better at paralysis strikes," he noted to Wuchang. "As many as there are, it'd make this faster."

"I'd offer instruction, but my condition makes such things impossible." Wuchang elbowed yet another man in the ear, the blow sending him reeling. "Unfortunate for our opponents, as I must use more painful methods."

A half-dozen more Niuhuru clansmen ran into the room from the back of the hall, dragging two struggling young women. The first was Yijin-mei, Yixiao's little sister. The second surprised him. "Gan Han?"

"You stinky brat," Gan Han snapped, spotting him and managing to get her mouth uncovered enough to curse. "You sent me back to China with just a hilt! Where's that sword of yours, anyway?"

"Ah. That." Yixiao had tricked Gan Han into thinking she had his saber when he realized she could somehow use it to trace him. It was an odd ability, likely part of her cultivation, but also an inconvenient one.

"That!? YOU HORRIBLE ROTTEN...." The rest of what Gan Han had to say was muted by her captor's gloved hand. Apparently he'd learned not to put bare fingers anywhere near her mouth.

"Master says, 'Save your breath for fighting.'" Yixiao suggested, then turned his attention to his sister. "You're all right, Mei-Mei? Mamas and Father?"

Since Yijin-mei wasn't making a fuss like Gan Han, her captor didn't cover her mouth. She smiled wanly at him. "I've been better, elder brother. Yourself?" At the same time she blinked at him, using the code they'd made up as children. She was fine and so were their parents. They were all ready to act; now the sorcerer was busy elsewhere. They just needed a distraction.

"Oh, I'm well enough, though dying of curiosity. Just why are our kinsmen here taking our father hostage? They surely don't think he'll get any concessions from the Emperor, do they?" The question wasn't actually aimed at Yijin-mei, but at the obvious leader of the group.

"Of course not," the man said. "I know as well as you that descendants of the traitor Heshen have no leverage with that idiot."

Yixiao could have pointed out that calling the Emperor an idiot was a treasonable offense, punished by death. Except he doubted this distant kinsman of his cared. "Let's see. I think I remember you. Alin-gu, wasn't it?"

"Honored you recall me, young lordling."

Yixiao sighed. "I'm not a lord, Alin-gu. My father is Duke of Jin but I hold no titles and never shall."

That made Gan Han sniff but they all ignored her. Instead, Alin-gu shrugged. "You are the grandson of our clan's Chief. You are yourself a warrior of distinction. You may not desire titles, but they are yours."

"We are not arguing this," Yixiao said firmly. "Tell me what you want."

"Quite simply put, I want your father to abdicate in my favor. Perhaps you can speak to him and change his mind on the matter."

Father? Abdicate? Yixiao was about to say that that made no sense. Except it did. Once Grandmother Lang died, his father would be Clan Chief, a title he didn't want and would gladly relinquish. The fact that he hadn't agreed was significant. "I trust my father's judgement in these matters. If you've earned the right, he'd have already given it to you."

"The entire country is falling apart around us. Rebels rise from every direction. The so-called Heavenly Kingdom seeks to supplant the Imperial Fool. Someone must take charge. That someone will be me!"

Yixiao shrugged. "Perhaps it will, perhaps it won't. But it won't be because you stepped over my father to get there." He took a deep breath, unslinging his saber from his shoulders, undoing the wrappings slowly, eyes on Alin-gu. As he revealed the blade he said, "Now, sister."

Yijin-mei's apparent cooperation ended in one short sharp strike to her captor's meridians, paralyzing the distracted man and dropping him. She struck again a moment later, sending the man holding Gan Han reeling, forcing him to let the girl go.

Before anyone else could react, Yixiao tossed his saber. "Gan Han, I loan it to you. No killing!"

"Always the 'no killing' with you," she snarled, though she caught the saber's tang, using the wrapping to hold the weapon fast.

At the same time Wuchang dodged past one of the other Niuhuru clansmen, slamming his fist into the man's belly and knocking him down.

The next few minutes were a confused mess. Yixiao caught glimpses of his sister using pinpoint strikes to incapacitate those Niuhuru too weak to withstand her skills. Glimpses of Gan Han using the back side of his saber to knock others out. Glimpses of Wuchang striking, kicking and cartwheeling towards the back halls. Good. He understood what Yixiao wanted and was on his way to protect the parents. No doubt he'd succeed.

As for Alin-gu, he made straight for Yixiao, howling the wolf-cry of the clan, trying to catch hold of Yixiao and break his back or neck for him. Yixiao dodged below, then leapt above the attacks, getting a feel for his speed and skill. Alin-gu was an excellent fighter: dangerously fast, frighteningly strong, surprisingly resilient. He took the lightning blows Yixiao dealt unflinchingly, pushing Yixiao back and back and further back.

Yixiao drew on every lesson he'd learned. He couldn't match Alin-gu's strength, but he was just a bit faster. Knowing he couldn't depend on his lightning whip here, he let himself be pushed a bit further, until he was at the door.

Seeing Yixiao falter, Alin-gu rushed him, only to nearly trip on the doorway to the courtyard. Yixiao sidestepped and gave the man a sharp kick to the buttocks, forcing him outside, onto his father's railroad track.

"You think you've a chance, Storm Hermit's disciple?" the man demanded. "There's not a cloud in the sky!"

"True," Yixiao agreed, reaching deep into himself. "I don't need one." He dropped to the ground, grasping a rail, and sent his power flowing down the metal.

Alin-gu barely had time to howl before the lightning struck him down.

⇒)(⇐

Shachen's dust ate at the mud Yuren summoned, drying it out and turning it to a weapon against her. If Disciple Lenghai weren't dropping huge flakes of damp snow into the courtyard, she'd have been forced back.

She rocked the earth, knocking Shachen backwards as the ground cracked. "Keep him contained," she ordered her companions. At the same time she raced past their enemy, forcing him to turn in her direction.

Following the rails, Yuren almost tripped on the rocks and logs supporting the things. Recovering herself, she forced the rocks behind her down and out. That just made Shachen scoff. "You think that's going to stop me?"

She backed away, Shachen balancing on one rail as he followed her. Showing off his strength. Showing off his skill. Showing off, yet still paying attention to the fight, keeping Yuren's power from shattering the dirt beneath him.

So focused was he on his surroundings he forgot to pay attention to Yuren's. She backed beneath the wooden structure. Reached deep into the earth. Felt for the structure's foundations. There. There they were. Four heavy stone blocks, the structure's posts tightly embedded in carved out holes.

"You don't think I'm fool enough to follow you under that water-tower, do you?" Shachen asked, stopping short a good twenty feet away. "I don't need to follow you to reach you."

As his dust swirled ahead of him, a wave of yellow and brown, Yuren grabbed the blocks with her power. "Indeed," she snapped. "Neither do I." With all her strength she tugged the stones out of the ground, toppling the water tower towards her enemy.

It crashed to the ground and she built a channel ahead of it, letting the water inside pour out in a flood that rushed along the bars and straight into Shachen. Startled, unprepared for that attack, the man was slammed backwards into a pile of logs. Trapped, partially submerged in the flood, he shrieked once, then fell silent.

As the dust storm and the dust-kin drifted to nothingness, Yuren checked her companions. None seemed hurt, for which she was devoutly grateful. "Brother Jigme, Disciple Lenghai, check the body. Sister Bianhua, we should go check on young Yixiao."

They turned, about to do that very thing, when the boy kicked a Northerner out of his father's house and into the courtyard. A moment later he grasped the rails, unleashing a flood of lightning from his bare hands, knocking the man cold.

Young Yixiao looked up and spotted Yuren. "Doctor. All well?"

Amused at the aplomb with which the boy spoke, Yuren chose to respond in kind. "Well enough. Your fight?"

"That's the leader. And from the sound of it, I think my companions have fin....OW!"

The last was because the young woman who helped care for Madam Lang came out of the house and rapped him over the head with a hiltless willow-leaf saber. She glared at him, shoving the weapon back into his hands. "We'll talk later, stinky boy. For now, here's this back."

"Yes, Gan Han. Whatever you say, Gan Han. I'm still not fighting you, Gan Han."

She made a rude gesture before going back inside, leaving young Yixiao grinning as he rubbed his head. At Yuren's raised brows, he added, "Her family wanted her to marry me. I don't plan on doing that, either."

Yuren had overhead bits and pieces of that particular family drama already and she was fairly sure young Yixiao was a great deal stubborner than Gan Han or her kinfolk. Rather than discuss it, she simply said, "That is a concern for later. For now, if you'd help me find a way to imprison Shachen...."

"Not necessary," Brother Jigme said from his position in the ankle-deep waters near where Shachen had fallen. "He's gone."

"Gone? Dead? Escaped?" Yuren hurried over, young Yixiao and Sister Bianhua close behind.

"This was another puppet," Brother Jigme told her, pointing at what lay sprawled amid the fallen logs and muddy water. "I think it was made of dust. The logs smashed its 'heart' and the water washed the dust away."

What remained were a twisted mess of clothes, a broken mask, and a skeleton of unliving metal. The shattered 'heart' lay in pieces inside the crushed ribs, its substance smoking as it melted away. "I don't understand."

"I begin to have a theory," young Yixiao said softly. "Just how many actual sorcerers are we dealing with?"

His statement made no sense and Yuren was about to ask when a voice called the boy's name. Lang Mianzhen, expression exhausted but joyful, his wives behind him, barely controlling their urge to run to young Yixiao. Not that they needed to. He was on his feet and rushing to them without hesitation or decorum; small blame to him anyway.

Yuren sighed. She wanted to know what strange idea the boy had come up with. Wanted to know if he had some plan that'd help her and her siblings fight their enemy. Wanted to know but could wait.

Because right then, after over a year apart, it was time for reunions.

Chapter 5
Green Dragon Seeks its Roots

September, 1851

Deceased: Gurun Princess Lang Hexiao, last surviving daughter of the Qianlong Emperor and Grand-Aunt to the Xianfeng Emperor, after a long illness.

Gurun Princess Hexiao was a fixture in Shanghai for most of her later years. Known for her charitable works, her strong opinions and her refusal to bend to any but the Emperor, her efforts to protect her people and ensure the continued stability of Shanghai will be long remembered and praised.

Gurun Princess Hexiao is survived by her son; Duke of Jin, Lang Mianzhen; his wives, Madam Tu Leilan and Madam Grace Smythe-Barnes; her adopted daughters Madam Li and Madam Xian; her three grandchildren, Magistrate Lang Yide, Priest Lang Yixiao, and Mistress Lang Yijin; as well as a number of great-grandchildren.

—Shanghai Times: English Edition

Grandmother Lang's death had been expected. Prepared for. Devastating. She'd been the center of the family's universe for so long. The center of the clan's power as well, which was another problem altogether.

Yixiao's father spent the days following Grandmother's death setting her business in order and dealing with both the government and the clan's concerns. The Xianfeng Emperor, Yixiao's cousin, worried that the White Wolf clan would take advantage of the Taiping Heavenly Kingdom Rebellion to push a new family to the throne. The White Wolf Clan, as part of the *jianghu,* feared Grandmother Lang's death would cause a new power struggle.

Neither were wrong but Yixiao wished they'd leave his father out of it. Aside from caring for his own little Duchy, Lang Mianzhen wanted nothing to do with governing. Indeed, their branch of the family was strictly banned from involving itself in Imperial matters, thanks to being descended from the traitor Heshen.

As for the *jianghu,* Father had no interest in that side of things either. Grandmother Lang had chosen her inheritor from the Western Gate Sect. That hadn't made the White

Wolf Clan happy, but their clan chief was several years younger than Yixiao and not mature enough to lead the *jianghu*. No doubt Alin-gu had meant to claim it in the boy's stead.

If not for Grandmother Lang's final orders, Yixiao would have remained with his family and assisted his father and brother in dealing with their problems. Instead he'd had his mother send for a guide to help them enter Khaitan. It'd take months to get there, even with the help of magic, but he needed to prepare the way for his family and make sure they'd be safe from the chaos about to erupt.

Kneeling before his grandmother's tablet, holding the incense straight, gazing ahead firmly, Yixiao prayed. Let his family be safe. Let his mission be successful. Let his grandmother look upon his actions with pride. He could not take her place in the *jianghu*. Could not return to that world ever again. But he would protect and he would guard and when the time came he would wander once again.

Having performed his last obeisances, Yixiao glanced sideways at his companion. Wuchang didn't have to join him but it was kind of him to do so. Especially since he owed the Lang family nothing, now the one who'd given him his orders was gone.

"Are you ready, then?"

"As much as I can be."

They set the incense in the bowl before Grandmother Lang's tablet. Rose. Bowed one last time. Then left the room just as Gan Han came up the hallway. To his surprise, she didn't demand a fight, or to come with them. Just said, "There you are, stinky boy. Your guide's in the Bamboo Courtyard," she told him. "Don't keep him waiting."

"That was fast. I heard Khaitan's caravanners had special skills, but I didn't expect him quite so soon."

Gan Han shrugged. "He says he's your guide and he's got the caravans to prove it." She frowned, adding, "Though I admit, he looks odd to me. Too young for the job. Barely fifteen, for all his hair's going grey."

"Pardon, Miss Gan, but Khaitanese do age differently," Wuchang reminded her.

That was true. Mother didn't look nearly as old as she actually was, and she only had a pinch of rabbit spirit blood in her. "They wouldn't send someone who couldn't do the job. Not with the situation in the south."

Gan Han looked dour. "Those madmen…"

The Taiping Rebels might well be mad but they had power and they had numbers on their side. The fact that their leader had tapped into his followers' intense desire to believe didn't help. "They're fanatics. Which can come down to the same thing. That doesn't make them safe to be around."

"No. I suppose not." Gan Han shook her head. "I still think you should wait out the mourning period. No one would fault you."

Yixiao would fault himself if he waited and couldn't get his family a promise of safety. Not when it looked like all China was about to be engulfed in internal and external troubles. But he'd argued that point with Gan Han and everyone else already. "The sooner I'm done, the sooner everyone's safe," he reminded her.

A sharp and disgusted sigh. "Fine. Are you coming to dinner?"

"After I've spoken with our guide. One last meal before we go." As Gan Han left him to tell the servants his plans, Yixiao headed for the Bamboo Courtyard. He was curious to meet the man who'd come to help them enter the magically hidden kingdom.

He just hoped the carter would be up to the challenge.

⋺⟩⟨⋲

Liu Yang settled silently in a small courtyard near the Lang family's kitchen. A tray of sweets and a pot of fragrant tea waited for him, brightening his mood.

Bowing, he murmured to the old servant who'd guided him there, "You honor me."

"Nonsense. You'll be keeping track of our Young Master and all his friends, from here to Khaitan. The least we can do is properly entertain you." The servant woman bowed and excused herself, adding, "It may take a while. Our Young Master is easily distracted."

Once he was alone, Yang sipped his tea and gazed curiously around. This was an attractive place, clearly meant for contemplation and meditation. Small stands of bamboo surrounded the courtyard, their leaves fluttering quietly in a soft breeze. Windows on all sides allowed passers by to look in, though at the moment the halls surrounding the courtyard were empty.

Yang corrected himself. There was a girl in servant's clothes watching him nervously. She wanted to say something to him and wasn't sure how to start.

Helpfully, he offered, "Hello. Am I needed somewhere?"

"You're the caravan master."

"Caravan's an awfully fancy title," he told her. "All I have are three carts, six horses, eight workers, and a foul-tempered camel named Guaiguai." He grinned. "Of course that last is redundant. Every camel I ever met has been foul-tempered."

She smiled, a sweet little-girl smile. "I'm sure there's at least one out there." Falling silent again, she continued to gaze at him curiously. Then, "You're so young."

"Now that I can't argue with." Not because she was right but because his memory started three years earlier. He'd no idea how old he really was and doubted it mattered. He knew his job and could do it well. "Would you like some tea?"

She came into the courtyard but refused a cup. Tremulously, she whispered, "I...this Feng hoped to ask you to hire me."

Taken aback, Yang stared. "Hire you."

"I can cook. I can help feed the animals. I'm strong." Absent-mindedly, she grasped hold of a twig of bamboo growing close to her and twisted it nervously.

She was a mere child. Small, slight and clearly not up to the rigors of the long trip across China. "I've enough assistants. No need, or room, for one more." Not wanting to be cruel, he suggested, "Second Young Master Lang will be bringing a group with him. Perhaps they'd need a servant."

"They say no!" she protested. "But I need to go west...my family needs me."

Much as Yang would like to help, he simply couldn't. "I hope you find a way, then. But I cannot help you."

"PLEASE!"

"Qu Feng, you shouldn't be bothering people this way. Didn't we already discuss the matter?" That came from the short young man standing at the doorway. Dressed in dark clothes, wearing a black band around his arm, with hair just barely to his shoulders, he almost had to be Second Young Master Lang.

The girl turned. Squeaked. "Young Master Yixiao!"

He smiled, kindly but firmly. "You know it's far too dangerous for you to be traveling in that region. Father's already told you he'll send someone to get your family to safety."

"But...."

"No means no, Feng-er. I understand your concern, but you are not going with us, either as part of my party or working for Mister...ah, Liu, was it?"

Yang inclined his head, feeling awkward. He didn't want to be caught in the middle of an argument like this. He hated arguments.

Lang Yixiao returned his attention to Feng-er. "You run along, now. I need to talk

" HELLO. AM I NEEDED SOMEWHERE ? "

with Mister Liu and you surely have work you're supposed to be doing."

As the girl ran off, sniffling, Yang stroked the damaged stem she'd left behind. It looked so sad, as if it too were weeping. He hoped she'd find the help she needed, but there was no way it could be him.

Standing, still petting the bamboo, Yang bowed. "This Liu Yang greets Young Master Lang and hopes he will be of service in the coming months."

"Please. No formality. I'm just a humble priest." Lang Yixiao gestured for Yang to sit, taking another seat and a cup of tea as he did so. "It's too late in the day to start traveling. But I'd like to discuss our path before we leave, if you don't mind."

Nothing would give Yang more pleasure. Without hesitation, he brought out his book of maps and set to explaining his plans.

⇒)(⇐

Gan Han had been right, saying Liu Yang didn't look old enough to be a caravanner. He was just a bit shorter than Yixiao, with sleek greying hair that didn't look right around a terribly youthful set of features. His enthusiasm when he set his maps out for Yixiao didn't help. He behaved like Yixiao's father and brother when they got all excited about train tracks.

"As long as we're outside Khaitan we'll have to travel at a more normal speed. I have shortcuts we can take, but we'll need to be careful."

Yixiao remembered some of those shortcuts from his last trip to Khaitan, over a decade ago. "I should say so. The one through that cavern system gave my brother nightmares for weeks."

"Oh, I know which one you mean. We won't be using that. The array was shattered a few years back. Something about a demonic sorcerer hunting an enemy, I'm told."

That was interesting. A few years back was when the Elemental Sorcerers had fled Khaitan to spread their enemy's forces. Yixiao would have to ask Doctor Yuren if she knew anything about the situation. He'd a feeling she did. "I'm not sure I like our going this way, though. It'll take us awfully close to the Taiping rebels' territory."

"Unfortunately we haven't a choice, unless you want to add half a year to our travels. The only other passage is up north."

Going too far north wouldn't be good either. Alin-gu probably wasn't the only clansman who wanted to force father to abdicate from a power he didn't possess. "No. That won't do. Well, we're a small group and all of us have some ability to protect ourselves." Liu Yang should be well enough, too. He wouldn't be a caravanner otherwise. "We'll be in your hands, then."

"I'll do my best to earn your trust."

They sat quietly for a few minutes longer, finishing the tea and resting in the cool greenness of the courtyard. Yixiao liked this garden great deal. It'd been a sanctuary in his younger days, when he'd needed quiet and calm to recover his temper. He didn't need a special hidden place for meditation anymore but he still enjoyed the moment.

From the looks of it, Liu Yang appreciated the silence too. He gazed at the stands of bamboo surrounding them, a small smile curving his lips as he stroked the slender twig of bamboo he'd been treating like a small child. He tilted his head, looking a bit like he was listening to a musician perform. For that matter, Yixiao almost heard a song himself, as if the leaves rustling in the stillness were singing to him.

At last Wuchang said, "Yixiao, I believe it's almost time for dinner."

"It is." Yixiao sighed. He'd have liked to sit here and rest longer, but he shouldn't make his parents wait for him. "Mister Liu, would you care to join us?"

"Ah, no, that would be impolite of me. An imposition on your family's time, just when you need to say goodbye. I will eat with the servants."

The caravanner was likely right. His family wouldn't be bothered but the servants probably would. They still clung to the idea of a place for everyone and everyone in their places.

"All right. Don't let them bully you."

Liu Yang released the twig of bamboo, letting it spring up behind him, its delicate leaves shining green in the late afternoon light. "I won't. I promise."

"I'll see you tomorrow morning, early. I and my companions."

"Until then."

As they left the man to himself, Yixiao frowned. A Khaitanese caravanner would, by nature, be an oddity among those outside his homeland. But he'd swear there was something niggling at the back of his mind. A thought that refused to properly catch hold.

Well, whatever it was, he'd have plenty of time in the coming months to try and figure it out.

ﾗ)(ﾐ

They set to traveling early the next morning. Eight assistants, human in appearance but built of metal and ceramics, powered by fire and water. Six passengers and their associated luggage in one cart, the other two carts full of goods. Western toys and fabrics, mostly. The sort of things seldom found in Khaitan because trade was so difficult. Yang would resell those goods, purchase Khaitanese items with the funds and take them outside to repeat the process.

Or that was what he'd usually do. This time he thought he'd do best to stay in Khaitan for a while. Either that or trade in Turkey instead. He'd a feeling he wouldn't be selling much in China. At least the only one he had to feed was his camel.

Yang usually didn't want to involve himself with his passengers. Quite often he'd never see them again, whichever direction they'd gone, and he didn't want to grow too attached. This group was different. Amusing. Friendly. Strangely familiar, except for Lang Yixiao and his friend Heibai Wuchang.

Yang kept finding himself wanting to sit with the other four. To laugh at jokes alongside them. To generally just be with them. It made no sense. He didn't know them. One in particular was both familiar and strange. Yet he wanted a connection he'd no right to.

Rather than force himself onto the others, Yang maintained his distance from the whole group. He'd check the borders of their camp at night, make sure his guards and Guaiguai were properly settled and on watch, then find a quiet place away from the fire to gaze at the night sky.

They'd travelled for almost a week when the routine changed. Yang had just sat down to await morning when he sensed a shadowy figure sneaking through the bushes. Whomever they were didn't notice him, at least until he spoke, "Miss Qu...Feng-er, you should not be here."

She startled. Fell over backwards and scrambled away from him, as if he was a bandit intending harm. "Stay away!"

"I'm not moving, Feng-er," he told her. "But the point remains. You shouldn't be here."

In the dim moonlight Feng-er's expression was full of grievance. "Mister Liu? I told you...."

"You did," he agreed. "And I told you I wouldn't hire you. I don't plan on changing my mind." He stood. Walked over to where she sprawled, eyes wide and frantic. "You'd best come with me, Miss."

She scooted backwards. Whimpered. Cried out for help she certainly didn't need. A cry that quickly drew Lang Yixiao over. By the feel of cold emptiness in the woods Heibai Wuchang waited and watched in case he was needed.

"Dear me. Whatever is going on here?" Lang Yixiao asked.

"He…he's going to beat me! Make me go away!"

Now that was ridiculous and Yang said as much. "At least the beating part," he added. "I'd be perfectly fine with your leaving, Miss. I'm not being paid to include you among my passengers."

Lang Yixiao considered the two of them. "Feng-er," he said after a moment. "Aren't you supposed to be back in Shanghai? Aren't you supposed to be cleaning…or whatever it is you do?"

The young woman's lips tightened. "I need…."

"You've said it quite frequently," Lang Yixiao agreed. "You need to get to your village. You need to make sure your family is all right. You need to go into a war-zone and put yourself at risk for the sake of filial piety."

She flushed, face darkening, expression tightening. "You don't understand filial piety!"

"I understand it quite well, Feng-er. Understand it well enough to know that putting yourself in harm's way just so you can see your elderly parents isn't piety. They need you to live. Not die struggling to reach them. Master says, 'A parent should not have to bury their child.'"

Quite suddenly on her feet, Feng-er snapped. "That isn't going to happen."

"Your family's home just inside the territory Tai Pan Heavenly Kingdom has claimed for themselves. Unless you know how to deal with those madmen, what makes you think you'll get through? More likely they'll use your family as tools."

She sobbed. "I have to!"

Lang Yixiao looked at Yang, who returned the gaze without expression. It wasn't up to him. The troubles of the world outside Khaitan weren't his and he'd no business involving himself. "I'm paid to carry you and your companions. If you wish to consider her part of your party, it's not my business."

With a sigh, Lang Yixiao told Feng-er, "I will not escort you to Dinghua village. I will not provide anything more than your basic needs while you're with us. But given you've come this far and given returning you to Shanghai would be difficult….very well. I will allow you to come with us as far as Xi Shan Town. After that, you're on your own."

She grasped his hand. Clung to him. "Master Yixiao!"

"No. I'm not your master. My father is and he won't be pleased with you for running off the way you have." Lang Yixiao gazed sternly down at the girl. "Nor am I interested in any rewards you might think to offer me. Come back to the campsite. You can use the third cart to sleep in."

As he walked away, the serving girl still trying to thank him profusely, Yang couldn't help wondering just what the young man was thinking. He'd only three years of memories to work with and even he recognized a set up when he saw it.

The question was, who was behind it, and why?

⇒)(⇐

"Did you know she was here?" Yixiao glanced at the cart where he'd settled Feng-er.

"I'm not even sure she is now." Wuchang's expression seldom showed much of what he was thinking but the slight frown creasing his forehead spoke volumes. "She has no sense of presence to her."

That made Yixiao turn a sharp stare on his companion. "Another of the Demonic Elementalists' puppets? Or our caravan master's interesting toys?" The latter were near perfect marionettes, dressed in the same simple style as Liu Yang's, their faces smooth. Delicate. Soft. Only their empty stares and utter silence made their nature obvious.

"No. Or if she is one of the enemy's puppets she's poorly designed. So far, I couldn't tell them from human."

Ah. Yes. Yixiao hadn't thought about that. "Was she that way back at the house?"

"I...can't quite recall. I'm sure I'd have said something if I'd noticed."

Knowing his friend was right, Yixiao leaned back against his bedding and considered the situation. "I could wish for a way to contact my family and find out if the real Feng-er is still at home. Lacking that, all I can think is to keep an eye on her and see what she tries to do."

"Under the circumstances, I can't see what else we can do." Wuchang smiled wanly. "For all I know, she's received the same treatment as I. I'd hate to err too far on the side of caution, given we don't know her real purpose."

The treatment Wuchang received involved an ancient form of necromancy that'd removed his still beating heart from his body and preserved it elsewhere. He claimed it hadn't been painful, just inconvenient.

It occurred to Yixiao that he'd never asked his friend about his condition, or even offered to help. Mostly he'd assumed Wuchang would have said something if he'd wanted to discuss the matter or if he wanted a change. Cautiously, he suggested, "Do you want to go looking for it, after this?"

That soft laugh deepened. "I've mixed feelings on the matter. There are things I'd have to deal with that I'm not sure I want to face. Perhaps some century I'll tire of my situation and act on it, but not yet." With a slight grin, Wuchang added, "Finding the one who did this and repaying him for his betrayals? That's a different story."

Yixiao made note of that desire. Wuchang had had no choice about following him to America and becoming his bodyguard. But they'd become friends and companions on the road. As such, he felt it only right to see to Wuchang's wishes as well as his own.

"We'll hope to run across him some day. For now we'd best rest. Tomorrow I'll discuss the situation with the others."

He settled himself for mediation, fully intending to do just that, only to sense yet another problem out in the trees surrounding their campsite. "Wuchang."

"Yes. A dozen men at least, headed our way."

As late and dark as it was, it was obvious the strangers weren't fellow travelers seeking a safe place to camp. Yixiao sighed. "It's a good thing I don't actually need to sleep anymore."

"I'll take my usual position." Wuchang didn't bother waiting for acknowledgement, slipping into the shadows and disappearing quickly.

Yixiao slid off his cart and went to the second one, where the others rested. Not that he needed to. They were awake and aware by the time he reached them.

"Thirteen to fourteen men. Xi Xuan isn't sure, but she thinks they're farmers," Disciple Lenghai told him before he could ask.

There were plenty of farms in this area, so that was no surprise. "Could she hear them talk?"

"They're speaking a dialect we don't recognize."

That made sense. They were in the Wuhan area and the dialect there was quite different from both Mandarin and Khaitanese.

"Do they appear to be cultivationists or sorcerers?" Brother Jigme asked.

"I don't think so. They're armed with bamboo spears and farm tools."

They might be locals supplementing their funds with a bit of highway robbery. They might be rebels looking to capture travelers for ransom. They might even have been instigated by the Demonic Elementalists, seeking to distract them while the real enemy snuck close.

"There's a girl in the other cart."

"En. A puppet of some kind. But not the same as the Demonic Elementalists." Doctor Song sounded absolutely certain on the matter and Yixiao gave her a curious look. "Like the elements we command, we each have a connection to two other elements. Mine is to wood and water. I sense the former from her, somehow."

That was something they'd have to explore, later. "In that case, keep an eye on her but don't overreact."

"Agreed. Besides, if she is related to our enemy, we're best off seeing what she does."

All reasonable. "And for now, do you wish to involve yourselves in this fight?"

"As many as there are, I don't see how we can't," Sister Bianhua told him. "Since they seem to be common-folk, we'll have to be careful, of course. So no drowning them in sea water or wrapping them up in metal coffins."

Both Disciple Lenghai and Brother Jigme looked mildly disappointed.

⋟)(⋞

The forest around them whispered warning, one Yang knew better than to ignore. He set orders on his drivers, and on Guaiguai, making sure they were ready to deal with whatever came.

It didn't take long. Within minutes of the strangers coming within range of his guards, the first three were moving quickly for the carts. Quickly and sneakily, as if they hoped to surprise those within.

Their hopes were dashed a moment later as Brother Jigme appeared from the shadows to strike at the first in the group. His movements were smooth and flexible, taking blows and bending with them. The style was familiar, though Yang had no idea why. A flicker of memory tried to rouse, a familiar but long forgotten voice intoning, 'Metal is malleable, yet hard as stone. Struck, it is reshaped and springs back.'

Other fighting styles raced through Yang's mind. Thoughts he forced back with desperate fury. It hurt. Tore at the empty place inside him and made him ache to reach out for what he could not have. He turned away. Focused on his own part in the fight. There were more people coming up from another direction. Part of the same group? They felt similar, as if their roots belonged in this place.

As far as Yang could tell, his passengers could handle their current attackers. Fifteen to twenty more coming from another direction might be a problem. He guided his guards to block the new group's path and heard someone shouting angrily about the camel.

He ignored the cries of dismay, focusing his attention on the job. Keeping so many guards working at once was wearing. So what if Guaiguai was involved? He'd trained her himself and she knew where her meals came from.

A man with a bamboo pitchfork rushed at him suddenly, catching him unawares.

This one had snuck in while he was distracted by his camel's success. Except a dozen or so bushes snagged at the man, trapping and tangling him.

Yang ignored the man's yelps, wondering how rose bushes had managed to grow out here in the forest. They usually liked open areas and sunlight.

Noticing one of the first group trying to slip away from the fight, Yang swung his jute whip, catching the man by the ankle and pulling him down. A moment later Lang Yixiao was on him, spinning the man onto his face and tying his wrists with some convenient vines.

One of their attackers sounded a retreat, rushing back the way they'd come without bothering to help their fallen compatriots.

"Do we follow?" Brother Jigme asked. A chorus of 'no's' came back, including Yang's. Really, didn't that child know better?

As Brother Jigme looked disappointed, Doctor Song told him, "What did Eldest Brother have to say about never running after a retreating foe?"

Her question was so exactly what Yang had been thinking that he couldn't help looking at her approvingly. He felt as if he should say something, but simply couldn't work out what. Instead, he asked, "Is everyone all right? Should I bring out the medical supplies?"

They checked each other for injuries. "Bamboo splinters, mostly. Farmers' weapons." Sister Bianhua's disdain was just audible in her voice. But, of course, she was the one in least danger from such things. "Easily burned."

"Properly hardened bamboo isn't so easy to burn," Yang couldn't help retorting, eliciting a startled glance, one that made him wave his hand dismissively as he went to check his guards and Guaiguai. He didn't want to discuss the matter.

Behind him he thought he heard the four talking quietly between themselves. Not that he cared because it wasn't his business what they said and did. He sent his guards back to their posts, settling them for the night, then went to feed the camel.

"You didn't say if you were hurt?" Lang Yixiao asked. He'd followed Yang over silently, not hiding his footsteps or trying to sneak up. "You and your devices had to handle that second group."

He continued working, not at all sure how to answer that. "They're puppets. I've had them for as long as I can remember."

Lang Yixiao assisted him in calming Guaiguai, wiping her damp hide with a cloth. "Not this young lady, though."

"No. I rescued her from her previous owners. She wasn't being fed, or well-treated."

"That's obviously not the case anymore."

Guaiguai scoffed derisively, clearly trying to decide if she wanted to bite or spit or just step on the overly confident stranger's foot. Aware of her thoughts, Lang Yixiao stepped backwards with a bright grin and dodged the glob aimed his way. "Might we talk later, Mr. Liu? I don't study Khaitanese sorcery, but my bump of curiosity is itching horribly right now."

Somehow, Yang had a feeling Lang Yixiao was one large bump of curiosity. "I'll happily answer whatever questions I can," he told the young man.

Of course, given how little he remembered about himself and how he'd come by his particular skills, he doubted he'd have much to say.

⇒)(⇐

Rather than question their captives after too little sleep and too much excitement, they bound and gagged the five men and stuck them under one of the carts. With bedding, of course. It was a cold night and it wouldn't do for the men to fall sick.

The next morning Wuchang dragged the men out and lined them up while Sister Bianhua and Brother Jigme made breakfast. They made sure to give their captives a good view of the proceedings because watching those two cook was a combination comedy and horror show.

"The fire is too hot."

"Not hot enough. Eggs won't puff."

"That hot they're going to be pure charcoal."

"Not if you cook them right. You never cook them right."

All this while Sister Bianhua heated the metal pan and Brother Jigme opened egg after egg into the bowl. This would have been a perfectly normal procedure if the pan hadn't been reshaped from the only iron tool the captives possessed, and if the heat weren't coming from Sister Bianhua's hand. Oh, yes, and Brother Jigme was cracking the eggs with a blade so fine the shells had perfectly smooth edges.

Despite the argument, breakfast turned out excellent. Puffy Cantonese style eggs, fried breads and congee. All basic and simple and requiring little in the way of cleanup. They set a portion aside in a pointed fashion, making it clear to their captives that they'd be fed, given they were cooperative.

Yixiao stayed away from the group, wanting to maintain the pretense that he was in charge, while his companions were servants. Fortunately, the elementalists cooperated. They might be cultivational siblings rather than related by blood, but they were a true family, up to and including the squabbling.

Beckoning Wuchang over, Yixiao asked, "Have they said anything?"

"Nothing intelligible. The local dialect is a bit difficult for me," Wuchang admitted.

Yixiao eyed him, a little amused. "You've had, what, centuries to learn it?"

"And I have. But this group have the thickest accent I've ever had the misfortune to listen to. To be honest, I'm not even sure it's Hunan."

Now that was interesting and possibly suggestive. Were they from some other, more distant, place and pretending to be local? Or was there some more innocent reason? "No time like the present to see if they can manage to communicate."

He approached the group with Wuchang, coming to a stop a good yard or so away. Near enough to speak, not so close they could try anything dangerous. "Would any of you like breakfast?" He spoke cheerfully, as if they were visitors on the road, rather than would-be bandits.

They glared at their feet angrily, muttering incomprehensibly amongst themselves. He caught a word or so of their complaints. He was tormenting them deliberately. Taunting them. No doubt they'd be dead long before they starved. There were suggestions of what he could do with himself, phrased so oddly he'd no idea what they were.

"Would any of you care to discuss your recent lack of manners?" Seeing no response, he glanced at Wuchang.

They'd played this game before. He the apparent fool, a rich man's child with no sense. Wuchang the put-upon guard whose job was to keep his idiot charge from walking too deep into the mire. With a faint flicker of a smile to acknowledge his role, Wuchang chose one of the men and lifted him in the air. "My master is asking you a question."

"Oh, don't be so rough, Wuchang."

Yixiao stepped closer, into the light, and was interrupted by the man's reaction. Their captive stared, eyes wide, gasping, "YOU!?"

Wuchang set the man on his feet, one hand holding him in place. It wasn't necessary because the man dropped to his knees, then flat to his face, gasping. "This one apologizes! This one knows he's wrong!"

A little startled, it occurred to Yixiao that the man must have seen the Emperor at some point in time. "I really should acquire a scar or a tattoo," he grumbled. "Get off your knees, man. I'm not who you think."

The man didn't move. Just trembled in place like a frightened animal. "This one is sorry!"

With a sigh, Yixiao knelt in front of the man and tugged him upright. "I promise you, sir. I am not the Emperor...."

That startled the man a moment. "Emperor? What Emperor? You're the Storm Hermit's disciple, aren't you? The one called The Wanderer?"

Wuchang laughed, a rare occurrence that sounded a bit like rock grating on rock. "I don't believe that's happened before, has it?"

"No, it has not." Yixiao tugged the man upright and set him back down on his butt. "I am the Storm Hermit's disciple, yes. I'm not sure how you know it, though."

"This one...."

"The Storm Hermit requires no formality and neither do I."

"Ah. Yes. I was in Hubei when you fought Embittered Sword. I saw the fight then. Saw what you can do."

Embittered Sword? At a loss, Yixiao glanced at Wuchang, who said, "Tang Wen. You killed him when he attacked your cousin, I believe."

Yixiao felt his cheeks warm. "Gods. That was back when I was still out of control. I hadn't wanted to kill anyone." The whole mess had been a mistake from start to finish. Bored with waiting for more teachings he'd slipped off with his cousin for entertainment.

But his cousin wasn't just anyone. His cousin had been Crown Prince at the time and a natural target. Tang Wen, an assassin from Chongqing, had attacked and Yixiao had killed the man with a poorly controlled lightning storm. Worse, if the Storm Hermit hadn't come after him he'd have flooded the town. To his immense surprise, the Storm Hermit had forgiven his mistake. He'd spent the next two years in seclusion for it, learning the control he'd failed to achieve before.

"But you're her disciple. You've her training. Her knowledge. Begging you, *Daozhang*, help us! Our village is in desperate trouble. Our river has dried up. Our fields burn and blow away in the wind. Our orchards rot away and our tools fall to pieces."

If he were the Storm Hermit he would be bound to offer assistance. Their sect's credo demanded it. That was why his Master had built a home so far from others. It meant you had to truly and desperately need her help to look for her. Yixiao didn't have that option. This man had called on him as a disciple and he must answer.

Of course, based on what he'd just been told, he didn't think this was a simple task. Indeed, he'd a feeling it was part of the one he'd set himself, agreeing to help the Elemental Masters against their enemy. Because from the sound of it, every one of the Demonic Elementalists had chosen this one village to focus on; either for purposes unknown or as a trap for their enemies.

The question was which?

⇒)(⇐

"I can take you to Dinghua village easily, Young Master Lang." Yang didn't understand why the young man wanted him to wait where they were. From the sound of it, the bandits - if one could truly call them that - were in a great deal of trouble. "You could use all the help you can get."

"I'd rather not have our caravan put in jeopardy. Especially given who's probably behind this mess. You might be targeted."

Ridiculous. "Who would target me? I'm just a caravanner. Not a particularly wealthy one, either."

The young man eyed him thoughtfully. "You don't know? Or won't admit?"

What in the name of the Eight Gods was the boy talking about? "Are you trying to tell me you know who I am?" No one knew who he was. He'd asked and asked and asked and no one had any answers. After three years trying, he'd finally become inured to the situation.

"Don't you?" The youngster considered him. "When you fight, every plant around you answers your call."

Yang scoffed. "I do not know what you're talking about."

They stared at each other; both silent, neither willing to give in. Then, with a sigh, Lang Yixiao said, "I can't make you stay out of this. But just be warned, my companions' enemies are likely yours. And their enemies are almost certainly waiting for us. For you."

It made no sense but Yang simply said, "Very well. I accept that possibility. And the risk."

Having established he was coming, Yang checked his drivers and guards, making sure they were all in good order and proper condition. He didn't know what Young Master Lang feared but he knew there was danger. Just not that he was its target.

A noise inside one of the caravans reminded him. Feng-er had been given space to sleep in there. He'd been so busy worrying about the attack and other matters that her existence had completely slipped his mind. Slipped everyone else's, too it seemed. Not even Young Master Lang had mentioned her again.

Poking his head into the caravan where Feng-er was resting, he found her curled up in the far corner, partly hidden behind the boxes. "Didn't anyone tell you it was safe to come out?"

"No."

Odd. And, thinking about it, why hadn't he done so himself? "Are you hungry? There's breakfast."

"I'm fine." She curled up tighter, clearly afraid he'd get too close. "Are we going?"

"That's what I wanted to tell you. It seems we're going to your village after all. Those men who attacked us last night were from there." A thought occurred to him. "Would you like to speak to them? Maybe you know them."

She pulled back. "...no...No, my family lives in the hills outside...we...we're not important. They wouldn't remember me anyway."

Some flicker of sense told Yang that there was something wrong with her claim. That people from a small village like Dinghua would know everyone else. He opened his mouth, about to say as much, but the thought slipped off and would not come back.

Aware something was wrong, just as his lost memory was wrong, Yang tried to recover his bearings. But Feng-er asked, "Why are we going to Dinghua anyway? I thought Young Master Lang said it was out of our way."

It was an easier question to answer than the one he was trying to recall, so Yang refocused. "Apparently the men we captured have asked him for help. Him being the Storm Hermit's disciple means it's his duty."

She thought about that. "But you don't have to go."

"There's no reason I shouldn't. And they might need help."

"You shouldn't put yourself in danger."

Yang shrugged off the advice. "I was hired to get Young Master Lang to Khaitan. If that means following him into a burning pit to drag him out of trouble, that's my job. My business, too, for that matter." Really, he didn't understand why all these people kept trying to protect him. "I'm not helpless."

"You're incomplete. Unready. Neither of us should go." At his dour expression she made up her mind. "Very well. I can't make you stay. I won't try. But…be careful."

Yang was always careful and he said as much, leaving Feng-er where she was to go back to the task of getting the caravan moving. As he climbed out of the cart, though, he found Heibai Wuchang watching him, a curious look on his face. "She doesn't want to go after all?"

The question confused him momentarily. Then, "Oh. Feng-er? She came from Dinghua. I don't see why she wouldn't want to go." He'd some vague sense that he'd talked to the girl about their plans. That he'd even argued. But like every memory that brought him close to other - more important - ones, the discussion faded from his thoughts. "She'll be fine."

"I've no doubt on that count," Heibai Wuchang murmured. "Her purpose, however, remains a curiosity."

Yang didn't understand and right that moment didn't care. He'd worry about it later, the way he worried about most troubling problems. He had a job to do and people to carry into possible battle.

And that was more important than anything else right now.

⇒)(⇐

"The maid from your household concerns me more; the longer she's with us."

Wuchang's comment made Yixiao blink. Maid? From his household? It took him a moment to remember Feng-er's existence. He shook himself, recalling Henrietta's interesting trick of making those around her think she belonged. "Just the fact that I needed you to remind me of her is worrisome."

"Indeed." Wuchang went silent, then with great reluctance, added, "I seem to have problems keeping her in my thoughts as well. You know how difficult that is."

That meant Feng-er's ability was stronger than Henrietta's had been. "Should we do something, do you think?"

"I'm not sure. I overheard her talking to our caravan master earlier. I almost think she's worried for him."

And there was another Yixiao had suspicions towards. Liu Yang's abilities resembled those of an Elementalist. But if he was the fifth of the Five Elemental Masters why hadn't his fellows acknowledged him? Why did he stay apart? Surely he'd wish to be reunited.

"Now we're aware of the effect, do you think we can block it?"

Another silent moment. "I think we'll be troubled. But we'll have to try. It wouldn't do to let her control our thoughts in the middle of a crisis. From the looks of things, that's exactly what we have."

Yixiao turned his attention forward. Wuchang was right, because the landscape ahead showed the damage their captives had described. He winced at the sight, staring around intently.

Dinghua was nestled at the foot of a small mountain east of Wuhan, a half-dozen miles north of the main road. Surrounded by rice-paddies and mountains, it seemed safe and remote from the troubles plaguing the rest of China. It wasn't impoverished but it wasn't so rich as to encourage banditry. Yixiao doubted it had much need for the Taiping Heavenly Rebellion, either.

"NEITHER OF US SHOULD GO."

It definitely didn't need the Demonic Elemental Masters, not this close to harvest. Rice paddies filled with ash. Others dried up, a thin greenish miasma rising above them. The faint sulfurous stench spoke of rot and rust. "One wouldn't expect that stink in the paddies," he muttered.

"The village looks well-off enough to afford iron tools," Wuchang suggested. "Possibly some were left behind when they fled the attack."

True enough. And ultimately unimportant. "Do you think you could scout ahead?"

"I was just about to suggest that very thing." Wuchang jumped off the cart and headed off to the northern side of the village.

Ordinarily, Yixiao would be doing the same and leaving someone else to take lead in this sort of game. There was no one else. Even if he was right about Liu Yang being the other elementalists' Eldest Brother, it was obvious the man was in no fit state to take charge. Worse, he couldn't be certain of Liu Yang's identity and therefore couldn't ask a total stranger to lead.

"Right," he muttered to himself. "Time to work, it seems."

He jumped from his side of the cart and sauntered forward, inclining his head at the four elementalists. "Be ready," he mouthed, though he knew he didn't need to.

The village itself consisted of about twenty small homes and a few larger buildings of unknown purpose. Storage or shops, perhaps. It was also suspiciously quiet, with a few staring eyes peeking out of windows and hurriedly backing away whenever they were noticed.

If things weren't so dangerous, Yixiao might have played the fool and waved or somersaulted or generally brought attention to himself. Right now he needed to focus and at least pretend to take this solemnly. A good thing, too, because the ones he'd pretty much expected were waiting for them in the village square.

A chair carved from rotted wood, somehow managing to stay functional despite the damage, sat at the middle of the square atop a platform, facing the entrance. Four people, or seeming people, stood in front, their appearance all too familiar.

"It seems our enemy fears to meet us," Sister Bianhua said from her position behind Doctor Song. "Given they're using more puppets."

"And the same ones they've used on us before. Or at least ones with the same appearance."

Yixiao gazed at the four. Now why go to the trouble of creating exact duplicates of the previous puppets? Surely it made the true nature of their tools obvious?

A faint flicker of an idea came to him, one he couldn't be sure of because magic wasn't his area of expertise. "Perhaps it takes more time and energy to create an entirely new puppet, instead of simply using the same design over and again. Unimaginative, perhaps, but expedient."

Something growled irritably and Yixiao turned his attention on the person in the seat. Old. Terribly old and twisted. Bald. Skin like aged wood, with small holes and broken chunks fallen in. They wore a shapeless robe covered in dead leaves and their teeth, what was left of them, were rotten chips of dark brown ivory. A faint ugly scent emanated from him, making Yixiao yearn to be sick.

Forcing himself to stand straight, he gazed directly at the person, asking, "You would be the Demonic Elemental Master of Rot, I presume?"

One of the four puppets struck out and Yixiao narrowly avoided the blow, leaning back just in time. She was Captain Brigid, or had been before Wusuo had stolen her shape. "Mannerless human. This has nothing to do with you."

"On the contrary," Yixiao argued. "This has everything to do with me now. I've been asked to help the people of this village and as the Storm Hermit's Disciple, I intend to do so."

Another of the puppets - Hui - snapped, "Dare speak so directly to our Master?" The perfect Khaitanese coming from a white man's lips was just as startling as Yixiao's British accent so often was to Europeans. "On your knees, human. Down before Fushi, Lord of Rot and Ruin!"

Ordinarily, Yixiao didn't pull rank. He made an exception this time. Gazing directly into Fushi's eyes, he said calmly, "All of you are wanted murderers in your homeland. Whereas this *Daozhang* is the great-grandson of the Qianlong Emperor and grandson of the Gatkiun King of Khaitan. This *Daozhang* is the inheritor of the Storm Hermit's teachings. And. This. *Daozhang*. Does. Not. Kneel. To. Criminals."

A moment of stunned silence followed. Then, inevitably, all four puppets launched themselves at Yixiao.

Lang Yixiao's sudden change in manner was surprising. It was also effective. Yang suspected the enemy had intended to drive him to some foolish, impetuous, move. Instead he'd let them cross the line first. Lightning flared around the youngster as he dodged, body lit blue and shadowed black by the intense light.

The others moved too, taking advantage of the enemy's focus on Lang Yixiao to choose their opponent. Fire against Mist. Water against Rust. Earth against Ash. Metal again Dust. Typical of elemental forms born of Chaos, there was no one way to defeat the others, but one was more effective than others.

Yang turned his attention on the leader of the Demonic Elementalists. Damaged. Badly damaged. It seemed he'd suffered setbacks in his attempt to overcome his enemies. That was the trouble with the sort of cultivation this lot used. Demonic elements fed off their source, destroying them in the process. But once the source they fed off of was gone, they faded, like shadows waning with the light.

When he said as much, Feng-er spoke from behind him, "And Fushi is weaker, now Wood is lost to him." It wasn't a question. It ought to have been a question. He ought to understand more. And it suddenly occurred to him that he understood too much.

"You're not an Elementalist," Feng-er murmured in his ear. "You're a wanderer, just like that boy out there. You aren't involved."

No. Not like Young Master Lang. Not like The Wanderer. Lang Yixiao wandered from choice, never lost because his place was everywhere and nowhere. Whereas Yang might know his physical location but he didn't know his own Self. Didn't know who he was or even what. "I still have to help."

"Why?"

He didn't know the answer to that question either. Only knew it to be true. "I can't answer that. 'Why' doesn't matter. This fight has to end."

"All things have a thing that feeds on them. All things cycle round to become something new. Perhaps it's better to fall and let the cycle continue."

If the Demonic Elementalists had a way to move on from where they were, Yang might have agreed. They didn't. "They destroy what they feed on, then fall to nothing. Decay, not change. There is no balance in their actions."

"Then it's a good thing you're not an Elementalist yourself," Feng-er told him. "Rot can't ruin wood if wood isn't there."

Yes. That was right. Yang turned his attention on his puppets. He'd made them from everything but wood. Ceramic flesh, with metal bones, water for blood and fire for life, they had nothing Fushi could touch. He focused his attention on them, sending them from their places to circle around the fight.

A cool wind blew around Yang, singing in his ear as if to give him courage and strength. All of which he needed because he'd no idea if he could do anything, as small and weak as he was compared to what he fought. Feng-er giggled at the wind's touch, her laugh giving him heart.

Fushi turned his attention on Yang's puppets. Creaked a curse as he leapt from his chair. Dodged first one, then another. His touch destroyed the first puppet's clothing, revealing pallid ceramic flesh. Another curse escaped his lips as he glared towards Yang. "You dare, human?"

Rust and Mist-born rushed at Yang, only to be smashed to nothing by Young Master Lang's lightning. The boy moved, taking position between the platform and Yang's caravan. Guaiguai screeched an insult as Dust and Ash-born raced at her. Kicking and spitting and screaming, she caught the things' cores in her mouth and bit down. She never did have much patience for monsters.

Sensing defeat approaching, Fushi tried to slip back and away, evading Yang's puppets by mere inches. They almost escaped, only to come face to face with Heibai Wuchang. The Hollowed Blade had circled around to the back of the village and was only now coming out to block him.

Fushi struck the platform below Heibai Wuchang's feet, rotting the wood and dropping him into the space below. Using the brief moment to rush forward, he almost escaped, only to drop as well when Heibai Wuchang cut the supports out from under him.

Seizing the chance, Yang sent his puppets leaping across the platform, catching hold of Fushi's flailing arms and dragging him from the hole. This forced the other Demonic Elemental puppets to try to protect him, only to be struck down by their opponents when they turned away from their own fights.

Clutched tight, unable to break free, Fushi shrieked and struggled, movements weaker and weaker. Watching him through the eyes of his puppets, Yang felt a painful mix of pity, compassion and hate. It was a difficult moment, not least because he felt he shouldn't kill out of hand. That he was neither judge nor executioner.

He didn't need to decide. The puppet containing Fushi's essence faltered, ruined body disintegrating in Yang's puppets' hands. Until all that was left was a peculiar mass of substance that might once have been part of a living creature and was now a dying thing, rotting away to nothingness. And with his decay, his tools fell also.

As the Demonic Elementalists' puppets crumpled to the ground, Feng-er leaned on Yang's shoulders and murmured softly, "Well now. That's done then." He turned a startled look on her, feeling her body fade to nothing as an intense warmth filled his chest.

Memory returned, a terrifying flood of pain, loss and desperation. So that was it. That was why he couldn't face the others. Why he'd lost his memory all those years ago. Why he'd wandered, slowly building the only weapons that could defeat Fushi.

It'd been his only escape from being consumed. His only defense. Split himself apart and set his two selves the task of preparing for his younger siblings' return. Because where Fushi could destroy Yang Zhengfeng - the Elemental Master of Wood - they'd no power over Liu Yang and Qu Feng.

And now Fushi was defeated Yang Zhengfeng could be one once more.

⇉)(⇇

Everything stank, but the fight was over. No one had been hurt, thank the Gods, though it was clear from his companions' expressions that they were too exhausted to do much more than lean against whatever they could find and rest.

Yixiao examined the remnants of the battle. The four Demonic Elementalists' puppets lay fallen around what little remained of Fushi, their faces blank and empty, their chests fallen in as if whatever had given them life had evaporated. As for what was left of Fushi, that was the strangest of all. A misshapen blob that might once have been a living person, albeit a living person whose arms and legs had been cut away.

He turned his attention on Wuchang. "You searched the village, I presume? Where are the other Demonic Elementalists?"

"Not to be found. I fear they may not be here after all."

Yixiao considered that, remembering how the puppets had fallen at the same moment Fushi had. "I wonder."

"How so?"

Examining the puppets more closely, Yixiao noted they lacked a part their counterparts had had before. "Where's the heartstone? We destroyed the ones belonging to the other puppets, but these should have their own." He pointed at the smoldering thing lying on the platform where Fushi had rotted away. "Look at the shape. A torso and a head. Nothing else. Is it possible the puppets we met were part of him?"

Sister Bianhua looked doubtful, opening her mouth to object, but Liu Yang approached before she could get a word out, saying, "That sounds likely, Young Master Lang. The part of me that retained its memory says the Demonic Elementalists were never five different people, but one, split apart to master their power separately."

They all turned to stare at him, for the quiet, meek, caravan driver had transformed. Clothing unchanged, appearance mostly the same, his speech was calm and direct, his manner had become studious and gently firm, the picture of a scholar or sect master. Yixiao eyed him, unsurprised at the change. "So you are the Elemental Master of Wood after all, sir?"

"This Master is, indeed, Yang Zhengfeng," he agreed and laughed as his younger siblings, all except Disciple Lenghai, rushed to him to grasp hold and cling tight. "Now, now. It's only been three years. A mere heartbeat in time."

"We should have known you from the first," Brother Jigme complained. "Why did you hide from us?"

"I was hiding from Fushi, little brother. He nearly killed me back then. The only thing I could do split myself in two and forget my existence. But now I'm whole and returned to you." Liu Yang...no, Yang Zhengfeng...turned his attention on Disciple Lenghai. "Come here, child."

Nervously, even more nervously than when he'd approached Doctor Song, Disciple Lenghai came closer. "I...This one is sorry. This one knows his fault...."

"Your predecessor's spirit says nothing was your fault and while she does tend to be more forgiving than most, I think I agree. You neither asked to be made, nor to be sent to harm her. And when she gave you her power, you became her heir without doubt or hesitation."

"I...wouldn't say that."

The wind whispered, *Don't argue*, and for a wonder Disciple...no...Brother Lenghai accepted Xi Xuan's chiding. He cupped his hands to Yang Zhengfeng, saying, "This youngest brother greets his elder and hopes to serve well."

"This elder brother greets his new youngest and is certain he will." Master Yang turned to Yixiao. "It seems to me we're done here, though I'm sure we should spend some time making sure the people of this village are safe and well. Does that meet with your approval, *Daozhang?*"

Now it was Yixiao's turn to bow. "It does. Though this *Daozhang* does have one question. What of Feng-er? Should I be concerned for her or about her? Or was her personal name significant?" Because the one thing Yixiao didn't like was a loose end, especially one that might find its way to stabbing one in the back.

"It was. As I said, I split myself in two to keep Fushi from finding me. Qu Feng was my other half, remembering everything I could not. Waiting until we could fight Fushi and win. And when you four returned, she knew that time had come."

Yixiao glanced at the ruined remains of their enemies...or enemy, rather...and reflected that Master Yang had been quite right. "Then let's finish cleaning up here," he said. "And tomorrow, when we're done, continue on to Khaitan. I'm sure you all look forward to going home and I have a mission to complete."

Preferably before all China exploded in civil war.

Chapter 6
Wanderer Circles Back to Home

"Greet you, your Majesty."

Five voices chorused; and one whispered. Five pairs of hands cupped; and air fluttered. Five knees bent; and a breeze sighed low.

Yixiao watched from his position of honor as the Five Elemental Masters, plus one fragile spirit, presented themselves to his aunt, the Chushenggan King. Ordinarily, Aunt Bi dispensed with formalities, but this time she wore the full regalia of her position; the Eight Colored robes and the dual crown. This was a significant moment, seeing as how Khaitan's cultivational defenders had finally returned.

King Bi inclined her head. "Rise." As the five and one obeyed, she murmured, "The land has needed you."

"This Master is at fault," Master Yang admitted readily. "He hoped to resolve the problem of Fall of Time quickly."

"You return with a new disciple in place of the old." King Bi examined Brother Lenghai thoughtfully, until the youngster blushed and tried to efface himself. "You will have to learn your duties quickly, young Master of Water. This Kingdom needs its protectors."

"This Lenghai will do his best."

Returning her attention to Master Yang, King Bi continued, "This King has been told you've defeated Fall of Time. Has an explanation been found for who that person was and what they wanted? Not to mention who their disciples were?"

Another bow. "Fall of Time was the only enemy we faced, your Majesty. He split his power five ways, creating tools who could best defeat the five of us."

"Then your enemy...our enemy...is defeated?"

"This Master believes so, your Majesty. Fall of Time extended himself too far. That and he was no match for us when we were supported by your nephew and his partner, Heibai Wuchang."

That made King Bi raise a brow and turn an interested gaze on Yixiao. "You didn't mention this."

"It was hardly worth mentioning, Your Majesty. This Wanderer's cultivation was just barely enough to turn the battle to our favor." Yixiao cupped his hands, bowing to his aunt, then to Master Yang and his martial siblings. "It was an honor to work with the Five Elemental Masters."

"And a privilege to be aided by *Daozhang* Yixiao," Master Yang said in turn.

"Still, you should be rewarded, just as I reward my Elemental Masters." King Bi gestured for a servant to come forward, a lacquer box in his hands. Turning to Master Yang, she added, "I'm of the understanding that no sect or temple roof is ever properly repaired. This should cover the expenses for that purpose for the next few years. Return to your place and your duties, my servants. Your King thanks you for your service."

As the five bowed and accepted their gift quietly, King Bi asked Yixiao, "And what would you have for a reward, nephew?"

"For myself? Nothing comes to mind, though I'm sure Wuchang and I could use some funds for when we return to our wandering. Food is seldom an issue, of course, but you'd be amazed at our clothing expenses." That got a slight chuckle from both his aunt and his companion.

"As for your request for your family. I know my brother-in-law well enough to know he won't want to stay."

That was only too true. "If they can take sanctuary here until I find them a safe place elsewhere, that may be the best possible solution."

King Bi agreed. "Then that, my wandering nephew, is what we shall do."

⋽)(⋶

Ten Years Later

Strikersport gleamed in the sunlight, a bustling town nestled against mountains, spanning a river running out to the ocean. The land had been a logging camp owned by Sebastian Krane once. But a series of fires had forced Krane to sell out to Zak Striker and his partner Jo Kraft. They, in turn, had built the mine that'd turned the place from a frontier camp to a bustling village.

The place had grown fast; gold and silver leaving town, sending food, farmers and workers back in its place. The Kranes built a farm, the Trendles a railway, the McLeods an engineering company. And, somewhere in all that, Mister Chang Yoon, owner of Jeen Loon Enterprises, claimed a small piece of land for himself and his employees.

Yixiao gazed at the rising walls of Strikersport's Chinatown with interest. "Mister Chang has gonads the size of a dragon's pearl, building a practical fortress here in America."

"He does," Wuchang agreed. "He can hardly be blamed, given current sentiment."

Passing through San Francisco had shown that much. The influx of Chinese miners in these last troubled years had increased prejudice and resulted in tightened restrictions. If Yixiao and Wuchang didn't have proof that they'd immigrated years earlier they might have found their return to California a great deal harder. Getting his family through had been more difficult, but Mister Chang had supplied all the necessary paperwork.

Once they'd made it through they'd reached Strikersport without issue. California had become a bit more civilized in the ten years since their last visit to the area. One hardly needed to fear bandits or wild animals, especially when one was riding a surprisingly comfortable train. Their real challenge had been keeping Yixiao's various family members from getting in the way, so fascinated were they by the whole business.

Noting Mister Chang waiting for them at the 'fortress' entrance, smiling blandly, Yixiao hurried to stop the man from bowing. "No need for that," he complained. "I'm just a wanderer."

"The Wanderer is our benefactor, Young Master Lang. Your grandmother's gifts to us in your family's name cannot be forgotten." Mister Chang glanced past Yixiao, watching the small horde of Langs wandering up the roadway, stopping to stare and point back at the steel tracks gleaming along the lower part of the mountainside. "Though it seems they're somewhat distracted."

No surprise Grandmother Lang had prepared the way for them. No surprise, either, that his family were dawdling along behind. Yixiao grinned. "As soon as your letters mentioned the railroad my parents were more than happy to leave Khaitan."

"Would that your brother had been willing to come. This old man admits to concern."

Yide-ge had stayed in China. As a magistrate he felt it his responsibility to remain home until a replacement could be found. Yixiao admitted to fearing for his older brother, yet understood Yide-ge's feelings on the matter.

All he could do was hope Yide-ge would stay safe, no matter how badly China's government was rocked. At least he'd sent his wife and children on ahead. Keeping them safe was just as important to him as duty.

As they waited for the others to join them, Mister Chang turned Yixiao's attention towards the mountain behind the walls of his small town. "You see the building up there?"

Yixiao peered upwards, catching sight of a wood and stone structure built near the top of the mountain. "I do."

"I've had a hermitage built for yourself and your partner. We hope you'll see fit to come down from its lofty heights to act as our priest, of course, but...."

"But you know how much we value solitude." Yixiao gazed up at the small building approvingly. Smiled. "Wuchang? What do you think?"

"Yixiao knows I need no home to be content," Wuchang murmured, a slight pleased smile flickering across his lips. "But I think that will do nicely."

It would, too. Overlooking the ocean to the west, overlooking the mountains stretching eastward from the coast. Remote but not too remote. Yixiao had no doubt he'd be called upon to wander again. No doubt he'd be needed to deal with the beings of this land, to protect and to guard against.

But having a place of his own, with his best friend to share it with; that was exactly the gift he needed. He returned his attention to Mister Chang. "Master says, 'Sooner or later you have to settle down.' I look forward to it."

And to a long and peaceful cultivation.

The End

About Our Creators

WRITER -

BARBARA DORAN - has been making up stories for as long as she can remember. From playing Ms. Marvel to her best friend's Captain Marvel to writing new stories for old characters (Hannibal King, X-Men, Green Hornet, The Saint, The Shadow and many others), to writing gaming and anime fanfiction online.

After ten years behind the keyboard as a software engineer, Barbara realized that her true love wasn't coding but making stuff up. So when she left that career in favor of dealing with two frequent interruptions of her life (namely her own personal Tiger and Dragon), she decided to use what little time they allowed her to work on writing. Her Long Suffering Husband, without whom she could never have managed such a goal, has been nothing if not supportive.

Along with reading every mystery, SF and fantasy book she could get her hands on, Barbara grew up watching Star Trek, Batman, Green Hornet, along with the usual Saturday morning cartoons. She became addicted to shows like Battle of the Planets and Doctor Who in her teens and discovered Run Run Shaw's martial arts flicks some years later. Those influences, along with a love of folklore and mythology, have become part of the world some small portion of her mind lives in. When, of course, she isn't chasing Tiger and Dragon from one school event to another.

Barbara can be contacted at <BarbaraDoran@sumergoscriptum.com>. Her website is <http://www.sumergoscriptum.com/barbaradoran/>.

INTERIOR ILLUSTRATIONS -

GARY KATO – was born in Honolulu, in 1949. He graduated from the University of Hawaii with a Bachelor in Fine Arts degree. His comic book work has appeared in such varied titles as Destroyer Duck, Thunderbunny, Ms. Tree and Mr. Jigsaw. He's also illustrated children's books such as The Menehune of Naupaka Village and the currently available Barry Baskerville Returns and Jamie and the Fish-Eyed Goggles. He's also been a contributor to the Children's Television Workshop magazines, 3-2-1 Contact and Kid City.

COVER ARTIST -

ROB DAVIS - began his professional art career doing illustrations for role-playing games in the late 1980's. Not long after he began lettering and inking, then penciling comics for a number of small black and white comics publishers—most notably for Eternity Comics, which eventually became Malibu Comics in the 1990's. It was on their book SCIMIDAR with writer R.A. Jones that he made his first impact in the industry. Branching out to other black and white publishers and eventually working at both DC and Marvel Rob worked on likeness intensive comics like TV adaptations of QUANTUM LEAP and STAR TREK's many incarnations. Most notably on the DEEP SPACE NINE comics for Malibu. At Marvel he worked on the Saturday morning cartoon adaptation PIRATES OF DARK WATER. After the comics industry implosion in the late 1990's Rob picked up work on video games, advertising illustration and

T-shirt design as well as some small press comics like ROBYN OF SHERWOOD for Caliber. Rob continues to do the occasional self-published comic book as well as publisher and designer for his small-press production REDBUD STUDIO COMICS. Rob is Art Director, Designer and Illustrator for the New Pulp production outfit AIRSHIP 27 partnered with writer/editor Ron Fortier. In 2021 Airship 27 was nominated for the prestigious Munsey Award given out a PulpFest in Pittsburg each year. Rob is the recipient of the PULP FACTORY AWARD for "Best Interior Illustrations" in 2010 and 2015 for his work on SHERLOCK HOLMES: CONSULTING DETECTIVE and has been nominated for the same award several times since. He works and lives in central Missouri with his wife and two grown children.

by the same author...

Trouble in Strikersport

When a mysterious evil force known only as the Voice begins to take control of the local mobs in the coast city of Strikersport, two new heroes appear on the scene. Their origin, the neighborhood streets of Chinatown. The masked Tiger and Dragon wield both science and magic in their battle to combat the forces of darkness. Soon several of the city's prominent citizens become players in this cataclysmic war. These include players from a wealthy family with roots to Strikersport history, a rookie cop and a crusading newspaper editor.

Writer Barbara Doran spins a classic pulp adventure with breakneck pacing, original characters and a tangled plot that will keep readers guessing to the very end. Mixing martial arts with Chinese mysticism, she offers a truly unique action mystery sure to entertain readers from beginning to end.

Mysteries of Shanghai

Shanghai in the 1930s is a place of excitement and intrigue... and magic. It is an international hotspot where foreign agents from around the world ply their trade. Brought to Shanghai to investigate a powerful new aircraft engine, young Conall McLeod becomes embroiled in a high-stakes game between gangs, spies and immortal beings. Together with his beloved Mudan Chang and hot-shot Chinese pilot, Feng Zhanchi, Conall must navigate the dangerous waters of the city's criminal undercurrents and help free a lost immortal from the clutches of evil.

Writer Barbara Doran spins a fantastic tale of action and mystery filled with some of the most memorable characters ever conceived. Whether deep within the city's maze of dark alleys or high atop an ancient castle of evil, none will be able to escape from *The Wings of the Golden Dragon!*

Havok in Strikersport

As the Feast of Hungry Ghosts begins in the northwest port city of Strikersport, monsters and actual ghosts begin appearing throughout the city causing all manner of chaos. Thus the city's twin protectors, Dragon and Tiger, enter the fray and set about uncovering the reason behind the sudden appearances.

Their revelations lead back in time to a horrendous massacre in the village of Batsu, a province of the magical kingdom of Khaitan. Have agents of ancient deities come to Strikersports to wreak vengeances on the guilty? And if so, what is the magical artifact and its connection to an animated shi shi lion roaming free through the city?

Once again Barbara Doran spins a tale of imaginative fantasy filled with colorful heroes, villains and oriental gods wielding amazing powers. It is a frenetic, pulp actioner fans will not be able to put to down.

www.ingramcontent.com/pod-product-compliance
Lightning Source LLC
Chambersburg PA
CBHW081227020726

47503CB00011B/2935